PIERS ANTHONY

The Continuing Xanth Saga

This 1996 edition is published by Wings Books,
a division of Random House Value Publishing, Inc.,
40 Engelhard Avenue, Avenel, New Jersey 07001,
by arrangement with Ballantine Books,
a division of Random House, Inc.

Wings Books and colophon are trademarks
of Random House Value Publishing, Inc.

Random House
New York • Toronto • London • Sydney • Auckland
http://www.randomhouse.com/

Printed and bound in the United States of America

Library of Congress Cataloging-in-Publication Data
Anthony, Piers.
[Selections]
The continuing Xanth saga / Piers Anthony.
p.   cm.
Contents: Centaur aisle — Ogre, ogre — Night mare.
ISBN 0-517-18337-4
1. Xanth (Imaginary place)—Fiction.   2. Fantastic fiction, American.
I. Title.
PS3551.N73A6   1997
813'.54—dc20
96-41490
CIP

8 7 6 5 4 3 2 1

Contents

PIERS ANTHONY

The Continuing Xanth Saga

A New Collection of Three Complete Novels

CENTAUR AISLE

OGRE, OGRE

NIGHT MARE

WINGS BOOKS

NEW YORK / AVENEL, NEW JERSEY

Centaur Aisle

The author thanks Jerome Brown for the notion of the "Spelling Bee" used in the first chapter, and the many other fans whose letters of encouragement have caused the Xanth trilogy to be expanded. May those who feel Xanth is sexist have pleasure in this novel, where Mundania is shown to be worse.

Contents

XANTH

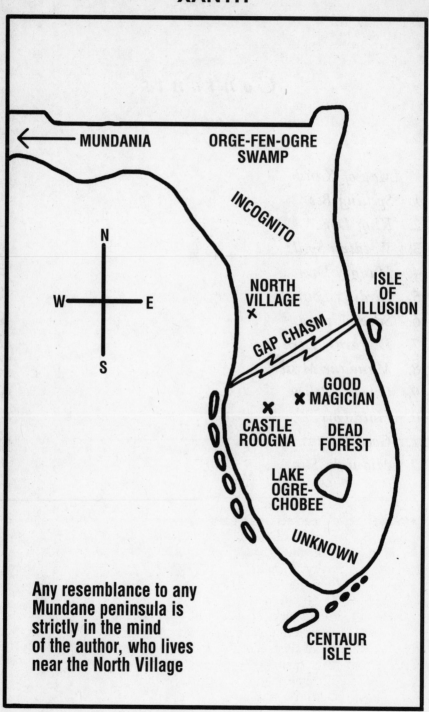

MUNDANIA ←

ORGE-FEN-OGRE SWAMP

INCOGNITO

N
W — E
S

NORTH VILLAGE ✕

ISLE OF ILLUSION

GAP CHASM

GOOD ✕ MAGICIAN

CASTLE ✕ ROOGNA

DEAD FOREST

LAKE OGRE-CHOBEE

UNKNOWN

CENTAUR ISLE

Any resemblance to any Mundane peninsula is strictly in the mind of the author, who lives near the North Village

Chapter 1

Spelling Bee

Dor was trying to write an essay, because the King had decreed that any future monarchs of Xanth should be literate. It was an awful chore. He knew how to read, but his imagination tended to go blank when challenged to produce an essay, and he had never mastered conventional spelling.

"The Land of Xanth," he muttered with deep disgust.

"What?" the table asked.

"The title of my awful old essay," Dor explained dispiritedly. "My tutor Cherie, on whom be a muted anonymous curse, assigned me a one-hundred-word essay telling all about Xanth. I don't think it's possible. There isn't that much to tell. After twenty-five words I'll probably have to start repeating. How can I ever stretch it to a whole hundred? I'm not even sure there are that many words in the language."

"Who wants to know about Xanth?" the table asked. "I'm bored already."

"I *know* you're a board. I guess Cherie, may a hundred curse-burrs tangle in her tail, wants to know."

"She must be pretty dumb."

Dor considered. "No, she's infernally smart. All centaurs are. That's why they're the historians and poets and tutors of Xanth. May all their high-IQ feet founder."

"How come they don't rule Xanth, then?"

"Well, most of them don't do magic, and only a Magician can rule Xanth. Brains have nothing to do with it—and neither do essays." Dor scowled at his blank paper.

"Only a Magician can rule any land," the table said smugly. "But what about you? You're a Magician, aren't you? Why aren't you King?"

"Well, I will be King, some day," Dor said defensively, aware that he was talking with the table only to postpone a little longer the inevitable struggle with the essay. "When King Trent, uh, steps down. That's why I have to be educated, he says." He wished all kinds of maledictions on Cherie Centaur, but never on King Trent.

He resumed his morose stare at the paper, where he had now printed THU LANNED UV ZANTH. Somehow it didn't look right, though he was sure he had put the TH's in the right places.

Something tittered. Dor glanced up and discovered that the hanging picture of Queen Iris was smirking. That was one problem about working in Castle Roogna; he was always under the baleful eye of the Queen, whose principal business was snooping. With special effort, Dor refrained from sticking out his tongue at the picture.

Seeing herself observed, the Queen spoke, the mouth of the image moving. Her talent was illusion, and she could make the illusion of sound when she wanted to. "You may be a Magician, but you aren't a scholar. Obviously spelling is not your forte."

"Never claimed it was," Dor retorted. He did not know what the word "forte" meant—perhaps it was a kind of small castle—but whatever it meant, spelling was not there. He did not much like the Queen, and the feeling was mutual, but both of them were constrained by order of the King to be reasonably polite to one another. "Surely a woman of your extraordinary talents has more interesting things to do than peek at my stupid essay," he said. Then, grudgingly, he added: "Your Majesty."

"Indeed I do," the picture agreed, its background clouding. She had of course noted the pause before he gave her title; it was not technically an insult, but the message was clear enough. The cloud in the picture had become a veritable thunderstorm, with jags of lightning shooting out like sparks. She would get back at him somehow. "But you would never get your homework done if not supervised."

Dor grimaced into the surface of the table. She was right on target there! Then he saw that ink had smeared all across his essay-paper, ruining it.

With an angry grunt he picked it up—and the ink slid off, pooled on the surface of the table, bunched together, sprouted legs, and scurried away. It leaped off the table like a gross bug and puffed into momentary vapor. It had been an illusion. The Queen had gotten back at him already. She could be extraordinarily clever in ugly little ways. Dor could not admit being angry about being fooled—and that made him angrier than ever.

"I don't see why anyone has to be male to rule Xanth," the picture said. That was of course a chronic sore point with the Queen. She was a Sorceress fully as talented as any Magician, but by Xanth law/custom no woman could be King.

"I live in the Land of Xanth," Dor said slowly, voicing his essay as he wrote, ignoring the Queen with what he hoped was insulting politeness. "Which is distinct from Mundania in that there is magic in Xanth and none in Mundania." It was amazing how creative he became when there was a negative aspect to it. He had twenty-three words already!

Dor cracked an eyelid, sneaking a peek at the picture. It had reverted to neutral. Good; the Queen had tuned out. If she couldn't bug him with crawling illusions, she wasn't interested.

But now his inspiration dehydrated. He had an impossible one hundred whole words to do, six times his present total. Maybe five times; he was not particularly apt at higher mathematics either. Four more words, if he counted the title. A significant fraction of the way through, but only a fraction. What a dreary chore!

Irene wandered in. She was King Trent and Queen Iris's daughter, the palace brat, often a nuisance—but sometimes not. It griped Dor to admit it, but Irene was an extremely pretty girl, getting more so, and that exerted an increasing leverage upon him. It made fighting with her awkward. "Hi, Dor," she said, bouncing experimentally. "What are you doing?"

Dor, distracted momentarily by the bounce, lost track of the sharp response he had planned. "Oh, come on," he grumped. "You know your mother got tired of snooping on me, so she assigned you to do it instead."

Irene did not deny it. "Well, *some*body has to snoop on you, dummy. I'd rather be out playing with Zilch."

Zilch was a young sea cow that had been conjured for her fifteenth birthday. Irene had set her up in the moat and used her magic to promote the growth of sturdy wallflowers to wall off a section of water, protecting Zilch from the moat-monsters while she grazed. Dor regarded Zilch as a great blubbery slob of an animal, but anything that distracted Irene was to some extent worthwhile. She took after her mother in certain annoying ways.

"Go ahead and play with the cow," Dor suggested disparagingly. "I won't tell."

"No, a Princess has to do her duty." Irene never spoke of duty unless it was something she wanted to do anyway. She picked up his essay-paper.

"Hey, give that back!" Dor protested, reaching for it.

"You heard him, snit!" the paper agreed. "Give me back!"

That only made Irene ornery. She backed away, hanging on to the paper, her eyes scanning the writing. Her bosom heaved with barely suppressed laughter. "Oh, say, this is something! I didn't think anybody could misspell 'Mundania' that badly?"

Dor leaped for her, his face hot, but she danced back again, putting the paper behind her. This was her notion of entertainment—teasing him, making him react one way or another. He tried to reach around her—and found himself embracing her, unintentionally.

Irene had always been a cute girl and socially precocious. In recent years nature had rushed to endow her generously, and this was quite evident at close range. Now she was a green-eyed, green-tint-haired—occurring naturally; she did not color her hair—buxom beauty. What was worse, she knew it, and constantly sought new ways to use it to her advantage. Today she was dressed in a green blouse and skirt that accentuated her figure and wore green slippers that enhanced her fine legs and feet. In short, she had prepared well for this encounter and had no intention of letting him write his essay in peace.

She took a deep breath, inflating herself against him. "I'll scream," she breathed in his ear, taunting him.

But Dor knew how to handle her. "I'll tickle," he breathed back.

"That's not fair!" For she could not scream realistically while giggling, and she was hyperticklish, perhaps because she thought it was fashionable for young ladies to be so. She had heard somewhere that ticklishness made girls more appealing.

Irene's hand moved swiftly, trying to tuck the paper into her bosom, where she knew he wouldn't dare go for it. But Dor had encountered this ploy before, too, and he caught her wrist en route. He finally got his fingers on the essay-paper, for he was stronger than she, and she also deemed it unladylike to fight too hard. Image was almost as important to her as mischief. She let the paper go, but tried yet another ploy. She put her arms around him. "I'll kiss."

But he was ready even for that. Her kisses could change to bites without notice, depending on her mercurial mood. She was not to be trusted, though in truth the close struggle had whetted his appetite for some such diversion. She was scoring on him better than she knew. "Your mother's watching."

Irene turned him loose instantly. She was a constant tease; but in her mother's presence she always behaved angelically. Dor wasn't sure why this was so, but suspected that the Queen's desire to see Irene become Queen after her had something to do with it. Irene didn't want to oblige her mother any more than she wanted to oblige anyone else, and expressing overt interest in Dor would constitute a compromising attitude. The Queen resented Dor because he was a full Magician while her daughter was not, but she was not about to let him make anyone else's daughter Queen. Irene, ironically, did want to be Queen, but also wanted to spite her mother, so she always tried to make it seem that Dor was chasing her while she resisted. The various facets of this cynical game became complex on occasion.

Dor himself wasn't sure how he felt about it all. Four years ago, when he was twelve, he had gone on an extraordinary adventure into Xanth's past and had occupied the body of a grown, muscular, and highly coordinated barbarian. He had learned something about the ways of men and women. Since he had had an opportunity to play with adult equipment before getting there himself, he had an inkling that the little games Irene played were more chancy than she knew. So he stayed somewhat clear, rejecting her teasing advances, though this was not always easy. Sometimes he had strange, wicked dreams, wherein he called one of her bluffs, and it wasn't exactly a bluff, and then the hand of an anonymous censor blotted out a scene of impending fascination.

"Dumbo!" Irene exclaimed irately, staring at the still picture on the wall. "My mother isn't watching us!"

"Got you off my case, though, didn't it?" Dor said smugly. "You want to make like Millie the Ghost, and you don't have the stuff." That was a double-barreled insult, for Millie—who had stopped being a ghost before Dor was born, but retained the identification—was gifted with magical sex appeal, which she had used to snare one of the few Magicians of Xanth, the somber Zombie Master. Dor himself had helped bring that Magician back to life for her, and now they had three-year-old twins. So Dor was suggesting to Irene that she lacked sex appeal and womanliness, the very things she was so assiduously striving for. But it was a hard charge to make stick, because Irene was really not far off the mark. If he ever forgot she was the palace brat, he would be in trouble, for what hidden censor would blot out a dream-turned-real? Irene could be awfully nice when she tried. Or maybe it was when she stopped trying; he wasn't sure.

"Well, you better get that dumb essay done, or Cherie Centaur will step on you," Irene said, putting on a new mood. "I'll help you spell the words if you want."

Dor didn't trust that either. "I'd better struggle through on my own."

"You'll flunk. Cherie doesn't put up with your kind of ignorance."

"I know," he agreed glumly. The centaur was a harsh taskmistress—which was of course why she had been given the job. Had her mate Chester done the tutoring, Dor would have learned much about archery, swordplay, and bare-knuckle boxing, but his spelling would have sunk to amazing new depths. King Trent had a sure hand in delegating authority.

"I know what!" Irene exclaimed. "You need a spelling bee!"

"A what?"

"I'll fetch one," she said eagerly. Now she was in her helpful guise, and this was especially hard to resist, since he did need help. "They are attracted by letter plants. Let me get one from my collection." She was off in a swirl of sweet scent; it seemed she had started wearing perfume.

Dor, by dint of phenomenal effort, squeezed out another sentence. "Everyone in Xanth has his one magic talent; no two are the same," he said as he wrote. Thirteen more words. What a deadly chore!

"That's not true," the table said. "My talent is talking. Lots of things talk."

"You're not a person, you're a thing," Dor informed it brusquely. "Talking isn't your talent, it's mine. I make inanimate things talk."

"Awww . . ." the table said sullenly.

Irene breezed back in with a seed from her collection and an earth-filled flowerpot. "Here it is." In a moment she had the seed planted—it was in the shape of the letter L—and had given it the magic command: "Grow." It sprouted and grew at a rate nature could not duplicate. For that was her talent—the green thumb. She could grow a giant acorn tree from a tiny seed in minutes, when she concentrated, or cause an existing plant to swell into monstrous proportions. Because she could not transform a plant into a totally different creature, as could her father, or give animation to lifeless things, as Dor and the Zombie Master could, she was deemed to be less than a Sorceress, and this had been her lifelong annoyance. But what she could do, she could do well, and that was to grow plants.

The letter plant sent its main stalk up the breadth of a hand. Then it branched and flowered, each blossom in the form of a letter of the alphabet, all the letters haphazardly represented. The flowers emitted a faint, odd odor a bit like ink and a bit like musty old tomes.

Sure enough, a big bee in a checkered furry jacket arrived to service the plant. It buzzed from letter to letter, harvesting each and tucking it into little baskets on its six legs. In a few minutes it had collected them all and was ready to fly away.

But Irene had closed the door and all the windows. "That was my letter plant," she informed the bee. "You'll have to pay for those letters."

"BBBBBB," the bee buzzed angrily, but acceded. It knew the rules. Soon she had it spelling for Dor. All he had to do was say a word, and the bee would lay down its flower-letters to spell it out. There was nothing a spelling bee couldn't spell.

"All right, I've done my good deed for the day," Irene said. "I'm going out and swim with Zilch. Don't let the bee out until you've finished your essay, and don't tell my mother I stopped bugging you, and check with me when you're done."

"Why should I check with you?" he demanded. "You're not my tutor!"

"Because I have to be able to say I nagged you until you got your stupid homework done, idiot," she said sensibly. "Once you clear with me, we're both safe for the day. Got it straight now, knothead?"

Essentially, she was proffering a deal; she would leave him alone if he didn't turn her in for doing it. It behooved him to acquiesce. "Straight, green-nose," he agreed.

"And watch that bee," she warned as she slipped out the door. "It's got to spell each word right, but it won't tell you if you have the wrong word." The bee zoomed for the aperture, but she closed it quickly behind her.

"All right, spelling bee," Dor said. "I don't enjoy this any more than you do. The faster we get through, the faster we both get out of here."

The bee was not satisfied, but buzzed with resignation. It was accustomed to honoring rules, for there were no rules more finicky and senseless than those for spelling words.

Dor read aloud his first two sentences, pausing after every word to get the spelling. He did not trust the bee, but knew it was incapable of misspelling a word, however much it might wish to, to spite him.

"Some can conjure things," he continued slowly, "and others can make a hole, or illusions, or can soar through the air. But in Mundania no one does magic, so it's very dull. There are not any dragons there. Instead there are bear and horse and a great many other monsters."

He stopped to count the words. All the way up to eighty-two! Only eight more to go—no, more than that; his fingers had run out. Twenty-eight to go. But he had already covered the subject. What now?

Well, maybe some specifics. "Our ruler is King Trent, who has reigned for seventeen years. He transforms people into other creatures." There were another seventeen words, bringing the total to—say, it was ninety-nine words! He must have miscalculated before. One more word and he'd be done!

But what one word would finish it? He couldn't think of one. Finally he made a special effort and squeezed out another whole sentence: "No one gets chased here; we fare in peace." But that was nine more words—eight more than he needed. It really hurt him to waste energy like that!

Sigh. There was no help for it. He would have to use the words, now that he had ground them out. He wrote them down as the bee spelled them, pronouncing each carefully so the bee would get it right. He was sure the bee had little or no sense of continuity; it merely spelled on an individual basis.

In a fit of foolish generosity, he fired off four more valuable words: "My tale is done." That made the essay one hundred and twelve words. Cherie Centaur should give him a top grade for that!

"Okay, spelling bee," he said. "You've done your part. You're free, with your letters." He opened the window and the bee buzzed out with a happy "BBBBBB!"

"Now I need to deliver it to my beloved female tutor, may fleas gnaw her coat," he said to himself. "How can I do that without her catching me for more homework?" For he knew, as all students did, that the basic purpose of instruction was not so much to teach young people good things as to fill up all their time unpleasantly. Adults had the notion that juveniles needed to suffer. Only when they had suffered enough to wipe out most of their naturally joyous spirits and innocence were they staid enough to be considered mature. An adult was essentially a broken-down child.

"Are you asking me?" the floor asked.

Inanimate things seldom had much wit, which was why he hadn't asked any for help in his spelling. "No, I'm just talking to myself."

"Good. Then I don't have to tell you to get a paper wasp."

"I couldn't catch a paper wasp anyway. I'd get stung."

"You wouldn't have to catch it. It's trapped under me. The fool blundered in during the night and can't find the way out; it's dark down there."

This was a positive break. "Tell it I'll take it safely out if it'll deliver one paper for me."

There was a mumble as the floor conversed with the wasp. Then the floor spoke to Dor again. "It's a fair sting, it says."

"Very well. Tell it where there's a crack big enough to let it through to this room."

Soon the wasp appeared. It was large, with a narrow waist and fine reddish-brown color: an attractive female of her species, marred only by shreds of dust on her wings. "WWWWWW?" she buzzed, making the dust fly off so that she was completely pretty again.

Dor gave her the paper and opened the window again. "Take this to the lady centaur Cherie. After that you're on your own."

She perched momentarily on the sill, holding the paper. "WWWWWW?" she asked again.

Dor did not understand wasp language, and his friend Grundy the Golem, who did, was not around. But he had a fair notion what the wasp was thinking of. "No, I wouldn't advise trying to sting Cherie. She can crack her tail about like a whip, and she never misses a fly." Or the seat of someone's pants, he added mentally, when someone was foolish enough to backtalk about an assignment. Dor had learned the hard way.

The wasp carried the paper out the window with a satisfied hum. Dor knew it would deliver; like the spelling bee, it had to be true to its nature. A paper wasp could not mishandle a paper.

Dor went out to report to Irene. He found her on the south side of the castle in a bathing suit, swimming with a contented sea cow and feeding the cow handfuls of sea oats she was magically growing on the bank. Zilch mooed when she saw Dor, alerting Irene.

"Hi, Dor—come in swimming!" Irene called.

"In the moat with the monsters?" he retorted.

"I grew a row of blackjack oaks across it to buttress the wallflowers," she said. "The monsters can't pass."

Dor looked. Sure enough, a moat-monster was pacing the line, staying just clear of the blackjacks. It nudged too close at one point and got tagged by a well-swung blackjack. There was no passing those trees!

Still, Dor decided to stay clear. He didn't trust what Zilch might have done in the water. "I meant the monsters on this side," he said. "I just came to report that the paper is finished and off to the tutor."

"Monsters on this side!" Irene repeated, glancing down at herself. "Sic him, Weedles!"

A tendril reached out of the water and caught his ankle. Another one of her playful plants! "Cut that out!" Dor cried, windmilling as the vine yanked at his leg. It was no good; he lost his balance and fell into the moat with a great splash.

"Ho, ho, ho!" the water laughed. "Guess that doused your fire!" Dor struck at the surface furiously with his fist, but it did no good. Like it or not, he was swimming in all his clothes.

"Hey, I just thought of something," Irene called. "That spelling bee—did you define the words for it?"

"No, of course not," Dor spluttered, trying to scramble out of the water but getting tangled in the tendrils of the plant that had pulled him in. Pride prevented him from asking Irene for help, though one word from her would tame the plant.

She saw the need, however. "Easy, Weedles," she said, and the plant eased off. Then she returned to her subject. "There may be trouble. If you used any homonyms—"

"No, I couldn't have. I never heard of them." Weedles was no longer attacking, but each time Dor tried to swim to the bank, the plant moved to intercept him. He had antagonized Irene by his monsters crack, and she was getting back at him mercilessly. She was like her mother in that respect. Sometimes Dor felt the world would be better off if the entire species of female were abolished.

"Different words that sound the same, dunce!" she said with maidenly arrogance. "Different spellings. The spelling bee isn't that smart; if you don't tell it exactly which word—"

"Different spellings?" he asked, experiencing a premonitory chill.

"Like wood and would," she said, showing off her vocabulary in the annoying way girls had. "Wood-tree, would-could. Or isle and aisle, meaning a bit of land in a lake or a cleared space between objects. No connection between the two except they happen to sound the same. Did you use any of those?"

Dor concentrated on the essay, already half forgotten. "I think I mentioned a bear. You know, the fantastic Mundane monster."

"It'll come out bare-naked!" she exclaimed, laughing. "That bee may not be smart, but it wasn't happy about having to work for its letters. Oh, are you ever in trouble, Dor! Wait'll Cherie Centaur reads that paper!"

"Oh, forget it!" he snapped, disgruntled. How many homonyms had he used?

"Bear, bare!" she cried, swimming close and tugging at his clothing. The material, not intended for water, tore readily, exposing half his chest.

"Bare, bare, bare!" he retorted furiously, hooking two fingers into the top of her suit and ripping it down. This material, too, came apart with surprising ease, showing that her body was fully as developed as suggested by the contours of her clothing. Her mother the Queen often made herself pretty through illusion; Irene needed no such enhancement.

"Eeeeek!" she screamed enthusiastically. "I'll get *you!*" And she ripped more of his clothing off, not stopping at his shirt. Dor retaliated, his anger mitigated by his intrigue with the flashes of her that showed between splashes. In a moment they were both thoroughly bare and laughing. It was as if they had done in anger something they had not dared to do by agreement, but had nevertheless wanted to do.

At this point Cherie Centaur trotted up. She had the forepart of a remarkably full-figured woman, and the rearpart of a beautiful horse. It was said that Mundania was the land of beautiful women and fast horses, or maybe vice versa on the adjectives; Xanth was the land where the two were one. Cherie's brown human hair trailed back to rest against her brown equine coat, with her lovely tail matching. She wore no clothing, as centaurs did not believe in such affectations, and she was old, despite her appearance, of Dor's father's generation. Such things made her far less interesting than Irene. "About this paper, Dor—" Cherie began.

Dor and Irene froze in place, both suddenly conscious of their condition. They were naked, half embraced in the water. Weedles was idly playing with fragments of their clothing. This was definitely not proper behavior, and was bound to be misunderstood.

But Cherie was intent on the paper. She shook her head, so that her hair fell down along her breasts—a mannerism that signaled something serious. "If you can interrupt your sexplay a moment," she said, "I would like to review the spelling in this essay." Centaurs did not really care what human beings did with each other in the water; to them, such interaction was natural. But if Cherie reported it to the Queen—

"Uh, well—" Dor said, wishing he could sink under the water.

"But before I go into detailed analysis, let's obtain another opinion." Cherie held the paper down so Irene could see it.

Irene was fully as embarrassed by her condition as Dor was about his. She exhaled to decrease her buoyancy and lower herself in the water, but in a moment she was gasping and had to breathe again—which caused her to rise once more, especially since her most prominent attributes tended to float anyway. But as her eyes scanned the paper, her mood changed. "Oh, no!" she exclaimed. "What a disaster!" she chortled. "You've outdone yourself this time, Dor!" she tittered. "Oh, this is the worst that ever was!" she cried gleefully.

"What's so funny?" the water asked, and its curiosity was echoed by the rocks, sand, and other inanimate things within range of Dor's talent.

Cherie disapproved of magic in centaurs—she was of the old-fashioned, conservative school that considered magic obscene in the civilized species of Xanth—but appreciated its uses in human beings. "I will read the essay to you, attempting to present the words as they are spelled," she said. She did—and somehow the new meanings came through even though the actual pronunciation of the words had not changed. Dor quailed; it was even worse than he had feared.

THE LAND OF XANTH
buy door

Eye live inn the Land of Xanth, witch is disstinked from Mundania inn that their is magic inn Xanth and nun inn Mundania. Every won inn Xanth has his own magic talent; know to are the same. Sum khan conjure things, and others khan make a whole ore illusions ore khan sore threw the heir. Butt inn Mundania know won does magic, sew its very dull. They're are knot any dragons their. Instead their are bare and hoarse and a grate many other monsters. Hour ruler is King Trent, whoo has rained four seventeen years. He transforms people two other creatures. Know won gets chaste hear; oui fair inn piece. My tail is dun.

By the end of it Irene was in tears from helpless laughter, the sea cow was bellowing bovine mirth, the water, beach, and stones were chortling, the blackjack oaks were zapping each other on the branches, and the moatmonsters were guffawing. Even Cherie Centaur was barely controlling a rebellious smirk. Dor was the only one who was unable to appreciate the excruciatingly funny nature of it; he wished he could tunnel through the bottom of the earth.

"O doesn't that beet awl!" Irene gasped. "Lets go two Mundania and sea a hoarse bare ore whatever!" And the creatures and landscape relapsed into a cacophony of fresh laughter. The stones themselves were squeezing out helpless tears of hilarity.

Cherie controlled her levity enough to form a proper frown. "Now I think you had better report to the King, Dor."

Oh, no! How much trouble could he get into in one afternoon? He'd be lucky if King Trent didn't transform him into a slug and drop him back in the moat. As if flunking his essay wasn't bad enough, getting caught naked with the King's daughter—

Dor wrapped his tatters of clothing about his midsection and scrambled out of the water. He would simply have to go and take his medicine.

He stopped off at home to get quickly into fresh clothing. He hoped his mother would be elsewhere, but she was cleaning house. Fortunately, she was in her nymph state, looking like a lovely doll, though in fact she was in the vicinity of forty. There was no one prettier than Chameleon when she was up, and no one uglier when she was down. But her intelligence varied inversely, so right now she was quite stupid. Thus she lacked the wit to inquire why he was wearing his clothing tied about his middle, sopping wet, while the objects in his path sniggered. But she was sensitive to the water. "Don't drip on the floor, dear," she warned.

"I'll be dry in a moment," he called reassuringly. "I was swimming with Irene."

"That's nice," she said.

Soon he was on his way to the King, who always interviewed him in the library. Dor's heart was beating as he hurried up the stairs. Cherie Centaur must have shown King Trent the paper before she came for Dor; maybe the King didn't know about the disaster in the moat.

King Trent was awaiting him. The King was a solid, graying, handsome man nearing sixty. When he died, Dor would probably assume the crown of Xanth. Somehow he was not eager for the post.

"Hello, Dor," the King said, shaking his hand warmly, as he always did. "You look fresh and clean today."

Because of the episode in the moat. That was one way to take a bath! Was the King teasing him? No, that was not Trent's way. "Yes, sir," Dor said uncomfortably.

"I have serious news for you."

Dor fidgeted. "Yes, sir. I'm sorry."

Trent smiled. "Oh, it has nothing to do with that essay. The truth is, I was none too apt in spelling in my own youth. That sort of thing is mastered in time." His face turned grave, and Dor quailed, knowing it had to be the other thing that perturbed the King.

Dor considered offering an explanation, but realized it would sound too much like an excuse. Kings and potential Kings, he understood, did not excuse themselves; it was bad for the image. So he waited in dreading silence.

"Please, Dor, be at ease," the King said. "This is important."

"It was an accident!" Dor blurted, his guilt overriding his resolve. It was so difficult to be Kingly!

"Are you by chance referring to that fall into the moat?"

Confirmation was as bad as suspicion! "Yes, sir." Dor realized that anything more he said could only put the blame on Irene, and that wouldn't be wise.

"Funniest splash I've seen in years!" King Trent said, smiling gravely. "I saw it all from the embrasure. She pulled you in, of course, and then tore into your clothes. This is ever the way of the distaff."

"You're not angry?"

"Dor, I trust you. You tend to come to grief in minor particulars, but you are generally sound in the major ones. And I have to admit my daughter is a provocative brat at times. But mainly, it is good to get into mischief while you're still young enough to profit from the experience. Once you are King, you are unlikely to have that luxury."

"Then that's not why you summoned me?" Dor asked, relieved.

"If I had the time and privacy, I would be splashing in that moat, too." Then the King's smile faded as he turned to business. "Dor, the Queen and I are making an official trip to Mundania. The excursion is scheduled to last one week. We have to go through a black body of water, up a great river, up to a beleaguered Kingdom in the mountains surrounded by hostile A's, B's, and K's. Normal trade has been largely cut off; they can't get out—or so my scout informs me. They have sent a message of welcome for our offer of trade. But the details remain obscure; I will have to work them out personally. I am the only one in authority here who has had sufficient experience in Mundania to cope. It is a small beginning, a cautious one—but if we establish a limited, viable, continuing trade with a section of Mundania, it will prove well worthwhile, if only for the experience. So we're investing this time now, while there is no crisis in Xanth. You will have to be King in that period of my absence, and rain—ah, reign over Xanth."

This caught Dor completely by surprise. "Me? King?"

"Commencing one week from today. I thought it best to give you warning."

"But I can't be King! I don't know anything about—"

"I would say this is an excellent time to learn, Dor. The Kingdom is at peace, and you are well regarded, and there are two other Magicians available to advise you." He winked solemnly. "The Queen offered to remain here to advise you, but I insisted I wanted the pleasure of her companionship myself. It is essential that you be prepared, in case the duty should come on you suddenly."

Despite his shock at this abrupt onset of responsibility, Dor appreciated the logic. If the Queen remained in Xanth, she would run the whole show and Dor would get no experience. The two remaining Magicians, Humfrey and the Zombie Master, would not interfere at all; neither participated voluntarily in the routine matters of Xanth. So Dor would have a free hand—which was exactly what King Trent wanted.

But the other reference—the duty coming on him suddenly? Was this a suggestion that something was amiss with King Trent? Dor was appalled at the thought. "But it'll be a long time before—I mean—"

"Do not be unduly concerned," King Trent said, comprehending Dor's poorly expressed notion, as he always did. "I am not yet sixty; I daresay you will be thirty before the onus falls on you. I remain in good health. But we must always be ready for the unexpected. Now is there anything you will need to prepare yourself?"

"Uh—" Dor remained numbed. "Can it be secret?"

"Kingship is hardly secret, Dor."

"I mean—does everyone have to know you're gone? From Xanth, I mean. If they thought you were near, that it was just a trial run—"

King Trent frowned. "You do not feel up to it?"

"Yes, sir. I don't."

The King sighed. "Dor, I am disappointed but not surprised. I believe you underestimate yourself, but you are young yet, and it is not my purpose to cause you unnecessary difficulties. We shall announce that the Queen and I are taking a week's vacation—a working vacation—and are allowing you to practice your future craft. I do not believe that is too great a deviation from the truth. We shall be working, and for me a visit to Mundania is a vacation. The Queen has never been there; it will be a novel experience for her. But you will know, privately, that we shall not be available to help you if there is any problem. Only the Council of Elders and the other Magicians will know where I am."

Dor's knees felt weak. "Thank you, sir. I'll try not to mess up."

"Do try that. See that you do not fall into the moat," King Trent said, smiling. "And don't let my daughter boss you around; it ill befits a King." He shook his head. "Hasn't she become a vixen, though? When you pulled her suit down—"

"Uh—" Dor said, blushing. He had hoped they were safely beyond this subject.

"She certainly asked for it! The Queen and I are entirely too lenient with her. I had to threaten to turn Iris into a cactus to keep her from interfering. And I proved correct; you two worked it out satisfactorily to yourselves."

Actually, Cherie Centaur had interrupted the struggle; otherwise there was no guessing where it might have led. For one of the few times in his life, Dor was thankful, in retrospect, for Cherie's intervention. Perhaps the King knew that, too.

"Uh, thanks, I mean, yes, sir," Dor agreed weakly. This was almost too much understanding; the Queen would certainly have dealt with him more harshly than this. Yet he knew the King had not been joking about the cactus; easy-going as he seemed, he tolerated absolutely no insubordination from anyone—which was of course one of his prime qualities of Kingship.

Unfortunately, Dor's own talent was not that forceful. He could not transform those who opposed him. If he gave an order, and someone refused to obey, what would he do? He had no idea.

"At any rate, you will work it out," King Trent said. "I am depending on you to carry through despite whatever hazards my daughter interposes."

"Yes, sir," Dor agreed without enthusiasm. "Do you really have to go?"

"We do have to go, Dor. I feel this can be an excellent opportunity for continuing trade. Mundania has vast and largely unexploited resources that would do us a great deal of good, while we have magic abilities that could help them equivalently. To date, our trade with Mundania has been sporadic, owing to difficulties of communication. We require a reliable, private connection. But we must exercise extreme caution, for we do not want the Mundanes invading Xanth again. So we are deliberately dealing with a small Kingdom, one unlikely to be able to mount such an offensive, should it ever choose to."

Dor could appreciate that. Xanth had a long history of being invaded by waves of Mundanes, until preventive measures had been taken. Actually, there was no firm route from Mundania to Xanth; Mundanian time seemed to be different, so that contacts were haphazard. Any Xanth citizen, in contrast, could go to Mundania merely by stepping beyond the region of magic. If he kept close track of his route, he could theoretically find his way back. That was academic, however; no one wanted to leave Xanth, for he would leave his magic talent behind.

No, Dor had to qualify that thought. His mother Chameleon had once sought to leave Xanth, before she met his father Bink, to eliminate her changes of phase. Also, the Gorgon had spent some years in Mundania, where her face did not turn people to stone. Perhaps there had been others. But that was a strategy of desperation. Xanth was so obviously the best place to be that very few would leave it voluntarily.

"Uh, suppose you get lost, Your Majesty?" Dor asked worriedly.

"You forget, Dor, I have been to Mundania before. I know the route."

"But Mundania changes! You can't go back to where you were!"

"Probably true. Certainly I would not take the Queen to the site of my first marriage." The King was silent a moment, and Dor knew this was a secret side of him he preferred not to discuss. King Trent had had a wife and child in Mundania, but they had died, so he had returned to Xanth and become King. Had his family lived, Trent would never have come back to Xanth. "But I believe I can manage."

Yet Dor was nervous. "Mundania is a dangerous place, with bears and horses and things."

"So your essay advised me. I do not pretend this trip is entirely without risk, Dor, but I believe the potential benefits make the risk worthwhile. I am an excellent swordsman and did have twenty years to perfect survival techniques, based on other things than magic. But I must confess that I do miss Mundania somewhat; perhaps that is the underlying motive for this excursion." The King pondered again, then broached a new aspect. "More tricky is the nature of the interface. You see, when we step through to Mundania, we may find ourselves at any point in its history. Until very recently, we could not select the point; this much has been chance. The Queen believes she has found a way to alleviate this problem. That is one reason I must negotiate a trade agreement personally. I can trust no one else to handle the vagaries of the transition. We may fail to reach our target Kingdom, or may reach it and return empty-handed; in that case I will have no one to blame except myself."

"But if you don't know where you'll arrive in Mundania, how do you know there's an opportunity? I mean, you might land somewhere else entirely."

"As I said, I do have a hint. I believe the time is now propitious to enter Mundania's medieval age, and the Queen has studied the matter and believes she can, as it were, fine-tune our entry to match the particular place-time our scout scouted. This spot should have copious natural resources like wood and cloth that we can work by magic into carvings and clothing they can't match. Perhaps something else will offer. Perhaps nothing. I believe a week will suffice to explore the situation. We can not afford to stand still; we must keep working to improve our situation. Magic is not enough to keep Xanth prosperous; the land also requires alert administration."

"I guess so," Dor agreed. But it seemed to him he would never be able to do the job King Trent was doing. Xanth was indeed doing well now, and the improvement had been steady from the time of Trent's ascension to power.

The Kingdom was well disciplined and well ordered; even the dragons no longer dared to maraud where men had staked their territory. Dor had a morbid fear that at such time as he, Dor, became King, the golden age would deteriorate. "I wish you well in Mundania, sir."

"I know you do, Dor," King Trent said affably. "I ask you to bear in mind this before all else—honesty."

"Honesty?"

"When you are in doubt, honesty is generally the best course. Whatever may happen, you will not have cause for shame if you adhere scrupulously to that."

"I'll remember," Dor said. "Honesty."

"Honesty," King Trent repeated with peculiar emphasis. "That's it."

Chapter 2

King Dor

In an instant, it seemed, the dread day came. Dor found himself huddled on the throne, feeling terribly alone. King Trent and Queen Iris had announced their vacation and disappeared into a cloud. When the cloud dissipated, they were gone; Iris' power of illusion had made them invisible. She had always liked dramatic entrances and exits.

Dor gritted his teeth and got into it. Actually, the business of governing was mostly routine. There was a trained palace staff, quite competent, whose members Dor had always known; they did whatever he asked and answered any questions he had. But they did not make important decisions—and Dor discovered that *every* decision, no matter how minor, seemed vitally important to the people it concerned. So he let the routine handle itself and concentrated on those areas that demanded the decision of the King, hoping his voluminous royal robe would conceal any tremor of his knees.

The first case concerned two peasants who had a difference about a plantation of light bulbs. Each claimed to be entitled to the brightest bulbs of the current crop. Dor questioned their wooden belt buckles and got the straight story, while both peasants stood amazed at this magic. Dor did this deliberately so they could see that he was, indeed, a Magician; they respected that caliber of magic and would be more likely to pay attention to him now.

Peasant A had farmed the field for many years with indifferent success; it belonged to him. Peasant B had been hired to help this season—and the field had brightened into the best crop in years, so that it never saw darkness. To whom, then, did the first choice of bulbs belong?

Dor saw that some diplomacy was called for here. He could of course make an arbitrary decision, but that would surely leave one party unsatisfied. That could lead to future trouble. He didn't want any of his decisions coming back to haunt King Trent in future months. "Peasant B obviously has the special touch that made this crop of bulbs glow so well," he said. "So he should be given his choice of the best, as many as he wants. After all, without him the crop would not be worth much." Peasant B looked pleased. "However, Peasant A does own the field. He can hire whomever he wants next year, so he can get to keep more of his crop." Peasant A nodded grim agreement. "Of course," Dor continued blithely, "Peasant A won't have much of a crop, and Peasant B won't have a job. The bulbs won't grow elsewhere, and won't brighten as well for anyone else, so both peasants will lose. Too bad. It would have been so simple to share the best bulbs equally, taking turns selecting each bulb, sharing the profit of the joint effort, and setting up for an even better future season . . ." Dor shrugged sadly.

The two peasants looked at each other, a notion dawning. Wasn't it, after all, more important to share many future harvests than run off with the best of only one? Maybe they could work this out themselves.

They departed, discussing the prospects with animation. Dor relaxed, his muscles unknotting. Had he done it the right way? He knew he could not make everyone happy in every case, but he did want to come as close as possible.

Dor woke next morning to discover a ghost standing beside the royal bed. It was Doreen, the kitchen maid. There had been half a dozen recognizable ghosts on the premises, each with his or her sad story, but most were close-mouthed about their living pasts. Dor had always liked Doreen because of the coincidence of names—Dor, Doreen—though apart from that they had little in common. Maybe he had been named after her, since she was a friend of Millie the Ghost, who had been his nursemaid during his early years. No one had seen fit to tell him, and the local furniture didn't know. There were many moderate little mysteries like that around this castle; it was part of its atmosphere. At any rate, Doreen was middle-aged and portly and often snappish, not having much to do with the living. Thus it was a surprise to find her here. "What can I do for you, Doreen?" he asked.

"Sir, Your Majesty King Dor," she said diffidently. "We just only merely wondered—I mean, maybe just possibly—since you're the Royal Monarch now, temporarily, for a while—"

Dor smiled. Doreen always found it hard to pinpoint the point. "Out with it, blithe spirit."

"Well, we, you know we haven't really quite seen very much of Millie since she passed on—"

To the ghosts, Millie's return to life was passing on. She had been one of their number for several centuries, and now was mortal again. "You miss her?"

"Yes, certainly, in a way we do, Your Majesty. She used to come see us every day, right after she, you know, but since she got herself in the matrimonial way she hasn't—she—"

Millie had married the Zombie Master and gone to share the castle now possessed by Good Magician Humfrey. It had been the Zombie Master's castle, eight hundred years before. "You'd like to see her again," Dor finished.

"Yes, sir, Your Majesty. You were her friend in life, and now that you're in the way of being the Royal King—"

"She hardly needs the King's approval to visit her old companions." Dor smiled. "Not that such approval would ever be withheld, but even if it were, how could anyone stop a ghost from going anywhere?"

"Oh, sir, *we* can't go anywhere!" Doreen protested. "We are forever bound by the site of our cruel demise, until our, you might say, to put it politely, our onuses are abated."

"Well, if you'd tell me your onuses, maybe I could help," Dor suggested.

It was the first time he had ever seen a ghost blush. "Oh, no, no, n-never!" she stammered.

Evidently he had struck a sensitive area. "Well, Millie can certainly come to see you."

"But she never, she doesn't, she won't seem to come," Doreen wailed. "We have heard, had information, we believe she became a mother—"

"Of twins," Dor agreed. "A boy and a girl. It was bound to happen, considering her talent."

Prudish Doreen let that pass. "So of course, naturally she's busy. But if the King suggested, intimated, asked her to visit—"

Dor smiled. "Millie was my governess for a dozen years. I had a crush on her. She never took orders from me; it was the other way around. Nobody who knows me takes me seriously." As he spoke, Dor feared he had just said something significant and damaging or damning; he would have to think about that in private.

"But now that you're King—" Doreeen said, not debating his point.

Dor smiled again. "Very well. I will invite Millie and her family here for a visit so you can meet the children. I can't guarantee they'll come, but I will extend the invitation."

"Oh, thank you, Your Majesty, sir!" Doreen faded gratefully out.

Dor shook his head. He hadn't realized the ghosts liked children. But of course one of them was a child, Button, so that could account for it. Millie's babies were only three years old, while Button was six—but of course in time the twins would grow to his age, while the ghost would not change. He had been six for six hundred years. Children were children. Dor had not met Millie's twins himself; a visit should be interesting. He wondered whether Millie retained her talent of sex appeal, now that she was happily married. Did any wife keep up with that sort of thing? He feared that by the time he found out, it would be too late.

Later that day, perhaps by no coincidence, Dor was approached by a zombie. The decrepit creatures normally remained comfortably buried in their graveyard near the castle, but any threat to the castle would bring them charging gruesomely forth. This one dropped stinking clods of earth and goo as it walked, and its face was a mass of pus and rot, but somehow it managed to talk. "Yhoor Mhajustee—" it pleaded loathsomely, spitting out a decayed tooth.

Dor had known the zombies well in his day, including zombie animals and a zombie ogre named Egor, so they no longer repulsed him as badly as they might have done. "Yes?" he said politely. The best way to deal with a zombie was to give it what it wanted, since it could not be killed or discouraged. Theoretically, it was possible to dismember one and bury the pieces separately, but that was hardly worth the trouble and still was not guaranteed effective. Besides, zombies were all right, in their place.

"Ohur Massssterr—"

Dor caught on. "You have not seen the Zombie Master in some time. I will ask him to visit here so you can get together and rehash old times. Must be many a graveyard you've patronized with him. I can't promise he'll come—he does like his privacy—but I'll make the effort."

"Thaaanks," the zombie whistled, losing part of its moldy tongue.

"Uh, remember—he has a family now. Two little children. You might find them scooping sand out of graves, playing with stray bones—"

But the zombie didn't seem concerned. The maggots squirmed alertly in its sunken eyes as it turned to depart. Maybe it was fun to have children play with one's bones.

Meanwhile, the daily chores continued. Another case concerned a sea monster invading a river and terrorizing the fish there, which caused a slack harvest. Dor had to travel there and make the ground in the vicinity rumble as if shaken by the passage of a giant. The inanimate objects went to it with a will; they liked conspiring to frighten a monster. And the sea monster, none too smart and not really looking for trouble, decided it was more at home in the deep sea, innocently gobbling down shipwrecked sailors and flashing at voyeuristic Mundane investigators of the supernatural. It made a "You'll be sorry when you don't have C. Monster to kick around any more!" honk and departed.

Again Dor relaxed weakly. This device would not work against a smart monster; he had been lucky. He was highly conscious of the potential for some colossal foulup, and felt it was only a matter of time before it occurred. He knew he didn't have any special talent for governing.

At night he had nightmares, not the usual kind wherein black female Mundane-type horses chased him, but the worse kind wherein he thought he was awake and made some disastrous decision and all Xanth went up in magic flames, was overrun by wiggle-worms, or, worst of all, lost its magic and became like drear Mundania. All somehow his fault. He had heard it said that the head that wore the crown was uneasy. In truth, not only was that crown wearing a blister into his scalp, making him quite uneasy; that head was terrified by the responsibility of governing Xanth.

Another day there was a serious theft in a northern village. Dor had himself conjured there; naturally Castle Roogna had a resident conjurer. The problem village was in central Xanth, near the Incognito territory largely unexplored by man, where dragons remained unchastened, and that made Dor nervous. There were many devastating monsters in Xanth; but as a class, the dragons were the worst because there were many varieties and sizes of them, and their numbers were large. But actually, it turned out to be a pleasant region, with most of the modern magic conveniences like soda-water springs and scented soapstones for laundry. This was fur-harvesting country, and this year there had been a fine harvest from the local stand of evergreen fur trees. The green furs had been seasoning in the sun and curing in the moon and sparkling in the stars, until one morning they were gone without trace.

Dor questioned the platform on which the furs had been piled, and learned that a contingent from another village had sneaked in and stolen them. This was one time his magic talent was superior to that of King Trent—the gathering of information. He then arranged to have the furs conjured back. No action was taken against the other village; those people would know their deed had been discovered, and would probably lie low for some time.

Through all this Irene was a constant nag. She resented Dor's ascension to the throne, though she knew it was temporary, and she kept hoping he would foul up. "My father could have done it better," she muttered darkly when Dor solved a problem and was hardly mollified when he agreed. "You should have punished that thieving village." And Dor wondered whether he had in fact been wishy-washy there, taking the expedient route instead of the proper one. Yet what could he do, except whatever seemed best at the time of decision? The crushing responsibility for error made him painstakingly cautious. Only experience, he suspected, could provide the necessary confidence to make excellent decisions under pressure. And that was exactly what King Trent, in his own experienced wisdom, had arranged for Dor to obtain here.

Dor, to his surprise, did not quite foul up. But the variety of problems he encountered strained his ingenuity, and the foreboding grew that his luck had to turn. He counted the passing days, praying that no serious problem would arise before King Trent returned. Maybe when Dor was Trent's age he'd be competent to run a kingdom full-time; right now it was such nervous business it was driving him to distraction.

Irene, at length perceiving this, flipflopped in girlish fashion and started offering support. "After all," she said consolingly, "it's not forever, even though it seems like it. Only two more days before the danger's over. Then we can all faint with relief." Dor appreciated the support, though he might have preferred a less pointed summation of his inadequacy.

He made it. The day of King Trent's return came, to Dor's immense relief and Irene's mixed gratification and subdued dismay. She wanted her father back, but had expected Dor to make more of a mess of things. Dor had escaped more or less unscratched, which she felt was not quite fair.

Both of them dressed carefully and made sure the Castle Roogna grounds were clean. They were ready to greet the returning royalty in proper style.

The expectant hours passed, but the King and Queen did not appear. Dor quelled his nervousness; of course it took time to travel, especially if a quantity of Mundane trade goods was being moved. Irene joined Dor for a lunch of number noodles and milk shakes; they tried to divert themselves by spelling words with numbers, but the milk kept shaking so violently that nothing held together. That fitted their mood.

"Where *are* they?" Irene demanded as the afternoon wore on. She was really getting worried. Now that she had a genuine concern, so that she wasn't concentrating her energy to embarrass Dor, she manifested as the infernally pretty girl she could be. Even the green tint of her hair was attractive; it did match her eyes, and after all, there was nothing wrong with plants.

"Probably they had stuff to carry, so had to go slow," Dor said, not for the first time. But a qualm was gnawing at him. He cuffed it away, but it kept returning, as was the nature of its kind.

Irene did not argue, but the green was spreading to her face, and that was less pretty.

Evening came, and night, without Trent and Iris's return. Now Irene turned to Dor in genuine apprehension. "Oh, Dor, I'm scared! What's happened to them?"

He could bluff neither her nor himself. He put his arm about her shoulders. "I don't know. I'm scared, too."

She clung to him for a moment, all soft and sweet in her anxiety. Then she drew away and ran to her own apartment. "I don't want you to see me cry," she explained as she disappeared.

Dor was touched. If only she could be like that when things were going well! There was a good deal more to her than mischief and sexual suggestion, if she ever let it show.

He retired and slept uneasily. The real nightmares came this time, not the sleek and rather pretty equines he had sometimes befriended, but huge, nebulous, misshapen creatures with gleaming white eyes and glinting teeth; he had to shake himself violently awake to make them leave. He used the royal chambers, for he was King now—but since his week was over, he felt more than ever like an imposter. He stared morosely at the dark hoofprints on the floor, knowing the mares were waiting only for him to sleep again. He was defenseless; he had geared himself emotionally for relief when the week expired, and now that relief had been negated. If the King and Queen did not return today, what would he do?

They did not return. Dor continued to settle differences and solve problems in the Kingly routine; what else could he do? But a restlessness was growing in the palace, and his own dread intensified as each hour dragged by. Everyone knew King Trent's vacation had been scheduled for one week. Why hadn't he returned?

In the evening Irene approached Dor privately. There was no mischief about her now. She was conservatively garbed in a voluminous green robe, and her hair was in disorder, as if overrun by weeds. Her eyes were preternaturally bright, as if she had been crying more than was good for her and had used vanishing cream to make the signs of it disappear. "Something's happened," she said. "I know it. We must go check on them."

"We can't do that," Dor said miserably.

"Can't? That concept is not in my lexicon." She had grown so used to using fancy words, she now did it even when distracted. Dor hoped he never deteriorated to that extent. "I can do anything I want, except—"

"Except rule Xanth," Dor said. "And find your parents."

"Where are they?" she demanded.

She didn't know, of course. She had not been part of the secret. He saw no way to avoid telling her now, for she was, after all, King Trent's daugher, and the situation had become serious. She did have the right to know. "In Mundania."

"Mundania!" she cried, horrified.

"A trade mission," he explained quickly. "To make a deal so Xanth can benefit. For progress."

"Oh, this is twice as awful as I feared. Oh, woe! Mundania! The awfullest of places! They can't do magic there! They're helpless!"

That was an exaggeration, but she was prone to it when excited. Neither Trent nor Iris was helpless in nonmagical terms. The King was an expert swordsman, and the Queen had a wonderfully devious mind. "Remember, he spent twenty years there, before he was King. He knows his way around."

"But he didn't come back!"

Dor could not refute that. "I don't know what to do," he confessed.

"We'll have to go find them," she said. "Don't tell me no again." And there was such a glint in her bright eyes that Dor dared not defy her.

Actually, it seemed so simple. Anything was better than the present doubt. "All right. But I'll have to tell the Council of Elders." For the Elders were responsible for the Kingdom during the absence of the King. They took

care of routine administrative chores and had to select a new King if anything happened to the old one. They had chosen Trent, back when the prior
monarch, the Storm King, had died. Dor's grandfather Roland was a leading
Elder.

"First thing in the morning," she said, her gaze daring him to demur.

"First thing in the morning," he agreed. She had forced this action upon
him, but he was glad for the decision.

"Shall I stay with you tonight? I saw the hoofprints."

Dor considered. The surest way to banish nightmares was to have compatible company while sleeping. But Irene was too pretty now and too accommodating; if he kissed her this night, she wouldn't bite. That made him
cautious. Once Good Magician Humfrey had suggested to him that it might
be more manly to decline a woman's offer than to accept it; Dor had not
quite understood that suggestion, but now he had a better inkling of its
meaning. "No," he said regretfully. "I fear the nightmares, but I fear you
more."

"Gee," she said, pleased. Then she kissed him without biting and left in
her swirl of perfume.

Dor sat for some time, wishing Irene were that way all the time. No
tantrums, no artful flashes of torso, no pretended misunderstandings, just a
sincere and fairly mature caring. But of course her niceness came only in
phases, always wiped out by other phases.

His decision had one beneficial effect: the nightmares foraged elsewhere
that night, letting him sleep in peace.

"Cover for me," he told Irene in the morning. "I would rather people
didn't know where I am, except for the conjurer."

"Certainly," she agreed. If people knew he was consulting privately with
an Elder, they would know something was wrong.

He went to see his grandfather Roland, who lived in the North Village,
several days' walk beyond the Gap Chasm. Kings of Xanth had once resided
here, before Trent restored Castle Roogna. He marched up the neat walk
and knocked on the humble door.

"Oh, grandfather!" Dor cried the moment the strong old man appeared.
"Something has happened to King Trent, and I must go look for him."

"Impossible," Roland said sternly. "The King may not leave Castle
Roogna for more than a day without appointing another Magician as successor. At the moment there are no other Magicians who would assume the
crown, so you must remain there until Trent returns. That is the law of
Xanth."

"But King Trent and Queen Iris went to Mundania!"

"Mundania!" Roland was as surprised as Irene had been. "No wonder he
did not consult with us! We would never have permitted that."

So there had been method in the manner King Trent had set Dor up for
this practice week. Trent had bypassed the Council of Elders! But that was

not Dor's immediate concern. "I'm not fit to govern, grandfather. I'm too young. I've got to get King Trent back!"

"Absolutely not! I am only one member of the Council, but I know their reaction. You must remain here until Trent returns."

"But then how can I rescue him?"

"From Mundania? You can't. He will have to extricate himself from whatever situation he is in, assuming he lives."

"He lives!" Dor repeated emphatically. He had to believe that! The alternative was unthinkable. "But I don't know how long I can keep governing Xanth. The people know I'm not really King. They think King Trent is nearby, just giving me more practice. They won't obey me much longer."

"Perhaps you should get help," Roland suggested. "I disapprove on principle of deception, but I think it best in this case that the people not know the gravity of the situation. Perhaps it is not grave at all; Trent may return in good order at any time. Meanwhile, the Kingdom need not be governed solely by one young man."

"I could get help, I guess," Dor said uncertainly. "But what about King Trent?"

"He must return by himself—or fail to. None of us can locate him in Mundania, let alone help him. This is the obvious consequence of his neglect in obtaining the prior advice of the Council of Elders. We must simply wait. He is a resourceful man who will surely prevail if that is humanly possible."

With that Dor had to be satisfied. He was King, but he could not go against the Elders. He realized now that this was not merely a matter of law or custom, but of common sense. Any situation in Mundania that was too much for King Trent to handle would be several times too much for Dor.

Irene was more positive than he had expected, when he gave her the news on his return. "Of course the Elders would say that. They're old and conservative. And right, I guess. We'll just have to make do until my father gets back."

Dor didn't quite trust her change of heart, but knew better than to inquire. "Who can we get to help?" He knew it would be impossible to exclude Irene from any such activity. King Trent was, after all, her father, the one person to whom her loyalty was unfailing.

"Oh, all the kids. Chet, Smash, Grundy—"

"To run a Kingdom?" he asked dubiously.

"Would you rather leave it to the Elders?"

She had a point. "I hope the situation doesn't last long," he said.

"You certainly don't hope it more than I do!" she agreed, and he knew that was straight from her heart.

Irene went off to locate the people mentioned so that Dor would not arouse suspicion by doing it himself. The first she found was Grundy the Golem. Grundy was older than the others and different in several respects. He had been created as a golem, animated wood and clay and string, and later converted to full-person status. He was only a handspan tall, and spoke all the languages of all living things—which was the useful talent for which he had been created. Grundy could certainly help in solving the routine problems of Xanth. But he tended to speak too often and intemporately. In other words, he was mouthy. That could be trouble.

"Now this is a secret," Dor explained. "King Trent is lost in Mundania, and I must run the Kingdom until he returns."

"Xanth is in trouble!" Grundy exclaimed.

"That's why I need your help. I don't know how much longer I'll have to be King, and I don't want things to get out of control. You generally have good information—"

"I snoop a lot," Grundy agreed. "Very well; I'll snoop for you. First thing I have to tell you is that the whole palace is sniggering about a certain essay someone wrote for a certain female tutor—"

"That news I can dispense with," Dor said.

"Then there's the gossip about how a certain girl went swimming in her birthday suit, which suit seems to have stretched some since her birth, along with—"

"That, too," Dor said, smiling. "I'm sure you comprehend my needs."

"What's in it for me?"

"Your head."

"He's King, all right," the golem muttered. One of the walls chuckled.

Irene brought in Chet. He was a centaur a little older than Dor, but he seemed younger because centaurs matured more slowly. He was Cherie's son, which meant he was highly educated but very cautious about showing any magic talent. For a long time centaurs had believed they lacked magical talents, because most creatures of Xanth either *had* magic or *were* magic. Modern information had dissipated such superstitions. Chet did have a magic talent; he could make large things small. It was a perfectly decent ability, and many people had fine miniatures he had reduced for them, but it had one drawback; he could not reverse the process. His father was Chester Centaur, which meant Chet tended to be ornery when challenged, and was unhandsome in his human portion. When he reached his full stature, which would not be for some years yet, he would be a pretty solid animal. Dor, despite the maledictions he heaped on the race of centaurs while sweating over one of Cherie's assignments, did like Chet, and had always gotten along with him.

Dor explained the situation. "Certainly I will help," Chet said. He always spoke in an educated manner, partly because he was unconscionably smart, but mostly because his mother insisted. Technically, Cherie was Chet's dam, but Dor refrained from using that term for fear Cherie would perceive the "n" he mentally added to it. Dor had sympathy for Chet; it was probably almost as hard being Cherie's son as it was trying to be King. Chet would not dare misspell any words. "But I am uncertain how I might assist."

"I've just barely figured out decent answers to the problems I've already dealt with," Dor said earnestly. "I'm bound to foul up before long. I need good advice."

"Then you should apply to my mother. Her advice is irrefutable."

"I know. That's *too* authoritative."

Chet smiled. "I suspect I understand." That was as close as he would come to criticizing his dam.

Later in the day Irene managed to bring in Smash. He was the offspring of Crunch the Ogre, and also not yet at full growth—but he was already about twice Dor's mass and strong in proportion. Like all ogres, he was ugly and not smart; his smile would spook a gargoyle, and he could barely pronounce most words, let alone spell them. That quality endeared him to Dor. But the ogre's association with human beings had made him more intelligible and sociable than others of his kind, and he was loyal to his friends. Dor had been his friend for years.

Dor approached this meeting diplomatically. "Smash, I need your help."

The gross mouth cracked open like caked mud in a dehydrated pond. "Sure me help! Who me pulp to kelp?"

"No one, yet," Dor said quickly. Again like all ogres, Smash was prone to rhymes and violence. "But if you could sort of stay within call, in case someone tries to pulp *me*—"

"Pulp me? Who he?"

Dor realized he had presented too convoluted a thought. "When I yell, you come help. Okay?"

"Help whelp!" Smash agreed, finally getting it straight.

Dor's choice of helpers proved fortuitous. Because they were all his peers and friends, they understood his situation better than adults would have and kept his confidences. It was a kind of game—run this Kingdom as if King Trent were merely dallying out of sight, watching them, grading them. It was important not to foul up.

A basilisk wandered into a village, terrorizing the people, because its stare caused them to turn to stone. Dor wasn't sure he could scare it away as he had the sea monster, though it was surely a stupid creature, for basilisks had exceedingly ornery personalities. He couldn't have a boulder conjured to squish it, for King Trent decreed the basilisk to be an endangered species. This was an alien concept the King had brought with him from Mundania— the notion that rare creatures, however horrible, should be protected. Dor did not quite understand this, but he was trying to preserve the Kingdom for Trent's return, so did it Trent's way. He needed some harmless way to persuade the creature to leave human villages alone—and he couldn't even talk its language.

But Grundy the Golem could. Grundy used a helmet and periscope—that was a magic device that bent vision around a corner—to look indirectly at the little monster, and told it about the most baleful she-bask he had ever heard of, who was lurking somewhere in the Dead Forest southeast of Castle

Roogna. Since the one Grundy addressed happened to be a cockatrice, the notion of such a henatrice appealed to it. It was no lie; there was a palace guard named Crombie who had the ability to point to things and he had pointed toward that forest when asked where the most baleful female basilisk resided. Of course, sex was mostly illusion among basilisks, since each was generated from the egg of a rooster laid in a dungheap under the Dog Star and hatched by a toad. That was why this was an endangered species, since very few roosters laid eggs in dungheaps under the Dog Star—they tended to get confused and do it under the Cat Star—and most toads had little patience with the seven years it normally required to hatch the egg. But like human beings, the basilisks pursued such illusions avidly. So this cock-bask took off in all haste—i.e., a fast snail's pace—for the Dead Forest, where the lonesome hen basked, and the problem had been solved.

Then there was an altercation in the Barracks—the village set up by the old soldiers of Trent's erstwhile Mundane army, dismantled when he came to power. Each had a farmstead, and many had Mundane wives imported to balance the sexual ratio. They could not do magic, but their children had talents, just like the real citizens of Xanth. The old soldiers entertained themselves by setting up a war-games spectacular, using wooden swords and engaging in complex maneuvers. King Trent allowed this sort of exercise, so long as no one was hurt; soldiers unable to stifle their murderous propensities were issued genuine bayonets from bayonet plants cultured for the purpose and were assigned to dragon-hunting duty. They went after those dragons who insisted on raiding human settlements. This tended to eliminate some of the dragons and most of the violent soldiers. It all worked out. But this time there was a difference of opinion concerning a score made by the Red team on the Green team.

The Reds had set up a catapult and fired off a puffball that puffed into lovely smoke at the apex of its flight. In the games, soldiers were not permitted to hurl actual rocks or other dangerous things at each other, to their frustration. The Reds claimed a direct score on the Greens' headquarters tent, wiping out the Green Bean and his Floozie of the Day. The Greens insisted that the Reds' aim had been off, so that they had not, after all, puffed Bean and Floozie. Since the Floozie was the brains of the outfit, this was a significant distinction. The Reds countered that they had surveyed in the positions of their catapult and the target tent, allowed for windage, humidity, air pressure, and stray magic, double-checked the azimuth, elevation, and charge with their Red Pepper and his Doll of the Day, and fired off the mock-shot in excellent faith. The victory should be theirs.

Dor had no idea how to verify the accuracy of the shot. But Chet Centaur did. Lower, middle, and higher math had been pounded into his skull by the flick of a horsewhip at his tail. He reviewed all the figures of the survey, including the Floozie and Doll figures, spoke with the military experts about corrected azimuths and trigonometric functions—which made Dor nervous; it wasn't nice to talk dirty in public—and concluded that the shot had been off-target by seven point three lengths of the Red Pepper's left foot. Presented with formal protests, he engaged in a brief debate in which obscure mathematical spells radiated like little whirlpools and nebulae from his head to clash with those of the Reds. A purple tangent spun into a yellow vector, breaking it in two; an orange cosine ground up a dangling cube root. The Red surveyors, impressed by Chet's competence, conceded the point. However, since the target tent had been twelve Pepper-foots in diameter, it was recognized that the probability of a glancing strike was high, even with due margin for error. The Greens were adjudged to have lost the services of the Floozie, and therefore to be at a serious disadvantage in the engagement. The maneuvers resumed, and Chet returned to Castle Roogna, problem solved.

Then a huge old rock-maple tree fell across one of the magic paths leading to Castle Roogna. This was a well-traveled path, and it was not safe to leave it, for beyond its protection the nickelpedes lurked. No one would risk setting foot into a nickelpede nest, for the vicious little creatures, five times the size and ferocity of centipedes, would instantly gouge out nickels of flesh. The tree had to be cleared—but the rock was far too heavy for any ordinary person to move.

Smash the Ogre took a hammer, marched down the path, and blasted away at the fallen trunk. He was as yet a child ogre, not more than half again as tall as Dor, so possessed of only a fraction of his eventual strength, but an ogre was an ogre at any age. The hammer clanged resoundingly, the welkin rang, the stone cracked asunder, dust flew up in clouds that formed a small dust storm wherein dust devils played, and fragments of maple shot out like shrapnel. Soon the little ogre had hewn a path-sized section through the trunk, so that people could pass again. The job had been simple enough for him, though as an adult, he would not have needed the hammer. He would merely have picked up the whole trunk and heaved it far away.

So it went. Another week passed—and still King Trent and Queen Iris did not return. Irene's nervousness was contagious. "You've got to *do* something, Dor!" she screamed, and several ornamental plants in the vicinity swelled up and burst, responding to her frustration.

"The Elders won't let me go after him," he said, as nervous as she.

"You do something right now, Dor, or I'll make your life completely miserable!"

Dor quailed anew. This was no empty bluff. She could make him miserable on her good days; how bad would it be when she really tried? "I'll consult with Crombie," he said.

"What good will that do?" she demanded. "My father is in Mundania; Crombie can't point out his location beyond the realm of magic."

"I have a feeble notion," Dor said.

When Crombie arrived, Dor put it to him: how about pointing out something that would help them locate King Trent? Crombie could point to anything, even an idea; if there were some device or some person with special information—

Crombie closed his eyes, spun about, flung out one arm, and pointed south.

Dor was almost afraid to believe it. "There really is something that will help?"

"I never point wrong," Crombie said with certainty. He was a stout, graying soldier of the old school, who had a wife named Jewel who lived in the nether caves of Xanth, and a daughter named Tandy of whom no one knew anything. Jewel had been a nymph of the rock; it was her job to salt the earth with all the diamonds, emeralds, sapphires, rubies, opals, spinels, and other gemstones that prospectors were destined eventually to find. She was said to be a lovely, sweet, and tolerant woman now, satisfied to see Crombie on those irregular occasions when he got around to visiting her. Dor understood that Jewel had once loved his father Bink, or vice versa— that had never been made quite clear—but that Crombie had captured her heart with a wish-spell. Love had transformed her from nymph to woman; that process, too, was not quite within Dor's comprehension. What was the distinction between a nymph and a girl like Irene? "Sometimes people interpret it wrong, but the point is always right," Crombie finished.

"Uh, do you have any idea how far it is?"

"Can't really tell, but pretty far, I think. I could triangulate for you, maybe." He went to another room of the castle and tried again. The point remained due south. "Too far to get a proper fix. Down beyond Lake Ogre-Chobee, I'd say."

Dor knew about that lake; it had been part of the geography Cherie Centaur had drilled into him. A tribe of fiends lived beneath it, who hurled curses at anyone who bothered them; they had driven off most of the ogres who had once resided on its shores. A number of those displaced ogres had migrated north, settling in the Ogre-fen-Ogre Fen; woe betide the curse-fiend who tried to follow them there! He didn't want to go to that lake; anything that could drive away a tribe of ogres was certainly too much for him to handle.

"But you're sure it will help us?" Dor asked nervously. "Not curse us?"

"You hard of hearing, Your Majesty? I said so before." Crombie was a friend of Dor's father and of King Trent; he did not put up with much nonsense from youngsters who had not even existed when he was sowing his wild oats. All he sowed now were tame oats; Jewel saw to that.

"*How* will it help us?" Irene asked.

"How should I know?" Crombie demanded. He was also a woman hater; this was another aspect of his personality whose consistency eluded Dor. How could a tamely married man hate women? Evidently Irene had changed, in Crombie's eyes, from child to woman; indeed, there was something in the way the old soldier looked at her now that made Irene tend to fade back. She played little games of suggestion with a harmless person like

Dor, but lost her nerve when confronted by a real man, albeit an old one like Crombie. "I don't define policy; I only point the way."

"Yes, of course, and we do appreciate it," Dor said diplomatically. "Uh, while you're here—would you point out the direction of any special thing I should be taking care of while I'm King?"

"Why not?" Crombie whirled again—and pointed south again.

"Ha!" Dor exclaimed. "I hoped that would be the case. I'm supposed to go find whatever it is that will help us locate King Trent."

Irene's eyes lighted. "Sometimes you border on genius!" she breathed, gratified at this chance to search for her parents.

"Of course I do," Crombie agreed, though the remark had not been directed at him. He marched off on his rounds, guarding the castle.

Dor promptly visited Elder Roland again, this time having Irene conjured along with him. She had never before been to the North Village, and found it quaint. "What's that funny-looking tree in the center court?" she inquired.

"That's Justin Tree," Dor replied, surprised she didn't know about it. "Your father transformed him to that form from a man, about forty years ago, before he went to Mundania the first time."

She was taken aback. "Why didn't he transform him back, once he was King?"

"Justin likes being a tree," Dor explained. "He has become a sort of symbol to the North Village. People bring him fresh water and dirt and fertilizer when he wants them, and couples embrace in his shade."

"Oh, let's try that!" she said.

Was she serious? Dor decided not to risk it. "We're here on business, rescuing your father. We don't want to delay."

"Of course," she agreed instantly. They hurried on to Roland's house, where Dor's grandmother Bianca let them in, surprised at Dor's return.

"Grandfather," Dor said when Roland appeared. "I have to make a trip south, according to Crombie. He points out a duty I have there, way down beyond Lake Ogre-Chobee. So the Elders can't say no to that, can they?"

Roland frowned. "We can try, Your Majesty." He glanced at Irene. "Would this relate to the absence of Magician Trent?"

"*King* Trent!" Irene snapped.

Roland smiled indulgently. "We Elders are just as concerned about this matter as you are," he said. He spoke firmly and softly; no one would know from his demeanor that he had the magic power to freeze any person in his tracks. "We are eager to ascertain Trent's present state. But we can not allow our present King—that's you, Dor—to risk himself foolishly. I'm afraid a long trip, particularly to the vicinity of Ogre-Chobee, is out of the question at this time."

"But it's a matter I'm supposed to attend to!" Dor protested. "And it's not exactly the lake; it's south of it. So I don't have to go near the fiends. If a King doesn't do what he's supposed to do, he's not fit to be King!"

"One could wish King Trent had kept that more firmly in mind," Roland said, and Irene flushed. "Yet at times there are conflicts of duty. Part of the art of governing is the choosing of the best route through seeming conflicts. You have done well so far, Dor; I think you'll be a good King. You must not act irresponsibly now."

"King Trent said much the same," Dor said, remembering. "Just before he left, he told me that when I was in doubt, to concentrate on honesty."

"That is certainly true. How strange that he did not do the honest thing himself, and consult with the Elders before he departed."

That was bothering Dor increasingly, and he could see that Irene was fit to explode. She hated denigration of her father—yet Roland's pique seemed justified. Had King Trent had some deeper motive than mere trade with Mundania? Had he, incredibly, actually planned not to return? "I'd like just to go to bed and hide my head under the blanket," Dor said.

"That is no longer a luxury you can afford. I think the nightmares would seek you out."

"They already have," Dor agreed ruefully. "The castle maids are complaining about the hoofprints in the rugs."

"I would like to verify your findings, if I may," Roland said.

There was a break while Dor arranged to have Crombie conjured to the North Village. Grandmother Bianca served pinwheel cookies she had harvested from her pinwheel bush. Irene begged a pinwheel seed from her; Irene had a collection of seeds she could grow into useful plants.

"My, how you've grown!" Bianca said, observing Irene.

Irene dropped her cookie—but then had it back unbroken. Bianca's magic talent was the replay; she could make time drop back a few seconds, so that some recent error could be harmlessly corrected. "Thank you," Irene murmured, recovering.

Crombie arrived. "I would like to verify your findings, if I may," Roland repeated to the soldier. Dor noted how the old man was polite to everyone; somehow that made Roland seem magnified in the eyes of others. "Will you point out to me, please, the greatest present threat to the Kingdom of Xanth?"

Crombie obligingly went through his act again—and pointed south again. "That is what I suspected," Roland said. "It seems something is developing in that region that you do indeed have to attend to, Dor. But this is a serious matter, no pleasure excursion."

"What can I do?" Dor asked plaintively. The horror of King Trent's unexplained absence was closing in on him, threatening to overwhelm his tenuous equilibrium.

"You can get some good advice."

Dor considered. "You mean Good Magician Humfrey?"

"I do. He can tell you which course is best, and if you must make this trip, he can serve in your stead as King."

"I don't think he'll agree to that," Dor said.

"I'm sure he won't," Irene agreed.

"There must be a Magician on the throne of Xanth. Ask Humfrey to arrange it, should he approve your excursion."

That was putting the Good Magician on the spot! "I will." Dor looked around, trying to organize himself. "I'd better get started. It's a long walk."

"You're the King, Dor. You don't have to walk there any more than you had to walk here. Have yourself conjured there."

"Oh. Yes. I forgot." Dor felt quite foolish.

"But first get the rest of us safely back to Castle Roogna," Irene told him, nibbling on another cookie. "I don't want to have to cross over the Gap Chasm on the invisible bridge and have the Gap Dragon looking up my skirt." She held the cookie up by the pin while she chewed around the wheel, delicately.

Chapter 3

𝕮𝖊𝖉𝖉𝖎𝖓𝖌 𝕾𝖕𝖊𝖑𝖑

Dor did not arrive inside Magician Humfrey's castle. He found himself standing just outside the moat. Something had gone wrong!

No, he realized. He had been conjured correctly—but the Good Magician, who didn't like intrusions, had placed a barrier-spell in the way, to divert anyone to this place outside. Humfrey didn't like to talk to anyone who didn't get into the castle the hard way. Of course he wasn't supposed to make the King run the gauntlet—but obviously the old wizard was not paying attention at the moment. Dor should have called him on a magic mirror; he hadn't thought of it, in his eagerness to get going. Which meant he deserved what he had gotten—the consequence of his own lack of planning.

Of course, he could probably yell loud enough to attract the attention of someone inside the castle so he could get admitted without trouble. But Dor had a slightly ornery streak. He had made a mistake; he wanted to work his way out of it himself. Rather, into it. He had forced his way into this castle once, four years ago; he should be able to do it now. That would prove he could recover his own fumbles—the way a King should.

He took a good look at the castle environs. The moat was not clear and sparkling as it had been the last time he was here; it was dull and noisome. The shape of the castle wall was now curved and slanted back, like a steep conical mountain. It was supremely unimpressive—and therefore suspect.

Dor squatted and dipped a finger in the water. It came up festooned with slime. He sniffed it. Ugh! Yet there was a certain familiarity about it he could not quite place. Where had he smelled that smell before?

One thing was certain: he was not about to wade or swim through that water without first ascertaining exactly what lurked in it. Magician Humfrey's castle defenses were intended to balk and discourage, rather than to destroy—but they were always formidable enough. Generally it took courage and ingenuity to navigate the several hazards. There would be something in the moat a good deal more unpleasant than slime.

Nothing showed. The dingy green gook covered the whole surface, unbroken by any other horror. Dor was not encouraged.

"Water, are there any living creatures lurking in your depths?" he inquired.

"None at all," the water replied, its voice slurred by the goop. Yet there was a tittery overtone; it seemed to find something funny in the question.

"Any inanimate traps?"

"None." Now little ripples of mirth tripped across the glutinous surface.

"What's so funny?" Dor demanded.

The water made little elongated splashes, like dribbles of spoiled mucus. "You'll find out."

The trouble with the inanimate was that it had very shallow notions of humor and responsibility. But it could usually be coaxed or cowed. Dor picked up a rock and hefted it menacingly. "Tell me what you know," he said to the water, "or I'll strike you with this stone."

"Don't do that!" the water cried, cowed. "I'll squeal! I'll spill everything I know, which isn't much."

"Ugh!" the rock said at the same time. "Don't throw me in that feculent sludge!"

Dor remembered how he had played the Magician's own defenses against each other, last time. There had been a warning sign, TRESPASSERS WILL BE PERSECUTED—and sure enough, when he trespassed he had been presented with a button with the word TRESPASSER on one side, and PERSECUTED on the other. The living-history tome that had recorded the episode had suffered a typo, rendering PERSECUTED into PROSECUTED for the sign, but not for the button, spoiling the effect of these quite different words. These things happened; few people seemed to know the distinction, and Dor's spelling had not been good enough to correct it. But this time there was no sign. He had to generate his own persecution. "Get on with it," he told the water, still holding the rock.

"It's a zombie," the water said. "A zombie sea serpent."

Now Dor understood. Zombies were dead, so it was true there were no living creatures in the moat. But zombies were animate, so there were no inanimate traps either. It made sudden sense—for Dor remembered belatedly that the Zombie Master was still here. When the Zombie Master appeared in the present Xanth, there had been a problem, since Good Magician Humfrey now occupied the castle the Zombie Master had used eight hundred years ago. The one had the claim of prior tenancy, the other the claim of present possession. Neither wanted trouble. So the two Magicians had agreed to share the premises until something better was offered. Evidently the Zombie Master had found nothing better. Naturally he helped out with the castle defenses; he was not any more sociable than Humfrey was.

As it happened, Dor had had experience with zombies. Some of his best friends had been zombies. He still was not too keen on the way they smelled, or on the way they dropped clods of dank glop and maggots wherever they went, but they were not bad creatures in their place. More important, they were hardly smarter than the inanimate objects Dor's magic animated, because their brains were literally rotten. He was confident he could fool a zombie.

"There should be a boat around here," he said to the rock. "Where is it?"

"Over there, chump," the rock said. "Now will you let me go?"

Dor saw the boat. Satisfied, he let the rock go. It dropped with a satisfied thunk to the ground and remained there in blissful repose. Rocks were basically lazy; they hardly ever did anything on their own.

He went to the boat. It was a dingy canoe with a battered double paddle—exactly what he needed. Dor walked away.

"Hey, aren't you going to use me?" the canoe demanded. Objects weren't supposed to talk unless Dor willed it, but they tended to get sloppy about the rules.

"No. I'm going to fetch my friend the zombie."

"Oh, sure. We see lots of that kind here. They make good fertilizer."

When Dor was out of sight of the castle, he stopped and stooped to grub in the dirt. He smeared dirt on his face and arms and over his royal robes. Naturally he should have changed to more suitable clothing for this trip, but of course that was part of his overall carelessness. He had not planned ahead at all.

Next, he found a sharp stone and used it to rip into the cloth of the robe. "Ooooh, ouch!" the robe groaned. "What did I ever do to *you* that you should slay me thus?" But the sharp stone only chuckled. It liked ripping off clothing.

Before long, Dor was a tattered figure of a man. He scooped several double handfuls of dirt into a fold of his robe and walked back to the castle. As he approached the moat, he shuffled in the manner of a zombie and dropped small clods to the ground.

He got into the canoe. "Oooooh," he groaned soulfully. "I hope I can make it home before I go all to pieces." And he used the paddle to push off into the scum of the moat. He was deliberately clumsy, though in truth he was not well experienced with canoes and would have been awkward anyway. The water slurped and sucked as the paddle dipped into the ooze.

Now there was a stirring as the zombie sea monster moved. The slime parted and the huge, mottled, decaying head lifted clear of the viscous surface. Globules of slush dangled and dripped, plopping sickly into the water. The huge, sloppy mouth peeled open, revealing scores of loose brownish teeth set in a jaw almost stripped of flesh.

"Hi, friend!" Dor called windily. "Can you direct me to my Master?" As he spoke he slipped forth a moist clod of dirt, so that it looked as if his lip were falling off.

The monster hesitated. Its grotesque head swung close to inspect Dor. Its left eyeball came loose, dangling by a gleaming string. "Sooo?" the zombie inquired, its breath redolent of spoiled Limberger.

Dor waved his arms, losing some more earth. One choice clod struck the monster on the nose with a dank squish. He was sorry he hadn't been able to find anything really putrid, like a maggoty rat corpse, but that was the luck of the game. "Whe-eere?" he demanded, every bit as stupid as a zombie. The big advantage to playing stupid was that it didn't take much intelligence. He knocked at his right ear and let fall another clod, as if a piece of his brain had been dislodged.

At last the serpent caught on. "Theeere," it breathed, spraying out several loose fragments of teeth and bone with the effort. Its snout seemed to be afflicted with advanced gangrene, and the remaining teeth were crumbling around their caries.

"Thaaanks," Dor replied, dropping another clod into the water. He took up the paddle again and scraped on toward the castle. "Hope I don't fall apart before I get there."

He had won the first round. The sea serpent was in poor condition, as most zombies were, but could have capsized the boat and drowned Dor in slime without difficulty. Had its brain been a better grade of pudding, it might have done just that. But zombies did not attack their own kind; that was too messy. Even the completeness of Dor's own body, conspicuously healthy under the tatters and dirt, did not count too much against him; fresh zombies were complete. It took time for most of the flesh to fall off.

He docked at the inner edge of the moat, where the castle wall emerged at its steep angle. Now Dor splashed a hole in the slime and cleared a section of halfway clean water he could wash in. His zombie ploy was over; he didn't want to enter the castle in this condition. The rents in his robe could not be repaired, but at least he would look human.

He got out of the canoe, but found it hard to stand on the sloping wall.

The surface was not brick or stone, as he had supposed, but glass—solid, translucent, seamless, cold hard glass. A mountain of glass.

Glass. Now he grasped the nature of the second challenge. The slope became steeper near the top, until the wall was almost vertical. How could he scale that?

Dor tried. He placed each foot carefully and found that he could stand and walk, slowly. He had to remain straight upright, for the moment he leaned into the mountain, as was his natural inclination, his feet began to skid. He could quickly get dumped into the awful moat if he let his feet slide out from under him. Fortunately, there was no wind; he could stand erect and step slowly up.

He noticed, however, a small cloud in the sky. As he watched, it seemed to extend rapidly. Oops—that surely meant rain, which would wash him out. That was surely no coincidence; probably the touch of his foot on the glass had summoned the storm. He had to hike to the top of the mountain before the cloud arrived. Well, the distance was not far. With care and good foot-friction, he could probably make it.

Then something came galloping around the mountain. It had four legs, a tail, and a funny horned head. But its chief oddity—

It was heading right for Dor, those horns lowered. The creature was no taller than he, and the horns were small and blunt, but the body was far more massive. Dor had to jump to get out of its way—and lost his footing and slid down to the brink of the water before stopping, his nose barely clear of the slime.

He stabilized himself while the zombie sea serpent watched with a certain aloof amusement. Dor wiped a dangle of goo from his nose. "What was that?"

"The Sidehill Hoofer," the glass responded.

"Something funny about that creature. The legs—"

"Oh, sure," the glass said. "The two left legs are shorter than the two rights. That's so she can charge around the mountain in comfort. It's natural selection; lots of the better mountains have them."

Shorter left legs—so the Hoofer could stay level while running on a slope. It did make a certain kind of sense. "How come I never heard of this creature before?" Dor demanded.

"Probably because your education has been neglected."

"I was tutored by a centaur!" Dor said defensively.

"The centaur surely told you of the Sidehill Hoofer," the glass agreed. "But did you listen? Education is only as good as the mind of the student."

"What are you implying?" Dor demanded.

"I rather thought you were too dense to grasp the implication," the glass said with smug condescension.

"You're a mountain of glass!" Dor said irately. "How bright can you be?"

"Thought you'd never ask. I'm the brightest thing on the horizon." And a beam of sunlight slanted down, avoiding the looming cloud, causing the mountain to glow brilliantly.

Dor had walked into that one! With the lifetime experience he had had, he still fell into the trap of arguing with the inanimate. He changed the subject. "Is the Hoofer dangerous?"

"Not if you have the wit to stay out of her way."

"I've got to climb to the top of this slope."

"Extraordinary fortune," the glass said brightly.

"What?"

The glass sighed. "I keep forgetting that animate creatures can not match my brilliance. Recognizing your handicap, I shall translate: Lots of luck."

"Oh, thank you," Dor said sarcastically.

"That's irony," the glass said.

"Irony—not glassy?"

"Spare me your feeble efforts at repartee. If you do not get moving before that cloud arrives, you will be washed right into the sea."

"That's an exaggeration," Dor grumped, starting back up the slope.

"That is hyperbole." The glass began humming a tinkly little tune.

Dor made better progress than before. He was getting the hang of it. He had to put his feet down flat and softly and will himself not to skid. But the Sidehill Hoofer came charging around the cone again, spooking him with a loud "Moooo!" and Dor slid down the slope again. He was no more partial to this bovine than he had been to Irene's sea cow.

The cloud was definitely closer, and playful little gusts of wind emanated from it. "Oh, get lost!" Dor told it.

"Fat chance!" it blew back, ruffling his hair with an aggravating intimacy.

Dor went up the slope a third time, by dint of incautious effort getting beyond the slight gouge in the mountain worn by the Hoofer's pounding hooves. The glass hummed louder and finally broke into song: "She'll be coming 'round the mountain when she comes."

Sure enough, the Sidehill Hoofer came galumphing around again, spied Dor, and corrected course slightly to charge straight at him. Her uneven legs pounded evenly on the incline, so that her two short horns were dead-level as they bore on him. Blunt those horns might be, but they were formidable enough in this situation.

Oh, no! It was no accident that brought this creature around so inconveniently; she was trying to prevent him from passing. Naturally this was the third barrier to his entry into the castle.

Dor jumped out of the way and slid down to the brink again, disgruntled. The Hoofer thundered by, disappearing around the curve.

Dor wiped another dribble of slime off his nose. He wasn't making much progress! This was annoying, because he had passed his first challenge without difficulty and faced only two comparatively simple and harmless ones— to avoid the Hoofer and scale the slippery slope. Either alone was feasible; together they baffled him. Now he had perhaps ten minutes to accomplish both before the ornery raincloud wiped him out. Already the forward edge of the cloud had cut off the sunbeam.

Dor didn't like leaning on his magic talent too much, but decided that pride was a foolish baggage at this point. He had to get inside the castle any way he could and get Good Magician Humfrey's advice—for the good of Xanth.

"Glass, since you're so bright—tell me how I can get past the Hoofer and up your slope before the cloud strikes."

"Don't tell him!" the cloud thundered.

"Well, I'm not so bright any more, now that I'm in your shadow," the glass demurred. This was true; the sparkle was gone, and the mountain was a somber dark mass, like the quiet depths of an ocean.

"But you remember the answer," Dor said. "Give."

"Take!" the storm blew.

"I've got to tell him," the glass said dolefully. "Though I'd much rather watch him fall on his as—"

"Watch your language!" Dor snapped.

"—inine posterior again and dip his nose in the gunk. But he's a Magician and I'm only silicon." The glass sighed. "Very well. Cogitate and masticate on—"

"What?"

"Give me strength to survive the monumental idiocy of the animate," the glass prayed obnoxiously. The cloud had let a gleam of sunlight through, making it bright again. "Think and chew on this: who can most readily mount the slope?"

"The Sidehill Hoofer," Dor said. "But that's no help. *I'm* the one who—"

"Think and chew," the glass repeated with emphasis.

That reminded Dor of the way King Trent had stressed the importance of honesty, and that annoyed Dor. This mountain was no King! What business did it have making oblique allusions, as if Dor were a dunce who needed special handling? "Look, glass—I asked you a direct question—"

"An indirect question, technically. My response reflects your approach. But surely you realize that I am under interdiction by another Magician."

Dor didn't know what "interdiction" meant, but could guess. Humfrey had told the mountain not to blab the secret. But the cloud was looming close and large and dense with water, and he was impatient. "Hey, I insist that you tell me—"

"That is of course the answer."

Dor paused. This too-bright object was making a fool of him. He reviewed his words. *Hey, I insist that you tell me*—how was that the answer? Yet it seemed it was.

"You'll never get it," the glass said disparagingly.

"Hey, now—" Dor started angrily.

"There you go again."

Hey, now?

Suddenly Dor got it. Hey—spelled H A Y. "Hay—now!" he cried. It was a homonym.

The zombie sea serpent, taking that for an order, swam across the moat and reached out to take a clumsy bite of dry grass from the outer bank. It brought this back to Dor.

"Thank you, serpent," Dor said, accepting the armful. He shook out the residual slime and dottle, and several more of the monster's teeth bounced on the glass. Zombies had an inexhaustible supply of fragments of themselves to drop; it was part of their nature.

He started up the slope yet again, but this time he wanted to meet the Hoofer. He stood there with his hay, facing her.

The creature came 'round the mountain—and paused as she sighted him. Her ears perked forward and her tongue ran over her lips.

"That's right, you beautiful bovine," Dor said. "This hay is for you. Think and chew—to chew on while you think. I noticed that there isn't much forage along your beat. You must use a lot of energy, pounding around, and work up quite an appetite. Surely you could use a lunch break before the rain spoils everything."

The Hoofer's eyes became larger. They were beautiful and soulful. Her square nose quivered as she sniffed in the odor of the fresh hay. Her pink tongue ran around her muzzle again. She was certainly hungry.

"Of course, if I set it down, it'll just slide down the slope and into the moat," Dor said reasonably. "I guess you could fish it out, but slime-coated hay doesn't taste very good, does it?" As he spoke, a stronger gust of wind from the eager storm swirled through, tugging at the hay and wafting a few strands down to the goo of the moat. The Hoofer fidgeted with alarm.

"Tell you what I'll do," Dor said. "I'll just get on your back and carry the hay, and feed it to you while you walk. That way you'll be able to eat it all, without losing a wisp, and no one can accuse you of being derelict in your duty. You'll be covering your beat all the time."

"Mmmooo," the Hoofer agreed, salivating. She might not be bright, but she knew a good deal when she smelled it.

Dor approached, gave her a good mouthful of hay, then scrambled onto her back from the uphill side. His left foot dragged, while his right foot dangled well above the surface of the glass, but he was sitting level. He leaned forward and extended his left hand to present another morsel of hay.

The Hoofer took it and chewed blissfully, walking forward. When she finished masticating that—Dor realized he had learned a new word, though he would never be able to spell it—he gave her more, again left-handedly. She had to turn her head left to take it, and her travel veered slightly that way, uphill.

They continued in this manner for a full circuit of the mountain. Sure enough, they were higher on the slope than they had been. His constant presentation of hay on the upward side caused the Hoofer to spiral upward. That was where he wanted to go.

The storm was almost upon them. *It* had not been fooled! Dor leaned forward, squeezing with his knees, and the Hoofer unconsciously speeded up. The second circuit of the mountain was much faster, because of the accelerated pace and the narrower diameter at this elevation, and the third was faster yet. But Dor's luck, already overextended, was running out. His supply of hay, he saw, would not last until the top—and the rain would catch them anyway.

He made a bold try to turn liabilities into assets. "I'm running out of hay—and the storm is coming," he told the Hoofer. "You'd better set me down before it gets slippery; no sense having my weight burden you."

She hesitated, thinking this through. Dor helped the process. "Anywhere will do. You don't have to take me all the way to the base of the mountain. Maybe there at the top, where I'll be out of your way; it's certainly closer."

That made good cow-sense to her. She trotted in a rapidly tightening spiral to the pinnacle, unbothered by the nearly vertical slope, where Dor stepped off. "Thanks, Hoofer," he said. "You do have pretty eyes." His experience with Irene had impressed upon him the advantage of complimenting females; they all were vain about their appearance.

Pleased, the Hoofer began spiraling down. At that point, the storm struck. The cloud crashed into the pinnacle; the cloud substance tore asunder and water sluiced out of the rent. Rain pelted down, converting the glass surface instantly to something like slick ice. Wind buffeted him, whistling past the needle-pointed apex of the mountain that had wounded the cloud, making dire screams.

Dor's feet slipped out, and he had to fling his arms around the narrow spire to keep from sliding rapidly down. The Hoofer had trouble, too; she braced all four feet—but still skidded grandly downward, until the lessening pitch of the slope enabled her to achieve stability. Then she ducked her head, flipped her tail over her nose, and went to sleep standing. The storm could not really hurt her. She had nowhere to go anyway. She was secure as long as she never tried to face the other way. He knew that when the rain abated, the Sidehill Hoofer would be contentedly chewing her cud.

So Dor had made it to the top, conquering the last of the hurdles. Only— what was he to do now? The mountain peaked smoothly, and there was no entrance. Had he gone through all this to reach the wrong spot? If so, he had outsmarted himself.

The water sluicing from the cloud was cold. His tattered clothing was soaked through, and his fingers were turning numb. Soon he would lose his grip and slide down, probably plunking all the way into the gook of the moat. That was a fate almost worse than freezing!

"There *must* be a way in from here!" he gasped.

"Of course there is, dumbbell," the spire replied. "You're not nearly as sharp as I am! Why else did you scheme your way up here? To wash off your grimy body? I trust I'm not being too pointed."

Why else indeed! He had just assumed this was the correct route, because it was the most difficult one. "Okay, brilliant glass—your mind has more of a cutting edge than mine. Where is it?"

"Now I don't have to tell you that," the glass said, chortling. "Any idiot, even one as dull as you, could figure that out for himself."

"I'm not just any idiot!" Dor cried, the discomfort of the rain and chill giving him a terrible temper.

"You certainly aren't! You're a prize idiot."

"Thank you," Dor said, mollified. Then he realized that he was being as gullible as the average inanimate. Furious, Dor bashed his forehead against the glass—and something clicked. Oops—had he cracked his skull?

No, he had only a mild bruise. Something else had made the noise. He nudged the surface again and got another click.

Oho! He hit the glass a third time—and suddenly the top of the mountain sprang open, a cap whose catch had been released. It hung down one side on stout hinges, and inside was the start of a spiral staircase. Victory at last!

"That's using your head," the glass remarked.

Dor scrambled into the hole. He entered headfirst, then wrestled himself around to get his feet on the steps. Then he hauled the pointed cap of the mountain up and over, at last closing off the blast of the rain. "Curses!" the cloud stormed as he shut it out.

He emerged into Humfrey's crowded study. There were battered leather-bound tomes of spells, magic mirrors, papers, and a general litter of indecipherable artifacts. Amidst it all, almost lost in the shuffle, stood Good Magician Humfrey.

Humfrey was small, almost tiny, and grossly wrinkled. His head and feet were almost as large as those of a goblin, and most of his hair had gone the way of his youth. Dor had no idea how old he was and was afraid to ask; Humfrey was an almost ageless institution. He was the Magician of Information; everything that needed to be known in Xanth, he knew—and he would answer any question for the payment of one year's service by the asker. It was amazing how many people and creatures were not discouraged by that exorbitant fee; it seemed information was the most precious thing there was.

"About time you got here," the little man grumped, not even noticing Dor's condition. "There's a problem in Centaur Isle you'll have to attend to. A new Magician has developed."

This was news indeed! New Magicians appeared in Xanth at the rate of about one per generation; Dor had been the last one born. "Who is he? What talent does he have?"

"He seems to be a centaur."

"A centaur! But most of them don't believe in magic!"

"They're very intelligent," Humfrey agreed.

Since centaurs did have magic talents—those who admitted it—there was no reason why there could not be a centaur Magician, Dor realized. But the complications were horrendous. Only a Magician could govern Xanth; suppose one day there were no human Magician, only a centaur one? Would the human people accept a centaur King? Could a centaur King even govern his own kind? Dor doubted that Cherie Centaur would take orders from any magic-working centaur; she had very strict notions about obscenity, and that was the ultimate. "You didn't tell me his talent."

"I don't know his talent!" Humfrey snapped. "I've been burning the midnight magic and cracking mirrors trying to ascertain it—but there seems to be nothing he does."

"Then how can he be a Magician?"

"That is for you to find out!" Obviously the Good Magician was not at all pleased to admit his inability to ascertain the facts in this case. "We can't have an unidentified Magician-caliber talent running loose; it might be dangerous."

Dangerous? Something connected. "Uh—would Centaur Isle be to the south?"

"Southern tip of Xanth. Where else would it be?"

Dor didn't want to admit that he had neglected that part of his geography. Cherie had made nonhuman history and social studies optional, since Dor was human; therefore he hadn't studied them. He had learned about the ogre migration only because Smash had been curious. His friend Chet lived in a village not far north of the Gap Chasm, in easy galloping range of Castle Roogna via one of the magic bridges. Of course Dor knew that there were other colonies of centaurs; they were scattered around Xanth just as the human settlements were. He just hadn't paid attention to the specific sites. "Crombie the soldier pointed out the greatest threat to Xanth there. Also a job I need to attend to. And a way to get help to rescue King Trent. So it all seems to fit."

"Of course it fits. Everything in Xanth makes sense, for those with the wit to fathom it. You're going to Centaur Isle. Why else did you come here?"

"I thought it was for advice."

"Oh, that. The Elders' face-saving device. Very well. Gather your juvenile friends. You'll be traveling incognito; no conjuring or other royal affectations. You can't roust out this hidden Magician if he knows you're coming. So the trip will take a week or so—"

"A week! The Elders won't let me be away more than a day!"

"Ridiculous! They made no trouble about King Trent going to Mundania for a week, did they?"

"Because they didn't know," Dor said. "He didn't tell them."

"Of course he told them! He consulted with me, and for the sake of necessary privacy I agreed to consult with the Elders and let him know if they raised any objections—and they didn't."

"But my grandfather Roland says he was never told," Dor insisted. "The truth is, he is somewhat annoyed."

"I told him myself. Here, verify it with the mirror." He gestured to a magic mirror on the wall. Its surface was finely crazed; evidently this was one of the ones that had suffered in the course of Humfrey's recent investigation of the centaur Magician.

"When did Magician Humfrey tell Elder Roland about King Trent's trip to Mundania?" Dor asked it carefully. One had to specify things exactly, for mirrors' actual depth was much less than their apparent depth, and they were not smart at all despite their ability to answer questions. "Garbage in, garbage out," King Trent had once remarked cryptically, apparently meaning that a stupid question was likely to get a stupid answer.

The tail of a centaur appeared in the marred surface. Dor knew that meant NO. "It says you didn't," he said.

"Well, maybe I forgot," Humfrey muttered. "I'm too busy to keep up with every trifling detail." And the front of the centaur appeared—a fetching young female.

No wonder there had been no protest from the Elders! Humfrey, distracted by other things, had never gotten around to informing them. King Trent, believing the Magician's silence meant approval from the Elders, had departed as planned. Trent had not intentionally deceived them. That gratified Dor; it had been difficult to think of the King as practicing deliberate deception. Trent had meant his words about honesty.

"I believe the Elders will veto my trip," Dor said. "Especially after—"

"The Elders can go—"

"Humfrey!" a voice called warningly from the doorway. "Don't you dare use such language on this day. You've already cracked one mirror that way!"

So that was how the mirror had suffered! Humfrey had uttered too caustic a word when balked on news of the new Magician.

Dor looked to the voice. It came from the nothingness that was the face of the Gorgon, an absolutely voluptuous, statuesque, shapely, and buxom figure of a lovely woman whose face no one could look at. Humfrey had put a temporary spell on it, ten or fifteen years ago, to protect society from the Gorgon's involuntary magic while he worked out a better way to solve the problem. It seemed he had never gotten around to that solution either. He was known to be a bit absent-minded.

Humfrey's brow wrinkled as if bothered by a pink mosquito. "What's special about this day?"

She seemed to smile. At least, the little serpents that were her hair writhed in a more harmonious manner. "It will come to you in due course, Magician. Now you get into your suit. The good one that you haven't used for the past century or so. Make the moth unball it for you." Her facelessness turned to Dor. "Come with me, Your Majesty."

Perplexed, Dor followed her out of the room. "Uh, am I intruding or something?"

She laughed, sending jiggles through her flesh. Dor squinted, to prevent his eyeballs from popping. "Hardly! You have to perform the ceremony."

Dor's bafflement intensified. "Ceremony?"

She turned and leaned toward him. It embarrassed him to look into her empty head, so he glanced down—and found himself peering through the awesome crevice of her burgeoning cleavage. Dor closed his eyes, blushing.

"The ceremony of marriage," the Gorgon murmured. "Didn't you get the word?"

"I guess not," Dor said. "A lot of words seem to get mislaid around here."

"True, true. But you arrived on schedule anyway, so it's all right. Only the King of Xanth can make it properly binding on that old curmudgeon. It has taken me a good many years to land him, and I mean to have that knot tied chokingly tight."

"But I've never—I know nothing about—" Dor opened his eyes again, and goggled at the mountains and valley of her bosom, and at the empty face, and retreated hastily back into darkness. Too little and too much, in such proximity!

"Do not be alarmed," the Gorgon said. "The sight of me will not petrify you."

That was what she thought. It occurred to him that it was not merely the Gorgon's face that turned a man to stone. Other parts of her could do it to other parts of him. But he forced his eyes open and up, from the fullness to the emptiness, meeting her invisible gaze. "Uh, when does it happen?"

"Not long after the nuptials," she said. "It will be a matter of pride with me to handle it without recourse to any potency spell."

Dor found himself blushing ferociously. "The—I meant the ceremony."

She pinched his cheek gently with her thumb and forefinger. "I know you did, Dor. You are so delightfully pristine. Irene will have quite a time abating your naïveté."

So his future, too, had been mapped out by a woman—and it seemed all other women knew it. No doubt there was a female conspiracy that continued from generation to generation. He could only be thankful that Irene had neither the experience nor the body of the Gorgon. Quite. Yet.

They emerged into what appeared to be a bedroom. "You'll have to change out of those soaking things," the Gorgon said. "Really, you young people should be more careful. Were you playing tag with a bayonet plant? Let me just get these tatters off you—"

"No!" Dor cried, though he was shivering in the wet and ragged robe.

She laughed again, her bosom vibrating. "I understand. You are such a darling boy! I'll send in the Zombie Master. You must be ready in half an hour; it's all scheduled." She turned and swept out, leaving Dor relieved, bemused, and guiltily disappointed. A woman like that could play a man like a musical instrument!

In a moment the gaunt but halfway handsome Zombie Master arrived. He shook hands formally with Dor. "I will never forget what I owe you, Magician," he said.

"You paid off any debt when you made Millie the Ghost happy," Dor said, gratified. He had been instrumental in getting the Zombie Master here, knowing Millie loved him; but Dor himself had profited greatly from the experience. He had, in a very real sense, learned how to be a man. Of course, it seemed that he had forgotten much of that in the ensuing years—the Gorgon had certainly set him in his place!—but he was sure the memory would help him.

"That debt can never be paid," the Zombie Master said gravely.

Dor was not inclined to argue. He was glad he had helped this Magician and Millie to get together. He remembered that he had promised to invite them both to visit Castle Roogna so that the ghosts and zombies could renew acquaintance.

"Uh—" Dor began, trying to figure out how to phrase the invitation.

The Zombie Master produced an elegant suit of clothing tailored to Dor's size, and set about getting him changed and arranged. "Now we must review the ceremony," he said. He brought out a book. "Millie and I will organize most of it; we have been through this foolishness before. You just read this service when I give the signal."

Dor opened the book. The title page advised him that this text contained a sample service for the unification of Age-Old Magicians and Voluptuous Young Maidens. Evidently the Gorgon had crafted this one herself. The service was plain enough; Dor's lines were written in black, the groom's in blue, the bride's in pink.

Do you, Good Magician Humfrey, take this lovely creature to be your bride, to love and cherish as long as you shall live? Well, it did make sense; the chances of him outliving her were remote. But this sort of contract made Dor nervous.

Dor looked up. "It seems simple enough, I guess. Uh, if we have a moment—"

"Oh, we have two or three moments, but not four," the Zombie Master assured him, almost smiling.

Dor broke into a full smile. This Magician had been cadaverously gaunt and sober when Dor had first known him; now he was better fleshed and better tempered. Marriage had evidently been good for him. "I promised the ghosts and zombies of Castle Roogna that your family would visit soon. I know you don't like to mix with ordinary people too much, but if you could see your way clear to—"

The Magician frowned. "I did profess a deep debt to you. I suppose if you insist—"

"Only if you want to go," Dor said quickly. "These creatures—it wouldn't be the same if it wasn't voluntary."

"I will consider. I daresay my wife will have a sentiment."

On cue, Millie appeared. She was as lovely as ever, despite her eight hundred and thirty-odd years of age. She was less voluptuous than the Gorgon, but still did have her talent. Dor became uncomfortable again; he had once had a crush on Millie. "Of course we shall go," Millie said. "We'll be glad to, won't we, Jonathan?"

The Zombie Master could only acquiesce solemnly. The decision had been made.

"It's time," Millie said. "The bride and groom are ready."

"The bride, perhaps," the Zombie Master said wryly. "I suspect I will have to coerce the groom." He turned to Dor. "You go down to the main chamber; the wedding guests are assembling now. They will take their places when you appear."

"Uh, sure," Dor agreed. He took the book and made his way down a winding stair. The castle layout differed from what it had been the last time he was here, but that was only to be expected. The outside defenses changed constantly, so it made sense that the inner schematic followed.

But when he reached the main chamber, Dor stood amazed. It was a grand and somber cathedral, seemingly larger than the whole of the castle, with stately columns and ornate arches supporting the domed glass ceiling. At one end was a dais whose floor appeared to be solid silver. It was surrounded by huge stained-glass windows, evidently another inner aspect of the exterior glass mountain. A jeweled chandelier supported the sun, which was a brilliantly golden ball, borrowed for this occasion. Dor had always wondered what happened to the sun when clouds blocked it off; perhaps now he knew. What would happen if they didn't finish the ceremony before the storm outside abated and the sun needed to be returned?

The guests were even more spectacular. There were hundreds of them, of all types. Some were human, some humanoid, and most were monsters. Dor spied a griffin, a dragon, a small sphinx, several merfolk in a tub of sea water, a manticora, a number of elves, goblins, harpies, and sprites; a score of nickelpedes, a swarm of fruitflies, and a needle cactus. The far door was dwarfed by its guardian—Crunch the Ogre, Smash's father, as horrendous a figure of a monster as anyone cared to imagine.

"What is this?" Dor asked, astonished.

"All the creatures who ever obtained answers from the Good Magician, or interacted significantly with him during the past century," the nearest window explained.

"But—but why?"

A grotesque bespectacled demon detached himself from conversation with a nymph. "Your Majesty, I am Beauregard, of the Nether Contingent. We are assembled here, in peace, not because we necessarily love the Good Magician, but because not one of us would pass up the chance to see him finally get impressed into bondage himself—and to the most fearsome creature known to magic. Come; you must take your place." And the demon guided Dor down the center aisle toward the dais, past as diversified an assortment of creatures as Dor had ever encountered. One he thought he recognized—Grundy the Golem, somehow spirited here for the unique occasion. How had all these creatures gotten past the castle defenses? No one had been around when Dor himself had braved them.

"Oh, you must be King Dor!" someone cried. Dor turned to discover a handsome woman whose gown was bedecked with a fantastic array of gems.

"You must be Jewel!" he exclaimed, as a diamond in her hair almost blinded him. It was the size of his fist, and cut in what seemed like a million facets. "The one with the barrel of gems—Crombie's wife."

"How did you ever guess?" she agreed, flashing sapphires, garnets, and giant opals. "You favor your father, Dor. So good of you to come in his stead."

Dor remembered that this woman had loved his father. Perhaps that explained why Bink wasn't here; a meeting, even after all these years, could be awkward. "Uh, I guess so. Nice to meet you, Jewel."

"I'm sorry my daughter Tandy couldn't meet you," Jewel said. "It would be so nice—" She broke off, and again Dor suspected he understood why. Jewel had loved Bink; Dor was Bink's son; Tandy was Jewel's daughter. It was almost as if Dor and Tandy were related. But how could that be said?

Jewel pressed a stone into his hand. "I was going to give this to Bink, but I think you deserve it. You will always have light."

Dor glanced down at the gift. It shone like a miniature sun, almost too bright to gaze at directly. It was a midnight sunstone, the rarest of all gems. "Uh, thanks," he said lamely. He didn't know how to deal with this sort of thing. He tucked the gem into a pocket and rejoined Beauregard, who was urging him on. As he reached the dais and mounted it, the hubbub diminished. The ceremony was incipient.

The music started, the familiar theme played only at nuptials. It gave Dor stage fright. He had never officiated at an affair like this before; the opportunities for blundering seemed limitless. The assembled creatures became absolutely quiet, waiting expectantly for the dread denouement. The Good Magician Humfrey was finally going to get his!

There was a scuffle to the side. The groom appeared in a dark suit that looked slightly motheaten; perhaps the guardian moth had not balled it properly. He was somewhat disheveled, and obliquely compelled by the Zombie Master. "I survived it; so can you!" the best man whispered, audible throughout the chamber. Somewhere in the Stygian depth of the audience, a monster chuckled. The expression on Humfrey's face suggested that he was in serious doubt about survival. More members of the audience grinned, showing assorted canine teeth; they liked this.

The music got louder. Dor glanced across and saw that the organist was a small tangle tree, its tentacles writhing expertly over the keys. No wonder there was a certain predatory intensity to the music!

The Zombie Master, dourly handsome in his funereal-tailed suit, straightened Humfrey's details, actually brushing him off with a little whisk broom. Then he put Humfrey in a kind of armlock and marched him forward. The music surged vengefully.

One demon in the front row twitched its tail and leaned toward another.

"A creature doesn't know what happiness is," he said, "until he gets married."

"And then it's too late!" half a dozen others responded from the next row back. There was a smattering of applause.

Magician Humfrey quailed, but the best man's grip was as firm as death itself. At least he had not brought his zombies to this ceremony! The presence of the walking dead would have been too much even for such a wedding.

Now the music swelled to sublime urgency, and the bridal procession appeared. First came Millie the Ghost, radiant in her maid-of-honor gown, her sex appeal making the monsters drool. Dor had somehow thought that an unmarried person was supposed to fill this office, but of course Millie had been unmarried for eight centuries, so it must be all right.

Then the bride herself stepped out—and if the Gorgon had seemed buxom before, she was amazing now. She wore a veil that shrouded the nothingness of her face, so that there was no way to tell by looking that she was not simply a ravishingly voluptuous woman. Nevertheless, few creatures looked directly at her, wary of her inherent power. Not even the boldest dragon or tangle tree would care to stare the Gorgon in the face.

Behind her trooped two cherubs, a tiny boy and girl. Dor thought at first they were elves, but realized they were children—the three-year-old twins that Millie and the Zombie Master had generated. They certainly looked cute as they carried the trailing end of the bride's long train. Dor wondered whether these angelic tots had manifested their magic talents yet. Sometimes a talent showed at birth, as had Dor's own; sometimes it never showed, as had Dor's father's—though he knew his father did have some sort of magic that King Trent himself respected. Most talents were in between, showing up in the course of childhood, some major, some minor.

Slowly the Gorgon swept forward, in the renewed hush of dread and expectation. Dor saw with a small start that she had donned dark glasses, a Mundane import, so that even her eyes behind the gauzy veil seemed real.

Now at last Humfrey and the Gorgon stood together. She was taller than he—but everyone was taller than Humfrey, so it didn't matter. The music faded to the deceptive calm of the center of a storm.

The Zombie Master nodded to Dor. It was time for the King to read the service, finally tying the knot.

Dor opened the book with trembling fingers. Now he was glad that Cherie Centaur had drilled him well in reading; he had the text to lean on, so that his blank mind couldn't betray him. All he had to do was read the words and follow the directions and everything would be all right. He knew that Good Magician Humfrey really did want to marry the Gorgon; it was just the ceremony that put him off, as it did all men. Weddings were for women and their mothers. Dor would navigate this additional Kingly chore and doubtless be better off for the experience. But his knees still felt like limp noodles. Why did experience have to be so difficult?

He found the place and began to read. "We are gathered here to hogtie this poor idiot—"

There was a stir in the audience. The weeping matrons paused in mid-tear, while males of every type smirked. Dor blinked. Had he read that right? Yes, there it was, printed quite clearly. He might have trouble spelling, but he could read well enough. "To this conniving wench—"

The demons sniggered. A snake stuck its head out over the Gorgon's veil and hissed. Something was definitely wrong.

"But it says right here," Dor protested, tapping the book with one forefinger. "The gride and broom shall—"

There was a raucous creaking sound that cut through the chamber. Then the Zombie Master's whisk broom flew out of his pocket and hovered before Dor.

Astonished, Dor asked it: "What are you doing here?"

"I'm the broom," it replied. "You invoked the gride and broom, didn't you?"

"What's a gride?"

"You heard it. Awful noise."

So a gride was an awful noise. Dor's vocabulary was expanding rapidly today! "That was supposed to be a bride and groom," Dor said. "Get back where you belong."

"Awww. I thought I was going to get married." But the broom flew back to the pocket.

Now Millie spoke. "Lacuna!" she said.

One of the children jumped. It was the little girl, Millie's daughter.

"Did you change the print?" Millie demanded.

Now Dor caught on. The child's talent—changing printed text! No wonder the service was fouled up!

The Zombie Master grimaced. "Kids will be kids," he said dourly. "We should have used zombies to carry the train, but Millie wouldn't have it. Let's try it again."

Zombies to attend the bride! Dor had to agree with Millie, privately; the stench and rot of the grave did not belong in a ceremony like this.

"Lacuna, put the text back the way it was," Millie said severely.

"Awww," the child said, exactly the way the whisk broom had.

Dor lifted the book. But now there was an eye in the middle of the page. It winked at him. "What now?" he asked.

"Eh?" the book asked. An ear sprouted beside the eye.

"Hiatus!" Millie snapped, and the little boy jumped. "Stop that right now!"

"Awww." But the eye and ear shrank and disappeared, leaving the book clear. Now Dor knew the nature and talent of the other twin.

He read the text carefully before reading it aloud. It was titled *A Manual of Simple Burial*. He frowned at Lacuna, and the print reverted to the proper text: *A Manual of Sample Wedding Services*.

This time he got most of the way through the service without disruption, ignoring ears and noses that sprouted from unlikely surfaces. At one point an entire face appeared on the sun-ball, but no one else was looking at it, so there was no disturbance.

"Do you, Good Magician Humfrey," he concluded, "take this luscious, faceless female Gorgon to be your—" He hesitated, for the text now read *ball and chain*. Some interpolation was necessary. "Your lawfully wedded wife, to have and to hold, to squeeze till she—uh, in health and sickness, for the few measly years you hang on before you croak—uh, until you both become rotten zombies—uh, until death do you part?" He was losing track of the real text.

The Good Magician considered. "Well, there are positive and negative aspects—"

The Zombie Master elbowed him. "Stick to the format," he muttered.

Humfrey looked rebellious, but finally got it out. "I suppose so."

Dor turned to the Gorgon. "And do you, you petrifying creature, take this gnarled old gnome—uh—" The mischievous text had caught him again. A monster in the audience guffawed. "Take Good Magician Humfrey—"

"I do!" she said.

Dor checked his text. Close enough, he decided. "Uh, the manacles—" Oh, no!

Gravely the Zombie Master brought forth the ring. An eye opened on its edge. The Zombie Master frowned at Hiatus, and the eye disappeared. He gave the ring to Humfrey.

The Gorgon lifted her fair hand. A snakelet hissed. "Hey, I don't want to go on that finger!" the ring protested. "It's dangerous!"

"Would you rather be fed to the zombie sea serpent?" Dor snapped at it. The ring was silent. Humfrey fumbled it onto the Gorgon's finger. Naturally he got the wrong finger, but she corrected him gently.

Dor returned to the manual. "I now pronounce you gnome and monst— uh, by the authority vested in me as King of Thieves—uh, of Xanth, I now pronounce you Magician and Wife." Feeling weak with relief at having gotten this far through despite the treacherous text, Dor read the final words. "You may now miss the gride." There was the awful banshee noise. "Uh, goose the tide." There was a sloppy swish, as of water reacting to an indignity. "Uh—"

The Gorgon took hold of Humfrey, threw back her veil, and kissed him soundly. There was applause from the audience, and a mournful hoot from the distance. The sea monster was signaling its sorrow over the Good Magician's loss of innocence.

Millie was furious. "When I catch you, Hi and Lacky—" But the little imps were already beating a retreat.

The wedding party adjourned to the reception area, where refreshments were served. There was a scream. Millie looked and paled, for a moment resembling her ghostly state. "Jonathan! You didn't!"

"Well, somebody had to serve the cake and punch," the Zombie Master said defensively. "Everyone else was busy, and we couldn't ask the guests."

Dor peered. Sure enough, zombies in tuxedos and formal gowns were serving the delicacies. Gobbets of rot were mixing with the cake, and yellowish drool was dripping in the punch. The appetite of the guests seemed to be diminishing.

The assembled monsters, noting that Humfrey had not been turned to stone despite being petrified, were now eager to kiss the bride. They were in no hurry to raid the refreshments. A long line formed.

Millie caught Dor's elbow. "That was very good, Your Majesty. I understand that my husband is to substitute for you during your journey to Centaur Isle."

"He is?" But immediately the beauty and simplicity of it came clear. "He's a Magician! He would do just fine! But I know he doesn't like to indulge in politics."

"Well, since we are going there for a visit anyway, to see the zombies and ghosts, it's not really political."

Dor realized that Millie had really helped him out. Only she could have persuaded the Zombie Master to take the office of King even temporarily. "Uh, thanks. I think the ghosts will like the twins."

She smiled. "The walls will have ears."

That was Hi's talent. "They sure will!"

"Let's go join the monsters," she said, taking his arm. Her touch still sent a rippling thrill through him, perhaps not just because of her magic talent. "How is Irene? I understand she will one day do with you what we women have always done with Magicians."

"Did it ever occur to any of you scheming conspirators that I might have other plans?" Dor asked, nettled despite the effect she had on him. Perhaps he was reacting in order to counter his illicit liking for her. She certainly didn't seem like eight hundred years old!

"No, that never occurred to any of us," she said. "Do you think you have a chance to escape?"

"I doubt it," he said. "But first we have to deal with this mysterious Magician of Centaur Isle. And I hope King Trent comes back soon."

"I hope so, too," Millie said. "And Queen Iris. She was the one who helped bring me back to life. She and your father. I'm forever grateful to them. And to you, too, Dor, for returning Jonathan to me."

She always referred to the Zombie Master by his given name. "I was glad to do it," Dor said.

Then a mishmash of creatures closed in on them, and Dor gave himself up to socializing, perforce. Everyone had a word for the King. Dor wasn't good at this; in fact, he felt almost as awkward as Good Magician Humfrey looked. What was it really like, getting married?

"You'll find out!" the book he still carried said, chuckling evilly.

Chapter 4

Hungry Dune

They had surveyed prospective routes and decided to travel down the coast of Xanth. Dor's father Bink had once traveled into the south-center region, down to the great interior Lake Ogre-Chobee, where the curse-fiends lived, and he recommended against that route. Dragons, chasms, nickelpedes, and other horrors abounded, and there was a massive growth of brambles that made passing difficult, as well as a region of magic-dust that could be hazardous to one's mental health.

On the other hand, the open sea was little better. There the huge sea monsters ruled, preying on everything available. If dragons ruled the wilderness land, serpents ruled the deep water. Where the magic ambience of Xanth faded, the Mundane monsters commenced, and these were worse yet. Dor knew them only through his inattentive geography studies—toothy alligators, white sharks, and blue whales. He didn't want any part of those!

But the coastal shallows excluded the larger sea creatures and the solid-land monsters. Chances were that with a strong youth like the ogre Smash along, they could move safely through this region without raising too much commotion. Had that not been the case, the Elders would never have permitted this excursion, regardless of the need. As it was, they insisted that Dor take along some preventive magic from the Royal Arsenal—a magic sword, a flying carpet, and an escape hoop. Irene carried a selected bag of seeds that she could use to grow particular plants at need—fruits, nuts, and vegetables for the food, and watermelons and milkweed if they had no safe supply of liquid.

They used a magic boat that would sail itself swiftly and quietly down any channel that was deep enough, yet was light enough to be portaged across sand bars. The craft was indefatigable; all they had to do was guide it, and in one full day and night it would bring them to Centaur Isle. This would certainly be faster and easier than walking. Chet, whose geographic education had not been neglected, had a clear notion of the coastal outline and would steer the boat past the treacherous shoals and deeps. Everything was as routine as the nervous Elders could make it.

They started in midmorning from the beach nearest Castle Roogna that had been cleared of monsters. The day was clear, the sea calm. Here there was a brief bay between the mainland and a long chain of barrier islands, the most secure of all waters, theoretically. This trip should not only be safe, but also dull. Of course nothing in Xanth could be taken for granted.

For an hour they traveled south along the bay channel. Dor grew tired of watching the passing islands, but remained too keyed up to rest. After all, it was a centaur Magician they were going to spy out—something never before known in Xanth, unless one counted Herman the Hermit Centaur, who hadn't really been a Magician, just a strongly talented individual who related to the Will-o'-Wisps.

Smash, too, was restive; he was a creature of physical action, and this free ride irked him. Dor would have challenged him to a game of tic-tac-toe, an amusement he had learned from the child of one of the soldier settlers, but knew he would win every game; ogres were not much on intellect.

Grundy the Golem entertained himself by chatting with passing fish and sea creatures. It was amazing, the gossip he came up with. A sneaky sawfish was cutting in on the time of the damselfish of a hammerhead, and the hammerhead was getting suspicious. Pretty soon he would pound the teeth out of the sawfish. A sea squirt was shoring himself up with the flow from an undersea fresh-water spring, getting tipsy on the rare liquid. A certain little oyster was getting out of bed at midnight and gambling with the sand dollars; he was building up quite an alluvial deposit at the central bank of sand. But when his folks found out, he would be gamboling to a different tune.

Irene, meanwhile, struck up a dialogue with the centaur. "You're so intelligent, Chet. How is it that your magic is so, well, simple?"

"No one is blessed with the selection of his personal talent," Chet said

philosophically. He was lying in the middle of the boat, so as to keep the center of gravity low, and seemed comfortable enough. "We centaurs less than most, since only recently has our magic been recognized. My mother—"

"I know. Cherie thinks magic is obscene."

"Oh, she is broad-minded about its presence in lesser creatures."

"Like human beings?" Irene asked dangerously.

"No need to be sensitive about it. We do not discriminate against your kind, and your magic does to a considerable extent compensate."

"How come we rule Xanth, then?" she demanded. Dor found himself getting interested; this was better than fish gossip anyway.

"There is some question whether humans are actually dominant in Xanth," Chet said. "The dragons of the northern reaches might have a different opinion. At any rate, we centaurs permit you humans your foibles. If you wish to point to one of your number and say, 'That individual rules Xanth,' we have no objection so long as that person doesn't interfere with important things."

"What's so important?"

"You would not be in a position to understand the nuances of centaur society."

Irene bridled. "Oh, yeah? Tell me a nuance."

"I'm afraid that is privileged information."

Dor knew Chet was asking for trouble. Already, stray wild seeds in Irene's vicinity were popping open and sending out shoots and roots, a sure sign of her ire. But like many girls, she concealed it well. "Yet humans have the best magic."

"Certainly—if you value magic."

"What would you centaurs say if my father started changing you into fruitflies?"

"Fruit neat," Smash said, overhearing. "Let's eat!"

"Don't be a dunce," Grundy said. "It's two hours yet till lunch."

"Here, I'll start a breadfruit plant," Irene said. "You can watch it grow." She picked a seed from her collection and set it in one of the earth-filled pots she had brought along. "Grow," she commanded, and the seed sprouted. The ogre watched its growth avidly, waiting for it to mature and produce the first succulent loaf of bread.

"King Trent would not do anything as irresponsible as that," Chet said, picking up on the question. "We centaurs have generally gotten along well with him."

"Because he can destroy you. You'd *better* get along!"

"Not so. We centaurs are archers. No one can get close enough to harm us unless we permit him. We get along because we choose to."

Irene adroitly changed the subject. "You never told me how you felt about your own magic. All your brains, but all you can do is shrink rocks."

"Well, it does relate. I render a stone into a calx. A calx is a small stone, a

pebble used for calculating. Such calculus can grow complex, and it has important ramifications. So I feel my magic talent contributes—"

"Monster coming," Grundy announced. "A little fish told me."

"There aren't supposed to be monsters in these waters," Dor objected.

Grundy consulted with the fish. "It's a sea dragon. It heard the commotion of our passage, so it's coming in to investigate. The channel's deep enough for it here."

"We'd better get out of the channel, then," Dor said.

"This is not the best place," Chet objected.

"No place is best to get eaten, dummy!" Irene snapped. "We can't handle a water dragon. We'll have to get out of its way. Shallow water is all we need."

"There are groupies in these shallows," Chet said. "Not a threat, so long as we sail beyond their depth, but not fun to encounter. If we can get farther down before diverging—"

But now they saw the head of the dragon to the south, gliding above the water. Its neck cut a wake; the monster was traveling fast. It was far too big for them to fight.

Smash, however, was game. Ogres were too stupid to know fear. He stood, making the craft rock crazily. "For me's to squeeze!" he said, gesturing with his meathooks.

"All you could do is gouge out handfuls of scales," Irene said. "Meanwhile, it would be chomping the rest of us. You know an ogre has to have firm footing on land to tackle a dragon of any type."

Without further argument, Chet swerved toward the mainland beach. But almost immediately the sand began to writhe. "Oh, no!" Dor exclaimed. "A sand dune has taken over that beach. We can't go there."

"Agreed," Chet said. "That dune wasn't on my map. It must have moved in the past few days." He swerved back the other way.

That was the problem about Xanth; very little was permanent. In the course of a day, the validity of a given map could be compromised; in a week it could be destroyed. That was one reason so much of Xanth remained unexplored. It had been traveled, but the details were not fixed.

The dune, noting their departure, reared up in a great sandy hump, its most typical form. Had they been so foolish as to step on that beach, it would have rolled right over them, buried them, and consumed them at leisure.

But now the water dragon was much closer. They cut across its path uncomfortably close and approached the island's inner shore. The dragon halted, turning its body to pursue them—but in a moment its nether loops ran aground in the shallows, and it halted. Jets of steam plumed from its nostrils; it was frustrated.

A flipper slapped at the side of the boat. "It's a groupie," Grundy cried. "Knock it off!"

Smash reached out a gnarled mitt to grasp the flipper and haul the thing up in the air. The creature was a fattish fish with large, soft extremities.

"That's a groupie?" Irene asked. "What's so bad about it?"

The fish curled about, got its flippers on the ogre's arm, and drew itself up. Its wide mouth touched Smash's arm in a seeming kiss.

"Don't let it do that!" Chet warned. "It's trying to siphon out your soul."

The ogre understood that. He flung the groupie far over the water, where it landed with a splash.

But now several more were slapping at the boat, trying to scramble inside. Irene shrieked. "Just knock them away," Chet said. "They can't take your soul unless you let them. But they'll keep trying."

"They're coming in all over!" Dor cried. "How can we get away from them?"

Chet smiled grimly. "We can move into the deep channel. Groupies are shallow creatures; they don't stir deep waters."

"But the dragon's waiting there!"

"Of course. Dragons eat groupies. That's why groupies don't venture there."

"Dragons also eat people," Irene protested.

"That might be considered a disadvantage," the centaur agreed. "If you have a better solution, I am amenable to it."

Irene opened her bag of seeds and peered in. "I have watercress. That might help."

"Try it!" Dor exclaimed, sweeping three sets of flippers off the side of the boat. "They're overwhelming us!"

"That is the manner of the species," Chet agreed, sweeping several more off. "They come not single spy, but in battalions."

She picked out a tiny seed. "Grow!" she commanded, and dropped it in the water. The others paused momentarily in their labors to watch. How could such a little seed abate such a pressing menace?

Almost immediately there was a kind of writhing and bubbling where the seed had disappeared. Tiny tendrils writhed outward like wriggling worms. Bubbles rose and popped effervescently. "Cress!" the mass hissed as it expanded.

The groupies hesitated, taken aback by this phenomenon. Then they pounced on it, sucking in mouthfuls.

"They're eating it up!" Dor said.

"Yes," Irene agreed, smiling.

In moments the groupies began swelling up like balloons. The cress had not stopped growing or gassing, and was now inflating the fish. Soon the groupies rose out of the water, impossibly distended, and floated through the air. The dragon snapped at those who drifted within its range.

"Good job, I must admit," Chet said, and Irene flushed with satisfaction. Dor experienced a twinge of jealousy and a twinge of guilt for that feeling. There was nothing between Chet and Irene, of course; they were of two different species. Not that that necessarily meant much, in Xanth. New composites were constantly emerging, and the chimera was evidently descended from three or four other species. Irene merely argued with Chet to try to bolster her own image and was flattered when the centaur bolstered it for her. And if there were something between them, why should he, Dor, care? But he did care.

They could not return to the main channel, for the dragon paced them alertly. It knew it had them boxed. Chet steered cautiously south, searching out the deepest subchannels of the bay, avoiding anything suspicious. But the island they were skirting was coming to an end; soon they would be upon the ocean channel the water dragon had entered by. How could they cross that while the dragon lurked?

Chet halted the boat and stared ahead. The dragon took a stance in mid-channel, due south, and stared back. It knew they had to pass here. Slowly, deliberately, it ran its long floppy tongue over its gleaming chops.

"What now?" Dor asked. He was King; he should be leader, but his mind was blank.

"I believe we shall have to wait until nightfall," Chet said.

"But we're supposed to make the trip in a day and night!" Irene protested. "That'll waste half the day!"

"Better waste time than life, green-nose," Grundy remarked.

"Listen, stringbrain—" she retorted. These two had never gotten along well together.

"We'd better wait," Dor said reluctantly. "Then we can sneak by the dragon while it's sleeping and be safely on our way."

"How soundly do dragons sleep?" Irene asked suspiciously.

"Not deeply," Chet said. "They merely snooze with their nostrils just above the water. But it will be better if there is fog."

"Much better," Irene agreed weakly.

"Meanwhile, we would do well to sleep in the daytime," Chet said. "We will need to post one of our number as a guard, to be sure the boat doesn't drift. He can sleep at night, while the others are active."

"What do you mean, *he?*" Irene demanded. "There's too much sexism in Xanth. You think a girl can't guard?"

Chet shrugged with his foresection and flicked his handsome tail about negligently. "I spoke generically, of course. There is no sexual discrimination among centaurs."

"That's what you think," Grundy put in. "Who's the boss in your family—Chester or Cherie? Does she let him do anything he wants?"

"Well, my mother *is* strong-willed," Chet admitted.

"I'll bet the fillies run the whole show at Centaur Isle," Grundy said. "Same as they do at Castle Roogna."

"Ha. Ha. Ha." Irene said, pouting.

"You may guard if you wish," Chet said.

"You think I won't? Well, I will. Give me that paddle." She grabbed the emergency paddle, which would now be needed to keep the boat from drift-ing.

The others settled down comfortably, using pads and buoyant cushions. Chet's equine portion was admirably suited for lying down, but his human portion was more awkward. He leaned against the side of the boat, head against looped arms.

"Say—how will I sleep when we're nudging past that dragon?" Irene asked. "My sleeping turn will come then."

There was a stifled chuckle from Grundy's direction. "Guess one sexist brought that on herself. Just don't snore too loud when we're passing under its tail. Might scare it into—"

She hurled a cushion at the golem, then settled resolutely into her guard position, watching the dragon.

Dor tried to sleep, but found himself too wound up. After a while he sat upright. "It's no use; maybe I'll sleep tomorrow," he said.

Irene was pleased to have his company. She sat cross-legged opposite him, and Dor tried not to be aware that in that position her green skirt did not fully cover her legs. She had excellent ones; in that limited respect she had already matched the Gorgon. Dor liked legs; in fact, he liked anything he wasn't supposed to see.

She sprouted a buttercup plant while Dor plucked a loaf from the bread-fruit, and they feasted on fresh bread and butter in silence. The dragon watched, and finally, mischievously, Dor rolled some bread into a compact wad and threw it at the monster. The dragon caught it neatly and gulped it down. Maybe it wasn't such a bad monster; maybe Grundy could talk to it and arrange for safe passage.

No—such a predator could not be trusted. If the dragon wanted to let them pass, it would go away. Better strategy would be to keep it awake and alert all day, so that it would be tired at night.

"Do you think this new centaur Magician will try to take over Xanth?" Irene asked quietly when it seemed the others were asleep.

Dor could appreciate her concern. Chet, who was a friend, was arrogant enough about centaur-human relations; what would be the attitude of a grown centaur with the power of a Magician? Of course the Magician would not be grown right now; it must be new-birthed. But in time it could become adult, and then it could be an ornery creature, like Chet's sire Chester, but without Chester's redeeming qualities. Dor knew that some centaurs did not like human beings; those tended to stay well clear of Castle Roogna. But Centaur Isle was well clear, and that was where this menace was. "We're on our way to investigate this matter," he reminded her. "There is help for King Trent there, too, according to Crombie's pointing. Maybe we just need to figure out how to turn this situation positive instead of negative."

She shifted her position slightly, unconsciously showing a little more of her legs, including a tantalizing flash of inner thigh. "You *are* going to try to help my father, aren't you?"

"Of course I'm going to try!" Dor said indignantly, hoping that if there was any flush on his face, she would assume it was because of his reaction to her words, rather than her flesh. Dor had in the past seen some quite lovely nymphs in quite scanty attire—but nymphs didn't really count. They were *all* well formed and scantily attired, so were not remarkable. Irene was a real girl, and that type ranged from lovely to ugly—in fact, his mother Chameleon covered that range in the course of each month—and Irene did not normally display a great deal of her body at a time. Thus each glimpse, beyond a certain perimeter, was special. But more special when the display was unintentional.

"I know if my father doesn't come back, you'll stay King."

"I'm not ready to stay King. In twenty years, maybe, I'll be able to handle it. Right now I just want King Trent back. He's your father; I think he's my friend."

"What about my mother?"

Dor grimaced. "Even Queen Iris," he said. "I'd rather face a lifelike illusion of a dragon than the real thing."

"You know, I never had any real privacy till she left," Irene said. "She was always watching me, always telling on me. I hardly dared even to think for myself, because I was afraid she'd slip one of her illusions into my mind and snitch on me. I used to wish something would happen to her—not anything bad, just something to get her out of my hair for a while. Only now that it has—"

"You didn't really want her gone," Dor said. "Not like this."

"Not like this," she agreed. "She's a bitch, but she is my mother. Now I can do anything I want—and I don't know what I want." She shifted position again. This time the hem of her skirt dropped to cover more of her legs. It was almost as if her reference to privacy from her mother's snooping around her mind had brought about privacy from Dor's surreptitious snooping around her body. "Except to have them back again."

Dor found he liked Irene much better this way. Perhaps her prior sharpness of tongue, back when her parents had been in Xanth, had been because of that constant feeling of being watched. Anything real might have been demeaned or ridiculed, so she never expressed anything real. "You know, I've had the opposite problem. I have privacy—but no one around me does. Because there's not much anybody does that I can't find out about. All I have to do is ask their furniture, or their clothing. So they avoid me, and I can't blame them. That's why I've found it easier to have friends like Smash. He wears nothing but his hair, and he thinks furniture is for bonfires, and he has no embarrassing secrets anyway."

"That's right!" she said. "I have no more privacy with you than I do with my mother. How come I don't feel threatened with you?"

"Because I'm harmless," Dor said with a wry chuckle. "Not by choice; it's just the way I am. The Gorgon says you have me all wrapped up anyway."

She smiled—a genuine, warm smile he liked a lot. "She snitched. She would. She naturally sees all men as creatures to be dazzled and petrified. Good Magician Humfrey never had a chance. But I don't know if I even want you. That way, I mean. My mother figures I've got to marry you so I can be Queen—but that's her desire, not necessarily mine. I mean, why would I want to grow up just like her, with no real power and a lot of time on my hands? Why make my own daughter as miserable as she made me?"

"Maybe you will have a son," Dor offered. This was an intriguing new avenue of exploration.

"You're right. You're harmless. You don't know a thing." She finished her bread and tossed the crumbs on the water. They floated about, forming evanescent picture patterns before drifting away.

Somehow the afternoon had passed; the sun was dropping into the water beyond the barrier island. There was a distant sizzle as it touched the liquid, and a cloud of steam; then it was extinguished.

The others woke and ate. Then Chet guided the boat to the island shore. "Anything dangerous to people here?" Dor asked it.

"Only boredom," the island replied. "Nothing interesting ever happens here, except maybe a seasonal storm or two."

That was what they wanted: a dull locale. They took turns leaving the boat in order to attend to sanitary needs. Irene also took time to grow a forgetme flower.

As the darkness closed, Dor reviewed the situation. "We're going to sneak by that dragon in the night. Irene will harvest some forgetme flowers to discourage memory of our passage; that way the reactions of fish in the area will not betray us. But that won't help us if the dragon sees us or hears us or smells us directly. We don't have any sight- or sound-blanking plants; we didn't anticipate this particular squeeze. So we must go extremely carefully."

"I wish I were string and clay again," Grundy said. "Then I couldn't be killed."

"Now we do have some other resources," Dor said. "The magic sword will make any person expert the moment he takes it in his hand. It won't help much against a pouncing dragon, but any lesser creature will be balked. If we get in serious trouble, we can climb through the escape hoop. The problem with that is that it leads to the permanent storage vat of the Brain Coral, deep under the earth, and the Coral doesn't like to release creatures. It happens to be my friend, but I'd rather not strain that friendship unless absolutely necessary. And there is the flying carpet—but that can only take one person at a time, plus Grundy. I think it could support Smash, but not Chet, so that's not ideal."

"I wouldn't fit through the hoop either," Chet said.

"Yes. So you, Chet, are the most vulnerable one in this situation, because of your mass. So we need to plan for another defense." Dor paused, for Irene was looking at him strangely. "What's the matter?"

"You're glowing," she said.

Startled, Dor checked himself. Light was streaming from one of his pockets. "Oh—that's the midnight sunstone Jewel gave me so I'll always have light. I had forgotten about it."

"We don't want light at the moment," she pointed out. "Wrap it up." She handed him a piece of cloth.

Dor wrapped the gem carefully, until its glow was so muted as to be inconsequential, and put it back in his pocket. "Now," he continued. "Irene has some seeds that will grow devastating plants—she really is Magician level, regardless of what the Elders say—but most of those plants would be as dangerous to us as to the enemy. We'd have to plant and run."

"Any that would block off the water so the dragon couldn't pursue?" Chet asked.

"Oh, yes," Irene said, glowing at Dor's compliment about her talent. "The kraken weed—"

"I see what Dor means," the centaur said quickly. "I don't want to be swimming in the same ocean with a kraken!"

"Or I could start a stunflower on the island here, but it would be likely to stun us, too." She considered. "Aha! I do have some popcorn. That's harmless, but it makes an awful racket. That might distract the dragon for a while."

"Grow me some of that," Chet said. "I'll throw it behind me if I have to swim."

"Only one problem," she said. "I can't grow that at night. It's a dayplant."

"I could unwrap the sunstone," Dor offered.

"That's too small, I think. We'd need a lot of light, radiating all about, not gleaming from tiny facets."

"What can you grow naturally at night?" Chet asked grimly.

"Well, hypno-gourds do well; they generate their own light, inside. But you wouldn't want to look in the peep-hole, because—"

"Because I'd be instantly hypnotized," Chet finished. "Grow me one anyway; it might help."

"As you wish," she agreed dubiously. She leaned over the side of the boat to drop a seed on the shore. "Grow," she murmured.

"Now if there is trouble," Dor said, "you, Irene, get on the flying carpet. You can drop a kraken seed near the dragon, while the rest of us use the hoop or swim for it. But we'll do our best to escape the notice of the dragon. Then we can proceed south without further trouble."

There was no objection. They waited until the hypno-gourd had fruited, producing one fine specimen. Chet wrapped it in cloth and tucked it in the boat. The craft started moving, nudging silently south toward the channel while the occupants hardly dared breathe. Chet guided it in an eastward curve, to intersect the main channel first, so that he could avoid the monster that was presumably waiting due south. In this silent darkness, they could not see it any more than it could see them.

But the dragon had outsmarted them. It had placed a sunfish in this channel that operated on a similar principle to the sunstone, but it was thousands of times as large. When they came near, the fish suddenly glowed like the sun itself, blindingly. The rounded fin projected above the surface of the water, and its light turned night to day.

"Oh, no!" Dor cried. He had so carefully wrapped his sunstone—and now this was infinitely worse.

There was a gleeful honk from the dragon. They saw its eyes glowing as it forged toward them. Water dragons did not have internal fire; the eyes were merely reflecting the blaze of the sunfish.

"Plant the kraken!" Dor cried.

"No!" Chet countered. "We can make it to the mainland shallows!"

Sure enough, the boat glided smoothly across the channel before the dragon arrived. The monster was silhouetted before the sunfish, writhing in frustration. It had planned so well, and just missed victory. It honked. "Curses!" Grundy translated. "Foiled again!"

"What about the sand dune?" Irene asked worriedly.

"They are usually quiescent by night," Chet said.

"But this isn't night any more," she reminded him, her voice taking on a pink tinge of hysteria.

Indeed, the dark mound was rippling, sending a strand of itself toward the water. The sand had enough mass, and the water was so shallow, that it was possible for the dune to fill it in. The ravenous shoreline was coming toward them.

"If we retreat from the dune, we'll come within reach of the dragon," Chet said.

"Feed goon to dune," Smash suggested.

"Goon? Do you mean the dragon?" Dor asked. The ogre nodded.

"Say, yes!" Irene said. "Talk to the dune, Dor. Tell it we'll lure the dragon within its range if it lets us go."

Dor considered. "I don't know. I'd hate to send any creature to such a fate—and I'm not sure the dune can be trusted."

"Well, string it out as long as you can. Once the dune tackles the dragon, it won't have time to worry about small fry like us."

Dor eyed the surging dune on one side, the chop-slurping dragon on the other, and noted how the region between them was diminishing. "Try reasoning with the dragon first," he told Grundy.

The golem emitted a series of honks, grunts, whistles, and tooth-gnashings. It was amazing how versatile he was with sounds—but of course this was his magic. In a moment the dragon lunged forward, trying to catch the entire boat in its huge jaws, but falling short. The water washed up in a small tsunami. "I asked if it it wouldn't like to let a nice group of people on the King's business like us go on in peace," Grundy said. "It replied—"

"We can see what it replied," Dor said. "Very well; we'll go the other route." He faced the shore and called: "Hey, dune!"

Thus hailed, the dune was touched by Dor's magic. "You calling me, tidbit?"

"I want to make a deal with you."

"Ha! You're going to be consumed anyway. What kind of deal can you offer?"

"This whole boatload is a small morsel for the likes of you. But we might arrange for you to get a real meal, if you let us go in peace."

"I don't eat, really," the dune said. "I preserve. I clean and secure the bones of assorted creatures so that they can be admired millennia hence. My treasures are called fossils."

So this monster, like so many of its ilk, thought itself a benefactor to Xanth. Was there any creature or thing, no matter how awful, that didn't rationalize its existence and actions in similar fashion? But Dor wasn't here to argue with it. "Wouldn't you rather fossilize a dragon than a sniveling little collection of scraps like us?"

"Oh, I don't know. Snivelers are common, but so are dragons. Size is not as important for the fossil record as quality and completeness."

"Well, do you have a water dragon in your record yet?"

"No, most of them fall to my cousin the deepsea muck, just as most birds are harvested by my other cousin, the tarpit. I would dearly like to have a specimen like that."

"We offer you that water dragon there," Dor said. "All you need to do is make a channel deep enough for the dragon to pass. Then we'll lure it in— and then you can close the channel and secure your specimen for fossilization."

"Say, that would work!" the dune agreed. "It's a deal."

"Start your channel, then. We'll sail down it first, leading the dragon. Make sure you let us go, though."

"Sure. You go, the dragon stays."

"I don't trust this," Irene muttered.

"Neither do I," Dor agreed. "But we're in a bind. Chet, can you apply your calculus?"

"The smallest of stones can be considered calculi," Chet said. "That is to say, sand. Now sand has certain properties . . ." He trailed off, then brightened. "You have seagrass seed?" he asked Irene.

"Lots of it. But I don't see how—" Then her eyes glowed. "Oh, I *do* see! Yes, I'll be ready, Chet!"

The sand began to hump itself into twin mounds, opening a narrow channel of water between them. Chet guided the boat directly down that channel. The dragon, perceiving their seeming escape, honked wrathfully and gnashed its teeth.

"Express hope the dragon doesn't realize how deep this channel is," Dor told Grundy. "In dragon talk."

Grundy smiled grimly. "I know my business!" He emitted dragon noises.

Immediately the dragon explored the end of the channel, plunging its head into it. With a glad honk it writhed on into the inviting passage.

Soon the dragon was close on their wake. Its entire body was now within the separation in the dune. "Now—close it up!" Dor cried to the dune.

The dune did so. Suddenly the channel was narrowing and disappearing as sand heaped into it. Too late the dragon realized its peril; it tried to turn, to retreat, but the way out was blocked. It honked and thrashed, but was in deep trouble in shallow water.

However, the channel ahead of the boat was also filling in. "Hey, let us out!" Dor cried.

"Why should I let perfectly good fossil material go?" the dune asked reasonably. "This way I've got both you and the dragon. It's the haul of the century!"

"But you promised!" Dor said plaintively. "We made a deal!"

"Promises and deals aren't worth the breath it takes to utter them—and I don't even breathe."

"I knew it," Chet said. "Betrayal."

"Do your stuff, Irene," Dor said.

Irene brought out two handfuls of seeds. "Grow!" she yelled, scattering them widely. On either side the grass sprouted rapidly, sending its deep roots into the sand, grabbing, holding.

"Hey!" the dune yelled, much as Dor had, as it tripped over itself where the grass anchored it.

"You reneged on our agreement," Dor called back. "Now you pay the penalty." For the sand in this region was no longer able to move; the grass had converted it to ordinary ground.

Enraged, the dune made one final effort. It humped up horrendously in the region beyond the growing grass, then rolled forward with such impetus that it spilled into the channel, filling it.

"It's swamping the boat!" Dor cried. "Abandon ship!"

"Some gratitude!" the boat complained. "I carry you loyally all over Xanth, risking my keel, and the moment things get rough, you abandon me!"

The boat had a case, but they couldn't afford to argue it. Heedless of its objection, they all piled out as the sand piled in. They ran across the remaining section of grass-anchorage while the boat disappeared into the dune. The sand was unable to follow them here; its limit had been reached, and already the blades of grass were creeping up through the new mound, nailing it down. The main body of the dune had to retreat and concentrate on the thrashing dragon that bid fair to escape by coiling out of the vanished channel and writhing back toward the sea.

The party stood at the edge of the bay. "We lost our boat," Irene said. "And the flying carpet, and escape hoop, and food."

"And my bow and arrows," Chet said mournfully. "All I salvaged was the gourd. We played it too close; those monsters are stronger and smarter than we thought. We learn from experience."

Dor was silent. He was the nominal leader of this party; the responsibility was his. If he could not manage a single trip south without disaster, how could he hope to handle the situation when he got to Centaur Isle? How could he handle the job of being King, if it came to that?

But they couldn't remain here long, whether in thought or in despair. Already the natives of the region were becoming aware of them. Carnivorous grass picked up where the freshly planted sea grass left off, and the former was sending its hungry shoots toward them. Vines trembled, bright droplets of sap-saliva oozing from their surfaces. There was a buzzing of wings; something airborne would soon show up.

But now at last the sunfish dimmed out, and night returned; the day creatures retreated in confusion, and the night creatures stirred. "If there's one thing worse than day in the wilderness," Irene said, shivering, "it's night. What do we do now?"

Dor wished he had an answer.

"Your plants have saved us once," Chet told her. "Do you have another plant that could protect us or transport us?"

"Let me see." In the dark she put her hand in her bag of seeds and felt around. "Mostly food plants, and special effects . . . a beerbarrel tree—how did that get in here? . . . water locust . . . bulrush—"

"Bulrushes!" Chet said. "Aren't those the reeds that are always in a hurry?"

"They rush everywhere," she agreed.

"Suppose we wove them into a boat or raft—could we control its motion?"

"Yes, I suppose, if you put a ring in the craft's nose. But—"

"Let's do it," the centaur said. "Anything will be better than waiting here for whatever is creeping up on us."

"I'll start the bulrushes growing," she agreed. "We can weave them before they're mature. But you'll have to find a ring before we can finish."

"Dor and Grundy—please question your contacts and see if you can locate a ring," the centaur said.

They started in, Dor questioning the nonliving, Grundy the living. Neither could find a ring in the vicinity. The weaving of the growing bulrushes proceeded apace; it seemed Chet and Irene were familiar with the technique and worked well together. But already the rushes were thrashing about, trying to free themselves to travel. The mass of the mat-raft was burgeoning; soon it would be too strong to restrain.

"Bring ring," Smash said.

"We're trying to!" Dor snapped, clinging to a corner of the struggling mat. The thing was hideously strong.

"Germ worm," the ogre said insistently. His huge hairy paw pushed something at Dor. The object seemed to be a loop of fur.

A loop? "A ring!" Dor exclaimed. "Where did you get it?"

"Me grow on toe," Smash explained. "Which itch."

"You grew the ring on your toe—and it itched?" Dor was having trouble assimilating this.

"Let me check," Grundy said. He made a funny sizzle, talking with something, then laughed. "You know what that is? A ringworm!"

"A ringworm!" Dor cried in dismay, dropping the hideous thing.

"If it's a ring, we need it," Chet said. "Before this mat gets away."

Chagrined, Dor felt on the ground and picked up the ringworm. He passed it gingerly to the centaur. "Here."

Chet wove it into the nose of the craft, then jerked several long hairs from his beautiful tail and twined them into a string that he passed through the ring. Suddenly the bulrush craft settled down. "The nose is sensitive," Chet explained. "The ring makes it hurt when jerked, so even this powerful entity can be controlled."

"Some come!" Smash warned.

Rather than wait to discover what it was that could make an ogre nervous, the others hastened to lead the now-docile bulrush boat to the water. Once it was floating, they boarded carefully and pushed off from the shore. The craft was not watertight, but the individual rushes were buoyant, so the whole business floated.

Something growled in the dark on the shore—a deep, low, throbbing, powerful, and ugly sound. Then, frustrated, it moved away, the ground shuddering. A blast of odor passed them, dank and choking. No one inquired what it might be.

Now Chet gave the bulrushes some play. The raft surged forward, churning up a faintly phosphorescent wake. Wind rushed past their faces.

"Can you see where we're going?" Irene asked, her voice thin.

"No," Chet said. "But the bulrushes travel best in open water. They won't run aground or crash into any monsters."

"You trust them more than I do," she said. "And I grew them."

"Elementary calculation of vegetable nature," the centaur said.

"May I lean against your side?" she asked. "I didn't sleep today, and your coat is so soft—"

"Go ahead," Chet said graciously. He was lying down again, as the woven fabric of the raft could not support his weight afoot. The rushes had swelled in the water, and Dor had succeeded in bailing it out; they were no longer sitting in sea water. Dor had not slept either, but he didn't feel like leaning against Chet's furry side.

The stars moved by. Dor lay on his back and determined the direction of travel of the raft by the stars' apparent travel. It wasn't even; the bulrushes were maneuvering to find the course along which they could rush most freely. They did seem to know where they were going, and that sufficed for now.

Gradually the constellations appeared, patterns in the sky, formations of stars that shifted from randomness to the suggestion of significance. There seemed to be pictures shaping, representations of creatures and objects and notions. Some resembled faces; he thought he saw King Trent peering down at him, giving him a straight, intelligent look.

Where are you now? Dor asked wordlessly.

The face frowned. *I am being held captive in a medieval Mundane castle,* it said. *I have no magic power here. You must bring me magic.*

But I can't do that! Dor protested. *Magic isn't something a person can carry, especially not into Mundania!*

You must use the aisle to rescue me.

What aisle? Dor asked, excited.

The centaur aisle, Trent answered.

Then a waft of ocean spray struck Dor's face, and he woke. The stellar face was gone; it had been a dream.

Yet the message remained with him. Center Isle? His spelling disability made him uncertain, now, of the meaning. How could he use an island to seek King Trent? The center of what? If it was centaur, did that mean Chet had something essential to do with it? If it was an aisle, an aisle between what and what? If this were really a message, a prophecy, how could he apply it? If it were merely a random dream or vision, a construct of his overtired and meandering mind, he should ignore it. But such things were seldom random in Xanth.

Troubled, Dor drifted to sleep again. What he had experienced could not have been a nightmare, for it hadn't scared him, and of course the mares could not run across the water. Maybe it would return and clarify itself.

But the dream did not repeat, and he could not evoke it by looking at the stars. Clouds had sifted across the night sky.

Chapter 5

Girding Loins

or woke again as dawn came. The sun had somehow gotten around to the east, where the land was, and dried off so that it could shine again. Dor wondered what perilous route it employed. Maybe it had a tunnel to roll along. If it ever figured out a way to get down without taking a dunking in the ocean, it would really have it made! Maybe he should suggest that to it sometime. After all, some mornings the sun was up several hours before drying out enough to shine with full brilliance; obviously some nights were worse than others. But he would not make the suggestion right now; he didn't want the sun heading off to explore new routes, leaving Xanth dark for days at a time. Dor needed the light to see his way to Centaur Isle. Jewel's midnight sunstone was not enough.

Centaur Isle—was that where he was supposed to find King Trent? No, the centaurs wouldn't imprison the King, and anyway, Trent was in Mundania. But maybe something at Centaur Isle related. If only he could figure out how!

Dor sat up. "Where are we now, Chet?" he inquired.

There was no answer. The centaur had fallen asleep, too, Irene in repose against his side. Smash and Grundy snored at the rear of the raft.

Everyone had slept! No one was guiding the craft or watching the course! The bulrushes had rushed wherever they wanted to go, which could be anywhere!

The raft was in the middle of the ocean. Bare sea lay on all sides. It was sheer luck that no sea monster had spied them and gobbled them down while they slept. In fact, there was one now!

But as the monster forged hungrily toward the craft, Dor saw that the velocity of the rushes was such that the serpent could not overtake the craft. They were safe because of their speed. Since they were heading south, they should be near Centaur Isle now.

No, that did not necessarily follow. Dor had done better in Cherie's logic classes than in spelling. He always looked for alternatives to the obvious. The craft could have been doing loops all night, or traveling north, and then turned south coincidentally as dawn came. They could be anywhere at all.

"Where are we?" Dor asked the nearest water.

"Longitude 83, Latitude 26, or vise versa," the water said. "I always confuse parallels with meridians."

"That doesn't tell me anything!" Dor snapped.

"It tells *me*, though," Chet said, waking. "We are well out to sea, but also well on the way to our destination. We should be there tonight."

"But suppose a monster catches us way out here in the sea?" Irene asked, also waking. "I'd rather be near land."

Chet shrugged. "We can veer in to land. Meanwhile, why don't you grow us some food and fresh-water plants so we can eat and drink?"

"And a parasol plant, to shield us from the sun," she said. "And a privacy hedge, for you-know."

She got on it. Soon they were drinking scented water from a pitcher plant and eating bunlike masses from puffball plants. The new hedge closed off the rear of the craft, where the expended pitchers were used for another purpose. Several parasols shaded them nicely. It was all becoming quite comfortable.

The bulrush craft, responsive to Chet's tug on the string tied to the ring in its nose, veered toward the east, where the distant land was supposed to be.

Smash the Ogre sniffed the air and peered about. Then he pointed. "Me see the form of a mean ol' storm," he announced.

Oh, no! Dor spied the roiling clouds coming up over the southern horizon. Smash's keen ogre senses had detected it first, but in moments it was all too readily apparent to them all.

"We're in trouble," Grundy said. "I'll see what I can do."

"What can you do?" Irene asked witheringly. "Are you going to wave your tiny little dumb hand and conjure us all instantly to safety?"

Grundy ignored her. He spoke to the ocean in whatever language its creatures used. In a moment he said: "I think I have it. The fish are taking word to an eclectic eel."

"A what?" Irene demanded. "Do you mean one of those shocking creatures?"

"An eclectic eel, dummy. It chooses things from all over. It does nothing original; it puts it all together in bits and pieces that others have made."

"How can something like that possibly help us?"

"Better ask it *why* it will help us."

"All right, woodenhead. Why?"

"Because I promised it half your seeds."

"Half my seeds!" she exploded. "You can't do that!"

"If I don't, the storm will send us all to the depths."

"He's right, Irene," Chet said. "We're over a barrel, figuratively speaking."

"I'll put the confounded golem in a barrel and glue the cork in!" she cried. "A barrel of white-hot sneeze-pepper! He has no right to promise *my* property."

"Okay," Grundy said. "Tell the eel no. Give it a shock."

A narrow snout poked out of the roughening water. A cold gust of wind ruffled Irene's hair and flattened her clothing against her body, making her look extraordinarily pretty. The sky darkened.

"It says, figuratively speaking, your figure isn't bad," Grundy reported with a smirk.

This incongruous compliment put her off her pace. It was hard to tell off someone who made a remark like that. "Oh, all right," she said, sulking. "Half the seeds. But I choose which half."

"Well, toss them in, stupid," Grundy said, clinging to the side of the craft as it pitched in the swells.

"But they'll sprout!"

"That's the idea. Make them all grow. Use your magic. The eclectic eel demands payment in advance."

Irene looked rebellious, but the first drop of rain struck her on the nose and she decided to carry through. "This will come out of your string hide, golem," she muttered. She tossed the seeds into the heaving water one by one, invoking each in turn. "Grow, like a golem's ego. Grow, like Grundy's swelled head. Grow, like the vengeance I owe the twerp . . ."

Strange things developed in the water. Pink-leaved turnips sprouted, turning in place, and tan tomatoes, and yellow cabbages and blue beets. Snap beans snapped merrily and artichokes choked. Then the flowers started, as she came to another section of her supply. White blossoms sprang up in great clusters, decorating the entire ocean near the raft. Then they moved away in herds, making faint *baa-aa-aas*.

"What's that?" Grundy asked.

"Phlox, ninny," Irene said.

Oh, flocks, Dor thought. Of course. The white sheep of flowers.

Firecracker flowers popped redly, tiger lilies snarled, honeybells tinkled, and bleeding hearts stained the water with their sad life essence. Irises that Irene's mother had given her flowered prettily in blue and purple. Gladiolas stretched up happily; begonias bloomed and departed even before they could be ordered to begone. Periwinkles opened their orbs to wink; crocuses parted their white lips to utter scandalous imprecations.

Grundy leaned over the edge of the raft to sniff some pretty multicolored little flowers that were vining upward. Then something happened. "Hey!" he cried suddenly, outraged, wiping golden moisture off his head. "What did they do that for?"

Irene glanced across. "Dummy," she said with satisfaction, "what do you expect sweet peas to do? You better stay away from the pansies."

On Dor's side there was an especially rapid development, the red, orange, and white flowers bursting forth almost before the buds formed. "My, these are in a hurry," he commented.

"They're impatiens," Irene explained.

The display finished off with a dazzling emergence of golden balls—marigolds. "That's half. Take it or leave it," Irene said.

"The eel takes it," Grundy said, still shaking pea out of his hair. "Now the eclectic eel will lead us through the storm to shore, in its fashion."

"About time," Chet said. "Everyone hang on. We have a rough sail coming."

The eel wriggled forward. The craft followed. The storm struck with its moist fury. "What do you have against us?" Dor asked it as the wind tore at his body.

"Nothing personal," it blew back. "It's my job to clear the seas of riffraff. Can't have flotsam and jetsam cluttering up the surface, after all."

"I don't know those people," Dor said. The raft was rocking and twisting as it followed the elusive eel, but they were somehow avoiding the worst of the violence.

A piece of planking floated by. "I'm flotsam," it said. "I'm part of the ship that wrecked here last month, still floating."

A barrel floated by on the other side, the battered trunk of a harvested jellybarrel tree. "I'm jetsam," it blew from its bung. "I was thrown overboard to lighten the ship."

"Nice to know you both," Dor said politely.

"The eel uses them for markers," Grundy said. "It uses anything it finds."

"Where's the riffraff?" Irene asked. "If the storm is here to clear it from the seas, there should be some to clear."

"I'm the raf'," the raft explained. "You must be the rif'." And it chuckled.

Now the rain pelted down full-strength. All of them were soaked in an instant. "Bail! Bail!" Chet screamed thinly through the wind.

Dor grabbed his bucket—actually, it was a bouquet Irene had grown, which his spelling had fouled up so that its nature had completely changed—and scooped out water. Smash the Ogre worked similarly on the other side, using a pitcher. By dint of colossal effort they managed to stay marginally ahead of the rain that poured in.

"Get low!" Grundy cried through the weather. "Don't let her roll over!"

"She's not rolling," Irene said. "A raft can't—"

Then the craft pitched horribly and started to turn over. Irene threw herself flat in the bottom of the center depression, joining Dor and Smash. The raft listed sickeningly to right, then to left, first throwing Irene bodily into Dor, then hurling him into her. She was marvelously soft.

"What are you doing?" Dor cried as his wind was almost knocked from him despite his soft landings.

"I'm yawing," the raft said.

"Seems more like a roll to me," Chet grumbled from the rear.

Irene fetched up against Dor again, hip to hip and nose to nose. "Dear, we've got to stop meeting this way," she gasped, attempting to smile.

In other circumstances Dor would have appreciated the meetings more. Irene was padded in appropriate places, so that the shocks of contact were pleasantly cushioned. But at the moment he was afraid for his life and hers. Meanwhile, she looked as if she were getting seasick.

The craft lurched forward and down, as if sliding over a waterfall. Dor's own gorge rose. "Now what are you doing?" he heaved.

"I'm pitching," the raft responded.

"We're out of the water!" Chet cried. His head remained higher despite his prone position. "There's something beneath us! That's why we're rolling so much!"

"That's the behemoth," Grundy said.

"The what?" Dor asked.

"The behemoth. A huge wallowing creature that floats about doing nothing. The eclectic eel led us up to it, to help weather the storm."

Irene unglued herself from Dor, and all of them crawled cautiously up and looked over the edge of the raft. The storm continued, but now it beat on the glistening blubbery back of the tremendous animal. The craft's perch seemed insecure because of the way it rolled and slid on the slick surface, but the enormous bulk of the monster provided security from the heaving ocean.

"But I thought behemoths were fresh-water creatures," Dor said. "My father encountered one below Lake Ogre-Chobee, he said."

"Of course he did. I was there," Grundy said superciliously. "Behemoths are where you find them. They're too big to worry about what kind of water it is."

"The eel just happened to find this creature and led us to it?" Chet asked. He also looked somewhat seasick.

"That's the eclectic way," Grundy agreed. "To use anything handy."

"Aw, you cheated," the storm howled. "I can't sink that tub." A whirling eye focused on Dor. "That's twice you have escaped me, man-thing. But we shall meet again." Disgruntled, it blew itself away to the west.

So that had been the same storm he had encountered at Good Magician Humfrey's castle. It certainly traveled about!

The behemoth, discovering that its pleasant shower had abated, exhaled a dusty cloud of gas and descended to the depths. There was no point in staying on the surface when the storm didn't want to play any more. The raft was left floating in a calming sea.

Now that he was no longer in danger of drowning, Dor almost regretted the passing of the storm. Irene was a good deal more comfortable to brace against than the reeds of the raft. But he knew he was foolish always to be most interested in what he couldn't have, instead of being satisfied with what he did have.

A monster showed on the horizon. "Get this thing moving!" Irene cried, alarmed. "We aren't out of the weather yet!"

"Follow the eel!" Grundy warned.

"But the eel's headed straight for the monster!" Chet protested.

"That must be the way, then." But even Grundy looked doubtful.

They forged toward the monster. It was revealed now as extremely long and flat, as if a sea serpent had been squeezed under a rolling boulder. "What is it?" Dor asked, amazed.

"A ribbonfish, dolt," Grundy said.

"How can that help us?" For the storm had taken up more of the day than it had seemed to; the sun was now at zenith, and they remained far from shore.

"All I know is the eel agreed to get us to land by nightfall," Grundy said.

They forged on. But now the pace was slowing; the bulrushes were losing their power. Dor realized that some of the material of the boat was dead now; that was why it had been able to speak to him, since his power related only to the inanimate. Soon the rushes would become inert, stranding the craft in mid-sea. They had no paddle; that had been lost with the first boat.

The ribbonfish brought its preposterously flat head down as the bulrush craft sputtered close. Then the head dipped into the water and slid beneath them. In a moment it emerged behind them, and the neck came up under the boat, heaving it right out of the water.

"Oh, no!" Irene screamed as they were carried high into the air. She flung her arms about Dor in terror. Again, he wished this could have happened when he wasn't terrified himself.

But the body of the ribbonfish was slightly concave; the raft remained centered, not falling off. As the head elevated to an appalling height, the boat began to slide down along the body, which was slick with moisture. They watched, horrified, as the craft tilted forward, then accelerated down the creature's neck. Irene screamed again and clung smotheringly to Dor as their bodies turned weightless.

Down they zoomed. But the ribbonfish was undulating, so that a new hump kept forming just behind them while a new dip formed ahead of them. They zoomed at frightening velocity along the creature, never getting down to the water.

"We're traveling toward land," Dor said, awed. "The monster's moving us there!"

"That's how it gets its jollies," Grundy said. "Scooping up things and sliding them along its length. The eel just made use of this for our benefit."

Perceiving that they were not, after all, in danger, Irene regained confidence. "Let go of me!" she snapped at Dor, as if he had been the one doing the grabbing.

The ribbonfish seemed interminably long; the raft slid and slid. Then Dor realized that the monster's head had looked down under the water and come up to follow its tail; the creature was running them through again. The land was coming closer.

At last the land arrived. The ribbonfish tired of the game and dumped them off with a jarring splash. The rushes had just enough power left to propel them to the beach; then they expired, and the raft began to sink.

The sun was well down toward the horizon, racing to cut off their day before they could travel anywhere further. Soon the golden orb would be quenched again. "From here we go by foot, I think," Chet remarked. "We will not achieve Centaur Isle this day."

"We can get closer, though," Dor said. "I've had enough of boats for now anyway." The others agreed.

First they paused to forage for some food. Wild fruitcakes were ripe and a water chestnut provided potable water; Irene did not have to expend any of her diminished store of seeds. In fact, she found a few new ones here.

Suddenly something jumped from behind a tree and charged directly at Dor. He whipped out his magic sword without thinking—and the creature stopped short, spun about, and ran away. It was all hair and legs and glower.

"What was that?" Dor asked, shaking.

"That's a jump-at-a-body," the nearest stone said.

"What's a jump-at-a-body?" Irene asked.

"I don't have to answer *you*," the stone retorted. "You can't take me for granite."

"Answer her," Dor told it.

"Awww, okay. It's what you just saw."

"That's not much help," Irene said.

"You aren't much yourself, doll," it said. "I've seen a better complexion on mottled serpentine."

Bedraggled and disheveled from the ocean run, Irene was hardly at her best. But her vanity had been pricked. "I can choke you with weeds, mineral."

"Yeah, greenie? Just try it!"

"Weeds—grow!" she directed, pointing to the rock. Immediately the weeds around it sprouted vigorously.

"Weed's the best that ever was!" the weeds exclaimed. Startled, Dor looked closely, for his talent did not extend to living things. He found that some sand caught in the plants had actually done the talking.

"Oh, for schist sake!" the rock said. "She's doing it!"

"Tell me what a jump-at-a-body is," Irene insisted.

The rock was almost hidden by vegetation. "All right, all right, doll! Just clear these junky plants out of my face."

"Stop growing," Irene told the weeds, and they stopped with a frustrated rustle. She tramped them down around the rock.

"You do have pretty legs," the rock said. "And that's not all."

Irene, straddling the rock, leaped away. "Just answer my question."

"They just jump out and scare people and run away," the rock said. "They're harmless. They came across from Mundania not long ago, when the Mundanes stopped believing in them, and don't have the courage to do anything bad."

"Thank you," Irene said, gratified by her victory over the ornery stone.

"I think the grass needs more tramping down," the rock suggested.

"Not while I'm wearing a skirt."

"Awww . . ."

They finished their repast and trekked on south. Very little remained of the day, but they wanted to find a decent place to camp for the night. Dor questioned other rocks to make sure nothing dangerous remained in the vicinity; this did seem to be a safe island. Perhaps their luck had turned, and they would reach their destination without further ill event.

But as dusk closed, they came to the southern border of the island. There was a narrow channel separating it from the next island in the chain.

"Maybe we'd better camp here for the night," Dor said. "This island seems safe; we don't know what's on the next one."

"Also, I'm tired," Irene said.

They settled in for the night, protected by a palisade formed of asparagus spears grown for the occasion. The jump-at-a-bodies kept charging the stockade and fleeing it harmlessly.

Chet and Smash, being the most massive individuals, lay at the outside edges of the small enclosure. Grundy needed so little room he didn't matter. Dor and Irene were squeezed into the center. But now she had room enough and time to settle herself without quite touching him. Ah, well.

"You know, that rock was right," Dor said. "You do have nice legs. And that's not all."

"Go to sleep," she said, not displeased.

In the morning a large roundish object floated in the channel. Dor didn't like the look of it. They would have to swim past it to reach the next island. "Is it animal or plant?" he asked.

"No plant," Irene said. She had a feel for this sort of thing, since it related to her magic.

"I'll talk to it," Grundy said. His talent applied to anything living. He made a complex series of whistles and almost inaudible grunts. Much of his communication was opaque to others, since some animals and most plants used inhuman mechanisms. In a moment he announced: "It's a sea nettle. A plantlike animal. This channel is its territory, and it will sting to death anyone who intrudes."

"How fast can it swim?" Irene asked.

"Fast enough," Grundy said. "It doesn't look like much, but it can certainly perform. We could separate, crossing in two parties; that way it could only get half of us, maybe."

"Perhaps you had better leave the thinking to those better equipped for it," Chet said.

"We have to get it out of there or nullify it," Dor said. "I'll try to lead it away, using my talent."

"Meanwhile, I'll start my stunflower," Irene said.

"Thanks for the vote of confidence." But Dor couldn't blame her; he had had success before in tricking monsters with his talent, but it depended on the nature and intelligence of the monster. He hadn't tried it on the water dragon, knowing that effort would be wasted. This sea nettle was a largely unknown quantity. It certainly didn't look smart.

He concentrated on the water near the nettle. "Can you do imitations?" he asked it. The inanimate often thought it had talent of this nature, and the less talent it had, the more vain it was about it. Once, years ago, he had caused water to imitate his own voice, leading a triton a merry chase.

"No," the water said.

Oh. "Well, repeat after me: 'Sea nettle, you are a big blob of blubber.' "

"Huh?" the water asked.

He *would* have to encounter a stupid quantity of water! Some water was volatile in its wit, with cleverness flowing freely; some just lay there in puddles. "Blob of blubber!" he repeated.

"You're another!" the water retorted.

"Now say it to the sea nettle."

"You're another!" the water said to the sea nettle.

The others of Dor's party smiled. Irene's plant was growing nicely.

"No!" Dor snapped, his temper shortening. "Blob of blubber."

"No blob of blubber!" the water snapped.

The sea nettle's spines wiggled. "It says thank you," Grundy reported.

This was hopeless. In bad temper, Dor desisted.

"The flower is almost ready," Irene said. "It's a bit like the Gorgon; it can't stun you if you don't look at it. So we'd better all line up with our backs to it—and don't look back. There'll be no returning this way; once a plant like this matures, I can't stop it."

They lined up. Dor heard the rustle of rapidly expanding leaves behind him. This was nervous business!

"It's blossoming," Grundy said. "It's beginning to feel its power. Oh, it's a bad one!"

"Sure it's a bad one," Irene agreed. "I picked the best seed. Start wading into the channel. The flower will strike before we reach the sea nettle, and we want the nettle's attention directed this way."

They waded out. Dor suddenly realized how constrictive his clothing would be in the water. He didn't want anything hampering him as he swam by the nettle. He started removing his apparel. Irene, apparently struck by the same thought, quickly pulled off her skirt and blouse.

"Dor's right," Grundy remarked. He was riding Chet's back. "You do have nice legs. And that's not all."

"If your gaze should stray too far from forward," Irene said evenly, "it could encounter the ambience of the stunflower."

Grundy's gaze snapped forward. So did Chet's, Smash's, and Dor's. But Dor was sure there was a grim smirk on Irene's face. At times she was very like her mother.

"Hey, the flower's bursting loose!" Grundy cried. "I can tell by what it says; it has a bold self-image. What a head on that thing!"

Indeed, Dor could feel a kind of heat on his bare back. The power of the flower was now being exerted.

But the sea nettle seemed unaffected. It quivered, moving toward them. Its headpart was gilled like a toadstool all around. Driblets of drool formed on its surface.

"The nettle says it will sting us all so hard—oooh, that's obscene!" Grundy said. "Let me see if I can render a properly effective translation—"

"Keep moving," Irene said. "The flower's incipient."

"Now the flower's singing its song of conquest," Grundy reported, and broke into the song: "I'm the one flower, I'm the STUNflower!"

At the word "stun" there was a burst of radiation that blistered their backs. Dor and the others fell forward into the channel, letting the water cool their burning flesh.

The sea nettle, facing the flower, stiffened. Its surface glazed. The drool crystallized. The antennae faded and turned brittle. It had been stunned.

They swam by the nettle. There was no reaction from the monster. Dor saw its mass extending down into the depths of the channel with huge stinging tentacles. That thing certainly could have destroyed them all, had it remained animate.

They completed their swim in good order, Chet and Grundy in the lead, then Dor, Smash, and finally Irene. He knew she could swim well enough; she was staying back so the others would not view her nakedness. She wasn't actually all that shy about it; it was mainly her sense of propriety, developing apace with her body, and her instinct for preserving the value of what she had by keeping it reasonably scarce. It was working nicely; Dor was now several times as curious about her body as he would have been had he seen it freely. But he dared not look; the stunning radiation of the stunflower still beat upon the back of his head.

They found the shallows and trampled out of the water. "Keep going until shaded from the flower," Irene called. "Don't look back, whatever you do!"

Dor needed no warning. He felt the heat of stun travel down his back, buttocks, and legs as he emerged from the water. What a monster Irene had unleashed! But it had done its job, when his own talent had failed; it had gotten them safely across the channel and past the sea nettle.

They found a tangle of purple-green bushes and maneuvered to put them between their bodies and the stunflower. Now Dor could put his clothing back on; he had kept it mostly dry by carrying it clenched in his teeth, the magic sword strapped to his body.

"You have nice legs, too," Irene said behind him, making him jump. "And that's not all."

Dor found himself blushing. Well, he had it coming to him. Irene was already dressed; girls could change clothing very quickly when they wanted to.

They moved on south, but it was a long time before Dor lost his nervousness about looking back. That stunflower . . .

Chet halted. "What's this?" he asked.

The others looked. There was a flat wooden sign set in the ground. On it was neatly printed NO LAW FOR THE LOIN.

It was obvious that no one quite understood this message, but no one wanted to speculate on its meaning. At last Dor asked the sign: "Is there any threat to us nearby?"

"No," the sign said.

They went on, each musing his private musings. They had come to this island naked; could that relate? But obviously that sign had been there long before their coming. Could it be a misspelling? he wondered. But his own spelling was so poor, he hesitated to draw that conclusion.

Now they came to a densely wooded marsh. The trees were small but closely set; Dor and Irene could squeeze between them, but Smash could not, and it was out of the question for Chet.

"Me make a lake," Smash said, readying his huge ham-fist. With the trees gone, this would be a more or less open body of murky water.

"No, let's see if we can find a way through," Dor said. "King Trent never liked to have wilderness areas wantonly destroyed, for some reason. And if we make a big commotion, it could attract whatever monsters there are."

They skirted the thicket and soon came across another sign: THE LOIN WALKS WHERE IT WILL. Near it was a neat, dry path through the forest, elevated slightly above the swamp.

"Any danger here?" Dor inquired.

"Not much," the sign said.

They used the path. As they penetrated the thicket, there were rustlings in the trees and slurpings in the muck below. "What's that noise?" Dor asked, but received no answer. This forest was so dense there was nothing inanimate in it; the water was covered with green growth, and the path itself was formed of living roots.

"I'll try," Grundy said. He spoke in tree language, and after a moment reported: "They are cog rats and skug worms; nothing to worry about as long as you don't turn your back on them."

The rustlings and slurpings became louder. "But they are all around us!" Irene protested. "How can we avoid turning our backs?"

"We can face in all directions," Chet said. "I'll go forward; Grundy can ride me facing backward. The rest of you can look to either side."

They did so, Smash on the left, Dor and Irene on the right. The noises stayed just out of sight. "But let's get on out of this place!" Irene said.

"I wonder how the loin makes out, since this seems to be its path," Dor said.

As if in answer to his question, they came upon another sign: THE LOIN IS LORD OF THE JUNGLE. Obviously the cog rats and skug worms didn't dare bother the loin.

"I am getting more curious about this thing," Irene said. "Does it hunt, does it eat, does it play with others of its kind? What *is* it?"

Dor wondered, too, but still hesitated to state his conjectures. Suppose it wasn't a misspelling? How, then, would it hunt, eat, and play?

They hurried on and finally emerged from the thicket—only to encounter another sign. THE LOIN SHALL LIE WITH THE LAMB.

"What's a lamb?" Irene asked.

"A Mundane creature," Chet said. "Said to be harmless, soft, and cuddly, but stupid."

"That's the kind the loin would like," she muttered darkly.

Still no one openly expressed conjectures about the nature of this creature. They traveled on down to the southern tip of this long island. The entire coastline of Xanth, Chet explained, was bordered by barrier reefs that had developed into island chains; this was as good and safe a route as they could ask for, since they no longer had a boat. There should be very few large predators on the islands, since there was insufficient hunting area for them, and the sea creatures could not quite reach the interiors of the isles. But no part of Xanth was wholly safe. All of them were ready to depart this Isle of the Loin.

As they came to the beach, they encountered yet another sign: A PRIDE OF LOINS. And a roaring erupted behind them, back along the path in the thicket. Something was coming—and who could doubt what it was?

"Do we want to meet a pride of loins?" Chet asked rhetorically.

"But do we want to swim through that?" Grundy asked.

They looked. A fleet of tiger sharks had sailed in while Dor's party stood on the beach. Each had a sailfin and the head of a tiger. They crowded in as close to the shore as they could reach, snarling hungry welcome.

"I think we're between the dragon and the dune again," Grundy said.

"I can stop the tiger sharks," Irene said. "I have a kraken seaweed seed."

"And I still have the hypno-gourd; that should stop a loin," Chet said. "Assuming it's a case of misspelling. There is a Mundane monster like the front half of a tiger shark, called a—"

"But there must be several loins in a pride," Grundy said. "Unless it's just one loin standing mighty proud."

"Me fight the fright," Smash said.

"A pride might contain twenty individuals," Chet said. "You might occupy half a dozen, Smash—but the remaining dozen or so would have opportunity to eat up the rest of us. If that is what they do."

"But we don't know there are that many," Irene protested uncertainly.

"We've got to get out of here!" Grundy cried. "Oh, I never worried about my flesh when I was a real golem!"

"Maybe you weren't as obnoxious then," Irene suggested. "Besides which, you didn't *have* any flesh then."

But the only way to go was along the beach—and the tiger sharks paced them in the water. "We can't escape either menace this way," Irene said. "I'm planting my kraken." She tossed a seed into the water. "Grow, weed!"

Chet held forward the hypno-gourd that he had retained through all their mishaps, one palm covering the peephole. "I'll show this to the first loin, regardless."

Smash joined him. "Me reckon the secon'," he said, his hamfists at the ready. "An' nerd the third."

"You're the Magician," Grundy told Dor. "Do something."

Dor made a wild attempt. "Anything—is there any way out of here?"

"Thought you'd never ask," the sand at his feet said. "Of course there's a way out."

"You know a way?" Dor asked, gratified.

"No."

"For goodness' sake!" Irene exclaimed. "What an idiot!"

"You'd be stupid, too," the sand retorted, "if your brains were fragmented mineral."

"I was referring to *him!*" she said, indicating Dor. "To think they call him a Magician! All he can do is play ventriloquist with junk like you."

"That's telling him," the sand agreed. "That's a real load of sand in his eyes."

"Why did you say there was a way out if you don't know it?" Dor demanded.

"Because my neighbor the bone knows it."

Dor spotted the bone and addressed it. "What's the way out?"

"The tunnel, idiot," the bone said.

The sound of the pride of loins was looming louder. The tiger sharks were snarling as the growing kraken weed menaced them. "Where's the tunnel?" Dor asked.

"Right behind you, at the shore," the bone said. "I sealed it off, took three steps, and fell prey to the loins."

"I don't see it," Dor said.

"Of course not; the high tide washes sand over it. Last week someone goosed the tide and it dumped a lot more sand. I'm the only one who can locate the tunnel now."

Dor picked up the bone. It resembled the thighbone of a man. "Locate the tunnel for me."

"Right there, where the water laps. Scrape the sand away." It angled slightly in his hand, pointing.

Dor scraped, and soon uncovered a boulder. "This seals it?" he asked.

"Yes," the bone said. "I hid my pirate treasure under the next island and tunneled here so no one would know. But the loins—"

"Hey, Smash," Dor called. "We have a boulder for you to move."

"Oh, I wouldn't," the bone cautioned. "That's delicately placed so the thieves can't force it. The tunnel will collapse."

"Well, how do we get in, then?"

"You have to use a sky hook to lift the boulder out without jarring the sides."

"We don't have a sky hook!" Dor exclaimed angrily.

"Of course you don't. That was my talent, when I was alive. No one but me could safely remove that boulder. I had everything figured, except the loin."

As the bone spoke, the kraken weed, having driven back the tiger sharks, was questing toward the shore. Soon it would be more of a menace to them than the tiger sharks had been.

"Any progress?" Chet asked. "I do not want to rush you, but I calculate we have thirty seconds before the loins, whatever they are, burst out of the forest."

"Chet!" Dor exclaimed. "Make this boulder into a pebble! But don't jar anything."

The centaur touched the boulder, and immediately it shrank. Soon it was a pebble that fell into the hole beneath it. The passage was open.

"Jump in!" Dor cried.

Irene was startled. "Who, me?"

"Close enough," Grundy said. "Want to stand there and show off your legs to the loins?"

Irene jumped in. "Say, this is neat!" she called from below, her voice echoing hollowly. "Let me just grow something to illuminate it—"

"You next," Dor said to Chet. "Try not to shake the tunnel; it's not secure." Chet jumped in with surprising delicacy, Grundy with him.

"Okay, Smash," Dor said.

"No go," the ogre said, bracing to face the land menace. "Me join the loin." And he slammed one huge fist into a hammy palm with a sound like a crack of thunder.

Smash wanted to guard the rear. Probably that was best. Otherwise the loins might pursue them into the tunnel. "Stand next to the opening," Dor said. "When you're ready, jump in and follow us. Don't wait too long. Soon the kraken will reach here; that will stop the loins, I think. Don't tangle with the kraken; we need it to stand guard after you rejoin us."

The ogre nodded. The bellow of the loins became loud. Dor jumped in the hole.

He found himself in a man-sized passage, leading south, under the channel. The light from the entrance faded rapidly. But Irene had thoughtfully planted starflowers along the way, and their pinpoint lights marked the progress of the tunnel. Dor paused to unwrap his midnight sunstone; its beam helped considerably.

As Dor walked, he heard the approach of the pride of loins outside. Smash made a grunt of surprise. Then there was the sound of contact. "What's going on?" Dor cried, worried.

"The ogre just threw a dandyloin to the kraken," the pebble in the mouth of the tunnel said. "Now he's facing up to their leader, Sir Loin Stake. He's tough and juicy."

"Smash, come on!" Dor cried. "Don't push your luck!"

The ogre's reply was muffled. All Dor heard was ". . . luck!"

"Oooo, what you said!" the pebble exclaimed. "Wash out your mouth with soapstone!"

In a moment Smash came lumbering down the tunnel, head bowed to clear the ceiling. A string of kraken weed was strewn across his hairy shoulder. Evidently he had held off the loins until the kraken took over the vicinity. "Horde explored, adored the gourd," he announced, cracking a smile like a smoking cleft in a lightning-struck tree. Those who believed ogres had no sense of humor were obviously mistaken; Smash could laugh with the best, provided the joke was suitably fundamental.

"What did the loins look like?" Dor asked, overcome by morbid curiosity.

Smash paused, considering, then uttered one of his rare nonrhyming utterances. "Ho ho ho ho ho!" he bellowed—and the fragile tunnel began to crumble around them. Rocks dislodged from the ceiling and the walls oozed moisture.

Dor and the ogre fled that section. Dor was no longer very curious about the nature of the loins; he just wanted to get out of this tunnel alive. They were below the ocean; they could be crushed inexorably if the tunnel support collapsed. A partial collapse, leading to a substantial leak, would flood the tunnel. Even an ogre could not be expected to hold up an ocean.

They caught up to the others. There was no crash behind them; the tunnel had not collapsed. Yet.

"This place makes me nervous," Irene said.

"No way out but forward," Chet said. "Quickly."

The passage seemed interminable, but it did trend south. It must have been quite a job for the pirate to excavate this, even with his sky hook to help haul out the refuse. How ironic that the loin should be his downfall, after he had finished the tunnel! They hurried onward and downward, becoming more nervous as the depth deepened. To heighten their apprehension, the bottom of the tunnel became clammy, then slick. A thin stream of water was flowing in it—and soon it was clear that this water was increasing.

Had the ogre's laugh triggered a leak, after all? If so, they were doomed. Dor was afraid even to mention the possibility.

"The tide!" Chet said. "The tide is coming in—and high tide covers the entrance. This passage is filling with water!"

"Oh, good!" Dor said, relieved.

Four pairs of eyes focused on him, perplexed.

"Uh, I was afraid the tunnel was collapsing," Dor said lamely. "The tide—that's not so bad."

"In the sense that a slow demise is better than a fast one," the centaur said.

Dor thought about that. His apprehension became galloping dread. How could they escape this? "How much longer is this tunnel?" Dor asked.

"You're halfway through," the tunnel said. "But you'll have trouble getting past the cave-in ahead."

"Cave-in!" Irene squealed. She tended to panic in a crisis.

"Oh, sure," the tunnel said. "No way around."

In a moment, with the water ankle-deep and rising, they encountered it—a mass of rubble that sealed the passage.

"Me bash this trash," Smash said helpfully.

"Um, wait," Dor cautioned. "We don't want to bring the whole ocean in on us in one swoop. Maybe if Chet reduces the pieces to pebbles, while Smash supports the ceiling—"

"Still won't hold," Chet said. "The dynamics are wrong. We need an arch."

"Me shape escape," Smash offered. He started to fashion an arch from stray chunks of stone. But more chunks rolled down to splash in the deepening water as he took each one.

"Maybe I can stabilize it," Irene said. She found a seed and dropped it in the water. "Grow."

The plant tried, but there was not enough light. Dor shone his sunstone on it; then the plant prospered. That was all it needed; Jewel's gift was proving useful!

Soon there was a leafy kudzu taking form. Tendrils dug into the sand; vines enclosed the rocks, and green leaves covered the wall of the tunnel. Now Smash could not readily dislodge the stones he needed to complete his arch without hurting the plant.

"I believe we can make it without the arch," Chet said. "The plant has secured the debris." He touched a stone, reducing it to a pebble, then touched others. Soon the tunnel was restored, the passage clear to the end.

But the delay had been costly. The water was now knee-deep. They splashed onward.

Fortunately, they were at the nadir. As they marched up the far slope, the water's depth diminished. But they knew this was a temporary respite; before long the entire tunnel would be filled.

Now they came to the end of it—a chamber in which there stood a simple wooden table whose objects were covered by a cloth.

They stood around it, for the moment hesitant. "I don't know what treasure can help us now," Dor said, and whipped off the cloth.

The pirate's treasure was revealed: a pile of Mundane gold coins—they had to be Mundane, since Xanth did not use coinage—a keg of diamonds, and a tiny sealed jar.

"Too bad," Irene said. "Nothing useful. And this is the end of the tunnel; the pirate must have filled it in as he went, up to this point, so there would be only the one way in. I'll have to plant a big tuber and hope it runs a strong tube to the surface, and that there is no water above us here. The tuber isn't watertight. If that fails, Smash can try to bash a hole in the ceiling, and Chet can shrink the boulders as they fall. We just may get out alive."

Dor was relieved. At least Irene wasn't collapsing in hysterics. She did have some backbone when it was needed.

Grundy was on the table, struggling with the cap of the jar. "If gold is precious, and gems are precious, maybe this is the most precious of all."

But when the cap came off, the content of the jar was revealed as simple salve.

"This is your treasure?" Dor asked the bone.

"Oh, yes, it's the preciousest treasure of all," the bone assured him.

"In what way?"

"Well, I don't know. But the fellow I pirated it from fought literally to the death to retain it. He bribed me with the gold, hid the diamonds, and refused to part with the salve at all. He died without telling me what it was for. I tried it on wounds and burns, but it did nothing. Maybe if I'd known its nature, I could have used it to destroy the loins."

Dor found he had little sympathy for the pirate, who had died as he had lived, ignominiously. But the salve intrigued him increasingly, and not merely because he was now standing knee-deep in water. "Salve, what is your property?" he asked.

"I am a magic condiment that enables people to walk on smoke and vapor," it replied proudly. "Merely smear me on the bottoms of your feet or boots, and you can tread any trail in the sky you can see. Of course, the effect only lasts a day at a time; I get scuffed off, you know. But repeated applications—"

"Thank you," Dor cut in. "That is very fine magic indeed. But can you help us get out of this tunnel?"

"No. I make mist seem solid, not rock seem misty. You need another salve for that."

"If I had known your property," the bone said wistfully, "I could have escaped the loins. If only I had—"

"Serves you right, you infernal pirate," the salve said. "You got exactly what you deserved. I hope you loined your lesson."

"Listen, greasepot—" the bone retorted.

"Enough," Dor said. "If neither of you have any suggestions to get us out of here, keep quiet."

"I am suspicious of this," Chet said. "The pirate took this treasure, but never lived to enjoy it. Ask it if there is a curse associated."

"Is there, salve?" Dor asked, surprised by the notion.

"Oh, sure," the salve said. "Didn't I tell you?"

"You did not," Dor said. How much mischief had Chet's alertness saved them? "What is it?"

"Whoever uses me will perform some dastardly deed before the next full moon," the salve said proudly. "The pirate did."

"But I never used you!" the bone protested. "I never knew your power!"

"You put me on your wounds. That was a misuse—but it counted. Those wounds could have walked on clouds. Then you killed your partner and took all the treasure for yourself."

"That was a dastardly deed indeed!" Irene agreed. "You certainly deserved your fate."

"Yeah, he was pur-loined," Grundy said.

The bone did not argue.

"Oops," Chet said. He reached down and ripped something from his foreleg, just under the rising waterline. It was a tentacle from the kraken.

"I was afraid of that," Irene said. "That weed is way beyond my control. It won't stop growing if I tell it to."

Dor drew his sword. "I'll cut off any more tentacles," he said. "They can't come at me too thickly here at the end of the tunnel. Go ahead and start your tuber, Irene."

She dipped into her seedbag. "Oh-oh. That seed must've fallen out somewhere along the way. It's not here."

They had had a violent trip on the raft; the seed could have worked loose anywhere. "Chet and Smash," Dor said without pause, "go ahead and make us a way out of here, if you can. Irene, if you have another stabilization plant—"

She checked. "That I have."

They got busy. Dor faced back down the dark tunnel as the water rose to thigh level, spearing at the dark liquid with his sword, shining the sunstone here and there. The sounds of the ogre's work grew loud. "Water, tell me when a tentacle's coming," he directed. But there was so much crashing behind him as Smash pulverized the rock of the ceiling that he could not hear the warnings of the water. A tentacle caught his ankle and jerked him off his feet. He choked on water as another tentacle caught his sword arm. The kraken had him—and he couldn't call for help!

"What's going on here?" Grundy demanded. "Are you going swimming while the rest of us work?" Then the golem realized that Dor was in trouble. "Hey, why didn't you say something? Don't you know the kraken's got you?"

The kraken seaweed certainly had him! The tentacles were dragging him back down the tunnel, half drowning.

"Well, somebody's got to do something!" Grundy said, as though bothered by an annoying detail. "Here, kraken—want a cookie?" He held out a gold coin, which seemed to weigh almost as much as he did.

A tentacle snatched the coin away, but in a moment discovered it to be inedible and dropped it.

Grundy grabbed a handful of diamonds. "Try this rock candy," he suggested. The tentacle wrapped around the gems—and got sliced by their sharp edges. Ichor welled into the water as the tentacle thrashed in pain.

"Now there's a notion," Grundy said. He swam to where Dor was still being dragged along, and sliced with another diamond, cutting into the tentacles. They let go, stung, though the golem was only able to scratch them, and Dor finally gasped his way back to his feet, waist-deep in coloring water.

"I have to go help the others," Grundy said. "Yell if you get in more trouble."

Dor fished in the water and recovered his magic sword and the shining sunstone. He was more than disheveled and disgruntled. He had had to be bailed out by a creature no taller than the span of his hand. Some hero he was!

But the others had had better success. A hole now opened upward, and daylight glinted down. "Come on, Dor!" Grundy called. "We're getting out of here at last!"

Dor crammed coins and diamonds into one pocket with the sunstone, and the jar of salve into another. Smash and Chet were already scrambling out the top, having had to mount the new passage as they extended it. The centaur was actually pretty good at this sort of climbing because he had six extremities; four or five were firmly braced in crevices while one or two were searching for new holds. Grundy had no trouble; his small weight allowed him to scramble freely. Only Dor and Irene remained below.

"Hurry up, slowpoke!" she called. "I can't wait forever!"

"Start up first," he called. "I'm stashing the treasure."

"Oh, no!" she retorted. "You just want to see up my skirt!"

"If I do, that's my profit," he said. "I don't want this hole collapsing on you." For, indeed, gravel and rocks were falling down as Chet's efforts dislodged them. The whole situation seemed precarious, despite the effort of the plant Irene had grown to help stabilize the wall.

"There is that," she agreed nervously. She started to climb, while Dor completed his stashing.

The kraken's tentacles, given respite from the attacks of sword and diamond, quested forward again. The water was now chest-high on Dor, providing the weed ample play. "There's one!" the water said, and Dor stabbed into the murky fluid. He was rewarded by a jerk on his sword that indicated he had speared something that flinched away. For a creature as bloodthirsty as the kraken, it certainly was finicky about pinpricks!

"There's another!" the water cried, enjoying this game. Dor stabbed again. But it was hard to do much damage, despite the magic skill the sword gave him, since he couldn't slash effectively through water. Stabbing only hurt the tentacles without doing serious damage. Also, the weed was learning to take evasive action. It wasn't very smart, but it did learn a certain minimum under the constant prodding of pain.

Dor started to climb, at last. But to do this he had to put away his sword, and that gave the tentacles a better chance at him. Also, the gold was very solid for its size and weighed him down. As he drew himself out of the water, a tentacle wrapped around his right knee and dragged him down again.

Dor's grip slipped, and he fell back into the water. Now three more tentacles wrapped themselves around his legs and waist. That kraken had succeeded in infiltrating this tunnel far more thoroughly than Dor had thought possible! The weed must be an enormous monster now, since this must be only a fraction of its activity.

Dor clenched his teeth, knowing that no one else could help him if he got dragged under this time, and drew his sword again. He set the edge carefully against a tentacle and sawed. The magically sharp edge sliced through the tender flesh of the kraken, cutting off the extremity. The tentacle couldn't flinch away because it was wrapped around Dor; its own greed anchored it. Dor repeated the process with the other tentacles until he was free in a milky, viscous pool of kraken blood. Then he sheathed the sword again and climbed.

"Hey, Dor—what's keeping you?" Irene called from halfway up.

"I'm on my way," he answered, glancing up. But as he did, several larger chunks of rock became dislodged, perhaps by the sound of their voices, and rattled down. Dor stood chest-deep in the water, shielding his head with his arms.

"Are you all right?" she called.

"Just stop yelling!" he yelled. "It's collapsing the passage!" And he shielded his head again from the falling rocks. This was hellish!

"Oh," she said faintly, and was quiet.

Another tentacle had taken hold during this distraction. The weed was getting bolder despite its losses. Dor sliced it away, then once more began his climb. But now ichor from the monster was on his hands, making his hold treacherous. He tried to rinse off his hands, but the stuff was all through the water. With his extra weight, he could not make it.

Dor stood there, fending off tentacles, while Irene scrambled to the surface. "What am I going to do?" he asked, frustrated.

"Ditch the coins, idiot," the wall said.

"But I might need them," Dor protested, unwilling to give up the treasure.

"Men are such fools about us," a coin said from his pocket. "This fool will die for us—and we have no value in Xanth."

It did make Dor wonder. Why was he burdening himself with this junk? Wealth that was meaningless, and a magic salve that was cursed. He could not answer—yet neither could he relinquish the treasure. Just as the kraken was losing tentacles by anchoring them to his body, he was in danger of losing his life by anchoring it to wealth—and he was no smarter about it than was the weed.

Then a tentacle dangled down from above. Dor shied away; had the weed found another avenue of attack? He whipped up his sword; in air it was far more effective. "You can't nab me that way, greedy-weedy!" he said.

"Hey, watch your language," the tentacle protested. "I'm a rope."

Dor was startled. "Rope? What for?"

"To pull you up, dumbbell," it said. "What do you think a rescue rope is for?"

A rescue rope! "Are you anchored?"

"Of course I'm anchored!" it said indignantly. "Think I don't know my business? Tie me about you and I'll rescue you from this foul hole."

Dor did so, and soon he was on his way, treasure and all. "Aw, you lucked out," the coin in his pocket said.

"What do you care?"

"Wealth destroys men. It is our rite of passage: destroy a man. We were about to destroy you, and you escaped through no merit of your own."

"Well, I'm taking you with me, so you'll have another chance."

"There is that," the coin agreed, brightening.

Soon Dor emerged from the hole. Chet and Smash were hauling on the rope, drawing him up, while Grundy called directions so that no snag occurred. "What were you doing down there?" Irene demanded. "I thought you'd never come up!"

"I had some trouble with the kraken," Dor said, showing off a fragment of tentacle that remained hooked to his leg.

It was now latening afternoon. "Any danger here?" Dor asked the ground.

"There's a nest of wyverns on the south beach of this island," the ground replied. "But they hunt only by day. It's quite a nest, though."

"So if we camp here at the north end we'll be safe?"

"Should be," the ground agreed grudgingly.

"If the wyverns hunt by day, maybe we should trek on past them tonight," Irene said.

Smash smiled. "We make trek, me wring neck," he said, his brute mitts suggesting what he would do to an unfortunate wyvern. The ogre seemed larger now, taller and more massive than he had been, and Dor realized that he probably *was* larger; ogres put on growth rapidly in their teen years.

But Dor was too tired to do it. "I've got to rest," he said.

Irene was unexpectedly solicitous. "Of course you do. You stood rearguard, fighting off the kraken, while we escaped. I'll bet you wouldn't have made it out at all if Chet hadn't found that vine-rope."

Dor didn't want to admit that the weight of the gold had prevented him from climbing as he should have done. "Guess I just got tired," he said.

"The fool insisted on bringing us gold coins along," the coin blabbed loudly from his pocket.

Irene frowned. "You brought the coins? We don't need them, and they're awful heavy."

Dor sat down heavily on the beach, the coins jangling. "I know."

"What about the diamonds?"

"Them, too," he said, patting the other pocket, though he wasn't sure which pocket he had put them in.

"I do like diamonds," she said. "I regard them as friends." She helped him get his jacket off, then his wet shirt. He had avoided the Kingly robes for this trip, but his garden-variety clothing seemed hardly better now. "Dor! Your arms are all scraped!"

"That's the work of the kraken," Grundy said matter-of-factly. "It hooked his limbs and dragged him under. I had to carve it with diamonds to make it let go."

"You didn't tell me it was that bad!" she exclaimed to Dor. "Krakens are dangerous up close!"

"You were busy making the escape," Dor said. Now the abrasions on his arms and legs were stinging.

"Get the rest of this clothing off!" she said, working at it herself. "Grundy, go find some healing elixir; we forgot to bring any, but a number of plants manufacture it."

Grundy went into the forest. "Any of you plants have healing juice?" he called.

Dor was now too tired to resist. Irene tugged at his trousers. Then she paused. "Oh, my—I forgot about that," she said.

"What?" Dor asked, not sure how embarrassed he should be.

"I'm certainly glad you brought that along!" she said. "Hey, Chet—look at this!"

The centaur came over and looked. "The salve!" he said. "Yes, that could be quite useful."

Dor relaxed. For a moment he had thought—but of course she had been talking about the salve.

Soon Irene had him stripped. "Your skin's abraded all over!" she scolded. "It's a wonder you didn't faint down there!"

"Guess I'll do it now," Dor said, and did.

Chapter 6

Silver Lining

Dor woke fairly well refreshed. Evidently Grundy had located a suitable balm, for the scraped skin was largely healed. His head was pillowed on something soft; after a moment he realized it was Irene's lap. Irene was asleep with her back against an ash tree, and a fine coating of ashes now powdered her hair. She was lovely in that unconscious pose.

He seemed to be wearing new clothing, too. They must have located a flannel plant, or maybe Irene had grown one from seed. As he considered that, he heard a faint bleat in the distance and was sure; newly shorn flannel plants did protest for a while. He decided not to dwell on how she might have measured or fitted him for the clothing she had made. Obviously she was not entirely naïve about such things. In fact, Irene was shaping up as a pretty competent girl.

Dor sat up. Immediately Irene woke. "Well, someone had to keep you from thrashing about in the sand until you healed," she said, embarrassed.

He had liked her better without the explanation. "Thank you. I'm better now."

Chet and Smash had gathered red and blue berries from colorberry bushes and tapped a winekeg tree for liquid. They got pleasantly high on breakfast while they discussed the exigencies of the day. "I don't think we had better try to walk by that wyverns' nest," Chet said. "But our most feasible alternative carries a penalty."

"The curse," Grundy said.

"Beware the air," Smash agreed.

Dor scratched his head. "What are you talking about?"

"The salve," Chet explained. "To walk on clouds."

"I don't want to perform some dastardly deed," Irene said. "But I don't want to get chewed up by wyverns either."

Now a shape loomed on the ocean horizon. "What's that?" Dor asked the sea.

"A big sea serpent," the water answered. "She comes by here every morning to clean off the beaches."

Now Dor noticed how clean this beach was. The sand gleamed as whitely as bone.

"I think our decision has just been made for us," Chet said. "Let's risk the curse and walk the vapors."

"But the clouds are way out of reach," Irene protested.

"Light a fire," Grundy said. "We can walk up the smoke."

"That ought to work," Chet agreed.

Hurriedly they gathered dry wood from the interior of the island while Irene grew a flame-vine. Soon the vine was blazing, and they set the wood about it, forming a bonfire. Several fine bons puffed into the sky, looking like burning bones; then smoke billowed up, roiling its way slantwise to the west. It seemed thick enough; but was it high enough?

The sea monster was looming close, attracted by the fire. "Let's move it!" Grundy cried. "Where's the salve?"

Dor produced the salve, and the golem smeared it on his little feet. Then he made a running leap for the smoke—and flipped over and rolled on the ground. "Lift me up to the top of it," he cried, unhurt. "I need to get it firmly under me, I think."

Smash lifted him up. Yes, the ogre was definitely taller than he had been at the start of their trip.

Now the golem found his footing. "Hey—it's hot!" he cried, dancing. He ran up the column—but the smoke was moving, making his footing uncertain, and in a moment he stumbled, fell—and plummeted through the smoke toward the ground.

Smash caught him before he struck. The golem disappeared entirely inside the ogre's brute hand. "Small fall," Smash commented.

"How about putting it on his hands, too?" Irene asked.

Dor did so, dabbing it on the golem with the tip of his little finger. They put Grundy up again. This time when the golem stumbled, he was able to catch himself by grabbing handfuls of smoke. "Come on up," he cried. "The vapor's fine!"

The sea monster was almost upon them. The others put salve on their hands and feet and scrambled onto the smoke. Chet, with four feet, balanced on the shifting surface fairly handily, but Smash, Irene, and Dor had trouble. Finally they scrambled on hands and feet, getting from the hot lower smoke to the cooler higher smoke. This was less dense, but the footing remained adequate.

The surface was spongy, to Dor's sensation, like a soft balloon that was constantly changing its shape. The smoke seemed solid to their soles and palms, but it remained gaseous in nature, with its own whorls and eddies. They could not stand still on it. Dor had to keep shifting his weight to maintain balance. It was a challenge—and became fun.

Now the sea monster arrived. She sniffed the beach, then followed her nose up to the smoke and the creatures on it. The wind was extending the smoke on an almost level course at this elevation, not quite beyond reach of the monster. The creature spied Irene up there, did a double take, then snapped at the girl—who screamed and jumped off the smoke.

For an instant Dor saw her there in midair, as if she were frozen, her shriek descending with her. He knew he could not reach her or help her. The fool girl!

Then a loop of rope snagged her and drew her back to the smoke. Chet had saved his rope, the one used to draw Dor up from the hole, and now had used it to rescue Irene from her folly. Dor's heart dropped back into place.

The sea monster, deprived of her morsel, emitted an angry honk and lunged again. But this time Irene had the wit to scramble away, and the huge snout bit into the smoke and passed through it harmlessly. The teeth made an audible clash as they closed on nothing.

However, the passage of the monster's head through the smoke disturbed the column, and Dor and Smash were caught on the side nearer the fire. They could not rejoin the others until the column mended itself.

Now the monster concentrated on the two of them, since they were closest to the ground. They could not move off the smoke, so she had a good shot at them. Her huge ugly snout oriented on Dor and lunged forward.

Dor had had enough of monsters. He danced aside and whipped out his magic sword. The weapon moved dazzlingly in his hand, slicing through the soft tissue of the monster's left nostril. The creature honked with pain and rage.

"Oooo, that's not ladylike!" Grundy called from upsmoke.

"Depends on the lady," Irene remarked.

Now the sea monster opened her ponderous and mottled jaws and advanced agape. Dor had to retreat, for the mouth was too big for him to handle; it could take him in with one chomp. The monsters of the ocean grew larger than those of the lakes!

But, stepping back, he stumbled over a fresh roil of smoke and sat down hard—on nothing solid. His seat passed right through, and he had to snatch madly with both hands to save himself. He was caught as if in a tub, supported only by his feet and hands.

The monster hissed in glee and moved in to take him in, bottom-first. But Smash stepped into her mouth, hamfists bashing into the giant teeth with loud clashing sounds, knocking chips from them. Startled, the monster paused, mouth still open. The ogre stomped on her tongue and jumped back to the smoke.

By the time Dor had regained his feet, the monster had retreated, and Smash was bellowing some rhyming imprecation at her. But the monster was not one of the shy little creatures of the inland lakes that gobbled careless swimmers; she was a denizen of the larger puddle. She had been balked, not defeated; she was really angry now.

The monster honked. "I have not yet begun to bite!" Grundy translated. She cast about for some better way to get at the smokeborne morsels—and spied the fire on the beach.

The monster was not stupid for her kind. The tiny wheels rotated almost visibly in her huge ugly head as she contemplated the blaze. Then she dropped her head down, gathered herself, and with her flippers swept a huge wash of water onto the beach.

The fire hissed and sent up a violent protest of steam, then ignominiously capitulated and died. The smoke stopped billowing up.

Dor and his friends were left standing on dissipating smoke. Soon they would be left with no visible means of support.

The remaining cloud of smoke coalesced somewhat as it shrank. Dor and Smash rejoined the other three. Now all were balancing on a diffusing mass; soon they would fall into the ocean, where the sea monster slavered eagerly.

"Well, *do* something!" Irene screamed at Dor.

Dor's performance under pressure had been spotty. Now his brain percolated more efficiently. "We must make more smoke," he said. "Irene, do you have any more flammable plants in your bag?"

"Just some torchflowers," she replied. "I lost so many good seeds to the eclectic eel! But where can I grow them? They need solid ground."

"Smear magic salve on the roots," Dor told her. "Let a torch grow in this smoke."

Her mouth opened in a cute O of surprise. "That just might work!" She took out a seed, smeared it in the salve Dor held out, and ordered it to grow.

It worked. The torch developed and matured, guttering into flame and smoke. The wind carried the smoke west in a thin, dark brown stream.

Irene looked at it with dismay. "I expected it to spread out more. It will take a balancing act to walk on that!"

"In addition to which," Chet said, "the smoke in which the torch is rooted is rapidly dwindling. When it falls into the ocean—"

"We'll have to root it in its own smoke," Dor said. "Then it will never fall."

"Can't," she protested. "The smoke won't curl down, and anyway it's always moving; the thing would go into a tailspin."

"It also smacks of paradox," Chet said. "This is a problematical concept when magic is involved; nevertheless—"

"Better do *something*," Grundy warned. "That sea monster's waiting open-mouthed beneath this cloud."

"Have you another torch-seed?" Dor asked.

"Yes, one more," Irene said. "But I don't see—"

"Grow it in smoke from this one. Then we'll play leap-frog."

"Are you sure that makes sense?"

"No."

She proceeded. Soon the second torch was blazing, rooted in the smoke of the first, and its own trail of smoke ran above and parallel to the first. "But we still can't balance on those thin lines," Chet said.

"Yes, we can. Put one foot on each."

Dubiously, Chet tried it. It worked; he was able to brace against the two columns, careful not to fall between them, and walk slowly forward. Irene followed, more awkwardly, for the twin columns were at slightly different elevations and varied in separation.

There was a honking chuckle from below. Irene colored. "That monster is looking up my skirt!" she exclaimed, furious.

"Don't worry," Grundy said. "It's a female monster."

"You can be sure your legs are the first it will chomp if it gets the chance," Dor snapped. He had little patience with her vanity at this moment.

Smash went out on the columns next, balancing easily; the ogre was not nearly as clumsy as he looked.

"Go on, Grundy," Dor said. "I'll move the first torch."

"How can you move it?" the golem demanded. "You can't balance on one column."

"I'll manage somehow," Dor said, though this was a complication he hadn't worked out. Once the first torch was moved, there would be no smoke from it for him to walk on.

"You're so busy trying to be a hero, you're going to wind up monster food," Grundy said. "Where is Xanth, if you go the way of King Trent?"

"I don't know," Dor admitted. "Maybe the Zombie Master will discover he likes politics after all."

"That dourpuss? Ha!"

"But those torches have to be moved."

"*I'll* move them," Grundy said. "I'm small enough to walk on one column. You go ahead."

Dor hesitated, but saw no better alternative. "Very well. But be careful."

Dor straddled the two columns. This felt more precarious than it had looked, but was far better than dropping to the water and monster below. When he had progressed a fair distance, he braced himself and looked back.

Grundy was laboring at the first torch. But the thing was about as big as the golem, and was firmly rooted in the remaining cloud of smoke from the erstwhile beach fire; the tiny man could not get it loose. The sea monster, perceiving the problem, was bracing herself for one good snap at the whole situation.

"Grundy, get out of there!" Dor cried. "Leave the torch!"

Too late. The monster's head launched forward as her flippers thrust the body out of the water. Grundy cried out with terror and leaped straight up as the snout intersected the cloud.

The monster's teeth closed on the torch—and the golem landed on the massive snout. The saucer-eyes peered cross-eyed at Grundy, who was no bigger than a mote that might irritate one of those orbs, while smoke from the torch drifted from the great nostrils. The effect was anomalous, since no sea monster had natural fire. Fire was the perquisite of dragons.

Then the sea monster's body sank back into the ocean. Grundy scrambled up along the wispy trail of smoke from the nostrils and managed to recover his perch on the original smoke cloud. But the torch was gone.

"Run up the other column!" Dor shouted. "Save yourself!"

For a moment Grundy stood looking down at the monster. "I blew it," he said. "I ruined it all."

"We'll figure out something!" Dor cried, realizing that everything could fall apart right here if every person did not keep scrambling. "Get over here now."

Numbly the golem obeyed, walking along the widening but thinning column. Dor saw that their problems were still mounting, for the smoke that supported the second torch was now dissipating. Soon the second column, too, would be lost.

"Chet!" Dor called. "Smear salve on your rope and hook it over one smoke column. Tie yourself to the ends and grab the others!"

"You have the salve," the centaur reminded him.

"Catch it!" Dor cried. He hefted the small jar in his right hand, made a mental prayer to the guiding spirit of Xanth, and hurled the jar toward the centaur.

The tiny missile arched through the air. Had his aim been good? At first its course seemed too high; then it seemed to drop too rapidly; then it became clear the missile was off to the side. He had indeed missed; the jar was passing well beyond Chet's reach. Dor, too, had blown his chance.

Then Chet's rope flung out, and the loop closed neatly about the jar. The centaur, expert in the manner of his kind, had lassoed it. Dor's relief was so great he almost sat down—which would have been suicidal.

"But this rope's not long enough," Chet said, analyzing the job he had to do with it.

"Have Irene grow it longer," Dor called.

"I can only grow live plants," she protested.

"Those vine-ropes live a long time," Dor replied. "They can root after months of separation from their parent-plants, even when they look dead. Try it." But as he spoke, he remembered that the rope had spoken to him when it came for him down the hole. That meant that it was indeed dead.

Dubiously, Irene tried it. "Grow," she called.

They all waited tensely. Then the rope grew. One end of it had been dormant; it must have been the other end that had been dead. Once more Dor's relief was overwhelming. They were skirting about as close to the brink of disaster as they could without falling in.

Once the rope started, it grew beautifully. Not only did it lengthen, it branched, becoming a full-fledged rope-vine. Soon Chet had enough to weave into a large basket. He smeared magic salve all over it and suspended it from the smoke column. Chet himself got into it, and Irene joined him, then Smash. It was a big basket, and strong; it had to be, to support both centaur and ogre. The two massive creatures clapped each other's hands together in victory; they liked each other.

Now the second torch lost footing and started to fall. Dor charged back along the two columns, dived down, reached out, and grabbed it. But his balance on one column was precarious. He windmilled his arms, but could not quite regain equilibrium.

Then another loop of rope flung out. Dor was caught under the arms just as he slipped off the column.

Chet hauled him in as he fell, so that he described an arc toward the water. The sea monster pursued him eagerly. Dor's feet barely brushed the waves; then he swung up on the far side of the arc.

"Sword!" Grundy cried, perched on smoke far above.

Dazedly, Dor transferred the torch to his left hand and drew his sword. Now he swung back toward the grinning head of the monster.

Chet heaved, lifting Dor up a body length. As a result, instead of swinging into the opening mouth, he smacked into the upper lip, just below the flaring nostrils. Dor shoved his feet forward, mashing that lip against the upper teeth. Then he stabbed forward with the sword, spearing the tender left nostril. "How's that feel, garlic-snoot?" he asked.

The snoot blasted out an angry gale of breath that was indeed redolent of garlic and worse. Creatures with the most objectionable qualities were often the ones with the most sensitive feelings about them. Dor was blown back out over the ocean, still rising as Chet hauled him up.

But now the smoke supporting the rope and basket was dissipating. Soon they would all fall—and the monster was well aware of this fact. All the pinpricks and taps on teeth and snout she had suffered would be avenged. She hung back for the moment, avoiding Dor's sword, awaiting the inevitable with hungry eagerness.

"The smoke!" Grundy cried.

Dor realized that the torch he held was pouring its smoke up slantingly. The breeze had diminished, allowing a steeper angle. "Yes! Use this smoke to support the rope!" he ordered.

Chet, catching on, rocked the rope-basket and set it swinging. As the smoke angled up, the basket swung across to intersect it. But that caused Dor to swing also, moving his torch and its smoke.

"Grow a beanpole!" he told Irene.

"Gotcha," Irene said. Soon another seed was sprouting: a bean in the form of a pole. Smash wedged this into the basket and bent it down so that Dor could reach the far tip. Dor grabbed it and hung on. Now the pole held him at an angle below the basket. Chet and Smash managed to rotate the whole contraption so that Dor was upwind from them. The smoke poured up and across, passing just under the basket, buoying it up, each wrinkle in the smoke snagging on the woven vines. The rising smoke simply carried the basket up with it.

The sea monster caught on that the situation had changed. It charged forward, snapping at Dor—but Dor was now just out of its reach. Slowly and uncertainly the whole party slid upward, buoyed by the smoke from the torch. The arrangement seemed too fantastic and tenuous to operate even with magic, but somehow it did.

The sea monster, seeing her hard-won meal escape, vented one terrible honk of outrage that caused the smoke to waver. This shook their entire apparatus. The sound reverberated about the welkin, startling pink, green, and blue birds from their island perches and sending sea urchins fleeing in childish tears.

"I can't even translate that," Grundy said, awed.

The honk had one other effect. It attracted the attention of the nest of wyverns. The empty nest flew up, a huge mass of sticks and vines and feathers and scales and bones. "What's this noise?" it demanded.

Oh, no! Dor's talent had to be responsible for this. He had been under such pressure, his magic was manifesting erratically. "The sea monster did it!" he cried, truthfully enough.

"That animated worm?" the nest demanded. "I'll teach it to disturb my repose. I'll squish it!" And it flew fiercely toward the monster.

The sea monster, justifiably astonished, ducked her head and dived under the water. Xanth was the place of many incredible things, but this was beyond incredibility. The nest, pursuing the monster, landed with a great splash, became waterlogged, and sank. "I'm all washed up!" it wailed desparingly as it disappeared.

Dor and the others stared. They had never imagined an event like this. "But where are the wyverns?" Chet asked.

"Probably out hunting," Grundy answered. "We'd better be well away from here when they return and find their nest gone."

They had by this devious route made their escape from the sea monster. As time passed, they left the monster far below. Dor began to relax again—

and his torch guttered out. These plants did not burn forever, and this one had expended all its smoke.

"Smoke alert!" Dor cried, waving the defunct torch. They were now so high in the air that a fall would be disastrous even without an angry monster below.

"So close to the clouds!" Chet lamented, pointing to a looming cloudbank. They had almost made it.

"Grow the rope some more," Grundy said. "Make it reach up to those clouds."

Irene complied. A new vine grew up, anchored in the basket. It penetrated the lowest cloud.

"But it has no salve," Chet said. "It can't hold on there."

"Give me the salve," Grundy said. "I'll climb up there."

He did so. Nimbly he mounted the rope-vine. In moments he disappeared into the cloud, a blob of salve stuck to his back.

The supportive smoke column dissipated. The basket sagged, and Dor swung about below it, horrified. But it descended only a little; the rope-vine had been successfully anchored in the cloud, and they were safe.

There was no way the rest of them could climb that rope, though. They had to wait suspended until a vagary of the weather caused a new layer of clouds to form beneath them, hiding the ocean. The new clouds were traveling south, in contrast to the westward-moving higher ones.

When the positioning was right, they stepped out and trod the billowy white masses, jumping over the occasional gaps, until they were safely ensconced in a large cloudbank. In due course this cleared away from the higher clouds, letting the sky open. The winds at different levels of the sky were traveling in different directions, carrying their burdens with them; this wind was bearing south. Since the basket was firmly anchored to the higher cloudbank, they had to unload it quickly so they would not lose their remaining possessions. They watched it depart with mixed emotions; it had served them well.

They sprouted a grapefruit tree and ate the grapes as they ripened. It was sunny and warm here atop the clouds; since this wind was carrying them south, there was no need for the travelers to walk. Their difficult journey had become an easy one.

"Only one thing bothers me," Chet murmured. "When we reach Centaur Isle—how do we get down?"

"Maybe we'll think of something by then," Dor said. He was tired again, mentally as well as physically; he was unable to concentrate on a problem of the future right now, however critical that problem might be.

They smeared salve on their bodies so they could lie down and rest. The cloud surface was resilient and cool, and the travelers were tired; soon they were sleeping.

Dor dreamed pleasantly of exploring in a friendly forest; the action was inconsequential, but the feeling was wonderful. He had half expected more nightmares, but realized they could not reach him up here in the sky. Not unless they got hold of some magic salve for their hooves.

Then in his dream he looked into a deep, dark pool of water, and in its reflection saw the face of King Trent. "Remember the Isle," the King told him. "It is the only way you can reach me. We need your help, Dor."

Dor woke abruptly, to find Irene staring into his face. "For a moment you almost looked like—" she said, perplexed.

"Your father," he finished. "Don't worry; it's only his message, I guess. I must use the Isle to find him."

"How do you spell that?"

Dor scratched his head. "I don't know. I thought—but I'm not sure. Island. Does aisle make sense?"

"A I S L E?" she spelled. "Not much."

"I guess I'm not any better at visions than I am at adventure," he said with resignation.

Her expression changed, becoming softer. "Dor, I just wanted to tell you—you were great with the smoke and everything."

"Me?" he asked, unbelieving. "I barely scrambled through! You and Chet and Grundy did all the—"

"You guided us," she said. "Every time there was a crisis and we froze or fouled up, you called out an order and that got us moving again. You were a leader, Dor. You had what it took when we really had to have it. I guess you don't know it yourself, but you *are* a leader, Dor. You'll make a decent King, some day."

"I don't want to be King!" he protested.

She leaned down and kissed him on the lips. "I just had to tell you. That's all."

Dor lay there after she moved away, his emotions mixed. The kiss had been excruciatingly sweet, but the words sweeter yet. He tried to review the recent action, to fathom where he might have been heroic, but it was all a nightmare jumble, despite the absence of the nightmares. He had simply done what had to be done on the spur of the moment, sometimes on the very jagged edge of the moment, and had been lucky.

He didn't like depending on luck. It was not to be trusted. Even now, some horrendous unluck could be pursuing them. He almost thought he heard it through the cloudbank, a kind of leathery swishing in the air—

Then a minor kind of hell broke loose. The head of a dragon poked through the cloud, uttering a raucous scream.

Suddenly the entire party was awake and on its feet. "The wyverns!" Chet cried. "The ones whose nest we swamped! They have found us!"

There was no question of avoiding trouble. The wyverns attacked the moment they appeared. In this first contact, it was every person for himself.

Dor's magic sword flashed in his hand, stabbing expertly at the vulnerable spots of the wyvern nearest him. The wyvern was a small dragon, with a barbed tail and only two legs, but it was agile and vicious. The sword went unerringly for the beast's heart, but glanced off the scales of its breast. The dragon was past in a moment; it was flying, while Dor was stationary, and contact was fleeting.

There were a number of the wyverns, and they were expert flyers. Smash was standing his own, as one ogre was more than a match for a dragon of this size, but Chet had to gallop and dodge madly to avoid trouble. He whirled his lasso, trying to snare the wyvern, but so far without success.

Irene was in the most trouble. Dor charged across to her. "Grow a plant!" he cried. "I'll protect you!"

A wyvern oriented on them and zoomed in, its narrow lance of fire shooting out ahead. Cloud evaporated in the path of the flame, leaving a trench; they had to scramble aside. "Some protection!" Irene snorted. Her complexion was turning green; she was afraid.

But Dor's magic sword slashed with the uncanny accuracy inherent in it and lopped off the tip of a dragon's wing. The wyvern squawked in pain and rage and wobbled, partly out of control, and finally disappeared into the cloud. There were sputtering sounds and a trail of smoke fusing with the cloud vapor where the dragon went down.

It was a strange business, with Dor's party standing on the puffy white surface, the dragons passing through it as if it were vapor—which of course it was. The dragons had the advantage of maneuverability and concealment, while the people had the leverage of a firm anchorage. But Dor knew the wyverns could undercut the people's footing by burning out the clouds beneath them; all the dragons needed to do was think of it. Fortunately, wyverns were not very smart; their brains were small, since any expendable weight was sacrificed in the interest of better flight, and what brains they had were kept too hot by the fire to function well. Wyverns were designed for fighting, not thinking.

Irene was growing a plant; evidently she had saved some salve for it. It was a tangler, as fearsome a growth as the kraken seaweed, but one that operated on solid land—or cloud. In moments it was big enough to be a threat to all in its vicinity. "Try to get the tree between you and the dragon," Irene advised, stepping back from the vegetable monster.

Dor did so. When the next wyvern came at him, he scooted around behind the tangler. The dragon, hardly expecting to encounter such a plant in the clouds, did a double take and banked off. But the tangler shot out a tentacle and hooked a wing. It drew the wyvern in, wrapping more tentacles about it, like a spider with a fly.

The dragon screamed, biting and clawing at the plant, but the tangler was too strong for it. The other wyverns heeded the call. They zoomed in toward the tangler. Chet lassoed one as it passed him; the dragon turned ferociously on him, biting into his shoulder, then went on to the plant. Three wyverns swooped at the tangler, jetting their fires at it. There was a loud hissing; foul-smelling steam expanded outward. But a tentacle caught a second dragon and drew it in. No one tangled with a tangler without risk!

"We'd better get out of here," Irene said. "Whoever wins this battle will be after us next."

Dor agreed. He called to Grundy and Smash, and they went to join Chet.

The centaur was in trouble. Bright red blood streamed down his left side, and his arm hung uselessly. "Leave me," he said. "I am now a liability."

"We're all liabilities," Dor said. "Irene, grow some more healing plants."

"I don't have any," she said. "We have to get down to ground and find one; then I can make it grow."

"We can't get down," Chet said. "Not until night, when perhaps fog will form in the lower reaches, and we can walk down that."

"You'll bleed to death by night!" Dor protested. He took off his shirt, the new one Irene had made for him. "I'll try to bandage your wound. Then—we'll see."

"Here, I'll do it," Irene said. "You men aren't any good at this sort of thing. Dor, you question the cloud about a fast way down."

Dor agreed. While she worked on the centaur, he interrogated the cloud they stood on. "Where are we, in relation to the land of Xanth?"

"We have drifted south of the land," the cloud reported.

"South of the land! What about Centaur Isle?"

"South of that, too," the cloud said smugly.

"We've got to get back there!"

"Sorry, I'm going on south. You should have disembarked an hour ago. You must talk to the wind; if it changed—"

Dor knew it was useless to talk to the wind; he had tried that as a child. The wind always went where it wanted and did what it pleased without much regard for the preferences of others. "How can we get down to earth in a hurry?"

"Jump off me. I'm tired of your weight anyway. You'll make a big splash when you get there."

"I mean safely!" It was pointless to get mad at the inanimate, but Dor was doing it.

"What do you need for safely?"

"A tilting ramp of clouds, going to solid land."

"No, none of that here. Closest we have is a storm working up to the east. Its turbulence reaches down to the water."

Dor looked east and saw a looming thunderhead. It looked familiar. He was about to have his third brush with that particular storm. "That will have to do."

"You'll be sor-ree!" the cloud sang. "Those T-heads are mean ones, and that one has a grudge against you. I'm a cumulus humilis myself, the most humble of fleecy clouds, but that one—"

"Enough," Dor said shortly. He was already nervous enough about their situation. The storm had evidently exercised and worked up new vaporous muscle for this occasion. This would be bad—but what choice did they have? They had to get Chet down to land—and to Centaur Isle—quickly.

The party hurried across the cloud surface toward the storm. The thunderhead loomed larger and uglier as they approached; its huge damp vortex eyes glared at them, and its nose dangled downward in the form of a whirling cone. New muscle indeed! But the slanting sunlight caught the fringe, turning it bright silver on the near side.

"A silver lining!" Irene exclaimed. "I'd like to have some of that!"

"Maybe you can catch some on the way down," Dor said gruffly. She had criticized him for saving the gold, after all; now she wanted silver.

A wyvern detached itself from the battle with the tangler and winged toward them. "Look out behind; enemy at six o'clock!" Grundy cried.

Dor turned, wearily drawing his sword. But this dragon was no longer looking for trouble. It was flying weakly, seeming dazed. Before it reached them it sank down under the cloud surface and disappeared. "The tangler must have squeezed it," Grundy said.

"The tangler looks none too healthy itself," Irene pointed out. She was probably the only person in Xanth who would have sympathy for such a growth. Dor looked back; sure enough, the tentacles were wilting. "That was quite a fight!" she concluded.

"But if the tangler is on its last roots," Dor asked, "why did the wyvern fly away from it? It's not like any dragon to quite a fight unfinished."

They had no answer. Then, ahead of them, the wyvern pumped itself above the cloud again, struggling to clear the thunderstorm ahead. But it failed; it could not attain sufficient elevation. It blundered on into the storm.

The storm grabbed the dragon, tossed it about, and caught it in the whirling cone. The wyvern rotated around and around, scales flying out, and got sucked into the impenetrable center of the cloud.

"I hate to see a storm feeding," Grundy muttered.

"That thing's worse than the tangler!" Irene breathed. "It gobbled that dragon just like that!"

"We must try to avoid that cone," Dor said. "There's a lot of vapor outside it; if we can climb down that, near the silver lining—"

"My hooves are sinking in the cloud," Chet said, alarmed.

Now they found that the same was happening to all their feet. The formerly bouncy surface had become mucky. "What's happening?" Irene demanded, her tone rising warningly toward hysteria.

"What's happening?" Dor asked the cloud.

"Your salve is losing its effect, dolt," the thunderhead gusted, sounding blurred.

The salve did have a time limit of a day or so. Quickly they applied more. That helped—but still the cloud surface was tacky. "I don't like this," Grundy said. "Maybe our old salve was wearing off, but the new application isn't much better. I wonder if there's any connection with the wilting tangler and the fleeing wyvern?"

"That's it!" Chet exclaimed, wincing as his own animation shot pain through his shoulder. "We're drifting out of the ambience of magic! That's why magic things are in trouble!"

"That has to be it!" Dor agreed, dismayed. "The clouds are south of Xanth—and beyond Xanth the magic fades. We're on the verge of Mundania!"

For a moment they were silent, shocked. The worst had befallen them.

"We'll fall through the cloud!" Irene cried. "We'll fall into the sea! The horrible Mundane sea!"

"Let's run north," Grundy urged. "Back into magic!"

"We'll only come to the edge of the cloud and fall off," Irene wailed. "Dor, *do* something!"

How he hated to be put on the spot like that! But he already knew his course. "The storm," he said. "We've got to go through it, getting down, before we're out of magic."

"But that storm hates us!"

"That storm will have problems of its own as the magic fades," Dor said.

They ran toward the thunderhead, who glared at them and tried to organize for a devastating strike. But it was indeed losing cohesion as the magic diminished, and could not concentrate properly on them. As they stepped onto its swirling satellite vapors, their feet sank right through, as if the surface were slush. The magic was certainly fading, and very little time remained before they lost all support and plummeted.

Yet as they encountered the silver lining, Dor realized there was an unanticipated benefit here. This slow sinking caused by the loss of effect of the salve was allowing them to descend in moderate fashion, and just might bring them safely to ground. They didn't have to depend on the ambience of the storm.

They caught hold of each other's hands, so that no one would be lost as the thickening winds buffeted them. Smash put one arm around Chet's barrel, holding him firm despite the centaur's useless arm. They sank into the swirling fog, feeling it about them like stew. Dor was afraid he would be smothered, but found he could breathe well enough. There was no salve on his mouth; cloud was mere vapor to his head.

"All that silver lining," Irene said. "And I can't have any of it!"

The swirl of wind grew stronger. They were thrown about by the buffets and drawn into the central vortex—but it now had only a fraction of its former strength and could not fling them about as it had the wyvern. They spiraled down through it as the magic continued to dissipate. Dor hung on to the others, hoping the magic would hold out long enough to enable them to land softly. But if they splashed into deep water—

After an interminably brief descent, they did indeed splash into deep water. The rain pelted down on them and monstrous waves surged around them. Dor had to let go of the hands he held, in order to swim and let the others swim. He held his breath, stroked for the surface of the current wave and, when his head broke into the troubled air, he cried, "Help! Spread the word!"

Did any magic remain? Yes—a trifle. "Help!" the wave echoed faintly. "Help!" the next wave repeated. "Help! Help! Help!" the other waves chorused.

A raft appeared. "Someone's drowning!" a voice cried. "Where are you?"

"Here!" Dor gasped. "Five of us—" Then a cruel wash of water smacked into his face, and he was choking. After that, all his waning energies were taken trying to stay afloat in the turbulence, and he was not quite succeeding.

Then strong hands caught him and hauled him onto a broad wooden raft. "The others!" Dor gasped. "Four others—"

"We've got them, King Dor," his rescuer said. "Waterlogged but safe."

"Chet—my friend the centaur—he's wounded—needs healing elixir—"

The rescuer smiled. "He has it, of course. Do you suppose we would neglect our own?"

Dor's vision cleared enough to take in the full nature of his rescuer. It was an adult centaur! "We—we made it—"

"Welcome to the waters of the coast of Centaur Isle, Your Majesty."

"But—" Dor spluttered. "You aren't supposed to know who I am!"

"The Good Magician Humfrey ascertained that you were in trouble and would require assistance when you touched water. The Zombie Master asked us to establish a watch for you in this locale. You are a most important person in your own land, King Dor! It is fortunate we honored their request; we do not ordinarily put to sea during a funnel-storm."

"Oh." Dor was abashed. "Uh, did they tell you what my mission was?"

"Only that you were traveling the Land of Xanth and making a survey of the magic therein. Is there something else we should know?"

"Uh, no, thanks," Dor said. At least that much had been salvaged. The centaurs would not have taken kindly to the notion of a Magician among them—a centaur Magician. Dor did not like deceit, but felt this much was necessary.

Irene appeared, soaked through, bedraggled, and unkempt, but still quite pretty. Somehow she always seemed prettiest to him when she was messed up; perhaps it was because then the artifice was gone. "I guess you did it again, Dor," she said, taking his hand. "You got us down alive."

"But you didn't get your silver lining," he reminded her.

She laughed. "Some other time! After the way that storm treated us, I don't want any of its substance anyway."

Then the centaurs led them into the dry cabin of the raft. Irene continued to hold his hand, and that pleased Dor.

Chapter 7

Dastardly Deed

It was dark by the time the centaurs' raft reached port. Chet was taken to a vet for treatment, as the wyvern's bite seemed to be resisting the healing elixir. Dor and his companions were given a good meal of blues and oranges and greens and conducted to a handsome stable for the night. It commanded a fine view of a succulent pasture, was adequately ventilated, and was well stocked with a water trough, hay, and a block of salt.

They stared at the accommodations for a moment; then Smash stepped inside. "Say, hay!" he exclaimed, and plunked himself down into it with a crash that shook the building.

"Good idea," Grundy said, and did likewise, only the shaking of the building was somewhat less. After another moment, Dor and Irene settled down, too. The hay was comfortable and sweetly scented, conducive to relaxation and thoughts of pleasant outdoors. Irene held Dor's hand, and they slept well.

In the morning a stately elder centaur male entered the stable. He seemed oddly diffident. "I am Gerome, the Elder of the Isle. King Dor, I am here to apologize for the error. You were not supposed to be bedded here."

Dor got hastily to his feet, brushing hay off his crumpled clothing while Irene straightened out her skirt and brushed brown hay out of her green hair. "Elder, we're so glad to be rescued from the ocean, and fed and housed, that these accommodations seem wonderful. We'll be happy to complete our business and go home; this was never intended as an official occasion. The stable was just fine."

The centaur relaxed. "You are gracious, Your Majesty. We maintain assorted types of housing for assorted types of guests. I fear a glitch got into the program; we try to fence them out, but they keep sneaking in."

"They infest Castle Roogna also," Dor said. "We catch them in humane glitch traps and deport them to the far forests, but they breed faster than we can catch them."

"Come," the centaur said. "We have attire and food for you." He paused. "One other thing. Some of our number attended the Good Magician's wedding. They report you performed splendidly in trying circumstances. Magician Humfrey had intended to give you an item; it seems the distractions of the occasion caused it to slip his mind." The centaur almost smiled.

"He does tend to be forgetful," Dor said, remembering the lapse about notifying the human Elders about King Trent's excursion to Mundania.

"Accordingly, the Gorgon asked one of our representatives to convey the item to you here." Gerome held out a small object.

Dor accepted it. "Thank you, Elder. Uh, what is it?"

"I believe it is a magic compass. Note that the indicator points directly to you—the one Magician on the Isle."

Dor studied the compass. It was a disk within which a needle of light showed. "This isn't pointing to me."

Gerome looked. "Why, so it isn't. But I'm sure it was until a moment ago; that is how I was certain it had reached its proper destination. Perhaps I misunderstood its application; it may have pointed to you only to guide us to you. Certainly it assisted our search for you yesterday afternoon."

"That must be it!" Dor agreed. The Good Magician might have anticipated the problem with the storm and sent down the one thing that would bring help to him unerringly. Humfrey was funny that way, doing things anachronistically. Dor tucked the compass in a pocket with the diamonds and sunstone and changed the subject. "Chet—how is he doing this morning?"

Gerome frowned. "I regret to report that he is not fully recovered. Apparently he was bitten near the fringe of magic—"

"He was," Dor agreed.

"And a Mundane infection got in. This is resistive to magic healing.

Perhaps, on the other hand, it was merely the delay in applying the elixir. We can not be certain. Odd things do happen at the fringe of magic. He is in no danger of demise, but I fear it will be some time before his arm is again at full strength."

"Maybe we can help him back at Castle Roogna," Dor said, uncomfortable. "He is our friend; without him, we could not have made it down here. I feel responsible—"

"He must not indulge in any further violence until he recovers completely," Gerome said gravely. "It is not at all wise to take a magic-resistive illness lightly. Come—he awaits you at breakfast."

On the way there, Gerome insisted they pause at the centaur clothier. Dor was outfitted with bright new trousers, shirt, and jacket, all intricately woven and comfortable. Irene got a dress set that set her off quite fetchingly, though it was not her normal shade of green. Even Smash and Grundy got handsome jackets. The ogre had never worn clothing before, but his jacket was so nice he accepted it with pride.

"This material," Irene said. "There's something magic about it."

Gerome smiled. "As you know, we centaurs frown on personal magic talents. But we do work with magic. The apparel is woven by our artisans from iron curtain thread, and is strongly resistant to penetration by foreign objects. We use it for vests during combat, to minimize injuries."

"But this must be very precious stuff!" Dor said.

"Your welfare is important to us, Your Majesty. Had you and Chet been wearing this clothing, the wyvern's teeth would not have penetrated his shoulder."

Dor appreciated the rationale. It would be a big embarrassment to the centaurs if anything happened to the temporary King of Xanth or his friends during their stay here. "Thank you very much."

They entered a larger room, whose tall ceiling was supported by ornate white columns. Huge windows let in the slanting morning sunlight, lending a pleasant warmth and brilliance. On an enormous banquet table in the center were goblets of striped sardonyx and white alabaster, doubly pretty in the sun. The plates were of green jadeite. "A King's ransom," Irene whispered. "I think they trotted out the royal crockery for you, Dor."

"I wish they hadn't," he whispered back. "Suppose something gets broken?"

"Keep an eye on Smash," she said. That made Dor more nervous than ever. How would the ogre handle the delicate tableware?

They were given high chairs, for the table was too tall for them. Several more centaurs joined them, male and female, introduced as the other Elders of the Isle. They stood at the table; centaurs had no way to use chairs, and the table was crafted to their height.

The food was excellent. Dor had been halfway fearful that it would be whole oats and cracked corn with silage on the side, but the glitch of the stable-housing was not repeated. There was a course of yellow cornmeal mush, from cornmeal bushes, and fine chocolate milk from cocoa-nuts. For sweetening there was an unusual delicacy called honey, said to be manufactured by a rare species of bees imported from Mundania. Dor had encountered sneeze-bees and the spelling bee, but it was odd indeed to think of honey-bees!

Smash, to Dor's surprise and relief, turned out to be a connoisseur of delicate stone. His kind, he informed them happily in rhyme, had developed their power by smashing and shaping different kinds of minerals. They could not turn out goblets as nice as these, but did produce pretty fair marble and granite blocks for walls and buildings.

"Indeed," Gerome agreed. "Some fine cornerstones here were traded from ogres. Those corners stand up to anything."

Smash tossed down another couple mugs of milk, pleased. Few other creatures recognized the artistic propensities of ogres.

Chet was there, looking somewhat wan and eating very little, which showed that his injury was paining him somewhat. There was nothing Dor could do except politely ignore it, as his friend obviously wanted no attention drawn to his weakness. Chet would not be traveling with them again for some time.

After the meal they were treated to a guided tour of the Isle. Dor was conscious of King Trent's reference to isle or aisle in the vision. If it were the only way Dor could reach him, he must be alert for the mechanism. Somewhere here, perhaps, was the key he needed.

The outside streets were broad, paved with packed dirt suitable for hooves, and were banked on the curves for greatest galloping comfort. At intervals were low wooden props that the centaurs could use to knock the dottle from their feet. The buildings were mixed; some were stables, while others were more like human residences.

"I see you are perplexed by our premises," Gerome said. "Our architecture derives from our origin; in due course you shall see our historical museum, where this will be made clear."

During their walk, Dor surreptitiously looked at the magic compass Good Magician Humfrey had sent him. He had believed he had figured out its application. "Compass—do you point to the nearest and strongest Magician who is not actually using you?" he asked.

"Sure," the compass replied. "Any fool knows that."

So it was now pointing to the centaur Magician. Once Dor got free of these formalities, he would follow that needle to the object of his quest.

They stopped at the extensive metalworking section of town. Here were blacksmiths and silversmiths and coppersmiths, fashioning the strange shoes that important centaurs used, and the unusual instruments they employed for eating, and the beautiful pots they cooked with. "*They* had no trouble harvesting plenty of silver linings," Irene commented enviously.

"Ah—you appreciate a silver lining?" Gerome inquired. He showed the way to another craftshop, where hundreds of silver linings were being fashioned as the fringes of jackets and such. "This is for you." And the centaur gave her a fresh fur with a fine silver lining sewn in, which gleamed with the splendor of sunlight after storm.

"Ooooh," Irene breathed, melting into it. "It's soft as cloud!" Dor had to admit, privately, that the decorative apparel did enhance her appearance.

One centaur was working with a new Mundane import, a strong light metal called aluminum. "King Trent's encouragement of trade with Mundania has benefited us," Gerome remarked. "We have no natural aluminum in Xanth. But the supply is erratic, because we never seem to be able to trade with the same aspect of Mundania twice in succession. If that problem could be ameliorated, it would be a great new day for commerce."

"He's working on it," Irene said. But she had to stop there; they had agreed not to spread the word about King Trent's situation.

They saw the weaving section, where great looms integrated the threads garnered from assorted sources. The centaurs were expert spinners and weavers, and their products varied from silkenly fine cloth to heavy ruglike mats. Dor was amazed; it had never occurred to him that the products of blanket trees could be duplicated artificially. How wonderful it would be to be able to make anything one needed, instead of having to wait for a plant to grow it!

Another section was devoted to weapons. Centaurs were superlative bowmen and spearmen, and here the fine bows and spears were fashioned, along with swords, clubs, and ropes. A subsection was devoted to armor, which included woven metal clothing as well as helmets, greaves, and gauntlets. Smash tried on a huge gauntlet and flexed it into a massive fist. "Me see?" he inquired hopefully.

"By all means," Gerome said. "There is a boulder of quartz we mean to grind into sand. Practice on it."

Smash marched to the boulder, lifted his fist high, and smashed it down upon the boulder. There was a crack of sound like thunder, and a cloud of dust and sand erupted from the point of contact, enveloping him. When it settled, they saw the ogre standing knee-deep in a mound of sand, a blissful smile cracking his ugly face. "Love glove," he grunted, reluctantly removing it. Wisps of smoke rose from its fingertips.

"Then it is yours, together with its mate," Gerome said. "You have saved us much labor, reducing that boulder so efficiently."

Smash was thrilled with the gift, but Dor was silent. He knew ogres were strong, but Smash was not yet grown. The metal gauntlet must have enhanced his power by protecting his hand. As an adult, Smash would be a truly formidable creature, with almost too much power. That could get him exiled from the vicinity of Castle Roogna. But more than that, Dor was disquieted by something more subtle. The centaurs were evidently giving choice gifts to each member of Dor's party—fine protective clothing, plus whatever else offered, such as Irene's silver lining and Smash's gauntlets. This might be a fine gesture of friendship—but Dor distrusted such largesse.

What was the purpose in it? King Trent had warned him once to beware strangers bearing gifts. Did the centaurs suspect Dor's mission, and were they trying to affect the manner he pursued it? Why? He had no ready answer.

They viewed the centaur communal kitchen, where foodstuffs from a wide area were cleaned and prepared. Obviously the centaurs ate very well. In fact, in most respects they seemed to be more advanced and to have more creature comforts than the human folk of the Castle Roogna area. Dor found this unsettling; he had somehow expected to find Centaur Isle inhabited by a few primitives galloping around and fighting each other with clubs. Now that he was here, Centaur Isle seemed more like the center of culture, while Castle Roogna appeared to be the hinterland.

The power of magic was surely weaker here near the fringe, which helped explain why most centaurs seemed to lack talents, while those farther toward the center of Xanth were showing them. How was it, then, that these deficient centaurs were doing so well? It was almost as if the lack of magic was an advantage, causing them to develop other skills that in the end brought more success than the magic would have. This was nonsense, of course; but as he viewed the things of the Isle, he almost believed it. Suppose, just suppose, that there *was* a correlation between success and the lack of magic. Did it then follow that Mundania, the land completely devoid of music, was likely to become a better place to live than Xanth?

That brought a puff of laughter. He had followed his thought to its logical extremity and found it ludicrous. Therefore the thought was false. It was ridiculous on the face of it to think of drear Mundania as a better place than Xanth!

The others were looking askance at him because of his pointless laughter. "Uh, just a chain of thought that snapped in a funny place," Dor explained. Then, fearing that wasn't enough to alleviate their curiosity, he changed the subject. "Uh, if I may inquire—since you centaurs seem to be so well organized here—certainly better than we humans are—how is it that you accept human government? You don't seem to need us, and if it ever came to war, you could destroy us."

"Dor!" Irene protested. "What a thing to say!"

"You are too modest, Your Majesty," Gerome said, smiling. "There are several compelling reasons. First, we are not interested in empire; we prefer to leave decisions of state to others, while we forward our arts, crafts, skills, and satisfaction. Since you humans seem to like the tedious process of government, we gladly leave it to you, much as we leave the shaping of granite stones to the ogres and the collection of diamonds to the dragons. It is far simpler to acquire what we need through trade."

"Well, I suppose so," Dor agreed dubiously.

"Second, you humans have one phenomenal asset that we generally lack," Gerome continued, evidently embarked on a favorite subject. "You can do magic. We utilize magic, but generally cannot perform it ourselves, nor would we wish to. We prefer to borrow it as a tool. Can you imagine one of us prevailing over King Trent in an altercation? He would convert us all to inchworms!"

"If he could get close enough," Dor said. He remembered that this matter had been discussed before; Chet had pointed out how the centaurs' skill with the bow and arrow nullified Trent's magic. Was there an answer to that? Dor would much prefer to believe that magic was the supreme force in Xanth.

"Who can govern from a distance?" Gerome inquired rhetorically. "Armies in the field are one thing; governing people is another. King Trent's magic enables him to govern, as does your own. Even your lesser talents are far beyond our capacities."

Was the centaur now gifting him with flattery? "But centaurs can do magic!" Dor protested. "Our friend Chet—"

"Please," Gerome said. "You humans perform natural functions, too, but we do not speak publicly of such things, in deference to your particular sensitivities. It is a fact that we centaurs were not aware of any personal magic talents through most of our history, and even now suspect manifestations are an aberration. So we have never considered personal magic as being available for our use and would prefer that no further mention of this be made."

"Uh, sure," Dor agreed awkwardly. It seemed the other centaurs were just as sensitive and unreasonable about this as Dor's tutor Cherie was. Humans were indeed finicky about certain natural functions, as the centaur Elder had reminded him, while centaurs were not; while humans were not finicky about the notion of personal magic the way the centaurs were. Probably one attitude made as much nonsense as the other.

But how would the citizens of Centaur Isle react to the news that a full Magician of their species was among them? Eventually Dor would have to tell them. This mission could be awkward indeed!

"Third, we honor an understanding dating from the dawn of our species," Gerome continued, leaving the distasteful subject of magic behind like a clod of manure. "We shall not indulge in politics, and will never compete with our human brethren for power. So even if we desired empire and had the ability to acquire it, we would not do so. We would never renege on that binding commitment." And the centaur looked so serious that Dor dared not pursue the matter further.

At last they came to the historical museum. This was an impressive edifice of red brick, several stories high, with small windows and a forbidding external aspect. But it was quite interesting inside, being crowded with all manner of artifacts. There were samples of all the centaurs' products, going back decade by decade to before the First Wave of human conquest. Dor could see how the earlier items were cruder; the craftsmen were still improving their skills. Everything was identified by neat plaques providing dates, places, and details of manufacture. The centaurs had a keen sense of history!

During the tour, Dor had continued to sneak glances at the magic compass. He was gratified to see that it pointed toward the museum; maybe the Magician was here!

"And this is our keeper of records," Gerome said, introducing a middle-aged, bespectacled centaur. "He knows where all the bodies are hidden. Arnolde the Archivist."

"Precisely," Arnolde agreed dourly, peering over his glasses. The demon Beauregard was the only other creature Dor had seen wearing such devices. "So nice to encounter you and your party, King Dor. Now if you will excuse me, I have a new shipment of artifacts to catalogue." He retreated to his cubby, where objects and papers were piled high.

"Arnolde is dedicated to his profession," Gerome explained. "He's quite intelligent, even by our standards, but not sociable. I doubt there is very much about Xanth natural history he doesn't know. Recently he has been picking up items from the fringe of magic; he made one trip to an island to the south that may have taken him entirely out of magic, though he denies this. Prior to the time King Trent dropped the shield that enclosed Xanth, such expeditions were impossible."

Dor remembered the shield, for his tutor had drilled him on it. Cherie Centaur was particularly strong on social history. The Waves of human conquerors had become so bad that one King of Xanth had finally put a stop to further invasion by setting up a magic shield that killed any living thing that passed through it. But that had also kept the inhabitants of Xanth in. The Mundanes, it seemed, came to believe that Xanth did not exist at all and that magic was impossible, since none of it leaked out any more. There had, it seemed, been many recorded cases of magic that Mundanes had witnessed or experienced; all these were now written off as superstition. Perhaps that was the Mundanes' way of reconciling themselves to the loss of something as wonderful as enchantment, to pretend it did not exist and never had existed.

But Xanth had suffered, too. In time it had become apparent that mankind in Xanth needed those periodic infusions of new blood, however violently they came, for without the Waves there was a steady attrition of pure human beings. First, people developed magic talents; later generations became magic themselves, either mating with animals to form various composite species like harpies or fauns or merfolk, or simply evolving into gnomes or giants or nymphs. So King Trent had lowered the shield and brought in a number of settlers from Mundania, with the understanding that these new people would be drawn on as warriors to repel any future violent invasion that might come. So far there had been none—but the Waves had been a pattern of centuries, not of decades, so that meant little. Immigration was an uncertain business, as it was far easier to go from Xanth to Mundania than the other way around, at least for individual people. But the human situation in Xanth did seem to be improving now. Dor could appreciate how an intelligent, inquisitive centaur would be eager to begin cataloguing the wonders of Mundania, which long had been a great mystery. It was still hard to accept the notion that here was a region where magic was inoperative, and where people survived.

They moved on down the narrow hall. Dor checked the compass again—and found that it pointed directly toward Arnolde the Archivist.

Could he be the centaur Magician, the threat to the welfare of Xanth, the important business Dor had to attend to? That didn't seem to make much sense. For one thing, Arnolde showed no sign of magic ability. For another, he was hardly the type to threaten the existing order; he was dedicated to recording it. For yet another, he was a settled, middle-aged person, of a species that lived longer than man. Magic talents might not be discovered early, but the evidence was that they existed from birth on. Why should this talent become an issue now, perhaps a century into Arnolde's life? So it must be a mistake; Dor's target had to be a young centaur, perhaps a newborn one.

Yet as Dor moved about the building, only half listening to the presentation, the compass pointed unerringly toward Arnolde's cubby.

Maybe Arnolde was married, Dor thought with exasperated inspiration. Maybe he had a baby centaur, hidden there among the papers. The compass could be pointing to the foal, not to Arnolde. Yes, that made sense.

"If you don't get that glazed look off your face, the Elder will notice," Irene murmured, jolting Dor's attention.

After that he concentrated and managed to assimilate more of the material. After all, there was nothing he could do about the Magician at the moment.

At length they completed the tour. "Is there anything else you would like to see, King Dor?" Gerome inquired.

"No, thank you, Elder," Dor replied. "I think I've seen enough."

"Shall we arrange to transport your party back to your capital? We can contact your conjurer."

This was awkward. Dor had to complete his investigation of the centaur Magician, so he was not ready to leave this Isle. But it was obvious that his mission and discovery would not be well received here. He could not simply tell the centaur Elders the situation and beg their assistance; to them that would be obscenity, and their warm hospitality would abruptly chill. A person's concept of obscenity was not subject to reasonable discussion, for of course the concepts of obscenity and reason were contradictory.

In fact, that might be the root of the centaurs' accommodation and generosity. Maybe they suspected his mission, so were keeping him reined at all times, in the guise of hospitality. How could he decline to go home promptly, after they had seemingly catered to his needs so conscientiously? They wanted him off the Isle, and he had little chance to balk their wish.

"Uh, could I talk with Chet before I decide anything?" Dor asked.

"Of course. He is your friend." Again Gerome was the soul of accommodation. That made Dor more nervous, ironically. He was almost sure, now, that he was being managed.

"And my other friends," Dor added. "We need to decide things together."

It was arranged. In the afternoon the five got together in a lovely little garden site of guaranteed privacy. "You all know our mission," Dor said. "It is to locate a centaur Magician and identify his talent—and perhaps bring him back to Castle Roogna. But the centaurs don't much like magic in themselves; to them it's obscene. They react to it somewhat the way we do to—well, like people looking up Irene's skirt."

"Don't start on that!" she said, coloring slightly. "I think the whole world has been looking up my skirt recently!"

"Your fault for having good legs," Grundy said. She kicked at him, but the golem scooted away. Dor noted that she hadn't tried very hard to tag Grundy; she was not really as displeased as she indicated.

"I happen to be in a position to understand both views," Chet said. His left arm was now in a sling, and he wore a packing of anti-pain potions. His outlook seemed improved, but not his immediate physical condition. "I admit that both centaur and human foibles are foolish. Centaurs do have magic talents and should be proud to display them, and Irene does have excellent limbs for her kind and should be proud to display them. And that's not all—"

"All *right!*" Irene snapped, her color deepening. "Point made. We can't go blabbing our mission to everyone on Centaur Isle. They just wouldn't understand."

"Yes," Dor said, glad to have this confirmation of his own analysis of the situation. "So now I need some group input. You see, I believe I have located the centaur Magician. It has to be the offspring of Arnolde the Archivist."

"Arnolde?" Chet asked. "I know of him. He's been at his job for fifty years; my mother speaks of him. He's a bachelor. He has no offspring. He's more interested in figures of the numerical persuasion than in figures of fillies."

"No offspring? Then it must be Arnolde himself," Dor said. "The magic compass points directly to him. I don't know how it is possible, since I'm sure no such Magician was known in Xanth before, but I don't believe Good Magician Humfrey would give me a bad signal on this."

"What's his talent?" Irene asked.

"I don't know. I didn't have a chance to find out."

"I could ask around," Grundy offered. "If there are any plants or animals around his stall, they should know."

"I can ask around myself," Dor said. "There are bound to be inanimate objects around his stall. That's not the problem. The Elders are ready to ship us home now, and I have no suitable pretext to stay. Even one night might be enough. But what do I tell them without lying or alienating them? King Trent told me that when in doubt, honesty is the best policy, but in this case I'm in doubt even about honesty."

"Again I perceive both sides," Chet said. "Honesty *is* best—except perhaps in this case. My kind can become exceedingly ornery when faced with an incompatible concept. While I would not wish to imply any criticism of my sire—"

The others knew what he meant. Chester Centaur's way to handle something he didn't like was to pick it up in a chokehold and shake the stuffing from it. The centaurs of Centaur Isle were more civilized, but just as ornery underneath.

"Tell them your business is unfinished and you need another day," Irene suggested. "That's the literal truth."

"That, simplistic as it sounds, is an excellent answer," Chet said. "Then go out at night and spy out Arnolde's talent. Have Grundy scout the route first, so you don't arouse suspicion. That way you can complete the mission without giving offense and go home tomorrow."

"But suppose we need to take him with us? A full Magician should come to Castle Roogna."

"No problem at all," Chet said. "I can tell you right now he won't come, and no Magician can be compelled. There's hardly a thing that could dislodge the archivist from his accustomed rounds."

"Knowing his talent should be enough," Irene said. "Our own Council of Elders can decide what to do about it, once they have the information."

Dor was relieved. "Yes, of course. Tonight, then. The rest of you can sleep."

"Fat chance," Irene said, and Smash grunted agreement. "We're in this mess together. You're certain to foul it up by yourself."

"I appreciate your vote of confidence, as always," Dor said wryly. But he also appreciated their support. He was afraid he would indeed foul it up by himself, but hadn't wanted to ask them to participate in what might be a nasty business.

That night they put their plot into execution. Grundy went out first, his tiny dark body concealed by the darkness. There was no trouble, and soon all of them left their comfortable human-style beds—Chet excepted, as he was separately housed and could not readily leave his stall unobserved—and moved into the moonlit evening. They had no difficulty seeing, because the moon was nearing full and gave plenty of light.

They found the museum without trouble. Dor had assumed it would be closed for the night, but to his dismay it was lighted. "Who is in there?" he asked the ground.

"Arnolde the Archivist," the ground replied. "You have to be pretty stupid not to know he's been working late all week, cataloguing those new Mundane artifacts, though what he finds so interesting about such junk—"

"What's his magic talent?"

"His what?" the ground asked, bewildered.

"You know of no magic associated with him?" Dor asked, surprised. Normally people were very free about what they did around only inanimate things, and it was hard to avoid the inanimate. That was what made Dor's own talent so insidious; the complete privacy people thought they had became complete disclosure in his presence. He tried not to pry into what did not rightly concern him, but most people, including his own parents, normally stayed clear of him, without making any issue of it. The people who had traveled with him were different, for their separate reasons; when he thought about it, he appreciated it immensely. Even Irene, who professed to value her privacy, was not truly uncomfortable in Dor's presence. She really didn't have to make any great play for him; gratitude would haul him into her orbit any time she wished. He knew she was accustomed to lack of privacy because of the way her mother was, but still found it easier to get along with her than with other girls. Others got unduly upset when their clothing started telling Dor their secrets.

Dor glanced at the large round moon again. It was amazing how that orb stimulated his thoughts along such lines!

Meanwhile, the ground had answered: "None at all. Centaurs don't do magic."

Dor sighed. "I guess we'll have to go in and brace him directly."

They went in. Arnolde had artifacts spread out all over a main table and was attaching tags to them and making notes. There were fragments of stone and crockery and rusted metal. "I wish the archaeologists would get these classified sooner," he grumbled. "This table is not available by day, so I have to tag them at night." Then he did a startled double take. "What are you doing here? The guest tour is over."

Dor considered making a bald statement of purpose and decided against it. He needed to get to know the centaur a little better before broaching so delicate a subject. "I have an important matter to discuss with you. A, uh, private matter. So I didn't bring it up during the tour."

Arnolde shrugged. "I have no inkling what the King of Xanth would want with me. Just keep your hands off the artifacts, and I will listen to what you have to impart. Mundane items are difficult to come by."

"I'm sure they are," Dor agreed. "We came here by air, riding the clouds, and almost went beyond the limit of magic. We were lucky we didn't fall. Mundania is no place for the creatures of Xanth."

"Oh?" the centaur said without much interest. "Did you see the southern island?"

"No. We weren't that far south. We came down in sight of Centaur Isle."

"There should have been plenty of magic. My raft was powered by a propulsion spell, and it never failed. I was needlessly concerned; evidently that island was Mundane historically, but is now magic." The centaur's hands were busy affixing each tag neatly and making careful entries in a ledger. He evidently liked his work, tedious as it seemed, and was conscientious.

"I think we were north of it, but we certainly had trouble," Dor said. "But there was a storm; that could have disrupted the magic."

"Quite possible," Arnolde agreed. "Storms do seem to affect it."

The centaur seemed sociable enough, now that they were not taking him away from his beloved work. But Dor still did not feel easy. "Uh, the Elder Gerome mentioned a—some kind of pact the centaurs made with my kind, back at the beginning. Do you have artifacts from that time?"

"Indeed I do," Arnolde said, growing animated. "Bones, arrowheads, the hilt of an iron sword—the record is fragmentary, but documents the legend. The full truth may never be known, sadly, but we do have a fair notion."

"Uh, if you're interested—I'm a Magician. I make things talk. If you'd like to question one of those old artifacts—"

Now Arnolde grew excited. "I had not thought of that! Magic is all right for you, of course. You're only human. I pride myself on being reasonably realistic. Yes, I would like to question an artifact. Are you familiar with the legend of centaur origin?"

"No, not really," Dor said, growing interested himself. "It would help me if I did know it; then I could ask the artifact more specific questions."

"Back CBP 1800—that's Circa Before Present one thousand, eight hundred years," the archivist intoned reverently, "the first man and first horse—you are aware of the nature of that animal? Front of a sea horse merged with the rear of a centaur—"

"Yes, like a nightmare, only in the day," Dor said.

"Exactly. These two, the first of each kind we know of, reached Xanth from Mundania. Xanth was already magic then; its magic seems to have existed for many thousands of years. The plants were already well evolved—you do know what I mean by evolution?"

"How nickelpedes developed from centipedes."

"Um, yes. The way individual species change with the times. Ah, yes, the King always has a centaur tutor, so you would have been exposed to such material. Back then the dragons dominated the land—one might term it the Age of Reptiles—and there were no human hybrids and no dwarves, trolls, goblins, or elves. This man saw that the land was good. He was able and clever enough to stay clear of the more predatory plants and to balk the dragons; he was a warrior, with a bow, sword, spear, club, and the ability to use them, and a valiant spirit.

"But though he found Xanth delightful, he was lonely. He had, it seemed, fled his home tribe—we like to think he was an honorable man who had run afoul of an evil King—such things do happen in Mundania, we understand—and could not safely return there. Indeed, in time a detachment of other warriors came after him, intent on his murder. There is an opacity about the manner Mundanes may enter Xanth; normally people from the same Mundane subsociety may enter Xanth only if they are grouped together, not separately, but it seems these ones were, after all, able to follow—I don't pretend to understand this, but perhaps it is a mere distortion of the legend—at any rate, they were less able than he and fell prey to the natural hazards of Xanth. All but two of them died—and these two, severely wounded, survived only because this first good man—we call him Alpha, for what reason the record does not divulge—rescued them from peril and put healing balm on their wounds. After that they declined to attack him any more; they owed life-debts to him, and swore friendship instead. There was a kind of honor in those days, and we have maintained it since.

"Now they were three men, with three fine mares they had salvaged. None of them could leave Xanth, for news of their betrayal had somehow spread, and enemies lurked just beyond the realm of magic. Or perhaps the Mundane culture had somehow become alien, one variant of the legend has reference to their attempt to return, and discovery of Babel—that they could no longer speak the language or comprehend the culture of the Mundanians. One of them had been a mercenary, a paid soldier, who it seemed spoke a different Mundanian dialect, but he spoke the same language as the others when they met in Xanth. We know this is a property of the magic of Xanth; all cultures and languages become one, including the written language; there is no language barrier between creatures of the same species. For whatever reason—I might wish that the legend was absolutely firm and clear, but must deal with a story line that fragments into mutually incompatible aspects, each of which has elements that are necessary to the continuation of the whole—a most intriguing riddle!—the three men and their mounts were safe, as long as they remained within the realm of magic they had come to understand and use so well—but they longed for the companionship of women of their kind. They wished to colonize the land, but could only live on it.

"Then, exploring deep in new territory, they came upon a spring on a lovely offshore island, and all three drank deeply and watered their horses. They did not know it was a spring of love that would compel instant love with the first creature of the opposite sex spied after drinking. And so it happened that each man, in that critical moment, saw first his good mare— and each mare saw her master. And so it was that the species of the centaur began. This is another of the perplexing distinctions between Xanth and Mundania; in the latter Kingdom representatives of different species are unable to interbreed to produce offspring, while in Xanth it is a matter of course, though normally individuals are most attracted to their own species. The offspring of these unions, perceiving that their parents differed from themselves and that the masters were human beings who were possessed of the greater part of the intellect while the mares possessed the greater part of the strength, learned to respect each species for its special properties. The men taught their offspring all the skills they knew so well, both mental and physical, and commanded in return the right to govern this land of Xanth. In time the mares died, after foaling many times, and eventually the men died, too, leaving only the continuing species of centaur on the island. But the tradition remained, and when, centuries later, other men came, and women, too, the centaurs accorded them the dominance of the Kingdom. So it continues to the present day."

"That's beautiful," Irene said. "Now I know why you centaurs have always supported us, even when our kind was unworthy, and why you served as our mentors. You have been more consistent than we have been."

"We have the advantage of cultural continuity. Yet it is a legend," Arnolde reminded her. "We believe it, but we have no detailed proof."

"Bring me an artifact," Dor said, moved by the story. He had no desire to mate with a creature of another species, but could not deny that love matches of many types existed in Xanth. The harpies, the merfolk, the manticora, the werewolves and vampire-bats—all had obvious human and animal lineage, and there were also many combinations of different animals, like the chimera and griffin. It would be unthinkable to deny the validity of these mixed species; Xanth would not be the same at all without them. "I'll get you the proof."

But now the centaur hesitated. "I thought I wanted the proof—but now I am afraid it would be other than the legend. There might be ugly elements in lieu of the beautiful ones. Perhaps our ancestors were not nice creatures. I sheer away; for the first time I discover a limit to my eagerness for knowledge. Perhaps it is best that the legend remain unchallenged."

"Perhaps it is," Dor agreed. Now at last he felt the time had come to express his real concern. "Since centaurs derive from men, and men have magic talents—"

"Oh, I suppose some centaurs do have some magic," Arnolde said in the manner of an open-minded person skirting a close-minded issue. "But it has no bearing on our society. We leave the magic, like the governing, to you humans."

"But some centaurs do—even Magician level—"

"Oh, you mean Herman the Hermit Centaur," Arnolde said. "The one who could summon the Will-o'-Wisps. He was wronged, I think; he used his power to save Xanth from the ravage of wiggles, and gave his life in that effort, eighteen years ago. But of course, though some magic has perforce been accepted recently in our society, if another centaur Magician appeared, he, too, would be outcast. We centaurs have a deep cultural aversion to obscenity."

Dor found his task increasingly unpleasant. He knew Cherie Centaur considered magic in her species to be obscene, though her mate Chester, Chet's father, had a magical talent. Cherie had adjusted to that situation with extraordinary difficulty. "There is one, though."

"A centaur Magician?" Arnolde's brow wrinkled over his spectacles. "Are you certain?"

"Almost certain. We have had a number of portents at Castle Roogna and elsewhere."

"I pity that centaur. Who is it?"

Now Dor was unable to answer.

Arnolde looked at him, the import dawning. "Surely you do not mean to imply—you believe it is I?" At Dor's miserable nod, the centaur laughed uncertainly. "That's impossible. What magic do you think I have?"

"I don't know," Dor said.

"Then how can you make such a preposterous allegation?" The centaur's tail was swishing nervously.

Dor produced the compass. "Have you seen one of these?"

Arnolde took the compass. "Yes, this is a magic compass. It is pointing at you, since you are a Magician."

"But when I hold it, it points to you."

"I can not believe that!" Arnolde protested. "Here, take it back, and stand by that mirror so I can see its face."

Dor did as bid, and Arnolde saw the needle pointing to himself. His face turned a shade of gray. "But it can not be! I can not be a Magician! It would mean the end of my career! I have no magic."

"It doesn't make sense to me," Dor agreed. "But Good Magician Humfrey's alarms point to a Magician on Centaur Isle; that's what brought me here."

"Yes, our Elders feared you had some such mischief in mind," Arnolde agreed, staring at the compass. Then, abruptly, he moved. "No!" he cried, and galloped from the room.

"What now?" Irene asked.

"We follow," Dor said. "We've got to find out what his talent is—and convince him. We can't leave the job half done."

"Somehow I'm losing my taste for this job," she muttered.

Dor felt the same. Going after an anonymous Magician was one thing; tormenting a dedicated archivist was another. But they were caught in the situation.

They followed. The centaur, though hardly in his prime, easily outdistanced them. But Dor had no trouble picking up the trail, for all he had to do was ask the surrounding terrain. The path led south to the ocean.

"He took his raft with the magic motor," Irene said. "We'll have to take another. He must be going to that Mundane island."

They pre-empted another raft, after Dor had questioned several to locate one with a suitable propulsion-spell. Dor hoped this would not be construed as theft; he had every intention of returning the raft, but had to catch up with Arnolde and talk to him before the centaur did something more foolish than merely fleeing.

The storm had long since passed, and the sea was glassy calm in the bright moonlight. The centaur's raft was not in sight, but the water reported its passage. "He's going for the formerly Mundane island," Grundy said. "Good thing it is magic now, since we're magical creatures."

"Did you suffer when the magic faded near the storm?" Irene asked.

"No, I felt the same—scared," Grundy admitted. "How about you, Smash?"

"This freak feel weak," the ogre said.

"In the knees," Irene said. "We all did."

"She's knees please me's," Smash agreed.

Irene's face ran a peculiar gamut from anger to embarrassment. She decided the ogre was not trying to tease her. He really wasn't that smart. "Thank you, Smash. Your own knees are like the boles on twisted ironwood trunks."

The ogre went into a small bellow of delight that churned up waves behind them and shoved the raft forward at a faster pace. She had found the right compliment.

The spell propelled them swiftly, and soon the island came into sight. Then progress slowed. "Something's the matter," Dor said. "We're hanging up on something."

But there was nothing; the raft was free in the water, unbothered by waves or sea creatures. It continued to slow, until it was hardly moving at all.

"We would get one with a defective go-spell," Irene complained.

"What's the matter with you?" Dor asked it.

"I—ugnh—" the raft whispered hoarsely, then was silent.

"The magic!" Irene cried. "We're beyond the magic! Just as we were during the storm!"

"Let's check this out," Dor said, worried. At least they were not in danger of falling from a cloud, this time! "Irene, grow a plant."

She took a bottleneck seed. "Grow," she ordered.

The seed began to sprout, hesitated, then fell limp.

"Is there anything you can talk to, Grundy?" Dor asked.

The golem spied some kelp in the water. He made strange sounds at it. There was no response.

"Smash, try a feat of strength," Dor said.

The ogre picked up one of his feet. "Uh, no," Dor said quickly. "I mean do something strong. Stand on one finger, or squeeze juice from a log."

Smash put one paw on the end of one of the raft's log-supports. He squeezed. Nothing happened. "Me unprepared, me awful scared," he said.

Dor brought out his midnight sunstone. Now it possessed only the faintest internal glimmer—and in a moment that, too, faded out.

"So that answers two questions," Dor said, trying to sound confident, though, in fact, he was deeply alarmed. "First, we are passing out of the region of magic; the propulsion-spell is defunct. I can't talk to the inanimate, and Irene can't grow plants magically. Second, it's only our magic that fades, not our bodies. Grundy can't translate the talk of other creatures, and Smash has lost his superhuman strength—but both are alive and healthy. Irene's plants won't grow, but she—" He paused, looking at her. "What happened to your hair?"

"Hair?" She took a strand and pulled it before her face. "Eeek, it's faded!"

"Aw, just the green's gone," Grundy said. "Looks better this way."

Irene, stunned, did not even try to kick at him. She, like Dor, had never realized that her hair tint was magical in nature.

"So Mundania doesn't hurt us," Dor continued quickly. "It just inconveniences us. We'll simply have to paddle the rest of the way to the island."

They checked the raft's supplies. The centaurs were a practical species; the raft was equipped with several paddles and a pole. Dor and Irene took the former and Smash the latter, and Grundy steadied the tiller. It was hard work, but they resumed progress toward the island.

"How did Arnolde ever get so far ahead alone?" Irene gasped. "He would have had an awful time paddling and steering."

Finally they reached the beach. There was Arnolde's raft, drawn up just out of the water. "He moved it along, all right," Grundy remarked. "He must be stronger than he looks."

"This is a fairly small island," Dor said. "He can't be far away. We'll corner him. Smash, you stand guard by the rafts and bellow if he comes back here; the rest of us will try to run him down."

They spread out and crossed the island. It had a distinctly Mundanian aspect; there was green grass growing that did not grab at their feet, and leafy trees that merely stood in place and rustled only in the wind. The sand was fine without being sugar, and the only vines they saw made no attempt to writhe toward them. How could the centaur have mistaken this for a spot within the realm of magic?

They discovered Arnolde at his refuge—a neat excavation exposing Mundane artifacts: the scholar's place of personal identification. Apparently he was more than a mere compiler or recorder of information; he did some field work, too.

Arnolde saw them. He had a magic lantern that illuminated the area as the moon sank into the sea. "No, I realize I can not flee the situation," he said sadly. "The truth is the truth, whatever it is, and I am dedicated to the truth. But I can not believe what you say. Never in my life have I evinced the slightest degree of magic talent, and I certainly have none now. Perhaps some of the magic of the artifacts with which I associate has rubbed off on me, giving the illusion of—"

"How can you use a magic lantern here in Mundania?" Irene asked.

"This is not Mundania," Arnolde said. "I told you that before. The limits of magic appear to have extended, reaching out far enough to include this island recently."

"But our magic ceased," Dor said. "We had to paddle here."

"Impossible. My raft spelled forward without intermission, and there is no storm to disrupt the magic ambience. Try your talent now, King Dor; I'll warrant you will discover it operative as always."

"Speak, ground," Dor said, wondering what would happen.

"Okay, chump," the ground answered. "What's on your slow mind?"

Dor exchanged glances with Irene and Grundy, astonished—and saw that Irene's hair in the light of the lantern was green again. "It's back!" he said. "The magic's back! Yet I don't see how—"

Irene threw down a seed. "Grow!" she ordered.

A plant sprouted, rising rapidly into a lively raspberry bush. "Brrrppp!" the plant sounded, making obscene sounds at them all.

"Is this really a magic island?" Grundy asked the nearest tree, translating into its language. The tree made a rustling response. "It says it is—now!" he reported.

Dor brought out the sunstone again. It was shining brightly.

"How could the magic return so quickly?" Irene asked. "My father always said the limit of magic was pretty constant; in fact, he wasn't sure it varied at all."

"The magic never left this island," Arnolde said. "You must have passed through a flux, an aberration, perhaps after all a lingering consequence of yesterday's storm."

"Maybe so," Dor agreed. "Magic is funny stuff. Ours certainly failed—for a while."

The centaur had a bright idea. "Maybe the magic compass was affected by a similar flux and thrown out of kilter, so it pointed to the wrong person."

Doubt nagged Dor. "I guess that's possible. Something's certainly wrong. If that's so, I must apologize for causing you such grief. It did seem strange to me that you should so suddenly manifest as a Magician when such power remains with a person from birth to death."

"Yes indeed!" Arnolde agreed enthusiastically. "An error in the instrument—that is certainly the most facile explanation. Of course I could not manifest as a Magician, after ninety years of pristine nonmagic."

So they had guessed correctly about one thing: the centaur was close to a century old. "I guess we might as well go back now," Dor said. "We had to borrow a raft to follow you, and its owner will be upset if it stays out too long."

"Feel no concern," Arnolde said, growing almost affable in his relief. "The rafts are communal property, available to anyone at need. However, there would be concern if one were lost or damaged."

They walked back across the island, the magic lantern brightening the vicinity steadily. As they neared the two rafts they saw Smash. He was holding a rock in both hands, squeezing as hard as he could, a grimace of concentration and disgust making his face even uglier than usual.

Suddenly the rock began to compress. "At length, my strength!" the ogre exclaimed as the stone crumbled into sand.

"You could never have done it, you big boob, if the magic hadn't come back," the sand grumbled.

"The magic returned—just now?" Dor asked, something percolating in the back of his mind.

"Sure," the sand said. "You should have seen this musclebrained brute straining. I thought I had him beat. Then the magic came back just as you did, more's the pity."

"The magic—came with us?" Dor asked.

"Are you dimwitted or merely stupid, nitbrain?" the sand asked with a gravelly edge. "I just said that."

"When was the magic here before?" Dor asked.

"Only a little while ago. Horserear here can tell you; he was here when it happened."

"You mean this is normally a Mundane island?"

"Sure, it's always been Mundane, except when ol' hoofleg's around."

"I think we're on to something," Grundy said.

Arnolde looked stricken. "But—but how can—this is preposterous!"

"We owe it to you and ourselves to verify this, one way or another," Dor said. "If the power of magic travels with you—"

"Oh, horrible!" the centaur moaned. "It must not be!"

"Let's take another walk around the island." Dor said. "Grundy, you go with Arnolde and talk to the plants and creatures you encounter; ask them how long magic has been here. The rest of us will spread out and wait for Arnolde to approach. If our magic fades out during his absence, and returns when he comes near—"

Grudgingly the centaur cooperated. He set out on a trot around the island, pretty spry for his age, the golem perching on his back.

No sooner were they on their way than Dor's magic ceased. His sunstone no longer shone, and he could no longer talk to the inanimate. It was evident that Irene and Smash were similarly discommoded.

In a few minutes the circuit was complete. They compared notes. "The magic was with us all along," Grundy reported. "But all the plants and shellfish said it had come only when we were there."

"When he go, me not rhyme," Smash said angrily. "Not even worth a dime."

That was extreme distress for the ogre. Dor had not realized that his rhyming was magic-related. Maybe frustration had flustered him—or maybe magic had shaped the lives of the creatures of Xanth far more than had been supposed. Irene's hair, Smash's rhymes . . .

"My potted petunia would not grow at all," Irene said. "But when the centaur came near, it grew and got roaring drunk."

"And my talent operated only when Arnolde was near," Dor said. "So my talent seems to be dependent on his presence here, as with the rest of you. Since I am a full Magician, what does that make him?"

"A Magician's Magician," Irene said. "A catalyst for magic."

"But I never performed any magic in my life!" Arnolde protested, still somewhat in shock. "Never!"

"You don't perform it, you promote it," Dor said. "You represent an island of magic, an extension of Xanth into Mundania. Wherever you go, magic is there. This is certainly a Magician's talent."

"How could that be true, when there was no indication of it in all my prior life? I can not have changed!"

But now Dor had an answer. "You left Xanth only recently, you said. You came to this Mundane island for research. Good Magician Humfrey's magic indicators never oriented on you before because you are completely camouflaged in Xanth proper; you are like a section of mist in the middle of a cloud. But when you left Xanth, your power manifested, triggering the alarms. Once the indicators had oriented on you, they continued to point you out; maybe your presence makes magic slightly more effective, since Centaur Isle is near the fringe of magic. It's like a bug on a distant leaf; once you know exactly where it is, you can see it. But you can't locate it when it sits still and you don't even know it exists."

Arnolde's shoulders slumped and his coat seemed to lose luster. He was an appaloosa centaur, with white spots on his brown flank, a natural blanket that made him quite handsome. Now the spots were fading out. "I fear you are correct. My associates always considered this to be a Mundane island; I thought them mistaken. But oh, what havoc this wreaks on my career! The profession of a lifetime ruined! I can never return to the museum."

"Do the other centaurs have to know?" Grundy asked.

"I may be contaminated by obscene magic," Arnolde said gravely. "But it is beneath me to prevaricate."

Dor considered the attitude of the various centaurs he had known. He realized Arnolde was right. The archivist could not conceal the truth, and the other centaurs would not tolerate a centaur Magician in their society. They had exiled Herman the Hermit in the past generation, then termed him a hero after he was dead. Some reward!

Dor's quest had gained him nothing and had destroyed the livelihood and pride of a decent centaur. He felt responsible; he had never wanted to hurt anyone this way.

The moon had been descending into the ocean. Now, just before it got soaked, it seemed to have swelled. Great and round and greenish, its cheese was tantalizingly close. Dor gazed at it, pondering its maplike surface. Could a column of smoke lead all the way up to the moon, and could they use the salve some day to—

Then he suffered an awful realization. "The curse!" he cried.

The centaur glanced dourly at him. "You have certainly cursed me, King Dor."

"The magic salve we used to tread the clouds—it had a curse attached. Whoever used it would do some dastardly deed before the next full moon. This is our deed; we have forced you out of your satisfied existence and made you into something you abhor. The curse made us do it."

"Such curses are a readily avoidable nuisance," the centaur remarked. "All that is requred is an elementary curse-counterspell. There are dozens in our archives; we don't even file them carefully. Ironic that this ignorance on your part should have such a serious consequence for me."

"Do something, Dor," Irene said.

"What is there to be done?" Arnolde asked disconsolately. "I am rendered at one fell stroke into an exile."

But Dor, cudgeling his brain under pressure, had a sudden explosion of genius. "You take magic with you anywhere you go," he said. "Right into Mundania. This relates in all the three ways we were warned. It is certainly a matter I must attend to, for the existence of any new Magician in Xanth is the King's business. It also could pose a threat to Xanth, for if you go out into Mundania on your own, taking that magic with you, bad people could capture you and somehow use your magic for evil. But most important, somewhere in Mundania is someone we fear is trapped or in trouble, who perhaps needs this magic to escape. Now if I were to take you into Mundania proper—"

"We could rescue my father!" Irene exclaimed, jumping up and down and clapping her hands in the manner of her kind. She bounced phenomenally, so that even the centaur paused to look, as if regretting his species and his age. "Oh, Dor, I could kiss you!" And without waiting for his reaction, she grabbed him and kissed him with joyful savagery on the mouth. In that moment of hyperanimation she became very special, radiant and compelling in the best sort of way; but by the time he realized it, she was already away and talking to the centaur.

"Arnolde, if you have to be exiled anyway, you might as well come with us. We don't care about your magic—not negatively, I mean—we all of us have talents. And think of the artifacts you can collect deep in Mundania; you can start your own museum. And if you help rescue my father, King Trent—"

The centaur was visibly wavering. Obviously he did not like the notion of exile, but could not return to his job on Centaur Isle. "And the centaurs around Castle Roogna are used to magic," Irene continued apace. "Chester Centaur plays a magic silver flute, and his uncle was Herman the Hermit. He would be glad for your company, and—"

"I believe I have little alternative," Arnolde said heavily.

"You will help us? Oh, thank you!" Irene cried, and she flung her arms about the centaur's forepart and kissed him, too. Arnolde was visibly startled, but not entirely displeased; his white spots wavered. Dor suffered a wash of jealousy, thinking of the legend of the origin of the centaurs. Kisses between different species were not necessarily innocent, as that legend showed. But it seemed Irene had convinced the centaur Magician to help, and that was certainly worthwhile.

Then Dor remembered another complication. "We can't just leave for Mundania. The Council of Elders would never permit it."

"How can they prevent it?" Irene asked, glancing meaningfully at him.

"But we must at least tell them—"

"Chet can tell them. He has to go home anyway."

Dor tried to dissemble. "I don't know—"

Then Irene focused her stare on him full-force, daring him to attempt to balk her; she was extremely pretty in her challenge, and Dor knew their course was set. She intended to rescue her father, no matter what.

Chapter 8

Mundane Mystery

They sailed the two rafts back to Centaur Isle that night. In the process they discovered that Arnolde's ambience of magic extended farthest toward the front, perhaps fifteen paces, and half that distance to the rear. It was least potent to the sides, going hardly beyond the centaur's reach. It was, in fact, less an isle of magic than an aisle, always preceding the centaur's march. Thus the second raft was able to precede Arnolde's raft comfortably, or to follow it closely, but not to travel beside it. They had verified that the hard way, having the magic propulsion fail, until Arnolde turned to face them.

Once they re-entered the main magic of Xanth, Arnolde's power was submerged. It seemed to make no difference how close he was or which way he faced; there was no enhancement of enchantment near him. But of course they had no way to measure the intensity of magic in his vicinity accurately.

Grundy sneaked in to wake Chet and explain the situation, while Arnolde researched in his old tomes for the best and swiftest route to Mundania. He reported that there was the tunnel the sun used to return from the ocean east to its position of rising, drying out and recharging along the way. This tunnel would be suitable by day, when the sun wasn't using it; they could trot right along it.

"But that would take us west," Irene protested. "My father left Xanth to the north."

Dor had to agree. "The standard route to Mundania is across the northwest isthmus. We must go there and hope to pick up traces of his passage. We can't use the sun's tunnel. But it's a long way to the isthmus, and I don't think we want to make another trip like the one down the coast; we might never get there. Are there any other good notions?"

"Well, tomorrow is destined to have intermittent showers," Arnolde said. "There should be a rainbow. There is a spell in the archives for traveling the rainbow. It is very fast, for rainbows do not endure long. There is some risk—"

"Speed is what we need," Dor said, remembering his dream-visions, where there had been a sensation of urgency. "I think King Trent is in trouble and needs to be rescued soon. Maybe not in the next day, but I don't think we can afford to wait a month."

"There is also the problem of mounting the rainbow," Arnolde said. Now that he had accepted the distasteful notion of his own magic, his mind was relating to the situation very readily. Perhaps it was because he was trained in the handling of information and knew how to organize it. "Part of the rainbow's magic, as you know, is that it appears equally distant from all observers, with its two ends touching the ground equally far from them, north and south. We must ascend to its top, then slide down quickly before it fades."

"The salve!" Grundy said. "We can mount smoke to a cloud, and run across the cloud to the top of the rainbow, if we start early, before the rainbow forms."

"You just don't understand," the centaur said. "It will seem just as far from us when we board the cloud. Catching a rainbow is one of the hardest things to do."

"I can see why," Dor muttered. "How can we catch one if it always retreats?"

"Excise the eyes," Smash suggested, covering his own gross orbs with his gauntleted mitts.

"Of course the monster is right," Arnolde said, not looking at Smash, whom he seemed to find objectionable. "That is the obvious solution."

It was hardly obvious to Dor. "How can covering our eyes get us to the rainbow?"

"It can hardly appear distant if you don't look at it," Arnolde said.

"Yes, but—"

"I get it," Grundy said. "We spot it, then close our eyes and go to where we saw it, and it can't get away because we aren't looking at it. Simple."

"But somebody has to look at it, or it isn't there," Irene protested. "Is it?"

"Chet can look at it," Grundy said. "He's not going on it anyway."

Dor distrusted this, but the others seemed satisfied. "Let's get some sleep tonight and see what happens tomorrow," he said, hoping it all made sense.

They slept late, but that was all right because the intermittent rain wasn't due until midmorning. Arnolde dutifully acquainted the centaur Elders with his situation; as expected, they encouraged him to depart the Isle forever at his very earliest convenience, without directly referring to the reason for his loss of status in their community. A Magician was not wanted here; they could not be comfortable with him. They would let it be known that Arnolde was retiring for reasons of health, so as to preserve his reputation, and they would arrange to break in a new archivist. No one would know his shame. To facilitate his prompt departure they provided him with a useful assortment of spells and counterspells for his journey, and wished him well.

"The hypocrites!" Irene exclaimed. "For fifty years Arnolde serves them well, and now, suddenly, just because—"

"I said you would not comprehend the nuances of centaur society," Chet reminded her, though he did not look comfortable himself.

Irene shut up rebelliously. Dor liked her better for her feeling, however. It was time to leave Centaur Isle, and not just because they had a new mission.

The intermittent clouds formed and made ready to shower. Dor set up a smudge pot and got a column of smudge angling up to intersect the cloud level. They applied the salve to their feet and hands, invoked the curse-counterspells Arnolde distributed, and marched up the column. Arnolde adjusted to this odd climb remarkably well for his age; he had evidently kept himself in traveling shape by making archaeological field trips.

For a moment they paused to turn back to face Chet, who was standing on the beach, watching for the rainbow. Dor found himself choking up, and could only wave. "I hope to see you again, cousin," Arnolde called. Chet was not related to him; what he referred to was the unity of their magic talents. "And meet your sire." And Chet smiled, appreciating the thought.

When they reached the cloud layer, they donned blindfolds. "Clouds," Dor said, "tell us where the best path to the top of the rainbow is. Don't let any of us step too near the edge of you."

"What rainbow?" the nearest cloud asked.

"The one that is about to form, that my friend Chet Centaur will see from the ground."

"Oh, *that* rainbow. It isn't here yet. It hasn't finished its business on the eastern coast of Xanth."

"Well, guide us to where it's going to be."

"Why don't you open your eyes and see it for yourself?" the canny cloud asked. The inanimate was often perverse, and the many folds and convolutions of clouds made them smarter than average.

"Just guide us," Dor said.

"Awww." But the cloud had to do it.

There was a popping sound behind them, down on the ground. "That's the popcorn I gave Chet," Irene said. "I told him to set it off when he saw the rainbow. Now that rainbow is fixed in place, as long as he looks at it and we don't; we must be almost upon it."

"Are we?" Dor asked the cloud.

"Yeah," the cloud conceded grudgingly. "It's right ahead, though it has no head. That's cumulus humor."

"Rainbow!" Dor called. "Sing out if you hear me!"

Back came the rainbow's song: "Tra-la-la-fol-de-rol!" It sounded beautiful and multicolored.

They hurried over to it. Once they felt its smooth surface projecting above the cloud and climbed upon it, they removed their blindfolds; the rainbow could no longer work its deceptive magic.

The rainbow was fully as lovely as it sounded. Bands of red and yellow, blue and green, extended lengthwise, and sandwiched between them, where ground observers couldn't see them, were the secret riches of the welkin: bands of polka-dot, plaid, and checkerboard. Some internal bands were translucent, and some blazed with colors seldom imagined by man, like fortissimo, charm, phon, and torque. It would have been easy to become lost in their wonders, and Irene seemed inclined to do just that, but the rainbow would not remain here long. It seemed rainbows had tight schedules, and this one was due for a showing somewhere in Mundania in half an hour. Some magic, it seemed, did extend to Mundania; Dor wondered briefly whether the Mundanes would have the same trouble actually catching up to a rainbow, or whether there it would stay firmly in place regardless how the viewers moved.

Arnolde brought out his rainbow-travel spell, which was sealed in a paper packet. He tore it open—and abruptly they began to slide.

The speed was phenomenal. They zoomed past the clouds, then down into the faintly rainy region below, plunging horrendously toward the sea to the north.

Below them was the Land of Xanth, a long peninsula girt by thin islands along the coastlines. Across the center of it was the jagged chasm of the Gap that separated the northern half of Xanth from the southern. It appeared on no maps because no one remembered it, but this was no map. It was reality, as viewed from the rainbow. There were a number of lakes, such as Ogre-Chobee in the south, but no sign of the human settlements Dor knew were there. Man had simply not made much of an impression on Xanth, physically.

"Fun begun!" Smash cried joyfully.

"Eeek—my skirt!" Irene squealed as the mischievous gusts whipped it up, displaying her legs to the whole world. Dor wondered why she insisted on wearing a skirt despite such constant inconveniences; pants of some kind would have solved the problems decisively. Then it occurred to him that she might not want that particular problem solved. She was well aware that her legs were the finest features of a generally excellent body and perhaps was not averse to letting the world know it also. If she constantly protested any inadvertent exposures that occurred, how could anyone blame her for showing herself off? She had a pretty good system going.

Dor and Grundy and Arnolde, less sanguine about violence than the ogre and less modest (?) than Irene, hung on to the sliding arc of the rainbow and stared ahead and down with increasing misgiving. How were they to stop, once the end came? The descent was drawing close at an alarming velocity. The northern shoreline of Xanth loomed rapidly larger, the curlicues of beaches magnifying. The ocean in this region seemed oddly reddish; Dor hoped that wasn't from the blood of prior travelers of the rainbow. Of course it wasn't; how could he think such a thought?

Then the travel-spell reversed, and they slid rapidly slower until, as they reached the water at the end of the rainbow, they were moving at no more than a running pace. They plunged into the crimson water and swam for the shore to the north. The color was not blood; it was translucently thin, up close. Dor was relieved.

Now that he could no longer see it from the air, Dor remembered other details of Xanth. The length of it was north-south, with the narrowest portion near where his grandfather Elder Roland's village was, in the middle north on the western side. At the top, Xanth extended west, linking to Mundania by the isthmus they were headed for—and somehow Mundania beyond that isthmus seemed huge, much larger than Xanth. Dor decided that must be a misimpression; surely Mundania was about the same size as Xanth, or somewhat smaller. How could a region of so little importance be larger, especially without magic?

Now they came to the shallows and waded through the dark red water to the beach. That crimson bothered him, as the color intensified near the tideline; how could the normally blue water change color here, in the Mundane quadrant? What magic could affect it here, where no magic existed?

"Maybe some color leaked from the rainbow," Irene said, following his thought.

Well, maybe. Of course there was the centaur aisle of magic now, so that wherever they were was no longer strictly Mundane. Yet the red water extended well beyond the area of temporary enchantment. It seemed to be a regular feature of the region.

They gathered on the beach, dripping pink water. Grundy and Smash didn't mind, but Dor felt uncomfortable, and Irene's blouse and skirt were plastered to her body. "I'm not walking around this way, and I'm not taking off my clothes," she expostulated. She felt in her seedbag, which she had refilled at Centaur Isle, and brought out a purple seed. It seemed the bag was waterproof, for the seed was dry. "Grow," she ordered it as she dropped it on the sand.

The thing sprouted into a heliotrope. Clusters of small purple flowers burst open aromatically. Warm dry air wafted outward. This plant did not really travel toward the sun; it emulated the sun's heat, dehydrating things in the vicinity. Soon their clothing was dry again. Even Smash and Grundy appreciated this, since both now wore the special jackets given them by the centaurs. Smash also shook out his gauntlets and dried them, and Irene spread her silver-lined fur out nearby.

"Do we know where we go from here?" Irene asked once she had her skirt and blouse properly fluffed out.

"Did King Trent pass this way?" Dor inquired of the landscape.

"When?" the beach-sand asked.

"Within the past month."

"I don't think so."

They moved a short distance north, and Dor tried again. Again the response was negative. As the day wore into afternoon and on into evening, they completed their traverse of the isthmus—without positive result. The land had not seen the King.

"Maybe the Queen still had an illusion of invisibility enchantment," Grundy suggested. "So nothing could see them."

"Her illusion wouldn't work here in Mundania, dummy," Irene retorted. She was still miffed at the golem because of the way Grundy had caused her to lose half her seeds to the eclectic eel. She carried a little grudge a long time.

"I am not properly conversant with King Trent's excursion," Arnolde said. "Perhaps he departed Xanth by another route."

"But I know he came this way!" Irene said.

"You didn't even know he was leaving Xanth," Grundy reminded her. "You thought he was inside Xanth on vacation."

She shrugged that off as irrelevant. "But this is the only route out of Xanth!" Her voice was starting its hysterical tremor.

"Unless he went by sea," Dor said.

"Yes, he could have done that," she agreed quickly. "But he would have come ashore somewhere. My mother gets seasick when she's in a boat too long. All we have to do is walk along the beach and ask the stones and plants."

"And watch for Mundane monsters," Grundy said, still needling her. "So they can't look up your—"

"I am inclined to doubt that countermagical species will present very much of a problem," Arnolde said in his scholarly manner.

"What he know, he hoofed schmoe?" Smash demanded.

"Evidently more than you, you moronic oaf," the centaur snapped back. "I have been studying Mundania somewhat, recently, garnering information from immigrants, and by most reports most Mundane plants and animals are comparatively shy. Of course there is a certain margin for error, as in all phenomena."

"What dray, he say?" Smash asked, perplexed by the centaur's vocabulary.

"Dray!" Arnolde repeated, freshly affronted. "A dray is a low cart, not a creature, you ignorant monster. I shall thank you to address me by my proper appellation."

"What's the poop from the goop?" Smash asked.

Dor stifled a laugh, turning it into a choking cough. In this hour of frustration, tempers were fraying, and they could not afford to have things get too negative.

Grundy opened his big mouth, but Dor managed to cover it in time. The golem could only aggravate the situation with his natural penchant for insults.

It was Irene who retained enough poise to alleviate the crisis. "You just don't understand a person of education, Smash. He says the Mundane monsters won't dare bother us while you're on guard."

"Oh. So," the ogre said, mollified.

"Ignorant troglodyte," the centaur muttered.

That set it off again. "Me know he get the place of Chet!" Smash said angrily, forming his gauntlets into horrendous fists.

So that was the root of the ogre's ire! He felt Arnolde had usurped the position of his younger centaur friend. "No, that's not so," Dor started, seeking some way to alleviate his resentment. If their party started fracturing now, before they were fairly clear of Xanth, what would happen once they got deep into Mundania?

"And he called you a caveman, Smash," Grundy put in helpfully.

"Compliments no good; me head like wood," the ogre growled, evidently meaning that he refused to be swayed by soft talk.

"Indubitably," Arnolde agreed.

Dor decided to leave it at that; a more perfect understanding between ogre and centaur would only exacerbate things.

They walked along the beach. Sure enough, nothing attacked them. The trees were strange oval-leafed things with brownish, inert bark and no tentacles. Small birds flitted among the branches, and gray animals scurried along the ground.

Arnolde had brought along a tome of natural history, and he consulted it eagerly as each thing turned up. "An oak tree!" he exclaimed. "Probably the root stock of the silver oak, the blackjack oak, the turkey oak, and the acorn trees!"

"But there's no silver, blackjacks, or acorns," Grundy protested.

"Or turkeys," Irene added.

"Certainly there are, in rudimentary forms," the centaur said. "Observe a certain silvery aspect to some leaves, and the typical shape of others, primitively suggestive of other, eventual divergencies. And I suspect there are also acorns, in season. The deficiency of magic prevents proper manifestation, but to the trained perception—"

"Maybe so," the golem agreed, shrugging. This was evidently more than he cared to know about oak trees.

Dor continued to query the objects along the beach, and the water of the sea, but with negative results. All denied seeing King Trent or Queen Iris.

"This is ridiculous!" Irene expostulated. "I *know* he came this way!"

Arnolde stroked his chin thoughtfully. "There does appear to be a significant discontinuity."

"Something doesn't fit," Grundy agreed.

As the sun set, they made camp high on the beach. Rather than post watches, they decided to trust in magic. Dor told the sand in their vicinity to make an exclamation if anything dangerous or obnoxious intruded, and the sand promised to do so. Irene grew a blanket bush for their beds and set a chokecherry hedge around them for additional protection. They ate beefsteak tomatoes that they butchered and roasted on flame-vines, and drank the product of wine-and-rain lilies.

"Young lady, your talent contributes enormously to our comfort," Arnolde complimented her, and Irene flushed modestly.

"Aw, he's just saying that 'cause she's pretty," Grundy grumbled. That only made Irene flush with greater pleasure. Dor was not pleased, but could not isolate the cause of his reaction. The hangups of others were easier for him to perceive than his own.

"Especially when her skirt hikes up over her knees," the golem continued. Irene quickly tugged down her hem, her flush becoming less attractive.

"Actually, there are few enough rewards to a mission like this," Arnolde said. "Had I my choice, I would instantly abolish my own magic and return to my sinecure at the museum, my shame extirpated."

And there was the centaur's fundamental disturbance, Dor realized. He resented their dastardly deed that had ripped him from his contented existence and made him an exile from his kind. Dor could hardly blame him. Arnolde's agreement to travel with them to Mundania to help rescue King Trent did not mean he was satisfied with his lot; he was merely making the best of what was for him an awful situation.

"Me help he go, with big heave-ho!" Smash offered.

"But we need his magic," Irene said, verbally interposing herself to prevent further trouble. "Just as we need your strength, Smash." And she laid her hand on the ogre's ponderous arm, pacifying him. Dor found himself resenting this, too, though he understood her motive. The peace had to be kept.

They settled down for the night—and the sand gave alarm. The monsters it warned of turned out to be sand fleas—bugs so small they could hardly even be seen. Arnolde dug a vermin-repulsor spell out of his collection, and that took care of the matter. They settled down again and this time slept. Once more the nightmares were unable to reach them, since the magic horses were bound to the magic realm of Xanth and could not cross the Mundane territory intervening. Dor almost felt sympathy for the mares; they had been balked from doing their duty to trouble people's sleep for several nights now, and must be very frustrated.

They resumed their march in the morning. But as the new day wore on, the gloom of failure became more pervasive. "Something certainly appears to be amiss," Arnolde observed. "From what we understand, King Trent had to have passed this vicinity—yet the objects here deny it. Perhaps it is not entirely premature to entertain conjectures."

Smash wrinkled his hairy brow, trying to figure out whether this was another rarefied insult. "Say what's on your mind, horsetail," Grundy said with his customary diplomacy.

"We have ascertained that the Queen could not have employed her power to deceive the local objects," Arnolde said didactically.

"Not without magic," Dor agreed. "The two of them were strictly Mundane-type people here, as far as we know."

"Could they have failed to come in from the sea?"

"No!" Irene cried emotionally.

"I have queried the sea," Dor said. "It says nothing like that is in it." Irene relaxed.

"Could they have employed a completely different route? Perhaps crossed to the eastern coast of Xanth and sailed north from there to intercept another region of Mundania?"

"They didn't," Irene said firmly. "They had it all planned, to come out here. Someone had found a good trade deal, and they were following his map. I saw it, and the route passed here."

"But if you don't know—" Dor protested.

"I didn't know they were going to travel the route, then," she said. "But I did see the map when their scout brought it in, with the line on it. *Now* I know what it meant. That's all I saw, but I am absolutely certain this was the way they headed."

Dor was disinclined to argue the point further. This did seem to be the only practical route. He had told the others all he knew about King Trent's destination, and this route certainly did not conflict with that information.

"Could they have been intercepted before leaving Xanth?" Arnolde continued, evidently with an intellectual conclusion in mind. "Waylaid, perhaps?"

"My father would have turned any waylayer into a toad," she said defiantly. "Anyway, inside Xanth, my mother's illusion would have made them impossible to identify."

"Then it seems we have eliminated the likely," Arnolde said. "We are thus obliged to contemplate the unlikely."

"What do you mean?" Irene asked.

"As I intimated, it is an unlikely supposition that I entertain, quite possibly erroneous—"

"Spit it out, brownfur," Grundy said.

"My dear vociferous construct, a civilized centaur does not expectorate. And my color is appaloosa, not mere brown."

Irene was catching on to her power over the centaur, and over males in general. "Please, Arnolde," she pleaded sweetly. "It's so important to me to know anything that might help find my lost father—"

"Of course, dear child," Arnolde agreed quickly, adopting an avuncular pose. "It is simply this: perhaps King Trent did not pass this region when we suppose he did."

"It had to be within this past month," she said.

"Not necessarily. That is the extraordinary aspect of this supposition. He may have passed here a century ago."

Now Dor, Irene, and Grundy peered at the centaur intently to see whether he was joking. Smash, less interested in intellectual conjectures, idly formed sandstone by squeezing handfuls of sand until the mineral fused. His new gauntlets evidently enabled him to apply his power in ways that were beyond his natural limits before, since even ogre's flesh was marginally softer than stone. A modest sandstone castle was developing.

"You happen to sleep with your head underwater last night?" the golem inquired solicitously.

"I have, as I have clarified previously, engaged in a modicum of research into the phenomena of Mundania," Arnolde said. "I confess I know only the merest fraction of what may be available, and must be constantly alert for error, but certain conclusions are becoming more credible. Through history, certain anomalies have manifested in the relationship between continuums. There is of course the matter of linguistics—it appears that there exist multiple languages in Mundania, yet all become intelligible in Xanth. I wonder if you properly appreciate the significance of—"

Irene was growing impatient. She tapped her small foot on the ground. "How could he have passed a century ago, when he wasn't even born then?"

"It is this matter of discontinuity, as I was saying. Time seems to differ; there may be no constant ratio. There is evidence that the several Waves of human colonization of Xanth originated from widely divergent subcultures within Mundania, and, in fact, some may be anachronistic. That is to say, the last Wave of people may have originated from a period in Mundania preceding that of the prior Wave."

"Now wait!" Dor exclaimed. "I visited Xanth of eight hundred years ago, and I guess that was a kind of time travel, but that was a special case. Since there's no magic in Mundania, how could people get reversed like that? Are their times mixed up?"

"No, I believe their framework is consistent in their world. Yet if the temporal sequence were reversed with respect to ours—"

"I just want to know where my father is!" Irene snapped.

"He may be in Mundania's past—or its future," the centaur said. "We simply do not know what law governs transfer across the barrier of magic, but it seems to be governed from Xanth's side. That is, we may be able to determine into what age of Mundania we travel, whereas the access of Mundania to Xanth is random and perhaps in some cases impossible. It is a most intriguing interface. It is as if Xanth were a boat sailing along a river; the passengers may disembark anywhere they choose, merely by picking their port, or a specific time on the triptych, so to speak, but the natives along the shores can take only that craft that happens to pass within their range. This is an inadequate analogy, I realize, that does not properly account for certain—"

"The King can be any*when* in Mundania?" Irene demanded skeptically.

"Marvelously succinct summation," Arnolde admitted.

"But he told me 'medieval,' " Dor protested.

"That does narrow it," the centaur agreed. "But it covers an extraordinary range, and if he was speaking figuratively—"

"Then how can we ever find him?" Irene demanded.

"That becomes problematical. I hasten to remind you that this is merely a theory, undocumented, perhaps fallacious. I would not have introduced it for consideration, except—"

"Except nothing else fits," Irene said. "Suppose it's right. What do we do now?"

"Well, I believe it would expedite things if we located research facilities in Mundania. Some institution where detailed records exist, archives—"

"And you're an archivist!" Dor exclaimed.

"Precisely. This should enable me to determine at what period in Mundania's history we have intruded. Since, as King Dor says, King Trent referred to a medieval period, that would provide a frame of reference."

"If we're in the wrong Mundane century," Irene said, "how do we get to him?"

"We should be required to return to Xanth and undertake a new mission to that century. As I mentioned, it seems feasible to determine the temporal locale from Xanth, and once in that aspect of Mundania, we would be fixed in it until returning to Xanth. However, this procedure is fraught with uncertainties and potential complications."

"I should think so," Dor said. "If we figured it wrong, we might get there before he did."

"Oh, I doubt that would happen, other than on the macroscopic scale, of course."

"The what?" Dor asked.

"I believe the times are consistent in particular circumstances. That is to say, within a given age, we could enter Mundania only with an elapsed period consonant with that of Xanth. Therefore—"

"We might miss by a century, but not by a day," Grundy said.

"That is the essence, golem. The particular channels appear to be fixed—"

"So let's go find the century!" Irene said, brightening. "Then all we'll need is the place."

"With appropriate research, the specific geography should also be evident."

"Then let's go find your archives," she said.

"Unfortunately, we have no knowledge of this period," Arnolde reminded her. "We are hardly likely to locate a suitable facility randomly."

"I can help there," Dor said. "It should be where there are a lot of people, right?"

"Correct, King Dor."

"Uh, better not call me King here. I'm not, really, and people might find it strange." Then Dor addressed the sand. "Which way to where most people live?"

"How should I know?" the sand asked.

"You know which direction most of them come from, and where they return."

"Oh, that. They mostly go north."

"North it is," Dor agreed.

They marched north, and in due course encountered a Mundane path that debouched into a road that became a paved highway. No such highway existed in Xanth, and Dor had to question this one closely to ascertain its nature. It seemed it served to facilitate the travel of metal and rubber vehicles that propelled themselves with some sort of magic or whatever it was that Mundanes used to accomplish such wonders. These wagons were called "cars," and they moved very rapidly.

"I saw something like that belowground," Grundy said. "The demons rode in them."

Soon the party saw a car. The thing zoomed along like a racing dragon, belching faint smoke from its posterior. They stared after it, amazed. "Fire it send from wrong end," Smash said.

"Are you sure there's no magic in Mundania?" Grundy asked. "Even the demons didn't have firebreathers."

"I am not at all certain," Arnolde admitted. "Perhaps they merely have a different name and application for their magic. I doubt it would operate for us. Perhaps this is the reason we believe there is no magic in Mundania—it is not applicable to our needs."

"I don't want any part of that car," Irene said. "Any dragon shooting out smoke from its rear is either crazy or has one awful case of indigestion! How could it fight? Let's find our archives and get out of here."

The others agreed. This aspect of Mundania was certainly inverted. They avoided the highway, making their way along assorted paths that paralleled it. Dor continued to query the ground, and by nightfall they were approaching a city. It was a strange sort of settlement, with roads that crisscrossed to form large squares, and buildings all lined up with their fronts right on the edges of the roads, so that there was hardly room for any forest there, jammed in close together. Some were so tall it was a wonder they didn't fall over when the wind blew.

Dor's party camped at the edge of the city, under a large umbrella tree Irene grew to shelter them. The tree's canopy dipped almost to the ground, concealing them, and this seemed just as well. They were not sure how the Mundanes would react to the sight of an ogre, golem, or centaur.

"We have gone as far as we can as a group," Dor said. "There are many people here, and few trees; we can't avoid being seen any more. I think Irene and I had better go in and find a museum—"

"A library," Arnolde corrected him. "I would love to delve eternally in a Mundane museum, but the information is probably most readily accessible in a library."

"A library," Dor agreed. He knew what that was, because King Trent had many books in his library-office in Castle Roogna.

"However, that is academic, no pun intended," the centaur continued. "You can not go there without me."

"I know I'll step out of magic," Dor said. "But I won't need to do anything special. Nothing magical. Once I find the library for you—"

"You have no certainty you can even speak their language," Arnolde said curtly. "In the magic ambience, you can; beyond it, this is problematical."

"I'm not sure we speak the same language in our own group, sometimes," Irene said with a smile. "Words like 'ambience' and 'problematical'—"

"I can speak their language," Grundy said. "That's my talent. I was made to translate."

"A magical talent," Arnolde said.

"Oooops," Grundy said, chagrined. "Won't work outside the aisle."

"But you can't just walk in to the city!" Dor said. "I'm sure they aren't used to centaurs."

"I would have to walk in to use the library," Arnolde pointed out. "Fortunately, I anticipated such an impediment, so obtained a few helpful spells from our repository. We centaurs do not normally practice inherent magic, but we do utilize particular enchantments on an *ad hoc* basis. I have found them invaluable when on field trips to the wilder regions of Xanth." He checked through his bag of spells, much the way Irene checked through her seeds. "I have with me assorted spells for invisibility, inaudibility, untouchability, and so forth. The golem and I can traverse the city unperceived."

"What about the ogre?" Dor asked. "He can't exactly merge with the local population either."

Arnolde frowned. "Him, too, I suppose," he agreed distastefully. "However, there is one attendant liability inherent in this process—"

"I won't be able to detect you either," Dor finished.

"Precisely. Some one of our number must exist openly, for these spells make the handling of books awkward; our hands would pass right through the pages. My ambience of magic should be unimpaired, of course, and we could remain with you—but you would have to do all the research unassisted."

"He'll never make it," Irene said.

"She's right," Dor said. "I'm just not much of a scholar. I'd mess it up."

"Allow me to cogitate," Arnolde said. He closed his eyes and stroked his chin reflectively. For a worried moment Dor thought the centaur was going to be sick, then realized that he had the wrong word in mind. Cogitate actually referred to thinking.

"Perhaps I have an alternative," Arnolde said. "You could obtain the assistance of a Mundane scholar, a qualified researcher, perhaps an archivist. You could pay him one of the gold coins you have hoarded, or perhaps a diamond; I believe either would have value in any frame of Mundania."

"Uh, I guess so," Dor said doubtfully.

"I tell you, even with help, he'll foul it up," Irene said. She seemed to have forgotten her earlier compliments on Dor's performance. That was one of the little things about her—selective memory. "You're the one who should do the research, Arnolde."

"I can only, as it were, look over his shoulder," the centaur said. "It would certainly help if I could direct the manner he selects references and turns the pages, as I am a gifted reader with a fine memory. He would not have to comprehend the material. But unless I were to abort the imperceptibility spells, which I doubt very much would be wise since I have no duplicates—"

"There's a way, maybe," Grundy said. "I could step outside the magic aisle. Then he could see me and hear me, and I could tell him to turn the page, or whatever."

"And any Mundanes in the area would pop their eyeballs, looking at the living doll," Irene said. "If anyone does it, I'm the one."

"So they can pop their eyes looking up your skirt," the golem retorted, miffed.

"That may indeed be the solution," Arnolde said.

"Now wait a minute!" Irene cried.

"He means the messenger service," Dor told her gently.

"Of course," the centaur said. "Since we have ascertained that the aisle is narrow, it would be feasible to stand quite close while Dor remains well within the forward extension."

Dor considered, and it did seem to be the best course. He had somehow thought he could just go into Mundania, follow King Trent's trail by querying the terrain, and reach the King without much trouble. This temporal discontinuity, as the centaur put it, was hard to understand and harder to deal with, and the vicarious research the centaur proposed seemed fraught with hangups. But what other way was there? "We'll try it," he agreed. "In the morning."

They settled down for the night, their second in Mundania. Smash and Grundy slept instantly; Dor and Irene had more trouble, and Arnolde seemed uncomfortably wide awake. "We are approaching direct contact with Mundane civilization," the centaur said. "In a certain sense this represents the culmination of an impossible dream for me, almost justifying the personal damnation my magic talent represents. Yet I have had so many confusing intimations, I hardly know what to expect. This city could be too primitive to have a proper library. The denizens could for all we know practice cannibalism. There are so many imponderabilities."

"I don't care what they practice," Irene said. "Just so long as I find my father."

"Perhaps we should query the surroundings in the morning," Arnolde said thoughtfully, "to ascertain whether suitable facilities exist here, before we venture any farther. Certainly we do not wish to chance discovery by the Mundanes unless we have excellent reason."

"And we should ask where the best Mundane archivist is," Irene agreed.

Dor drew a word in the dirt with one finger: ONESTI. He contemplated it morosely.

"This is relevant?" the centaur inquired, glancing at the word.

"It's what King Trent told me," Dor said. "If ever I was in doubt, to proceed with honesty."

"Honesty?" Arnolde asked, his brow wrinkling at the dirt.

"I think about that a lot when I'm in doubt," Dor said. "I don't like deceiving people, even Mundanes."

Irene smiled tiredly. "Arnolde, it's the way Dor spells the word. He is the world's champion poor speller. O N E S T I: Honesty."

"ONESTI," the centaur repeated, removing his spectacles to rub his eyes. "I believe I perceive it now. A fitting signature for a King."

"King Trent's a great King," Dor agreed. "I know his advise will pull us through somehow."

Arnolde seemed almost to smile, as if finding Dor's attitude peculiar. "I will sleep on that," the centaur said. And he did, lying down on the dirt-scratched word.

In the morning, after some problems with food and natural functions in this semipublic locale, they set it up. The centaur dug out his collection of spells, each one sealed in a glassy little globe, and Dor stepped outside the aisle of magic while the spells were invoked. First the party became inaudible, then invisible; it looked as if the spot were empty. Dor gave them time to get through the unfeeling spell, then walked back onto the lot. He heard, saw, and felt nothing.

"But I can smell you," he remarked. "Arnolde has a slight equine odor, and Smash smells like a monster, and Irene is wearing perfume. Better clean yourselves up before we get into a building."

Soon the smells faded, and after a moment Irene appeared, a short distance away. "Can you see me now?"

"I see you and hear you," Dor said.

"Oh, good. I didn't know how far out the magic went. I'm still the same to me." She stepped toward him and vanished.

"You've gone again," Dor said, hastening to the spot where she had been. "Can you perceive me?"

"Hey, you're overlapping me!" she protested, appearing right up against him, so that he almost stumbled.

"Well, I can't perceive you," he said. "I mean, *now* I can, but I couldn't before. Can you see the others when you're outside the aisle?"

She looked. "They're gone! We can see and hear you all the time, but now—"

"So you'll know when I can see you by when you can't see them."

She leaned forward, and her face disappeared, reminding him of the Gorgon. Then she drew back. "I could see them then. I'm really in the enchantment, aren't I?"

"You're enchanting," he agreed.

She smiled and leaned forward to kiss him—but her face disappeared and he felt nothing.

"Now I have to go find a library and a good archivist," he said, disgruntled, as she reappeared. "If you're with me, stay away from me."

She laughed. "I'm with you. Just don't try to catch me outside the aisle." And of course that was what he should have done, if he really wanted to kiss her. And he did want to—but he didn't want to admit it.

She walked well to the side of him, staying clear of the enchantment. "No sense you getting lost."

They walked on into the city. There were many cars in the streets, all zooming rapidly to the intersections, where they screeched to stops, waited a minute with irate growls and constant ejections of smoke from their posteriors, then zoomed in packs to the next intersections. They seemed to have only two speeds: zoom and stop. There were people inside the cars, exactly the way Grundy had described with the demon vehicles, but they never got out. It was as if the people had been swallowed whole and were now being digested.

Because the cars were as large as centaurs and moved at a constant gallop when not stopped, Dor was wary of them and tried to avoid them. But it was impossible; he had to cross the road sometime. He remembered how the nefarious Gap Dragon of Xanth lurked for those foolish enough to cross the bottom of the Gap; these cars seemed all too similar. Maybe there were some that had not yet consumed people and were traveling hungry, waiting to catch someone like Dor. He saw one car stopped by the side of the street with its mouth wide open like that of a dragon; he avoided it nervously. The strangest thing about it was that its guts seemed to be all in that huge mouth—steaming tubes and tendons and a disk-shaped tongue. Oddest of all, it had no teeth. Maybe that was why it took so long to digest the people.

He came to a corner. "How do I get across?" he asked.

"You wait for a light to stop the traffic," the street informed him with a contemptuous air of dust and car fumes. "Then you run-don't-walk across before they clip you, if you're lucky. Where have you been all your life?"

"In another realm," Dor said. He saw one of the lights the street described. It hung above the intersection and wore several little visors pointing each way. All sorts of colors flashed malevolently from it, in all sorts of directions. Dor couldn't understand how it made the car stop. Maybe the lights had some kind of stun-spell, or whatever it was called here. He played it safe by asking the light to tell him when it was proper to cross.

"Now," the light said, flashing green from one face and red from another.

Dor started across. A car honked like a sea monster and squealed like a sea-monster victim, almost running over Dor's leading foot. "Not that way, idiot!" the light exclaimed, flashing an angry red. "The other way! With the green, not the red! Haven't you ever crossed a street before?"

"Never," Dor admitted. Irene had disappeared; she must have re-entered the magic aisle to consult with the others. Maybe she found it safer within the spell zone; apparently the cars were unable to threaten her there.

"Wait till I tell you, then cross the way I tell you," the light said, blinking erratically. "I don't want any blood in *my* intersection!"

Dor waited humbly. "Now," the light said. "Walk straight ahead, keeping an even pace. Fast. You don't have all day, only fifteen seconds."

"But there's a car charging me!" Dor protested.

"It will stop," the light assured him. "I shall change to red at the last possible moment and force it to scorch rubber. I get a deep pleasure from that sort of thing."

Nervously, Dor stepped out onto the street again. The car zoomed terrifyingly close, then squealed to a stop a handspan's distance from Dor's shaking body. "Shook you up that time, you damned pedestrian," the car gloated through its cloud of scorched rubber. "If it hadn't been for that blinking light, I'd a had you. You creeps shouldn't be allowed on the road."

"But how can I cross the street if I'm not allowed on the road?" Dor asked.

"That's your problem," the car huffed.

"See, I can time them perfectly," the light said with satisfaction. "I get hundreds of them each day. No one gets through *my* intersection without paying his tax in gas and rubber."

"Go blow a bulb!" the car growled at the light.

"Go soak your horn!" the light flashed back.

"Some day we cars will have a revolution and establish a new axle," the car said darkly. "We'll smash all you restrictive lights and have a genuine free-enterprise system."

"You really crack me up," the light said disdainfully. "Without me, you'd have no discipline at all."

Dor walked on. Another car zoomed up, and Dor lost his nerve and leaped out of the way. "Missed him!" the car complained. "I haven't scored in a week!"

"Get out of my intersection!" the light screamed. "You never stopped!

You never burned rubber! You're supposed to waste gas for the full pause before you go through! How do you expect me to maintain a decent level of pollution here if you don't cooperate?"

"Oh, go jam your circuits!" the car roared, moving on through.

"Police! Police!" the light flashed. "That criminal car just ran the light! Rogue car! Rogue car!"

But now the other cars, perceiving that one was getting away with open defiance, hastened to do likewise. The intersection filled with snarling vehicles that crashed merrily into each other. There was the crackle of beginning fire.

Then the magic aisle moved out of the light's range, and it was silent. Dor was relieved; he didn't want to attract attention.

Irene reappeared. "You almost did it that time, Dor! Why don't you quit fooling with lights and get on to the library?"

"I'm trying to!" Dor snapped. "Where is the library?" he asked the sidewalk.

"You don't need a library, you clumsy oaf," the walk said. "You need a bodyguard."

"Just answer my question." The perversity of the inanimate seemed worse than ever, here in Mundania. Perhaps it was because the objects here had never been tamed by magic.

"Three blocks south, two east," the walk said grudgingly.

"What's a block?"

"Is this twerp real?" the walk asked rhetorically.

"Answer!" Dor snapped. And in due course he obtained the necessary definition. A block was one of the big squares formed by the crisscrossing roads. "Is there an archivist there?"

"A what?"

"A researcher, someone who knows a lot."

"Oh, sure. The best in the state. He walks here all the time. Strange old coot."

"That sidewalk sure understands you," Irene remarked smugly.

Dor was silent. Irene was safe from any remarks the sidewalk might make about her legs because she was outside the magic aisle. Dor knew Arnolde was keeping up with him, because his magic was operating. If Irene stepped within that region of magic, she would vanish. So she had the advantage and could snipe with impunity, for now.

A small group of Mundanes walked toward them, three men and two women. Their attire was strange. The men wore knots of something about their necks, almost choking them, and their shoes shone like mirrors. The women seemed to be walking on stilts. Irene continued blithely along, passing them. Dor hung back, curious about Mundane reactions to a citizen of Xanth.

The two females seemed to pay no attention, but all three males paused to look back at Irene. "Look at that creature!" one murmured. "What world is she from?"

"Whatever world it is, I want to go there!" another said. "Must be a foreign student. I haven't seen legs like that in three years."

"Her clothing is three centuries out of fashion, if it ever was *in* fashion," one of the women remarked, her nose elevated. Evidently she had after all paid attention. It was amazing what women could notice while seeming not to. Her own legs were unremarkable, though it occurred to Dor that the stilt-shoes might be responsible for deforming them.

"Men have no taste," the other woman said. "They prefer harem girls."

"Yeah . . ." the third man said with a slow smile. "I'd like to have her number."

"Over my dead body!" the second woman said.

The Mundanes went on, their strange conversation fading from Dor's hearing. Dor proceeded thoughtfully. If Irene were that different from Mundanes, what about himself? No one had reacted to him, yet he was dressed as differently from the males as Irene was from the females. He pondered that as he and Irene continued along the streets. Maybe the Mundanes had been so distracted by Irene's legs that they had skipped over Dor. That was understandable.

The library was a palatial edifice with an exceedingly strange entrance. The door went round and round without ever quite opening.

Dor stood near it, uncertain how to proceed. Mundane people passed him, not noticing him at all despite his evident difference. That was part of the magic, he realized suddenly, his contemplations finally fitting an aspect of the Mundane mystery together. He seemed to share their culture. Should he step outside the magic aisle, he would stand out as a complete foreigner, as Irene had. Fortunately, she was a pretty girl, so she could get away with it; he would not have that advantage.

At the moment, Irene was not in view; perhaps she had been more aware of the Mundane reaction, and preferred to avoid repetition. But as the Mundanes cleared the vicinity, she reappeared. "Arnolde believes that is a revolving door," she said. "There are a few obscure references to them in the texts on Mundania. Probably all you have to do is—" She saw another Mundane approaching, and hastily stepped into invisibility.

The Mundane walked to the door, put forth a hand, and pushed on a panel of the door. A chamber swung inward, and the man followed the compartment around. So simple, once Dor saw it in action!

He walked boldly up to the door and pushed through. It worked like a charm—that is, almost like a natural phenomenon of Xanth—passing him into the building. He was now in a large room in which there were many couches and tables, and the walls were lined with levels of books. This was a libary, all right. Now all he needed to do was locate the excellent researcher who was supposed to be here. Maybe in the history section.

Dor walked across the room, toward a wall of books. He could check those and see if any related. It shouldn't be too hard to—

He paused, aware that people were staring at him. What was the matter?

An older woman approached him, her face formed into stern lines. "Xf ibwf b esftt-dpef ifsf," she said severely, her gaze traveling disapprovingly from his unkempt hair to his dust-scuffed sandaled feet. It seemed she disapproved of his attire.

After a moment of confusion, Dor realized he had stepped beyond the magic aisle and was now being seen without the cushion of enchantment. Arnolde had been correct; Dor could not accomplish anything by himself.

What had happened to the centaur? Dor looked back toward the door—and saw Irene beckoning him frantically. He hurried back to her, the Mundane woman following. "Xf pqfsbuf a respectable library here," the Mundane was saying. "We expect a suitable demeanor—"

Dor turned to face her. "Yes?"

The woman stopped, nonplused. "Oh—I see you are properly dressed. I must have mistaken you for someone else." She retreated, embarrassed.

Dor's clothing had not changed. Only the woman's perception of it had, thanks to the magic.

"Arnolde can't get through the spinning door," Irene said.

So that was why Dor had left the aisle! He had walked well beyond the door. Of course those small chambers could not accommodate the mass of the centaur!

"Maybe there's another door," Dor suggested. "We could walk around the building—"

Irene vanished, then reappeared. "Yes, Arnolde says the spell fuzzes the boundaries of things somewhat, so his hands pass through Mundane objects, but his whole body mass is just too much to push through a solid Mundane wall. He might make it through a window, though."

Dor went back out the rotating door, then walked around the building. In the back was a double door that opened wide enough to admit a car. Dor walked through this and past some men who were stacking crates of books. "Hey, kid, you lost?" one called.

It had not taken him long to progress from "King" to "kid"! "I am looking for the archives," Dor said nervously.

"Oh, sure. The stacks. Third door on your left."

"Thank you." Dor went to the door and opened it wide, taking his time to pass through so that the others could get clear. He smelled the centaur and ogre, faintly, so knew they were with him.

Now they were in a region of long narrow passages between shelves loaded with boxes. Dor had no idea how to proceed, and wasn't certain the centaur could fit within these passages, but in a moment Irene appeared and informed him that Arnolde was right at home here. "But it would be better to consult with a competent archivist, he says," she concluded.

"There is one here," he said. "I asked." Then another thought came. "But suppose he sics the Mundane authorities on us? He may not understand our need."

"Arnolde says academics aren't like that. If there is a good one here, his scientific curiosity—I think that's what they call magic here—will keep him interested. Check in that little office; that looks like an archivist's cubby."

Reluctantly, Dor looked. He was in luck, of what kind he was not sure. There was a middle-aged, bespectacled man poring over a pile of papers. "Excuse me, sir—would you like to do some research?" Dor asked.

The man looked up, blinking. "Of what nature?"

"Uh, it's a long story. I'm trying to find a King, and I don't know where or when he is."

The man removed his spectacles and rubbed his tired eyes. "That would seem to be something of a challenge. What is the name of the King, and of his Kingdom?"

"King Trent of Xanth."

The man stood up and squeezed out of his cubby. He was fairly small and stooped, with fading hair, and he moved slowly. He reminded Dor of Arnolde in obscure ways. He located a large old tome, took it down, dusted it off, set it on a small table, and turned the brittle pages. "That designation does not seem to be listed."

Irene appeared. "He would not be a King in Mundania."

The scholar squinted at her with mild surprise. "My dear, I can not comprehend a word you are saying."

"Uh, she's from another land," Dor said quickly. Since Irene had to stand outside the magic aisle in order to be seen and heard, the magic translation effect was not operative for her. Since Dor had been raised in the same culture, he had no trouble understanding her. It was an interesting distinction. He, Dor, could understand both the others, and both seemed to be speaking the same language, but the two could not understand each other. Magic kept coming up with new wrinkles that perplexed him.

The scholar pondered. "Oh—she is associated with a motion picture company? This is research for a historical re-creation?"

"Not exactly," Dor said. "She's King Trent's daughter."

"Oh, it is a contemporary Kingdom! I must get a more recent text."

"No, it is a medieval one," Dor said. "Uh, that is—well, King Trent is in another time, we think."

The scholar paused thoughtfully. "The Kingdom you are re-creating, of course. I believe I understand." He looked again at Irene. "Females certainly have adequate limbs in that realm."

"What's he saying?" Irene demanded.

"That you have nice legs," Dor told her with a certain mild malice.

She ignored that. "What about my father?"

"Not listed in this book. I think we'll have to try another tack."

The scholar's eyes shifted from Irene's legs to Dor's face. "This is very odd.

You address her in English, and she seems to understand, but she replies in an alien tongue."

"It's complicated to explain," Dor said.

"I'd better check with Arnolde," Irene said, and vanished.

The Mundane scholar removed his spectacles and cleaned them carefully with a bit of tissue paper. He returned them to his face just in time to see Irene reappear. "Yes, that's definitely better," he murmured.

"Arnolde says we'll have to use some salient identifying trait to locate my father or mother." Irene said. "There may be a historical reference."

"Exactly what language is that?" the scholar asked, again fixing on Irene's legs. He might be old and academic, but he evidently had not forgotten what was what in female appearance.

"Xanthian, I guess," Dor said. "She says we should look for some historical reference to her parents, because of special traits they have."

"And what would these traits be?"

"Well, King Trent transforms people, and Queen Iris is mistress of illusion."

"Idiot!" Irene snapped. "Don't tell him about the magic!"

"I don't quite understand," the scholar said. "What manner of transformation, what mode of illusion?"

"Well, it doesn't work in Mundania," Dor said awkwardly.

"Surely you realize that the laws of physics are identical the world over," the scholar said. "Anything that works in the young lady's country will work elsewhere."

"Not magic," Dor said, and realized he was just confusing things more.

"How dumb can you get?" Irene demanded. "I'm checking with Arnolde." She vanished again.

This time the scholar blinked more emphatically. "Strange girl!"

"She's funny that way," Dor agreed weakly.

The scholar walked to the spot Irene had vacated. "Tubhf jmmvtjpo?" he inquired.

Oh, no! He was outside the magic aisle now, so the magic no longer made his language align with Dor's. Dor could not do anything about this; the centaur would have to move.

Irene reappeared right next to the scholar. Evidently she hadn't been paying attention, for she should have been able to see him while within the magic ambience. "Oh—you're here!" she exclaimed.

"Bnbajoh!" the scholar said. "J nvtu jorvjsf—"

Then the centaur moved. Irene vanished and the scholar became comprehensible. ". . . exactly how you perform that trick—" He paused. "Oops, you're gone again."

Irene reappeared farther down the hall. "Arnolde says we'll have to tell him," she announced. "About the magic and everything. Thanks to your bungling."

"Really, this is amazing!" the scholar said.

"Well, I'll have to tell you something you may find hard to believe," Dor said.

"At this stage, I'm inclined to believe in magic itself!"

"Yes. Xanth is a land of magic."

"In which people disappear and reappear at will? I think I would prefer to believe that than to conclude I am losing my sight."

"Well, some do disappear. That's not Irene's talent, though."

"That's *not* the young lady's ability? Then why is she doing it?"

"She's actually stepping in and out of a magic aisle."

"A magic aisle?"

"Generated by a centaur."

The scholar smiled wanly. "I fear you have the advantage of me. You can imagine nonsense faster than I can assimilate it."

Dor saw that the scholar did not believe him. "I'll show you my own magic, if you like," he said. He pointed to the open tome on the table. "Book, speak to the man."

"Why should I bother?" the book demanded.

"Ventriloquism!" the scholar exclaimed. "I must confess you are very good at it."

"What did you call me?" the book demanded.

"Would you do that again—with your mouth closed?" the scholar asked Dor.

Dor closed his mouth. The book remained silent. "I rather thought so," the scholar said.

"Thought what, four-eyes?" the book asked.

Startled, the scholar looked down at it, then back at Dor. "But your mouth was closed, I'm sure."

"It's magic," Dor said. "I can make any inanimate object talk."

"Let's accept for the moment that this is true. You are telling me that this King you are searching for can also work magic?"

"Right. Only he can't do it in Mundania, so I guess it doesn't count."

"Because he has no magic centaur with him?"

"Yes."

"I would like to see this centaur."

"He's protected by an invisibility spell. So the Mundanes won't bother us."

"This centaur is a scholar?"

"Yes. An archivist, like yourself."

"Then he is the one to whom I should talk."

"But the spell—"

"Abate the spell! Bring your centaur scholar forth. Otherwise I can not help you."

"I don't think he'd want to do that. It would be hard to get safely out of here without that enchantment, and we have no duplicate invisibility spell."

The scholar walked back to his cubby. "Mind you, I believe in magic no more than in the revelations of a hallucination, but I am willing to help you if you meet me halfway. Desist your parlor tricks, show me your scholar, and I will work with him to fathom the information you desire. I don't care how fanciful his outward form may be, provided he has a genuine mind. The fact that you find it necessary to dazzle me with ventriloquism, a lovely costumed girl who vanishes, and a mythological narrative suggests that there is very little substance to your claim, and you are wasting my time. I ask you to produce your scholar or depart my presence."

"Uh, Arnolde," Dor said. "I know it'll be awful hard to get out of here without the spells, but maybe we could wait till night. We really need the information, and—"

Abruptly the centaur appeared, facing the scholar's cubby. The ogre and golem stood behind him. "I agree," Arnolde said.

The scholar turned about. He blinked. "These are rare costumes, I admit."

Arnolde strode forward, his barrel barely clearing the shelves on either side, extending his hand. "I certainly do not blame you for being impatient with the uninitiate," he said. "You have excellent facilities here, and I know your time is valuable."

The scholar shook the hand, seeming more reassured by Arnolde's spectacles and demeanor than confused by his form.

"What is your specialty?"

"Alien archaeology—but of course there is a great deal of routine work and overlapping of chores."

"There certainly is!" the scholar agreed. "The nuisances I have to endure here—"

The two fell into a technical dialogue that soon left Dor behind. They became more animated as they sized up each other's minds and information. There was now no doubt they were similar types.

Irene, bored, grew a cocoa plant in the hall, and shared the hot cups of liquid with Dor, Smash, and Grundy. They knew it was important that Arnolde establish a good rapport so that they could gain the scholar's cooperation and make progress on their request.

Time passed. The two scholars delved into ancient tomes, debated excruciatingly fine points, questioned Dor closely about the hints King Trent had given him in both person and vision, and finally wound down to an animated close. The Mundane scholar accepted a mug of cocoa, relaxing at last. "I believe we have it," he said. "Will I see you again, centaur?"

"Surely so, sir! I am able to travel in Mundania, am fascinated by your comprehensive history, and am presently, as it were, between positions."

"Your compatriots found your magic as intolerable in you as mine would find a similar propensity in me! I shall not be able to tell anyone what I have learned this day, lest I, too, lose my position and possibly even be institutionalized. Imagine conversing with a centaur, ogre, and tiny golem! How I should love to do a research paper on your fantastic Land of Xanth, but it would hardly be believable."

"You could write a book and call it a story," Grundy suggested. "And Arnolde could write one about Mundania."

Both scholars looked pleased. Neither had thought of such a simple expedient.

"But do you know where my father is?" Irene demanded.

"Yes, I believe we do," Arnolde said. "King Trent left a message for us, we believe."

"How could he leave a message?" she demanded.

"He left it with Dor. That, and the other hints we had, such as the fact that he was going to a medieval region, in the mountains near a black body of water. There are, my friend informs me, many places in Mundania that fit the description. So we assume it is literal; either the water itself is black, or it is called black. As it happens, there is in Mundania a large body of water called the Black Sea. Many great rivers empty into it; great mountain ranges surround it. But that is not sufficient to identify this as the specific locale we seek; it merely makes it one possibility among many." Arnolde smiled. "We spent a good deal of time on geography. As it happens, there was historically a confluence of A, B, and K people in that vicinity in medieval times—at least that is so when their names are rendered into Xanth dialect. The Avars, the Bulgars, and the Khazars. So it does seem to fit. Everything you have told us seems to fit."

"But that isn't enough!" Dor cried. "How can you be sure you have the place, the time?"

"Honesty," Arnolde said. "O N E S T I." He pointed to a spot on an open book. "This, we believe, is the unique special hint King Trent gave you, to enable you and only you to locate him in an emergency."

Dor looked. It was an atlas, with a map of some strange Mundane land. On the map was a place labeled *Onesti.*

"There is only one such place in the world," Arnolde said. "It has to be King Trent's message to you. No one else would grasp the significance of that unique nomenclature."

Dor recalled the intensity with which King Trent had spoken of honesty, as if there had been a separate meaning there. He remembered how well aware the King had been of Dor's kind of spelling. It seemed no one else spelled it the obvious way, onesti.

"But if that's been there—that name, there in your maps and things—for centuries—that means King Trent never came back! We can't rescue him, because then the name would go."

"Not necessarily," Arnolde said. "The place-name does not depend on his presence. We should be able to rescue him without disturbing it. At any rate, we are never certain of the paradoxes of time. We shall simply have to go to that location and that time, circa AD 650, and try to find him."

"But suppose it's wrong?" Irene asked worriedly. "Suppose he isn't there?"

"Then we shall return here and do more research," Arnolde said. "I intend to visit here again anyway, and my friend Ichabod would like to visit Xanth. There will be no trouble about that, I assure you."

"Yes. You will be welcome here," the Mundane scholar agreed. "You have a fine and arcane mind."

"For the first time," Arnolde continued, "I look upon my exile from Centaur Isle and my assumption of an obscene talent with a certain equanimity. I have not, it seems, been excluded from my calling; my horizons have been inordinately expanded."

"And mine," Ichabod agreed. "I must confess my contemporaneous existence was becoming tiresome, though I did not recognize this until this day." Now the scholar sounded just like Arnolde. Perhaps some obscure wrinkle of fate had operated to bring these two together. Did luck or fate really operate in Mundania? Perhaps they did, when the magic aisle was present. "The prospect of researching in a completely new and mystical terrain is immensely appealing; it renovates my outlook." He paused. "Ah, would there by any chance be individuals of the female persuasion remotely resembling . . . ?" His glance flicked guiltily to Irene's legs.

"Nymphs galore," Grundy said. "A dime a dozen."

"Oh, you employ contemporaneous currency?" the scholar asked, surprised.

"Currency?" Dor asked blankly.

"A dime is a coin of small denomination here."

Dor smiled. "No, a dime is a tiny object that causes things passing over it to come to a sudden stop. When it has functioned this way twelve times, its enchantment wears out. Hence our saying—"

"How marvelous. I wonder whether one of my own dimes would perform similarly there."

"That's the idea," Grundy said. "Toss it in front of a troupe of gamboling nymphs, and grab the first one it stops. Nymphs don't have much brains, but they sure have legs." He moved farther away from Irene, who showed signs of kicking.

"Oh, I can hardly wait to commence research in Xanth!" the scholar exclaimed. "As it happens, I have a dime ready." He brought out a tiny silver coin, his gaze once again touching on Irene's limbs. "I wonder . . ."

Irene frowned. "Sometimes I wonder just how badly I really want to rescue my folks. I'll be lucky if my legs don't get blistered from all the attention." But as usual, she did not seem completely displeased. "Let's be on our way; I don't care what you do, once my father is back in Xanth."

Arnolde and Ichabod shook hands, two very similar creatures. On impulse, Dor brought out one of the gold coins he had so carefully saved from the pirate's treasure. "Please accept this, sir, as a token of our appreciation for your help." He pressed it on the scholar.

The man hefted the coin. "That's solid gold?" he exclaimed. "I believe it is a genuine Spanish doubloon! I can not accept it."

The centaur interceded. "Please do accept it, Ichabod. Dor is temporary King of Xanth; to decline would be construed as an offense to the crown."

"But the value—"

"Let's trade coins," Dor said, discovering a way through. "Your dime for my doubloon. Then it is an even exchange."

"An even exchange!" the scholar exclaimed. "In no way can this be considered—"

"Dimes are very precious in Xanth," Arnolde said. "Gold has little special value. Please acquiesce."

"Maybe a nymph would stop on a doubloon, too," Grundy suggested.

"She certainly would!" Ichabod agreed. "But not because of any magic. Women here are much attracted to wealth."

"Please," Irene put in, smiling beguilingly. Dor knew she only wanted to get moving on the search for her father, but her intercession was effective.

"In that case, I will exchange with you, with pleasure, King Dor," the scholar agreed, giving Dor his dime. "I only meant to protest that your coin was far too valuable for whatever service I might have provided, when in fact it was a pleasure providing it anyway."

"Nothing's too valuable to get my father back," Irene said. She leaned forward and kissed Ichabod on the cheek. The man froze as if he had glimpsed the Gorgon, an astonished smile on his face. It was obvious he had not been kissed by many pretty girls in his secluded lifetime.

It was now early evening. Ichabod delved into assorted cubbies and produced shrouds to conceal the bodies of the centaur and ogre. Then Arnolde and Smash walked out of the library in tandem, looking like two big workmen in togas, moving a covered crate between them. It turned out to be almost as good concealment as the invisibility spell; no one paid attention to them. They were on their way back to Xanth.

Chapter 9

Onesti's Policy

They did not go all the way back home. They trekked only to the northwest tip of Xanth, where the isthmus connected it to Mundania. Once they were back in magic territory, Irene set about replenishing her stock of seeds. Smash knocked down a jellybarrel tree, consumed the jelly, and fashioned the swollen trunk into a passable boat. Arnolde watched the terrain, making periodic forays into Mundania, just far enough to see whether it had changed. Dor accompanied him, questioning the sand. By the description of people the sand had recently seen, they were able to guess at the general place and time in Mundania.

For the change was continuous. Once a person from Xanth entered Mundania, his framework was fixed until he returned; but anyone who followed him might enter a different aspect of Mundania. This was like missing one boat and boarding the next, Arnolde explained; the person on the first boat could return, but the person on land could not catch a particular boat that had already departed. Thus King Trent had gone, they believed, to a place called "Europe," in a time called "Medieval." Dor's party had gone to a place called "America," in a time called "Modern." The shifting of places and times seemed random; probably there was a pattern to the changes that they were unable to comprehend. They simply had to locate the combination they wanted and pass through that "window" before it changed. Arnolde concluded, from their observations, that any given window lasted from five minutes to an hour, and that it was possible to hold a window open longer by having a person stand at the border; it seemed the window couldn't quite close while it was in use. Perhaps it was like the revolving door in the Mundanian library, whose turning could be temporarily stopped by a person in it—until some other person needed to use it.

On the third day it became tedious. Irene's seed collection was complete and she was restive; Smash had finished his boat and stocked it with supplies. Grundy had made himself a nest in the bow, from which he eavesdropped on the gossip of passing marine life. Arnolde and Dor walked down the beach. "What have you seen lately?" Dor inquired routinely of the same-yet-different patch of sand.

"A man in a spacesuit," the sand replied. "He had little antennae sprouting from his head, like an ant, and he could talk to his friends without making a sound."

That didn't sound like anyone Dor was looking for. Some evil Magician must have enchanted the man, perhaps trying to create a new composite-species. They turned about and returned to Xanth. This surely was not their window.

The sea changed color frequently. It had been reddish the first time they came here, and reddish when they returned, for they had been locked into that particular aspect of Mundania. But thereafter it had shifted to blue, yellow, green, and white. Now it was orange, changing to purple. When it was solid purple, they walked west again. "What have you seen lately?" Dor asked once more.

"A cavegirl swimming," the sand said. "She was sort of fat, but oooh, didn't she have—"

They walked east again, depressed. "I wish there were a more direct way to do this," Arnolde said. "I have been striving to analyze the pattern, but it has eluded me, perhaps because of insufficient data."

"I know it's not much of a life we have brought you into," Dor said. "I wish there had been some other way—"

"On the contrary, it is a fascinating life and a challenging puzzle," the centaur demurred. "It is akin to the riddles of archaeology, where one must have patience and fortune in equal measure. We merely must gather more data, whether it takes a day or a year."

"A year!" Dor cried, horrified.

"Surely it will be shorter," Arnolde said reassuringly. It was obvious that he had a far greater store of patience than Dor did.

As they re-entered Xanth, the sea turned black. "Black!" Dor exclaimed. "Could that be—?"

"It is possible," Arnolde agreed, reining his own excitement with the caution of experience. "We had better alert the remainder of our company."

"Grundy, get Smash and Irene to the boat," Dor called. "We just might be close."

"More likely another false alarm," the golem grumbled. But he scampered off to fetch the other two.

When they reached their usual spot of questioning, Dor noticed that there was a large old broad-leaved tree that hadn't been there before. This was certainly a different locale. But that in itself did not mean much; the landscape did shift with the Mundane aspects, sometimes dramatically. It was not just time but geography that changed; some aspects were flat and barren, while others were raggedly mountainous. The only thing all had in common was the beach line, with the sea to the south and the terrain to the north. Arnolde was constantly intrigued by the assorted significances of this, but Dor did not pay much attention. "What have you seen lately?" he asked the sand.

"Nothing much since the King and his moll walked by," the sand said.

"Oh." Dor turned to trek back to the magic section.

The centaur paused. "Did it say—?"

Then it sank in. Excitement raced along Dor's nerves. "King Trent and Queen Iris?"

"I suppose. They were sort of old."

"I believe we have our window at last!" Arnolde said. "Go back and alert the others; I shall hold the window open."

Dor ran back east, his heart pounding harder than warranted by the exertion. Did he dare believe? "We've found it!" he cried. "Move out now!"

They dived into the boat. Smash poled it violently forward. Then the ogre's effort diminished. Dor looked, and saw that Smash was striving hard but accomplishing little.

"Oh—we're out of the magic of Xanth, and not yet in the magic aisle," he said. "Come on—we've all got to help."

Dor and Irene leaned over the boat on either side and paddled desperately with their hands, and slowly the boat moved onward. They crawled up parallel to the centaur. "All aboard!" Dor cried, exhilarated.

Arnolde trotted out through the shallow water and climbed aboard with difficulty, rocking the boat. Some sea water slopped in. The craft was sturdy, as anything crafted by an ogre was bound to be, but still reeked of lime jelly, especially where it had been wet down.

The centaur stood in the center, facing forward; Irene sat in the front, her fair green hair trailing back in the breeze. It had faded momentarily when they were between magics, just now; perhaps that had helped give Dor the hint of the problem. It remained the easiest way to tell the state of the world around them.

Dor settled near the rear of the boat, and Smash poled vigorously from the stern. Now that they were within the magic aisle, the ogre's strength was full, and the boat was lively. The black waves coursed rapidly past.

"I wish I had known this was all we had to do to locate King Trent," Dor said. "We could have saved ourselves the trip into Modern Mundania."

"By no means," Arnolde protested, swishing his tail. "We might have discovered this window, true; but each window opens onto an entire Mundane world. We should soon have lost the trail and ourselves and been unable to rescue anyone. As it is, we know we are looking for Onesti and we know where it is; this will greatly facilitate our operation." The centaur paused. "Besides which, I am most gratified to have met Ichabod."

So their initial excursion did make sense, after all. "What sort of people do you see here?" Dor asked the water.

"Tough people with baggy clothes and swords and bows," the water said. "They're not much on the water, though; not the way the Greeks were."

"Those are probably the Bulgars," Arnolde said. "They should have passed this way in the past few decades, according to Ichabod."

"Who are the Bulgars?" Irene asked. Now that they were actually on the trail of her lost father, she was much more interested in details.

"This is complex to explain. Ichabod gave me some detail on it, but I may not have the whole story."

"If they're people my father met—and if we have to meet them, too—I want to know all about them." Her face assumed her determined look.

The boat was moving well, for the ogre's strength was formidable. The shoreline stretched ahead, curving in and out, with inlets and bays. "We do have a journey of several days ahead of us," the centaur said. "Time will doubtless weigh somewhat ponderously on our hands." He took a didactic breath and started in on his historical narrative, while the ogre scowled, uninterested, and Grundy settled down in his nest to sleep. But Dor and Irene paid close attention.

In essence it was this: about three centuries before this period, there had been a huge Mundane empire in this region, called—as Dor understood it—Roam, perhaps because it spread so far. But after a long time this empire had grown corrupt and weak. Then from the great inland mass to the east had thrust a formerly quiescent tribe, the Huns, perhaps short for Hungries because of their appetite for power, pushing other tribes before them. These tribes had overrun the Roaming Empire, destroying a large part of it. But when the Hungry chief, Attaboy, died of indigestion, they were defeated and driven partway back east, to the shore of this Black Sea, the very color of their mood. They fought among themselves for a time, as people in a black mood do, then reunited and called themselves the Bulgars. But the Buls were driven out of their new country by another savage tribe of Turks—no relation to the turkey oaks—called the Khazars. Some Buls fled north and some fled west—and this was the region the western ones had settled, here at the western edge of the Black Sea. They couldn't go any farther because another savage tribe was there, the Avars. The Avars had a huge empire in eastern Europe, but now it was declining, especially under the onslaught of the Khazars. At the moment, circa Mundane AD 650—the number referred to some Mundane religion to which none of these parties belonged—there was an uneasy balance in this region between the three powers, the Avars, Bulgars, and Khazars, with the Khazars dominant.

Somehow this was too complex for Dor to follow. All these strange tribes and happenings and numbers—the intricacies of Mundania were far more complicated than the simple magic events of Xanth! Easier to face down griffins and dragons than Avars and Khazars; at least the dragons were sensible creatures.

"But what has this to do with my father?" Irene demanded. "Which tribe did he go to trade with?"

"None of the above," the centaur said. "This is merely background. It would be too dangerous for us to deal with such savages. But we believe there is a small Kingdom, maybe a Gothic remnant, or some older indigenous people, who have retained nominal independence in the Carpathian Mountains, with a separate language and culture. They happen to be at the boundary between the Avars, Bulgars, and Khazars, protected to a degree because no one empire can make a move there without antagonizing the other two, and also protected by the roughness of the terrain. Hence the A, B, K complex King Trent referenced—a valuable clue for us. This separate region is the Kingdom of Onesti. It is ensconced in the mountains, difficult to invade, and has very little that others would want to take, which may help account for its independence. But it surely is eager for peaceful and profitable trade, and Ichabod's Mundane reference suggests that it did have a trade route that has been lost to history, which enabled the Kingdom to prosper for a century when their normal channels appeared to be blocked. That could be the trade route to Xanth that King Trent sought to establish."

"Yes, that does make sense," Irene agreed. "But suppose one of those other tribes caught my father, and that's why he never returned?"

"We shall trace him down," the centaur said reassuringly. "We have an enormous asset King Trent lacked—magic. All we need to do is go to Onesti and query the people, plants, animals, and objects. There will surely be news of him."

Irene was silent. Dor shared her concern. Now that they were on the verge of finding King Trent—how could they be certain they would find him alive? If he were dead, what then?

"Are we going to have to fight all those A's, B's, and K's?" Grundy asked. Apparently he had not been entirely asleep.

"I doubt it," Arnolde replied. "Actual states of war are rarer than they seem in historical perspective. The great majority of the time, life goes on as usual; the fishermen fish, the blacksmiths hammer iron, the farmers farm, the women bear children. Otherwise there would be constant deprivation. However, I have stocked a friendship-spell for emergency use." He patted his bag of spells.

They went on, the ogre poling indefatigably. Gradually the shoreline curved southward, and they followed it. When dusk came they pulled ashore briefly to make a fire and prepare supper; then they returned to the boat for the night, so as not to brave the Mundane threats of the darkness. There were few fish and no monsters in the Black Sea, Grundy reported; it was safe as long as a storm did not come up.

Now Arnolde expended one of his precious spells. He opened a wind capsule, orienting it carefully. The wind blew southwest, catching the small squat sail they raised for the purpose. Now the ogre could rest, while the boat coursed on toward their destination. They took turns steering it, Grundy asking the fish and water plants for directions, Dor asking the water, and Irene growing a compass plant that pointed toward the great river they wanted.

That reminded Dor of the magic compass. He brought it out and looked, hoping it would point to King Trent. But it pointed straight at Arnolde, and when Arnolde held it, it pointed to Dor. It was useless in this situation.

Sleep was not comfortable on the water, but it was possible. Dor lay down and stared at the stars, wide awake; then the stars abruptly shifted position, and he realized he had slept; *now* he was wide awake. They shifted again. Then he was wide awake again—when Grundy woke him to take his turn at the helm. He had, it seemed, been dreaming he was wide awake. That was a frustrating mode; he would almost have preferred the nightmares.

In the morning they were at the monstrous river delta—a series of bars, channels, and islands, through which the slow current coursed. Now Smash had to unship the two great oars he had made, face back, and row against the current. Still the boat moved alertly enough. Irene grew pastry plants and fed their pastry-flower fruits to the ogre so he would not suffer the attrition of hunger. Smash gulped them down entire without pausing in his efforts; Dor was almost jealous of the creature's sheer zest for food and effort.

No, he realized upon reflection. He was jealous of the attention Irene was paying Smash. For all that he, Dor, did not want to be considered the property of any girl, especially not this one, he still became resentful when Irene's attention went elsewhere. This was unreasonable, he knew; Smash needed lots of food in order to continue the enormous effort he was making. This was the big thing the ogre was contributing to their mission—his abundant strength. Yet still it gnawed at Dor; he wished *he* had enormous muscles and endless endurance, and that Irene was popping whole pies and tarts into his mouth.

Once, Dor remembered, he had been big—or at least had borrowed the body of a powerful barbarian—maybe an Avar or a Bulgar or a Khazar—and had discovered that strength did not solve all problems or bring a person automatic happiness. But at the moment, his selfish feelings didn't go along with the sensible thinking of his mind.

"Sometimes I wish I were an ogre," Grundy muttered.

Suddenly Dor felt better.

All day they heaved up the river, leaving the largest channel for a smaller one, and leaving that for another and still smaller one. There were some fishermen, but they didn't look like A's, B's, or K's, and they took a look at the size and power of the ogre and left the boat alone. Arnolde had been correct; the ordinary Mundane times were pretty dull, without rampaging armies everywhere. In this respect Mundania was similar to Xanth.

Well upstream, they drew upon the shore and camped for the night. Dor told the ground to yell an alarm if anything approached—anything substantially larger than ants—and they settled down under another umbrella tree Irene grew. It was just as well, for during the night it rained.

On the third day they forged up a fast-flowing tributary stream, ascending the great Carpath range. Some places they had to portage; Smash merely picked up the entire boat, upright, balanced it on his corrugated head, steadied it with his gauntleted hamhands, and trudged up through the rapids.

"If you don't have your full strength yet," Dor commented, "you must be close to it."

"Ungh," Smash agreed, for once not having the leisure to rhyme. Ogres were the strongest creatures of Xanth, size for size—but some monsters were much larger, and others more intelligent, so ogres did not rule the jungle. Smash and his parents were the only ogres Dor had met, if he didn't count his adventure into Xanth's past, where he had known Egor the zombie ogre; they were not common creatures today. Perhaps that was just as well; if ogres were as common as dragons, who would stand against them?

At last, on the afternoon of the third day, they came to the Kingdom of Onesti, or at least its main fortress, Castle Onesti. Dor marveled that King Trent and Queen Iris, traveling alone without magic, could have been able to get here in similar time. Maybe they underestimated the arduousness of the journey. Well, it would soon be known.

Dor tried to question the stones and water of the river, but the water wasn't the same from moment to moment and so could not remember, and the stones claimed that no one had portaged up here in the past month. Obviously the King had taken another route, probably an easier one. Perhaps the King of Onesti had sent an escort, and they had ridden Mundane horses up a horse trail. Yes, that was probably it.

They drew up just in sight of the imposing castle. Huge stones formed great walls, leading up to the front entrance. There was no moat; this was a mountain fastness. "Do we knock on the door, or what?" Irene asked nervously.

"Your father told me honesty is the best policy," Dor said, masking his own uncertainty. "I assume that wasn't just a riddle to suggest where he went. We can approach openly. We can tell them we're from Xanth and are looking for King Trent. Maybe they have no connection to whatever happened—*if* anything happened. But let's not go out of our way to tell them about our magic. Just in case."

"Just in case," she agreed tightly.

They marched up to the front entrance. That seemed to be the only accessible part of the edifice anyway; the wall passed through a forest on the south to merge cleverly with the clifflike sides of the mountain to the west and north. They were at the east face, where the approach was merely steep. "No wonder no one has conquered this little Kingdom," Irene murmured.

"I agree," Arnolde said. "No siege machinery could get close, and a catapult would have to operate from the valley below. Perhaps it could be taken, but it hardly seems worth the likely cost."

Dor knocked. They waited. He knocked again. Still no response. Then Smash tapped the door with one finger, making it shudder.

Now a window creaked open in the middle of the door. A face showed behind bars. "Who are you?" the guard demanded.

"I am Dor of Xanth. I have come to see King Trent of Xanth, who, I believe, is here."

"Who?"

"King Trent, imbecile!" one of the bars snapped.

The guard's head jerked back, startled. "What?"

"You got a potato in your ear?" the bar demanded.

"Stop it," Dor mumbled at the bars. The last thing he wanted was the premature exposure of his talent! Then, quickly, louder: "We wish to see King Trent."

"Wait," the guard said. The window slammed closed.

But Smash, tired from his two days' labors, was irritable. "No wait, ingrate!" he growled, and before Dor knew what was happening, the ogre smashed one sledgehammer fist into the door. The heavy wood splintered. He punched right through, then caught the far side of the door with his thick gauntleted fingers and hauled violently back. The entire door ripped free of its bolts and hinges. He put his other hand on the little barred window and hefted the door up and over his head, while the other people ducked hastily.

"Now see what you've done, you moronic brute," Arnolde said. But somehow the centaur did not seem completely displeased. He, too, was tired and irritable from the journey, and the welcome at Castle Onesti had not been polite.

The guard stood inside, staring, as the ogre hurled the great door down the mountainside. "Take us to your leader," Dor said calmly, as if this were routine. All he could do, after all, was make the best of the situation, and poise counted for a lot. "We don't want my friend to get impatient."

The guard turned about somewhat dazedly and led the way to the interior of the castle. Other guards came charging up, attracted by the commotion, swords drawn. Smash glared at them and they hastily faded back, swords sheathed.

Soon they came to the main banquet hall, where the King of Onesti held sway. The King sat at the head of an immense wooden table piled with puddings. He stood angrily as Dor approached, his huge belly bulging out over the table. "H cdlzmc sn jmnv sgd ldzmhmf ne sghr hmsqtrhnm—" he demanded, his fat face reddening impressively.

Then Arnolde's magic aisle caught up, and the King became intelligible. ". . . before I have you all thrown in the dungeon!"

"Hello," Dor said. "I am Dor, temporary King of Xanth while King Trent is away." Of course, the Zombie Master was temporary-temporary King now, while Dor himself was away, but that was too complicated to explain at the moment. "He came here on a trading mission, I believe, less than a month ago, and has not returned. So I have come to look for him. What's the story?"

The King scowled. Suddenly Dor knew this approach had been all wrong, that King Trent had not come here, that the people of Onesti knew nothing about him. This was all a mistake.

"I am King Oary of Onesti," the King said from out of his glower, "and I never saw this King Trench of yours. Get out of my Kingdom."

Despair struck Dor—but behind him Arnolde murmured: "That person is prevaricating, I believe."

"On top of that, he's lying," Irene muttered.

"Glib fib," Smash said. He set one hamhand down on the banquet table gently. The bowls of pudding jumped and quivered nervously.

King Oary considered the ogre. His ruddy face paled. His righteous anger dissolved into something like guilty cunning. "However, I may have news of him," he said with less bellicosity. "Join my feast, and I will query my minions."

Dor didn't like this. King Oary did not impress him favorably, and he did not feel like eating with the man. But the puddings looked good, and he did want Oary's cooperation. He nodded reluctant assent.

The servants hurried up with more chairs for Dor, Irene, and Smash. Grundy, too small for a chair, perched instead on the edge of the table. Arnolde merely stood. More puddings were brought in, together with flagons of beverage, and they all pitched in.

The pudding was thick, with fruit embedded, and surprisingly tasty. Dor soon found himself thirsty, for the pudding was highly spiced, so he drank— and found the beverage a cross between sweet beer and sharp wine from indifferent beerbarrel and winekeg trees. He hadn't realized that such trees grew in Mundania; certainly they did not grow as well. But the stuff was heady and good once he got used to it.

The others were eating as happily. They had all developed quite an appetite in the course of their trek up the mountain river, and had not paused to grow a meal of their own before approaching the castle. Smash, especially, tossed down puddings and flagons of drink with an abandon that set the castle servants gaping.

But the drink was stronger than what they were accustomed to. Dor soon found his awareness spinning pleasantly. Grundy began a little dance on the table, a routine he had picked up from a Mundane immigrant to Xanth. He called it the Drunken Sailor's Hornpipe, and it did indeed look drunken. King Oary liked it, applauding with his fat hands.

Arnolde and Irene ate more diffidently, but the centaur's mass required plenty of sustenance, and he was making good progress. Irene, it seemed, loved puddings, so she could not hold back long.

"Zmc vgn lhfgs xnt ad, ezhq czlrdk?" King Oary asked Irene pleasantly.

Oops—they were seated along the table, with the King at the end. The King was beyond the aisle of magic. But Arnolde grasped the problem quickly, and angled his body so that he now faced the King. That would extend the magic far enough.

Irene, too, caught on. "Were you addressing me, Your Majesty?" she asked demurely. Dor had to admit she was very good at putting on maidenly ways.

"Of course. What other fair damsels are in this hall?"

She colored slightly, looking about as if to spy other girls. She was getting more practiced at this sort of dissemblance. "Thank you so much, Your Majesty."

"What is your lineage?"

"Oh, I'm King Trent's daughter."

The King nodded sagely. "I'm sure you are prettier than your mother."

Did that mean something? Dor continued eating, listening, hoping Irene could get some useful information from the obese monarch. There was something odd here, but Dor did not know how to act until he had more definite information.

"Have you any news of my parents?" Irene inquired, having the wit and art to smile fetchingly at the King. Yet again Dor had to suppress his unreasoning jealousy. "I'm so worried about them." And she pouted cutely. Dor hadn't seen her use that expression before; it must be a new one.

"My henchmen are spying out information now," The King reassured her. "Soon we should have what news there is."

Arnolde glanced at Dor, a fleeting frown on his face. He still did not trust Oary.

"Tell me about Onesti," Irene said brightly. "It seems like such a *nice* little Kingdom."

"Oh, it is, it is," the King agreed, his eyes focusing on what showed of her legs. "Two fine castles and several villages, and some very pretty mountains. For centuries we have fought off the savages; two thousand years ago, this was the heartland of the battle-axe people, the Cimmerians. Then the Scyths came on their horses, driving the footbound Cimmerians south. Horses had not been seen in this country before; they seemed like monsters from some fantasy land."

The King paused to chew up another pudding. Monsters from a fantasy land—could that refer to Xanth? Dor wondered. Maybe some nightmares found a way out, and turned Mundane, and that was the origin of day horses. It was an intriguing speculation.

"But here at the mountains," the King resumed, wiping pudding crust from his whiskers, "the old empire held. Many hundreds of years later the Sarmatians drove out the Scyths, but did not penetrate this fastness." He belched contentedly. "Then came the Goths—but still we held the border. Then from the south came the horrible civilized Romans, and from the east the Huns—"

"Ah, the Huns," Irene agreed, as if she knew something about them.

"But still Onesti survived, here in the mountains, unconquered though beset by barbarians," the King concluded. "Of course we had to pay tribute sometimes, a necessary evil. Yet our trade is inhibited. If we interact too freely with the barbarians, there will surely be mischief. Yet we must have trade if we are to survive."

"My father came to trade," Irene said.

"Perhaps he got sidetracked by the dread Khazars, or their Magyar minions," King Oary suggested. "I have had some dealings with those; they are savage, cunning brutes, always alert for spoils. I happen to speak their language, so I know."

Dor decided he would have to do some searching on his own, questioning the objects in this vicinity. But not right now, while the King was watching. He was sure the King was hiding something.

"Have you been King of Onesti for a long time?" Irene inquired innocently.

"Not long," Oary admitted. "My nephew Omen was to be King, but he was underage, so I became regent when my brother died. Then Omen went out hunting—and did not return. We fear he strayed too far and was ambushed by the Khazars or Magyars. So I am King, until we can declare Omen officially dead. There is no hope of his survival, of course, but the old council moves very slowly on such matters."

So King Oary was in fact regent during the true King's absence—much as Dor was, in Xanth. But this King was eager to retain the throne. Had there been foul play by other than the Khazars?

Dor found his head on the table, contesting for space with a pudding. He must have gotten quite sleepy! "What's going on?" he mumbled.

"You've been drugged, you fool, that's what," the table whispered in his ear. "There's more in that rotgut than booze, I'll tell you!"

Dor reacted with shock, but somehow his head did not rise. "Drugged? Why?"

" 'Cause the Imposter King doesn't like you, that's why," the table said. "He always drugs his enemies. That's how he got rid of King Omen, and then that fake Magician King."

Magician King! It was funny, whispering with his head on the table, but fairly private. Dor's nose was almost under the pudding. "Was that King Trent?"

"That's what he called himself. But he couldn't do magic. He drank the drink, all-trusting the way they all are, the fools, and went to sleep just like you. You're all such suckers."

"Smash! Grundy!" Dor cried as loudly as he could, his head still glued to the table. "We've been betrayed! Drugged! Break out of here!"

But now many guards charged into the hall. "Remove this carrion," King Oary commanded. "Throw them in the dungeon. Don't damage the girl; she's too pretty to waste. Put the freak horse in the stable."

Smash, who had gulped huge quantities of the drugged drink, nevertheless had strength to rouse himself and fight. Dor heard the noise, but was facing the wrong way. Guards charged, and screamed, and retreated. "Give it to them, ogre!" Grundy cried, dancing on the table. "Tear them up!"

But then the violence abated. "Hey, don't slow down now!" Grundy called. "What's the matter with you?"

Dor knew what had happened. Smash had wandered outside the magic aisle, and lost his supernatural strength. Now the flagons of drugged drink took their toll, as they would on any normal creature. "Me sleep a peep," Smash said, the last of his magic expended in the rhyme.

Dor knew this fight was lost. "Get out of here, Grundy," he said with a special effort. "Before you sleep, too. Don't let them catch you." The unconsciousness overcame Dor.

Chapter 10

Hate Love

Dor woke with a headache. He was lying on sour-smelling hay in a dark cell. As he moved, something skittered away. He suspected it was a rat; he understood they abounded in Mundania. Maybe that was a blessing; the magic creatures of the night could be horrible in Xanth.

There was the sound of muted sobbing. Dor held his breath a moment to make certain it wasn't himself.

He sat up, peering through the gloom to find some vestige of light. There was a little, which grew brighter as his eyes acclimatized; it seemed to be a candle in the distance. But there was a wall in the way; the light filtered through the cracks.

He oriented on the sobbing. It was from an adjacent chamber, separated from his own by massive stone pilings and huge wood timbers. This must be the lower region of the castle, these cells hollowed out from around the foundations. There were gaps between the supports, big enough for him to pass his arm through but not his body.

"Irene?" he asked.

"Oh, Dor!" she answered immediately, tearfully. "I thought I was alone! What has become of us?"

"We were drugged and thrown in the dungeon," he said. "King Oary must have done the same to your parents, before." He couldn't quite remember where he had gotten that notion, or how he himself had been drugged; his memory was foggy on recent details.

"But why? My father came only to trade!"

"I don't know. But I think King Oary is a usurper. Maybe he murdered the rightful King, and your folks found out. Oary knew he couldn't fool us long, so he practiced his treachery on us, too."

"What do we do now?" she demanded hysterically. "Oh, Dor, I've never felt so horrible!"

"I think it's the drug," he said. "I feel bad, too. That should wear off. If we have our magic, we may be able to get free. Do you have your bag of seeds?"

She checked. "No. Only my clothing. Do you have your gold and gems?"

Dor checked. "No. They must have searched us and taken everything they thought was valuable or dangerous. I don't have my sword either." But then his questing fingers found something small. "I do have the jar of salve, not that it's much good here. And my midnight sunstone; it fell into the jacket lining. Let me see—" He brought it out. "No, I guess not. This has no light."

"Where are the others?"

"I'll check," he said. "Floor, where are my companions?"

There was no answer. "That means we have no magic. Arnolde must be in the stable." He seemed to remember something about that, foggily.

"What about Smash and Grundy?"

"Me here," the ogre said from the opposite cell. "Head hurt. Strength gone."

Now Dor had no further doubt; the magic was gone. The ogre wasn't rhyming, and no doubt Irene's hair had lost its color. Magic had strange little bypaths and side effects, where loss was somehow more poignant than that of the major aspects. But those major ones were vital; without his magic strength, Smash could probably not break free of the dungeon.

"Grundy?" Dor called inquiringly.

There was no answer. Grundy, it seemed, had escaped capture. That was about the extent of their good fortune.

"Me got gauntlets," Smash said.

Include one more item of fortune. If the ogre should get his strength back, those gauntlets would be a big help. Probably the castle guards had not realized the gauntlets were not part of the ogre, since Smash had used them for eating. The ogreish lack of manners had paid off in this respect.

Dor's head was slowly clearing. He tried the door to his cell. It was of solid Mundane wood, worn but far too tough to break. Too tough, too, for Smash, in his present condition; the ogre tried and couldn't budge his own door. Unless the centaur came within range, none of them had any significant lever for freedom.

The doors seemed to be barred by some unreachable mechanism outside: inside, the slimy stone floor was interrupted only by a disposal sump—a small but deep hole that reeked of old excrement. Obviously no one would be released for sanitary purposes either.

Smash banged a fist against a wall. "Oww!" he exclaimed. "Now me miss centaur!"

"He does have his uses," Dor agreed. "You know, Smash, Arnolde didn't really usurp Chet's place. Chet couldn't come with us anyway, because of his injury, and Arnolde didn't want to. We pretty much forced him into it, by revealing his magic talent."

"Ungh," the ogre agreed. "Me want out of here. No like be weak."

"I think we'll have to wait for whatever King Oary plans for us," Dor said grimly. "If he planned to kill us, he wouldn't have bothered to lock us in here."

"Dor, I'm scared, really scared," Irene said. "I've never been a prisoner before."

Dor peered out through the cracks in his door. Had the flickering candle shadow moved? The guard must be coming in to eavesdrop. Naturally King Oary would want to know their secrets—and Irene just might let out their big one before she realized. He had to warn her—without the guard catching on. They just might turn this to their advantage.

He went to the wall that separated them. "It will be a good idea to plan our course of action," he said. "If they question us, tell them what they want to know. There's no point in concealing anything, since we're innocent." He managed to reach his arm through the crevice in the wall nearest her. "But we don't want them to force us into any false statements."

His hand touched something soft. It was Irene. She made a stifled "Eeek!" then grasped his hand.

"Let me review our situation," Dor said. "I am King during King Trent's absence." He squeezed her hand once. "You are King Trent's daughter." He squeezed again, once. "Arnolde the Centaur is also a Prince among his people." This time he squeezed twice.

"What are you talking about?" she demanded. "Arnolde's not—" She broke off as he squeezed several times, hard. Then she began to catch on; she was a bright enough girl. "Not with us now," she concluded, and squeezed his hand once.

"If the centaur does not return to his people on schedule, they will proba-bly come after him with an army," Dor said, squeezing twice.

"A big army," she agreed, returning the two squeezes. "With many fine archers and spear throwers, thirsty for blood, and a big catapult to loft huge stones against the castle." She was getting into it now. They had their signals set; one squeeze for truth, two for falsehood. That way they could talk privately, even if someone were eavesdropping.

"I'm glad we're alone," he said, squeezing twice. "So we can talk freely."

"Alone," she agreed, with the double squeeze. Yes, now she knew why he was doing this. She was a smart girl, and he liked that; nymphlike proportions did not have to indicate nymphlike stupidity.

"We have no chance to break out of here ourselves," Dor said, squeezing twice. "We have no resources they don't already know about." Two.

"We don't have magical powers or anything," she agreed with an emphatic double squeeze.

"But maybe it would be better to let them *think* we have magic," Dor said, not squeezing. "That might make them treat us better."

"There is that," she agreed. "If the guards thought we could zap them through the walls, they might let us out."

"Maybe we should figure out something to fool them with," he said, this time squeezing once. "Something to distract them while the centaur army is massing. Like growing plants very fast. If they thought you could grow a tree and burst out the ceiling and maybe make this castle collapse—"

"They would take me out of this cell and keep me away from seeds," she said. "Then maybe I could escape and set out some markers so the centaurs can find us more quickly."

"Yes. But you can't just tell the Mundanes about growing things; it has to seem that they forced it out of you. And you'll need some good excuse in case they challenge you to grow something. You could say the time of the month is wrong, or—"

"Or that I have to do it in a stable," she said. "That would get me out of the heavily guarded area. By the time they realize it's a fake, and that I can't grow anything, I may have escaped."

"Yes." But had they set this up correctly? Would it trick the guards into taking Irene to the stable where Arnolde might be, or would they not bother? This business of deception was more difficult than he had thought.

Then she signaled alarm. "What about Smash? They'll want to know how he tore off the front gate, when he can't do a thing now."

Dor thought fast. "We have to hide from them the fact that the ogre is strong only when he's angry. The guard at the gate insulted Smash, so naturally he tore off the gate. But King Oary gave him a good meal, so he wasn't really angry despite getting drugged. Maybe we can trick a guard into saying something mean to Smash, or depriving him of food or water. When Smash gets hungry, he gets mean. And he has a big appetite. If they try starving him, watch out! He'll blow his top and tear this cellar apart!"

"Yes," she agreed. "That's really our best hope. Ill-treatment. We don't even need to trick anybody. All we have to do is wait. By midday tomorrow Smash will be storming. We'll all escape over the dead bodies of the guards who get in the way. We may not need the centaurs at all!"

Something caught Dor's eye. He squeezed Irene's hand to call her attention to it. The guard was quietly moving. No doubt a hot report was going upstairs.

"You're an idiot," Irene murmured, squeezing his hand twice. "You get these fool notions to fool our captors, and they'll never work. I don't know why I even talk to you."

"Because it's better than talking to the rats," he said without squeezing.

"Rats!" she cried, horrified. "Where?"

"I thought I saw one when I woke. Maybe I was wrong."

"No, this is the kind of place they like." She squeezed his hand, not with any signal. "Oh, Dor—we've got to get out of here!"

"They may take you out pretty soon, to verify that you can't grow plants." She squeezed his hand warningly. "They already know." Actually, the purpose of the fake dialogue had been to convince their captors that Dor and Irene had no magic. Then if they somehow got the chance to use magic, the guards would be caught completely by surprise. In addition, they had probably guaranteed good treatment for Smash—if their ruse had been effective.

Soon a wan crack of dawn filtered in through the ceiling near what they took to be the east wall. But the angle was wrong, and Dor finally concluded that they were incarcerated against the west wall, above the cliff, with the light entering only by crude reflection; it would have been much brighter on the other side. No chance to tunnel out, even if they had the strength; what use to step off the cliff?

Guards brought Smash a huge basket of bread and a barrel of water.

"Food!" the ogre exclaimed happily, and crunched up entire loaves in single mouthfuls, as was his wont. Then, perceiving that neither Dor nor Irene had been served, he hurled several loaves through to them. Dor squeezed one through the crevice to Irene.

The water was harder to manage. No cups had been provided, but Dor's thirst abruptly intensified, perhaps in reaction to the wine of the day before. He finally borrowed and filled one of the ogre's gauntlets and jammed that through to Irene.

"Tastes like sour sweat," she complained. But she drank it, then shoved the gauntlet back. Dor drank the rest of it, agreeing with her analysis of the taste, and returned the gauntlet to Smash with due thanks. Sweat-flavored water was much better than thirst.

"Give me your hand again," Irene said.

Thinking she had more strategy to discuss, Dor passed his right arm through the crack, gnawing on a loaf held in his left. "That was a mean thing you did, getting me food," she murmured, squeezing twice.

"Well, you know I don't like you," Dor told her, returning the double squeeze. He wasn't sure this mattered to their eavesdropper, but the reversals were easy enough to do.

"I never liked you," she returned in kind. "In fact, I think I hate you."

What was she saying? The double squeeze suggested reversal, the opposite of what she said. Reverse hate? "What would I want with an ugly girl like you anyway?" he demanded.

There was a long pause. Dor stared through the crack, seeing a strand of her hair, and, as he had expected, it had lost its green tint. Then he realized he had forgotten to squeeze. Belatedly he did so, twice.

"Ugly, huh?" She squirmed about, bringing something soft into contact with his palm. "Is that ugly?"

"I'm not sure what it is," Dor said. He squeezed experimentally.

"Eeek!" she yiped, and swatted his hand.

"Ugly as sin," he said, trying to picture female anatomy so as to ascertain what he had pinched. It certainly had been interesting!

"I'll bite your hand," she threatened, in their old game.

"There are teeth there?" he inquired, surprised.

For an instant she choked, whether on mirth or anger he could not quite tell. "With my mouth, I'll bite," she clarified. But only her lips touched his fingers.

"You wouldn't dare."

She kissed his hand twice more.

"Ouch!" Dor cried.

Now she bit him, lightly, twice. He wasn't sure what mood this signified.

It was a new variant of an old game, perhaps no more, but it caused Dor to think about his relationship with Irene. He had known her since childhood. She had always been jealous of his status as Magician and had always taunted him and sicked her plants on him—yet always, too, had been the underlying knowledge that they were destined for each other. He had resisted that as violently as she—but as they grew older, the sexual element had begun to manifest, at first in supposedly innocent games and accidental exposures, then more deviously but seriously. When he had been twelve and she eleven, they had kissed for the first time with feeling, and the experience had shaken them both. Since then their quarreling had been tempered by the knowledge that each could give a new kind of joy to the other, potentially, when conditions were right. Irene's recent development of body had intensified that awareness, and their spats had had a voyeuristic element, such as when they had torn the clothes off each other in the moat. Now, when they could not be sure of their fate, and in the absence of anything else to do, this relationship had become much more important. For the moment, almost literally, all he had was Irene. Why should they quarrel in what might be their last hours?

"Yes, I definitely hate you," Irene said, nipping delicately at the tip of one of his fingers twice, as if testing it for digestibility.

"I hate you, too," Dor said, trying to squeeze but only succeeding in poking his finger into her mouth. His whole being seemed to concentrate on that hand and whatever it touched, and the caress of her lips was excruciatingly exciting.

"I wish I could never see you again," she said, hugging his hand to her bosom.

This was getting pretty serious! Yet he found that he felt the same. He never wanted to leave her. They weren't even squeezing now, playing the game of reversal with increasing intensity and comprehension. Was this merely a reaction to the fear of extinction? He could not be sure—but was unable to resist the current of emotion. "I wish I could . . . hurt you," he said, having trouble formulating a properly negative concept.

"I'd hurt you back!" She hugged his hand more tightly.

"I'd like to grab you and—" Again the problem.

"And what?" she demanded, and once more he found his hand encountering strange anatomy, or something. His inability to identify it was driving him crazy! Was it limb or torso, above or below the waist—and which did he want it to be?

"And squeeze you to pieces," he said, giving a good squeeze. That moat-scene had been nothing, compared with this.

This time she did not make any sound of protest. "I wouldn't marry you if you were the last man alive," she whispered.

She had upped the ante again! She was talking of marriage! Dor was stunned, unable to respond.

She caressed his hand intimately. "Would you?" she prompted.

Dor had not thought much about marriage, despite his involvement in Good Magician Humfrey's wedding. He somehow thought of marriage as the perquisite of old people, like his parents, and King Trent, and Humfrey. He, Dor, was only sixteen! Yet in Xanth the age of consent coincided with the age of desire. If a person thought he was old enough to marry, and wished to do so, and had a willing bride, he could make the alliance. Thus a marriage could be contracted at age twelve, or at age one hundred; Magician Humfrey had hardly seemed ready even at that extreme!

Did he want to marry? When he thought of the next few hours, perhaps his last, he wanted to, for he had known he would have to marry before his life was out. It was a requirement of Kingship, like being a Magician. But when he thought of a lifetime in Xanth, he wasn't sure. There was a lot of time, and so much could happen in a lifetime! As Humfrey had said: there were positive and negative aspects. "I don't know," he said.

"You don't know!" she flared. "Oh, I hate you!" And she bit his hand, once, and her sharp teeth cut the flesh painfully. Oh, yes, this was getting serious!

Dor tried to jerk his hand away, but she clung to it. "You oaf! You in-grate!" she exclaimed. "You *man!*" And her face pressed against his hand, moistly.

Moistly? Yes, she was crying. Perhaps there was art to it; nevertheless this unnerved Dor. If she felt that strongly, could he afford to feel less? *Did* he feel less?

Then a tidal swell of emotion flooded him. What did it matter how much time there was, or how old he was, or where they were? He did love her.

"I—would not," he said, and tweaked her slick nose twice.

She continued crying into his hand, but now there was a gentler feeling to it. She was no longer angry with him; these were tears of joy.

It seemed they were engaged.

"Hey, Dor," a whisper came. It was from his own cell.

"Grundy!" Dor whispered back. He tried to signal Irene, but she seemed to have fallen asleep against his hand.

"Sorry I was so long," the golem said. "It took time to sleep off that knockout juice, and more time to find a good secret route here without running afoul of the rats. I talked to them—rat language seems to be much the same all over, so I didn't need the magic—but they're mean. I finally made myself a sword out of this big ol' hatpin, and after I struck a few they decided to cooperate." He brandished the weapon, a bent iron sliver; it did look deadly. Poked at a rat's eye, it would be devastating.

"Irene and I are engaged," Dor said.

The golem squinted at him to determine whether this was a joke and concluded it was not. "You are? Of all things! Why did you propose to her now?"

"I didn't," Dor confessed. "She proposed to me, I think."

"But you can't even touch her!"

"I can touch her," Dor said, remembering.

"Not where it counts."

"Yes, where it counts—I think."

The golem shrugged this off as fantasy. "Well, it won't make any difference, if we don't get out of here. I tried to talk to the animals and plants around here, but most of them I can't understand without magic. I don't think they know anything about King Trent and Queen Iris anyway. But I'm sure old King Oary's up to something. How can I spring you?"

"Get Arnolde into range," Dor said.

"That's not easy, Dor. They've got him in a stable, with a bar-lock setup like this, too heavy for me to force, and out of his reach. Crude but effective. If I could spring him, I could spring you."

"But we've got to get together," Dor whispered. "We need magic, and that's the only way."

"They aren't going to let him out," Grundy said. "They've got this fool notion that an army of warrior centaurs is marching here, and they don't want anyone to know there's a centaur in the castle."

Irene woke. "Are you talking to me, dear?" she asked.

"Dear!" Grundy chortled. "Hoo, has she lassoed you!"

"Quiet!" Dor whispered fiercely. "The guard is listening." But he wondered whether that was really his concern.

"Is that the golem?" Irene asked.

"Want to hold hands with me, dear?" Grundy called.

"Go unravel your string!" she snapped back.

"Anything but that," Grundy said, smiling mischievously. "I want to stick around and watch the nuptials. How are you going to make it through the wall?"

"Let me get at that big-mouthed imp!" Irene said. "I'll jam him down the sump headfirst."

"How did you get the poor sucker to accept the knot?" the golem persisted. "Did you scream at him, show him some forbidden flesh, and cry big green tears?"

"The sump is too good for him!" she gritted.

"If you both don't be quiet, the eavesdropping guard will learn everything," Dor warned, ravaged by worry and embarrassment.

Grundy looked at him. "Outside the magic ambience, they can't understand a word we say. How can they eavesdrop?"

Dor was stunned. "I never thought of that!" Had his entire ruse been for nothing?

"How come they fed Smash, then?" Irene demanded, forgetting her fury with the golem as she came to grips with this new question. "How come they heard about the centaur army? Seems to me you said—or did I dream that?"

"I said it, and it's true," Grundy said. "You mean *you* started that story? I overheard it when I was visiting Arnolde; then I could understand the Mundane speech."

"We started it," Dor agreed. "And we gave them the notion that Smash only has super strength when he's angry, and he gets angry when he's hungry. They brought him food very soon. So they must have understood. But how?"

"I think we're about to find out," Grundy said, fading into the shadow. "Someone's coming."

Irene finally let go of Dor's hand, and he drew it back through the wall. His arm was cramped from the hours in the awkward position, but Dor hardly regretted the experience. It was all right being engaged to Irene. He knew her well enough to know she would make a pretty good wife. She would quarrel a lot, but he was used to that, because that was the way his mother Chameleon was when she was in her smart phase. Actually, a smart woman who quarreled was not smart at all, but no one could tell her that. Irene, like her obnoxious mother, had a sense of the proprieties of the office. Queen Iris' mischief was never directed openly at the King. If Dor ever became King in fact as well as in name, Irene would never seek to undermine his power. That was perhaps a more important quality than her physical appearance. But he had to admit that she had acquired a most interesting body. Those touches she had used to tantalize him that Grundy had so acutely noted—they had been marvelously effective. Obviously she had been attempting to seduce him into acquiescence—and she had succeeded. As the Gorgon had intimated, Irene had him pretty well contained. What the Gorgon had not hinted was the fact that such captivity was quite comfortable to the captive, like a warm jacket on a cold day. Good Magician Humfrey was undoubtedly a happy man right now, despite his protestations. In fact, a man's objections to marriage were rather like Irene's objections to people looking at her legs—more show than substance.

Dor's attention was jerked back to the immediate situation by the arrival of the Mundanes. There were three guards, one carrying a crude iron bar. They stopped before Irene's cell and used the bar to pry up the wedged plank that barred it. Without that tool, evidently, the door could not be opened.

One of the guards went in and grabbed Irene. She did not resist; she knew as well as Dor did that this was the expected questioning. She would try to answer in such a way that they would take her to the stable where Arnolde was confined, if only to prove she was lying. Then she could pry up the bar on the centaur's stall, or start some devastating plant growing—

Except that she had no seeds. "Grundy!" he whispered. "Find Irene's seeds! She'll need them."

"I'll try." The golem scrambled through a crevice and was gone.

Now King Oary entered the dungeon. "Rn xnt'qd sgd Jhmf'r cztfgsdq," he said. "Vgzs hr xntq lzfhb?"

"I don't understand you," Irene said.

"His Highness King Oary asks what is your magic," one of the guards said. His speech was heavily accented, but he was intelligible.

"You know Xanth speech?" she asked, surprised. "How can that be?"

"You have no need to know," the guard said. "Just answer the question, wench."

So one of the Mundanes here spoke the language of Xanth! Dor's mind started clicking over. This explained the eavesdropping—but how could the man have learned it, however poorly? He had to have been in contact with people from Xanth.

"Go soak your snoot in the sump," Irene retorted.

Dor winced. She might be playing her role too boldly!

"The King will use force," the man warned. "Better answer, slut."

Irene looked daunted, as perhaps she was, but those insulting references to her supposed status made her angry. "You answer first, toady," she said, compromising.

The guard decided negotiation was the best course. "I met a spy from your country, tart. I am quick with languages; he taught me. Then he went back to Xanth."

"To report to my father, King Trent!" Irene exclaimed. "You promised him a trade agreement, didn't you, rogue, if he would come himself to negotiate it?"

"It is your turn to answer, hussy," the man said.

"Oh, all right, wretch. My magic is growing plants. I can make anything grow from seed to tree in moments."

Dor, peering out, could not see the man's face clearly, but was sure there was a knowing expression on it. The eavesdropper thought he knew better, but didn't want to betray his own secret snooping, so had to translate for the King. "Rgd fzud sgd khd," he said.

"H vzms sgd sqtsg!" Oary snapped.

"His Majesty suspects you are deceiving us," the guard said. "What is your real magic?"

"What does ol' fatso care? I'm not doing any magic now."

"You had magic when you came, trollop. The ogre used unnatural strength to destroy our front gate, and you all spoke our language. Now the ogre is weak and you speak your own language. What happened to the magic?"

The language! Dor cursed himself for overlooking that detail. Of course that had given away their secret! King Trent would have used an interpreter—probably this same man—and the ability of Dor's party to converse directly would have alerted cunning King Oary immediately. He had known they had operative magic and now wanted to discover the mechanism of it.

"Well, if you bring me some seeds, thug, maybe I can find out," Irene said. "I'm sure I can grow plants, if I just find the right place."

Bless her! She was still trying to get to the stable, where she really could perform.

But the Mundanes thought they knew better. "If the King says you lie, you lie, strumpet," the guard said. "Again I ask: what is your real magic? Can you speak in tongues, and cause others to do the same?"

"Of course not, villain!" she said. "Otherwise we wouldn't need you to translate to His Lowness King Puddingbelly here, would we? Plants are all I can enchant."

"Rgd vhkk mns sdkk," the guard said to the King.

"Vd rgzkk lzjd *ghl* sdkk," the King responded. "Snqstqd gdq hm eqnms ne ghl."

The other two guards grabbed Irene's arms and hauled her a few steps down the hall until they were directly in front of Dor's cell. "Prince Dor," the translator called. "You will answer our questions or see what we shall do."

Dor was silent, uncertain what to do.

"Qho nee gdq bknsgdr," the King ordered.

The two guards wrestled Irene's jacket and silver-lined fur off her body, while she struggled and cursed them roundly. Then the translator put his hand on her neckline and brutally ripped downward. The blouse tore down the front, exposing her fine bosom. Irene, shocked at this sudden physical violence, heaved with her arms, but the two men held her securely.

"Vdkk, knnj zs sgzs!" the King exclaimed admiringly. "H sgntfgs nmkx gdq kdfr vdqd fnnc!"

Dor could not understand a word of the language, but he grasped the essence readily enough. King, translator, and both guards were all gawking at Irene's revealed body. So was Dor. He had thought Irene did not match the

Gorgon in general architecture, but Irene had filled out somewhat since he had last looked. He had had the chance to see during the quarrel in the moat, but there had been other distractions then. During the journey south to Centaur Isle, Irene had kept herself fairly private, and perhaps her excellent legs had led his attention away from her other attributes. Now he saw that she was no longer reaching for bodily maturity; she had achieved it.

At the same time, he was furious with the King and his henchmen for exposing Irene in this involuntary manner. He determined not to tell them anything.

"Gd khjdr gdq, xnt snkc ld," the King said. "H bzm rdd vgx! Sgqdzsdm gdq zmc gd'kk szkj."

The King was plotting something dastardly! Dor hardly dared imagine what he might do to Irene. He couldn't stand to have her hurt!

The translator stood in front of Irene and formed a fist. He drew back his arm, aiming at her belly.

"Stop!" Dor cried. "I'll tell—"

"Shut up!" Irene snapped at him. One of her knees jerked up, catching the translator in the groin. The man doubled over, and the surprised guards allowed Irene to tear herself free, leaving shreds of cloth in their hands. Bare-breasted as any nymph, she ran a few steps, stooped to pick up the door-opening bar, and whirled to apply it to Dor's door.

"Run!" Dor cried. "Don't waste time on me!"

But it was already too late. Both guards had drawn their flat swords and were closing on Irene. She turned, raising the bar defensively, determined to fight.

"No!" Dor screamed, his voice breaking. "They'll kill you!"

But now there was a new distraction. Smash, snoozing before, had become aware of the situation. He rattled his door angrily. "Kill!" he bellowed.

Both guards and the King blanched. They believed the ogre's fantastic strength stemmed from his anger. If they hurt Irene while Smash watched—

The translator was beginning to recover from his injury; it probably had been a glancing blow. "Gdqc gdq hmsn gdq bdkk," he gasped to the other two guards. Then, to Irene: "Girl—go quickly to your cell and they won't hurt you."

Irene, realizing that she could not hope to escape the two swordsmen and knowing that the bluff of Smash's strength should not be called, edged toward her cell. The two guards followed cautiously. Smash watched, still angry, but with the sense not to protest as long as the guards were holding off. Then Irene stepped into her cell, the guards slammed the door shut and barred it, and the crisis was over.

"You should have run out of the dungeon!" Dor said with angry relief.

"I couldn't leave you," she replied. "Where would I find another like you?" Dor wasn't certain quite how to take that; was it a compliment or a deprecation?

King Oary himself seemed shaken. "Sgzs fhqk'r mns nmkx adztshetk, rgd

gzr ehfgshmf rohqhs," he said. "Cnm's gtqs gdq; H ltrs ehmc z trd enq gdq."
He turned about and marched out of the dungeon, followed by his henchmen. The translator, though still uncomfortable, had to remain where he
thought he was just out of sight, to eavesdrop some more. The dungeon
settled back into its normal gloom.

They were plotting something worse, Dor knew, but at least Irene had
escaped unhurt, and the secret of their magic had been preserved, at least in
part. The Mundanes knew the prisoners had magic, but still had not
fathomed its mechanism. It was a temporary respite, but much better than
nothing.

"I think we'd better get out of here soon," Irene said as the Mundanes
departed. "Give me your hand."

What was she contemplating this time? Dor passed his hand through the
crevice.

She took it in her own and kissed it. That was nice enough, though he
found himself obscurely disappointed. She had lost her jacket and blouse—

She took his wrist in her hand and had him spread his fingers. Then she
put something into his hand. Dor almost exclaimed with surprise, for it was
hard and cold and heavy.

It was the iron bar.

Of course! In their confusion, the guards had forgotten that Irene retained
the bar she had picked up. Now Dor had this useful tool or weapon. Maybe
he could lever open his door from the inside.

But a guard was in the hall, probably the translator, though there could
have been a change. Dor didn't dare try the door now; he would have to
wait. In fact, he could not risk prying at any other part of the cell, for the
noise would alert the guard and call attention to his possession of the bar.
So, for now, they had to wait—and there were things he wanted to tell
Irene.

"You were awfully brave," he said. "You faced up to those thugs—"

"I was scared almost speechless," she confessed. That was surely an over-
statement; she had traded gibes with the translator quite neatly. "But I knew
they'd hurt you if—"

"Hurt me! It was *you* they—"

"Well, I worry about you, Dor. You wouldn't be able to manage without
me."

She was teasing him—maybe. "I like your new outfit," he said. "But
maybe you'd better take my jacket."

"Maybe so," she agreed. "It's cool here."

Dor removed his centaur jacket and squeezed it through the crevice. She
donned it, and was quite fetching in it, though it tended to fall open in
front. Or perhaps that was why he found it so fetching. At least the jacket
would protect her from the cold and from the attack of instruments like
swords or spears, because it was designed to resist penetration. And it

wouldn't hurt to have her body concealed from the lecherous eyes of the King and his henchmen; Dor's jealousy of such things remained in force.

Grundy reappeared. "I got a seed," he said. "The bag's in the King's chamber, along with the magic sword. I knew it was safe to sneak in there, because the King was down here. But I couldn't carry the whole bag. Couldn't find the magic compass at all; they must have thrown that away. So I picked out what looked like a good seed."

"Give it here," Irene said eagerly. "Yes—this is a tangler. If I could start it and drop it in the hall—"

"But you can't," Dor said. "Not without—" He caught himself, for the eavesdropper was surely eavesdropping.

"I have an idea," Dor said. "Suppose we brought a part of you-know-who here—would it have a little magic, enough to start one seed?"

Irene considered. "A piece of hoof, maybe. I don't know. It's worth a try."

"I'm on my way," Grundy said.

"I always thought girls were supposed to be timid and sweet and to scream helplessly at the mere sight of trouble," Dor said. "But you—those guards—"

"You saw too much of Millie the Ghost. Real girls aren't like that, except when they want to be."

"You certainly aren't! But I never thought you'd risk your life like that."

"Are you disappointed?"

Dor considered. "No. You're a lot more girl—more woman than I thought. I guess I do need you. If I didn't love you before, I do now. And not because of your looks though when it comes to that—"

"Really?" she asked, sounding like an excited child.

"Well, I could be overreacting because of our imprisonment."

"I liked it better unqualified," she said.

"Oh, sure. Uh, I think you're beautiful. But—"

"Then we'd better check again after we get out of this, to see if we feel the same. No sense being hasty."

Dor was shaken. "You have doubts?"

"Well, I might meet a handsomer man—"

"Uh, yes," Dor said unhappily.

She laughed. "I'm teasing you. Girls are smarter about appearances than boys are. We go for quality rather than packaging. I have no doubt at all. I love you, Dor. I never intended to marry anyone else. But I refuse to take advantage of you when you're unsettled. Maybe when you get older you'll change your mind."

"You're younger than I am!"

"Girls mature faster. Hadn't you noticed?"

Now Dor laughed. "Just today, I noticed!"

She kissed his hand again. "Well, it's all yours, when."

When. Dor considered the ramification of that, and felt warm all over. She had a body, true—but what pleased him most was the loyalty implied. She would be with him, she would support him, whatever happened. Dor realized he needed that support; he really would foul up on his own. Irene was strong, when not jarred by an acute crisis; she had nerve he lacked. Her personality complemented his, shoring up his weakness. She was the one who had gotten them going on this rescue mission; her determination to rescue her father had never relented. With her at his side, he could indeed be King.

His reflections were interrupted by the return of the golem. "I got three hairs from his tail," he whispered. "He's very vain about his tail, like all his breed; it's his best feature. Maybe they'll be enough."

Did some magic adhere to portions of the centaur that were removed from his body? Dor brought out his midnight sunstone gem and held it close to the hairs. Almost, he thought, he saw a gleam of light, deep within the crystal. But maybe that was a reflection from the wan illumination of the cell.

"Take them in to Irene," Dor said, hardly allowing himself to hope.

Grundy did so. Irene set the seed down on the tail hairs and leaned close. "Grow," she breathed.

They were disappointed. The seed seemed to try, to swell expectantly, but could not grow. There was not enough magic.

"Maybe if I took it back to Arnolde," Grundy said.

Irene was silent, and Dor realized she was stifling her tears. She had really hoped her magic would work.

"Yes, try that," Dor told the golem. "Maybe the seed has been started. Maybe it just needs more magic now."

Grundy took the seed and the tail hairs and departed again. Dor reached through the crevice to pat Irene on the shoulder. "It was worth the try," he said.

She clutched his hand. "I need you, Dor. When I collapse, you just keep on going."

There was that complementary aspect again. She would soon recover her determination and nerve, but in the interim she needed to be steadied.

They remained that way for what seemed like a long time, and despite the despair they both felt, Dor would not have traded it. Somehow this privation enhanced their personal liaison, making their love burn more fiercely and reach deeper. What would happen after this day he could not know, but he was certain he had been changed by this experience of emotion. His age of innocence, in a fundamental and positive sense, had passed.

Then a commotion began in the distance. The sound electrified them. Was it possible—?

Grundy burst in on them. "It worked!" he cried. "That seed started growing. The moment I got it in the magic aisle, it heaved right out of its shell. It must have been primed by your command, in that bit of magic with the tail hairs. I had to throw it down outside the stall—"

"It worked!" Irene cried jubilantly. "I always knew it would!"

"I told Arnolde where we are, just in case," Grundy continued excitedly. "That tangler will rip apart his stall!"

"But can he get through all the locked doors?" Irene asked, turning worried. Her moods were swinging back and forth now. "He can't *do* magic himself, and there's no one with him to—"

"I'm way ahead of you, doll," the golem said. "I scouted all around. He can't get through those doors, but he can get out the main gate that Smash ripped off, 'cause they haven't fixed that yet, and there's a small channel outside the castle wall, and these cells are against the wall. Unless the outside wall is over his aisle-depth—"

"And if it is?" she prompted, as if uncertain whether to go into a scream of jubilation or of despair.

"I'm sure the wall isn't," Grundy said. "It's not more than six of your paces thick, and his aisle reaches twice that far forward. But we'll soon find out, because he'll soon be on his way."

The clamor continued. "I hope Arnolde doesn't get hurt," Dor said. "King Oary took our supply of healing elixir, too."

"Probably dumped it down a sump," Grundy said. "Make all the sick maggots healthy."

"Stand by the outer wall," Irene told him. "When you can talk to it, Dor, we'll know the centaur's here."

"I'll go check on his progress," Grundy said, and scurried away again.

"That tangler should be almost full-grown now," Irene said. "I hope Arnolde has the sense to stay away from its tentacles." Then she reconsidered. "But not so far away the lack of magic kills the tree. He's got to keep it in the aisle until it does its job. Once he leaves, it will die."

"Speak to me, wall," Dor said, touching the stone. There was no response.

"What's up?" Smash inquired from the next cell.

"Grundy took a sprouted tangler seed to Arnolde," Dor explained. "We hope the centaur's on his way here."

"At length, me strength," the ogre said, comprehending.

"Hey—you rhymed!" Dor cried. "He must be here!"

"Me see," Smash said. He punched his fist through the wall near Dor.

"You've got it!" Dor said. "Go rip open your door! Then you can free Irene and me!"

The ogre tramped to the front of his cell and gleefully smashed at his front door. "Ooo, that hurt!" he grunted, shaking his gauntleted fist. The door had not given way.

"His strength is gone again!" Irene said. "Something's wrong!"

Dor cudgeled his brain. What could account for this partial recovery? "Where is the centaur now?" he asked his back wall, fearing it would not answer.

"Right outside Irene's cell," it replied. "Clinging to a narrow track above a chasm, terrified."

Dor visualized the centaur's position. "Then he can't face directly into the castle?"

"He can only turn a little," the wall agreed. "Any more and he'll fall off. Soldiers are getting ready to put arrows in his tail, too."

"So his magic aisle slants in obliquely," Dor concluded. "It covers this wall, but not the front of our cells."

"Anybody can see that, idiot," the wall agreed smugly.

Dor used his sunstone to verify the edge of the aisle. The gem flashed and darkened as it passed outside the magic. The line was only a few handspans inside Dor's wall, projecting farther into Smash's cell.

"Hey, Smash!" Dor cried. "The magic's only at this end. Bash out the outer wall to let Arnolde in."

"Right site," Smash agreed. He aimed his huge, horny, gauntleted hamfist.

"Don't hit me!" the wall cried. "I support the whole castle!" But it was too late; the fist powered through the brick and stone. "Oooo, that smarts!"

The wall turned out to be double: two sections of stone, with a filling of rubble between. Smash ripped out the loose core, then pulverized the outer barrier, gaining enthusiasm as he went. In moments bright daylight shone through the cloud of dust.

The ogre ripped out more chunks, widening the aperture. Beyond was the back of the mountain, falling awesomely away into a heavily wooded valley.

"Good to see you, brute!" Arnolde's voice came. "Clear an entrance for me before these savages attack!"

Smash leaned out. He grabbed a stone. "Duck, cluck," he warned, and hurled his missile.

There was a thud and scream as someone was knocked off the ledge. "What did you do?" Irene cried, appalled.

Then Arnolde's front end appeared in the gap in the wall. Centaur and ogre embraced joyously. "I think he knocked off an enemy," Dor said.

Irene sounded weak with relief. "Oh. I guess they're friends now."

"We need both magic and power," Dor agreed. "Each is helpless without the other. They have come to understand that."

"We have all come to understand a lot of things," she agreed, smiling obscurely.

Now Arnolde faced the front door, putting it within the aisle, and Smash marched up and kicked it off its moorings. Then he took hold of the front wall and tore it out of the floor. Debris crashed down from the ceiling. "Don't bring the whole castle down on us!" Dor warned, while Irene choked on the voluminous dust.

"Me wrastle this castle," the ogre said, unworried. He hoisted one paw to the ceiling, and the collapse abated.

There was a stray guard in the hall. The man watched the progress of the ogre a few moments in silence, then fainted.

Grundy reappeared. "Troops coming," he reported. "We'd better move."

They moved. Doors and gates were locked, but Smash smashed them clear like so much tissue. When they encountered a wall, he burst right through it. They emerged into an inner court, where flowers grew. "Grow! Grow! Grow!" Irene ordered, and the plants exploded upward and outward.

"Where is our safest retreat?" Dor asked the next wall.

"The other side of me, dolt," it replied.

Smash opened another hole and they trooped out into a section of forest. Soon they had hidden themselves well away from the castle. They were together again and free, and it felt wonderful.

They paused, catching their breaths, assessing their situation. "Everybody all right?" Dor asked around. "No serious injuries?" There seemed to be none.

"So have you reconsidered?" Irene inquired. "You know how I abhor you."

He looked at her. She was still wearing his jacket over her bare upper torso, her hair was tangled, and dirt smudged her face. She seemed preternaturally lovely. "Yes," he said. "And the answer comes out the same. I still hate you." He took her in his arms and kissed her, and she was all eager and yielding in the manner of her kind—when her kind chose to be.

"If that be hate," Arnolde remarked, "I would be interested in witnessing their love."

"The idiots are engaged to each other," Grundy explained to the others. "It seems they saw the light in the darkness, or something."

"Or something," the centaur agreed dubiously.

Chapter 11

Good Omen

"Now we have arrived," Dor said, taking charge after reluctantly disengaging from Irene. "But we have not accomplished our mission. I believe this is the place King Trent and Queen Iris came to. I think the table told me they were here, just before I passed out from King Oary's drug. But I might have dreamed that; the memory is very foggy. Have we any solid proof?"

"Apart from the henchman who speaks the language of Xanth?" Grundy asked.

"That's circumstantial," Irene said. "It only proves he had contact with the Xanth scout, not that King Trent actually came here. We have to be sure."

"My evidence is rather tenuous," Arnolde offered. "It seems that the stable hands had difficulty thinking of me as a person of intellect, and spoke more freely in my vicinity than they might otherwise have done. I declined to speak to them, in what I confess might be construed as a fit of pique—"

"Chic pique," Smash chuckled.

"And so they did not realize that the magic in your vicinity caused their language to be intelligible to you, or that you had the wit to comprehend it," Dor put in, pleased. "We could not communicate with them without an interpreter, so it was natural for them to assume you couldn't either. That, combined with their tending to think of you as an animal—"

"Precisely. My pique may have been fortuitous. So I found myself overhearing certain things that were perhaps not entirely my affair." He smiled. "In one case, literally. It seems one of the cooks has a continuing liaison with a scullery maid—" He broke off, grimacing. "Right beside my stall! It was instructive; they are lusty folk. At any rate, there was at one point a reference to a certain alien King who, it seems, had claimed to be able to perform magic."

"King Trent!" Dor exclaimed. "My memory was right, then, not a dream! The table did say King Trent was here!"

"I think we always knew it!" Irene agreed, glowering in memory of the betrayal associated with that table.

"The translator knew about the magic of Xanth," Dor continued. "But of course no one could do magic here in Mundania, until we discovered you, Arnolde. King Trent would have said he could do magic *in Xanth,* and the qualification got dropped in translation."

"Certainly," the centaur agreed. "It seems that King Oary somehow anticipated magic that he thought might greatly enhance his power and was very angry when that magic did not materialize. So he arrested the alien King treacherously and locked him away, hoping to coerce him into performing, or into revealing the secret of his power."

"Where?" Irene demanded. "Where is my father?"

"I regret I did not overhear more than I have told you. The alien King was not named. I do not believe the people of the stables knew his identity, or believe in his power, or know where he may be confined. They merely gossip. The apparent magic of Smash's initial display of strength, and the manner we communicated with King Oary, caused a considerable ripple of interest around the castle, and indeed in the entire Kingdom of Onesti, which accounts for the gossip about similar cases. But already this interest is waning, since both strength and communication appeared to have been illusion. It is very easy to attribute phenomena to illusion or false memory when practical explanations are lacking, and Mundanes do this often." He smiled grimly. "I daresay a new round of speculation has commenced, considering the events of the past hour. Your tangle plant, Irene, was gratifyingly impressive."

"It sure was!" Grundy agreed enthusiastically. "It was grabbing people right and left, and it ripped the stall apart. But when Arnolde left, the tangler sank down dead."

"Magic plants can't function without magic, dummy," Irene said.

"Fortunately," Arnolde agreed. "On occasion it reached for me; then I angled away from it, depriving it of magic, and it desisted. After a time it ceased to bother me."

"Even a tangler isn't totally stupid!" Irene laughed.

"At least we have more to go on," Dor said. "We can be pretty sure King Oary imprisoned King Trent and Queen Iris, and that they remain alive. Oary's experience with us must have enhanced his conviction that anyone from Xanth is hiding magic from him, since we really did have magic, then stopped showing it when he imprisoned us. He probably intended to force us to tell him the secret of magic so he could do it, too, or at least compel the rest of us to perform for him."

"King Oary strikes me as a pretty cunning old rascal," Irene said. "Wrong-headed but cunning."

"Indeed," Arnolde agreed. "From my observation, he runs this Kingdom reasonably well, but unscrupulously. Perhaps that is what is required to maintain the precarious independence from the larger empires on three sides."

"We still need to locate King Trent," Dor said. "Arnolde, did you hear anything else that might remotely connect?"

"I am not sure, Dor. There was a reference to King Omen, Oary's predecessor who disappeared. It seems the common folk liked him and were sorry to lose him."

"He was King?" Dor asked. "I understood he was underage, so Oary was regent, and Omen never actually became King."

"I gather in contrast that he was indeed King, for about a year, before he disappeared," the centaur said. "They called him Good Omen, and believe the Kingdom of Onesti would have prospered under his guidance."

"Surely it would have," Dor agreed. He realized that King Oary might have preferred to minimize King Omen's stature in order to make his own position more secure. If the Kingdom of Onesti was well run, it could have been mostly King Omen's doing. "A trade agreement with Xanth could help both Kingdoms. Maybe King Omen was arranging that, then got deposed before King Trent arrived. King Oary's greed has cost him that chance."

"The peasants suspect that King Omen was illicitly removed," the centaur continued. "Some even choose to believe that he still lives, that King Oary imprisoned him by subterfuge and usurped power. This may of course be mere wish fulfillment—"

"And just may be the truth," Irene put in. "If King Oary deceived and imprisoned us and did the same with my parents, why not also with Good King Omen? It certainly fits his pattern."

"We are indulging in a great deal of supposition," Arnolde said warningly. "We could encounter disappointment. Yet if I may extend the rationale—it occurs to me that if King Trent and King Omen both survive, they may be confined together. We have already seen that the dungeons of Castle Onesti are not extensive. If there is another castle, and we find one confined there—"

"We find the other!" Irene finished. "And if we rescued them both, Good Omen would be King of Onesti again and all would be well. I'd sure like to depose hoary King Oary!"

"That was the extrapolation of my conjectures," Arnolde agreed. "Yet I reiterate, it is highly speculative."

"It's worth a try," Dor said. "Now let's plan our strategy. Probably only King Oary knows where King Trent and/or King Omen are incarcerated, and he won't tell. I could question the stones of the castle, but probably the Kings aren't here at all, and the stones wouldn't know anything about other places. If the local servants don't know anything about it, it probably isn't known. So the question is, how can we get him to tell?"

"He ought to have a guilty conscience," Irene said. "Maybe we could play on that."

"I distrust this," Dor said. "I encountered some bad people and creatures in another adventure, and I don't think their consciences troubled them, because they simply didn't believe they were doing anything wrong. Goblins and harpies—"

"Of course they don't have consciences," Irene snapped. "But Oary is a person."

"Human beings can be worst of all, especially Mundanes," Dor said. "Many of them have ravaged Xanth over the centuries, and King Oary may contemplate something similar. I just don't have much confidence in any appeal to his conscience."

"I perceive your point," Arnolde said. "But I think 'appeal' is not the appropriate term. A guilty conscience more typically manifests in the perception of nocturnal specters—"

"Not many specters running around this far from Xanth," Grundy pointed out.

"We could scare him into giving it away!" Irene exclaimed.

"Tonight," Dor decided. "We must rest and feed ourselves first—and hide from King Oary's troops."

They had no trouble avoiding the troops. It took Oary's forces some time to organize, after the devastation Smash had caused during the breakout, and only now, after the long discussion, was any real activity manifesting at the castle. Irene made vines grow, bristling with thorns; in their natural state these had been a nuisance, but now they were a menace. When the magic moved away, the vines died, for they had been extended far beyond their natural limits—but the tangle of thorns remained as a formidable barrier. That, coupled with the Mundanes' knowledge that the ogre lurked in the forest, kept the guards close to the castle even after they emerged. They were not eager for contact with the creature who had bashed all those holes in the massive walls.

At night, rested, Dor's party made its play. Grundy had scouted the castle, so they knew which tower contained the royal suite. King Oary was married, but slept alone; his wife couldn't stand him. He ate well and consumed much alcoholic beverage; this facilitated his sleep.

They had fashioned a platform that Smash carried to the base of the outer wall nearest the royal tower, which happened to be on the forest side. Arnolde mounted this, bringing his magic aisle within range of the King.

Irene had scouted for useful Mundane seeds and had assembled a small collection. Now she planted several climbing vines, and in the ambience of magic they assumed somewhat magical properties. They mounted wall and platform vigorously, sending their little anchor-tendrils into any solid substance they found, quickly binding the platform firmly in place. Arnolde had to keep moving his legs to avoid tendrils that swiped at his feet, until the growing stage passed that level. The plants ascended to the embrasure that marked the King's residence, then halted; the magic aisle extended more inward than upward.

Grundy used the sturdy vines to mount to that embrasure. He scrambled over, found himself a shrouded corner, and called quietly down: "I can see inside some, but I don't dare get close enough to cover the whole room."

"Talk to the plant," Irene said in her don't-be-dumb tone. She no longer used that on Dor, mute recognition of their changed situation, but obviously she retained the expertise.

"Say, yes," the golem agreed. "There's a vine that reaches inside." He paused, talking to the plant. "It says Oary's not alone. He's got a doxy in his bed."

"He would," Irene grumped. "Men like that will do anything."

It occurred to Dor that this could be the reason the translator had persisted in addressing Irene as "slut" and "strumpet." This was the type of woman King Oary normally associated with. But Dor decided not to mention this to Irene; she already had reason enough to hate Oary.

Dor climbed the vines, finding a lodging against the wall just beneath the embrasure. "Describe the room," he murmured to Grundy. "I've got to know exactly what's in it, and where."

The golem consulted with the plant. "There is this big feather bed to the right, two of your paces in from this wall. A wooden bench straight in from the embrasure, six paces, with her dress strewn on it. A wooden table to its left, one pace—and there's your sword on it, and Arnolde's bag of spells."

"Ha!" Dor exclaimed quietly. "I need that sword. Too bad it's not the variety that wields itself; I could call it right to me."

The golem continued describing the room, until Dor was satisfied he had the details properly fixed in his mind. He was able to picture it now—everything just so. "I hope my mind doesn't go blank," he called down.

"Don't you dare!" Irene snapped. "Save your fouling up for some other time. Do I have to come up there and prompt you?"

"That might help," Dor confessed. "You see, I can't make things say specific things. They only answer questions, or talk in response to my words.

Usually. And the inanimate is not too bright, and sometimes perverse. So I may indeed foul it up."

"For pity's sake!" Irene took hold of the vines and began climbing. "And don't look up my skirt!" she said to Arnolde.

"I wouldn't think of it," the centaur said equably. "I prefer to view equine limbs, and never did see the merit in pink panties."

"They're not pink!" she said.

"They're not? I must be colorblind. Let me see—"

"Forget it!" She joined Dor, gave him a quick kiss, wrapped her skirt closely about her legs, and settled in for the duration. Dor had worried about the strength of the vines, with all this weight on them, but realized she would have a better notion than he how much they could hold.

"Well, start," she whispered.

"But if I talk loud enough for the things to hear me, so will King Oary."

She sighed. "You *are* a dumbell at times, dear. You don't have to talk aloud to objects; just direct your attention to them. That's the way your magic works. As for King Oary—if that snippet with him knows her trade, he won't be paying any attention to what's outside the castle."

She was right. Dor concentrated, but still couldn't quite get it together. He was used to speaking aloud to objects. "Are they really not pink?" he asked irrelevantly.

"What?"

"Your—you-knows."

She laughed. "My panties? You mean you never looked?"

Dor, embarrassed, admitted that he had not.

"You're entitled now, you know."

"But I wasn't, back when I had a chance to see."

She released her grip on the vine with one hand and reached over to tweak his cheek, in much the manner the Gorgon had. "You're something sort of rare and special, Dor. Well, you get this job done right, and I'll show you."

"Will you get on with it?" Grundy demanded from above.

"But she says not till after this job's done," Dor said.

"I was referring to the job!" the golem snapped. "*I'll* tell you what color her—"

"I will wring your rag body into a tight little knot!" Irene threatened, and the golem was silent.

Prompted by this, Dor concentrated on the magic sword on the King's table. *Groan*, he ordered it mentally.

Obediently, the sword groaned. Naturally it hammed it up. "Grooooaan!" it singsonged in an awful key.

"The doxy just sat up straight," Grundy reported gleefully as the vine rustled the news to him. "Oh, she shouldn't have done that. She's stark, bare, nude naked!"

"Skip the pornography, you little voyeur!" Irene snapped. "It's the King we want to rouse." She nudged Dor. "You know the script we worked out. 'Let me free, let me free.' "

Dor concentrated again. *Sword, I have a game for you. If you play your part well, you can scare the pants off bad King Oary.*

"Hey, great!" the sword exclaimed. "Only they're already off him. Boy, is he fat!"

No. Don't talk to me! Talk to the King. Groan again and say, "Let me free, let me free!" The idea is you're the ghost of Good King Omen, coming back to haunt him. Can you handle that, or are you too stupid?

"I'll show you!" the sword exclaimed. It groaned again, with hideous feeling. It was definitely a ham.

"There's someone here!" the doxy screamed.

"There can't be," the King muttered. "The guards prevent anyone from getting through. They know I don't want to be disturbed when I'm conducting affairs of state."

"Affairs of state!" Irene hissed furiously.

"Affair, anyway," Dor said, trying to calm her.

"Let me free, let me free," the sword groaned enthusiastically.

"Then who's that?" the doxy demanded, hiding under the feathers.

"I am the ghooost of Goood King Ooomen," the sword answered. Dor no longer needed to prompt it.

The doxy emitted a half-stifled squeak and disappeared entirely into the feathers, according to Grundy's gleeful play-by-play report. The King clutched a feather quilt about him, causing part of the doxy to reappear, to her dismay.

"You *can't* be!" Oary retorted shakily, trying to see where the voice came from. The lone candle illuminating the room cast many wavering shadows, the plant reported, making such detection difficult.

"Coming back from the graaave to haaunt you!" the sword continued, really getting into it.

"Impossible!" But the King looked nervous, Grundy reported.

"He's a tough one," Irene murmured. "He should be terrified, and he's only worried. We're only scaring the doxy, who doesn't matter. Girls can be such foolish creatures!" Then she reconsidered. "When they want to be."

Dor nodded, worried himself. If this ruse didn't work—

"Yooou killed me," the sword said.

"I did not!" Oary shouted. "I only locked you up until I figured out what to do with you. I never killed you."

The doxy's face reappeared, replacing the rounder portion of her that had showed before. "You locked up Good Omen?" she asked, surprised.

"I had to, or I never would have gotten the throne," the King said absently. "I thought he would foul up as King, but he didn't, so there was no way to remove him legitimately." As he talked, he hoisted his porcine torso from the bed, wrapped the quilt about it, and stalked the voice he heard.

"But I didn't kill him. I am too cautious for that. It is too hard to undo a killing, if anything goes wrong. So this can't be his ghost."

"Then whose ghost is it?" the doxy demanded.

"No ghost at all," the King said. "There's no one there." He picked up the sword. "Just this sword I took from the Xanth Prince. I thought it was magic, but it isn't. I tried it out, and there's nothing remarkable about it except a fine edge."

"That's not true!" the sword cried. "Unhand me, varlet!"

Unnerved at last, the King hurled it out the embrasure. "The thing talks!" he cried.

"Well, that's one way to recover my weapon," Dor murmured.

"Try for my bag of seeds," Irene suggested. "I can do a lot with genuine magic plants."

Grundy had located the seeds, carelessly thrown in a corner; no doubt Oary had been disappointed when he discovered the bag did not contain treasure, though he should have been satisfied with the gold and diamonds Dor had carried. Greed knew no restraint! "You can't get rid of me that way," the seedbag said as Dor mentally prompted it. "My ghost will haunt you forever."

"I tell you, I didn't kill you!" Oary said, looking for the new voice that sounded seedy. "You're just making that up."

"Well, I might as well be dead," the seedbag said. "Locked up here alone—it's awful."

"What do you mean, alone?" Oary demanded. "The Xanth King is in the next cell, and the sharp-tongued Xanth Queen in the third. They wanted to know what had happened to you, and wouldn't deal with me, so now they know."

Irene's free hand clutched Dor's shoulder. "Confirmation!" she whispered, thrilled.

Dor was equally gratified. The talking objects had hardly terrorized Oary, but they had evoked his confession nevertheless. Dor continued to concentrate. *But you're way out in nowhere,* he thought to the bag.

"But we're way out in nowhere," the bag dutifully repeated. Dor was getting better at this as he went. He had never before used his talent in quite this way; it was a new aspect.

"Nowhere?" The King pounced on the bag and shook it. "You're in the Ocna dungeon! The second biggest castle of the Kingdom! Plenty of company there! I'd be proud to be in that dungeon myself! Out, you ungrateful bag!" And he hurled it out the embrasure.

"What?" the doxy demanded. She had evidently heard only the last few words.

"Out, you ungrateful bag," the table repeated helpfully. "That's what he said."

"Well, I never!" the doxy said, flushing wrathfully.

"Don't tell *me* you never!" the feather quilt she had retained said. "I was right here when you—"

The doxy slapped the quilt, silencing it, then wrapped it about her and stalked out. "Help!" the quilt cried. "I'm being kidnapped by a monster!" Then it was beyond the magic aisle and said no more.

"Guards!" the King bellowed. "Search the premises! Report anything remarkable."

There was a scream from the hall, and the sound of someone being slapped. "He said premises, not mistresses!" the doxy's voice cried.

There was a guttural laugh. "But we do have something remarkable to report."

"He's seen it before!" she retorted. Her footfalls moved on away.

Guards charged into the room. Quickly they ascertained that no one except the King was in the tower. Then they spied the tip of the vine that had grown into the embrasure. They investigated it—while Dor and Irene scrambled down the wall. Grundy leaped from above them, dropping to the centaur's back. "Take off!" he cried.

Arnolde in turn launched himself from the platform, landing with heavy impact on the dark ground and galloping off. The platform was shoved violently by the back thrust of his hooves, so that the vines holding it in place were wrenched from the wall. Suddenly Irene was falling, her support gone, while Dor dangled tenuously from his vine, his grip slipping.

But Smash the Ogre was there below. He snatched Irene out of the air and whirled her around, absorbing the shock of her fall. Her skirt flew out and up—and now at last Dor saw her panties. They were green. Then Smash deposited her gently on the ground while Dor slid down as quickly as he could, weak with relief. "I'm glad you were there!" Dor gasped.

"Me glad centaur was still near," Smash said. "He out of range now."

Which meant that the ogre's magic strength was gone again. Irene had fallen in those few seconds that the rear extension of the aisle remained. Now Smash's nonrhyming showed that the Mundane environment had closed in.

"Someone's out there!" King Oary cried from the embrasure. "After him!" But the guards had no good light for the purpose, and seemed loath to pursue a magic enemy in the moonlight.

"You sword," Smash said, pressing it into Dor's hand. "You seeds," he said to Irene, giving her the bag he had rescued.

"Thanks oodles, Smash," she said. "Now let's get away from here."

But as they moved out, a small gate opened in the castle wall and troops poured forth bearing torches. "Oary must have caught on that it was our magic," Dor said as they scrambled away.

Soon they caught up, to the centaur, who had stopped as soon as he realized what was happening. Dor felt no different as they re-entered the magic aisle, but Smash's panting alleviated; his strength had returned.

Quickly Dor summarized their situation. "We're together; we have our magic things, except for Arnolde's spells, and we know King Trent, Queen Iris, and King Omen are alive in Castle Ocna. Oary's troops are on our trail. We had better hurry on to rescue the three, before the troops catch us. But we don't know the way."

"Every plant and rock must know the way to Ocna," Grundy said. "We can ask as we go along."

The guards were spreading out and combing through the forest. Whatever virtues King Oary lacked, he evidently compelled obedience when he really wanted it. Dor's party had to retreat before them. But there were two problems: this section of forest was small, so that they could not remain concealed long; and they were being herded the wrong way. For it turned out that Ocna was half a day's walk northwest of Onesti, while this forest was southeast. They were actually moving toward the village settlement, where the peasants who served the castle dwelt. That village would, in the course of centuries, expand into the town of Onesti, whose designation on the map had given them the hint where to find King Trent. They didn't want to interfere with that!

"We've got to get on a path," Irene said. "We'll never make it to Ocna tonight traveling cross-country. But the soldiers will be patrolling the paths."

"Maybe there's a magic seed for this," Grundy suggested.

"Maybe," Irene agreed. "Another tangler would do—except I don't have one. I do have a cherry seed—"

"The kind that grows cherry bombs? That would do it!"

"No," Arnolde said.

"What's the matter, horsetail?" the golem demanded nastily. "You'd rather get your rump riddled with arrows than throw a few cherries at the enemy?"

"Setting aside the ethical and aesthetic considerations—which process I find objectionable—there remain practical ones," the centaur said. "First, we don't want a pitched battle; we do want to elude these people, if possible, leaving them here in a fruitless search while we proceed unchallenged to Ocna. If we fight them, we shall be tied down indefinitely, until their superior numbers overwhelm us."

"There is that," Dor agreed. Centaurs did have fine minds.

"Second, we must keep moving if we are to reach Ocna before dawn. A half-day's march for seasoned travelers by day, familiar with the route, will be twice that for us at night. A cherry tree can't travel; it must be rooted in soil. And since it is magic—"

"We'd have to stay with it," Irene finished. "It'd die the moment we left. Anything magic will be no good away from the magic aisle."

"However," the centaur said after a moment, "it might be possible to grow a plant that would distract them, even if it were dead. Especially if it were dead."

"Cherry bombs won't work," Grundy said. "They don't exist in Mundania. They wouldn't explode outside the aisle."

"Oh, I don't know," Irene said defensively. "Once they are mature and ready to detonate, it seems to me they should be able to explode anywhere. I'd be willing to try them, certainly."

"Possibly so," the centaur said. "However, I was thinking of resurrection fern, whose impact would extend beyond the demise of the plant itself."

"I do have some," Irene said. "But I don't see how it can stop soldiers."

"Primitives tend to be superstitious," the centaur explained. "Especially, I understand, Mundanes, who profess not to belive in ghosts."

"That's ridiculous!" Dor protested. "Only a fool would not believe in ghosts. Some of my best friends are—"

"I'm not certain all Mundanes are fools," Arnolde said in his cautious way. "But these particular ones may be. So if they encountered resurrection fern—"

"It could be quite something, for people who didn't know about it," Irene agreed.

"And surely these Mundanes don't," Arnolde said. "I admit it is a bit of a dastardly deed, but our situation is desperate."

"Dastardly deed," Dor said. "Are you sure that counter-spell we used with the salve worked?"

The centaur smiled. "Certainly I'm sure! We do not *have* to do such a deed, but we certainly can if we choose to."

Irene dug out the seed. "I can grow it, but you'll have to coordinate it. The wrong suggestion can ruin it."

"These primitives are bound to have suffered lost relatives," the centaur said. "They will have repressed urgings. All we shall have to do is establish pseudo-identities."

"I never talked with resurrection fern," Grundy complained. "What's so special about it? What's this business about lost relatives?"

"Let's find a place on a road," Arnolde said. "We want to intercept the Mundanes, but have easy travel to Ocna. They will pursue us when they penetrate the deception."

"Right," Irene agreed. "I'll need time to get the fern established so it can include all of us."

"Include us all in *what?*" the golem demanded.

"Resurrection fern has the peculiar property of—" the centaur began.

"Near here!" Smash called, pointing. Ogres had excellent night vision.

Sure enough, they had found a path, a rut worn by the tread of peasants' feet and horses' hooves.

"Do you go to Ocna?" Dor asked the path.

"No. I merely show the way," it answered.

"Which way is it?"

"That way," the section of path to their west said. "But you'll have trouble traveling there tonight."

"Why?"

"Because there is something wrong with me. I feel numb, everywhere but here. Maybe there's been a bad storm that washed me out."

"Could the path be aware of itself beyond the region of magic?" Irene asked Dor.

"I'm not sure. I don't think so—but then, it does know it goes to Ocna, so maybe it does have some awareness. I'm not used to dealing with things that straddle magic and nonmagic; I don't know all the rules."

"I believe it is reasonably safe to assume the path is animate only within the aisle," Arnolde said. "In any event, this is probably as good a place for our purpose as any. The soldiers are surely using this path, and will circle around here. It is better to meet them in a manner of our choosing than to risk an accidental encounter. Let us begin our preparations."

"Right," Irene said. "Now the fern will grow in the dark, but needs light to activate its magic. The soldiers will have torches, so it should be all right."

"I have the sunstone," Dor reminded her. "That can trigger the fern, if necessary. Or we could clear out some trees to let the moonlight in."

"Good enough," she agreed. She planted several seeds. "Grow."

"But what does it *do?*" Grundy asked plaintively.

"Well, it relates to the psychology of the ignorant spectator," Arnolde explained. "Anyone who comprehends its properties soon penetrates the illusion. That is why I feel it will be more effective against Mundanes than against citizens of Xanth. Thus we should be able to deceive them and nullify the pursuit without violence, a distinct advantage. All we have to do is respond appropriately to their overtures, keeping our own expectations out of it."

"What expectations?" the golem demanded, frustrated.

Dor took a hand. "You see, resurrection fern makes figures seem like—"

"Refrain!" Smash whispered thunderingly. "Mundane!" Ogres' hearing was also excellent.

They waited by the growing fern. In a moment three Onesti soldiers came into view, their torches flashing between the trees, casting monstrous shadows. They were peering to either side, alert for their quarry.

Then the three spied the five. The soldiers halted, staring, just within the magic aisle. "Grandfather!" one exclaimed, aghast, staring at Smash.

The ogre knew what to do. He roared and made a threatening gesture with one hamfist. The soldier dropped his torch and fled in terror.

One of the remaining soldiers was looking at Irene. "You live!" he gasped. "The fever spared you after all!"

Irene shook her head sadly. "No, friend. I died."

"But I *see* you!" the man cried, in an agony of doubtful hope. "I hear you! Now we can marry—"

"I am dead, love," she said with mournful firmness. "I return only to warn you not to support the usurper."

"But you never cared for politics," the soldier said, bewildered. "You did not even like my profession—"

"I still don't," Irene said. "But at least you worked for Good King Omen. Death has given me pause for thought. Now you work for his betrayer. I will never respect you, even from the grave, if you work for the bad King who seeks to send Good King Omen to his grave."

"I'll renounce King Oary!" the soldier cried eagerly. "I don't like him anyway. I thought Good Omen dead!"

"He lives," Irene said. "He is in the dungeon at Castle Ocna."

"I'll tell everyone! Only return to me!"

"I can not return, love," she said. "I am resurrected only for this moment, only to tell you why I can not rest in peace. I am dead; King Omen lives. Go help the living." She moved back to hide behind the centaur, disappearing from the soldier's view.

"Beautiful," Arnolde whispered.

"I feel unclean," she muttered.

The third man focused on Grundy. "My baby son—returned from the Khazars!" he exclaimed. "I knew they could not hold you long!"

The golem had finally caught on to the nature of resurrection fern: it resurrected the memories of important figures in the viewers' lives. "Only my spirit escaped," he said. "I had to warn you. The Khazars are coming! They will besiege Onesti, slay the men, rape the women, and carry the children away into bondage, as they did me. Warn the King! Fetch all troops into the castle! Barricade the access roads! Don't let more families be ravaged. Don't let my sacrifice be in vain! Fight to the last—"

Dor nudged the golem with his foot. "Don't overdo it," he murmured. "Mundanes are ignorant; they aren't necessarily stupid."

"Let's move out," Irene whispered. "This should hold them for a while."

They moved out cautiously. The two soldiers remained by the fern, absorbed by their thoughts. Before rounding a curve in the path, Dor glanced back—and saw a giant, pretty spider, of the kind that ranged about rather than forming a web. The decorations on its body resembled a greenish face, and it had eight eyes of different sizes.

"Jumper!" he exclaimed—then stifled himself. Jumper had died of old age years ago. He had been Dor's closest friend, when the two had seemed to be the same size within the historical tapestry of Castle Roogna, but their worlds were different. The spider's descendants remained by the tapestry, and Dor could talk to them if he arranged for translation, but it wasn't the same. They seemed like interlopers, taking the place of his marvelous friend. Now he saw Jumper himself.

But of course it was only a resurrection, not the real friend. As Dor reminded himself of that, the image reduced to the standing soldier. How Dor wished it could have been genuine! This new separation, albeit from a phantom, was painfully poignant.

"So the fern resurrects precious memories," Grundy said as they got clear.

"The person looking sees what is deepest-etched in his experience. He really should know better."

"Oh, what do you know about it?" Irene said irritably. "It's an awful thing to do to a person, even a Mundane."

"You looked back, too?" Dor asked.

"I saw my father. I know he isn't dead, but I saw him." She sounded choked. "What a torment it would have been if that were all I would ever see of him."

"We'll soon find him," Dor said encouragingly. This, too, he found he liked about her—her human feeling and loyalty to her father, who had always been a large figure in Dor's own life.

She flashed him a grateful smile in the moonlight. Dor understood her mood; his vision of his long-gone friend had wrenched his emotion. How much worse had it been for the Mundanes, who lacked knowledge of the mechanism? It was indeed a dastardly thing they had done; perhaps the violence of ogre and sword would have been gentler.

Soon, however, they heard the commotion of pursuit. The resurrection fern had perished, or at least had become inactive after the magic aisle left it; there would be no more visions there. The stories of the three affected soldiers would spread alarm, but there would also be many who still followed their orders to capture Dor's party.

They stepped from the path, hiding in the brush—and the troops rushed on past. A snatch of their dialogue flung out: ". . . Khazars coming . . ." It seemed the golem's information had been taken to heart!

"I think they've forgotten us," Irene said as they stepped back on the path. "The resurrections gave them other things to think about. Now they aren't even looking for us. So maybe we can travel to Ocna safely."

"It was a good move we made, strategically," Dor said. "A dirty one, perhaps, and I wouldn't want to do it again, but effective."

"First we must pass Castle Onesti," Arnolde reminded them.

They got past Onesti by following the directions the path gave. There was a detour around that castle, for peasants had fields to attend to, wood to fetch, and hunting to do well beyond the castle, and the immediate environs were forbidding.

This path angled down below the clifflike western face of the peak the castle stood on, wending its way curvaceously through pastures and forest and slope. Several parties of soldiers passed them, but were easily avoided. It seemed these people took the Khazars seriously!

Beyond the castle the way grew more difficult. This was truly mountainous country, and there was a high pass between the two redoubts. Dor and the others were not yet fully rested from their arduous climb to Onesti of a day or so ago; now the stiffness of muscles was aggravated. But the path assured them there was no better route. Perhaps that was its conceit—but they had no ready alternative. So they hauled themselves up and up, until near midnight they came to the highest pass. It was a narrow gap between jags.

It was guarded by a select detachment of soldiers. They could not conveniently circle around it, and knew the soldiers would not let them through unchallenged.

"What now?" Irene asked, too tired even to be properly irritable.

"Maybe I can distract them," Dor said. "If I succeed, the rest of you hurry through the pass."

They worked their way as close to the pass as they could without being discovered. Arnolde oriented himself so that the magic aisle was where they needed it. Then Dor concentrated, causing the objects to break into speech.

"Ready, Khazars?" an outcropping of rock cried.

"Ready!" came a chorused response from several loose rocks.

"Sneak up close before firing your arrows," the outcropping directed. "We want to get them all on the first volley."

"Save some for our boulder!" the upper face of the cleft called. "We have a perfect drop here!"

The Onesti soldiers, at first uneasy, abruptly vacated the cleft, glancing nervously up at the crags. It seemed impossible for anyone to have a boulder up there, but the voice had certainly been convincing. They charged the rocks, swords drawn. "Move out!" Dor cried.

Arnolde and Grundy charged for the pass. Smash and Irene hesitated. "Go on!" Dor snapped. "Get through before the magic ends!"

"But what about you?" Irene asked.

Dor concentrated. "Retreat, men!" the outcropping cried. "They're on to us!" There was the sound of scrambling from the rocks.

"I'm not going without you!" Irene said.

"I've got to keep them distracted until the rest of you safely clear the pass!" Dor cried, exasperated.

"You can't keep on after—"

Then the voices stopped. The magic aisle had passed.

"After Arnolde gets out of range," she finished lamely.

The soldiers, baffled by the disappearance of the enemy, were turning about. In a moment they would spy the two; the moonlight remained too bright for effective concealment in the open.

"I grew a pineapple while we waited," Irene said. "I hate to use it on people, even Mundanes, but they'll kill us if—"

"How can a magic pineapple operate outside the aisle?" he demanded, knowing this argument was foolish, but afraid if they moved that the soldiers would spy them.

She looked chagrined. "For once you're right! If cherry bombs are uncertain, so is this!"

Smash was standing in the cleft. "Run!" he cried.

But the soldiers were closing in. Dor knew they couldn't make it through in time. He drew his sword. Without its magic, it felt heavy and clumsy, but it was the best weapon he had. He would be overwhelmed, of course, but he would die fighting. It wasn't the end he would have chosen, had he a reasonable choice, but it was better than nothing. "Run to Smash," he said. "I'll block them off."

"You come, too!" she insisted. "I love you!"

"Now she tells me," he muttered, watching the soldiers close in.

Irene threw the pineapple at them. "Maybe it'll scare them," she said.

"It can't. They don't know what—"

The pineapple exploded, sending yellow juice everywhere. "It detonated!" Dor exclaimed, amazed.

"Come *on!*" Arnolde called, appearing behind the ogre. Suddenly it made sense; the centaur had turned about and come back when they hadn't followed. That had returned the magic to the vicinity, just in time.

They ran to the cleft. The Mundanes were pawing at their eyes, blinded by pineapple juice. There was no trouble.

"You were so busy trying to be heroes, you forgot common sense," Arnolde reproved them. "All you needed to do was follow me while the Mundanes' backs were turned. They would never have known of our passage."

"I never was strong on common sense," Dor admitted.

"That's for sure," Irene agreed. "That juice won't hold them forever. We'll have to move far and fast."

They did just that, their fatigue dissipated by the excitement. Now the path led downhill, facilitating progress somewhat. But it was treacherous in the darkness at this speed, for the mountain crags and trees shadowed it, and it curved and dropped without fair warning. Soon the soldiers were in pursuit.

But Dor used his talent, making the path call out warnings of hazards, so that they could proceed more rapidly than other strangers might. His midnight sunstone helped, too, casting just enough light to make pitfalls almost visible. But he knew they couldn't remain on the path long, because the soldiers were more familiar with it, and had their torches, and would surely catch up. They would have to pull off and hide—and that might not be enough, this time. There was too little room for concealment, and the soldiers would be too wary.

Then disaster loomed. "The bridge is out!" the path warned.

"What bridge?" Dor panted.

"The wooden bridge across the cut, dummy!"

"What happened to it?"

"The Onesti soldiers destroyed it when they heard the Khazars were coming."

So Dor's party had brought this mischief on itself! "Can we cross the cut some other way?"

"See for yourself. Here it is."

They halted hastily. There, shrouded by darkness and fog, was a gap in the mountain—a fissure four times the full reach of a man, extending from the clifflike face of the peak above down to the deep valley below, shrouded in nocturnal fog. Here the moonlight blazed down, as if eager to show the full extent of the hazard.

"A young, vigorous centaur could hurdle that," Arnolde said. "It is out of the question for me."

"If we had the rope—" Irene said. But of course Chet had that, wherever he was now.

Ascent of the peak seemed virtually impossible, and there was no telling what lay beneath the fog. The bridge had been the only practical crossing— and only fragments of that remained. This had become a formidable natural barrier—surely one reason the Khazars had been unable to conquer this tiny Kingdom. Any bridge the enemy built could readily be hacked out or fired.

But now the torches of the garrison of the upper pass were approaching. That was the other pincer of this trap. A few men could guard that pass, preventing retreat. The slope was steep here, offering little haven above or below the path. If the soldiers didn't get them, nature would.

"The salve," Irene said. "See the fog—we've got to use the salve!"

"But the curse—we've lost the counterspell!" Dor protested. "We'll have to do some dastardly deed"

"Those soldiers will do some dastardly deed to *us* if we don't get away from here fast," she pointed out.

Dor looked at her, standing in the moonlight, wearing his jacket, her fine-formed legs braced against the mountain. He thought of the soldiers doing a dastardly deed to her, as they had started to do in the dungeon. "We'll use the salve," he decided.

They scrambled down the steep slope to reach the level of the mist. They had to cling to trees and saplings, lest they slide into the cleft involuntarily.

Dor felt in his pocket for the jar—and found the dime he had obtained from Ichabod in Modern Mundania. He had forgotten that; it must have slipped into another crevice of his pocket and been overlooked. It was of course of no use now. He fumbled farther and found the jar.

Quickly they applied the salve to their feet. The supply was getting low; this was just about the last time they would be able to use it. Then they stepped cautiously out onto the fog.

"Stay close to Arnolde," Dor warned. "And in line. Anyone who goes outside the magic aisle will fall through."

Now the soldiers reached the cut. They were furious when they discovered no victims there. But almost immediately they spied the fugitives. "Cnvm adknv!" one cried. "Sgdx'qd nm sgd bkntc." Then he did a double take.

For a moment the soldiers stared. "Sgdx can't do that!" one protested as the rear of the magic aisle swung around to intersect him.

But their leader found the answer. "They're sorcerers! Spies sent by the Khazars. Shoot them down!"

Numbly responsive to orders, the soldiers nocked arrows to their bow-strings. "Run!" Dor cried. "But stay with Arnolde!"

"This time I'll bring up the rear, just to be sure," the centaur said. "Lead the way, the rest of you."

It made sense. The main part of the magic aisle was ahead of the centaur, and this way Arnolde could angle his body to keep them all within it. Dor and Irene and Smash charged forward as the first volley of arrows came at them. Grundy rode the centaur; it was the best way to keep him out from underfoot. They crossed the fog-filled cut, coming to the dense forest at the far side.

"Aaahh!" Arnolde screamed.

Dor paused to look back. An arrow had struck the centaur in the rump. Arnolde was crippled, trying to move forward on three legs.

Smash was leading the way. He reached out to grab the branch of a tree that projected through the fog. He ripped that branch out of its trunk and hurled it uphill and across the cut toward the soldiers. His aim was good; the soldiers screamed and flung themselves flat as the heavy branch landed on them, and one almost fell into the chasm.

Then Smash charged back across the cloud. He ducked down, grabbed the centaur by one foreleg and one hindleg, and hefted him to shoulder height. "Oh, I say!" Arnolde exclaimed, amazed despite his pain.

But within the ambience of magic, there was no strength to match that of the ogre. Smash carried Arnolde to the slope and set him down carefully where the ground rose out of the fog. This place was sheltered from the view of the soldiers; there would be no more shooting.

"But the arrow," the centaur said bravely. "We must get it out!"

Smash grabbed the protruding shaft and yanked. Arnolde screamed again—but suddenly the arrow was out. It had not been deeply embedded, or the head would have broken off.

"Yes, that was the appropriate way to do it," the centaur said—and fainted.

Irene was already sprouting a seed. They had lost their healing elixir with Arnolde's bag of spells, but some plants had curative properties. She grew a balm plant and used its substance on the wound. "This won't cure it all the way," she said. "But it will deaden the pain and start the healing process. He should be able to walk."

Smash paced nervously. "Yet—Chet," he said. "Mundane, the pain—"

Dor caught on to the ogre's concern. "We don't know that a Mundane wound will always become infected the way Chet's did. That was probably Chet's bad luck. Also, he was bitten by a wyvern, so there might have been poison, while Arnolde was struck by an arrow. This is a different situation— I think." Still, the coincidence of a second centaur getting wounded bothered Dor. Could it be part of the salve's curse? The centaurs had had to use twice as much salve, since they had four feet, and perhaps that made them more susceptible to the curse.

Arnolde soon woke and agreed that the agony of the wound was much abated. That was a relief, for at least two reasons. Nevertheless, Dor decided to camp there for the remainder of the night. Their chance of approaching Castle Ocna secretly was gone anyway, and the recovery of their friend was more important. After all, the centaur's aisle of magic was essential to their welfare in Mundania.

Chapter 12

Midnight Sun

In midday, weary but hopeful, they reached Castle Ocna. This was less imposing than Castle Onesti, but still formidable. The outer wall was far too high for them to scale. "Me bash to trash," Smash offered confidently.

"No," Dor said. "That would alert the whole castle and bring a hundred arrows down on us." He glanced at Arnolde, who seemed to be doing all right; no infection was in evidence. But they wanted no more arrows! "We'll wait until night and operate quietly. They'll be expecting our attack, but won't know exactly what form it will take. If we can bring the magic aisle to cover King Trent, he'll be able to take it from there."

"But we don't know where in the castle he is," Irene protested anxiously.

"That's my job," Grundy said. "I'll sneak in and scout about and let you know by nightfall. Then we'll wrap this up without trouble."

It seemed like a good idea. The others settled themselves for a meal and a rest, while the golem insinuated his way into the castle. Arnolde, perhaps more greatly weakened by his injury than he showed, slept. Smash always conked out when he had nothing physical to do. Dor and Irene were awake and alone again.

It occurred to Dor that bringing the magic aisle to bear on King Trent might not necessarily solve the problem. King Trent could change the jailor to a slug—but the cell would still be locked. Queen Iris might make a griffin seem to appear—but that would not unlock the cells. More thinking needed to be done.

They lay on the slope, in the concealment of one of the huge ancestral oaks, and the world was deceptively peaceful. "Do you really think it will work?" Irene asked worriedly. "The closer I get, the more I fear something dreadful will happen."

Dor decided he couldn't afford to agree with her. "We have fought our way here," he said. "It can't go for nothing."

"We have had no omens of success—" She paused. "Or *have* we? Omen—King Omen—can he have anything to do with it?"

"Anything is possible with magic. And we have brought magic to this Kingdom."

She shook her head. "I swing back and forth, full of hope and doubt. You just keep going on, never suffering the pangs of uncertainty, and you do generally get there. We'll make a good match."

No uncertainty? He was made of uncertainty! But again, he didn't want to undermine what little confidence Irene was grasping for. "We have to succeed. Otherwise I would be King. You wouldn't want that."

She rolled over, fetching up next to him, shedding leaves and grass. She grabbed him by the ears and kissed him. "I'd settle for that, Dor."

He looked at her, startled. She was disheveled and lovely. She had always been the aggressor in their relationship, first in quarreling, more recently in romance. Did he really want it that way?

He grabbed her and pulled her back down to him, kissing her savagely. At first she was rigid with surprise; then she melted. She returned his kiss and his embrace, becoming something very special and exciting.

It would have been easy to go on from there. But a note of caution sounded in Dor's mind. In the course of assorted adventures he had come to appreciate the value of timing, and this was not the proper time for what offered. "First we rescue your father," he murmured in her ear.

That brought her up short. "Yes, of course. So nice of you to remind me."

Dor suspected he had misplayed it, but as usual, all he could do was bull on. "Now we can sleep, so as to be ready for tonight."

"Whatever you say," she agreed. But she did not release him. "Dear."

Dor considered, and realized he was comfortable as he was. A strand of Irene's green-tinted hair fell across his face, smelling pleasantly of girl. Her breathing was soft against him. He felt that he could not ask for a better mode of relaxation.

But she was waiting for something. Finally he decided what it was. "Dear," he said.

She nodded, and closed her eyes. Yes, he was learning! He lay still, and soon he slept.

"Now aren't we cozy!" Grundy remarked.

Dor and Irene woke with a joint start. "We were just sleeping together," she said.

"And you admit it!" the golem exclaimed.

"Well, we are engaged, you know. We can do what we like together."

Dor realized that she was teasing the golem, so he stayed out of it. What did it matter what other people thought? What passed between himself and the girl he loved was their own business.

"I'll have to tell your father," Grundy said, nettled.

Suddenly Dor had pause to reconsider. This was the daughter of the King!

"I'll tell him myself, you wad of string and clay!" Irene snapped. "Did you find him?"

"Maybe I shouldn't tell a bad girl like you."

"Maybe I should grow a large flytrap plant and feed you to it," Irene replied.

That fazed the golem. "I found them all. In three cells, the way the three of you were, one in each cell. Queen Iris, King Trent, and King Omen."

Irene sat up abruptly, disengaging from Dor. "Are they all right?"

Grundy frowned. "The men are. They have been through privation before. The Queen is not pleased with her situation."

"She wouldn't be," Irene agreed. "But are they all right physically? They haven't been starved, or anything?"

"Well, they were a bit close-mouthed about that," the golem said. "But the Queen seems to have lost weight. She was getting fat anyway, so that's all right, but I guess she hasn't been fed much. And I saw a crust of bread she left. It was moldy. The flies are pretty thick in there, too; must be a lot of maggots around."

Irene got angry. "They have no right to treat royalty like that!"

"Something else I picked up," Grundy said. "The guard who feeds them— it seems he eats what he wants first, and gives them the leavings. Sometimes he spits on it, or rubs dirt in it, just to aggravate them. They have to eat the stuff anyway or starve. Once he even urinated in their drinking water, right where they could see him, to be sure they knew what they were drinking. He doesn't speak, he just shows his contempt by his actions."

"I have heard of this technique," Arnolde said. "It is the process of degradation. If you can destroy a person's pride, you can do with him what you will. Pride is the backbone of the spirit. Probably King Oary is trying to get

King Omen to sign a document of abdication, just in case there is ever any challenge to King Oary's legitimacy."

"Why is he keeping the others alive, then?" Dor asked, appalled by both the method and the rationale. Mundanes played politics in an ugly fashion.

"Well, we have seen how he operates. If he lets the three spend time together and become friends, then he can use the others as leverage against King Omen. Remember how you told me he was going to torture Irene to make you talk?"

"He's going to torture my parents?" Irene demanded, aghast.

"I dislike formulating this notion, but it is a prospect."

Irene was silent, smoldering. Dor decided, regretfully, to tackle the problem of freeing the prisoners. "I hoped King Trent could use his power to break out, but I'm not sure how transformation of people can unlock doors. If we can figure out a way—"

"Elementary," Arnolde said. "The King can transform the Queen to a mouse. She runs out through a crevice. Then he transforms her back, and she opens the cells from the outside. If there are guards, he can transform her to a deadly monster to dispatch them."

So simple! Why hadn't he, Dor, thought of that?

Irene shifted gears, in the manner of her sex, becoming instantly practical. "Who is in the cell closet to the wall?"

"The Queen." The golem frowned. "You know, I think she's the only one the magic aisle can reach. The wall's pretty thick in that region."

"So my father probably can't transform anyone," Irene said.

Trouble! Dor considered, trying to come up with an alternate suggestion. "The Queen does have powerful magic. It should be possible for her to free them by means of illusion. She can make them see the cells as empty, or containing dead prisoners, so that the guards open the gates. Then she can generate a monster to scare them away."

"There are problems," Arnolde said. "The aisle, as you know, is narrow. The illusion will not operate outside it. Since two cells are beyond—"

"The Queen's illusion will have very limited play," Dor concluded. "We had better warn her about that. She should be able to manage, if she has time to prepare."

"I'm on my way," Grundy said. "I don't know how this expedition would function without me!"

"There isn't one of us we can do without," Dor said. "We've already seen that. When we get separated, we're all in trouble."

As the night closed, they moved to the castle, trying to reach the spot nearest the Queen's cell as described by the golem. Again there was no moat, just a glacis, so that they had to mount a kind of stone hill leading up to the wall. Dor could appreciate how thick that wall might be, set on a base this massive.

Castle Ocna was alert, fearing the invasion of the Khazars; torches flickered in the turrets and along the walls. But Dor's party was not using the established paths and remained unobserved. People who lived in castles tended to be insulated from events outside, and to forget the potential importance of the exterior environment. It occurred to Dor that this also applied to the whole land of Xanth; few of its inhabitants knew anything about Mundania, or cared to learn. Trade between the realms, hitherto a matter of erratic chance, should be established, if only to facilitate a more cosmopolitan awareness. King Oary was evidently not much interested in trade, to the detriment of his Kingdom; he regarded the Xanth visitors as a threat to his throne. As indeed they were—since he was a usurper.

"Now we can't plan exactly how this will work," Dor said in a final review. "I hope the Queen will be able to make an illusion that will cause the guards to release her, and then she can free the others."

"She'd love to vamp a guard," Irene said. "She'll make herself look like the winsomest wench in all Mundania. Then when he comes close, she'll turn into a dragon and scare him to death. Serve him right."

Dor chuckled. "I think I know how that works."

She whirled on him in mock fury. "You haven't begun to see how it works!" But she couldn't hold her frown. She kissed him instead.

"The lady appears to have given fair warning," Arnolde remarked. "You won't see the dragon until you are securely married."

"He knows that," Irene said smugly. "But men never learn. Each one thinks he's different."

Arnolde set himself against the wall, changing his orientation by small degrees so that the aisle swung through the castle. "Grundy will have to report whether we intercept the Queen," he said. "I can not perceive the use of the aisle."

"If anything goes wrong," Irene said, "Smash will have to go into action, and I'll grow some plant to mess them up."

They waited. The centaur completed a sweep through the castle without event. He swept back, still accomplishing nothing. "I begin to fear we are, after all, beyond range," he said.

Smash put one cauliflower ear to the wall. "Go down for crown."

"Of course!" Dor agreed. "They are in the dungeon! Below ground level. Aim down."

With difficulty, Arnolde bent his forelegs, leaving his hindlegs extended, tilting his body down. He commenced another sweep. This was quite awkward for him, because of the position and his injury. Smash joined him, lifting him up and setting him down at a new angle, making the sweep easier.

"But if they are too far inside for the aisle to reach—" Irene murmured tensely.

"Grundy will let us know," Dor said, trying to prevent her from becoming hysterically nervous. He knew this was the most trying time for her—this period when they would either make contact or fail. "We may catch Queen

Iris, then sweep on past, and it will take a while for the golem to relay the news."

"That could be it," she agreed, moving into the circle of his arm. He turned to kiss her and found her lips eager to meet his own. Once she had declared her love, she made absolutely no secret of it. Dor realized that even if their mission failed, even if they perished here in Mundania, it was privately worth it for him in this sense. He had discovered love, and it was a universe whose reaches, pitfalls, and potential rewards were more vast than all of Mundania. He held the kiss for a long time.

"Is this how you behave when unchaperoned?" a woman's voice demanded sharply.

Dor and Irene broke with a start. There beside them stood the Queen. "Mother!" Irene cried, half in relief, half in chagrin.

"Shamefully embracing in public!" Queen Iris continued, frowning. She had always been the guardian of other people's morals. "This must come to the attention of—"

The Queen vanished. Arnolde, turning as well as he could to face her image, had thereby shifted the magic aisle away from Iris' cell, so that the Queen's magic was interrupted. She could no longer project her illusion-image.

"Beg pardon," the centaur said. He shifted back.

Queen Iris reappeared. Before she could speak again, Irene did so. "That's nothing, Mother. This afternoon Dor and I slept together."

"You disreputable girl!" Iris exclaimed, aghast.

Dor bit his tongue. He had never really liked Queen Iris and could hardly have thought of a better way to prick her bubble.

The centaur tried to reassure her. "Your Majesty, we all slept. It—"

"You, too?" Iris demanded, her gaze surveying them with an amazing chill. "And the ogre?"

"We're a very close group," Irene said. "I love them all."

This was going too far. "You misunderstand," Dor said. "We only—"

Irene tromped his toe, cutting him off. She wanted to continue baiting her mother. But Queen Iris, no fool, had caught on. "They only saw up your skirt, of course. How many times have I cautioned you about that? You have absolutely no sense of—"

"We bring the King?" Smash inquired.

"The King!" Iris exclaimed. "By all means! You must march in and free us all."

"But the noise—" Dor protested. "If we alert the soldiers—"

"You forget my power," Queen Iris informed him. "I can give your party the illusion of absence. No one will hear you or see you, no matter what you do."

Such a simple solution! The Queen's illusion would be more than enough to free them all. "Break in the wall, Smash," Dor called. "We can rescue King Trent ourselves!"

With a grunt of glee, the ogre advanced on the wall. Then he disappeared. So did the centaur. Dor found himself embracing nothing. He could neither see nor feel Irene, and heard nothing either—but there was resistance where he knew her to be. Experimentally he shoved.

Something shoved him back. It was like the force of inertia when he swung around a corner at a run, a force with no seeming origin. Irene was there, all right! This spell differed from the one the centaur had used; it made the people within it undetectable to each other as well as to outsiders. He hoped that didn't lead to trouble.

A gap appeared in the wall. Chunks of stone fell out, silently. The ogre was at work.

Dor kept his arm around the nothingness beside him, and it moved with him. Curious about the extent of the illusion, he moved his hand. Portions of the nothingness were more resilient than others. Then he found himself stumbling; a less resilient portion had given him another shove. Then something helped steady him; the nothingness was evidently sorry. He wrapped his arms about it and drew it in close for a kiss, but it didn't feel right. He concluded he was kissing the back of her head. He grabbed a hank of nothingness and gave it a friendly tug.

Then Irene appeared, laughing. "Oh, am I going to get even for that!" Then she realized she could perceive him in the moonlight. She wrapped the jacket about her torso—it had fallen open during their invisible encounter— and drew him forward. "We're getting left be—" She vanished and silenced.

They had re-entered the aisle. Dor kept hold of her nothing-hand and followed the other nothings into the hole in the wall.

For a moment they all became visible. Arnolde was ahead, negotiating a pile of rubble; Smash had broken through to the lower level, but the path he made was hardly smooth. The centaur, realizing that the aisle had shifted away from the Queen, hastily corrected his orientation. They all vanished again.

Castle personnel appeared, gaping at the rubble, unable to fathom its cause. One stepped into the passage—and vanished. That created another stir. As yet the Mundanes did not seem to associate this oddity with an invasion.

The ogre's tunnel progressed apace. Soon enough it broke into the Queen's cell, then into King Trent's and finally King Omen's. At that point the parties became visible again. There was ambient light, courtesy of the Queen's illusion. Dor was uncertain at what point illusion became reality, since light was light however it was generated, but he had learned not to worry unduly about such distinctions.

Irene lurched forward and flung herself into King Trent's arms. "Oh, daddy!" she cried with tears of joy.

Now Dor experienced what he knew to be his most unreasonable surge of jealousy yet. After all, why should she not love her father? He glanced about—and saw Queen Iris watching her husband and daughter with what appeared to be identical emotion. She, too, was jealous—and unable to express it.

For the first time in his life, Dor felt complete sympathy with the Queen. This was one shame he shared with her.

The King set Irene down and looked about. Suddenly it was incumbent on Dor to make introductions and explanations. He hurried up. "Uh, we've come to rescue you, King Trent. This is Arnolde the Centaur—he's the one who made the magic aisle—that's his talent—and this is Smash the Ogre, and Irene—"

King Trent looked regal even in rags. "I believe I know that last," he said gravely.

"Uh, yes," Dor agreed, flustered, knowing he was really fouling it up. "I— uh—"

"Do you know what he did, father?" Irene asked King Trent, indicating Dor.

"I did not!" Dor exclaimed. Teasing the Queen was one thing; teasing the King was another.

"Anyway, Dor and I are—" Irene's voice broke off as she spied the third prisoner.

He was a stunningly handsome young man who radiated charisma, though he, too, was dressed in rags. "King Omen," King Trent said with his customary gravity. "My daughter Irene."

For the first time Dor saw Irene girlishly flustered. King Omen strode forward, picked up her limp hand, and brought it to his lips. "Ravishing," he murmured.

Irene tittered. Dor felt a new surge of jealousy. Obviously the girl, so ardent toward Dor a moment ago, was now smitten by the handsome Mundane King. She was, after all, fifteen years old; constancy was not her nature. Yet it hurt to be so suddenly forgotten.

Dor turned his eyes away—and met the gaze of the Queen. Again there was a flash of understanding.

"Now we have business to accomplish," King Trent said. "My friend King Omen must be restored to his throne. To make that secure, we must separate the loyal citizens of Onesti from the disloyal."

Dor forced his mind to focus on this problem. "How can anyone in this castle be loyal? They kept their King prisoner in the dungeon."

"By no means," King Omen said resonantly. "Few were aware of my presence. We were brought in manacled and hooded, and the only one who sees us is a mute eunuch who is absolutely loyal to Oary the Usurper. No doubt the castle personnel were told we were Khazar prisoners of war."

"So only the mute knew your identity?" Dor asked, remembering Grundy's description of the man's activities. But the golem sometimes exaggerated for effect. "At least he brought you food."

"Food!" the Queen cried. "That slop! Irene, grow us a pie tree! We haven't had a decent meal since this happened."

Irene wrenched her eyes off King Omen long enough to dig out and sprout a seed. Quickly the plant grew, leafing out in the illusion of daylight and developing big circular buds that burst into assorted fruit pies.

King Omen was amazed. "It's magic!" he exclaimed. "What an ability!"

Irene flushed, pleased. "It's my talent. Everyone in Xanth does magic."

"But I understood no magic would work here in the real world. How is it possible now?"

Evidently Dor's introduction of Arnolde had not been sufficient for one who was completely unused to magic. "That's the centaur's talent," he explained. "He's a full Magician. He brings magic with him in an aisle. In that aisle, everyone's talent works. That's why we were able to come here."

King Omen faced King Trent as they bit into their pies. "I apologize, sir, for my nagging doubt about your abilities. I have never believed in magic, despite the considerable lore of our superstitious peasants. Now I have seen the proof. Your lovely wife and lovely daughter have marvelous talents."

Irene flushed again, inordinately thrilled.

"King Omen is really a fine young man," Queen Iris remarked to no one in general.

Dor felt cold. The Queen's favor was not lightly gained; she had extremely strict and selfish notions of propriety, and these were focused largely on her daughter. Queen Iris had evidently concluded that King Omen was a suitable match for Irene. Of course the final opinion was King Trent's; if he decided on King Omen, Dor was lost. But King Trent had always supported Dor before.

Suddenly a huge fat man burst upon them. His eyes rounded with amazement as he spied the visitors in the dungeon and the pie tree. Then he drew his sword. He charged upon King Omen.

Irene screamed as the man passed near her father. Then the Mundane turned into a purple toad, his sword clattering to the floor. King Trent had transformed him.

"Who was that?" Dor asked, his startlement subsiding raggedly.

"The mute eunuch guard," King Omen said, picking up the fallen sword. "We bear him no love." He considered the toad speculatively. It was covered with green warts. "Yes, your magic is impressive! Will he remain that way?"

"Until I transform him again," King Trent said. "Or until he leaves the region of magic. Then, I believe, he will slowly revert to his normal state. But that process may take months and be uncomfortable and awkward, if someone does not take him for a monster and kill him before it is complete."

"A fitting punishment," King Omen said. "Let him begin it." He urged the toad on out of the magic aisle by pricking it with the point of the sword.

"Now let's consider prospects," King Trent said. "We have achieved a significant breakthrough here, regaining our magic. But very soon the usurper's picked private troops, comprised largely of Avar mercenaries, will lay siege to us here, and we have no magic that will stop a flight of arrows. We are certain that the general populace will rally gladly to King Omen, once they realize he is alive; but most of the people are outside the castles, and we are in danger of being wiped out before that realization prevails. We must plan our strategy carefully."

"I must advise you that the magic associated with me is in a fairly narrow aisle," Arnolde said. "It extends perhaps fifteen paces forward, and half that distance back, but only two to either side. Therefore the Queen's illusion will be limited to that ambience, and any person outside it will be immune."

"But a lot can be done within the aisle," Dor said. "When Irene and I lagged outside the aisle, we reappeared—but the rest of you remained invisible to us. We weren't immune to the illusion, just outside it. So the Queen can keep us all from the perception of the Mundanes. That's a considerable asset."

"True," the centaur agreed. "But now that they know about our magic, we can not prevent them from firing their arrows into this region in a saturation pattern that is bound to wipe us out. I have already had experience with this tactic." He rubbed his flank ruefully. The healing had continued nicely, but he still walked slightly stiffly.

"We must take cover, of course," King Trent agreed. "There is now plenty of rubble to shield us from arrows. But we can not afford to remain confined here. The problem will be the elimination of the enemy forces."

"Maybe we can lure them in here and ambush them," King Omen suggested. "We now have two swords, and I am impressed with the ogre's strength."

"No good," Grundy said. He had reappeared during their feast on the pies and now took a small pie for himself. "The Avar commander is a tough, experienced son of a buzzard who knows you have magic. He is heating a cauldron of oil. Soon he'll pour it down the dungeon steps. Anyone hiding here, with or without magic, will be fried in oil."

"Impossible to fill this chamber with oil," Queen Iris said. "It would all leak out."

"But it will cover the whole floor first," Grundy said. "You'll all get hotfeet."

Dor looked down at his sandals nervously. He did not like the notion of splashing through a puddle of boiling oil.

Trent considered. "And an ambush waits outside the dungeon?"

"Sure thing," Grundy agreed. "You don't think they let you sit here and gorge on pies just because they like you, do you?"

"Turn us all into birds, father," Irene suggested. "We'll fly out before they know it."

"Two problems, daughter," King Trent said. "You will have trouble when you fly outside the magic aisle. I'm not sure how you will function, but probably poorly, as you won't be able to change back, yet the magic will be gone. Also, I can not transform myself."

"Oh—I forgot." She was chagrined, since the rescue of her father had been her whole purpose.

"We have to get you safely out of here, sir," Dor said. "The Land of Xanth needs you."

"I have every present intention of returning," King Trent said with a smile. "I am now merely pondering mechanisms. I can deal with the Avars readily enough, provided I can get close enough to them with my magic power intact. That means I shall have to remain with Magician Arnolde."

"And with me," Queen Iris said. "To keep you invisible. And the ogre, to open doors."

"And me," Irene said loyally.

"You I want safely out of the way," her father said.

There was a bubbling noise. "The oil!" Grundy cried. "We've got to move!"

Smash went into action. He started bashing out a new channel.

They became invisible. But Dor had a mental picture of where each person was; King Trent, Arnolde, and the Queen were near the ogre, ready to follow in his new tunnel and avoid the spilling oil. But Irene and the golem were on the far side of the chamber. The oil was already flowing between them and the ogre. They would be trapped—and as the centaur moved away, they would become visible and vulnerable, even if they avoided the oil.

Dor ran across to pick up a fragment of rubble. He tossed it into the flowing oil. He grabbed more chunks and tossed them, forming a dam. But it wasn't enough; he wasn't sure Irene could make it through.

Then the pieces started flying into place at double the rate he was throwing them. Someone else was helping. Dor could not tell who, or communicate directly; he simply continued tossing stones, damming off the hot oil. Soon it formed a reluctant pool. Dor filled in the crevices of the dam with sand, and the way was clear. The oil ploy had been abated, and Irene could cross to safety.

Now a troop of guards charged down the steps, swords drawn. They wore heavy boots, evidently to protect them from the oil they thought would be distracting their quarry. It should have been a neat double trap. They didn't know the quarry had departed.

Still, the Avars could use their bows to fire arrows up the new tunnel, doing much harm. Dor leaped across to guard the tunnel entrance, trusting that the others had by now safely passed through it. An invisible guardian could hold them off long enough, perhaps.

Then he saw his own arms. The magic aisle had left him vulnerable!

The soldiers spied him in the torchlight. They whirled to attack him.

Another sword flashed beside him. King Omen! *He* was the other person who had helped dam the hot oil!

No words were exchanged. They both knew what had to be done; they had to guard this entrance from intrusion by the enemy until King Trent could handle his task.

The ogre's new passage was too narrow to allow them to fight effectively while standing inside, and the dungeon chamber was too broad; soldiers could stand against the far wall, out of sword range, and fire their arrows down the length of the tunnel. So Dor and Omen moved out into the chamber, standing back to back near the wilting pie tree, and dominated the entire chamber with their two swords. Dor hoped King Omen knew how to use his weapon.

The Avars, no cowards, came at them enthusiastically. They were of a wild Turk nomad tribe, according to Arnolde's secondhand information, dissatisfied with their more settled recent ways, and these mercenaries were the wildest of the bunch. Their swords were long, single-edged, and curved, made for vigorous slashing, in contrast with Dor's straight double-edged sword. Here in the somewhat confined region of the dungeon, the advantage lay with the defenders. Omen cut great arcs with his curved blade, keeping the ruffians at bay, and Dor stabbed and cut, severing an Avar's hand before the soldiers learned respect. Dor's sword was not magic now; he had to do it all himself. But he had been taught the rudiments of swordplay, and these now served him well.

Several bats shot out of the tunnel and flew over the heads of the Avars, who mostly ignored them. One bat, as if resentful of this neglect, hovered in the face of the Avar leader, who sliced at it with his sword. The bat gave up and angled out of the chamber.

But swordplay was tiring business, and Dor was not in shape for it. His arm soon felt leaden. Omen, too, was in a poor way, because of his long imprisonment. The Avars, aware of this, pressed in harder; they knew they would soon have the victory.

One charged Dor, blade swinging down irresistibly. Dor tried to step aside and counter, but slipped on blood or oil and lost his footing; the blade sliced into his left hip. Dor fell helplessly headlong. "Omen!" he cried. "Flee into the tunnel! I can no longer guard your back!"

"Xnt zqd gtqs!" Omen exclaimed, whirling.

The Avars, seeing their chance, charged. Omen's blade flashed in another circle, for the moment daunting them, while Dor fought off the pain of his wound and floundered for his lost sword. His questing fingers only encountered something mushy; a spoiled chocolate pie from the dead pie tree.

Two Avars stepped in, one countering King Omen while the other ducked low to slice at Omen's legs. Dor hefted the pie and smashed it into the Avar's face. It was a perfect shot; the man dropped to his knees, pawing at his mud-filled eyes, while the stink of rotten pie filled the chamber.

King Omen, granted this reprieve, dispatched the remaining Avar. But already another was charging, and Dor had no other pie within reach. Omen hurled his sword at the bold enemy, skewering him, then bent to take hold of Dor and haul him back to the tunnel.

"This is crazy!" Dor cried. Despite the peril of their situation, he noticed that Omen, too, had been wounded; a slash on his left shoulder was dripping bright blood, and it was mixing with the gore from Dor's own wound. "Save yourself!"

Then the Avars were closing for the final assault, knowing they faced two unarmed and injured men, taking time to aim their cuts. Even if Omen got them to the tunnel, he would be doomed. He had been a fool to try to save Dor—but Dor found himself rather liking the man.

Suddenly a dragon shot out of the tunnel, wings unfurling as it entered the dungeon chamber. It snorted fire and hovered in the air, raising gleaming talons, seeking prey. The Avars fell back, amazed and terrified. One made a desperate slash at the monster—and the sword passed right through the dragon's wing without resistance or damage.

Illusion, of course! The magic had returned, and now the Queen was fighting in her spectacular fashion. But the moment the Avars realized that the dragon had no substance—

It worked the opposite way. The Avar, discovering that he could not even touch the dragon, screamed and fled the chamber. He was far more afraid of a spiritual menace than of a physical one.

King Omen, too, stared at the dragon. "Where did that come from?" he demanded. "I don't believe in dragons!"

Dor smiled. "It's an illusion," he explained. They were able to converse again, because of the ambience of magic. "Queen Iris is quite an artist in her fashion; she can generate completely credible images, with smell and sound and sometimes touch. No one in all the history of Xanth has ever been able to do it better."

The dragon spun to face them. "Why, thank you, Dor," it said, dissolving into a wash of color that drifted after the departing Avars.

Now Irene appeared, as the Avars scrambled to escape the dragon. "Oh, you're hurt!" she cried. Dor wasn't sure whether she was addressing him or Omen.

"King Omen saved my life," he said.

"You were the only one with sense enough to dam off the oil to save the girl," Omen replied. "Could I do less than help?"

"Thanks," Dor said, finding himself liking this bold young King more than ever. Rival he might be, but he was a good man.

They shook hands. Dor didn't know whether this was a Mundane custom, but King Trent had evidently explained Xanth ways. "Now our blood has mingled; we are blood brothers," Omen said gravely.

Irene and Iris were tearing up lengths of cloth from somewhere, fashioning bandages. Irene got to Omen first, leaving Dor for her mother. "I suspect I underestimated you, Dor," the Queen murmured as she worked efficiently on his wound, cleaning and bandaging it after applying some of the plant healing extract. "But then, I also underestimated your father."

"My father?" Dor asked, bewildered.

"That was a long time ago, before I met Trent," she said. "None of your business now. But he did have mettle in the crunch, and so do you."

Dor appreciated her compliment, but regretted that her modification of attitude had come too late. Irene had focused on King Omen. He tried to stop himself from glancing across to where Irene was working on the Mundane King, but could not help himself.

The Queen caught the glance. "You love her," she said. "You did not before, but you do now. That's nice."

Was she taunting him? "But you endorse King Omen," Dor said, his emotion warring within himself.

"No. Omen is a fine young man, but not right for Irene, nor she for him. I support your suit, Dor; I always did."

"But you said—"

She smiled sadly. "Never in her life did my daughter do what I wished her to. Sometimes subtlety is necessary."

Dor stared at her. He tried to speak, but the thoughts stumbled over themselves before reaching his tongue. Instead, he leaned forward and kissed her on the cheek.

"Let's get you on your feet," the Queen said, helping him up. Dor found that he could stand, though he felt dizzy; the wound was not as critical as it had seemed, and already was magically healing.

King Trent appeared. "You did good work, men. Thanks to your diversion, I was able to get close to the majority of the Avar soldiers. I turned them into bats."

So that was the origin of the bats Dor had seen! One bat had tried to warn the remaining Avars, without success.

"But the Avars are not the only enemies," King Omen said. "We need to weed out the other collaborators, lest assassins remain among us."

"Magic will help there," King Trent said. "Iris and Dor will see to it."

"We will?" Dor asked, surprised.

"Of course," the Queen said. "Can you walk?"

"I don't know," Dor said. His feelings about Irene's mother had just been severely shaken up, and it would take some time for them to settle into a new pattern. He stepped forward experimentally, and she gripped his arm and steadied him. He half wished it were Irene lending him support.

The Avars, however, had discovered that the dragon did not follow beyond the dungeon. They were not yet aware that their backup contingent had been eliminated. Now they charged back into the chamber.

"They're catching on to the illusion," Grundy said. "We'd better get out of here."

True enough. The Avars were stopping just outside the magic aisle and nocking arrows to strings. They had found the way to fight magic.

Smash went back into action. He ripped a boulder out of the foundation and hurled it at the Avars. His strength existed only within the aisle, but the boulder, once hurled, was just as effective beyond it as the arrows were within it. The troops dived out of the way.

The party moved back up the tunnel, Dor limping. Dragons flew ahead and behind, a ferocious honor guard.

In due course they reached the main hall of Castle Ocna. A number of the castle personnel were there, huddled nervously at one end. The Avars had spread out and used other routes, and now were ranged all around the hall. The castle staff were afraid of the Avars, and did not yet know King Omen lived. Thus the castle remained in King Oary's power despite King Omen's release.

"The ogre and I will guard King Omen," King Trent said. "Irene, grow a cherry tree; you and the golem will be in charge of defensive artillery. Magician Centaur, if you please, stand in the center of the hall and turn rapidly in place several times as soon as I give the signal. Iris and Dor, your powers reach farther than mine; you will rout out the lurking Avars."

"You see, I know how my husband's mind works," Queen Iris murmured. "He's a genius at tactics."

"But the Avars are beyond the magic aisle!" Dor protested. "And they know about your illusions. They're pretty smart, in their fashion. We can't fool them much longer."

"We don't need to," Iris said. "All you have to do is have any stones in the magic aisle call out the position of any lurking Avars. The rest of us will take it from there."

"Ready, Irene?" Trent inquired.

Irene's tree had grown rapidly, and now had a number of bright red cherries ripening. "Ready, father," she said grimly.

Dor was glad King Trent was a good tactician, for he, Dor, had only the haziest notion what was developing. When Arnolde turned, it might bring some Avars within the magic aisle, but most would remain outside. How could those others be nullified before they used their bows?

"Now it gets nervy," King Trent said. "Be ready, ogre. King Omen, it's your show."

King Omen mounted a dais in the center of the hall. He was pale from loss of blood, and carried his left arm awkwardly, but still radiated an aura of Kingliness. Irene picked several of the ripe cherries, giving some to Grundy, who stood beside a pile of them. Smash lifted a solid wooden post to his shoulder.

Arnolde, in response to Trent's signal, began turning himself about in place. Dor concentrated, willing the stones in the hall to cry out if any Avars were hiding near them. Queen Iris fashioned an illusion of extraordinary grandeur; the dais became a solid gold pedestal, and King Omen was clothed in splendid royal robes, with a halo of light about his body.

"Hearken to me, minions of Castle Ocna and loyal citizens of the Kingdom of Onesti," the King declaimed, and his voice resonated throughout the chamber. "I am King Omen, your rightful monarch, betrayed and imprisoned by the usurper Oary. Now my friends from the magic Land of Xanth have freed me, and I call upon you to renounce Oary and resume your rightful homage to me."

"Mknn jko!" the Avar leader cried in his own language. "Ujqqv jko fqyp!"

An arrow flew toward King Omen. Smash batted it out of the air with his stake. "Oww!" the arrow complained. Dor's talent was operating too effectively. "I was only doing my duty."

As Arnolde turned, the magic aisle rotated, reaching to the farthest extent of the hall. "Here's an Avar!" a stone cried as the magic engaged it. "He shot that arrow!"

"Shut up, you invisible tattletale!" the Avar snapped, striking at what he assumed was there.

Now a winged dragon launched toward the Avar, belching forth fire. "You, too, you fake monster!" the man cried. He drew his sword and slashed at the dragon.

Irene threw a cherry. It struck the floor at the Avar's feet and exploded. The man was knocked back against the wall, stunned and soaked with red cherry juice.

Arnolde had hesitated, facing the action. Now he resumed his turning. Another stone cried out: "There's one behind me!" The dragon, flying in the moving aisle, sent out another column of flame, rich and red. This time Irene timed her throw to coincide, and the cherry bomb detonated as the dragon's apparent flame struck. That made the dragon seem real, Dor realized.

"All of you—shoot your cttqyu!" the Avar leader called as the magic aisle passed by him. "Vjg oqpuvgtu ctg lwuv knnwukqpu!" But his men hesitated, for two of their number had been stunned by something that was more than illusion. The cherry bombs did indeed detonate outside the ambience of magic; maybe there were, after all, such things in Mundania.

Arnolde continued to turn, and the stones continued to betray the Avars. The lofted cherries commanded respect among the Avars that King Omen did not. The ogre's bat prevented their arrows from scoring, and the Queen's illusions kept them confused. For the flying dragon became a giant armored man with a flashing sword, and the man became a pouncing sphinx, and the sphinx became a swarm of green wasps. Thunder sounded about the dais, the illusion of sound, punctuating King Omen's speech. Soon all the remaining Avars had been cowed or nullified.

"Now the enemy troops are gone," King Omen said, his size increased subtly by illusion. "Loyal citizens of the Kingdom of Onesti need have no fear. Come before me; renew your allegiance." Stars and streamers floated down around him.

Hesitantly, the castle personnel came forward. "They're afraid of the images," Grundy said.

The Queen nodded. Abruptly the monsters vanished, and the hall became a region of pastel lighting and gentle music—at least within the rotating aisle. Heartened, the people stepped up more boldly. "Is it really you, Your Majesty Good Omen?" an old retainer asked. "We thought you dead, and when the monsters came—"

"Hold!" a strident voice called from the archway nearest the castle's main entrance.

All turned. There stood King Oary, just within the aisle. Dor realized the man must have ridden to Castle Ocna by another route, avoiding the path with the bridge out. Oary had figured out where Dor's party was heading, had known it meant trouble, and hastened to deal with the situation before it got out of control. Oary had cunning and courage.

"There is the usurper!" King Omen cried. "Take him captive!"

But Oary was backed by another contingent of Avar mercenaries, brought with him from the other castle. The ordinary servitors could not readily approach him. He stood just at the fringe of the magic aisle, so that his words were translated; he had ascertained its limit. He could step out of it at any moment.

"Fools!" Oary cried, his voice resounding throughout the hall. "You are being deluded by illusion. Throng to me and destroy these alien intruders."

"Alien intruders!" King Omen cried, outraged. The stars exploded around him, and gloriously indignant music swelled in the background. "You, who drugged me and threw me into the dungeon and usurped my throne—you dare call me this?"

The people of the castle hesitated, looking from one King to another, uncertain where their loyalty should lie. Each King was imposing; Oary had taken time to garb himself in full regalia, his royal cloak, crown, and sword rendering his fat body elegant. King Omen was enhanced by Queen Iris' magic to similar splendor. It was obviously hard for the ordinary people to choose between them, on the basis of appearance.

"I call you nothing," Oary roared, with the sincerity of conviction that only a total scoundrel could generate. "You do not even exist. You died at the hands of Khazar assassins. You—"

The stars around Omen became blinding, and now they hissed, sputtered, and roared with the sound of the firmament being torn asunder. The noise drowned out Oary's words.

"Nay, let the villain speak," King Omen said. "It was ever our way to let each person present his case."

"He'll destroy you," Queen Iris warned. "I don't trust him. Don't give him a chance."

"It is Omen's choice," King Trent said gently.

With that, the illusion stopped. Not in the slightest way did Queen Iris ever oppose her will to King Trent's—at least in public. There was only the Mundane court, silent and drab, with its huddled servants facing the knot of Avars.

"You are no more than an illusion," Oary continued boldly, grasping his opportunity. "We have seen how the aliens can fashion monsters and voices from nothing; who doubts they can fashion the likeness of our revered former King?"

Queen Iris looked pained. "Master stroke!" she breathed. "I knew we shouldn't have let that cockatrice talk!"

Indeed, the castle personnel were swayed. They stared at King Omen as if trying to fathom the illusion. The very facility of Queen Iris' illusions now worked against King Omen. Who could tell reality from image?

"If King Omen somehow returned from the dead," King Oary continued, "I would be the first to welcome him home. But woe betide us all if we proffer loyalty to a false image!"

King Omen stood stunned by the very audacity of Oary's ploy. In their contest of words, the usurper had plainly scored a critical point.

"Destroy the impersonator!" Oary cried, seizing the moment. The people started toward King Omen.

Now King Omen found his voice. "How can you destroy an illusion?" he demanded. "If I am but a construct of air, I will laugh at your efforts."

The people paused, confused again. But once more Oary rushed into the gap. "Of course there's a man there! He merely *looks* like King Omen. He's an imposter, sent here to incite you to rebellion against your real King. Then the ogre can rule in my stead."

The people shuddered. They did not want to be ruled by an ogre.

"Imposter?" King Omen exclaimed. "Dor, lend me your sword!" For in the confusion Dor had recovered his sword, while King Omen had lost his.

"That will settle nothing," King Trent said. "The better swordsman is not necessarily the rightful King."

"Oh, yes, he is!" Omen cried. "Only the royalty of Onesti are trained to fine expertise with the sword. No peasant imposter could match Oary. But I am a better swordsman than the usurper, so can prove myself no imposter."

"Not so," Oary protested. "Well I know that is an enchanted sword your henchman has given you. No one can beat that, for it makes any duffer skilled."

The man had learned a lot in a hurry! It had never occurred to Dor that King Oary would be so agile in debate. Evidently his head was not filled with pudding.

Omen glanced at the sword, startled. "Dor did not evince any particular skill with it," he said with unconscious disparagement of Dor's technique.

"It is nevertheless true," King Trent said. "Dor was outside the magic aisle when he used it."

"That's right," Dor agreed reluctantly. "In the aisle, with that sword, anyone could beat anyone. Also, the Queen's illusion could make King Trent look like you, King Omen—and he is probably a better swordsman than you are." Dor wondered just after he said it whether he had made that comparison because he smarted from Omen's disparagement of his own skill. Yet King Trent was the finest swordsman in Xanth, so his point was valid.

"You fools!" Queen Iris expostulated. "Victory in your grasp, and you squander it away on technicalities!"

"It's a matter of honesty," Dor said. "O N E S T I."

King Omen laughed, able to grasp the spelling pun within the centaur's range. "Yes, I understand. Well, I will fight Oary outside the magic aisle."

"Where your wound will weaken you, and you will have the disadvantage of using a straight sword when you are trained to a curved one," Queen Iris said. "If those aren't enough, the imposter's Avars will put an arrow in your back. Don't be even more of a fool than you need to be. Oary's trying to maneuver you into a position where his treachery can prevail. I tell you, I know the type."

Dor was silent. The Queen knew the type because she *was* the type. That made her a good adviser in a situation like this.

"But how can I prove my identity?" King Omen asked somewhat plaintively.

"Let the castle personnel come to you and touch you and talk with you," King Trent suggested. "Surely many of them know you well. They will be able to tell whether you are an imposter."

Oary tried to protest, but the suggestion made too much sense to the castle personnel. King Trent's ability to maneuver had foiled Oary's stratagems. Non-Avar guards appeared, reaching for their weapons, and they were more numerous than the Avars. It seemed that news of this confrontation had spread, and the true Onesti loyalists were converging.

Seeing himself losing position, Oary grudgingly agreed. "I will join the line myself!" he declared. "After all, I should be the first to welcome King Omen back, should he actually return, since it is in his stead I hold the throne of Onesti."

Queen Iris scowled, but King Trent gestured her to silence. It was as if this were a game of moves and counter-moves, with limiting rules. Oary was now going along with King Trent's move, and had to be accommodated until he made an open break. Dor noted the process; at such time as he himself had to be King for keeps, this might guide him.

"Come, King," King Trent said, taking Omen by the arm. "Let us all set aside our weapons and form a receiving line." Gently he took the magic sword and passed it over to Queen Iris, who set it carefully on the floor.

Oary had to divest himself of his own weapon, honoring this new move. His Avars grumbled but stayed back. Smash the Ogre moved nearer them, retaining his post. This encouraged them to keep the peace.

The line formed, the palace personnel coming eagerly forward to verify the person of King Omen. The first was an old man, slow to move but given the lead because of the respect of the others.

"Hello, Borywog!" King Omen said, grasping the man's frail arm. "Remember what a torment I was when a child, and you my tutor? Worse than my father was! You thought you'd never teach me to spell! Remember when I wrote the name of our Kingdom as HONESTY?"

"My Lord, my Lord!" the old man cried, falling to his knees. "Never did I tell that abomination to a soul! It has to be you, Your Majesty!"

The others proceeded through the line. King Omen knew them all. The case was becoming conclusive. King Trent stood behind him, smiling benignly.

Suddenly one of the men in the line drew a dagger and lunged at Omen. But before the treacherous strike scored, the man became a large brown rat, who scurried away, terrified. A palace cat bounded eagerly after it. "I promised to stand bodyguard," King Trent said mildly. "I have had a certain experience in such matters."

Then Oary was at the head of the line. "Why, it *is* Omen!" he exclaimed in seeming amazement. "Avars, sheathe your weapons; our proper King has returned from the dead. What a miracle!"

King Omen, expecting another act of treachery, stood open-mouthed. Again King Trent stepped in. "So nice to have your confirmation, King Oary. We always knew you had the best interests of the Kingdom of Onesti at heart. It is best to resolve these things with the appearance of amicability, if possible. Dor, why don't you conduct King Oary to a more private place and work out the details?"

Now Dor was amazed. He stood unspeaking. Grundy appeared, tapping Dor on the leg. "Take him into an anteroom," the golem whispered. "I'll get the others."

Dor composed himself. "Of course," he said with superficial equilibrium. "King Oary, shall we adjourn to an anteroom for a private discussion?"

"By all means," Oary said, the soul of amicability. He seemed to understand the rules of this game better than Dor did.

They walked sedately to the anteroom, while King Omen continued to greet old friends and the Avars fidgeted in their isolated mass. Without Oary to command them, the Avars were ineffective; they didn't even speak the local language.

Dor's thoughts were spinning. Why had Oary welcomed Omen, after trying to deny him and have him assassinated? Why did he pretend not to know where Omen had been? And why did King Trent, himself a victim of Oary's treachery and cruelty, go along with this? Why, finally, had King Trent turned the matter over to Dor, who was incompetent to understand the situation, let alone deal with it?

Irene, Smash, and Arnolde joined them in the anteroom. Oary seemed unperturbed. "Shall we speak plainly?" the Mundane inquired.

"Sure," Irene retorted, drawing her jacket close about her. "I think you stink!"

"Do you folk comprehend the situation?" Oary asked blithely.

"No," Dor said. "I don't know why King Trent didn't turn you into a worm and step on you."

"King Trent is an experienced monarch," Oary said. "He deals with realities, rather than emotions. He goes for the most profitable combination, rather than simple vengeance. Here is reality: I have one troop of Avars here who could certainly create trouble. I have more at the other castle. It would take a minor civil war to dislodge those mercenaries, whose captains are loyal to me—and that would weaken the Kingdom of Onesti at a time when the Khazar menace is growing. It would be much better to avoid that nuisance and keep the Kingdom strong. Therefore King Omen must seek accommodation with me—for the good of Onesti."

"Why not just—" Irene started, but broke off.

"You are unable to say it," Oary said. "That is the symptom of your weakness, which you will have to eliminate if you hope to make as effective a Queen as your mother. Why not just kill me and be done with it? Because your kind lacks the gumption to do what is necessary."

"Yeah?" Grundy demanded. "Why didn't you kill King Omen, then?"

Oary sighed. "I should have, I suppose. I really should have. But I liked the young fool. No one's perfect."

"But you tried to have him killed just now," Dor said.

"A desperate measure," Oary said. "I can't say I'm really sorry it failed. The move came too late; it should have been done at the outset, so that Omen never had opportunity to give proof of his identity. Then the game would have been mine. But that is the measure of my own inadequacy. I didn't want to retain my crown enough."

Dor's emotions were mixing. He knew Oary to be an unscrupulous rascal, but the man's candor and cleverness and admission of civilized weakness made it hard to dislike him totally. "And now we have to deal with you," Dor said. "But I don't see how we can trust you."

"Of course you can't trust me!" Oary agreed. "Had I the option, I would have you right back in the dungeon, and your horse-man would be touring the Avar empire as a circus freak."

"Now see here!" Arnolde said.

"If we can't kill him, and can't trust him, what can we do with him?" Dor asked the others.

"Throw him in the same cell he threw King Omen," Irene said. "Have a sadistic mute eunuch feed him."

"Smash destroyed those cells," Grundy reminded her. "Anyway, they aren't safe. One of his secret henchmen might let him out."

"But we've got to come up with a solution for King Omen!" Dor said. "I don't know why this was put in my hands, but—"

"Because you will one day be King of Xanth," Oary said. "You must learn to make the hard decisions, right or wrong. Had I had more experience before attaining power, I would have acted to avoid my present predicament. Had Omen had it, he would never have lost his throne. You have to learn by doing. Your King Trent is one competent individual; it was my misfortune to misjudge him, since I thought his talk about magic indicated a deranged mind. Usually only ignorant peasants really believe in sorcery. By the time you are King, you will know how to handle the office."

This made brutal sense. "I wish I *could* trust you," Dor said. "You'd make an excellent practical tutor in the realities of governing."

"This is your practical tutoring," Oary said.

"There are two customary solutions, historically," Arnolde said. "One is mutilation—the criminal is blinded or deprived of his extremities, so he can do no further harm—"

"No!" Dor said, and Irene agreed. "We are not barbarians."

"You are not professional either," Oary said. "Still you balk at expedient methods."

"The other is banishment," the centaur continued. "People of your species without magical talents used to be banished from Xanth, just as people of my species *with* such talents are banished. It is a fairly effective device."

"But he could gather an army and come back," Dor protested. "King Trent did, way back when he was banished—"

"But he did not conquer Xanth. The situation had changed, and he was invited back. Perhaps in twenty years the situation will be changed in Onesti, and Oary will be needed again. At any rate, there are precautions. A selective, restricted banishment should prevent betrayal while keeping him out of local mischief. It would be advisable not to call it banishment, of course. That would suggest there was something untoward about the transfer of power, instead of an amicable return of a temporarily lost King. He could be assigned as envoy or ambassador to some strategic territory—"

"The Khazars!" Grundy cried.

"Hey, I don't want to go there!" Oary protested. "Those are rough people! It would take all my wit just to survive."

"Precisely," the centaur said. "Oary would be something of a circus freak in that society, tolerated but hardly taken seriously. It would be his difficult job to maintain liaison and improve relations with that empire, and of course to advise Onesti when any invasion was contemplated. If he did a good enough job for a long enough period, he might at length be pardoned and allowed to retire in Onesti. If not—"

"But the Khazars are bound to invade Onesti sooner or later," Oary said. "How could I prevent—"

"I seem to remember that at this period the Nordic Magyars were nominally part of the Khazar empire," Arnolde said. "They remained, however, a discrete culture. Oary might be sent to the Magyar court—"

"Where he would probably foment rebellion against the Khazars!" Dor said. "Just to keep the action away from Onesti. It would take constant cunning and vigilance—"

"What a dastardly deed!" Irene exclaimed gleefully.

Surprised, they all exchanged glances. "A dastardly deed . . ." Dor repeated.

"We were cursed to do it," Irene said. "Before the moon got full—and it's very nearly full now. Let's go tell the others how Ambassador Oary is going to the Magyars."

"Purely in the interest of serving the Kingdom I love so well, to promote the interests of my good friend and restored liege, King Omen," Oary said philosophically. "It could have been worse. I thought you'd flay me and turn me loose to beg naked in the village."

"Or feed you to the ogre," Grundy said. "But we're soft-headed, and you're too clever to waste."

They trooped out. "Oary has graciously consented to be your ambassador to the Magyar court of the Khazar empire," Dor told King Omen, who had finally completed the receiving line. "He wants only what is best for the Kingdom of Onesti."

"Excellent," King Omen said. He had evidently been briefed in the interim. "And who will be Xanth's ambassador to Onesti?"

"Arnolde Centaur," King Trent said promptly. "We realize that his enforced absence from his home in Centaur Isle is a personal sacrifice for him, but it is evident we need a certain amount of magic here, and he is uniquely qualified. He can escort specially talented Xanth citizens, such as my daughter, when trade missions occur."

Arnolde nodded, and Dor saw how King Trent was facilitating things for the centaur, too. Arnolde had no future at Centaur Isle anyway; this put a different and far more positive face on it. Naturally Arnolde would not spend all his time here; he would have time to visit his friend Ichabod in the other aspect of Mundania, too. In fact, he would be able to do all the research he craved. There was indeed an art to governance, and King Trent was demonstrating it.

"Ah, your daughter," King Omen said. "You told me about her, during our long days of confinement, but I took it for the fond imaginings of a parent. Now I think it would be proper to seal the alliance of our two Kingdoms by a symbolic personal merger."

Dor's heart sank. King Omen certainly wasn't reticent! He moved boldly to obtain what he wanted—as a King should. Dor doubted that he himself would ever be that type of person. The irony was that he could not oppose King Omen in this; he liked the man and owed him his life, and Irene liked him, too, and was probably thrilled at the notion. The alliance did seem to make sense, politically and personally. If there were benefits to being in line for the Kingship, there were also liabilities; Dor had to give way to what was best. But he hated this.

King Trent turned to Irene. "How do you feel about it? You do understand the significance."

"Oh, I understand," Irene agreed, flushing becomingly. "It makes a lot of sense. And I'm flattered. But there are two or three little points. I'm young—"

"Time takes care of that," King Omen said. It was evident that her youth did not repel him, any more than the youthfulness of the doxy had repelled King Oary. "In fact, women age so quickly, here in Onesti, that it is best to catch them as young as possible, while they remain attractive."

Irene paused, as if tracking down an implication. In Xanth, women remained attractive a long time, with the aid of minor magic. "And I would have trouble adjusting to a life with no magic—" she continued after a moment.

"A Queen does not need magic!" King Omen said persuasively. "She has power. She has authority over the entire kitchen staff."

Irene paused again. "That much," she murmured. It was evident that men dominated the society of Onesti, while in Xanth the sexes were fairly even, except for the rule about who could be King.

Dor thought of living the rest of his life in Mundania, unable to utilize his own magic or participate in the magic of others. The notion appalled him. He doubted Irene could stand it long either.

"And I'm in love with another man," Irene finished.

"But the girl's love has nothing to do with it!" King Omen protested. "This is a matter of state." His eyes traveled along the length of her legs.

King Trent considered. "We conduct such matters differently in Xanth, but of course compromise is essential in international relations. If you really desire my daughter—"

"Father!" Irene said warningly.

"Now don't embarrass your father," Queen Iris said. Irene reacted with a rebellious frown that she quickly concealed. It was the old syndrome; if her mother pushed something, Irene did the opposite. Dor's secret ally had struck again. Bless the Queen!

King Trent's gaze passed across them all, finishing with the Queen, who made the slightest nod. "However," he continued, "I understand that in some societies there is a certain premium on the, shall we say, pristine state—"

"Virginity," Irene said clearly.

"But we never—" Dor started, just before she stomped on his toe."

King Omen had caught the motion. "Ah, I did not realize it was you she loved, blood brother! You came all the way here at great personal risk to help restore my throne; I can not—"

"Yet a liaison would certainly be appropriate," King Trent mused.

"Father!" Irene repeated sharply. Queen Iris smiled somewhat smugly in her daughter's direction. It was strange, Dor reflected, how the very mannerisms that had annoyed him in the past now pleased him. Irene would never go with King Omen now.

"Yet there is that matter of pristinity," King Omen said. "A Queen must be above—"

"Do you by chance have a sister, King Omen?" King Trent inquired. Dor recognized the tone; Trent already knew the answer to his question. "Dor might—"

"What?" Irene screeched.

"No, no sister," Omen said, evidently disgruntled.

"Unfortunate. Perhaps, then, a symbolic gesture," King Trent said. "If

Prince Dor, here, is taking something of value to King Omen, or perhaps has already compromised the value—"

"Yes," Irene said.

"Shame!" Queen Iris said, glaring at Dor with only the tiniest quirk of humor twitching at one lip.

"But—" Dor said, unwilling to confess falsely.

"Then some token of recompense might be in order," King Trent concluded. "We might call it a gift, to preserve appearance—"

"The midnight sunstone!" Dor exclaimed. After all, it was just about midnight now. Without waiting for King Trent to take the matter further, Dor drew it from his pocket. "King Omen, as a sincere token of amity between the Kingdom of Xanth and the Kingdom of Onesti and of my appreciation for the manner you saved my life, allow me to present you with this rarest of gems. Note that it shines in the presence of magic—but turns dull in the absence of magic. Thus you will always know when magic is near." He gave the gem to King Omen, who stepped out of the magic aisle, then back in, fascinated by the manner the gem faded and flashed again.

"Oh, yes," King Omen agreed. "I shall have this set in my crown, the most precious of all my treasures!"

But now Irene was angry. "I will not be bought for a gem!" she exclaimed.

"But—" Dor said helplessly, stepping toward her. Right when he thought things had fallen into place, they were falling out again.

"Stay away from me, you slaver!" she flared, retreating.

"I think I am well off," King Omen murmured, smiling.

Dor did not want to chase her. It was undignified and hardly suited to the occasion. Also, he could not move rapidly; his fresh wound inhibited him. Yet he was in a sense on stage; he could not let her walk out on him now.

Then he remembered the dime. He had a use for it after all! He clutched it out of his pocket and threw it at her moving feet.

Irene came to an abrupt stop, windmilling her arms and almost falling. "What—" she demanded.

Then Dor caught up to her and took her in his arms.

"The dime!" she expostulated. "You made me stop on a dime! That's cheating!"

Dor kissed her—and found an amazingly warm response.

But even amidst the kiss, he realized that Arnolde was facing in another direction. Irene had been outside the magic aisle when she stalled on the dime. "But—" he began, his knees feeling weak.

She bit lightly on his ear. "Did the Gorgon let go of Magician Humfrey?" she asked.

Dor laughed, somewhat nervously. "Never."

"Another dastardly deed performed in the light of the midnight sunstone," Grundy said. And Dor had to hold Irene delightfully tight to prevent her from kicking the golem.

Ogre, Ogre

For Cheryl-
my daughter,
whose tantrums really
aren't that bad.

Contents

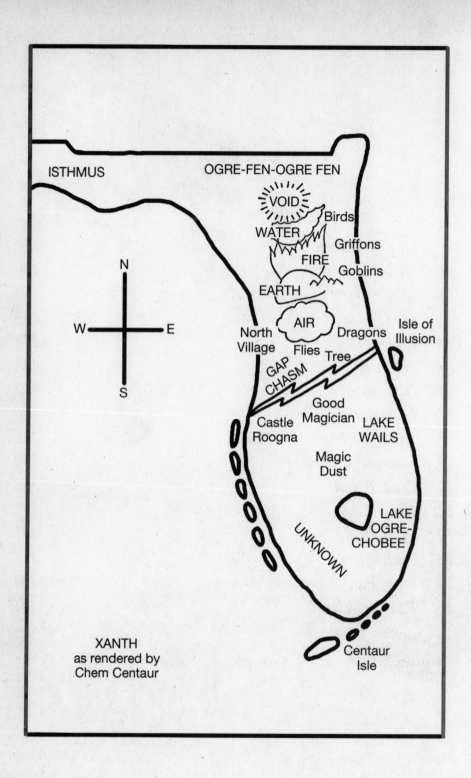

ISTHMUS

OGRE-FEN-OGRE FEN

VOID

WATER

Birds

Griffons

FIRE

Goblins

EARTH

N

AIR

Dragons

Isle of
Illusion

W — E

North
Village

Flies

Tree

S

GAP
CHASM

Good
Magician

LAKE
WAILS

Castle
Roogna

Magic
Dust

LAKE
OGRE-
CHOBEE

UNKNOWN

XANTH
as rendered by
Chem Centaur

Centaur
Isle

Chapter 1

Nightmare

andy tried to sleep, but it was difficult. The demon had never actually entered her private bedroom, but she was afraid that one night he would. This night she was alone; therefore she worried.

Her father Crombie was a rough soldier who had no truck with demons. But he was away most of the time, guarding the King at Castle Roogna. Crombie was fun when he was home, but that was rare. He claimed to hate women, but had married a nymph, and tolerated no interference by other males. Tandy remained a child in his eyes; his hand would have hovered ominously near his sword if he even suspected any demon was bothering her. If only he were here.

Her mother Jewel was on a late mission, planting orange sapphires in a stratum near the surface. It was a long way away, so she rode the Diggleworm, who could tunnel through rock without leaving a hole. They would be back after midnight. That meant several more hours, and Tandy was afraid.

She turned over, wrapped the candy-striped sheet about her in an uncomfortable tangle, and put the pink pillow over her head. It didn't help; she still feared the demon. His name was Fiant, and he could dematerialize at will. That meant he could walk through walls.

The more Tandy thought about that, the less she trusted the walls of her room. She was afraid that any unwatched wall would permit the demon to pass through. She rolled over, sat up, and peered at the walls. No demon.

She had met Fiant only a few weeks ago, by accident. She had been playing with some large, round, blue rubies, rejects from her mother's barrel—rubies were supposed to be red—and one had rolled down a passage near the demons' rum works. She had run right into a rum wrap a demon was using, tearing it so that it became a bum wrap. She had been afraid the demon would be angry, but instead he had simply looked at her with a half-secret half-smile—and that had been worse. Thereafter that demon had shown up with disturbing frequency, always looking at her as if something demoniacally special was on his mind. She was not so naïve as to be in doubt about the nature of his thought. A nymph would have been flattered—but Tandy was human. She sought no demon lover.

Tandy got up and went to the mirror. The magic lantern brightened as she approached, so that she could see herself. She was nineteen years old, but she looked like a child in her nightie and lady-slippers, her brown tresses mussed from constant squirming, her blue eyes peering out worriedly. She wished she looked more like her mother—but of course no human person could match the pretty faces and fantastic figures of nymphs. That was what nymphdom was all about—to attract men like Crombie who judged the distaff to be good for only one thing. Nymphs were good for that thing. Human girls could be good for it, too, but they really had to work at it; they fouled it up by assigning far more meaning to it than the nymphs did, so were unable to proceed with sheer delighted abandon. They were cursed by their awareness of consequence.

She peered more closely at herself, brushing her tresses back with her hands, rearranging her nightie, standing straighter. She was no child, whatever her father might choose to think. Yet she was not exactly buxom, either. Her human heritage had given her a good mind and a soul, at the expense of voluptuousness. She had a cute face, with a pert, upturned nose and full lips, she decided, but not enough of the rest of it. She couldn't make it as a nymph.

The demon Fiant obviously thought she would do, however. Maybe he didn't realize that her human component made her less of a good thing. Maybe he was slumming, looking for an intriguing change of pace from the dusky demonesses who could assume any form they chose, even animal forms. It was said that sometimes they would change to animal form in the middle of the act of—but no human girl was supposed to be able to imagine anything like that. Tandy couldn't change form, in or out of bed, and certainly she didn't want any demon's attention. If only she could convince him of that!

There was nothing to do but try to sleep again. The demon would come or he wouldn't; since she had no control over that, there was no sense worrying.

She lay down amidst the mess her bed had become and worried. She closed her eyes and remained still, as if sleeping, but remained tensely awake. Maybe after a while her body would be fooled into relaxing.

There was a flicker at the far wall. Tandy spied it through almost-closed eyes and kept her small body frozen. It was the demon; he really had come.

In a moment Fiant solidified inside the room. He was large, muscular, and fat, with squat horns sprouting from his forehead and a short, unkempt beard that made him look like a goat. His hind feet were hooflike, and he had a medium-length tail at his posterior, barbed at the tip. There was a dusky ambience about him that would have betrayed his demonic nature, no matter what form he took. His eyes were like smoky quartz shielding an internal lava flow, emitting a dull red light that brightened when his attention warmed to something. By diabolic standards, he was handsome enough, and many a nymph would have been deliciously happy to be in Tandy's place.

Tandy hoped Fiant would go away, after perceiving her asleep and disordered, but knew he wouldn't. He found her attractive, or at least available, and refused to be repulsed by her negative response. Demons expected rejections; they thrived on them. It was said that, given a choice between rape and seduction, they would always choose the rape. The females, too. Of course, it was impossible to rape that kind; she would simply dematerialize if she didn't like it. Which might be another explanation for Fiant's interest in Tandy; *she* couldn't dematerialize. Rape was possible.

Maybe if she were positive, welcoming him, that would turn him off. He was obviously tired of willing females. But Tandy couldn't bring herself to try that particular ploy. If it didn't work, where would she be?

Fiant approached the bed, grinning evilly. Tandy kept her eyes screwed almost shut. What would she do if he touched her? She was sure that screaming and fighting would only encourage him and make his eyes glow with preternatural lust—but what else was there?

Fiant paused, looming over her, his paunch protruding, the light from his eyes spearing down through slits. "Ah, you lovely little morsel," he murmured, a wisp of smoke curling from his mouth as he spoke. "Be thrilled, you soft, human flesh. Your demon lover is here at last! Let me see more of you." And he snatched the sheet away.

Tandy hurled the pillow at him and bounced off the bed, her terror converting to anger. "Get out of here, foul spirit!" she screamed.

"Ah, the tender morsel wakes, cries welcome! Delightful!" The demon strode toward her, the blue tip of his forked tongue rasping over his thin lips. His tail flicked similarly.

Tandy backed away, her terror/anger intensifying. "I loathe you! Go away!"

"Presently," Fiant said, his tail stiffening as it elevated. "Hone your passion to its height, honey, for I will possess its depth." He reached for her, his horns brightening in the reflected glare of his eyes.

Desperate, Tandy wreaked her ultimate. She threw a tantrum. Her body stiffened, her face turned red, her eyes clenched shut, and she hurled that tantrum right at the demon's fat chest.

It struck with explosive impact. The demon sundered into fragments, his feet, hands, and head flying outward. His tail landed on the bed and lay twitching like a beheaded snake.

Tandy chewed her trembling lip. She really hadn't wanted to do that; her tantrums were devastating, and she wasn't supposed to throw them. Now she had destroyed the demon, and there would be hell to pay. How could she answer to hell for murder?

The pieces of the demon dissolved into smoke. The cloud coalesced—and Fiant formed again, intact. He looked dazed. "Oh, that kiss was a beauty," he said, and staggered through the wall.

Tandy relaxed. Fiant wasn't dead after all, but he was gone. She had the best of both situations. Or did she? He surely would not stay gone—and now they both knew her tantrums would not stop him. She had only postponed her problem.

Nevertheless, now she was able to sleep. She knew there would be no more trouble this night, and her mother would be home the next few nights. Fiant, for all his boldness when he had his victim isolated, stayed clear when a responsible person was in the neighborhood.

Next day Tandy tried to talk to her mother, though she was pretty sure it wouldn't help. "Mother, you know that demon Fiant, who works at the rum refinery? He—"

"Oh, yes, the demons are such nice people," Jewel said, smelling of mildly toasted sulfur. That was her magic: her odor reflected her mood. "Especially Beauregard, doing his research paper—"

"Which he has been working on since before I was born. He's a nice demon, yes. But Fiant is another kind. He—"

"They never make any trouble for me when I have to set gems in their caves. The demons are such good neighbors." The sulfur was getting stronger, beginning to crinkle the nose; Jewel didn't like to hear criticisms.

"Most are, Mother." Naturally the demons didn't bother Jewel; without her, there would be no gems to find, and the demons were partial to such trinkets. "But this one's different. He—"

"Everyone's different, of course, dear. That's what makes Xanth so interesting." Now she smelled of freshly blooming orange roses.

"Maybe different isn't quite what I mean. He comes to my room at night—"

"Oh, he wouldn't do that! That wouldn't be right." The wrongness of such a thing showed in the smell of an overripe medicine ball; even immature medicine balls smelled unpleasantly of illness, and aging intensified the effect.

"But he *did!* Last night—"

"You must have dreamed it, dear," Jewel said firmly. And the aroma of carrion of a moderately sated dragon showed how distasteful any such notion was to Jewel. "Sometimes those nightmares carry irresponsible dreams."

Tandy saw that her mother did not want to become aware of the truth. Jewel had been a nymph and retained many of her nymphal qualities despite the burden of experience that marriage and motherhood had imposed on her. She had no real understanding of evil. To her, all people and all creatures were basically good neighbors, including demons. And in truth, the demons had been tolerably well behaved, until Fiant had taken his interest in Tandy.

Her father Crombie would understand, though. Crombie was not only human, he was a man of war. Well did he understand the ways of males. But he hardly ever had time off, and she had no way to advise him of her situation, so he couldn't help now.

As she thought of her father, Tandy abruptly realized that Jewel could not afford to lose her faith in people, because then she would have to question Crombie's fidelity. That could only disrupt her life. Evidently Jewel's thoughts were to some extent parallel to Tandy's because now there was the disturbing odor of a burning field of wild oats.

So Tandy couldn't actually talk to her mother about this. It would have to be her father, in private. That meant she had to get to him, since he would not be home in time to deal with the demon. It was said that no man could stand against a demon in combat, but Crombie was more than a man: he was her father. She had to reach him.

That was a problem in itself. Tandy had never been to Castle Roogna. She had never even been to the surface of Xanth. She would be lost in an instant if she ever left the caves. In fact, she was afraid to try. How could she travel all the way to her father's place of employment, alone? She had no good answer.

The demon did not come the following night. The nightmares visited instead. Every time she slept, they trotted in, rearing over her bed, hooves flashing, ears flat back, snorting the scary vapors that were the bad dreams they bore. She woke in justified terror, and they were gone—only to return as she slept again. That was the way of such beasts.

Finally she became so desperate she threw a tantrum at one of them. The tantrum struck it on the flank. The mare squealed with startled pain, her hindsection collapsing, and her companions fled.

Tandy was instantly sorry, as she generally was after throwing a tantrum; she knew the dark horse was only doing its duty and should not be punished. Tandy woke completely, tears in her eyes, determined to help the animal—

but of course it was gone. It was almost impossible to catch a nightmare while awake.

She checked where the mare had stood. The floor was scuffled there, and there were a few drops of blood. Tandy hoped the mare had made it safely home; it would be several nights before this one was fit for dream-duty again. It was a terrible thing to lash out at an innocent creature like that, no matter how bothersome it might be, and Tandy resolved not to do that again.

Next time she slept, she watched for the nightmares, trying to identify the one she had hurt. But they were a long time in coming, as if they were now afraid of her, and she could hardly blame them for that. But at last they came, for they were compelled to do their job even when it was dangerous to them. Timidly they approached with their burdens of dreams, and these now related to the harming of equines. They were making her pay for her crime! But she never saw the hurt one, and that made her feel increasingly guilty. She was sure that particular nightmare was forever wary of her, and would not come again. Maybe it was lying in a stall wherever such creatures went by day, suffering. If only she had held her temper!

It was the job of nightmares to carry the unpleasant dreams that sleepers were scheduled to have, just as it was Jewel's job to place the gems people were destined to find. Since the dreams were ugly, they could not be trusted to voluntary participation. Thus nightmares had a bad reputation, in contrast with the invisible daymares who brought in pleasant daydreams. People tried to avoid nightmares, and this made the horses' job more difficult. Tandy wasn't sure what would happen if the bad dreams did not get delivered, but was sure there would be trouble. It was generally best not to interfere with the natural order. She wondered idly what dreams the nightmares themselves had when they slept.

A few days later, when Tandy was settling down, the demon Fiant came again. He walked right through the wall, a lascivious grin on his face. "Open up, cutie; I'm here to fulfill your fondest fancies and delve into your deepest desires." His tail was standing straight up, quivering.

For a moment Tandy froze, unable even to speak. She had been bothered by this creature before; now she was terrified. Staring-eyed, she watched his confident approach.

Fiant stood over her, as before, his eyes glowing like red stars. "Lie back, spread out, make yourself comfy," he gloated. "I shall exercise your extreme expectations." He reached for her with a long-nailed diabolic hand.

Tandy screamed.

This night, Jewel was home; she rushed in to discover what was the matter. But the demon marched calmly out through the wall before Jewel arrived, and Tandy had to blame her scream on the nightmares. That provided her with a fresh burden of guilt, for of course the mares were innocent.

Tandy knew she had to do something. Fiant was getting bolder, and soon he would catch her alone—and that would be worse than any nightmare. He had proved he could survive one of her tantrums, so Tandy had no protection. She would have to go to her father Crombie—soon. But *how?*

Then she had an inspiration. Why not catch a nightmare and ride her to Castle Roogna? The creature would surely know the way, as the mares had the addresses of all people who slept.

But there were problems. Tandy had no experience riding horses; she had sometimes ridden the Diggle behind her mother, traveling to the far reaches of Xanth to place emeralds and opals and diamonds, but this was different. The Diggle moved slowly and evenly, phasing through the rock as long as someone made a tune it liked. The nightmares, she was sure, moved swiftly and unevenly. How could she catch one—and how could she hold on?

Tandy was an agile girl. She had climbed all over the caverns, swinging across chasms on rope-vines, squeezing through tiny crevices—good thing she was small!—swimming the chill river channels, running fleetly across sloping rockslides, throwing chunks at the occasional goblins who pursued her. If a nightmare got close enough, she was confident she could leap onto its back and hang on to its flowing mane. It would not be a comfortable ride, but she could manage. So all she really had to worry about was the first step—catching her mare.

The problem was, the nightmares came only during a person's sleep. She might pretend sleep, but she doubted she would fool them—and if she grabbed one while awake, it would surely dissipate like demon-smoke, leaving her with nothing but a fading memory. Nightmares were, after all, a type of demon; they could dematerialize in much the way Fiant did. That was how they passed through walls to reach the most secure sleepers. In fact, she suspected they became material only in the presence of a sleeper.

She would have to ride the nightmare in her sleep. Only that would keep it material, or enable her to dematerialize with it.

Tandy set about her task with determination. It was not that she relished the prospect of such a ride, but that she knew what would happen to her at the hands—or whatever—of the demon if she did not ride. She set up a bolster on two chairs and practiced on it, pretending it was the back of a horse. She lay on her bed, then abruptly bounced off it and leaped astride the bolster, grabbing a tassle where the mane should be and squeezing with her legs. Over and over she did this, drilling the procedure into herself until it became fast and automatic. She got tired and her legs got sore, but she kept on, until she could do it in her sleep—she hoped.

This took several days. She practiced mostly when her mother was out setting jewels, so that there would be no awkward questions. The demon did not bother her by day, fortunately, so she was able to snatch some sleep then, too.

When she was satisfied, and also when she dared delay no longer, because of Fiant's boldness and her mother's upcoming overnight journey to set diamonds in a big kimberlite pipe—a complex job—she acted.

She wrote a note to her mother, explaining that she had gone to visit her father and not to worry. Nymphs tended not to worry much anyway, so it should be all right. She gathered some sleeping pills from the recesses where they slept, put them in her pockets, and lay down. One pill was normally good for several hours before it woke, and she had several; they should keep her in their joint sleep all night.

But as the power of the pills took their magic effect on her body, drawing her into their slumber, Tandy had an alarming thought: suppose no nightmares came tonight? Suppose Fiant came instead—and she was locked in slumber, unable to resist him? That thought disturbed her so much that the first nightmare rushed to attend to her the moment she slept.

Tandy saw the creature clearly in her dream: a midnight-colored equine with faintly glowing eyes—there was the demon stigma!—set amidst a flaring forelock. The mane was glossy black, and the tail dark ebony; even the hooves were dusky. Yet she was a handsome animal, with fine features and good musculature. The black ears perked forward, the black nostrils flared, and the dark neck arched splendidly. Tandy knew this was an excellent representative of the species.

"I'm alseep," she reminded herself. "This is a dream." Indeed it was. A bad dream, full of deep undertow currents and grotesque surgings and fear and shame and horror, making her miserable. But she fought it back, nerved herself, and leaped for the dark horse.

She made it. Her tedious rehearsals had served her well. She landed on the nightmare's back, clutched the sleek mane, and clasped its powerful body with her legs.

For an instant the mare stood still, too surprised to move. Tandy knew that feeling. Then the creature took off. She galloped through the wall as if it were nothing—and indeed it felt like nothing, for they had dematerialized. The power of the nightmare extended to her rider, just as the sleeping power of the pills extended to their wearer. Tandy remained asleep, in the dream-state, fastened to her steed.

The ride was a terror. Walls shot by like shadows, and open spaces like daylight, as the mare galloped headlong and tailshort. Tandy hung on to the mane, though the strands of it cut cruelly into her hands, because she was afraid to let go. How hard would she fall, where would she be, if she lost purchase now? This was a worse dream than any before—and the sleeping pills prevented her from waking.

They were already far away from her mother's neat apartment. They cruised through rock and caverns, water and fire, and the lairs of large and small monsters. They galloped across the table where six demons were playing poker, and the demons paused a moment as if experiencing some chill doubt without quite seeing the nightmare. They zoomed by a secret conclave of goblins planning foul play, and these, too, hesitated momentarily as the ambience of bad visions touched them. The nightmare plowed through the deepest recess, where the Brain Coral stored the living artifacts of Xanth, and the artifacts stirred restlessly, too, not knowing what moved them.

Tandy realized that when a nightmare passed a waking creature, she caused a brief bad thought. Only in sleep did those thoughts have full potency.

Now Tandy had another problem. She had to guide this steed—and she didn't know how. If she had known how, she still wouldn't have known the way to Castle Roogna. Why hadn't she thought of this before?

Well, this was a dream, and it didn't have to make sense. "Take me to Castle Roogna!" she cried. "Then I'll let you go!"

The nightmare neighed and changed course. Was that all there was to it? It occurred to Tandy that the steed was as frightened as Tandy herself was. Such horses weren't meant for riding! So maybe the mare would cooperate, just to be rid of her rider.

They burst out of the caverns and onto the upper surface of Xanth. Tandy was used to strange things in dreams, but was nevertheless awed. Her eyes were open—at least they seemed to be, though this could be merely part of the dream—and she saw the vastness of the surface night. There were spreading trees and huge empty spaces and rivers without cave-canyons, and above was a monstrous ceiling full of pinpoints of light in great patches. She realized that these were stars, which her father had told her about—and she had thought he was making it up, just as he made up tales of the heroic deeds of the men of legendary Xanth's past—and that where there were none was because of clouds. Clouds were like the vapor surrounding water-falls, loosed to ascend to the heavens. Turn a cloud loose, and naturally it did whatever it wanted.

Then from behind a cloud came a much larger light, surely the fabled sun, the golden ball that tracked across the sky, always in one direction. No, not the sun, for that chose to travel, for reasons of its own, only during the day. Jewel had told her that, though Tandy wasn't sure Jewel herself had ever seen the sun. When Tandy had asked her father whether it was true, Crombie had just laughed, which she took to be affirmation of the orb's diurnal disposition. Of course things didn't need sensible reasons for what they did. Maybe the sun was merely afraid of the dark, so stayed clear of night.

No, this must be the moon, which was an object of similar size but dimmer because it was made of green cheese that didn't glow so well. Evidently, high-flying dragons had eaten most of it, for only a crescent remained, the merest rind. Still, it was impressive.

The mare pounded on. Tandy's hands grew numb, but her hold was firm. Her body was bruised and chafed by the bouncing; she would be sore for days! But at least she was getting there. Her bad dream slipped into oblivion for a while, as dreams tended to, fading in and out as the run continued.

Abruptly she woke. A dark castle loomed in the fading moonlight. They had arrived!

Barely in time, too, for now dawn was looming behind them. The night-mare could not enter the light of day. In fact, the mare was already fading out, for regardless of dawn, it was no longer bound when Tandy left the dream-state. The sleeping pills must have finished their nap, and Tandy had finished hers with them. No—the stones were mostly gone; they must have bounced out one at a time in the course of the rough ride, and now only one was left, not enough to do the job.

In a moment the mare vanished entirely, freed by circumstance, and Tandy found herself sprawled on the ground, battered and wide-eyed.

She was stiff and sore and tired. It had not been a restful sleep at all. Her legs felt swollen and numb from thigh to ankle. Her hair was plastered to her scalp with the cold sweat of nocturnal fear. It had been a horrendous ordeal. But at least she was in sight of her destination.

She got painfully to her feet and staggered toward the edifice as the blinding sun hefted itself ambitiously above the trees. The Land of Xanth brightened about her, and the creatures of day began to stir. Dew sparkled. It was all strangely pretty.

But as she came to the moat and saw that there was the stirring of some awful creature within it, orienting on her, she had a horrible revelation. She knew what Castle Roogna looked like, from descriptions her father had made. He had told her wonderful stories about it, from the time she was a baby onward, about the orchard with its cherry-bomb trees, bearing cherries a person dared not eat, and shoes of all types growing on shoe trees, and all manner of other wonders too exaggerated to be believed. Only an idiot or a hopeless visionary would believe in the Land of Xanth, anyway! Yet she almost knew the individual monsters of the moat by name, and the same for the guardian zombies who rested in the graveyard, awaiting the day when Xanth needed defense. She knew the spires and turrets and all, and the ghosts who dwelt within them. She had a marvelously detailed mental map of Castle Roogna—and this present castle did not conform.

This was the wrong castle.

Oh, woe! Tandy stood in dull, defeated amazement. All her effort, her last vestige of strength and hope, and her deviously laid plans to reach her father lay in ruins. What was she to do now? She was lost in Xanth, without food or water, so tired she could hardly move, with no way to return home. What would her mother think?

Something stirred within the castle. The drawbridge lowered, coming to rest across the small moat. A lovely woman walked out of the castle, subduing the reaching monster with a trifling gesture of her hand, her voluminous robe blowing in the morning breeze. She saw Tandy and came toward her—and Tandy saw with a new shock of horror that the woman had no face. Her hood contained a writhing mass of snakes, and emptiness where human features should have been. Surely the nightmare had saved the worst dream for last!

"Dear child," the faceless woman said. "Come with me. We have been expecting you."

Tandy stood frozen, unable even to muster the energy for a tantrum. What horrors lay within this dread castle?

"It is all right," the snake-headed woman said reassuringly. "We consider

s of their fine leather suffusing the pie, which
riffin. This was an ideal meal for an ogre.
othering to employ any stealth. The griffin
gs, issuing a warning squawk. Nobody in his
feeding griffin, except a sufficiently large and

ight mind. No ogre ever was. There was simply
right. "Me give he three, leave sight of me," he
inane rhyme and lacked facility with pronouns,
le roots. But ogres generally made themselves
sh fashion.
prior experience with an ogre. That was its for-
ogres in these parts. The griffin opened its eagle
warning challenge.
called. That was unfortunate, because no ogre was
th dimwitted joy, he rose to the prospect of may-
unting off on his smallest hamfinger. The griffin

earch, he found another finger.
enough of this. It gave a raucous battle cry and
t as well, for Smash had lost count. This sort of
s horrendously difficult for his kind; his head hurt
mb. But now he was released from the necessity of
three, and that was a great relief.
fin by its bird beak and lion's tail, whirled it around,
r the forest in a cloud of small feathers and fur. The
reception, spread its wings, oriented, circled, decided
een a fluke, and started to come in for another engage-
have a monopoly on stupidity!
lion-bodied bird. "Scram, ham!" he bellowed.
bellow tore out half a dozen pinfeathers and two flight
the griffin spinning out of control. The creature righted
s time decided to seek its fortune elsewhere. Thus did it
sag halfway smart, yielding the stupidity title to the ogre.
tcying leap into the center of the shoefly pie. Leatherlike
p. The ogre grabbed a big handful of the delicious mess and
in maw. He slurped noisily on a boot, chewed the tongue in
mated on a pleasantly tough heel. Oh, it was good! He grabbed
e hals, crunching soles and sucking on laces and spitting the
elets like seeds. Soon all the pie was gone. He burped up a few
ils, satisfied.
gorge, he went to a stream and slurped a few gallons of shivering
er. he lifted his head, he heard a faint call. "Help! Help!"
look about, his ears rotating like those of the animal he was, to
the ound. It came from a nearby brambleberry bush. He parted

that your phenomenal effort in catching and riding the nightmare consti-
tutes sufficient challenge to reach this castle. You will not be subject to the
usual riddles of admission."

They were going to take her inside! Tandy tried to run, but her strength
was gone. She was a spunky girl, but she had been through too much this
night. She fainted.

Chapter 2

Smash Ogre

Smash tromped through the blackboard jungle of Xanth, looking at the pictures on the blackboards because, like all his kind, he couldn't read the words. He was in a hurry because the foul weather he was enjoying showed signs of abating, and he wanted to get where he was going before it did. When he encountered a fallen beech tree across the path, he simply hurled it out of the way, letting the beech-sand fall in a minor sandstorm. When he discovered that an errant river had jumped its channel and was washing out the path and threatening to clean the grunge off his feet and make his toenails visible for the first time in weeks, he grabbed that stream by its tail and flexed it so hard that it splatted right back into its proper channel and lay there quivering and bubbling in fear. When an ornery bullhorn blocked the way, threatening to ram its horn most awkwardly into the posterior of anyone who distracted it, Smash did more than wardly into the posterior of anyone who distracted it, Smash did more than

that. He picked
turned the crea
travelers on that

This sort of th
and stupid of all ?
nervously when he
prudent to catch err
fled with indecent h
any wit at all wanted

He was twice the he
his knots of hairy musc
Some creatures might
imaginative individuals.
stretch of imagination cou
Smash was an appalling sp
revolting creature on this

Yet Smash, like most po
rior, hidden deep inside wh
raised among human beings,
Princess Irene, and had made
somewhat civilized by his envi
people believed that no ogre wa
belief to hold.

Yet Smash was no ordinary ogr
without some faint reason and tha
somewhat stifled. This was a sad cc
moderately well. Now he had a mi

The bad weather cleared. The
lovely shafts of sunlight slant down,
shook out their feathers and trilled j
and pleasant.

Smash snorted with disgust. How co
to camp for the afternoon and night and

He was hungry, for it took huge an
sustain an ogre in proper arrogance. He ca
massive enough to sustain him, such as a
applesauce or a mossy rock-candy boulder,
had already been scavenged out.

Then he heard the squawk of a contented
of delicious pie. The perceptions of ogres w
oddly; though the griffin was some distance aw
by sound and odor. He tromped toward it. Th
had cleaned out all the edibles of this region.

The griffin had captured a monstrous shoefly

been cooked juice
massed abou the
Smash not b
whirled, ha s wir
right mind h a
hungry drag
But Sma his
not enough be
said. All og in
which the edi
plain enou rut
The gri ad
tune. The w
beak wide d
Smash's n
smart eno W
hem. "On
didn't mo
"Two."
The gr
charged,
intellectu
and his f
counting
He gra
and hurle
griffin, st
the even
ment. Og
Smash
The b
feathers,
itself aga
finally d
Smash
pastry cr
stuffed i
half, and
two mo
metal ev
metal n
After
cool wa
Smash
orient

the foliage with one gross finger and peered in. There was a tiny manlike creature. "Help, please!" it cried.

Ogres had excellent eyesight, but this person was so small that Smash had to focus carefully to see him. Her. It was naked and had—well, it was a tiny female imp. "Who you?" he inquired politely, his breath almost knocking her down.

"I'm Quieta the Imp," she cried, rearranging her hair, which his breath had violently disarrayed. "Oh, ogre, ogre—my father's trapped and will surely perish if not rescued soon. Please, I beseech you most prettily, help him escape, and I will reward you in my fashion."

Smash did not care one way or another about imps; they were too small to eat; anyway, he was for the moment full. This one was hardly more massive than one of his fingers. He did, however, like rewards. "Okay, dokay," he agreed.

"My name's Quieta, not Dokay," she said primly. She led him to a spot under a soapstone boulder. It was, of course, a very clean place, and the soap had been carved into interesting formations. There was her father-imp, caught in an alligator clamp. The alligator's jaws were slowly chewing off his little leg.

"This is my father Ortant," Quieta said, introducing them. "This is big ugly ogre."

"Pleased to meet you, Bigugly Ogre," Imp Ortant said as politely as the pain in his leg permitted.

Smash reached down, but his hamfingers were far too big and clumsy to pry open the tiny clamp. "Queer ear," he told the imps, and obediently both covered their minuscule ears with miniature hands.

Smash let out a small roar. The alligator clamp yiped and let go, scrambling back to the farthest reach of its anchor-chain, where it cowered. The imp was free.

"Oh, thank you, thank you so much, ogre!" Quieta exclaimed. "Here is your reward." She held out a tiny disk.

Smash accepted it, balancing it on the tip of one finger, his gross brow furrowing like a newly plowed field.

"It's a disposable reflector," Quieta explained proudly. Then, seeing that he did not comprehend: "A mirror, made from a film of soap-bubble. That's what we imps do. We make pretty, iridescent bubbles for the fairies, and lenses for sunbeams, and sparkles for the morning dew. Each item works only once, so we are constantly busy, I can tell you. We call it planned obsolescence. So now you have a nice little mirror. But remember—you can use it only one time."

Smash tucked the mirror into his bag, vaguely disappointed. Somehow, for no good reason, he had expected more.

"Well, you saved my father only once," Quieta said defensively. "He's not very big, either. It's a perfect mirror, you know."

Smash nodded, realizing that small creatures gave small rewards. He wasn't quite sure what use the mirror would be to him, since ogres did not look at their own ugly faces very much, because their reflections tended to break mirrors and curdle the surfaces of calm lakes; in any event, this mirror was far too small and frail to sustain his image. Since it could be used only once, he would save it for an important occasion. Then he tromped to a pillow bush, pounded it almost flat and lumpy, and snored himself to sleep while the jungle trembled.

The weather was unconscionably fair the next day, but Smash tromped on regardless until he reached the castle of the Good Magician Humfrey. It was not particularly imposing. There was a small moat he could wade through, and an outer wall he could bash through—practically an open invitation.

But Smash had learned at Castle Roogna that it was best to be polite around Magicians, and not to bash too carelessly into someone's castle. So he opened his bag of belongings and donned his finest apparel: an orange jacket and steely gauntlets, given to him four years ago by the centaurs of Centaur Isle. The jacket was invulnerable to penetration by a weapon, and the gauntlets protected his hamfists from the consequence of their own power. He had not worn these things before because he didn't want them to get dirty. They were special.

Now, properly dressed, he cupped his mug and bellowed politely: "Some creep asleep?" Just in case the Good Magician wasn't up yet.

There was no response. Smash tried again. "Me Smash. Me bash." That was letting the Magician know, delicately, that he was coming in.

Still no answer. It seemed Humfrey was not paying attention. Having exhausted his knowledge of the requirements of human etiquette as he understood them, Smash proceeded to act. He waded into the water of the moat with a great and satisfying splash. Washing was un-ogrish, but splashing wasn't. In a moment the spume dimmed the sunlight and caused the entire castle to shine with moisture.

A sea monster swam to intercept him. Mostly that kind did not frequent rivers or moats, but the Good Magician had an affinity for the unusual. "Hi, fly," Smash said affably, removing a gauntlet and raising a hairy hamfist in greeting. He generally got along all right with monsters, if they were ugly enough.

The monster stared cross-eyed for a moment at the huge fist under its snout, noting the calluses, scars, and barnaclelike encrustations of gristle. Then the creature turned tail and swam hastily away. Smash's greetings sometimes affected other creatures like that; he wasn't sure why.

He redonned the gauntlet and forged on out of the moat, reaching a brief embankment from which the wall rose. He lifted one gauntleted hamfist to bash a convenient hole—and spied something on the stone. It was a small lizard, dingy blah in color, with medium sandpaper skin, inefficient legs, a truncated tail, and a pungent smell. Its mean little head swiveled around to fix on the ogre.

Smash's gauntleted hand snapped out, covering the lizard, blocking its head off from view. Ogres were stupid but not suicidal. This little monster was no ordinary lizard; it was a basilisk! Its direct glance was fatal, even to an ogre.

What was he to do? Soon the creature's poisonous body would corrode the metal of the gauntlet, and Smash would be in trouble. He couldn't remain this way!

He remembered that Prince Dor had had a problem with a basilisk that was a cockatrice. Dor had sent news of a baleful henatrice, and the cocklizard had hurried off at a swift crawl to find her. But Smash had no such resource; he didn't know where a hen might be, and realized that this one might even *be* a henatrice. It was hard to look closely enough to ascertain the sexual status of such a creature without getting one's eyeballs stoned. And if he had happened to know where a basilisk of the opposite sex might be, how could he tell that news to this one? He didn't speak the language. For that he needed the assistance of his friend Grundy the Golem, who could speak any language at all.

Then he remembered the imp's disposable reflector. He fished in his bag with his left mitt and, after several clumsy tries, brought it out. He stuck it to the tip of his gauntleted finger and poked it toward the region where the basilisk's head should be.

Carefully he withdrew his right hand, averting his gaze. This was delicate work! If he aimed the mirror wrong, or if it fell off his finger, or if the basilisk didn't look—

There was a plop on the ground at his feet. Oh, no! The mirror had fallen! Dismayed, he looked.

The basilisk lay stunned. It had seen its own reflection in the mirror and suffered the natural consequence. It would recover after a while—but by then Smash would be out of its range.

The mirror had not dropped. It had shattered under the impact of the basilisk's glare. But it had done its job. Quieta's little reward had proved worthwhile.

Smash scooped out a handful of dirt and dumped it over the body of the basilisk so that he would not accidentally look at it. As long as that mound was intact, he would know he was safe.

Now he hefted his right fist and smashed it into the stone wall. Sand fragments flew outward from the impact with satisfying force. This was sheer joy; only when exercising the prerogative of his name did Smash feel truly happy. Smash! Smash! Smash! Dust filled the air, and a pile of rubble formed about him as the hole deepened.

Soon he was inside the castle. There was a second wall, an arm's reach inside the first. Oh, goody! This one was a lattice of bars, not nearly as substantial as the first, but much better than nothing.

For variety, Smash used his left fist this time. After all, it needed fun and exercise, too. He smashed it into the bars.

The fist stopped short. Oooh, ouch! Only the gauntlet preserved it from injury, but it still smarted. This was much tougher stuff than stone or metal!

Smash took hold of the bars with both hands and heaved. His power should have launched the entire wall toward the clouds, but there was nary a budge. This was the strongest stuff he had encountered!

Smash paused to consider. What material could resist the might of an ogre?

Thinking was hard for his kind. His skull heated up uncomfortably, causing the resident fleas to jump off with hot feet. But in due course he concluded that there was only one thing as tough as an ogre, and that was another ogre. He peered at the bars. Sure enough—these were ogres' bones, lashed together with ogres' sinews. No wonder he had found them impervious!

This was a formidable barrier. He could not bash blithely through it—nor would he wish to, for the bones of ogres were sacred to ogres. Little else was.

Smash pondered some more. His brain was already sweating from the prior effort; now there was a scorched smell as the fur of his head grew hot. Ogres were creatures of action, not cerebration! But again his valiant and painful effort was rewarded; he rammed through a notion.

"Oh, ogres' bones," he said. "Me know zones of deep, deep ground where can't be found."

The wall of bones quivered. All bad ogres craved indecent burial after death; it was one of their occasional links with the species of man. The best interment was in a garbage dump or toxic landfill for the disposal of poisonous plants and animals, but ordinary ground would do if properly cursed and tromped down sufficiently hard.

"Me pound in mound with round of sound," Smash continued, arguing his case with extraordinary eloquence.

That did it. The wall collapsed into an expectant pile. Smash picked up a bone, set it endwise against the ground, and, with a single blow of his gauntleted fist, drove it so deep in the earth that it disappeared. He took another and did the same. "Me flail he nail," he grunted, invoking an ogrish ritual of disposal. He was nailing the ground.

Soon all the bones were gone. "Me fling he string," he said, poking the tendons down after the bones with his finger and scooping dirt over the holes. Then he stomped the mound, his big flat feet making the entire region reverberate boomingly. Stray stones fell from the walls of the castle, and the monster of the moat fled to the deepest muck.

At last it was time for the concluding benediction. "Bone dark as ink, me think he stink!" he roared, and there was a final swirl of dust and grit. The site had been cursed, and the burial was done.

But now a new hazard manifested. This was a kind of linear fountain, the orange liquid shooting up high and falling back to flow into a channel like a small moat. It was rather pretty—but when Smash started to push through it, he drew back his hand with a grunt. That was not water—it was firewater!

He tried to walk around it, but the ring of fire surrounded the inner castle. He tried to jump over, but the flames leaped gleefully higher than he could, licking up to toast his fur. Ogres could not be hurt by much, but they did feel pain when burned. This was awkward.

He tried to pound out a tunnel under the fire, but the water flowed immediately into it and roasted him some more. It danced with flickering delight, with evilly glittering eyes forming within its substance, winking, mocking him, and fingers of flame elevating in obscene gestures. This was in fact a firewater elemental, one of the most formidable of spirits.

Smash pondered again. The effort gave him a splitting headache. He held his face together with his two paws, forcing the split back together, squeezing his skull until the bone fused firm, and hurried back to the moat to soak his head.

The cool shock of water not only got his head back together, it gave him an idea. Ideas were rare things for ogres, and not too valuable. But this one seemed good. Water not only cooled heads, it quenched fire. Maybe he could use the moat to break through the wall of fire.

He formed his paw into a flipper and scooped a splash through the hole in the outer wall toward the firewall. The splash scored—but the fire did not abate. It leaped higher, crackling mirthfully. He scooped again, wetting the whole region, but with no better effect. The firewall danced unharmed, mocking him with foul-smelling noises.

Ogres were slow to anger, because they lacked the wit to know when they were being insulted. But Smash was getting there. He scooped harder, his paw moving like a crude paddle, hurling a steady stream of moatwater at the wall. Still the fire danced, though the water flooded the region. Smash labored yet harder, feeling the exhilaration of challenge and violence, until the level of the moat lowered and the entire cavity between the outer wall and the firewall surged with muddy fluid. The sea monster's tail was exposed by the draining water; it hastily squiggled deeper. Still the fire danced, humming a hymn of victory; it could not be quenched. Water was as much its element as fire. It merely flickered on the surface, spreading wider, reaching toward Smash. Was there no way to defeat it?

"Hooo!" Smash exclaimed, frustrated. But the blast of his breath only made the flame bow concavely and leap yet higher. It liked hot air as well as cool water.

Smash couldn't think of anything better to do, so he kept shoveling water. The flood level rose and backwater coursed out through the gap. Smash tried to dam it up with rubble, but the level was too high. The fire still flickered merrily on the surface, humming a tune about an old flame.

Then the ogre had one more smart notion, a prohibitively rare occurrence for his kind. He dived forward, spread his arms, and swam under the fire. It couldn't reach him *below* the moatwater. He came up beyond it, the last hurdle navigated.

"Ccurrssess!" the firewater hissed furiously, and flickered out.

Now Smash stood within a cluttered room. Books overflowed shelves and piled up on the floor. Bottles and boxes perched everywhere, interspersed with assorted statuettes and amulets and papers. In the middle of it all, like another item of clutter, hunched over a similarly crowded wooden desk, was a little gnome of a man. Smash recognized him—the Good Magician Humfrey, the man who knew everything.

Humfrey glanced up from his tome. "Don't drip on my books, Smash," he said.

Smash fidgeted, trying not to drip on the books. There was hardly room for him to stand upright, and hardly a spot without a book, volume, or tome. He started to drip on an amulet, but it crackled ominously and he edged away. "Me no stir, Magician sir," he mumbled, wondering how the Good Magician knew his name. Smash knew of Humfrey by description and reputation, but this was the first time the two had met.

"Well, out with it, ogre," the Magician snapped irritably. "What's your Question?"

Now Smash felt more awkward than ever. The truth was, he did not know what to ask. He had thought his life would be complete when he achieved his full growth, but somehow he found it wasn't. Something was missing— and he didn't know what. Yet he could not rest until the missing element was satisfied. So he had tromped to see the Good Magician, because that was what creatures with seemingly insoluble problems did—but he lacked the intellect to formulate the Question. He had hoped to work it out during the journey; but, with typical ogrish wit, he had forgotten all about it until this moment. There was no getting around it; there were some few occasions when an ogre was too stupid for his own good. "No know," he confessed, standing on one of his own feet.

Humfrey scowled. He was a very old gnome, and it was quite a scowl. "You came here to serve a year's service for an Answer—and you don't have a Question?"

Smash had a Question, he was sure; he just didn't know how to formulate it. So he stood silent, dripping on stray artifacts, like the unsmart oaf he was.

Humfrey sighed. "Even if you asked it, it wouldn't be the right Question," he said. "People are forever asking the wrong Questions, and wasting their efforts. I remember not long ago a girl came to ask how to change her nature. Chameleon, her name was, except she wasn't called that then. Her nature was just fine; it was her attitude that needed changing." He shook his head.

As it happened, Smash knew Chameleon. She was Prince Dor's mother, and she changed constantly from smart to stupid and from beautiful to ugly. Humfrey was right: her nature was just fine. Smash liked to talk with her when she was down at his own level of idiocy, and to look at her when she was at his level of ugliness. But the two never came together, unfortunately. Still, she was a fairly nice person, considering that she was human.

"Very well," Humfrey said in a not-very-well voice. "We are about to have a first: an Answer without a Question. Are you sure you wish to pay the fee?"

Smash wasn't sure, but did not know how to formulate that uncertainty, either. So he just nodded affirmatively, his shaggy face scaring a cuckoo bird that had been about to signal the hour. The bird signaled the hour with a terrified dropping instead of a song, and retreated into its cubby.

"So be it," the Magician said, shrugging. "You will discover what you need among the Ancestral Ogres." Then he got up and marched to the door. "Come on; my effaced wife will see about your service."

Numbly, Smash followed. Now he had his Answer—and he didn't understand it.

They went downstairs—apparently, somehow, in a manner that might have been intelligible to a creature of greater wit, Smash had gotten upstairs in the process of swimming under the firewall and emerging in the Good Magician's study—where Humfrey's wife awaited them. This was the lovely, faceless Gorgon—faceless because if her face were allowed to show, it would turn men instantly to stone. Even faceless, she was said to have a somewhat petrifying effect. "Here he is," Humfrey said, as if delivering a bag of bad apples.

The Gorgon looked Smash up and down—or seemed to. Several of the little serpents that substituted for her hair hissed. "He certainly looks like an ogre," she remarked. "Is he housebroken?"

"Of course he's not housebroken!" Humfrey snapped. "He dripped all over my study! Where's the girl?"

"Tandy!" the Gorgon called.

A small girl appeared, rather pretty in a human way, with brown tresses and blue eyes and a spunky, turned-up nose. "Yes'm?"

"Tandy, you have completed your year's service this date," the Gorgon said. "Now you will have your Answer."

The little girl's eyes brightened like noontime patches of clear sky. She squiggled with excitement. "Oh, thank you, Gorgon. I'm almost sorry to leave, but I really should return home. My mother is getting tired of only seeing me in the magic mirror. What is my Answer?"

The Gorgon nudged Humfrey, her voluptuous body rippling as she moved. "The Answer, spouse."

"Oh. Yes," the Good Magician agreed, as if this had not before occurred to him. He cleared his throat, considering.

"Also say, what me pay," Smash said, not realizing that he was interrupting an important cogitation.

"The two of you travel together," Humfrey said.

Smash stared down at the tiny girl, and Tandy stared up at the hulking ogre. Each was more dismayed than the other. The ogre stood two and a half times the height of the girl, and that was the least of the contrast between them.

"But I didn't ask—" Tandy protested.

"What me task?" Smash said simultaneously. Had he been more alert, he might have thought to marvel that even this overlapping response rhymed.

The Gorgon seemed to smile. "Sometimes my husband's pronouncements need a little interpretation," she said. "He knows so much more than the rest of us, he fails to make proper allowance for our ignorance." She pinched Humfrey's cheek in a remarkably familiar manner. "He means this: the two of you, Smash and Tandy, are to travel through the wilds of Xanth together, fending off hazards together. That is the ogre's service in lieu of a year's labor at this castle—protecting his companion. It is also the girl's Answer, for which she has already paid."

"That's exactly what I said," Humfrey grumped.

"You certainly did, dear," the Gorgon agreed, planting a faceless kiss on the top of his head.

"But it doesn't make sense!" Tandy protested.

"It doesn't have to make sense," the Gorgon explained. "It's an Answer." Oh. Now Smash understood, as far as he was able.

"May I go back to my tome?" the Good Magician asked petulantly.

"Why, of course you may," the Gorgon replied graciously, patting his backside as he turned. The Good Magician climbed back up toward his study. Smash knew the man had lost valuable working time, but somehow the Magician did not seem unhappy. Naturally the nuances of human inter-relations were beyond the comprehension of a mere ogre.

The Gorgon returned her attention to them. "He's such a darling," she remarked. "I really don't know how he survived a century without me." She focused, seemingly, on Tandy. "And you might, if you would, do me a favor on the way," the Gorgon said. "I used to live on an island near the Magic Dust Village, which I think is right on your route to Lake Ogre-Chobee. I fear I caused some mischief for that village in my youth; I know I am not welcome there. But my sister the Siren remains in the area, and if you would convey my greetings to her—"

"But how can I travel with an ogre?" Tandy protested. "That's not an Answer; that's a punishment! He'll gobble me up the first time he gets hungry!"

"Not necessarily so," the Gorgon demurred. "Smash is no ordinary ogre. He's honest and halfway civilized. He will perform his service correctly, to the best of his limited understanding. He will not permit any harm to come to you. In fact, you could hardly have a better guardian while traversing the jungles of Xanth."

"But how does this solve my problem, even if I'm not gobbled up?" Tandy persisted. Smash saw that her spunky nose was a correct indication of her character; she had a fighting spirit despite her inadequate size. "Traveling won't solve a thing! There's nowhere I can go to—"

The Gorgon touched the girl's lips with a forefinger. "Let your problem be private for now, dear. Just accept my assurance. If my husband says traveling will solve your problem, then traveling will solve it. Humfrey knew an ogre would be coming here at this time, and knew you needed that sort of protection, since you have so little familiarity with the outside world. Believe me, it will turn out for the best."

"But I don't have anywhere to go!"

"Yes, but Smash does. He is seeking the Ancestral Ogres."

"A whole tribe of ogres? I'm absolutely doomed!"

The Gorgon's expression was facelessly reproving. "Naturally you do not have to follow the advice you paid for, dear. But the Good Magician Humfrey really does know best."

"I think he's getting old," Tandy said rebelliously. "Maybe he doesn't know as much as he used to."

"He likes to claim that he's forgotten more than he ever knew," the Gorgon said. "Perhaps that is so. But do not underestimate him. And don't misjudge this ogre."

Tandy pouted. "Oh, all right! I'll go with the monster. But if he gobbles me up, you'll be responsible! I'll never speak to you again."

"I accept the responsibility," the Gorgon agreed. "Now Smash is hungry." She turned to him. "Come to the kitchen, ogre, for a peck or two of raw potatoes. They haven't been cleaned, and some have worms; you'll like them."

"You're joking!" Tandy said. Then she looked again at Smash, who was licking his chops. "You're *not* joking!"

"Well spoke; no joke," Smash agreed, hoping there would also be a few barrels of dirty dishwater to glug down with the potatoes. Tandy grimaced.

Chapter 3

Eye Queue

They traveled together, but it was no pleasure for either. Smash had to take tiny slow steps to enable the girl to keep up, and Tandy made it plain she considered the ogre to be a monstrous lout. She refused to let him carry her, as he could readily have done; despite the Gorgon's assurances, she was afraid of getting gobbled. She seemed to have a thing about monsters, and male monsters in particular; she hated them. So they wended their tedious way south toward Lake Ogre-Chobee—a journey that should have taken Smash alone a single day, but promised to take several days with Tandy. The Good Magician had certainly come up with a bad chore in lieu of his year's service for an Answer! And Smash still didn't know what Question had been answered.

The scenery was varied. At first they crossed rolling hills; it took some time for Tandy to get the hang of walking on a hill that rolled, and she took several tumbles. Fortunately, the hills were covered with soft, green turf, so that the girl could roll with the punches, head over feet without much damage. Smash did note, as a point of disinterest, that his companion was not the child she seemed. She was very small even for her kind, but in the course of her tumbles she displayed well-formed limbs and torso. She was a little woman, complete in every small detail. Smash knew about such details because he had once traveled to Mundania with Prince Dor and Princess Irene, and that girl Irene had somehow managed to show off every salient feature of her sex in the course of the adventure, all the while protesting that she wanted no one to see. Tandy had less of each, but was definitely of a similar overall configuration. And her exposures, it seemed, were genuinely unintentional, rather than artful. She evidently had no notion of what to wear on such a trip. In fact, she seemed amazingly ignorant of Xanth terrain. It was as if she had never been here before—which, of course, was nonsense. Every citizen of Xanth had lived in Xanth, as had even the zombies and ghosts, who no longer lived, but remained active.

After they passed the rolling hills they came to a more stable area, where a tangle tree held sway. Tanglers were like dragons and ogres in this respect: no sensible creature tangled voluntarily with one. Smash didn't even think about it; he just stepped around it, letting it sway alone.

But Tandy walked straight down the neat, clear path that always led to such trees, innocently sniffing the pleasant fragrance of the evil plant. She was almost within its quiveringly hungry embrace before Smash realized that she really didn't know what it was.

Smash dived for the girl, trying to snatch her out of the grasp of the twitching tentacles. "No go!" he bellowed.

Tandy saw him. "Eeek! The monster's going to gobble me!" she cried. But it was Smash she meant, not the real menace. She scooted on inside the canopy of the dread tree.

With a gleeful swish, the hanging tentacles pounced. Five of them caught her legs, arms, and head. The girl was hauled up and carried toward the slavering wooden orifice in the base of the trunk. She screamed foolishly, as was her kind's wont in such circumstances.

Smash took only a moment to assess the situation. Thought with his brain was tedious and fatiguing and none too effective, but thought with his muscles was swift and sure. He saw Tandy in midair, wearing a pretty red print dress and matching red slippers; tentacles were grabbing at these, assuming them to be edible portions. One tentacle was tugging at her hair, dislodging the red ribbon in it. In a moment the tree would realize that the red was only the wrapping, and would tear that away and get down to serious business.

Smash could handle a small tangler; he was, after all, an ogre. But this was a big tangler. It had a hundred or more pythonlike tentacles, and a personality to match its strength. There was no way to negotiate or to reason with it; Smash had to fight.

The ogre charged in. That wasn't hard; tanglers wanted creatures to enter their turf. It was the getting out again that was difficult. He grabbed the mass of tentacles that had wrapped around the terrified and struggling girl. "Tree let be," he grunted, hauling the works back away from the sap-drooling orifice.

Now, tanglers were ferocious, but not unduly stupid. This tree was full-sized—but so was the ogre. Very few things cared to cross an ogre. The tree hesitated, and its coils about the girl loosened.

Then the tree decided that it could, after all, handle this challenge and gain a respectable meal in the bargain. It attacked Smash with its remaining tentacles.

Smash had been wary of this, but was stuck for it. He grabbed a tentacle in each hand and yanked—but the material was flexible and stretchable, and moved with him. He lacked the leverage to rip the tentacles out. Meanwhile, Tandy was being carried back to the orifice, trailing torn swatches of red cloth.

Smash tried a new tactic: he squeezed. Now the tree keened in vegetable pain as its two tentacles were constricted into jelly, dripped and spurted juice, and finally were lopped off. But the thing expected to take some losses, and it could always grow new tentacles; Tandy was almost at the glistening maw. A limber fiber tongue was tasting the red fabric. By the time Smash could truncate all the tentacles, the girl would be long digested.

Smash hurled himself at the orifice. He smashed his gauntleted fists into it, breaking off the wooden teeth. Sap splashed, burning his fur where it struck. The tree roared with a sound like sundering timber, but the tentacles kept coming.

The ogre braced himself before the orifice, blocking the entry of the girl. She banged into him before the tree realized this, and he was able to grab a couple more tentacles and pinch them off. Now the tree could not consume her until it dealt with him—and he was turning out to be tougher than it had anticipated. In fact, he was turning out tougher than *he* had anticipated; he had thought the tree had the advantage, but he was faring pretty well.

It was a bad thing in Xanth when a predator misjudged its foe. The tree was now in trouble, but had to fight on. As new tentacles converged, Smash caught them, twisted several together, and tied their tips into a great raveled knot that he shoved into the orifice in the trunk. The maw closed automatically, squirting digestive sap—and the tree suffered a most unpleasant surprise. The keening of agony magnified piercingly.

During this distraction, Smash unwrapped the girl, squeezing each tentacle until it let go. Soon Tandy stood on the ground, disheveled, shaken, but intact. "So—go," Smash said, catching other questing tentacles to clear her escape.

The girl scooted out. She might be small and ignorant, but she didn't freeze long in a crisis! Now Smash retreated cautiously, glaring at hovering tentacles to discourage renewed attack. But the tree had had enough; the ogre had defeated it. There was no further aggression.

Smash stepped out, privately surprised. How was it he had been able to foil a tangler this size? He concentrated, with effort, and managed to come to a conclusion; he had grown since the last time he had tangled with a tangler. Before, he would not have been strong enough to handle it; now, with his larger mass and the gauntlets, he had the advantage. His self-image had not kept pace with his physical condition. He knew his father Crunch could have handled this tree; he, Smash, was now as powerful as that.

Tandy was waiting for him down the path. She was sadly bedraggled, her dress in tatters, and bruises on her body, but her spirit remained spunky. "I guess I have to apologize to you, Smash," she said. "I thought—never mind what I thought. You risked your life to save me from my folly. I was being childish; you were mature."

"Sure—mature," Smash agreed, uncertain what she was getting at. People did not apologize to ogres, so he had no basis for comprehension.

"Well, next time you tell me 'no go,' I'll pay better attention," she concluded.

He shrugged amenably. That would make things easier.

The day was getting on, and they were tired. Battling tangle trees tended to have that effect. Smash located a muffin bush with a number of fresh ripe muffins, and used his finger to punch a hole in a lime-soda tree so they could drink. Then he found a deserted harpy nest in a tree, long since weathered out, so that the filth and smell were gone. He harvested a blanket from a blanket bush and used it to line the nest. This was for Tandy to sleep in. It took her some time to catch on, but as darkness loomed across the land in the grim way it had in the wilderness, and the nocturnal noises began, she was glad enough to clamber to it and curl up in it. He noted that she was good at climbing, though she hardly seemed to know what a tree was. He settled down below, on guard.

Tandy did not sleep immediately. Curled in her nest, she talked. Apparently this was a human trait. "You know, Smash, I've never been out on the surface of Xanth on foot before. I was raised in the caverns, and then I rode a nightmare to the Good Magician's castle. That was an accident; I really wanted to go to Castle Roogna to see my father, Crombie. But dawn came too soon, and I was out of sleeping pills, and—well, I sort of had to ask a Question so as to have a nice place to stay until I figured out what to do. I spent a whole year working inside the castle; I never even set foot beyond the moat, because I was afraid a certain party would be lurking for me. So it's not surprising I don't know about things like rolling hills and tangle trees."

That explained a lot. Smash realized he would have to watch her more closely, to be sure she did not walk into a lethal trap. The Magician's rationale for having her travel with him was making more sense. She certainly could not safely travel alone.

"I'm sorry I distrusted you, Smash," she continued in her talkative way. "You see, I was raised near demons, and in some ways you resemble a demon. Big and strong and dusky. I was prejudiced."

Smash grunted noncommittally. He had not met many demons, but doubted they could powder rock in the manner of ogres.

"I certainly have a lot to learn, don't I?" she continued ruefully. "I thought trees were sweet plants and ogres were bad brutes, and now I know they aren't."

Oops. "Ogre. No—grrr!" Smash exclaimed emphatically.

Tandy was quick to catch on; she had the ready intelligence of her kind. "You mean I shouldn't trust all ogres? That they really do gobble people?"

"Ogres prone to crunch bone," Smash agreed.

"But you didn't—I—mean—" she grew doubtful.

"Smash work hard, girl to guard."

"Oh, you mean because the Good Magician charged you with my protection," she said, relieved. "Your service for your Answer. So ogres do gobble people and crunch bones, but they also honor their obligations."

Smash didn't follow all of the vocabulary, but it sounded about right, so he grunted assent.

"Very well, Smash," she concluded. "I'll trust you, but will be wary of all other ogres. And all other things of Xanth, too, especially if they seem too nice to be true."

That was indeed best. They lapsed into sleep.

No one bothered them in the night. After all, the nightmares had to be wary of Tandy, after she had ridden one of them, and he wasn't sure whether the mares knew how to climb trees. As for himself—it was always the best policy to let a sleeping ogre lie.

They breakfasted on sugar sand and cocoa-nut milk. Tandy had never before drunk cocoa and was intrigued by the novelty. She was also amazed by the way Smash literally shoveled the sugar into his mouth, hardly pausing to chew, and crunched up whole cocoa-nuts, husks and all. "You really are a monster," she said, half admiringly, and Smash grunted agreement, pleased.

Then they resumed their trek south, encountering only routine creatures. A toady was hopping north, looking for some important person to advise; when told that Castle Roogna was many days of hopping distant, it contorted its broad and warty mouth into a scowl. "I hope I don't croak before I get there," it said, and moved on. Croaking, it seemed, was bad form for toadies.

Then there was the quack, with a wide bill and webbed feet and a bag of special magic medicines. He was, he explained, looking for a suitable practice, where his marvelous remedies would be properly appreciated. Meanwhile, did they happen to know where Pete was? Pete was a bog, very good for delving. Since Pete wasn't north, where Tandy and Smash had come from, and probably wasn't south, where the Magic Dust Village was supposed to be, and wasn't west, where the quack had come from, it had to be east, by elimination. The quack coughed and, his mind jogged by the term, deposited some genuine fresh birdlime on the ground. Flies instantly materialized, having a taste for lime, and Smash and Tandy moved on.

By noon they were in rougher territory. Sweaters swarmed about them, causing them to perspire, until Smash got fed up and issued a bellowing roar that blew them all away. Unfortunately, it also blew the leaves off the nearest trees, and several more tatters from Tandy's dress.

Then they encountered a region of curse-burrs—little balls of irritation that clung tenaciously to any portion of the body they encountered. Smash's face lit up in a horrendous smile. "Me remember here!" he cried. "Me whelped near."

"You were born here? Amidst these awful burrs?" Tandy smiled ruefully. "I should have known."

Smash laughed. It sounded like a rockslide in a canyon. "Me sire Crunch, best of bunch." He looked avidly about, whelphood memories filtering back into his thick skull. Later, his family had moved to the vicinity of Castle Roogna, because his lovely mother, whose hair was like nettles and whose face would make a zombie blush, had felt their cub should have some slight exposure to civilization. Crunch, the slave of love, had acceded to this un-ogrish notion; who could resist the blandishments of such a mushface as Smash's mother?

"Oh, this is awful!" Tandy protested. "These burrs are getting in my hair." It seemed human girls were sensitive to that sort of thing.

"Could be worse," Smash said helpfully. "She make curse."

"Curse?" she asked blankly.

Smash demonstrated. "Burr—grrr!" he growled. A burr dropped lifelessly off his gross nose.

"I don't think I can make such rhymes," Tandy said. Then a burr stuck her finger. "Get away, you awful thing!" she exploded.

The burr dropped off. Tandy looked at it, comprehending. She was certainly intelligent! "Oh, I see. You just have to curse them away!"

Even so, it was not easy, for Tandy had been raised as a nice girl and did not know many curses. They hurried out of the burr region.

Now they came to a dead forest. The trees stood gaunt, petrified in place. "I'd like to know how that happened," Tandy remarked. Smash knew, but it was a long story involving the romantic meeting of his parents, and it was hard for him to formulate it properly, so he let it go.

In the afternoon they came to a region of brambles. These were aggressive plants with glistening spikes. Smash could wade through them imperviously, for his skin was so tough he hardly felt the few thorns they dared to stick him with. It was quite another matter for Tandy, who had delicate and sweet-smelling skin, the kind that was made to be tormented by thorns.

There were neatly cleared paths through the brambles that Tandy was inclined to use, but Smash cautioned her against this. "Lion, ant, between plant."

Her small brow wrinkled. "I don't see anything."

Then an ant-lion appeared. It had the head of a lion and the body of an ant, and massed about as much as the girl did; it was, of course, ten times as ferocious as anything a nice girl could imagine. It roared when it spied her, striding forward aggressively.

Smash roared back. The ant-lion hastily reversed course; it had been so distracted by the luscious prey that it had not before seen the unluscious guardian. But Smash knew that soon many more would arrive and would swarm over the intruders. This was no safe place, even for the likes of himself.

"Now I understand," Tandy said, turning pale. "Smash, let's get out of here!"

But already there were rustlings behind them. The ant-lions had surrounded them. There would be no easy escape.

"Me know path, avoid ant wrath," Smash said, looking upward. How fortunate that he had been raised in this vicinity, so that useful details of geography were coming back to his slow memory!

"Oh, I couldn't swing from branch to branch through the trees the way I'm sure you can," Tandy said. "I'm agile, but not that agile. I'd be sure to fall."

But the ant-lions were closing in, a full pride of them. Smash had to pick Tandy up to get her out of their reach. Thus burdened, he was unable to fight effectively. Realizing this, the ants grew bolder, closing in, growling and snapping. The situation was getting awkward.

Then Smash spied what he was looking for—the aereal path. "Take care. Go there," he said, boosting the girl up by her pert bottom.

"But it's sidewise!" she protested, peering at the path with dismay. "I'd fall off!"

"Stand tall. No fall," he insisted.

Tandy obviously didn't believe him. But an ant-lion leaped for her, jaws gaping, large front pincers snapping, so she reached up to grab for the high path.

Suddenly she landed on it—sidewise. "I'm level!" she cried, amazed. "The world has turned!" She stood up, or rather sidewise, her body parallel to the ground.

Smash didn't worry about it. He knew the properties of the path, having played on it as a cub. It was always level—to the person on it. He was now far too massive to use it himself, since the aereal path was getting old and brittle, but he didn't need to. He was now unencumbered, free to deal with the lions his own way.

The lions, angered at the escape of the lesser prey, pounced on the greater prey. That was foolish of them. Smash emitted a battle bellow that tore their whiskers back and clogged their pincers with debris, then began stomping and pounding. Lions yowled as the gauntleted fists connected, and screeched as the hairy feet found flesh. Then Smash picked up two ants by their narrow waists and hurled them into the nettles. He took a moment to rip a small hemlock tree out of the ground, shaking the locks from its hem, and bit off its top, forming a fair club from the remaining trunk. Soon the path was clear; the ant-lions, like the tangle tree, had learned new respect for ogres.

"You're really quite something, Smash!" Tandy called, clapping her hands. "You're a real terror when you get worked up. I'll bet there's nothing more formidable than an angry ogre!" She had an excellent view of the proceedings from the elevated path, dodging when an ant flew past. Ant-lions did not normally fly; this was a consequence of being hurled out of the way. Ants were now stuck in a number of the jungle trees.

"Me know who," Smash grunted, pleased. "Ogres two."

She laughed. "That figures. The only thing tougher than one ogre is two ogres." She was now standing inverted, her brown tresses hanging naturally about her shoulders as if she were upright. She looked about, from her vantage. "The ants aren't gone, just backed off, Smash," she reported. "Can you come up here?"

Smash shook his head no. But he wasn't worried. He could use the ant paths. If the ants wanted a little more ogre-type fun, he would gladly accommodate them.

They proceeded south, Tandy tilting with the orientation of the aereal path, sometimes upright, sometimes not, enjoying the experience. "There is nothing much in the caverns like this!" she commented.

Smash tromped along the ant highways, tearing through nettles when he needed to change paths. Soon the nettles and ants were left behind, but the high path continued, so Tandy stayed on it. Smash knew it terminated at the Magic Dust Village, and since they had to pass there anyway, this was convenient. According to Castle Roogna information, the Magic Dusters had once had a population problem, not being able to hold on to their males, so they had constructed the skyway to encourage immigration. Now there were plenty of people at the village, so the path didn't matter, but no one had bothered to take it down. Smash and Tandy made excellent progress.

Now they passed a region of hanging vines. They were twined, almost braided, like queues, and seemed to have eyes looking out from their recesses. Smash distrusted unfamiliar things in general and dangling vines in particular, so he avoided the Eye Queues. They could be harmless, or they could be bloodsuckers. This was beyond the region of his cubhood familiarity, and anyway, things could have changed in the interim. One could never take magic for granted.

He also kept an eye on Tandy, above, to make sure she did not brush against any vines. As a result, he didn't pay close enough attention to his big feet—and stumbled over a minor boulder that was damming a streamlet, much to the streamlet's annoyance.

The boulder dam shattered, of course; it was only stone. The streamlet gladly flowed through, with a burble of thanks to its deliverer. But Smash suffered a momentary loss of balance, his feet sinking into the sodden riverbed, and he lurched headlong into a hanging vine.

The thing wrapped disgustingly around his head. He snatched at it, but already it was sinking into his fur and his flesh and hurting terribly when he tried to scrape it loose. Since an ogre's course was generally that of most resistance, Smash put both hands to his scalp and scraped—and the burgeoning agony made him reel.

"Stop, Smash, stop!" Tandy screamed from above. "You'll rip off your head!"

Smash stopped. "I concur. There is no sense in that."

Tandy stared down at him. "What did you say?"

"I said there is no sense in mortifying my flesh, since the queue does not appear to have seriously incapacitated me."

"Smash—you're not rhyming!"

"Why—so I am not!" he agreed, startled. "That must be the curse of the Eye Queue; it has disrupted my natural mechanism of communication."

"It's done more than that!" Tandy exclaimed. "Smash, you sound smart!"

"That must be a fallacious impression. No ogre is unduly intelligent."

"Well, you sure *sound* smart!" she insisted. "That Eye Queue, as you call it, must have added some brains to your head."

"That seems reasonable," he agreed, after cogitating momentarily without effort. "The effect manifested concurrently with my contact with that object. Probability suggests a causal connection. This, of course, is much worse than any purely physical attack would have been; it has temporarily unogred me. I must expunge it from my system!"

"Oh, no, don't do that," she protested. "It's sort of interesting, really. I don't mind you being smart, Smash. It's much easier to talk with you."

"In any event, I seem unable for the moment to deactivate it," Smash said. "It seems I must tolerate this curse for the time being. But I assure you I shall be alert for an antidote."

"Okay," she said. "If that's the way you feel."

"Indubitably."

They went on—and now Smash noted things that hadn't interested him before. He saw how erosion had caused rifts in the land, and how the forest stratified itself, with light-indifferent vegetation and fungi at the nether levels and bright, broad leaves above to catch the descending light of the sun. The entire jungle was a cohesive unit, functioning compatibly with its environment. All over Xanth, things were integrating—in his new awareness. How blind he had been to the wonders of magic, all his life!

As dusk closed, the aereal path descended to the ground, and they arrived at the Magic Dust Village. A troll came forth to meet them. "Ogre, do you come in peace or mayhem?" the creature inquired, standing poised for flight while other villagers hastily manned the fortifications and cleared children and the aged from the region.

"In peace!" Tandy said quickly. "I am Tandy; this is Smash, who is protecting me from monsters."

The troll's eyes gaped. This was an unusual expression, even for this type of creature. "Protecting you from—?"

"Yes."

"Now, we have no prejudice against monsters here," the troll said, scratching his long and horny nose with a discolored claw. "I'm a monster myself, and some of my best friends are monsters. But only a fool trusts an ogre."

"Well, I'm a fool," Tandy said. "This ogre fought a tangle tree to save me."

"Are you sure you aren't a kidnap victim? You certainly do look good enough to eat."

Smash did not appreciate the implication, which would have passed him by had he not suffered the curse of the Eye Queue vine. "My father is Crunch, the vegetarian ogre," he said gruffly. "My family has not kidnapped anyone in years."

The troll looked at him, startled. "You certainly don't sound like an ogre! Did the Transformer-King transform you to this shape?"

"I was whelped an ogre!" Smash insisted, the first traces of roar coming into his voice.

Then the troll made a connection. "Ah, yes. Crunch married a curse-fiend actress. You have human lineage; that must account for your language."

"It must," Smash agreed drolly. He found he didn't care to advertise his misadventure with the vine. He would be laughed out of the village if its inhabitants learned he was intelligent. "But I should advise you, purely in the interest of amity, that I have been known to take exception to the appellation 'half-breed.' I am a true ogre." He picked up a nearby knot of green wood and squeezed it in one hand. The green juice dripped as the wood pulped, until at last there was a pool of green on the ground and the knot had become a lump of coal.

"Yes, indeed," the troll agreed hastily. "No one here would think of using that term. Welcome to our table for supper; you are surely hungry."

"We are only passing through," Tandy said. "We're going to Lake Ogre-Chobee."

"You can't get there from here," the troll said. "The Region of Madness intervenes."

"Madness?" Tandy asked, alarmed.

"From the airborne magic dust we process. Magic is very potent here, and too much of it leads to alarming effects. You will have to go around."

They did not argue the case. Smash's inordinate intelligence, coupled with his memories of this region, corroborated the information; he knew it would be impossible for him to protect Tandy in the Region of Madness. There were tales of the constellations of the night coming to life, and of reality changing dangerously. In Xanth, things were mostly what they seemed to be, so that illusion was often reality. But illusion could be taken too far in the heightened magic of the Madness. Smash was now too smart to risk it.

They joined the villagers' supper. Creatures of every type came forth to feed, all well behaved: elves, gnomes, goblins, a manticore, fauns, nymphs, fairies, human beings, centaurs, griffins, and assorted other creatures. The hostess was the troll's mate, Trolla. "It is much easier to arrive than to depart," she explained as she served up helpings of smashed potatoes and poured out goblets of mead. "We have never had opportunity to construct an exit ramp, and our work mining the source of magic is important, so we stay. You may choose to remain also: we labor hard, but it is by no means a bad life."

Smash exchanged a glance with Tandy, since it occurred to him that this might be the sort of situation she was looking for. But she was negative. "We have a message from the sister of a neighbor of yours. We must get on and deliver it."

"A neighbor?" Trolla asked.

"She is called the Siren."

There was a sudden hush.

"You know," Tandy said. "The sister of the Gorgon."

"You are friend to the Gorgon?" Trolla asked coldly.

"I hardly know her," Smash said quickly, remembering that this village had suffered at the Gorgon's hands—or rather, her face, having had all the men turned to stone. Fortunately, that mischief had been undone at the time of the loss of magic, when all Xanth had become as drear as Mundania, briefly. Numerous spells had been aborted in that period, changing Xanth in ways that were still unraveling. "I had to see Good Magician Humfrey, and she's his wife. She asked us to say hello to the Siren."

"Oh, I see." Trolla relaxed, and the others followed her example. There were murmurs of amazement and awe. "The Good Magician's wife! And she turned *him* to stone?"

"Not anywhere we could see," Tandy said, then blushed. "Uh, that is—"

Trolla smiled. "He's probably too old for such enchantment anyway, so the sight of her merely stiffens his spine, or whatever." She gulped a goblet of mead. "The Siren no longer lures people, since a smart centaur broke her magic dulcimer. She is not a bad neighbor, but we really don't associate with her."

They finished their repast, Smash happily consuming all the refuse left after the others were done. The villagers set them up with rooms for the night. Smash knew these were honest, well-meaning folk, so he didn't worry about Tandy's safety here.

As he lay on his pile of straw, Smash thought about the place of the Magic Dust Village in the scheme of Xanth. Stray references to it bubbled to the surface of his memory—things he had heard at different times in his life and thought nothing of, since ogres thought nothing of everything. From these suddenly assimilating fragments he was now able to piece together the role of this village, geologically. Here it was that the magic dust welled to the surface from the mysterious depths. The villagers pulverized it and employed a captive roc-bird to flap its wings and waft huge clouds of the dust into the air, where it caused madness close by, technicolor hailstorms farther distant, and magic for the rest of Xanth as it diluted to natural background intensity. If the villagers did not perform this service, the magic dust would tend to clump, and the magic would be unevenly distributed, causing all manner of problems.

Certainly the Magic Dusters believed all this, and labored most diligently to facilitate the proper and even spreading of the dust. Yet Smash's Eye Queue-infected brain obnoxiously conjured caveats, questioning the realities the villagers lived by.

If the magic really came from the dust, it should endure as long as the dust did, fading only slowly as the dust wore out. Yet at the Time of No Magic, all Xanth had been rendered Mundane instantly. That had happened just before Smash himself had been whelped, but his parents had told him all about it. They had considered it rather romantic, perhaps even a signal of their love. Crunch had lost his great strength in that time, but other creatures had been affected far more, and many had died. Then the magic had returned, as suddenly as it had departed, and Xanth had been as it was before. There had been no great movements of dust then, no dust storms. That suggested that the magic of Xanth was independent of the dust.

The dust came from below, and if it brought the magic, the nether regions must be more magical than the surface. Tandy had lived below, yet she seemed normal. She did not even appear to have a magic talent. So how could the magic be concentrated below?

But Smash decided not to raise these questions openly, as they would only make things awkward for the villagers. And perhaps the belief of the Dusters was right and his vine-sponsored objections were wrong. After all, what could a Queue of Eyes understand of the basic nature of Xanth?

His thought turned to a bypath. A magic talent—that must be what Tandy was questing for! He, as an ogre, was fortunate; ogres had strength as their talent. When Smash had gone to Mundania, outside the magic ambience of Xanth, he had lost his strength and his rhyme, distressingly. Now he had lost his rhymes and his naïveté, but not his strength.

Was the infliction of the curse of the Eye Queue really so bad? There were indeed pleasures in the insights this artificial intelligence afforded him. Yet ogres were supposed to be stupid; he felt sadly out of place.

Smash decided to keep quiet, most of the time, and let Tandy do the talking. He might no longer be a proper ogre in outlook, but at least he could *seem* like an ogre. If he generated an illusion of continuing stupidity, perhaps in time he would achieve it again. Certainly this was worth the hope. Meanwhile, his shame would remain mostly secret.

Chapter 4

Catastrophe

In the morning they walked along an old groundbound path to the small lake that contained the Siren's isle. It was pretty country, with few immediate hazards, and so Smash found it dull, while Tandy liked it very well.

The Siren turned out to be a mature mermaid who had probably been stunning in her youth and was not too far from it even now. She evidently survived by fishing and seemed satisfied with her lot, or more correctly, her pond.

"We bring greetings from your sister the Gorgon," Tandy called as they crossed the path over the water to the island.

Immediately the mermaid was interested. She emerged from the water and changed to human form—her fish-tail simply split into two well-formed legs—and came to meet them, still changing. She had been nude in the water, but it hardly mattered since she was a fish below the waist. But as she dried, the scales that had covered her tail converted to a scale-sequin dress that nudged up to cover the upper portion of her torso. For a reason that had never been clear to Smash, it was all right for a mermaid to show her breasts, but not all right for a human woman to do the same. The finny part of her flukes became small shoes. It was minor but convenient magic; after all, Smash thought, she might otherwise get cold feet. "My sister!" she exclaimed, her newly covered bosom heaving. "How is she doing?"

"Well, she's married to the Good Magician Humfrey—"

"Oh, yes, I had news of that! But how is she recently?"

"Recently?" Tandy's brow furrowed.

Smash caught on to the nature of the Siren's question. "She wants to know whether the Gorgon is pregnant," he murmured.

Tandy was startled. "Oh—I don't know about that. I don't think so. But she does seem happy, and so does the Magician."

The Siren frowned. "I'm so glad she found hers. I wish I had found mine." And Smash now perceived, from this close range and the magnification of his interpretive intellect, that the Siren was not happy at all. She had lost her compelling magic twenty years ago and had very little left.

Such things had not before been concerns of Smash's. Ogres hardly cared about the nuances of the lifestyles of nymphal creatures. Now, thanks to the curse of the Eye Queue, Smash felt the Siren's problem, and felt the need to alleviate it. "We are going to Lake Ogre-Chobee. Perhaps if you went there, you would find yours."

The Siren brightened. "That's possible."

"But we are having trouble finding the way," he said. "The Madness intercedes."

"It's a nuisance," the Siren agreed. "But there are ways around it."

"We would like to know of one."

"Well, there's the catapult. Yet you have to pay the cat's price."

"What is the cat's price?" Tandy asked warily. "If it's a kind of demon, we might not like it."

"It likes catnip—and that's not easy to get."

"Smash could get it," Tandy said brightly. "He fought a tangle tree and a pride of ant-lions."

"Well, he's an ogre," the Siren agreed matter-of-factly. "That sort of thing is routine for them."

"Why don't you come with us and show us where the catnip is?" Tandy suggested. "Then we can all go to the catapult and on to Lake Ogre-Chobee."

The Siren considered. "I admit I don't seem to be accomplishing much here. I never thought I'd travel with an ogre!" She faced Smash. "Are you tame? I've heard some bad things about ogres—"

"They're all true!" Smash agreed. "Ogres are the worst brutes on two legs. But I was raised in the environs of Castle Roogna, so am relatively civilized."

"He's really very nice, when you get to know him," Tandy said. "He doesn't crunch the bones of friends."

"I'll risk it," the Siren decided. "I'll lead you to the catnip." She adjusted her dress, packed a few fish for nibbling on the way, and set off, leading them east of the lake.

The catnip grew in a section of the jungle separated by a fiercely flowing stream. They had to use a narrow catwalk past a cataract that was guarded by a catamount. "Don't fall into the water," the Siren warned. "It's a catalyst that will give you catarrh, catatonia, and catalepsy."

"I don't understand," Tandy said nervously. "Is that bad?"

"A catalyst is a substance that facilitates change," Smash explained, drawing on his new Eye Queue intellect. "In the case of our living flesh, this is likely to mean deterioration and decay such as catarrh, which is severe inflammation inside the nose, catatonia, which is stupor, and catalepsy, which is loss of motion and speechlessness. We had better stay out of this water; it is unlikely to be healthy."

"Yes, unlikely," Tandy agreed faintly. "But the catamount is on the cat-walk! It will throw us off."

"Oh, I wouldn't be concerned about that," Smash said. He strode out on the catwalk. It dipped and swayed under his mass, but he had the sure balance of his primitive kind and proceeded with confidence.

"No violence!" Tandy pleaded.

The catamount was a large reddish feline with long whiskers and big paws. It snarled and stalked toward Smash, its tail swishing back and forth. No violence?

A fright would have been fun, but Smash realized now that the girls would worry, so he used his intellect to ponder on a peaceful option. What about the one he had used on the moat-monster at the Good Magician's castle? "I want to show you something, kitty," he said. He leaned forward and held out his right hand. The catamount paused distrustfully.

Smash carefully closed his gauntleted hamfingers into a huge, gleaming fist. Shafts of sunlight struck down to elicit new gleams as Smash slowly rotated his fist. It was amazing how each shaft knew exactly where to go!

Smash nudged this metallic hamfist under the catamount's nose. "Now kitty," he said quietly. "if you do not vacate this path expeditiously, you are apt to have a closer encounter with this extremity. Does this eventuality meet with your approval?"

The feline's ears twitched as if it suffered indigestion; it seemed to have a problem with the vocabulary. It considered the extremity. The fist sent another barrage of glints of reflected sunlight out, seeming to grow larger. The ogre stood perfectly balanced and at ease, muscles bulging only slightly, fur lying almost unruffled. After a moment, snarling ungraciously, the cata-mount decided not to dispute the path this time. It backed away.

Well, well, Smash thought. His bluff had worked—now that he had the wit to bluff. Of course, it would have been fun to hurl the catamount into the water below and see what happened to it, but that pleasure was not to be, this time.

A catbird sailed down out of the sky. It had the body of a crow and the head of a cat. "Meow!" it scolded the catamount, and issued a resounding catcall. Then it wheeled on Smash, claws extended cat-as-catch-can.

The ogre's mitt moved swiftly. The hamfingers caught the catbird, who screeched piteously. Smash brought it down, pulled out one large tailfeather, and lofted the creature away. The catbird flew awkwardly, its rudder malfunctioning. The fight had been taken out of it, along with much of the flight.

A catfish protested from below. It lifted its cat-head from the flowing water and yowled. Its voice had a nasal quality; the creature did indeed seem to be suffering from catarrh and perhaps catalepsy, though probably it had built up a certain immunity to the curses of the water. Smash hurled the feather down into its mouth. The catfish choked and sneezed, disappearing.

Now Smash, Tandy, and the Siren crossed without impediment. "Sometimes it's really handy having an ogre along," Tandy remarked. She seemed to have swung from absolute distrust to absolute support, and Smash was not displeased.

The path led through a field of cattails growing in catsup where cattle grazed, fattening up in case some cataclysm came. It terminated at a catacomb. "The catnip grows in there," the Siren said, pointing to the teeth of the comb that barred the entrance. "But it's dangerous to enter, because if the cataclysm comes, the cattle will stampede into it."

"Then I will go alone," Smash said. He brushed the comb aside and marched on down. The way soon became dark, but ogres had good night vision, so he wasn't much bothered.

"Don't invite catastrophe!" the Siren called after him.

"I certainly hope not," Smash called back, though in truth he wouldn't have minded a little of that to make things interesting. "I will be pusillanimously careful."

Deep inside the cave, he found a garden of pleasantly scented, mintlike plants with felinely furry leaves. Each had a spike of blue flowers. These must be the catnips.

Smash took hold of one and pulled it up by the roots, being uncertain which part of the plant he needed, and stuffed it into his bag. The flowers nipped at him, but lacked the power even to be annoying. He grabbed and crammed more plants, until he felt he had enough.

He turned to depart—and spied a dimly glowing object. It was set in the cave wall beside the exit, framed in stone set with yellow cat's-eye gems. It was a furry hump with a tail descending from it: evidently the posterior of some sort of feline. A pussy-willow? No, too large for that. Smash recalled reference to one of the barbarian customs of the Mundanes, in which they killed animals and mounted their heads on walls. That was stupid—perfectly edible heads going to waste! Someone must have done the same for this cat's rear.

Smash considered, then decided to take the trophy along. It certainly wasn't doing any good here in the dark. Perhaps the girls would like to see it. Smash realized that it was a measure of the degradation foisted on him by the Eye Queue that he even thought of showing something interesting to others, but he was stuck with it.

He reached out to grab the stone frame. The cat's-eyes blinked warningly. The thing was firmly set, so he applied force. The frame ripped out of the wall—and the roof collapsed.

Puzzled, Smash put one fist up over his head. The rock fell on this and cracked apart, piling up on either side. Smash climbed up through the rubble, toting his bag of plants, but was unable to bring the posterior-trophy. In a moment he reached daylight.

"Oh, you're all right!" Tandy cried. "I was so afraid—"

"Rockfalls can't hurt ogres," Smash said. "I tried to take a trophy, but the roof fell in." He dusted himself off.

"A trophy?" Tandy asked blankly.

"The rear end of some kind of cat, mounted in the wall."

"That was the catastrophe!" the Siren cried. "I told you not to invite it!"

Catastrophe—a trophy of the rear of a cat. Now Smash understood. He had not properly applied his new intelligence, and had done considerable damage to the catnip garden as a result. He would try to be more careful in the future. As long as he was cursed with intellect, he might as well use it.

"I had better clear the rocks out of the garden," Smash said. This, too, was an un-ogrish sentiment, but the Eye Queue and the presence of the girls seemed to have that effect on him.

"No, don't bother," the Siren said. "You wouldn't know how to set it right. The caterpillar will take care of that after we leave. It likes to push rocks around."

They crossed the catwalk past the cataract again and proceeded to the catapult. This was a feline creature the size of a small sphinx, crouched in a clearing. Its tail expanded into a kind of netting at the end, large enough for a boulder to rest on. There was a basket nearby, just that size.

The Siren approached the catapult. "Will you hurl us to Lake Ogre-Chobee, please?" she asked. "We have some catnip for you."

The cat brightened. It nodded its whiskered head. They laid the catnip plants down before it, then moved the basket to the expanded tail. The three of them climbed in and drew the wicker lid over, enclosing themselves.

The cat sniffed the catnip. Its tail stiffened ecstatically. Then it nipped the catnip. As the potent stuff took effect, the tail suddenly sprang up, carrying the basket along. Suddenly the party of three was flying.

They looked out between the slats. Xanth was cruising by beneath them, all green and blue and yellow. There were scattered, low-hanging clouds around them, white below, all other colors above, where they couldn't be seen from the ground. Some were rainclouds, shaped like pools, brimming with water. Stray birds were taking baths in them, and flying fish were taking breathers there, too. The basket clipped the edge of one of these rainclouds and tore a hole in it; the water poured out in a horrendous leak. There was an angry uproar from below as the unscheduled deluge splashed on the forest. But this was the Region of Madness anyway; no one would be able to prove the difference.

Now it occurred to Smash to wonder about their descent. They had risen smoothly enough, but the fall might be less comfortable.

Then some sort of material popped out of the lid of the basket. It spread into a huge canopy that caught the air magically and held back the basket. The descent became slow, and they landed by the shore of Lake Ogre-Chobee.

They opened the basket and stepped out. "That was fun!" Tandy exclaimed girlishly. "But how will the catapult get its basket back?"

An orange creature hurried up, vaguely catlike. "I'll take that," it said.

"Who are you?" Tandy asked.

"I am the agent of this region. It is my job to see that things get where they belong. The catapult has a contract for the return of its baskets."

"Oh. Then you had better take it. But I don't know how you'll be able to carry that big basket through that thick jungle, or past the Region of Madness."

"No problem. I'm half mad already." The orange agent picked up the basket and trotted north. The vegetation wilted and died in the creature's vicinity, making a clear path.

"Oh—that's its magic talent," Tandy said. "Agent Orange kills plants."

They turned to Lake Ogre-Chobee. It was a fine blue expanse of water with a whirlpool in the center. "Don't go there," the Siren cautioned. "The curse-fiends live there."

"What is wrong with the curse-fiends?" Smash asked. "My mother was one."

The Siren turned her gaze on him, startled. "Oh—I understood you were an ogre. The curse-fiends are of human derivation. I didn't mean to—"

"My mother is an actress. She had to play the part of an ogress in an adaptation of *Prince Charming*, a Mundane tale. Naturally she was the ingénue."

"Naturally," the Siren agreed faintly.

"But my father Crunch happened onto the set, innocently looking for bones to crunch, and spied her and was instantly smitten by her horribleness and carried her away. Naturally she married him."

"Yes, of course," the Siren agreed, looking wan. "I am jealous of her fortune. I'm of human derivation myself."

"The curse-fiends fired off a great curse that killed a huge forest," Smash continued. "But my parents escaped the curse by becoming vegetarians. Most ogres crunch bones, so this confused the curse and caused it to misfire."

"You were raised in a non-bone-crunching home!" Tandy exclaimed.

"I'm still an ogre," he said defensively.

"I'm glad it worked out so well," the Siren said. "But I think it would be wise to avoid the curse-fiends. They might not appreciate your position."

"I suppose so," Smash admitted. "But they are excellent actors. No one ever confused my mother for a human being."

"I'm sure they didn't," the Siren agreed. "I saw one of the curse-fiends' plays once. It was very well done. But it can be awkward associating with someone who throws a curse when aggravated."

Smash laughed. "It certainly can be! I acted un-ogrish once, letting a wyvern back me off from an emerald I had found—"

"My mother set that emerald in place!" Tandy exclaimed.

"And my mother threw a curse at me," he continued. "It scorched the ground at my feet and knocked me on my head. I never let any monster back me off again!"

"That was cruel," Tandy said. "She shouldn't have cursed you."

"Cruel? Of course not. It was ogre love, the only kind our kind understands. She cursed my father once, and it was two days before he recovered, and the smile never left his face."

"Well, I don't know," Tandy said, and she seemed unusually sober. Did she have some connection to the curse-fiends? Smash filed the notion for future reference.

They walked around a portion of Lake Ogre-Chobee, trying not to attract attention. There were no ogres in evidence, and no traces of their presence—no broken-off trees or fragmented boulders or flat-stomped ground.

There seemed to be no threats, either; the entire lake was girded, as far as they could see, by a pleasant little beach, and the water was clear and free of monsters. Evidently the curse-fiends had driven away anything dangerous.

"Look at the noses!" Tandy cried, pointing across the water. Smash looked. There were scores of nostrils swimming in pairs toward the shore, making little waves. As they drew near, he saw that the nostrils were the visible tips of more extensive snouts, which continued on into long reptilian bodies.

"Oh—the chobees," the Siren said, relaxing. "They're mostly harmless. Chobees aren't related to other kinds of bees; they don't sting. Once in a while one strays up to my lake."

"But what big teeth they have!" Tandy said.

"They're imitation teeth, soft as pillows."

A chobee scrambled out onto the beach. It had short, fat, green legs and a green corrugated skin. The Siren petted it on the head, and the chobee grinned. She touched one of its teeth, and the tooth bent like rubber, snapping back into place when released.

But Smash had a nagging doubt. "I remember something my father said about the chobees. Most of them are innocent, but some—"

"Oh, yes, that's right," the Siren agreed. "A few, a very few, have real teeth. Those kind are dangerous."

"Let's stay away from the bad ones, then," Tandy said. "What do they look like?"

"I don't know," the Siren admitted.

"They look just like the nice ones," Smash said slowly, dredging his memory.

"But then any of these could be a bad one," Tandy said, alarmed.

"True," Smash agreed. "Unless the curse-fiends got rid of them."

"How could the curse-fiends tell the difference, if we can't?" Tandy asked.

"If a chobee eats a curse-fiend, it's probably a bad one," the Siren said, smiling obscurely.

"Do we need to tell the chobees apart the same way?" Tandy asked worriedly.

The Siren laughed musically. Her voice was only a shadow of what it must have been when she had her luring magic, but it remained evocative. "Of course not, dear. Let's avoid them all." That seemed easy enough to do, as the three of them could walk faster than the reptiles could. Soon the chobees gave up the chase and nosed back into the water, where they buzzed away toward the deeper portions of the lake. Tandy watched the wakes their nostrils left with relief.

At one point the lake become irregular, branching out into a satellite lake that was especially pretty. A partial causeway crossed the narrow connection between the large and small lakes. "I'll wade across!" Smash said, delighting in the chance to indulge in some splashing.

"I don't know," Tandy said. "The nice paths can be dangerous." She had learned from her experience with the tangler and the ant-lions; now she distrusted all the easy ways.

"I will explore the water," the Siren said. "I will be able to tell very quickly whether there are dangerous water creatures near. Besides, I'm hungry; I need to catch some fish." She slid into the small lake, her legs converting to the sleekly scaled tail, her dress fading out.

"If you find a monster, send it my way," Smash called. "I'm hungry, too!"

She smiled and dived below the surface, a bare-breasted mernymph swimming with marvelous facility. In a moment her head popped up, tresses glistening. "No monsters here!" she called. "Not even any chobees. I believe that causeway is safe; I find no pitfalls there."

That was all Smash needed. "Too bad," he muttered. He waded in, sending a huge splay of water to either side.

But Tandy remained hesitant. "I think I'll just walk around it," she said.

"Good enough!" Smash agreed, and forged on into deeper water. The causeway dropped lower, but never deeper than chest height on him. He conjectured that it might have been constructed by the curse-fiends to prevent large sea monsters from passing; they preferred deep water and avoided shallows. Maybe the smaller lake had been developed as a resort region. This suggested that there could be monsters in Lake Ogre-Chobee; they just happened to be elsewhere at the moment. Maybe they represented an additional protection for the fiends, converting the whole of the large lake into a kind of moat. It really didn't matter, since he had no business with the curse-fiends. After all, they had not let his mother go willingly to marry his father. She had had no further contact with her people after she had taken up with Crunch the Ogre, and it occurred to Smash that this could not have made her feel good. So his attitude toward the fiends was guarded; he would not try to avoid them, but neither would he try to seek them out. Neutrality was the watchword. He had never thought this out before—but he had not suffered the curse of the Eye Queue before, either. He still hoped to find some way to be rid of it, as these frequent efforts of thought were not conducive to proper ogrish behavior.

He glanced across the water of the little lake. Tandy was picking her way along the beach, looking very small. He felt un-ogrishly protective toward her—but, of course, this was his service to the Good Magician. Ogres were gross and violent, but they kept their word. Also, the Eye Queue curse lent him an additional perception of the virtue of an ethical standard. It was a bit like physical strength; the ideal was to be strong in all respects, ethical as well as physical. And Tandy certainly needed protection. Besides which, she was a nice girl. He wondered what she was looking for in life and how it related to his journey to seek the Ancestral Ogres. Had old Magician Humfrey finally lost his magic, and had to foist Tandy off on an ogre in lieu of a genuine Answer? Smash hoped not, but he had to entertain the possibility. Suppose there was in fact no Answer for Tandy—or for himself?

Smash had no ready answer for that, even with his unwanted new intelligence, so had to let the thought lapse. But it was disquieting. High intelligence, it seemed, posed as many questions as it answered; being smart was not necessarily any solution to life's problems. It was much easier to be strong and stupid, bashing things out of the way without concern for the consequences. Disquiet was no proper feeling for an ogre.

Now he got down in the water and splashed with all limbs. *This* was proper ogre fun! The spray went up in a great cloud, surrounding the sun and causing its light to fragment into a magic halo. The whole effect was so lovely that he continued splashing violently until pleasantly winded. When he stopped, he discovered that the water level of the small lake had dropped substantially, and the sun was hastening across the sky to get out of the way, severely dimmed by all the water that had splashed on it.

But his thorough washing did not clear the Eye Queue from the fur of his head. Somehow the Queue had sunk into his brain, and the braided Eyes were providing him new visions of many kinds. It would be hard indeed to get those Eyes out again.

At last he waded out at the far side. The Siren swam up, converted her tail to legs, and joined him on the warm beach. "You made quite a splash, Smash," she said. "Had I not known better, I would have supposed a thunderstorm was forming."

"That good!" he agreed, well satisfied. Of course it wasn't all good; he was now unconscionably clean. But a few good rolls in the dirt would take care of that.

"That bad," the Siren said with a smile.

He studied her as she gleamed wetly, her scale-suit creeping up to cover the fullness of her front. She seemed to be turning younger, though this might be inconsequential illusion. "I think the swim was good for you, too, Siren. You look splendid." Privately, he was amazed at his words; she did look splendid, and her affinity to the voluptuous Gorgon was increasingly evident, but no ordinary ogre would have noticed, let alone complimented her in the fashion of a human being. The curse of the Queue was still spreading!

"I do feel better," she agreed. "But it's not just the swim. It's the companionship. I have lived alone for too long; now that I have company, however temporarily, my youth and health are returning."

So that explained it! People of human stock had need for the association of other people. This was one of the ways in which ogres differed from human beings. Ogres needed nobody, not even other ogres. Except to marry.

He looked again at the Siren. Her nymphlike beauty would have dazzled a man and led him to thoughts of moonlight and gallivanting. Smash, however, was an ogre; full breasts and smoothly fleshed limbs appealed to him only aesthetically—and even that was a mere product of the Eye Queue. An uncursed ogre would simply have become hungry at the sight of such flesh.

Which reminded him—he needed something to eat. He checked around for edibles and spied some ripe banana peppers. He stuffed handfuls of them into his mouth.

Something nagged him as he chewed. Flesh—female—hunger—ah, now he had it. A girl in danger of being eaten. "Where's Tandy?" he asked.

"I haven't seen her, Smash," the Siren said, her fair brow furrowing. "She should be here by now, shouldn't she? We had better go look for her, in case—well, let's just see. I'll swim; you check the beach."

"Agreed." Smash crammed another double fistful of peppers into his face and started around the beach, concerned. He blamed himself now for his selfish carelessness. He knew that Tandy was unfamiliar with the surface of Xanth, liable to fall into the simplest trap. If something had happened to her—

"I find nothing here," the Siren called from the water. "Maybe she went off the beach for a matter of hygiene."

Good notion. Smash checked the tangled vines beyond the beach—and there, in due course, he found Tandy. "Hi-ho!" he called to her, waving a hamhand.

Tandy did not respond. She was kneeling on the turf, looking at something. "Are you all right?" Smash asked, worry building up like a sudden storm. But the girl neither moved nor answered.

The Siren came out of the water, dripping and changing in the effective way she had, and joined Smash. "Oh—she's fallen prey to a hypnogourd."

A hypnogourd. Smash remembered encountering that fruit before. Anyone who peeked in the peephole of such a gourd remained mesmerized until some third party broke the connection. Naturally Tandy had not been aware of this. So she had peeked, being girlishly curious—and remained frozen there.

Gently, the Siren removed the gourd, breaking the connection. Tandy blinked and shook her head. But her eyes did not quite focus. Her features coalesced into an expression of vacant, continuing horror.

"Hey, come out of it, dear," the Siren said. "The bad vision is over. It ended when you lost contact with the gourd. Everything's all right."

Yet the girl seemed numb. The Siren shook her, but still Tandy did not respond.

"Maybe it's like the Eye Queue," Smash said. "It stays in the mind until removed."

"The gourds aren't usually that way," the Siren said, perplexed. "Of course, I have not had much personal experience with them, since I have lived alone; there's no one to break the trance for me, so I have stayed clear. But I met a man once, a Mundane, back when I was able to lure men with my music. He said the gourds were like computer games—that seems to be something he knew about in Mundania, one of their forms of magic—only more compelling. He said some people got hooked worse than others."

"Tandy was raised in the caves. She has no experience with most of Xanth. She must be susceptible. Whatever she saw in there maintains its grip on her mind."

"That must be it. Usually people have no memory of what they see inside, but maybe that varies also. That same Mundane spoke of acidheads, which I think are creatures whose heads—well, I can't quite visualize that. But it seems they suffered flashbacks of their mad dreams after their heads were back in normal shape. Maybe Tandy is—"

"I'll go into that gourd and destroy whatever is bothering her," Smash said. "Then she'll be free."

"Smash, you may not have your body in there! I have never looked into a gourd, but I don't think the same rules apply as those we know. You could get caught there, too. It could be catastrophe."

"I will be more careful to avoid that trophy, this time," Smash said with an ogrish grimace. He applied his eye to the peephole.

He was in a world of black and white. He stood before a black wooden door set in a white house. There was no sound at all, and the air was chill. Faintly ominous vibrations wafted in from the near distance. There was the diffuse odor of spoiling carrion.

Smash licked his lips. Carrion always made him hungry. But he did not trust this situation. Tandy was not here, of course, and he saw nothing that could account for her condition. Nothing to frighten or horrify a person. He decided to leave.

However, he perceived no way out. He had arrived full-formed within this scene; there was no obvious exit. He was locked into this vision—unless he had entered through this door and turned about to face it without realizing, and could depart through it. Doors generally did lead from one place to another.

He took hold of the black metal doorknob. The thing zapped him with a small bolt of lightning. He tried to let go, but his hand was locked on. He wore no gauntlets; evidently he had left them behind. The electric pain pulsed through his fingers, locking the muscles clenched with its special magic. There was a wash of pain, literally; his black hand was now glowing with red color, in stark contrast with the monochrome of the rest of the scene.

Smash yanked hard on the knob. The entire door ripped off its hinges. The pain stopped, the red color faded, his fingers relaxed at last, and he hurled the door away behind him.

Before him was a long, blank hall penetrating the somber house. From the depths of it came a horrendous groan. This did not seem to be the way out; he was sure he had not walked any great distance inside the gourd. But it did seem pleasant enough, and was the only way that offered. Smash stepped inside.

A chill draft rustled the fur on his legs. The odor of putrefaction intensified. The floor shuddered as it took his weight. There was another groan.

Smash strode forward, impatient to get out of this interestingly drear but pointless place, worried about Tandy. He needed to consult with the Siren, to work out some strategy by which he might find whatever had scared Tandy and deal with it. Otherwise he would have felt free to enjoy the further entertainments of this house. Had he realized what kind of scene was inside the gourd, he would have entered it years ago.

Something flickered before him. Smash squinted, and saw it was a ghost. "You trapped, too?" he asked sympathetically, and walked through it.

The ghost made an angry moan and flickered to his frontside again. "Boooooo!" it boooooooed.

Smash paused. Was this creature trying to tell him something? He had known very few ghosts, as they did not ordinarily associate with ogres. There were several at Castle Roogna, attending to routine hauntings. "Do I know you?" he asked. "Do we have any mutual acquaintances?"

"Yoowwell!" the ghost yoweled, its hollow eyes flashing darkness.

"I'd help you if I could, but I'm lost myself," Smash said apologetically, and brushed on through it again. The ghost, disgusted for some obscure reason, faded away.

The passage narrowed. This was no illusion; the walls were closing on either side, squeezing together. Smash didn't like to be crowded, so he put one hamhand on each wall and pushed outward, exerting ogre force. Something snapped; then the walls slid apart and lay tilted at slightly odd angles. It would probably be a long time before they tried to push another ogre around!

At the end of the hall was a rickety staircase leading up. Smash pressed one hairy bare foot on the lowest step and shoved down, testing it. The step bowed and squeaked piteously, but supported his weight. Smash took another step—and suddenly the entire stairway began to move, carrying him upward. Magic stairs! What would this enjoyable place think of next?

The stairs accelerated. Faster and faster they went, making the dank air breeze past Smash's face. At the top of the flight they ended abruptly, and he went sailing out into blank space.

Ogres liked lots of violent things, but were not phenomenally partial to falling. However, they weren't unduly concerned about it, either. Smash stiffened his legs. In a moment he landed on hard concrete. Naturally it fractured under the impact of his feet. He stepped out of the rubble and looked about.

He seemed to be in some sort of deep well, or oubliette. The circular wall narrowed above, making climbing out difficult. Then a shape appeared in silhouette, holding a big stone over its head. The figure had horns and looked like a demon. Smash was not especially partial to demons, but he greeted this one courteously enough. "Up yours, devil!" he called.

The demon dropped the stone down the well. Smash saw the dark shape looming, but had no room to step out of the way.

Then light flared. Smash blinked. It was broad daylight in the forest of Xanth. "Are you all right?" the Siren asked. "I didn't dare let you stay out too long."

"I am all right," Smash said. "How is Tandy?"

"Unchanged, I'm afraid. Smash, I don't think you *can* destroy what is bothering her, because the horror is now in her mind. We could smash the gourd and it still wouldn't help her."

Smash considered. His skull no longer heated up when he did that. "I believe you are correct. I saw nothing really alarming in there. Perhaps I should go into the gourd with her and show her that it's not so bad."

The Siren frowned. "I suspect ogres have different definitions of bad. Just what happened in there?"

"Only a haunted house. Shocking doorknob. Ghost. Squeezing walls—I suppose those could have been awkward for a human person. Moving stairs. A demon dropping a rock down a well."

"Why would a demon do that?"

"I don't know. I happened to be below at the time. Maybe it didn't like my greeting."

Tandy stirred. Her eyes swung loosely about. Her lips pursed flaccidly. She looked disturbingly like a ghost. "No, no house, no demon. A graveyard . . ." She lapsed into staring, her mouth beginning to drool.

"Evidently you had separate visions," the Siren said, using a puff from a puffball growing nearby to clean up the girl's face. "That complicates it."

"Maybe if we go in together, we'll share a vision," Smash conjectured.

"But there is only one peephole."

Smash poked his littlest hamfinger into the rind of the gourd. "Two, now."

"You ogres are so practical!"

They set the gourd before Tandy, who immediately peered into the first peephole. Then Smash squatted so that he could peer into the second.

He was back in the well. The rock was plunging at his head. Hastily he raised a fist, since he didn't want a headache. The rock shattered on the fist, falling around him in the form of fragments, pebbles, and gravel. So much for that. If the demon would just drop a few more stones down, Smash would soon have this well filled up with rubble and could step out.

But the demon did not reappear. Too bad. Smash looked around the gloom. Tandy was not with him. He was in the same vision he had left, picking it up in the same moment he had left it. He was using a different peephole, but that didn't seem to matter. Probably Tandy was back in her original vision, at the same point it had been interrupted, getting scared by whatever had scared her before. It seemed the gourd programmed each vision separately.

However, it was all the same gourd. Tandy had to be somewhere in here, and he intended to find her, rescue her from her horror, and smash that horror into a quivering pulp so it wouldn't bother her again. All he had to do was make a sufficient search.

He took hold of a stone in the wall of the well and yanked it out. Three more stones fell out with it. Smash took another; this time five more fell. This old well was not well constructed! He stood on these and drew out more stones. The well filled in beneath him steadily, and before long he was back at the surface. There was no sign whatsoever of the demon who had dropped the first rock on him. That was just as well, for Smash might have treated that demon a trifle unkindly, perhaps snapping its tail like a rubber band and launching the creature on a flight to the moon. The least that demon could have done was to stay around long enough to drop a few more useful boulders down the well.

Now he stood in a chamber surrounded by doors. He heard a faint, despairing scream. Tandy!

He went to the nearest door and grasped the knob. It shocked him, so he ripped the door out of its socket and threw it away. The room inside was a bare chamber: a false lead. He tried the next door, got shocked again, and ripped it out, too. Another bare chamber. He went to the third door—and it didn't shock him. The doors were learning! He opened this one gently. But it led only to another decoy chamber.

Finally he opened one that showed an outdoor walk. He hurried down this, hurdling a square that he recognized as a covered pitfall—ogres naturally knew about such things, having had centuries of ancestral experience avoiding such traps set for them by foolish men—and emerged into a windy graveyard.

Battered gravestones were all around, marking sunken graves. Some stones tilted forward precariously, as if trying to peer into the cavities they demarked. It occurred to Smash that the buried bodies might have climbed out and gone elsewhere, accounting for the sunkenness of the graves and the suspicions of the headstones, but this was not his concern.

The odor of carrion was stronger out here. Maybe some of the corpses had not been buried deep enough. A wind came up, cutting around the stone edges with dismal howling. Smash breathed deeply, appreciating it, then concentrated on the business at hand. "Tandy!" he called. "Where are you?" For she had said she was in a graveyard, and this must be the place.

He heard a faint sobbing. Carefully he traced down the source. It was slow work, because the sound was carried by the wind, and the wind curved around the gravestones in cold blue streams, searching out the best edges for making moaning tunes. But at last he found the huddled figure, cowering behind a white stone crypt.

"Tandy!" he repeated. "It's I. Smash, the tame ogre. Let me take you away from all this."

She looked up, pale with fright, as if hardly daring to recognize him. Her mouth opened, but only drool came out.

He reached out to take her arm, to help her to her feet. But she was as limp as a rag doll and would not rise. She just continued sobbing. She seemed little different from her Xanth self. Something was missing.

Smash considered. For once he was thankful for the Eye Queue, because now he could ponder without pain. What would account for the girl's lethargy and misery? He had thought it was fear, but now that he was here, she should have no further cause for that. It was as if she had lost something vital, like eyesight or—

Or her soul. Suddenly Smash remembered how vulnerable souls could be, and knew that if anyone were likely to blunder into a soul-hazardous situation, Tandy was the one. She knew so little of the ways of Xanth! No wonder she was desolate and empty.

"Your soul, Tandy," he said, holding her so that she had to look into his face. "Where is it?"

Listlessly she nodded toward the crypt. Smash saw that it had a heavy, tight stone door. Scrape marks on the dank ground indicated it had recently been opened. She must have gone inside, perhaps trying to escape the graveyard—and had been ejected without her soul.

"I will recover it," he said.

Now she bestirred herself enough to react. "No, no," she moaned. "I am lost. Save yourself."

"I agreed to protect you," he reminded her. "I shall do it." He set her gently aside and addressed the crypt. The door had no handle, but he knew how to deal with that. He elevated his huge bare fist and smashed it brutally forward into the stone.

Ouch! Without his gauntlets, his hands were more tender. He could not safely apply his full force. But his blow had accomplished its purpose; the stone door had cracked marginally and jogged a smidgen outward. He applied his horny fingernails and hauled the door unwillingly open.

A dark hole faced him. As his eyes adjusted, he saw a white outline. It was the skeleton of a man. It reached for him with bone-fingers.

Smash realized where the bodies in the sunken graves had gone. They had been recruited for guard duty and were walking about this crypt. But he was not in the mood for nuisance. He grabbed the skeleton by the bones of its arm and hauled it violently out of the crypt. The thing flew through the air and landed as a jumble of bones. The ogre proceeded on into the hole.

Other skeletons appeared, clustering about him, their connections rattling. Smash treated them as he had the first, disconnecting their foot-bones from their leg-bones and other bones, causing the bonepile to grow rapidly. Soon the remaining skeletons reconsidered, not wishing to have him roll their bones, and left him alone.

Deep in the ground the ogre came to a dark coffin. The smell was mouth-wateringly awful; something really rotten was in there. Was Tandy's soul in there, too? He picked up the box and shook it.

"All right, all *right!*" a muffled voice came from the coffin. "You made your point, ogre. You aren't afraid of anything. What do you want?"

"Give back Tandy's soul," Smash said grimly.

"I can't do that, ogre," the box protested. "We made a deal. Her freedom for her soul. I let her out of this world; I keep her soul. That's the way we deal here; souls are the currency of this medium."

"The Siren let her out by removing the gourd," Smash argued. "She never had to pay."

"Coincidence. I permitted it, once the deal was struck. The negotiation is sealed."

Smash had lived and thought like an ogre a lot longer than he had lived and thought intelligently. Now he reverted to convenient old habits. He roared, picked up the coffin, and hurled it against the wall. The box fell to the floor, somewhat sprung, and several ceiling stones dropped on it. Nauseating goo dribbled from a crack in it. Dirt sifted down from the chamber wall to smooth the outlines.

"Maybe further negotiation is possible after all," the voice from the coffin said, somewhat shaken. "Would you consider trading souls?"

Smash readied his hamfist again. "Wait!" the voice cried, alarmed. It evidently wasn't used to dealing with real brutes. "I merely collect souls; I don't have the authority to give them back. If you want the girl's soul now, your only option is to trade."

The ogre considered. He might smash the coffin and its occupant to pieces, but that would not necessarily recover the soul. If Tandy's soul were in there, it could get hurt in the battering. So maybe it was better to bargain. "Trade what?"

"Another soul, of course. How about yours?"

This box thought he was a typically stupid ogre. "No."

"Well, someone else's. What about that buxom mature nymph out in Xanth, with the sometime fish-tail? She probably has a luscious, bouncy, juicy soul."

Smash considered again. He decided, with an un-ogrish precision of ethics, that he could not make any commitments on behalf of the Siren. "Not her soul. And not mine."

"Then the girl's soul must remain."

Smash got another whiff of the stench from the coffin and knew that Tandy's soul could not be allowed to rot there. He still did not consider the deal by which the coffin had gotten Tandy's soul to be valid. He stooped to pick up the battered coffin again.

"Wait!" the voice cried. "There is one other option. You could accede to a lien."

The ogre paused. "Explain."

"A lien is a claim on the property of another as security for a debt," the coffin explained. "A lien on your soul would mean that you agree to replace the girl's soul with another soul—and if you don't, then your own soul is forfeit. But you keep your soul in the interim, or most of it."

It did seem to make sense. "How long an interim?"

"Shall we say thirty days?"

"Six months," Smash said. "You think I'm stupid?"

"I did think that," the coffin confessed. "After all, you are an ogre, and it is well known that the brains of ogres are mostly in their muscles. In fact, their brains *are* mostly muscles."

"Not true," Smash said. "An ogre's skull is filled with bone, not muscle."

"I stand corrected. My skull is filled with necrosis. How about sixty days?"

"Four months."

"Split the difference: ninety days."

"Okay," Smash agreed. "But I don't agree you are entitled to keep *any* soul, just because you tricked an innocent girl into trading it off for nothing."

"Are you sure you're an ogre? You don't sound like one."

"I'm an ogre," Smash affirmed. "Would you like me to throw you around some more to prove it?"

"That won't be necessary," the coffin said quickly. "If you disagree with the assessment, you must deal with the boss: the Night Stallion. He makes decisions of policy."

"The Dark Horse?"

"Close enough; some do call him that. He governs the herd of nightmares."

It began to fall into place. "This is where the nightmares live? By day, when they're not out delivering bad dreams to sleepers?"

"Exactly. All the bad dreams are generated here in the gourd, from the raw material of people's fundamental fears—loss, pain, death, shame, and the unknown. The Stallion decides where the dreams go, and the mares take them there. Your girlfriend abused a mare, so it took a lien on her soul, and when she came here, that lien was called due. So her soul is forfeit, and now we have it, and only the Night Stallion can change that. Why don't we set you up for an appointment with the Stallion, and you can settle this directly with him?"

"An appointment? When?"

"Well, he has a full calendar. Bad dreams aren't light fancies, you know. There's a lot of evil in the world that needs recognition. It's a lot of work to craft each dream correctly and designate it for exactly the right person at the right time. So the Stallion is quite busy. The first opening is six months hence."

"But my lien expires in three months!"

"You're smarter than the average ogre, for sure! You might force an earlier audience, but you'd have to find the Stallion first. He certainly won't come to you within three months. I really wouldn't recommend the effort of locating him."

Smash considered again. It seemed to him that this coffin protested too profusely. Something was being concealed here. Time for the ogre act again. "Perhaps so," he said. "There is therefore no point in restraining my natural inclination for violence." He picked up a rock and crumpled it to chips and sand with one hand. He eyed the coffin.

"But I'm sure you can find him!" the box said quickly. "All you have to do is seek the path of most resistance. That's all I can tell you, honest!"

Smash decided that he had gotten as much as he could from the coffin. "Good enough. Give me the girl's soul, and I'll leave my three-month lien and meet the Stallion when I find him."

"Do you think a soul is something you can just carry in your hand?" the coffin demanded derisively.

"Yes," Smash said. He contemplated his hand, slowly closing it into a brutishly ugly fist that hovered menacingly over the coffin.

"Quite," the coffin agreed nervously, sweating another blob of stinking goo. The soul floated up, a luminescent globe that passed right through the wood. Smash cupped it carefully in his hand and tromped from the gloomy chamber. Neither coffin nor skeletons opposed him.

Tandy sat where she had been, the picture of hopeless girlish misery. "Here is your soul," Smash said, and held out the glowing globe.

Unbelievingly, she reached for it. The globe expanded at her touch, becoming a ghost-shape that quickly overlapped her body and merged. For an instant her entire body glowed, right through the tattered red dress; then she was her normal self. "Oh, Smash, you did it!" she exclaimed. "I love you! You recovered my soul from that awful corpse!"

"I promised to protect you," he said gruffly.

"How can I reward you?" She was actually pinching herself, amazed by her restoration. Smash, too, was amazed; he had not before appreciated how much difference a person's soul made.

"No reward," he insisted. "It's part of my job, my service for my Answer."

She considered. "Yes, I suppose. But how ever did you do it? I thought there was no way—"

"I had to indulge my natural propensities slightly," he admitted, glancing at the pile of bones he had made. The bones shuddered and settled lower, eager to avoid his attention.

"Oh. I guess you were more terrible than the skeletons were," she said.

"Naturally. That is the nature of ogres. We're worse than anything." Smash thought it best not to inform her of the actual nature of his deal. "Let's get out of here."

"Oh, yes! But how?"

That was another problem. He could bash through walls, but the force holding Tandy and himself inside the gourd was intangible. "I think we'll have to wait for the Siren to free us. All she has to do is move the gourd so we can't look into it any more, but she doesn't know when we'll be finished in here."

"Oh, I don't want to stay another minute in this horrible place! If I had known what would happen when I peeked into that funny little hole—"

"It's not a bad place, this," Smash said, trying to cheer her. "It can even be fun."

"Fun? In this awful graveyard?"

"Like this." Smash had spied a skeleton poking around a grave, perhaps looking for a new convert. He sneaked up behind it. Ogres didn't have to shake the earth when they walked; they did it because they enjoyed it. "BOOO!" he bellowed.

The skeleton leaped right out of its foot-bones and stumbled away, terrified. Tandy had to smile. "You're pretty scary, all right, Smash," she agreed.

They settled down against a large gravestone. Tandy huddled within the protection of the ogre's huge, hairy arm. It was the only place the poor little girl felt safe in this region.

Chapter 5

Prints of Wails

The Siren greeted them anxiously as they woke to the outer afternoon of Xanth. "I gave you an hour this time, Smash; I just didn't dare wait longer," she said. "Are you all right?"

"I have my soul back!" Tandy said brightly. "Smash got it for me!"

The Siren had been looking her age, for her human stock caused her to be less than immortal. Now relief was visibly restoring her youthfulness. "That's wonderful, dear," she said, hugging her. Then, looking at Smash, the Siren sobered again. "But usually souls can't be recovered without hell to pay—ah, that is, some sort of quid pro quo. Are you sure—"

"I've got mine," Smash said jovially. "Such as it is. Ogres do have souls, don't they?"

"As far as I know, only people of human derivation have souls," the Siren said. "But all of those do, even if their human ancestor was many generations ago, and so we three qualify. I'm sure yours is as good as any, Smash, and perhaps better than some."

"It must be stronger and stupider, anyway," he said.

"I'm so glad it's all right," the Siren said, seeming not entirely convinced. She evidently suspected something, but chose not to make an issue of it at this time. Older females tended to be less innocent than young ones, he realized, but also more discreet.

They considered their situation. There seemed to be no ogres and no merfolk at Lake Ogre-Chobee, despite its name.

"Now I remember," Smash said. "The curse-fiends drove the ogres away. They migrated north to the Ogre-fen-Ogre Fen. I don't know why I didn't think of that before!"

"Because you weren't cursed by the Eye Queue before, silly," Tandy said. "You weren't very smart. But that's all right; we'll just go up to the Ogre Fen and find your tribe."

"But that's the entire length of Xanth!" the Siren protested. "Who knows what horrors lie along the way?"

"Yes, fun," Smash said.

"Funny, the Good Magician didn't remind you about the ogres' change of residence," the Siren said. "Well, there's certainly not much doing here. I would like to travel with you a little longer, if I may, at least until I find a lake inhabited by merfolk."

"Sure, come along, we like your company," Tandy said immediately, and Smash shrugged. It really made little difference to him. He was partially preoccupied by his problem with the lien on his soul. He would soon have to find a pretext to go back into the gourd to search for the Night Stallion and fight for his soul.

"But first, let's abolish this menace once and for all," the Siren said. She picked up the hypnogourd and lifted it high overhead, throwing it violently to the ground.

"No!" Smash cried. But before he could move, the gourd had smashed to earth. It fragmented into pinkish pulp, black seeds, and translucent juice. There was no sign of the world he and Tandy had toured within it; the magic was gone.

The ogre stood staring at the ruin. Now, how could he return to that world to settle his account? Somehow he knew his lien had not been abated by the destruction of the gourd; his avenue to that world had merely been closed. It would take time to manifest, but he knew he was in very bad trouble.

"Is something wrong?" the Siren asked. "Did you leave something in there?"

"It doesn't matter," Smash said brusquely. After all, she had meant well, and there was nothing to be done now. No point in upsetting the girls, no matter how privately satisfying it might have been to rant and rave and stomp, ogre-style, until the whole forest and lake trembled and roiled with reaction to the violence.

They trekked north through the variegated jungle and tundra and intemperate zones of Xanth. Most of the local flora and fauna left the party alone, wisely not wishing to antagonize an ogre. Upon occasion, some gnarled old bull-spruce would paw the earth with a branch-hoof and poke a limb-horn into the way, but a short, sharp blow with Smash's gauntleted fist taught such trees manners. Progress was good.

They were just considering where to spend the night when they heard something. There was a thin, barely audible screaming, and a cacophony of ugly pantings, breathings, and raspings. "Something unpleasant is going on," the Siren said.

"I'll investigate," Smash said, glad for the chance for a little relaxing violence. He tromped toward the commotion.

A crowd of multilegged things was chasing a little fairy lass, who seemed to have hurt one of her gossamer wings. She was running this way and that, but wherever she went, creatures like squished caterpillars with tentacles moved to block the way, dribbling hungry drool. The fairy was screaming with fright and horror, and the pursuers were reveling in her discomfort, playing cruelly with her before closing for the kill.

"What's this?" Smash demanded.

One of the creatures turned toward him, though it was hard to tell which side was its front. "Stay out of what does not concern you, trashface," it said insolently.

Now, Smash normally did not involve himself in what did not concern him, but his recent experience with Tandy in the gourd had sensitized him to the plight of small, pretty females in distress. Also, he did not like being told to stay out, despite the compliment to his face. Therefore he reacted with polite force. "Get out of here, you ghastly parody."

"Oho!" the ghastly cried. "So the dumb brute needs a lesson, too!"

Immediately the creatures oriented on Smash. From a distance they were repulsive; from up close, they were worse. They launched purple spittle at him, belched obscenely all over their bodies, and scratched at him with dirty claws. But several still chased the hapless fairy lass.

Smash became moderately perturbed. Now it seemed the reputation of ogres was on the line. He picked up a ghastly. It defecated on his paw. He heaved it into the forest. It scurried back. He pounded another into the ground—but it merely squished flat, then rebounded. He tore one apart, but it just stretched impossibly, and snapped back to its normal shapelessness when he let go, leaving a slug of smelly slime on his fingers.

Now the fairy screamed louder. The ghastlies had almost caught her. Smash had to act quickly or he would be too late to help her. But what would stop these creatures?

Fortunately, his new intelligence assisted. If throwing, pounding, and stretching didn't work, maybe tying would. He grabbed two ghastlies and squeezed and squished them together, tying a knot in their infinitely stretch-able limbs. Then he tied in a third, and a fourth, and a fifth. Soon he had a huge ball of tied ghastlies, since they kept coming stupidly at him. Their rebounding and stretching didn't do them much good; it merely tightened the knots. In due course, all the ghastlies were balled together, spitting, hissing, scratching, and pooping on each other constantly.

Smash dropped the ball, wiped himself off on some towel-leaves, and checked on the fairy. She was as frightened of him as she had been of the ghastlies. He did not chase her; he had only wanted to make sure she was not too badly hurt.

When the fairy saw him stop, she stopped. She was a tiny thing, hardly half the height of Tandy, a nude girl form with sparklingly mussed hair and thin, iridescent wings with scenic patterns. "You aren't chasing me, ogre?"

"No. Go your way in peace, fairy."

"But why did you tie all the ghastlies in a knot, if you didn't want to gobble me up?"

"To help you escape."

She had difficulty assimilating this. "I thought you were an ogre, but you neither sound nor act like one."

"We all have our off days," Smash said apologetically.

Tandy and the Siren arrived. "He's a gentle ogre," the Siren explained. "He helps the helpless." She introduced the three of them.

"I'm John," the fairy said. Then, before they could react, she continued. "I know, I know it's not a proper name for the like of me, but my father was away when I was born, and the message got garbled, and I was stuck with it. So now I'm on a quest for my proper name. But I got tossed by a gust and hurt my wing, and then the ghastlies—"

"Why don't you travel with us?" Tandy asked. "Until your wing gets better. Monsters don't bother us much. We have one of our own." She gripped Smash's dangling ham-hand possessively.

John considered, evidently uncertain about traveling with a monster. Then the ball of ghastlies began working loose, and she decided. "Yes, I will go with you. It should take only a day or so for my wing to mend."

Smash did not comment. He had not asked for any companions, but Tandy had been forced on him, and she had a propensity for inviting others. Perhaps it was because Xanth was so new to her that she felt the company of others who were more familiar with it would improve things. Maybe she was right; the Siren had certainly helped them get out of the gourd. It didn't really matter; Smash could travel with three as well as with one.

Now night came. Smash foraged for food and found a patch of spaghetti just ripening near a spice tree. He harvested several great handfuls, shook the spice on them, and proffered this for their repast. The girls seemed a trifle doubtful at first, but all were hungry, and soon they were consuming the delicious, slippery stuff, ogre-style, by the handful and slurpful. Then

they found a basket palm with enough stout hanging baskets for all, and
spent a reasonably comfortable night.

But before they slept, the Siren questioned John about the kind of name
she was looking for. "Why don't you just take any name you like and use it?"

"Oh, I couldn't," John said. "I can answer only to the name I was given.
Since I was given the wrong one, I must keep it until I recover the right
one."

"How can you be sure there *is* a right one? If your father was mis-
informed—"

"Oh, no, he knew who I was. He sent back a good name, but somehow it
got lost, and the wrong name arrived instead. By the time he got home, it
was too late to fix it."

Smash understood the Siren's perplexity. He, like her, had not been
aware that names were so intricately tagged.

"Does that mean that someone else got your name?" the Siren asked.

"Of course. Some male fairy got my name, and must be as unhappy with it
as I am with his. But if I find him, we can exchange them. Then everything
will be just fine."

"I see," the Siren said. "I hope you find him soon."

In the morning they breakfasted on honeydew that had formed on the
leaves of the basket tree, then resumed the trek north. John buzzed her
healing wing every so often, and the pattern on it seemed to come alive in a
three-dimensional image, like flowers blooming, but she could not yet fly.
She had to be content to walk. She was a cheery little thing, good company,
and full of cute anecdotes about life among the fairies. It seemed the Fairy
Kingdom was a large one, with many principalities and interstate commerce
between groups, and internecine trade wars.

They started to climb. None of them was familiar with this section of
Xanth, which was east of the Region of Madness, so they merely proceeded
directly north. With luck, it wouldn't be too bad.

But it was bad. The mountain became so steep it was impossible to climb
normally. They could not go around it, because the sides of the channel they
traveled had risen even more steeply. They had either to proceed forward or
to retreat all the way to the base and try another approach. None was willing
to retreat.

Smash used his gauntleted fists to break out sections of rock, making
crude steps for the others. Fortunately, the really steep part was not extensive, and by noon they stood at the top.

It was a lake, hardly on the scale of Ogre-Chobee but impressive enough,
brimful with sparkling water. "This must be an old volcano," John said. "I
have flown over similar ones, though not this big. We must beware; water
dragons like such lakes, especially if they are hot on the bottom."

Smash grimaced. He didn't like water dragons, because they tended to be
too much for an honest ogre to handle. But he saw no sign of such a creature
here. No droppings, no piles of bones, no discarded old scales or teeth.

"What are those?" Tandy inquired, pointing.

There were marks on the surface of the water. They were roughly circular indentations, with smaller indentations on one side of each large one. "They look like prints," the Siren said. "As if some creature walked on the water. Is that possible?"

Smash put one foot on the water. It sank through. The ripples moved across the prints, erasing them. "Not possible," he decided.

Still, they decided to stay clear of the water until they knew more about it. Seemingly minor mysteries could be hazardous to their health in Xanth. They walked around the west side of the lake, following one of those suspiciously convenient paths because there was no other route between the deep water and the clifflike outer face of the mountain.

But as they bore north, following the curve of the cone, they encountered an outcropping of spongy rock. "Magma," Smash conjectured, forcing another subterranean memory to the surface, slightly heated.

"I don't care who it is, it's in our way," Tandy complained. Indeed, the rock blotted out the path, forcing them to attempt a hazardous scramble.

"I shall remove it," Smash decided. He readied his hamfist and pounded one good pound on the magma.

The rock responded with a deafening reverberation. They all clapped their hands over their ears while the mountain shook and the lake made waves.

Finally the awful noise died away. "That magma comes loud!" the Siren said.

"Magma cum laude," the ogre agreed, not hearing well yet.

"It sure is some sound," Tandy said, looking dizzy. The fairy agreed.

They decided they didn't like the sound of it, and would try the other side of the lake, where the way might be quieter. As they walked the path back, an awful moan slid across the water. "What is that?" Tandy demanded anxiously.

"The wailing of whatever made the prints," the Siren conjectured.

"Oh. So these are the prints of wails."

"Close enough." The Siren grimaced. "I hope we don't meet the wail, though. I've had some experience with music on water, and this makes me nervous."

"Yes, you ought to know," Tandy agreed. "My father said you could bring any man to you from afar, if he heard you."

"Yes, when I had my magic," she said sadly. "Those days are gone, and perhaps it is just as well, but I do get lonely."

They approached the east side of the lake. But here they encountered more trouble. An ugly head lifted on a serpentine neck. It was not exactly a dragon's head, and not exactly a sea monster's head, but it had affinities with both. It was not large as monster heads went, but it hissed viciously enough.

Smash was tired of being balked. He did not mess with this minor monster; he reached out with one hand and caught the neck between gauntleted thumb and forefinger.

Immediately another head appeared, similar to the first and just as aggressive. Smash caught this one in his other glove.

Then a third came. This was getting awkward! Had he stumbled onto a whole nest of serpents? Hastily Smash smashed the first two heads together, crushing both, and reached for the third.

"They all connect!" the Siren exclaimed. "It's a many-headed serpent!"

Indeed it was! Four more heads rose up, making seven in all. Smash crushed two more, but had to move quickly to prevent the remaining three from burying their fangs in his limbs. He rose to the need, however, by catching one under his feet and the last two in his hands. In a moment all had been crushed, and he relaxed.

"Smash, look out!" Tandy cried. "More heads!"

Apparently a couple of the ones he had dealt with had not been completely destroyed, and had revived. This was unusual; things seldom recovered from the impact of ogre force. He grabbed these—and discovered they sprouted from the same neck. Their junction formed a neat Y. He was sure he hadn't encountered this configuration before.

"More heads!" Tandy screamed.

"Now there were six more, in three pairs. New heads were growing from the old ones!

"It's a hydra!" the Siren cried. "Each lost head generates two more! You can never get ahead of it!"

"I've got too many heads of it!" Smash muttered, stepping back. The hydra was generating a small forest of hissing heads, each lunging and snapping at anything in range. Two were squaring off at each other.

"You can't kill a hydra," the Siren continued. "Its essence is immortal. It draws its strength from the water."

"Then I shall remove the water," Smash said. "It will be easy to bash a hole in this rim and let the lake out."

"Oh, please don't do that!" the Siren protested. "I'm a creature of water, and I hate to see it mistreated. You would ruin a perfectly lovely lake, and drown many innocent creatures below, and kill many innocent lake denizens. There is an entire ecology in any such body—"

Was the mermaid becoming the conscience of the group? Smash hesitated.

"That's true," John admitted. "Pretty lakes should be left alone. Most of them have much more good than evil in them."

Smash looked at Tandy. "I agree," she said. "We don't want to harm others, and this water *is* nice."

The ogre shrugged. He didn't want trouble with his friends. As he thought about it, with his amplified Eye Queue intelligence—which remained a nuisance—he realized they were right. Wanton destruction could only beget a deterioration of the environment of Xanth, and that would, in the long run, damage the prospects of ogres. "No harm to others," he agreed gruffly. If any other ogres ever heard of this, he would be in trouble! Imagine *not* destroying something!

"Oh, I could kiss you," Tandy said. "But I can't reach you."

Smash chuckled. "Good thing. Now we'll have to swim across the lake. Do all of you know how to swim?"

"Oh, I couldn't swim," John said. "My wings would break."

"Maybe you can fly now," the Siren suggested.

"Maybe." The fairy tried, buzzing her pretty wings, making the flower-pattern blossoms again. She seemed to lighten as the downdraft of air dusted dirt out from the ridge, but she did not quite take off. Then she jumped. A gust of wind passed at that moment, carrying her out over the rim. She agitated her wings furiously, but could not sustain elevation and began to fall.

Smash reached out and caught her before she crashed into the rocky slope. She screamed, then realized he was helping her, not attacking her. He set her carefully back on the ledge, where she stood panting prettily and quivering with reaction.

"Not yet, it seems," the Siren said. "But you might sit on Smash's back while he swims."

"I suppose," the fairy agreed faintly. Her little bare bosom was heaving. It occurred to Smash that the loss of the ability to fly might be quite disturbing to a creature whose natural mode of travel was flight. He might react similarly if he lost his ogre strength.

They entered the water. Tandy could swim well enough, and, of course, the Siren converted to mermaid form and was completely at home. John perched nervously on Smash's head and was so light he hardly felt her weight. He began stroking across the lake, careful not to splash enough to cause trouble, despite his pleasure in splashing. Some sacrifices were necessary when one traveled in company.

The Siren led the way, easily outdistancing the others. That creature certainly could swim; she was in her element.

Then something loomed from the north. It was huge and dark, like a low-flying thundercloud, scooting across the water. Simultaneously the awful wailing came again, and now Smash realized it came from the cloud-thing. There was also a pattering drumbeat punctuating the wails.

The Siren paused in place. "I don't like this," she said. "That thing is trotting on the surface of the water; I feel the vibrations of its footfalls. And it's headed for us. I could outdistance it, I think; but Tandy can't, and Smash can't do much without imperiling John. We had better get out of the water."

"It's coming too fast," John said. "It will catch us before we get back to shore."

She was right. The monster loomed rapidly onward, casting a dark shadow. It was not actually a cloud, but was composed of gray-blue foam, with a number of holes through which the wailing passed, and hundreds of little feet that touched the water. When it moved to one side, they saw the prints left on the surface, just like the ones they had seen before. The prints of wails.

"Oh, we are doomed!" John cried. "Save yourself, Smash; dive under the water, hide from it!"

An ogre hide from a monster? Little did the fairy grasp the magnitude of the insult she had innocently rendered. "No," Smash said. "I'll fight it."

"It's too big to fight!"

"It probably smothers its prey by surrounding it," Tandy said. She was being practical. She seemed much less afraid of things since having discovered the ultimate nature of fear inside the gourd. Monsters were only monsters, when one's soul was intact. "You can't fight fog or jelly."

Smash realized she was probably right. These assorted girls were making more sense than he would have thought before he came to know them. In the water, with a delicate and flightless fairy on his head, he could not fight efficiently anyway—and if there was nothing really solid to punch out, his fists would be of little use. It galled him to concede that there were monsters that an ogre couldn't handle, but in this case it seemed to be so. Curse this Eye Queue that made him see reason!

"I'll lead it away!" the Siren cried. She was hovering in the water, her powerful tail elevating her body, so that it was as if she stood only waist-deep. She would have been a considerable sight, that way, for a human male. It seemed to Smash that she should have no trouble attracting a merman, at such time as she found one. "You swim on across the lake," the Siren continued. She set off toward the west, moving with amazing velocity. She was like a bird in flight across the surface of the lake.

When she was a fair distance away, she paused and began to sing. She had a beautiful voice, with an eerie quality, a little like the wailing of the monster. Perhaps she was deliberately imitating it.

The monster paused. Then it rotated grandly and ran toward the Siren, its little feet striking the water without splashing, leaving the prints. That mystery had been solved, though Smash did not understand how the prints remained after the wailing monster moved on. But, of course, the effects of magic did not need any explanation.

Once the monster had cleared the area, lured away by the Siren, Smash and Tandy swam on across. It was a fair distance, and Tandy tired, slowing them; it seemed there were not many lakes this big in the underworld. Finally Smash told her to grab hold of one of his feet so he could tow her. The truth was, he was getting tired himself; he would have preferred to wade, but the water was far too deep for that. It would have been un-ogrish to confess any weakness, however.

They made it safely to the north lip. They drew themselves out and rested, hoping the Siren was all right.

Soon she appeared, swimming deep below the surface. Her tail gave her a tremendous forward thrust, and she was a thing of genuine beauty as she slid through the water, her hair streaming back like bright seaweed, her body as sleek and glossy as that of a healthy fish. Then she came up, her head bursting the surface, her hands rising automatically to brush back her wet tresses, mermaidlike. "My, that was interesting!" she said, flipping out of the water to sit on the rim, her tail hidden in the water, so that now she most resembled a healthy nymph.

"The monster was friendly?" Tandy asked doubtfully.

"No, it tried to consume me. But it couldn't reach below the water because its magic prints keep it above. It tried to lure me close, but I'm an experienced hand at luring creatures, and was too careful to be taken in."

"Then you were in real danger!" Tandy was now very sensitive to danger from monsters that lured their victims, whether by an easy access path or a convenient peephole.

"No danger for me," the Siren said, flinging her damp hair out as she changed to human legs and climbed the rest of the way from the water. "Few creatures can catch my kind in our element. Not that there are many quite like me; most merfolk can't make legs. That's my human heritage. Of course, my sister the Gorgon never was able to make a tail; it was her face that changed. Magical heredity is funny stuff! But I talked briefly with the monster. He considers himself a whale."

"A whale of a what?" Smash asked.

"Just a whale."

"Isn't that a Mundane monster?" John asked. It was generally known in Xanth that the worst monsters were Mundane, as were the worst people.

"Yes. But this one claims some whales migrated to Xanth, grew legs so they could cross to inland waters, and then kept the legs for lake-running. Some find small lakes; they're puddle-jumpers. Some find pools of rum; they're rum-runners. He says he's of the first water, a royal monster, a Prince of his kind."

"A Prince of Whales," Tandy said. "Is he really?"

"I don't think so. That's why he wails."

"Life is hard all over," Smash said without much sympathy. "Let's get down off this mountain."

Indeed, the sun was losing strength and starting to fall, as it did each day, never learning to conserve its energy so that it could stay aloft longer. They needed to get to a comfortable place before night. Fortunately, the slope on this side was not as steep, so they were able to slide down it fairly readily.

As they neared the northern base, where the forest resumed, a nymph came out to meet them. She was a delicate brown in color, with green hair fringed with red. Her torso, though slender and full in the manner of her kind, was gently corrugated like the bark of a young tree, and her toes were rootlike. She approached Tandy, who was the most human of the group. "Please—do you know where Castle Roogna is?"

"I tried to reach Castle Roogna a year ago," Tandy said. "But I got lost. I think Smash knows, though."

"Oh, I wouldn't ask an ogre!" the nymph exclaimed.

"He's a halfway tame ogre," Tandy assured her. "He doesn't eat many nymphs."

Smash was getting used to these slights. He waited patiently for the nymph to gain confidence, then answered her question as well as he could. "I have been to Castle Roogna. But I'm not going there at the moment, and the way is difficult. It is roughly west of here."

"I'll find it somehow," the nymph said. "I've got to." She faced west.

"Now wait," Tandy protested, as Smash had suspected she would. The girl had sympathy enough to overflow all Xanth! "You can't get there alone! You could easily get lost or gobbled up. Why don't you travel with us until we find someone else who is going there?"

"But you're going north!" the nymph protested.

"Yes. But we travel safely, because of Smash." Tandy indicated him again. "Nobody bothers an ogre."

"There is that," the nymph agreed. "I don't want to bother him myself." She considered, seeming somewhat tired. "I could help you find food and water. I'm good at that sort of thing. I'm a hamadryad."

"Oh, a tree-nymph!" the Siren exclaimed. "I should have realized. What are you doing out of your tree?"

"It's a short story. Let me find you a place to eat and rest, and I will tell it."

The dryad kept her promise. Soon they were ensconced in a glade beside a large eggplant whose ripe eggs had been hard-boiled by the sun. Nearby was a sodapond that sparkled effervescently. They sat in a circle cracking open eggs, using the shells to dip out sodawater. Proper introductions were made, and the dryad turned out to be named Fireoak, after her tree.

She was, despite her seeming youth, over a century old. All her life had been spent with her fireoak tree, which had sprouted from a fireacorn the year she came into being. She had grown with it, as hamadryads did, protecting it and being protected by it. Then a human village had set up nearby, and villagers had come out to cut down the tree to build a firehouse. Fireoak made fine fire-resistant wood, the dryad explained; its own appearance of burning was related to Saint Elmo's fire, an illusion of burning that made it stand out beautifully and discouraged predatory bugs except for fireants. In vain had the dryad protested that the cutting of the oak would kill both it and her; the villagers wanted the wood. So she had taken advantage of the full moon that night to weave a lunatic fringe that shrouded the tree, hiding it from them. But that would last only a few days; when the moon shrank to a crescent, so would the fringe, betraying the tree's location. She had to accomplish her mission before then.

"But how can a trip to Castle Roogna help?" John asked. "They use wood there, too, don't they?"

"The King is there!" Fireoak replied. "I understand he is an environmentalist. He protects special trees."

"It is true," Smash agreed. "He protects rare monsters, too." Now for the first time he realized the probable basis for King Trent's tolerance of an ogre family near Castle Roogna: they were rare wilderness specimens. "He always looks for the solution of least ecological damage."

The dryad looked at him curiously. "You certainly don't talk like an ogre!"

"He blundered into an Eye Queue vine," Tandy explained. "It cursed him with smartness."

"How are you able to survive away from your tree?" the Siren asked. "I thought no hamadryad could leave for more than a moment."

"That's what I thought," Fireoak said. "But when death threatened my tree, desperation gave me extraordinary strength. For my tree I can do what I must. I feel terribly insecure, however. My soul is the tree."

Tandy and Smash jumped. The analogy was too close for comfort. It was no easy thing to be separated from one's soul.

"I know the feeling," the Siren said. "I lived all my life in one lake. But I suddenly realized that it had become a desolate place for a lone mermaid. So I am looking for a better lake. But I do miss my original lake, for it contains all my life's experience, and I wonder whether it misses me, too."

"How will you know the new lake won't be desolate for you, too?" Fireoak asked.

"It won't be if it has the right merman in it."

The dryad blushed, her face for an instant showing the color of the fire of her tree. "Oh."

"You're a hundred years old—and you have no experience with men?" Tandy asked.

"Well, I'm a dryad," Fireoak said defensively. "We just don't have much to do with men—only with trees."

"What sort of experience have you had?" the Siren asked Tandy.

"A demon—he—I'd rather not discuss it." It was Tandy's turn to blush. "Anyway, my father is a man."

"Most fathers are," the Siren said.

"Mine isn't!" Smash protested. "My father is an ogre."

She ignored that. "I inherited my legs from my father, my tail from my mother. She was not a true woman, but he was a true man."

"You mean human men really do have, uh, dealings with mermaids?" Tandy asked.

"Human men have dealings with any maid they can catch," the Siren said with a wry smile. "I understand my mother wasn't hard to catch; my father was a very handsome man. But he had to leave when my sister the Gorgon was born."

After a pause, Fireoak resumed her story. "So if I can just talk to the King and get him to save my tree, everything will be all right."

"What about the other trees?" John asked.

Fireoak looked blank. "Other trees?"

"The other ones the villagers are cutting down. Maybe they don't have dryads to speak for them, but they don't deserve destruction."

"I never thought of that," Fireoak said. "I suppose I should put in a word at Castle Roogna for them, too. It would be no bad thing to lobby for the trees."

They found good locations in the trees and settled down for the night. Smash spread himself out on the glade ground; no one would bother him. His head was near the liquidly flowing trunk of a water oak Fireoak had chosen; he overheard the hamadryad's muted sobbing. Evidently her separation from her beloved home tree was harder on her than she showed by day, and the threat to that tree was no distant concern. Smash hoped he could find a way to help her. If he had to, he could go and stand guard over her tree himself. But he didn't know how long that would take. He didn't want to delay his own mission too long, lest the time for the Good Magician's Answer should run out. There was also the matter of the gourd-coffin's lien on his soul; anything he had to do, he had better get done within three months. Already he felt not quite up to snuff, as if part of his soul had been leached away, taking some of his strength with it.

Next day the five of them marched north. The land leveled out, but hazards remained. Tandy blundered into a chokecherry bush, and Smash had to rip the entire plant out of the ground before its vines stopped choking her. Farther along they encountered a power plant, whose branches swelled out into strange angular configurations and hummed with power; woe betide the creature who blundered into that!

Around midday they discovered a lovely vegetable tree, on whose branches grew cabbages, beans, carrots, tomatoes, and turnips, all in fine states of ripeness. Here were all the ingredients for an excellent salad! But as Smash approached it, Tandy grew nervous. "I smell a rat," she said, sniffing the air. "There are big rats down in the caves where I live; I know their odor well. They always mean trouble."

Smash sniffed. Sure enough, there was the faint aroma of rats. What were they doing here?

"I smell it, too," John said. "I hate rats. But where are they?"

The Siren was walking around the tree. "Somewhere in or near the vegetable tree," she announced. "I fear this plant is not entirely what it appears."

Fireoak approached it. "Let me check. I'm good with trees." She was showing no sign of the agony of her separation from her tree, but Smash knew it remained. Her night in a tree must have restored her somewhat, though of course it wasn't *her* tree.

The hamadryad stood close to the vegetable tree. Slowly she touched a leaf. "This is a normal leaf," she said. Then she touched a potato—and one of its eyes blinked. "Get away from here!" Fireoak screamed. "It's a rat!"

Then the fruits and vegetables exploded into action. Each one sprouted legs, tail, and snout and dropped to the ground. A major swarm of rats had camouflaged itself by masquerading as vegetables, luring the unwary into contact—but the smell had given them away. Once a rat, always a rat, by the smell of it.

The Siren, Tandy, and John scurried back in time to avoid the first surge of the rat-race. But Fireoak stood too close. The beasties swarmed around her, biting at her legs, causing her to trip and fall.

Smash leaped across, swooping down with one hand to lift the hamadryad clear of the ground. Several rats came up with her, chewing savagely at her barklike skin. She screamed and tried to brush them off, but they clung tenaciously and bit at her hands.

Smash shook her, but hesitated to do it vigorously enough to fling away the rats, lest it hurt her. As it was, bits of bark and leaf were flying off. Smash had to pinch the rats off one by one, and their claws and teeth left scratches on the dryad's body. By the time the last was gone, she was in an awful state, oozing sap from several scrapes. The swarm of rats surrounded Smash and tried to bite his feet and climb his hairy legs.

Smash stomped ferociously, shaking the glade and crushing several rats with each stomp. But there were hundreds of the little monsters, coming at him from every direction, moving rapidly. They threatened to get on him no matter how fast he stomped. He didn't dare set the dryad down, lest the same fate befall her. His great strength hardly availed against these relatively puny enemies.

"Get away from him!" Tandy screamed from a safe distance. "Leave him alone, you rats!" She seemed really angry. It was almost as if she were trying to defend him from the enemy; that, of course, was a ludicrous reversal of their situation, yet it touched him oddly.

Smash stomped away from the tree, but the rats stayed with him. In order to run he would have to do two things: move the dryad back and forth as his arms pumped and flee a known danger. The one seemed physically hazardous to another person, while the other was emotionally distasteful. So he moved slowly, stamping, while the rats began climbing his legs.

Then Tandy's arm shot out as if hurling a rock. Her face was red, her teeth bared, her body rigid, as if she were in a state of absolute fury—but there was no rock in her hand. She was throwing nothing.

Something exploded at Smash's feet. He was knocked off them, barely catching his balance. All around him the rats turned belly-up, stunned.

He stared at the carnage, standing still because his legs were numb. He set down the hamadryad, who stepped daintily over the bodies. "What happened?"

Tandy sounded abashed. "I threw a tantrum."

Smash left the twitching rats and went to join her. His feet felt as if they were nothing but bones, with the flesh melted off, though this was not the case. "That's a spell?"

"That's bad temper, my talent," she said, eyes downcast. "When I get mad, I throw a tantrum. Sometimes it does a lot of damage. I'm sorry; I should have controlled my emotion."

"Sorry?" Smash said, bewildered, looking back at the ruin of the rat-swarm. "That's a wonderful talent!"

"Oh, sure," she replied with irony.

"My mother had a similar talent. Of course, she was a curse-fiend; they all throw curses."

"Maybe I have curse-fiend ancestry," Tandy said sourly. "My father Crombie came from a long line of soldiers, and they do get around quite a bit."

Now the others came up. "You did that, Tandy?" Fireoak asked. "You saved me a lot of misery! If Smash had put me down amidst those awful rats, or if they had climbed up him and gotten to me, as they were trying to—" She winced, feeling her wounds. She was obviously in considerable discomfort.

"That's an extremely useful talent for the jungles of Xanth," the Siren said.

"You really think so?" Tandy asked, brightening. "I always understood it wasn't nice to be destructive."

"It isn't?" Smash asked, surprised.

Then they all laughed. "Sometimes perhaps it is," the Siren concluded.

They found some genuine vegetables for lunch, then resumed the march. But soon they heard a ferocious snuffling and snorting ahead, low to the ground. "Oh, that might be a dragon with a cold," John said worriedly. "I can't say I really like dragons; they're too hot."

"I will go see," Smash said. He discovered he was rather enjoying this journey. Violence was a natural part of his nature—but now he had people to protect, so there was a certain added justification to it. It was more meaningful to bash a dragon to save a collection of pretty little lasses than it was to do it merely for its own sake. The Eye Queue caused him to ponder the meaning of the things he did, and so it helped to have at least a little meaning present. At such time as he got free of the curse, he could forget about these inconvenient considerations.

He rounded a brush-bush and faced the snorting monster, hamfists at the ready—and paused, dismayed.

It was no dragon. It was a small oink, with a squared-off snout and a curled-up tail. But it snorted like a huge fire-breathing monster.

Smash sighed. He picked up the oink by the tail and tossed it into the brush. "All clear," he called.

The others appeared. "It's gone?" Tandy asked. "But we didn't hear any battle."

"It was only a short snort," the ogre said, disgusted. He had so looked forward to a good fight!

"Another person might have represented it as the most tremendous of dragons," the Siren said.

"Why?"

"To make it seem he had done a most valiant deed."

"Why do that?" Smash asked, perplexed.

She smiled. "Obviously you don't suffer from that syndrome."

"I suffer from the Eye Queue curse."

"Cheer up, Smash," Tandy said. "We're bound to encounter a real dragon sometime."

"Yes," the ogre agreed, cheering as directed. After all, the thing to do with disappointments was to rise above them. The Eye Queue told him that.

"Speaking of dragons," John said, "there is a story that circulates among fairies about dragons and their parts, and I've always wondered whether it was true."

"I've met some dragons," Smash said. "What's the story?"

"That if a dragon's ear is taken off, you can listen to it and hear wondrous things."

Smash scratched his head. Several fleas jumped off, startled. Since his skull no longer heated much when he tried to think, the fleas had no natural control. "I never tried that."

"It must be sort of hard to get a dragon's ear," Tandy remarked. "I doubt they part with them willingly."

Fireoak considered. "There are stories the mockingbirds tell, to mock the ignorant. They would nest in my tree sometimes and talk of marvelous things, and I never knew how much to believe. One did once mention such a quality of a dragon's ear. It said the ear would twitch when anything of interest to the holder was spoken anywhere, so one would know to listen. But often the news was not pleasant, for dragons have ears for bad news. And as Tandy says, dragons' ears are very hard for normal people to come by."

"Next dragon I slay, I will save an ear," Smash said, intrigued.

They continued north till dusk, with only minor adventures, avoiding tangle trees, clinging vines, and strangler figs, scaring off tiger lilies and dogwood, and ignoring the trickly illusions spawned by assorted other plants. Swarms of biting bugs converged, but Smash blew them away in his usual fashion with selected roars. By nightfall the party was close to something significant, but Smash couldn't remember what.

They located a forest of black, blue, and white ash trees whose shedding ashes covered the forest floor. Any recent footprints showed; and, because each color of tree spread its ashes at a different hour, it was possible to know how recently any creature had passed. White prints were the most recent, blue prints were older and somehow more intricate, with maplike traceries on them, and black prints dated from the night. Some ashes had been hauled, but no dragons or other dangerous creatures had been here in the past few hours.

Amidst this forest was a handsome cottonwood that provided cotton for beds for them all. "I always thought camping out would be uncomfortable," Tandy remarked. "But this is getting to be fun. Now if only I knew where I was going!"

"You don't know?" the Siren asked, surprised.

"Good Magician Humfrey answered my Question by telling me to travel with Smash," Tandy said. "So I'm traveling. It's a pretty good trip, and I'm learning a lot and meeting nice new people, but that's not my Answer. Smash is looking for the Ancestral Ogres, but I doubt that's what I'm looking for."

"I understand the Good Magician is getting old," the Siren said.

"He's pretty old," Tandy agreed. "But he knows an awful lot, and your sister the Gorgon is making him young again."

"She would," the Siren said. "I am jealous of her power over men. In my heyday I used to summon men to my isle, but she always took them away, and, of course, they never looked at other women after she was through with them."

Because they had turned to stone, Smash knew. The fact was, the Gorgon had been as lonely as the Siren, despite her devastating power. The Gorgon had been smitten by the first man who could nullify her talent, Magician Humfrey, so she had gone to him with a Question: would he marry her? He had made her serve a year as housemaid and guardian in his castle before giving her his Answer: he would. Evidently that was the sort of man it required to capture the heart of the Gorgon. Smash understood that their wedding, officiated by Prince Dor when he was temporary King, had been the most remarkable occasion of the year, attended by all the best monsters. Smash's father Crunch had been there, and Tandy's mother Jewel. By all accounts, the marriage was a reasonably happy one, considering the special nature of its parties.

"I wonder what it is like to be with a man?" Fireoak said, in a half-wistful question. Her injuries of the day had fatigued her greatly, perhaps making her depressed. Evidently their conversation of the preceding night had remained on her mind.

"My friends always told me men were difficult to get along with," John said. "A girl can't live with them, and she can't live without them."

"Well, I've tried living without," the Siren said. "I'm ready to try with. Good and ready! At least it shouldn't be dull. First pool I find with an available merman, watch out!"

"Poor merman!" the fairy said.

"Oh, I'm sure he'll deserve whatever I give him. I don't think he'll have cause to complain, any more than Magician Humfrey has with my sister. We draw on similar lore."

"All girls do. But it seems terribly original to each innocent man." There was general laughing agreement.

"You speak as if no man is here," Tandy said, sounding faintly aggrieved.

"There's a man here, listening to our secrets?" Fireoak cried, alarmed.
"Smash."

There was another general titter. "Don't be silly," John said. "He's an ogre."

"Can't an ogre also be a man?"

The tittering subsided. "Yes, of course, dear," the Siren said reassuringly. "And a good one, too. We take Smash too much for granted. None of us could travel freely here without his formidable protection. We ought to thank him, instead of imposing on him."

Smash lay still. He had not intended to feign sleep, but thought it best not to join in this conversation. It was interesting enough without his participation. He had not known about this conspiracy of the females of Xanth, but now he could remember how he had seen it in action when Princess Irene snared Prince Dor, and even when his mother pacified his father. It did seem that the distaff knew things that the males did not and used them cleverly to achieve their desires.

"What's a lady ogre like?" Tandy asked.

"One passed my tree once," Fireoak said. "She was huge and hairy and had a face like a bowl of overcooked mush someone had sat on. I never saw anything so ugly in all my life."

"Well, she was an ogress," the Siren said. "They have different standards of beauty. You can bet they know what bull-ogres like, though! I suppose an ogre wants a wife who can knock down her own trees for firewood—no offense, Fireoak—and kill her own griffins for stew so he doesn't have to interrupt his dragon hunting for trifles."

They laughed again, and their chatter meandered across other femalish subjects, recipes, prettifying spells, jungle gossip, and such, until they all drifted off to sleep. But the images they had conjured enchanted Smash's imagination. An ogress who could knock down her own trees and slay her own griffins—what an ideal mate! And a face like squashed mush—what sheerest beauty! How wonderful it would be to encounter such a creature!

But the only ogress he had met was his mother—who wasn't really an ogress, but a curse-fiend acting the part. She acted very well, but when she forgot her makeup, her face no longer looked like mush. Smash had always pretended not to notice how distressingly fair her face and form became in those unguarded moments, so as not to embarrass her. The truth was, had his mother the actress chosen to pass among females like these Smash now traveled with, she could have done so without causing alarm. And, of course, as soon as she prepared herself, she was the compleat ogress again, as brutish and mean as any ogre could ask for. Certainly his father Crunch loved her and would move mountains for her, despite her secret shame of an un-ogrish origin. One of those mountains had been moved to rest near their home so that she could climb it and look out across Xanth when the mood took her.

At last Smash slept. He still wasn't used to doing so much thinking, and it tired him despite the amplification the Eye Queue provided. He had never had to work things out so rationally before, or to see the interrelationships among diverse things. Well, one day he would win free of the curse and be a true brute of an ogre again. He slept.

Chapter 6

Dire Strait

Next morning they came up against the barrier Smash had been unable to remember. It was a huge crevice in the earth, a valley so deep and steep that they shrank back from it. It extended east and west; there seemed to be no end to it, no way around.

"How can we go north?" Tandy asked plaintively. "This awful cleft is impossible!"

"Now I remember it," Smash said. "It crosses all of Xanth. Down near Castle Roogna there are magic bridges."

"Castle Roogna?" Fireoak asked. She looked wan, as if she had not been eating well, though she had been provided with all she wanted. Smash suspected her absence from her beloved tree was like an ordinary person's need for water. She would have to return to it soon, or die. She was suffering from deprivation of soul, and would soon become as Tandy had been within the gourd, if not helped. Her rat wounds only aggravated the condition, hastening the process.

"That's right," Tandy said brightly. "If this crack passes near Castle Roogna, you can follow it there! Your problem is solved."

"Yes, solved," the hamadryad agreed wanly.

Now the Siren noticed her condition. "Dear, are you well?"

"As well as I can be," the dryad replied gamely. "The rest of you must go on across the chasm; I will find my own way to Castle Roogna."

"I think you have been away from your tree too long," the Siren said. "You had better return to it, to restore your strength, before attempting the long trip to Castle Roogna."

"But there is not time!" Fireoak protested. "The moon is waning, night by night; soon the lunatic fringe will sunder, and my tree will be exposed."

"Yet if you perish on the way to see the King, you can do your tree no good," the Siren pointed out.

"It is indeed a dire strait," the dryad agreed, sinking to the ground.

The Siren looked at Smash. "Where is your tree, dear?" she asked Fireoak.

"North of the chasm. I had forgotten about—"

"But how did you cross?"

"A firebird helped me. Because I am associated with a fireoak. But the bird is long gone now."

"I think we must nevertheless cross over soon and return you to your tree," the Siren said. Again she looked meaningfully at Smash.

"We will go with you, to guard your tree," Smash said, catching on.

Tandy clapped her hands. "Oh, how wonderful to think of that, Smash! We can help her!"

Smash said nothing. The Siren had really thought of it, but he was amenable. They couldn't let Fireoak perish from neglect—and she surely would, otherwise. They could certainly guard her tree from harm; no one would come near an ogre.

But first they had to get to the tree—and that meant crossing the chasm—in a hurry. How were they going to do that?

"You chipped steps in the prints-of-wails mountain," Tandy suggested.

"But that was slow," the Siren said. "It could take several days. We must cross today."

They stared into the chasm, baffled. There seemed to be no way to cross it rapidly—yet they had to, somehow. For now all could see how the hamadryad was failing. Fireoak's surface had turned from lightly corrugated skin to deeply serrated bark, from young nymph to old tree trunk. Her green hair was wilting, and the tinge of red was turning black. Her fire would soon be out.

"There must be a path," John said. "If we just spread out and look, surely we'll find it."

That was a positive idea. They commenced their search for the path.

There was the sound of galloping hooves from the west. The group ran back together, and Smash faced the sound, ready for whatever might come.

Two centaurs appeared, moving rapidly. One was male, the other female. Centaurs could be good news or bad, depending. Smash was conscious of his orange jacket and steel gauntlets, gifts of the centaurs of Centaur Isle, but knew that there could be rogue centaurs in this wilderness. What were these two doing here?

Then Smash recognized them. "Chet! Chem!" he exclaimed.

The two drew up, panting, a light sheen of sweat on their human and equine portions. Smash embraced each in turn, then turned to make introductions. "These are friends of mine from the Castle Roogna region." He faced the other way. "And these are friends of mine from all over Xanth."

"Smash!" the filly centaur exclaimed. "What happened to your rhymes?"

"I'm cursed with intelligence, among other things."

"Yes, I can see the other things," Chet said, contemplating the assorted females. "I never knew you were interested."

"We sort of imposed on him," Tandy said.

"Yes, Smash is impose-able," Chem agreed. She was young, so lacked the imposing proportions of her mother; the last time Smash had seen her, she had been playing children's galloping games. In another year or so she would be looking for a mate. He wondered why she was not still in centaur-schooling, as her mother was very strict about education. "We came here to do the same."

"The same?" Smash asked. "We're traveling north."

"Yes," Chem said. "Good Magician Humfrey told me where to intercept you. You see, I'm doing a thesis on the geography of uncharted Xanth, completing my education, but my folks won't let me travel alone through that region, so—"

"And so I escorted my little sister this far," Chet finished. He was a handsome centaur, with noble features, a fine coat, and excellent muscles on both his human and equine portions. But a purple scar marred his left shoulder, where a wyvern had once bitten him, causing serious illness. "I know she'll be safe with you, Smash. You're a big ogre now."

"Safe? We're about to try to cross this gulf!" Smash protested. "And we don't know how."

"Oh, yes. The Gap Chasm. I brought you a rope." Chet presented a neat coil. "Humfrey said you would need it."

"A rope!" Suddenly their way down into the chasm was clear. Centaur rope was always strong enough for its purpose.

"I'll help get you down," Chet said. "But I'm not supposed to go myself. I have to return immediately to Castle Roogna with a message or two. What's the message?"

Smash's curse of intelligence enabled him to catch on. "A village is about to cut down a fireoak tree for timber. The tree's hamadryad will die. The King must save the tree."

"I'll tell him," Chet agreed. "Where is it?"

Smash turned to Fireoak, who sat listlessly on the ground. "Where is your tree?"

The hamadryad made a feeble motion with her hand.

"This is no good," Chet said. "Chem, let's use your map."

The filly walked over to Fireoak. "Show me on my picture," she said.

An image formed between them. It was a contour map of the Land of Xanth, a long peninsula with the Gap Chasm across its center and the ocean around it. "Show me where the tree is," Chem repeated.

Fireoak looked, slowly orienting on the scene. "There," she said, pointing to a region near the northern rim of the Gap.

Chem nodded. "There is a human village there, just setting up. That's already on my chart." She looked at her brother. "Got it, Chet?"

"Got it, Chem," the male centaur replied. "You always do make the scene. Smash, the moment you're down in the Gap, I'll gallop back and tell the King. I'm sure he'll handle the business about the tree. But it will take me a couple days to get there, so you'll have to protect the tree until then." He glanced about. "Was there any other message? It seems there should be more than one."

The people looked around at each other. Finally Tandy said, "I'd like to send a greeting to my father Crombie, if that's all right."

Chet tapped his head, making a mental note. "One greeting to Crombie from daughter. Got it." He looked more carefully at Tandy. "He always bragged he had a cute daughter. I see he was correct."

Tandy blushed. She hadn't known her father had said that about her.

They tied the rope to the trunk of a steelwood tree. Chem insisted on going down first. "That will prove the rope is safe," she explained. "Even Smash doesn't weigh more than I do." Of course she was correct, for though her human portion was girlishly slender, her equine portion was as solid as a horse.

She backed down, her four hooves bracing against the steep side of the chasm. The rope looped once about her small human waist, just below her moderate bosom, and she used her hands to give herself slack by stages. When she got down to where the slope leveled out enough to enable her to stand, she released the rope.

The Siren went down next, having less trouble because she had so much less mass. Then Tandy, followed by the fairy, who fluttered her wings to make herself even lighter than she was. Smash then made a harness out of the end of the rope, set Fireoak in it, and stood on the brink to lower her carefully to Chem's waiting arms.

Finally Smash himself descended, merely applying one gauntlet to the rope and sliding rapidly down. Chet undid the upper end from the steelwood tree and dropped it into the chasm. They would need the rope again on the north slope.

"I'm on my way with one and a half messages," Chet called, and galloped off. "Remember: two days."

The slope continued to level, until they stood at the base. Here grass grew, but no trees. It was pleasant enough, and the north slope was visible a short distance away. They walked across, studying the rise for the most suitable place to ascend.

It certainly wasn't good for climbing with a party of girls. The ground sloped gently up to a corner; from there the cliff went almost straight up a dizzying height, beyond the reach of the rope, even if there were any place or way to anchor it.

"We must do what we started to do before," the Siren said. "Spread out and look for a suitable place to climb."

"I believe there are paths here and there," Chem said. "I don't have them on my map, because few people remember the Gap Chasm; it has an enduring forget-spell on it. But there has been enough travel in Xanth so that people have to have crossed it, and not just at the magic bridges."

"A forget-spell," the Siren said. "How interesting. That accounts for Fireoak's forgetting it. And I'm sure Smash has been here before, too. I hope that's the extent of the spell."

"What do you mean?" Tandy asked.

"Oh, I'm just a worrier over nothing."

"I don't think so," Tandy said. "If there's any danger, you should warn us."

The Siren sighed. "You're right. Yet if there is danger here, it's too late for us to avoid it, since we're already here. It's only that once I heard something about a big dragon in a chasm—and this is a chasm. It would be hard to escape a monster here. But of course that's far-fetched."

"Let's look for good hiding places, too," Tandy said. "Just in case."

"Just in case," John agreed, overhearing. "Oh, suddenly I don't really like this place!"

"So we must try to get out of this chasm as fast as we can," Smash said, though the prospect of danger did not bother him. There really had not been much violence on this journey.

Chem trotted east, while Smash lumbered west, since these were the two fastest movers of the group. The girl, Siren, and fairy spread out in between. They left the hamadryad in the shade of a bush, since she was now too weak to walk.

The cliff face changed, sloping at different angles and different heights, but Smash found nothing that would really help. It looked as if he would have to bash out a stairway of sorts, tedious as that would be. But could he get the party up that way within two days, let alone in time to save the hamadryad and her tree?

There was a commotion to the east. Chem was galloping back, her lovely brown hair-mane flinging out, tail swishing nervously. "Dragon! Dragon!" she cried breathlessly.

The Siren's concern had been justified! "I'll stop it," Smash said enthusi-astically, charging east.

"No! It's big. It's the Gap Dragon!"

Now Smash remembered. The Gap Dragon ranged the Gap Chasm, trap-ping and consuming any creatures foolish enough to stray here. The forget-spell had deceived him again. The monster really profited from that spell, since no one remembered the danger. But it was coming back to him now. This was a formidable menace.

The Siren, Tandy, and John were running west. Behind them whomped the monster. It was long and low, with a triple pair of stubby legs. Its scales were metallic, glistening in the sunlight, and clouds of steam puffed out of its nostrils. Its body was the thickness of a good-sized tree trunk, but exceed-ingly limber. It moved by elevating one section and whomping it forward, then following through with another, because its legs were too short for true running. But the clumsy-seeming mechanism sufficed for considerable veloc-ity. In a moment the Gap Dragon would overtake the Siren.

Smash lumbered to the fray. He stood much taller than the dragon, but it reached much longer than he. Thus they did not come together with a satis-fying crash. The dragon scooted right under Smash, intent on the nymphlike morsel before it.

The ogre screeched to a stop, literally, his calloused hamfeet churning up mounds of rubble. He bent forward and grabbed the dragon's tail as it slid westward. He lifted it up, holding it tightly in both hands. This would halt the monster!

Alas, he had underestimated the dragon. The creature whomped onward. The tail lost its slack—but such was the mass and impetus of the monster that it wrenched the ogre into a somersault. He flipped right over, hanging on to that tail, and landed with a whomp of his own on his back—on the dragon's tail.

But Smash's own mass was not inconsiderable. The shock of his landing traveled along the body of the dragon in a ripple. When the ripple passed a set of legs, they were wrenched momentarily off the ground; when it arrived at the head, the mouth snapped violently. The jaws, reaching close to the desperately fleeing Siren, fell short.

Now Smash had the Gap Dragon's baleful attention. The dragon let out a yowl of discomfort and whipped its head around. Its tail, pinned under the ogre, thrashed about, so that Smash had trouble regaining his feet.

The dragon's neck curved in a sharp U-turn, bonelessly supple. The head traveled smoothly back along the length of the body. The monster hardly needed its legs for this sort of maneuver. In a moment the spreading jaws were at Smash's own head, ready to take it in.

The ogre, still flat on his back, stabbed upward with a gauntleted fist. The jaws closed on it, but the fist continued inexorably, punching past the slurp-wet tongue and into the back of the throat. The dragon's head was so large that Smash's whole arm was engulfed—but that strike in the throat caused the monster to gag, and the jaws parted again. Smash recovered his arm before it got chomped.

The ogre sat up, but remained in the midst of the coils of the dragon. The two grotesque heads of ogre and dragon faced each other, snout to snout. Smash realized that this time he had gotten himself into an encounter whose outcome he could not know. The Gap Dragon was his match.

Delightful! For the first time since attaining his full strength, Smash could test his ultimate. But at the moment they were all tangled up in an ineffective configuration, unable to fight decisively.

Smash made a face, bulging his eyes and stretching his mouth wide open. "Yyrwll!" he yyrwlled.

The Gap Dragon made a face back, wrinkling up its snout horrendously and crossing its eyes so far that the pupils exchanged places. "Rrooarw!" it rrooarwed.

Smash made a worse face, swallowing his nose and part of his low forehead. "Ggrummf!" he ggrummffed.

The dragon went him one better, perhaps two better, swallowing its snout up past the ears and partway down its neck. "Sstth!" it ssstthed.

The monster was outdoing him. Petulantly, Smash bit into a rock and spit out a stream of gravel. The dragon's teeth were pointed, so it could not match that. Instead, it hoisted a petard of steam at him, the greasy ball of vapor curling the hairs of his face and clogging his nostrils.

So much for the niceties. Now the real action commenced. Smash threw himself into the sheer joy of combat, the fundamental delight of every true ogre. It had been some time since he had crunched bones in earnest. Of course, this dragon was mostly boneless, but the principle remained.

He punched the dragon in the snoot. This sort of punch could put a fist-sized hole in an ironwood tree, but the dragon merely gave way before the force of it and was only slightly bloodied. Then the dragon struck back, snapping sidewise at Smash's arm. That sort of bite could lop a mouthful of flesh from a behemoth, but the gauntlet extended back far enough to catch the edge of the bite and strike sparks from the teeth.

Then Smash boxed the dragon's right ear with his left fist—and the ear squirted right off the skull and flew out of sight. The dragon winced; that smarted! But the monster hardly needed that ear, and came back with a blast of steam that cooked the outer layer of the ogre's head. Smash's thick skull stopped the heat from penetrating to the Eye Queue-corrupted brain—more was the pity, he thought.

So much for the second exchange of amenities. Smash had had slightly the better of it this time, but the fight was only warming up. Now the pace intensified.

Smash took hold of the dragon's upper jaw with one hand, the lower jaw with another, and slowly forced the two apart. The dragon resisted, and its jaw muscles were mighty, well leveraged, and experienced, but it could not directly withstand the full brute force of a concentrating ogre. Slowly the jaws separated.

The dragon whipped its body about. In a moment the sinuous length of it was wrapped about the ogre's torso, engulfing him anew. While Smash forced open the jaws, the dragon tightened its coils, constricting him.

All this was in slow motion, yet it was a race. Would Smash rip the head apart first, or would the dragon squeeze the juice out of him? The answer was uncertain. Smash was having trouble breathing; he was beginning to lose strength. It seemed to him that this should not be happening, or at least not this fast. But the dragon's jaws were now quite far apart, and should soon break.

Neither ogre nor dragon would give. They remained, their strength in balance. The jaws were on the verge of breaking, the torso on the verge of smothering. Who would succumb first? It occurred to Smash that he might break open the dragon's jaw, but be unable to extricate himself from its convulsed coils and smother because he couldn't breathe. Or the dragon might crush him—but suffer a broken jaw in Smash's dying effort. Both could lose this encounter.

In the good old days before the Eye Queue vine had fallen on him, Smash would not have wasted tedious thought on such a thing; he would merely have bashed on through, to kill and/or be killed, hardly caring which. Now he was cursed with the notion of meaning. To what point was this violence if neither participant survived?

It was discomfiting and un-ogrish, but Smash found he had to change his tactic. This one had little promise of success, since it would not free him from the serpent's toils. He was in a dire strait, and bulling ahead would only worsen it.

He drew the dragon's head forward, toward his own face. The dragon thought this meant Smash was weakening, and went forward eagerly. In a moment, the dragon believed, it could chomp the ogre's face off. Its breath steamed out, its woodsmoke fragrance toasting Smash's skin. He tried to sneeze, but was unable to inhale because of the constriction in which he was held.

Sure of victory now, the dragon cranked its jaws marginally closer together and lunged. Smash deflected the thrust as much as he could and jerked his head to the side. The dragon's head plunged down as Smash's hands let go—and the huge wedge-teeth chomped savagely on the uppermost coil. This was a device Smash had used on the tangle tree with good effect.

It took the Gap Dragon a moment to catch on. Meanwhile, it chewed. It surely felt the bite, but did not yet realize that this was its own doing, or that its teeth had not contacted ogre flesh. It took a while for the difference in taste to register. The dragon wrenched its supposed prey upward, driving the teeth in deeper. The coil loosened, giving Smash half a gasp of breath.

Then at last the dragon realized what it was doing. Its jaws began to open, to free itself from its own bite and to emit a honk of sheer pain and frustration—but Smash's two gauntleted hamhands came down on either side of it, clasping the snout, pressing it firmly closed on the meat. The jaw muscles were weaker this way; the dragon could not release its bite. Still, the ogre could not use his hands for further attack, for the moment he let go, the jaws would open. It was another position of stalemate.

Blood welled out around the dragon's lower fangs and dripped off its chin, coating Smash's gauntlet. The fluid was a deep purple hue, thick and gooey, smelling of ashes and carrion. It probably had caustic properties, but the gauntlet protected Smash's flesh, as it had when he held the basilisk. The centaur gifts were serving him well.

Now it was the dragon's turn to scheme. Dragons were not the brightest creatures of Xanth; but, as with ogres, their brains were largely in their muscles, and they were cunning fighters. The dragon knew it could get nowhere unless it freed itself from its own bite, and knew that its own coils anchored the ogre in place so that he could put his clamp on that bite. By and by, it realized that if it released the ogre, the ogre would lack anchorage and could then be thrown off. So the dragon began laboriously uncoiling.

Smash held on, gasping more deeply as the constriction abated. His strategy was getting him free—but it would free the dragon, too. This fight was a long way from over!

At last the coils were gone. The dragon wrenched its forward section away—and Smash's lower hand slipped on the blood coating it, and he lost his hold.

Now they faced each other again, the dragon with bloodied jaw and little jets of purple goo spurting from the deep fang-holes in its body, the ogre panting heavily from sore ribs. On the surface Smash had had the better of this round, but inside he doubted it. His rib cage was made of ogre's bones; nevertheless, it was hurting. Something had been bent if not broken. He was no longer in top fighting condition.

The dragon evidently had found the ogre to be stiffer competition than anticipated. It made a feint at Smash, and Smash raised a fist. Then the dragon dived abruptly back, as if fleeing. Suspicious, Smash paused—then saw that the dragon was going after Fireoak the Hamadryad, who was still lying helplessly on the ground.

This was very bad form. It suggested that Smash was no longer worth noticing as an opponent. His temper heated and bent toward the snapping point.

Chem Centaur leaped to Fireoak's defense, intercepting the dragon before Smash reoriented. She reared, her forehooves flashing in the air, striking at the dragon's snout. But she could not hope to balk such a monster for long. The Siren and John were running up to help, but Smash knew they could only get themselves in trouble.

He grabbed the dragon's tail again, this time bracing himself firmly against the rocky ground so as not to be flipped over. The moving body took up the slack again with a heavy shock that transmitted straight to the ogre's braced feet. The feet plowed into the ground, throwing up wakes of dirt and stones, then driving down deeper. When the dragon finally halted, Smash was braced knee-deep at an angle in the ground. He was strong, but the dragon had mass that mere strength couldn't halt instantly.

The dragon's nose had stopped a short distance from the hamadryad. Infuriated at this balk, the creature turned again, lunging at the ogre.

Smash exploded out of the ground, kicking dirt in the dragon's snoot. He reached for the jaws, but this time the dragon was wise enough to keep its mouth shut; it wanted no more prying open! It drove at the ogre with sealed jaws, trying to knock him down before taking a bite.

Smash boxed at the head, denting the metal scales here and there and rebloodying, the smashed ear-socket, but could do no real damage. The dragon weaved and bobbed, presenting a tricky target, while gathering itself for some devastating strike.

The ogre looked toward the assembled girls. "Get away from here!" he bellowed. He wanted no more distractions from the main event; one of them was sure to get incidentally gobbled by the dragon.

From the other side Tandy called, "I've found a ledge! It's out of reach of the dragon! We can use the rope to climb to it while Smash destroys the dragon!"

She had boundless confidence in his prowess! Smash knew he was in the toughest encounter of his life. But he could proceed with greater confidence the moment he knew the girls were safe. He looked where Tandy pointed and saw the ledge, about halfway up the steep slope. There was a pining tree on it, its mournful branches drooping greenly, the sad needles hanging down. They would be able to loop the rope about the trunk of this tree and haul themselves up to it.

Then the dragon, taking advantage of Smash's distraction, leaped at him. The ogre ducked, throwing up a fist in his standard defensive ploy, but the dragon's mass bore him down. The huge metal claws of the foremost set of feet raked at his belly, attempting to dismember him. Smash had to fall on his back to avoid them—and the weight of the dragon landed on him. Now the stubby legs reached out on either side, the claws clutching the earth, anchoring the long body. Smash was pinned.

He tried to get up, but lacked leverage. He reached out to grab a leg, but the dragon cunningly moved it out of reach. Meanwhile, the sinuous body was moving elsewhere along its line, bringing another set of legs to bear. These would soon attack the pinned ogre. It would be easy for these free claws to spear through his flesh repeatedly, and sooner or later they would puncture a vital organ.

But Smash had resources of his own. He reached up to embrace the serpentine segment. He was just able to complet the circuit, his fingers linking above it. Now he had his leverage. He squeezed.

Ogres were notorious for several things: the manner in which their teeth crunched bones into toothpicks, the way their fists pulverized rocks, and the power of their battle embrace. A rock-maple tree would have gasped under the pressure Smash now applied. So did the Gap Dragon. It let out a steam-whistle of anguish.

But its body was flexible and compressible. When it had been squeezed down to half its original diameter, Smash could force it no farther without taking a new grip—and the moment he released his present one, the body would spring out again. His compression was not enough. The dragon was in pain, but still able to function; now it was again bringing its other claws into play. That would be trouble, for the outsides of Smash's arms were exposed. They could be clawed to pieces.

He drew on another weapon—his teeth. They did not compare with those of the dragon, but they were formidable enough in their own fashion. He pretended the underbelly before him was a huge, tasty bone and started in.

The first chomp netted him only a mouthful of scales. He spit them out and bit again. This time he reached the underlayer of reptilian skin, still pretty tough, but no match for an ogre's teeth. He ripped out a section, exposing the muscular layer beneath. He sank his teeth into that.

Again the monster whistled with pain. It struggled to draw back—but Smash's embrace held it firm. The compression made it worse; the ogre's teeth could take in twice as much actual flesh with each bite.

The dragon's claws ripped out of the ground. It humped its midsection, lifting Smash into the air. The huge head swung around, blasting forth steam. Now the ogre had to let go, for the back of his neck could not withstand much steam-cooking. He dropped off, spitting out a muscle. It would have been nice to chew the thing up and swallow it, but he needed his teeth clear for business, not pleasure.

The dragon was doubly bloodied now, yet still full of fight. It snorted a voluminous and slightly blood-flecked cloud of steam, charged Smash—and sheered off at the last moment, leaving the ogre smiting air with his fists. The serpentine torso whizzed by faster and faster, until the tail struck with a hard crack against Smash's chest.

It was quite a smack. Smash was rocked back. But his orange centaur jacket was made to protect him from physical attack and it withstood the lash of the sharp tail. Otherwise Smash could have been badly gashed, or even cut in half. The tail, at its extremity, was long and thin, like a whip, with edges like a feathered blade. Smash wanted no more of that.

He spied a boulder half buried in the ground. He ripped it from its mooring and hurled it at the dragon. The dragon dodged, but Smash threw another, and a third. Eventually he was bound to score, and the dragon knew it.

The dragon ducked behind a small ridge of rock and disappeared. Smash lobbed a boulder at it without effect. Cautiously he moved up and peered behind the ridge—and found nothing. The dragon was gone.

He bent to study the ground. Ah—there was a hole slanting down—a tunnel the diameter of the dragon. The monster had fled underground!

He dislodged a larger boulder and rolled it to cover the hole. That would seal in the dragon, at least until Tandy and the others could vacate the Gap Chasm. It was too bad he hadn't been able to finish the fight, but it had been an excellent one, and such ironies did occur in the wilds of Xanth.

Then two sets of claws came down from behind him. The dragon had emerged from another hole and ambushed him from the rear! That was what came of getting careless in the enemy's home territory.

Smash tried to turn, but the claws landed on his shoulder and hauled him backward to the opening jaws. This time he could not attack those jaws with his hands; he could not reach them. He was abruptly doomed.

Tandy appeared beside the boulder. "Look out, Smash!" she cried unnecessarily.

"Get away from here!" Smash shouted as he felt the dragon's steam on the back of his neck.

But Tandy's face was all twisted up in terror or horror or anger; her eyes were squeezed almost shut, and her body was stiff. She paid no attention to him. Then her arm moved as she threw something invisible. Smash, realizing her intent almost too late, dropped to his knees, though the talons dug cruelly into his shoulder.

The tantrum brushed over his head, making his fur stand on end. The dragon caught the full brunt of it in the snoot and froze in place, half a jet of steam stuck in one nostril.

Smash turned and stood. The Gap Dragon's eyes were glazed. The monster had been stunned by the tantrum. "Quick, run!" Tandy cried. "It won't hold that dragon long!"

Run? That was hardly the way of an ogre! "You run; I shall bind the dragon."

"You lunkhead!" she protested. "Nothing will hold it long!"

Smash picked up the dragon's whiplike tail. He threaded the tip of it into the smash-ruined ear, through the head, and out the other ear, drawing a length of it through. Then he used a finger to poke a hole in the boulder, and a second hole angling in to meet the first inside the stone. He passed the tail tip in one hole and out the other, exactly as if this were another dragonhead. Then he fashioned an ogre hangknot and tied the tail to itself. "Now I'll go," he said, satisfied.

They walked to the cliff face. Behind them the Gap Dragon revived. It shook its head to clear itself of confusion—and discovered it was tied. It tried to draw back—and the tail pulled taut against the boulder.

"A little puzzle for the dragon," Smash explained. Privately, he was nettled because he had had to have help to nullify the monster; that was not an ogre's way. But the infernal common sense foisted on him by the Eye Queue reminded him that without an ogre the girls would have very little chance to survive and the hamadryad's tree would be cut down. So he beat down his stupid pride and proceeded to the next challenge.

Chem, John, Fireoak, and the Siren rested on the ledge. The rope dangled down carelessly.

"All right, girls, it's over," Tandy called. "Ready for us to come up?"

No one answered. It was as if they were asleep.

"Hey, wake up!" Tandy cried, irritated. "We have to be on our way, and there's a long climb ahead!"

The Siren stirred. "What does it matter?" she asked dolefully.

Smash and Tandy exchanged glances, one cute girl glance for one brute ogre glance. What was this?

"Are you all right, Siren?" Smash called.

The Siren got to her feet, standing precariously near the edge of the ledge. "I'm so sad," she said, wiping a tear. "Life has no joy."

"No joy?" Tandy asked, bewildered. "Smash tied the dragon. We can go on now. That's wonderful!"

"That's nothing," the Siren said. "I will end it all." And she stepped off the ledge.

Tandy screamed. Smash leaped to catch the Siren. Fortunately, she was coming right toward him; all he had to do was intercept her fall and swing her about and set her safely on her feet.

"She tried to kill herself!" Tandy cried, appalled.

Something was definitely wrong. Smash looked up at the pining tree. The other tree sat drooping, like the tree itself.

Then he caught on. "The pining tree! It makes people pine!"

"Oh, no!" Tandy lamented. "They've been there too long, getting sadder and sadder. Now they're suicidal!"

"We must get them down from there," Smash said.

The Siren stirred. "Oh, my—I was so sad!"

"You were near the pining tree," Tandy informed her. "We didn't realize what it did."

The Siren mopped up her tear-stained face. "So that was it! That's a crying shame."

"I'll climb up and carry them down," Smash said.

"Then *you'll* get sad," Tandy said. "We don't need a suicidal ogre falling on our heads."

"It does take a while for full effect," the Siren said. "The longer I sat, the sadder I got. It didn't strike all at once."

"That's our answer," Tandy said. "I'll go up and push people off the ledge, and Smash can catch them. Quickly, before I get too sad myself."

"What about Chem?" the Siren asked. "She's too heavy for Smash to catch safely."

"We'll have to lower her on the rope."

They decided to try it. Tandy climbed the rope, picked up the weeping John, and threw her down. Smash caught the fairy with one hand, avoiding contact with her delicate wings. Then Tandy pushed Fireoak off the ledge. Finally she tied the end of the rope about the centaur's waist, passed the rope behind the tree, and forced her to back down while Smash played out the other end of the rope gradually. It was slow, but it worked.

Except for one thing. Tandy remained beside the tree, since the rope was now taken up by the centaur, and the tree was getting to her. She wandered precariously near the edge, her tears flowing. Then she stepped off.

If Smash moved to catch her, he would let Chem fall. If he did not—

He figured it out physically before solving it mentally. He held the rope in his right hand while jumping and reaching out with his left hand. He caught Tandy by her small waist and drew her in to his furry body without letting Chem slip.

Tandy buried her face in his pelt and cried with abandon. He knew it was only the effect of the pining tree, but he felt sorry for her misery. All he could do was hold her.

"That was a nice maneuver, Smash," the Siren said, coming up to take the girl from his arm.

"I couldn't let her fall," he said gruffly.

"Of course you couldn't." But the Siren seemed thoughtful. It was as if she understood something he didn't.

Now they were all down and safe—but unfortunately at the bottom of the Gap Chasm. The Gap Dragon was still twitching, trying to discover a way to free itself without pulling out either its brains or its tail. Which was more important wasn't clear.

John revived. "Oh, my, that was awful!" she exclaimed. "Now I feel so much better, I could just fly!" And she took off, flying in a loop.

"Well, *she* can get out of the chasm," the Siren said.

Smash looked at the fairy, and at the dragon, and at the pining tree. There was a small ironwood tree splitting the difference between the pining tree and the top of the cliff wall. He had an idea. "John, can you fly to the top of the chasm carrying the rope?"

The fairy looked at the rope. "Way too heavy for me."

"Could you catch it and hold it if I hurl the end up to you?"

She inspected it again. "Maybe, if I had something to anchor me," she said doubtfully. "I'm not very strong."

"That ironwood tree."

"I could try."

Smash tied an end of the rope to a rock, then hurled the rock up past the ironwood tree. John flew up and held the rope at the tree. Now Smash walked over to the Gap Dragon, which was still trying to free itself from the boulder without hurting its head or its tail in the process. Smash knocked it on the head with a fist, and it quieted down; the dragon was no longer in fighting condition and couldn't roll with the punch.

Smash untied the tail, disconnected it from the boulder, unthreaded the head, and tied the tip of the tail to the nether end of the rope. Then he dragged the inert dragon to the base of the chasm wall and placed its tail so that it reached well up toward the top.

"Now drop that stone," he called.

The fairy did so. The rock pulled the slack rope up and around the ironwood trunk. When it began to draw on the dragon's tail, the weight of the rope wasn't enough. The fairy flew down and sat on the rock, adding weight, and it dropped down farther. Finally Smash was able to jump and catch hold of it.

John flew back to the ground while Smash hauled the dragon up by the tail. But soon the weight was too much; instead of hauling the dragon up, Smash found himself dangling. This was a matter of mass, not strength.

"We can solve that," Chem said, shaking off her remaining melancholy. She had received a worse dose of pining than the others, perhaps because of her size and because she had been closest to the tree. "Use the boulder for ballast."

Smash rolled the boulder over. He hooked a toe in the hole he had punched in it, then drew on the rope again. This anchorage enabled him to drag the dragon farther up the slope. When it got to the point where both ogre and boulder were dangling in the air. Chem added her considerable weight to the effort by balancing on the boulder and clinging to Smash. "I'll bet you've never been hugged like this before," she remarked.

Smash pondered that while he hauled on the rope, trying to get the dragon up. Actually, he had embraced his friend Chet, her older brother, and Arnolde the Archivist, the middle-aged centaur who was now in charge of liaisons with Mundania. But those had been males, and his recent company had attuned him somewhat more to the difference of females. Chem was not of his species, of course, but she was clinging to him with extraordinary constriction because it was hard for her human arms to support her equine body. She was pleasant to be close to; her present hug was almost like that of an ogress.

All these girls were pleasant to be close to, he realized as the Eye Queue curse enabled him to think the matter through. Each had her separate female fashion, sort of rounded and soft, structured for holding. But it seemed best not to let them know that he noticed. They allowed themselves to get close to him only because they regarded him as a woolly monster who had no preception of their nonedible attributes.

He hauled on the rope, bringing the dragon up another notch. Now Smash was approaching the limit of his strength, for the dragon was a heavy monster and there was a long way to haul. When the job got near the end, ogre, boulder, and centaur were all getting light; any more and they would be swinging in the air.

But at last it was done. Now the Gap Dragon was suspended by its tail from the ironwood tree, its snout just touching the level ground at the base of the chasm. Smash climbed the rope to the tree, caught the trailing tip of the dragon's tail, and knotted it about the tree. Then, clinging to the tree, he untied the rope and flung it upward over the tip of the cliff. He had had the foresight to leave Chem and the boulder anchoring the rope at ground level before doing this.

John flew up and caught the rope. She dragged the end to a tree beyond the chasm and tied it firmly with a fairy knot. Smash climbed the rest of the way up and stood at last on the northern side of the Gap Chasm. Now they had their escape route.

"Climb the dragon, climb the rope," he called down. His voice echoboomed back and forth across the chasm, but finally settled down to the bottom, where they could hear it.

Tandy came up, placing her feet carefully against the dragon's metal scales, which tended to fold outward because of its inverted position, making the footing better. The Siren followed, not quite as agile.

Chem and Fireoak were more of a problem. The centaur had let herself down readily enough, but lacked the muscle either to climb the dragon vertically or to haul herself up along the rope to the top. And the hamadryad was too weak even to make the attempt.

Smash could handle that. He slid down the rope and dragon, picked up the dryad, and carried her to the top. Then he returned for the centaur. He had her hold on to him again, circling her arms about his waist while he hauled himself up by hands and feet. Progress was slow, for her hooves could not grip the dragon's scales comfortably, but eventually they made it to the ironwood tree.

At this point the nature of the problem changed. The rope went straight up to the overhanging lip, and Smash doubted Chem could hold on to him while he climbed that. Also, he was tiring, and might be unable to haul himself and her up, using only his arms. So he parked her, wedged between the ironwood trunk and the cliff, while he rested and considered.

But he was not provided much time for either. The Gap Dragon, quiescent until now, stirred. It was a tough animal, and even a punch in the head by the fist of an ogre could not put it to sleep indefinitely. It twisted about, trying to discover what was happening.

"I think you had better climb back up your rope now," Chem said.

"Tie the end about your waist; I will draw you up from above."

"I will make a harness," she decided. She looped the rope around her body in various places. "This way I can defend myself."

Smash clambered up the taut rope while the dragon thrashed about with increasing vigor. As Smash crossed the cliff lip, he saw the dragon's head coming back up along its body, toward the centaur filly. That could certainly be trouble!

Atop the cliff, Smash took hold of the rope and drew it up. The weight was great, but the rope was magically strong. He had to brace carefully, lest he be pulled back over the cliff. Again he was reminded that strength alone was not sufficient; anchorage was at times more important. He solved the problem by looping the rope about his own waist so that he could not be drawn away from the tree and could exert his full force.

John was hovering near the lip. "That dragon has spotted Chem," she announced with alarm. "It's reaching up. I don't know whether it can . . ."

Smash kept on hauling. He could go only so fast, since he had to take a fresh grip each time and tense for the renewed effort. He hated to admit it, even to himself, but he was tiring more rapidly. What had become of his ogre endurance?

"Yes, the dragon can reach her," John reported. "It's lunging, snapping. She's fending it off neatly with her hooves, but she's swinging around without much leverage. She can't really hurt it. It's trying again—you'd better lift her up higher, Smash!"

Smash was trying, but now his best efforts yielded only small, slow gains. His giant ogre muscles were solidifying with fatigue.

"Now the dragon is trying to climb its own tail, to get higher, so it can chomp the rope apart or something," the fairy said. "This time she won't be able to stop it. Pull her up quickly!"

But try as he might, Smash could not. The rope began to slip through his exhausted hands.

The Siren leaped up. "I have a knife!" she cried. "I'll go down and cut off the dragon's tail so it will drop to the bottom of the chasm, out of reach!"

"No!" Tandy protested. "You'll have no way to get up again!"

"I'll do it!" John said. "Quick—give me the knife!"

The Siren gave her the knife. The fairy dropped out of sight beyond the ledge. Smash tried to rouse himself to resume hauling on the rope, but his body was frozen into a deathlike rigor. He could only listen.

The Siren lay on the bank, her head over the cliff, looking down. "The dragon's head is almost there," she reported. "John is down near the tree. She's afraid of that monster; I can tell by the way she skirts it. But she's approaching the tied tail. Now she's sawing on it with the knife. She's not very strong, and those scales are tough. The dragon doesn't see her; it's orienting on Chem. Oops—now it sees John. That knife is beginning to hurt it as she digs through the scales. It's slow work! The dragon is turning its head about, opening its jaws. Chem is slipping down farther. She's kicking at the dragon's neck with her forefeet, trying to distract it. Now she's throwing dirt at it from the chasm wall. John is still sawing at the tail. I think she's down to real flesh now. The dragon is really angry. It's blasting out steam— Oh!" She paused, horrified.

"What happened?" Tandy demanded, her face pale with strain.

"The steam—John—" The Siren took a ragged breath. "The steam shriveled her wings, both of them. They're just tatters. John's clinging to the tree trunk. Still sawing at the tail. What awful courage she has! She must be in excruciating pain."

The fairy had lost her newly recovered wings and was suffering terribly— because of Smash's failure. In an agony of remorse, he forced strength through his frozen muscles and hauled again on the rope. Now it came up, its burden seeming lighter, and soon the centaur was over the lip of the chasm and scrambling to safety. But what of John?

"There goes the dragon!" the Siren cried. "She did it! She cut through the tail! There's dragon blood all over her and she's lost the knife, but the dragon's bouncing down the slope in a cloud of dust and steam. Now the monster's rolling at the base. It's galumphing away!"

"What of John?" Tandy cried.

"She's sitting there by the ironwood tree. Her eyes are closed. I don't think she quite comprehends what has happened. Her wings—"

Tandy was fashioning the rope into a smaller harness. "Lower this to her. We'll draw her up!"

Smash merely stood where he was, listening. His brief surge of strength had been exhausted; now he could do nothing. He felt ashamed for his weakness and the horrible consequence of it, but had no further resource. John had thought she would be safe in the company of an ogre!

Chem drew the fairy up. Smash saw John huddled in the harness. Her once-lovely wings, with the blossoming flower patterns, were now melted amorphous husks, useless for flying. Would they ever grow back? It seemed unlikely.

"Well, we crossed the chasm," Tandy said. She was not happy. None of them was. One of their number had lost her invaluable wings, another was too wasted to stand, and Smash was too tired to move. If this was typical of the hazards they faced, traversing central Xanth, how would they ever make it the rest of the way?

"Well, now," a new voice declared.

Smash turned his head dully to view the speaker. It was a gnarled, ugly goblin—at the head of a fair-sized troop of goblins.

Goblins hated people of any type. The strait had become yet more dire.

Chapter 7

Lunatic Fringe

"If you fight, we'll shove you all over the brink without your rope," the goblin leader said. He was a stunted black creature about John's height, with a huge head, hands, and feet. His short limbs seemed twisted, as if the bones had been broken and reset many times, and his face was similarly uneven, with one eye squinting, the other round, the nose bulbous, and the mouth crooked. By goblin standards, he was handsome.

The goblins spread out to surround the party. They peered at the ogre, centaur, hamadryad, fairy, Siren, and girl as if all were supreme curiosities. "You crossed the Gap?" the leader asked.

Tandy took it upon herself to answer. "What right have you to question us? I know your kind from the caves. You don't have any useful business with civilized folk."

The leader considered her. "Whom do you know in the caves, girl-thing?"

"Everybody who is anybody," she retorted. "The demons, the Diggle-worm, the Brain Coral—"

The leader seemed fazed. "Who are you?"

"I am Tandy, daughter of Crombie the Soldier and Jewel the Nymph. You know who sets out those black opals you goblins steal to give to your goblin girls! My mother, that's who. Without her there wouldn't be any gems of any kind to find anywhere."

There was a muttering commotion. "You have adequate connections," the goblin leader grudged. "Very well, we won't eat you. You may go, girl-thing."

"What of my friends?" Tandy asked suspiciously.

"They have no such connections. Their mothers don't plant gems in the rocks. We'll cook them tonight."

"Oh, no, you won't! My friends go with me!"

"If that's the way you want it," the goblin said indifferently.

"That's the way I want it."

"Come this way, then. You'll all go in the pot together."

"That's not what I meant!" Tandy cried.

"It isn't?" The goblin seemed surprised. "You said you wanted to be with your friends."

"But not in the pot!"

The goblin shook his head in confusion. "Females change their minds a lot. Exactly what do you want?"

"I want us all to continue our trip north through Xanth," Tandy said, enunciating clearly. "I can't do it alone. I don't know anything about surface Xanth. I need the ogre to protect me. If he weren't worn out from fighting the Gap Dragon and hauling us all up out of the Gap, he'd be cramming all of *you* into the pot!"

"Nonsense. Ogres don't use pots."

Tandy huffed herself up into the resemblance of a tantrum. But before she completed the process, a goblin lieutenant sidled up to whisper in the leader's ear. The leader nodded. "Maybe so," he agreed. He turned back to Tandy. "You are five females, guarded by the tired ogre?"

"Yes," Tandy agreed guardedly.

"How many others has he eaten?"

"None!" Tandy responded indignantly. "He doesn't eat friends!"

"He can't be much of an ogre, then."

"He beat up the Gap Dragon!"

The goblin considered. "There is that." He came to a decision. "My name is Gorbage Goblin. I control this section of the Rim. But I have a daughter, and we are exogamous."

"What?" Tandy asked, bewildered.

"Exogamous, twit. Girls must marry outside their home tribes. But there is no contiguous goblin tribe; we are apart from the main nation of goblins.

The dragons extended their territory recently, cutting us off." He scowled. "The other goblins keep forgetting us, the slugbrains. I don't know why."

Smash knew why. It was the forget-spell laid on the Gap Chasm. These goblins lived too close to it, so suffered a peripheral effect.

"So my daughter Goldy Goblin must cross to another tribe," Gorbage grumbled. "But travel beyond our territory is now hazardous to the health. She needs a guard."

Tandy's face lighted with eventual comprehension. "You want us to take your daughter with us?"

"To the next goblin tribe, north of here. Beyond the dragons, in the midst of the five forbidden regions, near the firewall. Yes."

Five forbidden regions? Firewall? Smash wondered about that. It didn't sound like the sort of territory to take five or six delicate girls through.

"You will let us go if we do that?" Tandy asked.

"You and the ogre."

Tandy's face set. She was a very stubborn girl at times. "*All* of us."

The goblin leader wavered. "That's a lot to ask. We haven't had fresh meat in several days."

"I don't care if you never have fresh meat again!" the girl flared. "You can cook up zombies if you get hungry. I want all my friends."

"It's only one daughter you're taking north, after all."

"Remember the feminine wiles," the Siren murmured.

Tandy considered. "The ogre can't do all the guarding," she said reasonably. "When he fights off a big dragon or a tangle tree or something, he gets tired. Then he has to rest, and someone else stands guard, like the centaur. If we cross a lake, the Siren scouts it out first. We never know whose skill will be useful." She paused, then with an effort turned on extra charm. "If you really want your daughter to travel safely—"

Gorbage capitulated with bad grace. "Oh, very well. All of you go. It's a bad deal for me, but Goldy will slaughter me if I don't get her matched soon. She's a cussheaded lass, like all her kind."

Smash was amazed. Tandy had, with a little timely advice from the Siren, talked them out of disaster and gotten them all free passage through goblin-infested territory. Already his own strength was filtering back; all he needed was a little rest. But there was no longer any need for violence.

Goldy Goblin turned out to be a petite, amazingly pretty lass. The goblin females were as lovely as the goblin males were ugly. "Thank you so much for taking me," she said politely. "Is there anything I can do in return?"

Tandy had the grace to take this seriously. "We have to stop by a fireoak tree in this vicinity. If you could show us the best route to it—"

"Certainly. There's only one fireoak hereabouts, with a resident hama-dryad nymph—" Goldy paused, spying Fireoak. "Isn't that she?"

"Yes. She's trying to save her tree. We must get her back to it as soon as possible."

"I know the way. But the path to it goes by a hypnogourd patch. So you have to be careful."

"I don't want to go near the gourds!" Tandy cried, horrified.

But Smash remembered his contact with the coffin inside the other gourd. Was it possible that—? "I want a gourd," he said.

The Siren was perplexed. "Why would you want a terrible thing like that?"

"Something I may have forgotten in there."

The Siren frowned but dropped the subject.

They trekked on, Smash carrying the hamadryad. He tried not to show it, but his strength had returned only partially. Fireoak was light, the kind of burden he could normally balance on his little finger without effort, but now he had to control his breathing, lest he pant so loudly he call attention to himself. He would be no help at all if they happened on another dragon. Maybe he just needed a good meal and a night's sleep. Yet it had never before taken him so long to recover from exertion. He suspected something was wrong, but he didn't know what.

They came to the region of hypnogourds. The vines sprawled abundantly, and gourds were all about. Smash stared at them, half mesmerized. He had thought his soul lost when the Siren smashed the other gourd—but was it possible that the gourd had been a mere window on the otherworld reality? His Eye Queue was crazy enough to think this was so. Could he use another gourd to return to that world and fight for his soul?

He felt small hands on his arm. "What is it, Smash?" Tandy asked. "I'm deathly afraid of those things, but you seem fascinated. What's with you and those awful gourds?"

He answered, not fully conscious of his situation. "I must go fight the Night Stallion."

"A Dark Horse?"

"The ruler of the nightmares. He has a lien on my soul."

"Oh, no! Is that how you rescued my soul?"

Smash snapped out of it. He hadn't meant to say anything about the lien to Tandy. "I'm gibbering. Ignore it."

"So that's why you wanted another gourd," the Siren said. "You had unfinished business there! I didn't realize . . ."

Now the goblin girl approached. "The ogre's been into a gourd? I've seen that happen before. Some people escape unscathed; some lose their souls; some get only halfway free. We lost a lot of goblins before we caught on. Now we use those gourds as punishment. Thieves are set at a peephole for an hour; they usually escape with a bad scare and never thieve again. Murderers are set there for a day; they often lose their souls. It varies; some people are cleverer than others, and some luckier. The lien is like a delayed sentence; a month or two and it's all over."

"A lien!" the Siren said. "How long for you, Smash?"

"Three months," he replied glumly.

"And you said nothing!" she cried indignantly. "What kind of a creature are you?" But she answered herself immediately. "A self-sacrificing one. Smash, you should have told us."

"Yes," Tandy agreed faintly. "I never realized—"

"How can a person nullify such a lien?" the Siren asked, getting practical.

"He has to go back in and fight," Goldy said. "If he doesn't, he just gets weaker, bit by bit, as the Stallion calls in the soul. It's too late to fight, once the lien is due. He has to do it early, while he has most of his strength."

"But a person can redeem himself if he goes in early?" the Siren asked.

"Sometimes," the goblin girl said. "Maybe one out of ten. One of our old goblins is supposed to have done it a long time ago in his youth. We're not sure we believe him. He mumbles about trials of fear and pain and pride and such-like, making no sense at all. But it is theoretically possible to win."

"So that's why Smash has gotten so weak," the Siren said. "He was using his strength as if he had plenty to spare, but he has an illness of the soul."

"I know about that," Fireoak breathed.

"I didn't know!" Tandy said, clouding up. "Oh, it's all my fault! I never would have taken my soul back if—"

"I didn't know, either," the Siren said, calming her. "But I should have suspected. Maybe I did suspect; I just didn't pursue the thought fast enough. I forgot that Smash is no longer a simple-minded ogre; he has the devious Eye Queue contamination, making him react more like human folk."

"The curse of human intellect, replacing the primeval beastly innocence," Tandy agreed. "I, too, should have realized—"

"Tandy, we've got to help Smash destroy that lien!"

"Yes!" Tandy agreed emphatically. "We can't leave him to the law of the lien."

Smash almost smiled, despite the seriousness of the situation. During his travels with Prince Dor, he had encountered the law of the loin; was this related?

"I'll help," Goldy said.

The Siren frowned. "What is your interest? Your tribe was going to eat us all."

"How can I get to another goblin tribe if I don't have a strong ogre to clear the way? I do know a little bit about the matter."

"I suppose you do have a practical interest," the Siren agreed. "We all need the ogre, until we find our own individual situations. What do you know about the gourds that might help?"

"Our people have reported details of the gourd geography. It's the same for every gourd; they're all identical inside. But each person enters at a different place, and it's possible to get lost. So it is best to carry a line of string to mark the way."

"But a person is out the moment his contact with the peephole is broken! How can he get lost?"

"It's not that sort of lost," Goldy said. "There's a lot of territory in there, and some pretty strange effects. Some talk of graves, others of mirrors. A person always returns to the spot he left, and the time he left, no matter how long he's been away from it; a break in the sequence is only an interruption, not a change. If he's lost in gourdland, he's still lost when he returns there, even if he's been a long time out of his gourd. He doesn't know where he's going because he doesn't know where he's been. But if he strings the string, it'll mark where he's been, and he'll know the moment he crosses his trail. And that's the secret."

Smash was getting quite interested. He had been out of his gourd for some time, but apparently could still return. "What secret?"

"The Night Stallion is always in the last place a person looks, in the gourd," the goblin girl explained. "So all you have to do to reach him is always look in a new place—never in a place you've been before; that's a waste of time and effort. You are apt to get caught in an endless loop, and then you are really lost. You may never find him if you rehash your old route."

"You *do* know something about it!" Tandy agreed. "But suppose Smash threads the maze, finds the Night Stallion—and is too weak to fight him?"

"Oh, it's not that sort of strength he needs," the goblin girl said. "We've had physically strong goblins go in, and physically weak ones, and the weak ones do just as well. All kinds lose in the gourd. Physical strength may even be a liability. Destroying the facilities does not destroy the commitment. Only defeating the Stallion does that, on the Stallion's own terms."

"What are the Stallion's terms?"

Goldy shrugged. "No one knows. Our one surviving goblin refuses to tell, assuming he knows. He just sort of turns a little grayer. I think there is no way to find out except to face the creature."

"I think we have enough to go on," Tandy said. "Let's take a gourd along. We have to get to the fireoak tree before the lunatic-fringe-spell gives out." She went to harvest a gourd, her concern for Smash overriding her fear of the thing.

"I think the peephole is a lunatic fringe," the Siren muttered.

They moved on. Smash pondered what the goblin girl had said. If physical strength was not important in the struggle with the Night Stallion, why was it important to join this contest early, before weakness progressed too far? Was that a contradiction or merely a confusion? He concluded that it was the latter. There was weakness of the body and of the spirit; both might fade together, but they were not identical. Smash was physically weak now because he had overextended himself; otherwise it should have taken him three months to fade. His soul had probably suffered relatively little so far. But if he waited till the end of the lien term to meet the Stallion, then his soul would be weak, and he would lose the nonphysical contest. Yes, that seemed to make sense. Things didn't have to make sense, with magic, but it helped.

They arrived at a pleasant glade. Within it was a crazy sort of shimmer that made Smash feel a little crazy himself; he turned his eyes away.

"My tree!" the hamadryad cried, suddenly reviving.

Smash set her down. "Where?"

"There! Behind the lunatic fringe!" She seemed to grow stronger instant by instant and in a moment pranced into the glade. Her body wavered and vanished.

"I guess the spell is still holding," Tandy said. She followed Fireoak, carrying the gourd, and disappeared similarly. The others went the same route.

When Smash contacted the fringe, he felt a momentary surge of dizziness; then he was through. There before him was the tree, a medium-large fireoak, its leaves blazing in the late afternoon sunlight. The hamadryad was hugging its trunk in ecstasy, her body almost indistinguishable from it, and her color was returning. She had rejoined her soul. The tree, too, seemed to be glowing, and leaves that had been wilting were now forging back into health. Evidently it had missed her also. There was something very touching about the love of nymph and tree for each other.

Tandy approached him, her blue eyes soulful. "Smash, if I had known—" She choked up. She shoved the gourd at him.

"We'll let you go into it until the lunatic fringe fades and the people attack this tree," the Siren said. "Maybe you'll have time to conquer the Night Stallion and regain your full strength." She produced a ball of string that the hamadryad must have had stored in her tree. "Use this so you won't get lost in there."

"But first eat something," Chem said, bringing an armful of fruits. "And get a night's sleep."

"No. I want to settle this now," Smash said.

"Oh, please do at least eat something!" Tandy pleaded. "You can eat a lot in a hurry."

True words—and he was hungry. Ogres were usually hungry. So he crammed a bushel of whole fruits into his mouth and gulped them down, ogre-fashion, and drank a long pull of water from the spring at the base of the tree.

As the sun dropped down behind the forest, singeing the distant tips of trees, Smash took leave of the six females as if setting out on a long and hazardous trek. Then he settled down against the trunk of the tree, put the gourd in his lap, and applied his right eye to the peephole.

Instantly he was back in the gourd world. He stood before the crypt, having just gotten up from his snooze. Tandy was not there; for a moment he had feared that she would be locked into this adventure with him, since she had been here before, but of course she was free now.

A chill wind cut around the stonework, ruffling his fur. The landscape was bleak: all gravestones and dying weeds and dismal dark sky. "Beautiful!" he exclaimed. "I would like to stay here forever."

Then his Eye Queue, in its annoying fashion, forced him to amend his statement mentally. He would like to stay here forever after he rescued his soul from the lien and regained his full strength and saved the hamadryad's tree and had gotten Tandy and all the others to wherever they were going and found his Answer from the Good Magician. After these details, then this paradise of the gourd would be a nice retirement spot.

He had been afraid he would find himself somewhere else and be unable, after all, to pursue his quest to its close. Despite what the goblin girl had said, this was a different gourd, and might not know where his adventure in the last gourd had ended. Now he was reassured, and confident that he could locate the Night Stallion and abate the lien. After all, he was an ogre, wasn't he?

He held his ball of string, since he had willed it to accompany him, but again he had forgotten to bring his gauntlets or orange jacket. He backtracked to the back of the haunted house and anchored one end of the string to a post, then crossed the graveyard to the far gate, letting the string unravel behind. It was a good-sized ball, so he was confident he would have plenty to mark his way.

A skeleton came out to see what was going on; Smash made a horrendous face at it, and the thing fled so fast its bones rattled. Yes, the bone-folk remembered him here!

Beyond the gate was a broad, bleak, open plain illuminated by ghastly, pale white moonlight. Black, ugly clouds scudded horrendously across the dismal sky, forming dark picture-shapes that resembled trolls, goblins, and ogres. Naturally the other creatures were fleeing before the ogre-shapes. Smash was delighted; this was an even better scene than the last! Whoever had set up this gourd world had had ogre tastes in mind.

Where should he go now? It was not his purpose to dally amidst the delights of the terrain, but to locate the Night Stallion. Yet he knew that he would have to cover a lot of territory before he reached the last place to look. So he had better move rapidly anywhere, getting the ground covered.

He tromped forth, straight across the beautifully barren plain. The cracked ground shuddered pleasantly under the impact of his feet. He was regaining his strength. Yet now he knew, thanks to the goblin girl, that physical strength was not necessarily what it took to prevail here. He had used it to cow the voice in the coffin, forcing it to release Tandy's soul—but had suffered the compromise of his own soul. Probably the coffin had given him nothing that had not already been allocated; he had fooled himself, thinking an ogre's power would scare the dead. The curse of the Eye Queue was making him see uncomfortable truths!

Yet perhaps he should not take this revelation on faith, either. He could go back and rattle the coffin some more, and determine just how much it feared his violence. After all, the skeletons now fled from him. No—that was a temptation to be avoided, for it would cause him to backtrack his own trail, the one thing he needed to avoid doing. Smash continued resolutely forward.

Black dots appeared on the bleak horizon. Quickly they expanded, racing toward him on beating hooves. The nightmares! This was where they stayed by day—here, where night was eternal.

The mares were handsome animals, absolutely black, with flaring manes, flying tails, and darkly glowing eyes. Their limbs were sleekly muscular, and they moved with the velocity of thought. In moments they surrounded him, galloping around him in a circle, squealing warningly. They did not want him going the way he was going. But since the Night Stallion did not seem to be among them, he had to proceed.

Smash ignored their warning. He tromped onward—and their circle stayed with him despite his speed. Experimentally he dodged to one side, and the circle remained centered on him. He leaped, and the circle leaped with him. Just as he had thought, these were magical creatures, orienting magically; the feet of a dream-horse had no essential connection with the ground. Prince Dor had once mentioned escaping the nightmares by sleeping on a cloud, beyond their reach, but probably Prince Dor had not had any bad dreams scheduled that night. The mares could go anywhere, and Smash could not escape their circle by running.

Not that he wanted to. He liked these fine, healthy animals. They were an ogre's type of creature. He remembered how one of them had given Tandy a ride to the Good Magician's castle—which had perhaps been a better destination for her than the one she had sought. The Good Magician had provided Tandy a home for a year, and a solution to her problem— maybe. Her father Crombie, the soldier at Castle Roogna, might not have been much help. Smash knew the man casually. Crombie was getting old, no longer the fighter he used to be. He was also a woman hater who might not have taken his daughter's problem seriously. But if he had taken it seriously—what could he have done, without leaving his post at Castle Roogna?

And the nightmares—one had helped Tandy travel, but then had put in for a lien on her soul, causing her awful grief. Some help that had been! Maybe these nightmares needed to feel the weight of an ogre's displeasure.

Still he did not know enough to act. What was Tandy's problem that the Magician had answered? She had never quite said. Did it relate to that nightmare lien on her soul? But she had incurred that lien in order to reach the Good Magician. That hardly seemed profitable. Also, she had not been aware of the lien, so she would not have put a Question about it.

How would traveling with an ogre abate her problem? Had it been the Magician's intent that Smash redeem that girl's lost soul with his own? That was possible—but his understanding of the Magician's mode of operations argued against it. Humfrey did not need to fool people about the nature of their payments for their Answers. He should not pretend the service was merely protection duty when, in fact, it was soul substitution. So that, too, remained an enigma.

So far, Tandy had recruited fellow travelers with abandon, and now there were six females in the party. That was probably as unlikely a group as existed at the moment in Xanth. Normally such maidens fled ogres, and for good reason—ogres consumed such morsels. Were it not for Smash's commitment not to indulge his natural appetites because of the service he owed the Good Magician—

He shook his head, flinging loose a few angry fleas. No, he could not be sure of his motive there. His father Crunch was a vegetarian ogre, married to a female of human derivation, so Smash had been raised in an atypical ogre home. His folks had been permitted to associate with the people of Castle Roogna as long as they honored human customs. Smash himself had not operated under the restriction of oath or of human taste—but had always known he would be banished from human company if he ever reverted to the wild state. Anyone who made trouble for King Trent ran the risk of being transformed to a toad or a stinkbug, for Trent was the great transformer. It had been easy to conform. So Smash had not actually crunched many human bones, and had carried away no delicious human maidens. Perhaps he had been missing something vital—but he remained unwilling to gamble that one good meal would be more satisfying than the human friendships he had maintained. So perhaps it was more than the Good Magician's service that protected Tandy and the others. Ogres weren't supposed to need companionship, but the curse of the Eye Queue showed him that he was, to that extent, atypical of his kind. Like the Siren, he now knew he would be lonely alone.

Smash suddenly realized that the ring of mares was only half the diameter it had been. While he tromped forward, thinking his slew of un-ogrish thoughts, they had been constricting their loop. Soon they would be almost within reach of him.

And if they closed on him all the way—what then? Mere horses could hardly hurt an ogre. Each weighed about as much as he did, but they were only mares, with the foreparts of sea horses and the rear parts of centaurs. They were basically pretty and gentle. True, their ears were flat back against their skulls, and their manes flared like dangerous spikes, their tails flicked like weapons, their teeth showed white in the moonlight, and their eyes stared slantwise at him as if he were prey instead of monster—but he knew he could throw any of them far out across the plain, if he chose, when he had his normal ogre strength. Why should they want to come within his reach?

In a moment he had the answer. These were standard nightmares, used to carry bad dreams to their proper dreamers. They had not been cursed with the Eye Queue; they had no super-equine intelligence. They were giving him the standard treatment, crowding him, trying to scare him—

Smash burst out laughing. Imagine anything scaring an ogre!

The mares broke ranks, startled. This was not S. O. P. The victim was not supposed to laugh. What was wrong?

Smash was sorry. "I didn't mean to mess up your act, mares," he said apologetically. "Circle me again, and I'll pretend to be frightened. I don't want you to get in trouble with your Stallion. In fact, I'd like to meet him myself. I don't suppose you could take me to him?"

Still the mares milled about. Their formation was in a shambles. They were not here to play a game, but to terrify. Since that had failed, they had other business to attend to. After all, night had been drawing nigh when he entered the gourd. The group began breaking up. Probably they would be all over Xanth within the next hour, bearing their burdensome dreams.

"Wait!" Smash cried. "Which of you gave Tandy a ride?"

One mare hesitated, as if trying to remember. "A year ago," Smash said. "A small human girl, brown hair, throws tantrums."

The black ears perked forward. The mare remembered!

"She sends her thanks," Smash said. "You really helped her."

The mare nickered, seeming interested. Did these creatures really care about the welfare of those on whom they visited the bad dreams? Yet his Eye Queue warned him that it was not safe to judge any creature by his or her job. Some ogres did not crunch bones; some mares might not hate girls.

"Did you mean to destroy her?" he asked. "By taking a lien on her soul?"

The mare's head lifted back, nostrils flaring.

"You didn't know?" Smash asked. "When she wandered into the gourd, the coffin-creep stole her soul, on the pretext she owed it for the ride."

The mare snorted. She hadn't known. That made Smash feel better. Life was a jungle inside the gourd as well as in Xanth, with creatures and things grasping whatever they could get from the unwary. But some were innocent.

"She might visit here again," he continued. "You might see her following my string." He pointed to the line he had laid out behind him. "If you like, you could give her another ride and sort of explain things to her. It would help her catch up to me quickly. But no more liens!"

The mare snorted and pawed the ground. She was not interested in giving rides.

"Maybe I can make a deal with you," Smash said. "I don't want Tandy getting in trouble here." Not at the risk of her soul, certainly! "Is there anything I can do for you, outside?"

The mare considered. Then she brightened. She licked her lips.

"Something to eat?" Smash asked, and the mare nodded. "Something nice?" She agreed again. "Rock candy?" She neighed nay.

Smash played the guessing game, but could not quite come up with the correct item. All the other mares had departed, and this one was fidgeting; he could not hold her longer. "Well, if I find it, maybe I'll know it," Smash said. "Maybe Tandy will know, and bring it with her, if she comes. You keep in touch, okay?"

The nightmare nodded, then turned and trotted off. No doubt she was going to pick up her load of unpleasant dreams for delivery to her clientele of sleepers. Maybe some of them were his friends at the fireoak tree. "Good luck!" Smash called after her, and she flicked her tail in acknowledgement.

Alone again, he wondered whether he had been foolish. What business did he have with nightmares? What would a nightmare want from a person, that the mare could not pick up for herself on her rounds? He was an ogre who loved violence and horror, and he was here on a personal mission. Yet somehow he felt it was best to get along with any creature he could; perhaps something would come of it.

This confounded Eye Queue! Not only did it set him to trying un-ogrish things, it rendered him confused about the meaning of these things and full of uncomfortable self-doubt. What a curse it was!

He faced resolutely forward and resumed his tromping. He saw something new on the horizon and proceeded toward it. Soon it manifested as a build-ing—no, as a castle—no, larger yet, an entire city, enclosed by a forbidding wall.

As he drew close, he discovered the city was solid gold. Every part of it scintillated in the moonlight, shades of deep yellow. But when he drew closer yet, he found that it was not gold but brass—just as shiny, but not nearly as precious. Still it was a marvel.

The outer wall was unbroken, riveted metal, gleaming at every angle. The front gate was the same, so large it dwarfed even Smash's monstrous propor-tions. This was the sort of city giants would inhabit!

Smash considered that. The little knobs of the haunted house had shocked him; how much worse would this one be? He was not at all sure he could rip this door from its moorings; it was big and strong, and he was now relatively weak. This was not a situation he liked to admit, but he was no longer properly stupid about such things.

He pondered, drawing on the full curse of the Eye Queue. What he needed was insulation—something to protect him from shock. But there was nothing near; the city wall rose out of sand. He might use his orange jacket—but he was not wearing it, here in the gourd. All he had was the string, and that wasn't suitable.

No help for it. He would have to touch the metal. Actually, there might be a metal floor inside that he would have to walk on; if he were going to get shocked, it would happen with every step. Might as well find out now. He extended a hamfinger and touched the knob.

There was no shock. He grasped and turned the knob. It clicked, and the door swung inward. It wasn't locked!

There was a bright metal hall leading from the gate into the city. Smash walked down it, half expecting the door to slam shut behind him. It did not. He continued through the hall, his bare, furry soles thumping on the cool metal.

He emerged into an open court with a paving of brass, the moonlight bearing down preternaturally. All was silent. No creatures roamed the city.

"Ho!" Smash bellowed, loud enough to disturb the dead, as seemed appro-priate in this realm.

No dead were disturbed. If they heard, they were ignoring him. The city seemed to be empty. There was an eerie quality to this that Smash liked. But he wondered who had made this city and where those people had gone. It seemed like far too interesting a place to desert. If ogres built cities, this was the sort of city they would build. But of course no ogre was smart enough to build a single building, let alone a city, certainly not a lovely city of brass.

He tromped through it, his big, flat feet generating a muted booming on the metal street. Brass buildings rose on either side, their walls making blank brass faces at precise right angles to the street. He looked up and saw that the tops were squared off, too. There were no windows or doors. Of course that didn't matter to the average ogre; he could always bash out any windows when and where he wanted. All was mirror-shiny; he could see his appalling reflection in every surface that faced him. Brass ogres paced him to either side, and another walked upside down under the street.

Smash remembered the story his father Crunch had told of entering a sleeping city and discovering the lovely mushfaced ogress who had become Smash's mother. This city of brass was pleasantly reminiscent of that. Was there an ogress here for him? That was an exciting prospect, though he hoped she wasn't made of brass.

He traversed the city, but found no entrance to any building. If an ogress was sleeping here, she was locked away where he couldn't reach her. Smash banged on a wall, making it reverberate; but though the sound boomed pleasantly throughout the city, no one stirred. He punched harder, trying to break a hole in the wall. It was no good; he was too weak, the brass was too strong, and he lacked his protective gauntlets. His fist smarted, so he stuck it in his mouth.

Smash was beginning to be bothered. Before there had been halfway interesting things like walking skeletons, electrified doors, and nightmares. Now there was just brass. What could he accomplish here?

He invoked the curse of the Eye Queue yet again and did some solid thinking. So far, each little adventure within the gourd had been a kind of riddle; he had to overcome some barrier or beat some sort of threat before he could continue to the next event. So it was probably not enough just to enter this empty city and depart; that might not count. He had to solve the riddle, thus narrowing the options, reducing the remaining places for the Night Stallion to hide. Straight physical action did not seem to be the requirement here. What, then, was?

There must be a nonphysical way to deal with this impassive place, perhaps to bring it to life so it could be conquered. Maybe a magical spell. But Smash did not know any spells, and somehow this city seemed too alien to be magical. What else, then?

He paced the streets, still unreeling his string, careful never to cross his own path. And, in a little private square directly under the moon, he discovered a pedestal. Significant things were usually mounted on pedestals directly under the moon, he remembered. So he marched up to it and looked.

He was disappointed. There was only a brass button there. Nothing to do except to press it. There might be serious consequences, but no self-respecting ogre worried about that sort of thing. He turned his big hamthumb down and mashed the button. With luck, all hell would break loose.

As it happened, luck was with him. Most of hell broke loose.

There was a pleasantly deafening klaxon alarm noise that filled all this limited universe with vibrations. Then the metal buildings began shifting about, moving along the floor of the city, squeezing the streets and the court. In a moment there would be no place remaining for him to stand.

This was more like it! At first Smash planned to brace himself and halt the encroaching buildings by brute ogre strength. But he lacked his full power now, and anyway, it was better to use his brain. Perhaps the Eye Queue was gradually subverting him, causing him to endorse its nature; already it seemed like less of a curse, and he knew—because, ironically, of the intelligence it provided him—that this was a significant signal of corruption. Mental power tended to corrupt, and absolute intelligence tended to corrupt absolutely, until the victim eschewed violence entirely in favor of smart solutions to stupid problems. Smash hoped he could fight off the curse before it ever ruined him to that extent! If he stopped being stupid, brutal, and violent, he would no longer be a true ogre.

Nevertheless, the expedience of the moment forced him to utilize his mind. He knew that a block that moved one way had to leave a space behind it, unless it happened to be expanding rapidly. He zipped between buildings, emerging from the narrowing aisle just before the two clanged together. Sure enough, there was a new space where a building had stood. It was perfectly smooth brass except for a cubic hole where the center of the building had been. Probably that was the anchoring place, like part of a lock mechanism; a heavy bolt would drop down from the building to wedge in that hole and keep the building from sliding about when it wasn't supposed to. When he had pressed the brass button, the lock bolts had lifted, freeing the buildings. Buildings, like clouds, bashed about all over the place when given the freedom to do so. The klaxon had sounded to warn all crushable parties that motion was commencing, so they could either get out of the way or pick their favorite squishing-spot. It all made a sort of violent sense, his Eye Queue informed him. He liked this city better than ever.

Now the building blocks were bouncing back, converging on him. Smash moved again, avoiding what could be a crushing experience. He found himself in a new open space, with another anchorage slot.

But the blocks were moving more quickly now, as if getting warmed up. Because they were big, he needed a certain amount of time to run between them. If they speeded up much more, he would not have time to clear before they clanged. That could be awkward.

"Well, brain, what do you say to this?" he asked challengingly. "Can you outsmart two buildings that plan to catch me and squish me flat?"

His vine-corrupted brain, thus challenged, rose to the occasion. "Get in the pit," it told him.

Smash thought this was crazy. But already the brass was moving, sounding off with its tune of compression, and he had to act. He leaped into the pit as the blank metal face of the building charged him.

Too late, it occurred to him, or to his Eye Queue—it became difficult at times to distinguish ogre-mind from vine-mind—that he could be crushed when the bolt dropped down to anchor the building. But that should happen only when the building was finished traveling and wanted to settle down for a rest. He would try to be out by then. If he failed—well, squishing was an ogrish kind of demise.

It was dark there as the metal underbody of the building slid across. He felt slightly claustrophobic—another weakness of intelligence, since a true ogre never worried about danger or consequence. What would happen if the building did not move off?

Then light flashed down from above. Smash blinked and discovered that the center of the building was hollow, glowing from the inner walls. He had found his way inside!

He scrambled up and stood on the floor, still holding his ball of string. The building was still moving, but there was no way it could crush him now. The building floor covered everything except the square where the anchorage hole would be when it lay at anchor, so he could simply ride along with it.

He looked about—and spied an army of brass men and women, each individual fully formed, complete with brass facial features, hair, and cloth- ing—the men fully clothed, the women less so. But they were statues, erected on platforms that, like the floor, moved with the building. Nothing here was of interest to an ogre. He knew brass wasn't good to eat.

Then he spied another brass button.

Well, why not? Maybe this one would make the building stop moving. Of course, if this one stopped and the other buildings did not, there would be a horrendous crash. Smash jammed his thumb down on the button.

Instantly the brass statues animated. The metal people spied the ogre and converged on him. And Smash—

Found himself leaning against the fireoak tree. Tandy stood before him, holding the gourd. She had broken his line of vision to the peephole. "Are you all right, Smash?" she asked with her cute concern.

"Certainly!" he grumped. "Why did you interrupt me? It was just getting interesting."

"The lunatic fringe is tearing," she said worriedly. "The human villagers are in the area and will soon discover the tree."

"Well, bring me back when they do," Smash said. "I have metal men to fight inside."

"Metal men?"

"And women. Solid brass."

"Oh," she said, uncomprehending. "Remember, you're in there to fight for your soul. I worry about you, Smash."

He guffawed. "You worry about me! You're human; I'm an ogre!"

"Yes," she agreed, but her face remained drawn. "I know what it's like in there. You put your soul in peril for me. I can't forget that, Smash."

"You don't like it in there," he pointed out. "I do. And I agreed to protect you. This is merely another aspect." He took the gourd back and applied his eye to the peephole.

The brass people were converging, exactly where they had been when he left. They seemed not even to be aware of his brief absence. The building was moving, too—but it had not moved in the interim. His Eye Queue-cursed brain found all this interesting, but Smash had no time for that nonsense at the moment. The brassies were almost on him.

The first one struck at him. The man was only half Smash's height, but the metal made him solid. Smash hauled him up by the brassard and threw him aside. Smash still lacked the strength to do real damage, but at least he could fight weakly. In his strength he would have hurled the brass man right through the brass wall of the building.

A female grabbed at him. Smash hooked a forefinger into her brassiere and hauled her up to his eye level. "Why are you attacking me?" he asked, curious rather than angry.

"We're only following our program," she said, kicking at him with a pretty brass foot.

"But if you fight me, I shall have to fight you," he pointed out. "And I happen to be a monster."

"Don't try to reason with me, you big hunk of flesh; I'm too brassy for that." She swung at him with a metal fist. But he was holding her at his arm's length, so she could not reach him.

Something was knocking at his knee. Smash looked down. A man was striking at him with his brass knuckles. Smash dropped the brass girl on the brass man's brass hat, and the two crashed to the floor in a shower of brass tacks. They cried out with the sound of brass winds.

Now a half-dozen brassies were grabbing at Smash's legs, and he lacked the strength to throw them all off at once. So he reached down to pluck them off one at a time—

He was under the tree again. He saw the problem immediately. Half a dozen brassies—no, these were men and women of the human village—were converging on the tree, bearing wicked-looking axes. The hamadryad was screaming.

Smash had no patience with this. He stood up, towering over the villagers, ogre-fashion. He roared a fine ogre roar.

The villagers turned and fled. They didn't know Smash was short of strength at the moment. Otherwise they could have attacked him and perhaps put him in difficulty, in the same way the brassies were doing in the gourd. He had replaced the illusion of the lunatic fringe with the illusion of his own formidability.

The hamadryad dropped from her tree, her hair glowing like fire, catching him about the neck. She was now a vibrant, healthy creature. "You great big wonderful brute of a creature!" she exclaimed, kissing his furry ear. Smash was oddly moved; as the centaur had noted, ogres were seldom embraced or kissed by nymphs.

He handed the hamadryad back into her tree, then settled down for another session in the gourd. None of them had anywhere to go until the King got the news and acted to protect the tree permanently, and he wanted to wrap up this gourd business.

"Wake me at need," he said, noting that the shimmer of the lunatic fringe was now almost gone. If trees had ogres to protect them instead of cute but helpless hamadryads, very few trees would be destroyed. Of course, ogres themselves were prime destroyers of trees, using them to make toothpicks and such, so he was in no position to criticize. He applied his left eye to the peephole this time, giving his right orb a rest.

He stood in an alley between buildings. What was this? The sequence was supposed to pick up exactly where it had left off. What had gone wrong?

The two buildings slid toward him, forcing him to scoot out of the way. Smash emerged into a new space—and saw his line of string. He was about to cross his own path! But he couldn't retreat; the buildings were clanging behind him.

Still, his cursed Eye Queue wouldn't let him leave well enough alone. It wanted to know why the gourd scene had slipped a notch. Was the gourd getting old, beginning to rot, breaking down its system? He didn't want to be trapped in a rotting gourd.

The buildings separated, starting to converge on a new spot. The alley reopened, the string he had just set out running down its length—and stopping.

Smash ran to the end of it. The string had been severed cleanly; it ended at the point he had re-entered the vision.

But as the buildings separated, Smash saw another cut end of string. That must be where he had been before, just a little distance away. He had jumped no farther than he could have bounded by foot. But he hadn't jumped physically; he had left the scene, then returned to it slightly displaced. Why?

The buildings reversed course and closed on him again. They certainly wasted no time pondering questions! Smash ran back, his mind working. And suddenly it came to him—he had switched eyes! His left eye was a little apart from his right eye—and though that distance was small in the real world of Xanth, it was larger in the tiny world of the gourd. So there had been a shift, and a break in his string.

Well, that had freed him of the brass folk. But Smash couldn't accept that. He didn't want to escape, he wanted to win, to conquer this setting and go on to the next, knowing he had narrowed the Night Stallion's options. He wanted to do his job right, leaving no possible loophole for the loss of his soul. So he had to go back to the place he had left off, and resume there.

He followed his prior line, dragging his new line behind him. He found the square pit as the building moved off it, and he got down into it. The building swung back, and the interior light came on. Smash climbed out and ran to the end of his string.

The brass folk saw him and came charging in. Smash tied the two ends of string together, making his line complete, then stood as half a dozen people grabbed him. This was where he had left off; now it was all right.

He resumed plucking individual brass folk off. One of them was the girl in the brassiere. "You again?" he inquired, holding her up by one finger, as he had done before. It was really the best place, since she was flailing all her limbs wildly. "Do I have to drop you again?"

"Don't you dare drop me again!" she flashed, her brass surface glinting with ire. She took an angry breath—which almost dislodged her, for she had a full brassiere and his purchase on it was slight. "I have a dent and three scratches from the last time, you monster!" She pointed at her arms. "There's a scratch. There's another. But I won't show you the dent."

"Well, you did kick at me," Smash said reasonably, wondering where the dent was.

"I told you! We have to—"

Then he was back in Xanth again. Smash saw the problem immediately; a cockatrice was approaching the tree. The baby basilisk had evidently been recently hatched and was wandering aimlessly—but remained deadly dangerous.

"Put me down, you lunk!"

Startled, Smash looked at the source of the voice. He was still holding the brass girl, dangling by her brassiere hooked on his finger. She had been brought out of the gourd with him!

Hastily Smash set her down, carefully so she would not dent. He had a more immediate matter to attend to. How could he get rid of the cockatrice?

"Oh, look," the brass girl said. "What a cute chick!" She stepped over to the terrible infant, reaching down.

"Don't touch it!" the Siren cried. "Don't even look at it!"

Too late. The brass girl picked up the baby monster. "Oh, aren't you a sweet one," she cooed, turning it in her hand so she could look it in the snoot.

"No!" several voices cried.

Again they were too late. The brass girl stared deeply into the monster's baleful eyes. "Oh, I wish I could keep you for my very own pet, along with my other pets," she said, touching her pert nose to its hideous schnozzle. "I don't have anything like you in my collection."

The chick hissed and bit—but its tiny teeth were ineffective against the brass. "Oh, how nice," the girl said. "You like me, don't you!"

Apparently the little monster's powers were harmless against the metal girl. She was already harder than stone.

"Uh, miss—" the Siren said.

"I'm called Blyght," the brass girl said. "Of Building Four, in the City of Brass. Who are you?"

"I'm called the Siren," the Siren said. "Blythe, we would appreciate it if—"

"Blyght," the girl corrected her brassily.

"Sorry. I misheard. Blyght. If you would—"

"But I think I like Blythe better. This place is so much softer than I'm used to. So you can use that, Sirn."

"Siren. Two syllables."

"That's all right. I prefer one syllable, Sirn."

"You can change names at will?" John asked incredulously.

"Of course. All brassies can. Can't you?"

"No," the fairy said enviously.

"Blythe, that animal—" the Siren broke in. "It's deadly to us. So if you would—"

Smash had been looking around to see if there were any other dangers. At this point his eye fell on the gourd—and even from a distance his consciousness was drawn into the peephole, and he was back among the brassies. This time he stood within the building, but apart from the crowd, and his string had been interrupted again. He was using his right eye.

The brass folk spied him and charged. This was getting pointless. "Wait!" he bellowed.

They paused, taken aback. "Why?" one inquired.

"Because I accidentally took one of your number out of the gourd, and if anything happens to me, she'll be forever stranded there."

They were appalled, almost galvanized. "That would be a fate worse than death!" one cried. "That would be—" He paused, balking at the awful concept.

"That would be—*life*," another brass man whispered. There was a sudden hush of dread.

"Yes," Smash agreed cruelly. "So I have to fetch her back. And I will. But you'll have to help me."

"Anything," the man said, his brass face tarnishing.

"Tell me how to get out of here, on my own."

"That's easy. Take the ship."

"The ship? But there's no water here!"

Several brassies smiled metallically. "It's not that kind of ship. It's the Luna-fringe-shuttle. You catch it at the Luna triptych building."

"Show me to it," Smash said.

They showed him to a brass door that opened to the outside. "You can't miss it," they assured him. "It's the biggest block in the city."

Smash thanked them and stepped out. The buildings were still moving, but now he had the experience and confidence to travel by their retreating sides, avoiding collisions. He glanced back at the building he had left and saw the number 4 inscribed on the side, but there was no sign of the door he had exited by. Apparently it was a one-way door that didn't exist from this side.

Soon he spied a building twice the size of the others. That had to be the one. He ducked into an anchor hole as the building approached, and in a moment was inside. There was the fringe-shuttle, like a monstrous arrowhead standing on its tail. It had a porthole in the side big enough to admit him, so he climbed in.

He found himself in a tight cockpit that the cock seemed to have vacated. There was only one place to sit comfortably, a kind of padded chair before a panel full of dinguses. So he sat there, knowing he could bash the dinguses out of the way if they bothered him. There was another brass button on the panel, and he punched it with his thumb.

The porthole clanged closed. A wheel spun itself about. Air hissed. Straps rose up from the chair and wrapped themselves around his body. A magic mirror lit up before his face. An alarm klaxon sounded. The ship shuddered, then launched upward like a shot from a catapult, punching through the roof.

In moments the mirror showed clouds falling away ahead. Then the moon came into view, growing larger and brighter each moment. It was now a half-circle. Of course—that was why the lunatic fringe no longer shrouded the fireoak tree—not enough moon left to sustain it. But the half that remained seemed solid enough, except for the round holes in it. Of course, cheese did have holes; that was its nature.

Now it occurred to him that the brassies might have misconstrued his request. They had shown him the way out of the City of Brass—but not out of the gourd. Well, nothing to do now but carry this through. Maybe the ship could get him back to the fireoak tree.

He didn't really want to go to the moon, though the view of all that fresh cheese made him hungry. After all, it had been at least an hour since he had eaten that bushel of fruit. So he checked the panel before him and found a couple of projecting brass sticks. He grabbed them, wiggling them about.

The moon veered out of the mirror-picture, and Smash was flung about in his chair as if tossed by a storm. Fortunately, the straps held him pretty much in place. He let go of the sticks—and after a moment the moon swung back into view. Evidently he had messed up the ship's program. His Eye Queue curse caused him to ponder this, and he concluded that the sticks controlled the ship. When they were not in use, the ship sailed where it wanted, which was evidently a hole in the cheese of the moon. Maybe this Luna shuttle was the mechanism by which the moon's cheese was brought to Xanth, though he wasn't sure what use metal people would have for cheese.

Smash took hold of the sticks again and wiggled more cautiously. Ogres were clumsy only when it suited them to be so; they could perform delicate tasks when no one was watching. The moon danced about but did not leave the screen. He experimented some more, and soon was able to steer the ship where he wanted and to make it go at any speed he wanted.

Fine—now he would take it back to Xanth and land beside the fireoak tree. Then he could turn it over to Blythe Brassie so she could fly back to her city and building.

Then blips appeared on the screen. They were shaped like little curse-burrs and were hurtling toward him. What did they want?

Then flashes of light came near him. The ship shook. The screen flared red for a moment, as if it had been knocked half silly. Smash understood this sort of thing. It was like getting knocked in the snoot by a fist and having stars and planets fly out from one's head. The entire night sky was filled with the stars flung out from people's heads in the course of prior fights, but Smash didn't care to have his own lights punched out. The thing to do was to hit back and destroy the enemy.

He checked the panel again, enjoying the prospect of a new type of violence. There was a big button he hadn't noticed before. Naturally he thumbed it.

A flash of light shot toward the blips, evidently from his own ship. It was throwing its sort of rocks when he told it to. Very well, in this strange gourd world, he could accept the notion of a fist made of light. But it wasn't aimed well, and missed the blips. It lanced on to blast a chunk of cheese out of the moon. Grated cheese puffed out into space in a diffuse cloud, where some of the blips went after it; no doubt they were hungry, too.

Smash pressed the button again, sending out another fist of light. This one missed both blips and moon. But he was getting the feel of it; he had to have his target in the very center of the mirror, where there was a faint intersection of lines like the center of a spider web. Funny place for a spider to work; maybe it had been trying to catch stray stars or blips or bits of blasted cheese.

To center the target, he had to work the two sticks in a coordinated fashion. He did so, after glancing nervously about to make quite sure no one was near to see him being so well coordinated. Of course, it took more than strength to balance his whole body on a single hamfinger or to smash a rock into a particular grade of gravel with one blow, but that was an ogre secret. It was fashionable to appear clumsy.

When he had a blip centered, he pushed the button with his big left toe so he wouldn't have to stop maneuvering. This time his aim was good; the beam speared out and struck the blip, which exploded with lovely violence and pretty colors.

This was fun! Not as much fun as physical bashing would be, but excellent vicarious mayhem. Ogres could appreciate beauty, too—the splendor of bursting bodies or of blips flying apart, forming intricate and changing patterns in the sky. He oriented on another blip, but it took evasive action.

Meanwhile, all the other blips were nearer, and their light-fists were striking closer. He had to dodge them, and that interfered with his own strikes.

Well, he was not an ogre for nothing! He licked his chops, worked his sticks, looped about, oriented, fired, dodged, and oriented again. Two more blips exploded beautifully.

Then the fight intensified. But Smash loved combat of any kind and was good at it; he didn't have to use physical fists. He almost liked this form of fighting better, because it was less familiar and therefore more of a challenge. He knocked out blip after blip, and after a while the remaining blips turned tail and fled past the moon. He had won the battle of the Luna fringe!

He was tempted to pursue the blips, so as to continue the pleasure of the fight a little longer, but realized that if he wiped them all out at this time, they would not have a chance to regenerate and return for future battles. Better to let them go, for the sake of more fun on future days. Also, he had other business.

He turned the ship about and headed for Xanth—which resembled a small disk from this vantage, like a greenish pie. That made him hungry again. Well, he would be careful not to miss it. He accelerated, zooming happily onward.

Chapter 8

Dragon's Ear

He was back in Xanth. "Smash, something else is coming!" Tandy cried.

"That's all right," he said. "I've won another battle. I feel stronger." And he did; he knew he was winning the gourd campaign, getting closer to the Night Stallion, and recovering physical strength in the process. It had been in large part his former hopelessness that had weakened him. He had believed his soul was doomed, until learning that he could fight for it in another gourd.

Blythe Brassie was still here. Now he wondered—how had she been carried out with him, when he had not been physically *in* the gourd?

His Eye Queue curse provided him with the answer to a question any normal ogre would not even have thought of. Blythe was here in spirit, just as he had been inside the gourd in spirit. It was very hard to tell such spirit from reality, but each person knew his own reality and was not fooled. No doubt Blythe Spirit's real body remained in the gourd, in a trance-state; since the brassies spent much of their time as statues anyway, waiting for someone to come push their button, no one had noticed the difference. Or rather, they had noticed, and been alarmed because she remained a statue while they were animate. So they knew that her vital element, her soul, was elsewhere. Yes, it all made sense. Everything in Xanth made sense, once a person penetrated the seeming nonsense that masked it. Different things made different sorts of sense for different people.

He would have to take the brass girl back. His curse not only forced intelligence on him, it forced un-ogrish moral awareness. At the moment he wasn't even certain that such awareness was a bad thing, inconvenient as it might be when there was mayhem to be wreaked.

But the tree-chopping attack party was coming again. Smash oriented on the group as it galloped just beyond view. The villagers must have gotten reinforcements. The individuals were larger than basilisks—evidently Blythe had deposited the chickatrice safely elsewhere—but smaller than sphinxes. They were hoofed. In fact—

"That's my brother!" Chem exclaimed. "Now I recognize his hoofbeat. But there's something with him—not a centaur."

Smash braced himself for what could be a complicated situation. If some monster were riding herd on his friend Chet . . .

They hove into view. "Holey cow!" the Siren breathed.

That was exactly what it was—a cow as full of holes as any big cheese. She had holes in her body every which way through which daylight showed. She was worse than the moon! A big one was in her head, about where her brain should have been; evidently that didn't impede her much. Even her horns and tail had little holes. Her legs were so holey they seemed ready to collapse, yet she functioned perfectly well.

In fact, she carried two human riders who braced their hands and feet in her holes. She was a big cow, and her gait was bumpy, so these handholds and footholds were essential.

Now Smash recognized the riders. "Dor! Irene!" he cried happily.

"*Prince* Dor?" the Siren asked. "And his fiancée?"

"Yes, they are taking forever about working up to marriage," Chem murmured with a certain equine snideness. "It's been four years now . . ."

"And Grundy the Golem!" Smash added, spying the tiny figure perched on the back of the centaur. "All my friends!"

"We're your friends, too," Tandy said, nettled.

The party drew abreast of the fireoak tree. "What's this?" the golem cried. "Snow White and the Seven Dwarves?"

Smash stood among the damsels, towering over them, not comprehending the reference. But the Eye Queue curse soon clarified it, obnoxiously. Some of the Mundane settlers in Xanth had a story by that title, and, compared with Smash the Ogre, the seven females were dwarvishly short, as was even Chem the Centaur.

"It seems you have a way with women, Smash," Prince Dor said, dismounting from the holey cow and coming to greet him. "What's your secret?"

"I only agreed not to eat them," Smash said.

"To think how much simpler my life would have been if I had known that," Dor said. "I thought girls had to be courted."

"You never courted me!" Princess Irene exclaimed. She was a striking beauty by human standards, nineteen years old. The other girls all took jealously deep breaths, watching her. "I courted you! But you never would marry me."

"You never would set the date!" Dor retorted.

Her mouth opened in a pretty O of indignation. "*You* never set the date! I've been trying to—"

"They've been fighting about the date since before there was anything to date," Grundy remarked. "He doesn't even know what color her panties are."

"I don't think she knows herself," Dor retorted.

"I do, too!" Irene flashed. "They're—" She paused, then hiked up her skirt to look. "Green."

"It's only a pretext to show off her legs," Smash explained to the others.

"So I see," Tandy said enviously.

"And her panties," John said. She, like Fireoak, the Siren, and Chem, didn't wear panties, so couldn't show them off. Blythe's panties were copper-bottoms.

"You creatures are getting too smart," Irene complained. Then she did a double take, turning to Smash. "What happened to your rhymes?"

"I got cursed by the vine," the ogre explained. "It deprived me of both rhyme and stupidity in one swell foop."

"In a foop? Oh, you poor thing," she said sympathetically.

"Now that incorrigible ogre charm is working on Irene, too," Prince Dor muttered.

"Of course it is, idiot," she retorted. "All women have a secret passion for ogres." She turned to Smash. "Now you had better introduce us all."

Smash did so with dispatch. "Tandy, Siren, John, Fireoak, Chem, Goldy, and Blythe—these are Dor, Irene, Grundy, and Chet, and vice versa."

"Moooo!" lowed the holey cow, each O with a big round hole in it.

"And the Holey Cow," Smash amended. Satisfied, the bovine swished her tattered tail and began to graze. The cropped grass fell out the holes in her neck as fast as she swallowed it, but she didn't seem to mind.

"I delivered your message," Chet said. "King Trent has declared this tree a protected species, and all the other trees in sight of it, and sent Prince Dor to inform the village. There will be no more trouble about that."

"Oh, wonderful!" the hamadryad cried. "I'm so happy!" She danced a little jig in air, hanging by one hand from a branch. The tree's leaves seemed to catch fire, harmlessly. Both nymph and tree were fully recovered from the indisposition of their recent separation. "I could just kiss the King!"

"Kiss me instead," Dor said. "I'm the messenger."

"Oh, no, you don't!" Irene flashed, taking him firmly by the ear.

"Kiss me instead of Dor," Chet offered. "There's no shrew guarding me."

The hamadryad dropped from her branch, flung her arms about the centaur, and kissed him. "Maybe I have been missing something," she commented. "But I don't think there are any males of my species."

"You could take up with one of the woodland fauns," Princess Irene suggested. "You do have pretty hair." The hamadryad's hair, under its red fringe, was green—as was Irene's hair.

"I'll consider it," Fireoak agreed.

"How did you gather such a bevy?" Prince Dor asked Smash. "They certainly seem affectionate, unlike some I have known." He moved with agility to avoid Irene's swift kick.

"I just picked them up along the way," the ogre said. "Each has her mission. John needs her correct·name, the Siren needs a better lake—"

"They all need men," the golem put in.

"I need to go home," Blythe said.

"Oh. I'll take you there now." Smash reached for the gourd.

"She's from a hypnogourd?" Princess Irene asked. "This should be interesting. I always wondered what was inside one of those things."

Smash hooked his finger into Blythe's brassiere and lifted her high.

"Well, that's one way to pick up a girl," Dor remarked. "I'll have to try that sometime."

"Won't work," Irene said. "I don't wear a—"

"Not even a green one?" Tandy asked, brightening.

Smash looked into the gourd's peephole.

The two of them were in the brass spaceship, descending rapidly toward Xanth.

"Oh!" Blythe exclaimed, terrified. She flung her brass arms about Smash. "I'll fall! I'll fall! Save me, ogre!"

"But I have to bring it down to return to your building," Smash said. He was having difficulty because there was hardly room for two. He grabbed for a control stick, jerked it around—and the brass girl jumped.

"What are you doing with my knee?" she cried.

Oh. Smash saw now that he had hold of the wrong thing. But it was almost impossible to operate the controls with her limbs in the way. The ship veered crazily, which set Blythe off again. Her nerves certainly were not made of steel! The more she kicked and screamed, the worse the ship spun, and the more frightened she became. They were now plunging precipitously toward ground.

Then they were back under the fireoak tree. "We thought you had enough time to drop her off," Tandy said. Then she paused, frowning.

Blythe was wrapped around Smash, her metal arms hugging his neck desperately, her legs clasping his side. He had firm hold of one of her knees.

"I think we interrupted something," Princess Irene remarked sardonically.

Blythe's complexion converted from brass to copper. Smash suspected his own was doing much the same, as his Eye Queue now made him conscious of un-ogrish proprieties. The two disengaged, and Smash set the brass girl down on the ground, where she sat and sobbed brass tears. "We were crashing," Smash explained lamely.

"Oh—Mundane slang," Chet said. "But I think she wasn't quite ready for it."

"It's really no business of ours what you call it," Grundy said, smirking.

"Oh, don't be cruel!" the Siren said. "This poor girl is terrified, and we know Smash wouldn't hurt her. Something is wrong in the gourd."

In due course they worked it out. Smash would have to return to the brass building first, then come back for Blythe, who, it seemed, was afraid of interplanetary heights.

But now dawn was coming, and other business was pressing. They had to inform the local village of the protected status of the tree and its environs, and then Chet and his party had to return to Castle Roogna. In addition, Blythe was no longer so eager to jump into the gourd, with or without the ogre. If she went alone, she might find herself crashing in the ship, and have no way to get back outside, since she was not an outside creature. It would be better to send her back later, once things were more settled.

"Oh," Chet said. "Almost forgot. I gave Tandy's message to Crombie, and he made a pointing—that's his talent, you know, pointing out things—and he concluded that if you went north, you'd face great danger and lose three things of value. But when he did a pointing back where you came from, there was something else you'd lose that was even more important. He couldn't figure out what any of the things were, but thought you'd better be advised. He says you're a spunky girl who will probably win through in the manner of your kind."

Tandy laughed. "That's my father, all right! He hates women, and he knows I'm growing up, so he's starting to hate me, too. But I'm glad to have his advice."

"What's back at your home that's worse than the jungle of Xanth?" Chet asked.

Tandy remembered the demon Fiant. "Never mind. I'm not going home until that danger is nullified. I'll just take my chances with the three things I'll lose in the jungle." But she found the message disquieting. She had no things to lose—but she knew her father never made a mistake when he pointed something out.

Princess Irene's talent was growing plants. She grew a fine, big, mixed-fruit bush, and they dined on red, green, blue, yellow, and black berries, all juicy and luscious. Smash had always liked Irene, because no one remained hungry in her presence, and she did have excellent legs. Not that an ogre should notice, of course—yet it was hard not to imagine how delicious such firmly fleshed limbs would taste.

"Uh, before you go," the Siren said. "I understand you have a way with the inanimate, Prince Dor."

"Whatever gave you that idiotic notion, fish-tail?" a rock beside the Prince inquired. The Siren was sitting next to a bucket of water and was soaking her tail; she got uncomfortable when she spent too long out of the water.

"I picked up something, and I think it may be magical," the Siren continued. "But I'm not sure in what way, and don't want to experiment foolishly." She brought out a bedraggled, half-metallic thing.

"What are you?" Prince Dor asked the thing.

"I am the Gap Dragon's Ear," it answered. "The confounded ogre bashed me off the dragon's head."

Smash was surprised. "How did you get that?"

"I picked it up during the fight, then forgot about it, what with the pining tree and all," the Siren explained.

"The Gap Chasm does have a forgetful property," Irene said. "I understand that's Dor's fault."

"But the Gap's been forgotten for centuries, hasn't it?" the Siren asked. "We can only remember it now because we're still quite close to it; we'll forget it again when we go on north. How can Dor possibly be responsible?"

"Oh, he gets around," Irene said, giving the Prince a dark look. "He's been places none of us would believe. He even used to live with Millie, the sex-appeal maid."

"She was my governess when I was a child!" Dor protested. "Besides, she was eight hundred years old."

"And looked seventeen," Irene retorted. "You weren't conscious of that?"

Dor concentrated on the Ear. "What is your property?" he asked it.

"I hear anything relevant," it said. "I twitch when my possessor should listen. That's how the Gap Dragon always knew when prey was in the Gap. I heard it for him."

"Well, the Gap Dragon still has one ear to hear with," Dor said. "How can *we* hear what you hear?"

"Just listen to me, dummy!" the Ear said. "What else do you do with an ear?"

"That's a mighty impolite item," Tandy said, bothered.

"Can we test it?" the Siren asked. "Before you go, Prince Dor?"

"Oh, let me try," John said. She seemed much recovered, though her wings remained nubs. It would be long before she flew again, if ever.

The Siren gave her the Ear. John held it to her own tiny ear. She listened intently, her face showing puzzlement. "It's a rushing sound, maybe like water flowing," she reported. "Is that relevant?"

"Well, I didn't twitch," the Ear grumped. "You take your chances when there's nothing much on."

"How is that rushing noise relevant?" Dor asked the Ear.

"Obvious, stupid," the Ear said. "That's the sound of the waterfall where the fairy she wants is staying."

"It *is?*" John demanded, so excited that her wing-stubs fluttered. "The one with my name?"

"That's what I said, twerp."

"Do you tolerate insults from the inanimate?" the Siren asked the Prince.

"Only stupid things insult others gratuitously," Dor said.

"That's for sure, you moron," the rock agreed. Then it reconsidered. "Hey—"

The Siren laughed. "Now I understand. You have to consider the source."

Prince Dor smiled. "You resemble your sister. Of course, I've never seen her face."

"The rest will do," the Siren said, flattered. "Do only smart people compliment others gratuitously?"

"Perhaps," he agreed. "Or observant ones. But I do obtain much useful information from the inanimate. Now we must go talk with the villagers and head back to Castle Roogna. It has been nice to meet all of you, and I hope you all find what you wish."

There was a chorus of thank-yous. Prince Dor and Princess Irene remounted the holey cow. Chet kissed Chem good-bye, and Grundy the Golem scrambled onto his back. "Get moving, horsetail!" Then Grundy paused thoughtfully, exactly as the rock had. They moved off toward the village.

"Dor will make a fine King one day," the Siren remarked.

"But Irene will run the show," Chem said. "I know them well."

"No harm in that," the Siren said, and the other girls laughed, agreeing.

"We'd better get started north," Tandy said. "Now that the tree is safe."

"How can I ever thank you?" Fireoak exclaimed. "You saved my life, my tree's life. Same thing."

"Some things are simply worth doing for themselves, dear," the Siren said. "I learned that when Chem's father Chester destroyed my dulcimer, so I couldn't lure men any more." Her sunshine hair clouded momentarily.

"My father did that?" Chem asked, surprised. "I didn't know!"

"It stopped me from being a menace to navigation," the Siren said. "I was doing a lot of damage, uncaringly. It was a necessary thing. Likewise it was necessary to save the fireoak tree."

"Yes," Chem agreed. But she seemed shaken.

They bade farewell to the hamadryad, promising to visit her any time any of them happened to be in the vicinity, and started north.

At first they passed through normal Xanth countryside—carnivorous grasses, teakettle serpents whose kisses were worse than their fires, poisonous springs, tangle trees, sundry spells, and the usual ravines, mountains, river rapids, slow and quicksand bogs, illusions, and a few normally foul-mouthed harpies, but nothing serious occurred. They foraged along the way for edible things and took turns listening to the Gap Dragon's Ear, though it was not twitching; this became more helpful as they gradually learned to interpret it. The Siren heard a kind of splashing, as of someone swimming. She took this to be the merman she wanted to find. Goldy heard the sounds of a goblin settlement in operation: where she was going. Smash heard the rhyming grunts of ogres. Blythe, persuaded to try it, jumped as the Ear twitched in her hands, and she actually heard herself mentioned. The brassies missed her and feared the ogre had betrayed their trust. "I must go back!" she cried. "As soon as I recover enough of my courage. My nerves aren't iron, you know."

But when Chem tried it, her face sobered. "It must be out of order. All I get is a faint buzzing."

The Siren took back the Ear. "That's funny. I get the buzzing, too, now."

They passed the Ear around. Everyone heard the same thing, and it twitched for none of them.

Smash applied his Eye Queue curse to the Ear. "Either it is malfunctioning," he decided, "or the buzzing is somehow relevant to all of us, without being specific to any of us. No one is talking about us, no one is lurking for us, so it is just something we should know about."

"Let's assume it's not malfunctioning," Tandy said. "The last thing we need is a glitching Ear, especially when my father says there is danger ahead. So we'd better watch out for something that buzzes. It seems to be getting louder as we go."

Indeed it was. Now there were variations in it, louder buzzes in front of background ones, an elevating and lowering of pitch. It was, in fact, a whole collection of buzzes, sounding three-dimensional, as some pitches became louder and clearer, while others faded back and some faded out entirely. What did it mean?

They came across a wall made from paper. It traveled roughly east/west and reached up to the top level of the trees, too high for Smash to surmount. It was opaque; he could not see through it at all.

However, a wall of paper could hardly impede an ogre. He readied a good punch.

"Careful!" John cried. "That looks like—"

Smash's fist punched through the wall. The paper separated readily, but glued itself to his arm.

"Flypaper," the fairy concluded.

Smash tried to pull the sticky stuff off, but it stuck to his other hand when he touched it. The more he worked at it, the more places it adhered to. Soon he was covered with the stuff.

"Slow down, Smash," Chem said. "I'm sure hot water will clean that off. I saw a hotspring a short distance back."

She took him to the hotspring and washed him off, and it did clean him up. Her hands were efficient yet gentle; Smash discovered he liked having a female attend to him this way. But of course he couldn't admit it; he was an ogre. "Next time use a stick to poke through that paper," the centaur advised.

But when they returned to the wall, they found the others had already thought of that. They had poked and peeled a hole big enough for anyone to pass through. "But there's one thing," Tandy warned. "There are swarms of flies over there."

So that was what the Ear had warned them of. They were going to pass through a region of flies.

That didn't bother Smash; he normally ignored flies. Blythe was also unworried; no fly could sting brass. But Tandy, Chem, Goldy, John, and the Siren were concerned. They didn't want stinging flies raising welts on their pretty skins. "If only we had some repellent," Tandy said. "In the caves there are some substances that drive them off—"

"Some repellent bushes do grow in these parts," Goldy said. "Let me look." She scouted about and soon located one. "The only problem is, they smell awful." She held out the leaves she had plucked.

She had not overstated the case. The stench was appalling. No wonder the flies stayed clear of it!

They discussed the matter and decided it was better to stink than to suffer too great a detour in their route north. They held their breath and rubbed the foul leaves over their bodies. Then, reeking of repellent, they stepped through the rent in the flypaper and proceeded north.

There was a sound behind them. Marching along the paper wall was a monstrous fly in coveralls, toting a cart. It stopped at the rent, unrolled a big patch of paper, and set it in place, sealing it over with stickum. Then the flypaper hanger moved on to the east, following the wall.

"We're sealed in," Tandy muttered.

A dense swarm of stingflies spotted them and zoomed in—only to bank off in dismay as the awful odor smote it. Good enough; Smash's nose was already acclimating or getting deadened to the smell, which wasn't much worse than that of another ogre, after all.

They walked on, watching the flies. There were many varieties, and some were beautiful with brightly colored, patterned wings and furry bodies. John became very quiet; obviously she missed her own patterned wings. There were deerflies and horseflies and dragonflies, looking like winged miniatures of their species; the deerflies nibbled blades of grass, the horseflies kicked up their heels as they galloped, and the dragonflies even jetted small lances of fire. At one spot there was music; fiddler flies were playing for damselflies to dance. It seemed to be a real fly ball.

This became a pleasant trip, since there seemed to be no dangerous creatures here; the flies had driven them all away. But then the sky clouded and rain fell. It was a light fall—but it washed away their repellent. Suddenly they were in trouble, having failed to take immediate shelter.

The first flies to discover this were sweat-gnats. Soon a cloud of them hovered about each person except Blythe, causing everyone to sweat uncom-

volunteer to be the first eaten. But I think you alone among us are secure from that fate."

"I wonder," the brassie said thoughtfully.

Already the first dragon was arriving. It was a huge eight-legged land rover, snorting smoke. Smash strode forward to meet it, knowing it would have been too much for him even when he had his full strength. It wasn't the dragon's size so much as its heat; it could roast him long before he hurt it. But the dragon would attack regardless of whether he fought, and it was an ogre's way to fight. Maybe he could hurl some boulders at it and score a lucky conk on its noggin.

Then Blythe ran past him, intercepting the dragon. The dragon exhaled, bathing her in flame, but brief heat could not hurt her. She continued right on up to its huge snout. "Eat me first, dragon!" she cried.

The dragon did not squat on ceremony. It opened its monstrous jaws and took her in one bite.

And broke half a dozen teeth on her hard metal.

Blythe frowned amidst the smoke and piled fragments of teeth. "You can do better than that, dragon!" she urged indignantly.

The dragon tried again—and broke six more teeth.

"Come on, creature!" Blythe taunted. "Show your mettle on my metal. I've received worse dents just from being dropped—but I won't say where."

Now several more dragons arrived. They paused, curious about the holdup. Another snatched Blythe away, crunching down hard on her body—and it, too, lost six teeth.

The brass girl was insulted. "Is that all there is to it? What kind of experience is that? Here I visit this great big, soft, slushy, living world at great inconvenience, and you monsters aren't doing a thing!"

Abashed, the dragons stared at her. She still looked like a clothed flesh person. Finally a third one tried—and lost its quota of teeth.

"If you dumb dragons can't eat one little girl when she's cooperating, what good are you?" Blythe demanded, disgusted. She shook tooth fragments off her body, marched up to one of the largest monsters, and yanked at a whisker. "You—eat me or else!"

The dragon exhaled a horrendous belch of flame. It burned Blythe's remaining flypaper to ashes, but didn't hurt her. Seeing that, the monster backed off, dismayed. If a thing couldn't be chomped or scorched, it couldn't be handled.

"You know, I think we have had a stroke of luck," the Siren said. "The dragons naturally assume we are all like that."

"Luck?" John asked. "Blythe knows what she's doing! She knows she needs us to get her back to her world. She's helping us get out of a fix."

Smash's Eye Queue operated. "Maybe we can benefit further. We need a nice, steady stream of steam to melt off the flypaper."

"A steam bath," the Siren agreed. "But very gentle."

Blythe tried it. She approached a big steam-turbine dragon. "Bathe me, monster, or I'll make you eat me," she said imperiously.

Cowed, the dragon obeyed. It jetted out a wash of rich white steam and vapor. In a moment the brass girl stood shining clean, well polished, the fly ash all sogged off.

"Now my friends," Blythe ordered. "A little lower on the heat; they're tougher than I am and don't need so much."

She was playing it cool! Nervously the others stood in place while the dragon sent forth a cooler blast. Smash and the girls stepped into it. The vapor was as hot as John could stand, but since she had already lost her wings, it didn't hurt her. The others had no trouble. All the flypaper was steamed off.

Smash also became aware that his fleas were gone. Now that he thought about it, he realized that he hadn't been scratching since entering the Kingdom of the Flies. Those fly-repellent leaves must have driven off the fleas, too!

Now a dragon approached with an elf on a leash. "Do any of you freaks speak human?" the elf asked.

Smash exchanged glances with the others. Blythe Brassie had been speaking to these monsters all along, and they had understood. Didn't this elf know that? Better to play it stupid. "Me freak, some speak," he said, emulating his former ogre mode.

The elf considered him. The little man's expression ran a brief gamut from fear of a monster to contempt for the monster's wit. "What are you doing here with these six females?"

"Me anticipate girls taste great," Smash said, slurping his tongue over his chops.

Again the fearful contempt. "I *know* ogres eat people. But what are you doing here in Dragonland?"

Smash scratched his hairy head as if confused. "Me criticize buzzing flies."

"Oh. They booted you." The elf made crude growls at his dragon, and Smash realized he was translating, much as Grundy the Golem did for the King of Xanth. Maybe Blythe had gotten through to the dragons mainly by force of personality.

The dragon growled back. "You'll have to check in with the Dragon Lady."

"Dragon Lady not afraidy?" Smash asked stupidly.

The elf sneered. "Of the like of you? Hardly. Come on now, ignoramus."

Ignoramus? Smash smiled inwardly. Not while he remained cursed with the Eye Queue! But he shuffled behind the dragon, gesturing the girls to follow.

The Siren fell in beside Smash as they walked. "I've been listening to the Ear," she murmured. "The voice that talked about us before was the elf's; the Dragon Lady knows about us already. Now the Ear is roaring like a terrible storm. I don't know what that means."

"Maybe we have to get to that storm," Smash whispered. Then the elf turned, hearing him talk, and the conversation had to end.

They came to a huge tent fashioned of dragonet. Inside the net was the Dragon Lady—a scintillatingly regal Queen of her species. She reclined, half supine, in her huge nest of glittering diamonds; whenever she twitched, the precious stones turned up new facets, like the eyes of the Lord of the Flies, reflecting spots of light dazzlingly. She switched her barbed, blue tail about restlessly, growling, and arched her bright red neck. It was really quite impressive. She had been reading a book of Monster Comics, and seemed not too pleased to be interrupted.

"Her Majesty the Illustrious Dragon Lady demands further information, oaf," the elf said, becoming imperious in the reflected glory of his mistress.

Oaf, eh? Smash played stupider than ever. "Me slow, no know," he mumbled.

"Is it true you are impossible to eat?"

Smash held out a gauntleted fist. The Dragon Lady reached delicately forward with her snout and took a careful nip. The metal balked her gold-tinted teeth, and she quickly desisted. She growled.

"If you aren't edible, what use are you, Her Majesty wants to know?" the elf demanded.

"What a question!" Tandy cried indignantly. "People-creatures rule Xanth!"

"*Dragon*-creatures rule Xanth," the elf retorted. "Dragons tolerate other creatures only as prey." Nonetheless, the Dragon Lady's growl was muted. Smash suspected that she was not eager to incite a war with the Transformer-King of the human folk.

In response to another growl from his mistress, the elf turned again to Smash. "What are we to do with you?" he demanded.

Smash shrugged. "Me only distrust place where me rust." Actually, neither his stainless steel gauntlets nor Blythe's brass rusted; water was more likely to cause trouble with the fires of the dragons. But he was mindful of the Ear's storm-signal; if he could trick the Dragon Lady into casting them into the storm, their chances should be better than they were here.

"Metal—rust," the elf mused as the Dragon Lady growled. "True, our iron-scaled dragons do have a problem in inclement weather." He glanced suspiciously at Smash. "I don't suppose you could be fooling us?"

"Me ghoul, big fool," Smash said amiably.

"Obviously," the elf agreed with open contempt.

So the Dragon Lady ordered the inedible party dumped into the Region of Air, since the Region of Water did not border Dragonland. An abrupt demarcation established the border; the near side was green turf and trees, the far side a mass of rolling stormcloud. Smash didn't like this, for he knew the others could not endure as much punishment as he could. But now they were committed, and it did seem better than staying among the dragons.

They took the precaution of roping themselves together with Chem's rope so that no one would blow away.

They stepped across the line. Instantly they were in the heart of the wind, choking on dust. It was a dust storm, not a rainstorm! The flying sand cut cruelly into their skins. Smash picked up several girls and hunched his gross body over them, protecting them somewhat as he staggered forward. Then he tripped, for he could not see his own flat feet in this blinding sand, and fell and rolled, holding himself rigid so as not to crush the girls.

He fetched up in a valley formed in the lee of a boulder. Chem thumped to a stop beside them. Here the sand bypassed the party, mostly, and it was possible for each person to pry open an eye or two. Thanks to the rope, all were present, though battered.

"What do we do now?" Tandy asked, frightened.

The Siren sat up and put the Ear to her ear. "Nothing here," she reported. "But maybe the noise of this sandstorm is drowning it out."

Smash took the Ear and listened. "I hear the brass spaceship," he said.

Blythe took it. "I hear my own folk! They're playing the brass band! I must be ready to go home!"

"Are you sure?" the Siren asked.

"Yes, I think I am now," the brass girl said. "I have experienced enough of your world to know I like mine better. You are all nice enough people, but you just aren't brass."

"All too true," the Siren agreed. "We must find another gourd so Smash can take you back. We might all prefer your world at this moment."

"Maybe that's the silence you heard," Tandy said. "A gourd."

"No, there's lots of noise in the gourd," Smash said. "It's an ogrishly fun place."

"Let's find that gourd!" Blythe exclaimed. She was hardly bothered by the sand; she was merely homesick.

"Not until this storm dies down," the Siren said firmly. "Gourds don't grow in this weather."

"But this is the Region of Air; the wind will never die," Blythe protested.

Chem nodded agreement. "I have, as you know, been mapping the inner wilds of Xanth; that's why I'm here. My preliminary research, augmented by certain references along the way, suggests that there are five major elemental regions in Unknown Xanth: those of Air, Earth, Fire, Water, and the Void. This certainly seems to be Air—and probably the storm never stops here. We'll just have to plow on out of it."

"I can plow!" Blythe said eagerly. She milled her brass hands and began tunneling through the mounded sand. In moments she had started a tunnel.

"Good idea!" Tandy exclaimed. "I'll help!" She shook sand out of her hair and fell in behind the brass girl, scooping the sand farther back. Soon the others were helping, too, for as the tunnel progressed, the sand had longer to go before it cleared.

Finally they were all doing it, in a line, with Smash at the tail end packing the sand into a lengthening passage behind. Progress was slow but relatively comfortable. Periodically Blythe would tunnel to the surface to verify that the storm was still there. When they came to a sheltering cliff, they emerged and made better time on the surface.

The landscape was bleak: all sand and more sand. There were dunes and valleys, but no vegetation and no water. The wind was indefatigable. It howled and roared and whistled. It formed clouds and swirls and funnels, doing its peculiar sculpture in the sky. Every so often a funnel would swoop in near the cliff, trying to suck them into its circular maw, but it could not maintain itself so close to the stone. Smash was aware that this must be a great frustration to the funnels, which were rather like ogres in their way— all violence and brainlessness.

Then they came to another demarcation. As they stepped across it, the winds abruptly ceased. The air cleared miraculously. But this was no improvement, for the violence of the air was replaced by the violence of the land. The ground shuddered, and not by any ogre's tread. It was an earthquake!

"Oh, I don't like this!" Chem said. "I've always been accustomed to the firmness of ground beneath my hooves."

Smash glanced at her. The centaur girl was standing with her forelegs braced awkwardly in different directions, her brown coat dulled by the recent sand-scouring, her tail all atremble, and her human breasts dancing rather appealingly. "Maybe the ground is firmer farther north," he suggested.

They turned north—and encountered an active volcano. Red-hot lava boiled out of it and flowed down the slope toward them. "Oh, this is worse yet!" Chem complained, slapping at a spark that landed in her pretty tail. She was really shaken; this was just not her type of terrain.

The Siren listened to the Gap Dragon's Ear again. "Say!" she said. "The sounds differ, depending on which way I face!" she rotated, listening intently. "To the north, it's a horrendous crashing; that's the volcano we see. I can hear the sound as I see it belch. To the south, it's the roaring of winds. We've already been there. To the west, a sustained rumble—the main part of the earthquake. To the east—" She smiled beautifully. "A lovely, quiet, still silence."

"Graves are silent," Tandy said with a shudder.

"Better a graveyard than this," Chem said. "We can walk on through a cemetery."

"Sometimes," Tandy agreed.

They turned east. The ground shifted constantly beneath them as if trying to prevent progress, but they were determined to get free of this region.

As the sun set tiredly beyond the volcano, fortunately not landing inside it, they reached another demarcation of zones. Just beyond it was a patch of hypnogourds. The silence was not of the grave, but of a garden area.

"I never thought I'd be glad to see a patch of those," Tandy said grimly.

"This is where we spend the night," the Siren said. "While we're at it, let's find out whether those gourds are edible."

"Save one! Save one!" Blythe cried.

"Of course, dear. Try this one." The Siren handed the brass girl a nice big gourd.

Blythe hesitated, then looked into the peephole. She looked back up. "There's nothing there," she said.

"Nothing there?" It had not occurred to Smash that any of the gourds could be inoperative. He took the gourd from Blythe and looked in.

And found himself in the spaceship, spinning toward the ground. Hastily he grabbed the controls and tilted it back to equilibrium. Without the brass girl entangling him, he could manage just fine.

In moments he brought the ship back to the City of Brass and to the launching building. He managed to turn it around and land fairly neatly. Then he got out and made his way through the moving buildings to the one where Blythe lived, Number Four, following his string back. He wondered idly whether he had left a trail of string strewn all over the sky, near the moon. He had lost that string in Xanth, but retained it here. Good enough.

The brassies clustered around him. "Where is Blyght?" they demanded. "We're rehearsing with our brass band, and we need her."

"Blythe. She changed her name. She'll be back as soon as I can fetch her. She heard you practicing, and said she would come back very soon. I had to find my way back here, because spaceships scare her."

"Of course; we are afraid of heights. We dent when we fall too far. Blyght already had a dent in her—"

"Don't speak of that to a stranger!" a brass girl told the male brassie.

"So give me some time," Smash said, "and I'll return her. Now I know how to do it."

They were not quite satisfied with this, but let him be. Smash settled down in a niche that moved with the wall, and snoozed.

Chapter 9

Gourmet Gourd

e woke in Xanth, where Tandy had taken away the gourd.
"I never know how long to give you," she said. "I'm very
nervous about leaving you in there." She lifted the Gap
Dragon's Ear. "I kept listening in this, and when it got pretty quiet, I
thought maybe it was time to bring you out. I wasn't sure it was you I was
listening to, but since your health is relevant to mine—"

Smash took the Ear. He heard a guttural voice, saying, "Mirror, mirror on
the wall, pass this fist or take a fall," followed by a tinkling crash.

"It's not quiet now," Smash reported. "Sounds like me talking."

She smiled. "Talk all you want, Smash. You're my mainstay in this strange
surface world. I do worry when you're gone."

Smash put his huge, hairy paw over her tiny human hand. "I appreciate
that, Tandy. I know it would be bad for you if you got stranded alone in

wilderness Xanth. But I am learning to handle things in the gourd, and I am getting stronger."

"I hope so," she said. "We all do need you, and not just for protection from monsters. Chem says there seems to be a mountain range to the north that we can't scale; the dragons are to the east, and the air storm to the south. So we'll have to veer west, back through the Region of Earth—and that volcano is still spewing hot lava."

"We shall just have to wait till the lava stops," Smash said.

"Yes. But we don't know how long that will be—and it will have to cool so we can walk over it. I guess we're here in the melon patch for a while yet."

"So be it," Smash said. He released her hand, lest the inordinate weight of his own damage it. "Did you say these gourds are edible?"

"Oh, yes, certainly. You can eat all you want. We're all full; they're very good, just so long as you don't look in the peephole. Funny thing is, there's no sign of any world in there, no graveyard or anything." She handed him a gourd, peephole averted.

Smash took a huge bite. It was indeed good, very sweet and seedy and juicy. It did seem strange that something that could affect his consciousness could also be such good eating—but, of course, that was the nature of things other than gourds. A dragon could be a terrible enemy—but was also pretty good eating, once conquered.

"That gourd I just looked into—" Smash said between gulps. "Why didn't it return Blythe when she looked?"

"We discussed that while you were out," Tandy said. She was the only one of the girls who remained awake; the others were sleeping, including the brass girl. Smash wondered briefly why a person made of metal needed to sleep, then realized this was no more remarkable than a person of metal becoming animate at the punch of a button. "We concluded that she is merely a representation, like you when you're in the gourd. So she can't cross through by herself; she has to be taken by one of us. Then her pretend-body will vanish here, just as yours vanishes there."

"Makes sense," Smash agreed, consuming another gourd in a few bites. "Did she disappear when I took her aboard the Luna shuttle ship?"

"Yes. You remained, holding nothing. Then she reappeared when we took the gourd away, hugging you—"

"There was no room in that cockpit," Smash explained.

"I understand," she said, somewhat distantly.

"I'm out of the ship now, and back in her building. There won't be any trouble this time."

"That's nice. But please rest before you go back in there," Tandy said. "There is time, while we wait for the lava to stop. And—"

Smash glanced at her. She was mostly a silhouette in the wan moonlight, rather pretty in her pensiveness. "Yes?"

She shrugged. "Take care of yourself, Smash."

"Ogres do," he said, cracking a smile. It seemed to him that she had meant to say something more. But, of course, girls changed their minds readily, especially small girls, whose minds were small. Or whatever.

When he was comfortably stuffed, Smash stretched out among the gourds and slept. Tandy settled against his furry forearm and slept, too. He was aware of her despite his unconsciousness, and found he rather liked her cute little company. He was becoming distressingly un-ogrish at times; he would have to correct that.

As dawn brightened, the lava dulled. The volcano was quiescent. The Siren listened to the Ear and reported silence, which she took to mean that they should wait for further cooling. Periodically she tossed damp fragments of gourd on the nearest hardening lava flow; as long as it sizzled and steamed, the time was not yet right.

"Are you ready to go home, Blythe?" Smash asked the brass girl, knowing the answer. "I'm back in the building."

"Good and ready, ogre," she agreed with alacrity. She turned to the others. "No offense to you folk; I like you. But I don't understand this wide-open land. It's so much more secure in a brass building."

"I'm sure it is, dear," the Siren said, embracing her. "Maybe in due course the rest of us will find our own brass buildings."

"And the way you have to sleep here, instead of getting turned off by a button—that's strange."

"All creatures are strange in their own fashion," Chem said. "And we want to thank you for what you did with the dragons. You may have saved our hides."

"I took no risk," Blythe said. But she flushed copper, pleased.

Then Smash picked Blythe up by her brassiere. "And keep your hand off her knee!" Tandy warned.

Everyone laughed, and he looked into a delicious-seeming gourd.

This time it worked. They were both in the brass building.

The brassies spied them and clustered around. There was a flurry of welcomings. Blythe was certainly glad to be home.

"Now if you folk can tell me some other way out of here, I will depart," Smash said. "I don't want the spaceship; there must be some land route."

"Oh, there is!" Blythe said eagerly. "I'll show you."

"Haven't you had enough of me?" Smash asked.

"I feel I owe it to you to help you on your way," she said defensively. "I'll show you the way to the paper world."

"As you wish," Smash agreed. "But you helped us considerably, what with the tunneling and such."

Her face clouded, turning leaden. "The dragons wouldn't eat me!"

Smash did not argue the point. Evidently the brass girl had more than one motive for her scene with the dragons.

Blythe led him out a concealed door, into a smaller chamber. Smash had to hunch over to fit in this one. Then the room jerked and moved, causing him to bump into a wall. "This is an elevator," Blythe explained. "It leads to the paper works, but it takes a little while."

"I'll wait," Smash said, squatting down and leaning into a corner so he would not be bumped around too much."

Blythe sat on one of his knees. "Smash—"

He suffered déjà vu. His Eye Queue insisted on running down the relevance immediately, instead of allowing it to be the pleasant mystery nature intended. Tandy had addressed him in much the same way last night. "Yes?"

"I wanted to talk to you a moment, alone," she confessed. "That's why I volunteered to show you the way. There's something you should know."

"Where your dent is?"

"I can't show you that; your knee's in the way. It's something else."

"You know something about the Night Stallion?" he asked, interested.

"No, not that," she said. "It's about Xanth."

"Oh."

"Smash, I'm not part of your world. But maybe I see something you don't. Those girls like you."

"And I like them," he admitted, voicing the un-ogrish sentiment with a certain embarrassment. How was he ever going to find his Answer in life if he kept losing his identity? "They're nice people. So are you."

Again she coppered. "I like them, too. I never knew flesh people before. But that's not what I mean. They—they're not just friends to you. It's hard for me to say, because my own heart's made of brass. They're female; you're male. So—"

"So I protect them," Smash agreed. "Because females aren't very good at surviving by themselves. I'll help as long as they are with me and need protection."

"That, too. But it's more than that. Tandy, especially—"

"Yes, she needs a lot of protection. She hardly knows more of Xanth than you do, and she's not made of metal."

The brass girl seemed frustrated, but she kept smiling. Her little teeth were brass, too. "We talked, some, while you were in the gourd—that's funny, to think of my whole world as a gourd!—and Tandy told us why she left home. I may be violating a confidence, but I really think you ought to know."

"Know what?" Smash asked. His Eye Queue informed him he was missing something significant; that was an annoying part of the curse. A true ogre wouldn't have worried!"

"Why she left home. You see, there was this demon, named Fiant, who was looking for a wife. Well, not a wife, exactly—you know."

"A playmate?"

"You could call it that. But Tandy didn't want to play. I gather a demon is like an ifrit, not nice at all. She refused to oblige him. But he pursued her and tried to rape her—"

"What is that?" Smash asked.

"Rape? You actually don't know?"

"I'm not made of brass," he reminded her. "There's lots I don't know. There is a kind of plant in Xanth by that name that girls shy away from—"

She sighed. "The Siren's right. You are hopelessly naïve. Maybe all males worth knowing are. But, of course, that's why females exist; someone has to know what's what. Look, Smash—do you know the way of a man with a woman?" Her brass face was more coppery than ever, and he realized this was an awkward subject for her.

"Of course not," he reassured her. "I'm an ogre."

"Well, the way of an ogre with an ogress?"

"Certainly." What was she getting at?

She paused. "I'm not sure we're communicating. Maybe you'd better tell me what is the way of an ogre with an ogress."

"He chases her down, screaming, catches her by a rope of hair, hauls her up by one leg, bashes her head against a tree a few times, throws her down, sets a boulder on her face so she can't get away, then—"

"That's rape!" Blythe cried, appalled.

"That's fun," he countered. "Ogresses expect it, and give back little ogres. It's the ogre mode of love."

"Well, it isn't the human mode of love."

"I know. Human beings are so gentle, it's a wonder they even know what they're doing. Prince Dor and Princess Irene have taken four years trying to get around to it. Now, if they had a little more ogre heritage, four seconds might be enough to—"

"Ah . . . yes," she agreed. "Well, this demon tried to—to make ogre love to Tandy—"

"Oh, now I understand! Tandy wouldn't like that!"

"True. She's no ogress. So she left her home and sought help. And the Good Magician told her to travel with you. That way the demon can't get her."

"Sure. If she wants that demon smashed, I'll do it. That's my name."

"That's not exactly what she wants. You see, she does want to marry— someone other than the demon. And she has a lot to offer the right male. So she hopes to find a suitable husband on this journey. But—"

"That's wonderful!" Smash said in the best un-ogrish tradition. "Maybe we'll find a nice human man, just right for her."

"You didn't wait for my but, Smash."

"Your butt?" he asked, looking at her brass posterior. "Where your dent is?"

"But, B U T," she clarified. "As in however."

"However has a dent?"

She paused briefly. "Forget the dent. However she likes you."

"Certainly, and I like her. So I will help her find herself a man."

"I don't think you understand, Smash. She may not want to go with her ideal human man, if she finds him, if she likes you too well first."

He chortled. "Nobody likes an ogre too well!"

The brass girl shook her head doubtfully. "I'm not sure. You are no ordinary ogre, they inform me. For one thing, they told me you're much smarter than most of your kind."

"That's because of the curse of the Eye Queue. Once I get rid of that, I'll be blissfully stupid again. Just like any other ogre. Maybe more so."

"There is that," Blythe agreed. "I don't think Tandy would like you to be just like any other ogre."

The room stopped moving, after a jolt that bounced her off his knee. "Well, here we are at the paper world," she said.

The elevator opened onto a literal world of paper. Green-colored fragments of paper served for a lawn; brown and green paper columns were trees; a flat paper sun hung in the painted blue sky. At least this world had color, in contrast with the monochrome of most of the rest of the gourd.

"This is as far as I go," Blythe said as Smash stepped out. "If it's any comfort, I think that in some ways you're still pretty stupid, even with the Eye Queue."

"Thank you," Smash said, flattered.

" 'Bye, ogre." The door closed and she was gone. Smash turned to the new adventure that surely awaited him.

Paper was everywhere. Smash saw a bird; idly he caught it out of the air in a paw, not to hurt it but to look at it, because it seemed strange. It turned out to be strange indeed; it, too, was made of paper, the wings corrugated, the body a cylinder of paper, the beak a stiffened, painted triangle of cardboard. he let it go and it flew away, peeping with the rasp of stiff paper.

Curious, he caught a bug. It was only an intricate convolution of paper, brightly painted. When he released it, the paper reconvoluted and the bug buzzed away. There were butterflies, also of paper. The bushes and stones and puddles were all colored paper. It seemed harmless enough.

Then a little paper machine charged up. Smash had seen machines during a visit to Mundania and didn't like them; they were ornery mechanical things. This one was way too small to bother him seriously, but it did bother him lightly. It fired a paper spitball at him.

The spitball stung his knee. Smash smiled. The miniature machine had a name printed on its side: TANK. It was cute.

The ogre stomped on. The tank followed, firing another damp paper ball. It stung Smash on the rump. He frowned. The humor was wearing thin. He didn't care to have a dent to match that of the brass girl.

He turned to warn the tank away—and its third shot plastered his nose.

That did it. Smash lifted one brute foot and stomped the obnoxious machine flat. It was only paper; it collapsed readily. But an unexpended spitball stuck to the ogre's toe.

Smash tromped on, seeking whatever challenge this section offered. But now three more of the paper tanks arrived. Burp—burp—burp! Their spit-balls spit in a volley at the ogre, sticking to his belly like a line of damp buttons. He stamped all three paper vehicles flat.

Yet more tanks arrived, and these were larger. Their spitballs stung harder, and one just missed his eye. Smash had to shield his face with one hand while he stomped them.

He heard something behind. A tank was chewing up his line of string! That would prevent him from knowing when he crossed his own trail, and he could get lost. He strode back and picked up the tank, looking closely at it.

The thing burped a huge splat of a spitball at him that plugged a nostril. Smash sneezed—and the tank was blown into a flat sheet of paper. Words were printed on it: GET WITH IT, DOPE.

Funny—Smash had never learned how to read. No ogre was smart enough for literacy. But he grasped this message perfectly. This must be another facet of the curse of the Eye Queue. He pretended he did not fathom the words.

He turned again—and saw a much bigger paper tank charging down on him. He grabbed the tip of the cardboard cannon and pinched it closed just as the machine fired. The backpressure blew up the tank in a shower of confetti.

But more, and yet larger, tanks were coming. This region seemed to have an inexhaustible supply! Smash cast about for some way to stop them once and for all.

He had an idea. He bent to scoop through the paper-turf ground. Sure enough, it turned to regular dirt below, with rocks. He found a couple of nice quartz chunks and bashed them together to make sparks. Soon he struck a fire. The paper grass burned readily.

The tanks charged into the blaze—and quickly caught fire themselves. Their magazines blew up in violent sprays of spit. Colored bits of paper flew up in clouds, containing pictures and ads for products and all the other crazy things magazines filled their pages with. Soon all the tanks were ashes.

Smash tromped on. A paper tiger charged from the paper jungle, snarling and leaping. Smash caught it by the tail and shook it into limp paper, the black and orange colors running. He dipped this into a fringe of the fire and used the resulting torch to discourage other paper animals. They faded back before his bright-burning tiger, and he proceeded unhampered. Apparently there was nothing quite so fearful as a burning tiger. If this had been a battle, he had won it.

Now he came to a house of cards. Smash knew what cards were; he had seen Prince Dor and Princess Irene playing games with them at Castle Roogna, instead of getting down to basics the way ogres would. Sometimes they had constructed elaborate structures from the cards. This was such a structure—but it was huge. Each card was the height of Smash himself, with suit markings as big as his head and almost as ugly.

He paused to consider these. At the near side was the nine of hearts. He knew what hearts were: the symbol of love. This reminded him irrelevantly of what the brass girl had told him about Tandy. Could it be true that the tiny human girl liked him more than was proper, considering that ogres weren't supposed to be liked at all? If so, what was his responsibility? Should he growl at her, to discourage her? That did seem best.

He entered the house of cards, careful not to jostle it. These structures collapsed very readily, and after all, this might be the way out of the paper land. He felt he was making good progress through the worlds of the gourd, and he wanted to go on to the last station and meet the Dark Horse.

The inner wall showed the two of clubs. Clubs were, of course, the ogre's favorite suit. There was nothing like a good, heavy club for refreshing violence! Then there was the jack of diamonds, symbolizing the wealth of dragons. His curse of intellect made symbolism quite clear now. He remembered how many of the bright little stones the Dragon Lady had had; this was probably her card. Then there was the two of spades, with its shovel symbol. The suit of farmers.

In the center of the house of cards was the joker. It depicted a handsomely brutish ogre with legs that trailed into smoke. Of course! Smash pushed against it, assuming it to be his door to the next world—and the whole structure collapsed.

The cards were not heavy, of course, and in a moment Smash's head poked above the wreckage. He looked about.

The scene had changed. The paper was gone. The painted sky and cardboard trees existed no longer. Now there was a broad and sandy plain, like that of the nightmares' realm, except that this one was in daylight, with the sun beating down hotly.

He spied an object in the desert. It glinted prettily, but not like a diamond. Curious, Smash stomped over to it. It was a greenish bottle, half buried in the sand, fancily corked. He found himself attracted to it; a bottle like that, its base properly broken off, could make a fine weapon.

He picked it up. Inside the bottle was a hazy motion, as of slowly swirling mist. The cork had a glossy metallic seal with a word embossed: FOOL.

Well, that was the nature of ogres. He was thirsty in this heat; maybe the stuff in the bottle was good to drink. Smash ripped off the seal and used his teeth to pop the cork. After all, he was uncertain how long it would be before he came across anything potable, here in the gourd. But mainly, his action was his Eye Queue's fault; because of it, he was curious.

As the cork blasted free, vapor surged out of the bottle. It swelled out voluminously. Too bad—this was neither edible nor potable, and it smelled of sulfur. Smash sneezed.

The vapor formed a big greenish cloud, swirling about but not dissipating into the air. In a moment, two muscular arms projected from it, and the remainder formed into the head and upper torso of a gaseous man-creature about Smash's own size.

"Who in the gourd are you?" Smash inquired.

"Ho, ho, ho!" the creature boomed. "I be the ifrit of the bottle. Thou has freed me; as thy reward, I shall suffer thee to choose in what manner thou shalt die."

"Oh, one of those," Smash said, unimpressed. "A bottle imp." He now recognized, in retrospect, this creature as the figure on the joker card. He had taken it to be an ogre, but, of course, ogres had hairy legs and big flat feet, rather than trailing smoke.

"Dost thou mock me, thou excrescence of excrement?" the ifrit demanded, swelling angrily. "Beware, lest I squish thee into a nonentitious cube and make bouillon soup of thee!"

"Look, ifrit, I don't have time for this nonsense," Smash said, though the mention of the bouillon cube made him hungry. He had squished a bull into a bouillon cube once and made soup with it; he could use some of that now! "I just want to find the Night Stallion and vacate the lien on my soul. If you aren't going to help, get out of my way."

"Surely I shall destroy thee!" the ifrit raged, turning dusky purple. He reached for the ogre's throat with huge and taloned hands.

Smash grabbed the ifrit's limbs, knotted them together in much the way he had tied the extremities of the ghastlies, and jammed the creature head-first back into the green bottle. "Oaf! Infidel!" the ifrit screamed, his words somewhat distorted since his mouth was squeezed through the bottle's neck. "What accursed mischief be this?"

"I warned you," Smash said, using a forefinger to tamp more of the ifrit into the container. "Don't mess with ogres. They have no sense of humor."

Struggle as he might, the ifrit could not prevail against Smash's power. "Ooo, ouch!" the voice came muffled from the glass. "OooOOoo!" For Smash's finger had rammed into the creature's gasous posterior.

Then a hand came back out of the bottle. It waved a white flag.

Smash knew that meant surrender. "Why should I pay attention to you?" he asked.

"Mmph of mum genuine free wish," the voice cried from the depths of the bottle.

That sounded promising. "But I don't need a wish about how I will die."

"Mmmph oomph!"

"Okay, ifrit. Give me one positive wish." Smash removed his finger.

The ifrit surged backward out of the bottle. "What is thy wish, O horrendous one?" he asked, rubbing his rear.

"I want to know the way to the next world."

"I was about to send thee there!" the ifrit exclaimed, aggrieved.

"The next gourd scene. How do I get there?"

"Oh." The ifrit considered. "The closest be the mirror world. But that be no place for the like of thee. Thy very visage would shatter that scene."

This creature was trying to lull him with flattery! "Tell me anyway."

"On thy fool head be it." The ifrit made a dramatic gesture. There was a blinding flash. "Thou wilt be sorree!" the creature's voice came, fading away with descending pitch as if retreating at nearly the speed of sound.

Smash pawed his eyes, and gradually sight filtered back.

He stood among a horrendous assortment of ogres. Some were much larger than he, some much smaller; some were obesely fat, some emaciatedly thin; some had ballooning heads and squat feet, others the other way around.

"What's this?" he asked, scratching his head, though it had no fleas now.

"This . . . this . . . this . . . this," the other ogres chorused in diminishing echo, each scratching his head.

The Eye Queue needed only that much data to formulate an educated hypothesis. "Mirrors!"

"Ors . . . ors . . . ors . . . ors," the echoes agreed.

Smash walked among the mirrors, seeing himself pacing himself in multiple guises. The hall was straight, but after a while the images repeated. Suspicious, he used a horny fingernail to scratch a corner of one mirror, then walked farther down the hall, checking corners. Sure enough, he came across another mirror with a scratch on it, just where he had made his mark. It was the same one, surely. This hall was an endless reflection, like two mirrors facing each other. One of those endless loops he had been warned about. In fact, now he saw three lines of string: he had been retracing his course. He was trapped.

The ifrit had been right. This was no place for the like of him. Already he was hungrier, and there was no food here. How could he get out?

He could smash through a mirror and through the wall behind it, of course—but would that accomplish anything? There were situations in which blind force was called for—but other situations, his Eye Queue curse reminded him obnoxiously, called for subtler negotiation. The trick was to tell them apart. One could not conquer a mirror by breaking it; one could only forfeit the game.

Smash stared into the scratched mirror, and his distorted image stared back. The image was almost as ugly as he was, but the distortion hampered it, making it less repulsive than it should have been. Probably that was why it was snarling.

He turned and contemplated the three strands of string on the floor. He saw where the first one started: it came from another mirror. So he had entered here through a mirror. Surely that was also the way to leave. If he found some means to make another blinding flash, would he be able to step through, as before? But he had no flash-material.

Then he remembered what he had heard in the Gap Dragon's Ear. Could that relate? It had sounded like his voice, talking about a mirror. He decided to try it.

He positioned himself squarely before the mirror. He elevated his hamfist. "Mirror, mirror on the wall," he intoned, imitating his own voice as well as he could. "Pass this fist or take a fall." Then he punched forward.

His fist smashed through the glass and into the wall behind it. The mirror tinkled in pieces to the floor.

Smash leaned forward to peer through the hole in the wall. It opened on another hall of mirrors. Sure enough, there was no escape there; he was caught among the mirrors until he found the proper way out.

He tromped to the next mirror. He raised his fist again and spoke his rhyme. Then he punched through, with the same result.

This did not seem to be working. But it was the only clue he had. Maybe when the other mirrors saw what was happening, they would capitulate. After all, this technique had been effective with the shocking doorknobs. The inanimate tended to be stupid, as Prince Dor had shown, but it did eventually learn what was good for it.

The change happened sooner than anticipated. His fist did not strike the third mirror; it passed through without resistance. His arm and body followed it, and he did a slow fall through the aperture.

He rolled on something soft and sat up. He sniffed. He looked. He salivated.

He sat on a huge bed of cake, replete with vanilla icing. Pastries and sweets were all about him, piled high: doughnuts, strudel, éclairs, tarts, cookies, creampuffs, gingerbread, and more intricate pastries.

Smash had been growing hungry before; it had been well over an hour since he had last filled up. Now he was ravenous. But again the damned curse of the Eye Queue made him pause. The purpose of these worlds inside the gourd seemed to be to make him unhappy. This food did not fit that purpose—unless there were something wrong with it. Could it be poisoned? Poison did not bother ogres much, but was best avoided.

One way to find out. Smash scooped up a glob of floor and crammed it in his big mouth. The cake was excellent. Then he got up and explored the region, keeping himself busy while waiting for the poison to act. He had not eaten enough to cause real damage to the gross gut of an ogre, but if he felt discomfort, he would take warning.

He was in a large chamber completely filled with the pastries. There was no apparent exit. He punched experimentally through a wall of fruitcake, but the stuff seemed to have no end. He suspected he could punch forever and only tear up more cake. There appeared to be no reasonable limit to the worlds that fit inside the gourd. How, then, was he to escape this place?

His stomach suffered nothing but the ravages of increasing hunger, so he concluded the food was not poisoned. Still he hesitated. There had to be some trap, something to make him hurt. If not poison, what? There seemed to be no threat, no spitball-shooting tanks, no ifrit, not even starvation from delay.

Well, suppose he fell to and ate his fill? Where would he be? Still here, with no way out. If he remained long enough, stuffing himself at will, he would lose his soul by default in three months. No point in that.

Yet, no sense in going hungry. He grabbed a hunk of angelcake and gulped it down. He felt angelic. That was no mood for an ogre! He chomped some devilsfood, and felt devilish. That was more like it. He gulped some dream pie, and dreamed of smiting the Night Stallion and recovering the lien on his soul.

Wait. He forced himself to stop eating, lest he sink immediately into the easy slough of indulgence. Better to keep hungry and alert, his cursed task-master of an Eye Queue told him. What did the Eye Queue care about hunger? It didn't have to eat! But he went along with it for the moment, knowing it would give him no peace otherwise. He would reward himself only for making progress in solving this particular riddle. That was discipline no ordinary ogre could master, infuriating as it was.

Still, time was passing, and he had no idea how to proceed. There had to be *something*. After all, it wasn't as if he could simply eat his way out of here.

That thought made him pause. Why *not* eat out? Chew a hole in the wall until he ran out of edibles—which would be another world.

No. There would be too much cake for even an ogre to eat. Unless he knew exactly where a weak spot was—

Weak spot. Surely so. Something that differed from the rest of this stuff.

Smash started a survey course of eating, looking for the difference. All of it was excellent. A master pastry chef had baked this chamber.

Then he encountered a vein of licorice. That was one confection Smash didn't like; it reminded him of manure. True, some ogres could eat and like manure, but that just wasn't Smash's own taste. Naturally he avoided this vein.

Then his accursed, annoying, and objectionable Eye Queue began perco-lating again. The Eyes of the vine saw entirely too much, especially what wasn't necessarily there. Manure. What would leave manure in the form of a confection?

Answer: some creature in charge of a chamber of confections. The Night Stallion, perhaps. When the Stallion departed, he would leave his token of contempt. Big brown balls of sweet manure.

What exit would the Stallion use? How could that exit be found?

Answer: the trail of manure would show the way. Horses hardly cared where they left it, since it was behind them. They left it carelessly, thought-lessly, often on the run.

Smash started digging out the licorice. But when he did, the foul stuff melted into other cake, transforming it into licorice, too. That obscured the trail. He had to do something about that.

He cast about, but came up with only the least pleasant solution. He would have to eat it. That was the only way to get rid of it. To consume the manure of the Stallion.

Fortunately, ogres didn't have much pride about what they ate. He nerved himself and bit in. The licorice-cake was awful, truly feculent, but he gulped it down anyway.

Now his gorge was rising violently inside him. Ogres were supposed never to get sick, no matter how rotten the stuff they ate. But this was manure! He ate on.

Smash came to a round hole in the material of the chamber. The dung had led him to it—since this was the exit the Stallion had taken. Smash scrambled through the passage, knowing that if he could just choke down his revolted, revolting stomach a little longer, he would win this contest, too.

He came to a drop-off and tumbled out, spinning and turning in air. Now he was falling through darkness.

That last jolt of weightlessness was too much. His stomach burst its constraints and heaved its awful contents violently out. The reaction sent him zooming backward through space. Smash puked, it seemed, for eons, and worked up a velocity to rival that of the brass spaceship. He hoped he didn't get lost in space beyond the stars.

Chapter 10

Fond Wand

He was retching into the gourd patch. Apparently he had jetted himself right out of the gourd! Chem was using the hardened rind of an empty gourd to scoop the vomit away, making room for more as it flowed voluminously from Smash's mouth.

As he realized where he was, his sickness abated. He looked about.

The girls were in a sorry state. All five of them were spattered. "We decided to get you out of the gourd before it got worse," Tandy said apologetically. "What happened?"

"I ate a lot of horse—er, manure," Smash said. "Instead of cake and pastry."

"Ogres do have unusual tastes," John remarked.

Smash chuckled weakly. "Where's some decent food? I don't want to eat any more gourds, and I'm going to be hungry as soon as I feel better."

"There'll be food at Goblinland," Goldy Goblin said.

"How far is that?"

Chem produced her map. "As I make it, we're close. From what Goldy tells me, the main tribe of goblins is not far from here, as the dragon flies. Just a few hours' walk, except that there's a mountain in the way, so we have to go around—across the Earth works. That complicates it. But I think the lava is cool enough now. We had better get over it before more comes."

"Like hot vomit," Goldy muttered.

Smash looked at the conic mountain. It steamed a little, but was generally quiescent. "Yes—let's cross quickly."

They started across. Goldy knew a little foot-cooling spell used by goblins and taught it to them. It wasn't real magic, but rather an accommodation to the local landscape. Smash's Eye Queue was cynical, suspecting that any benefit from the spell was simply illusion, the belief in cooler feet. Yet his feet did feel cooler.

They had to skirt the volcano's eastern slope. The cone rumbled, annoyed, but was in its off-phase and could not mount any real action.

The ground, however, was rested. It had energy to expend. It shook, making their travel difficult. The shaking became more violent, causing the hardened lava to craze, to crack, to break up, and to form fissures, exposing the red-hot rock down below.

"Hurry!" Chem cried, her hooves dancing on the shifting rocks. Smash remembered that insecure footing made her nervous. Now it made him nervous, too.

"Oh, I wish I could fly again!" John cried, terrified. She stumbled and started to fall into a widening crack.

Chem caught her. "Get on my back," she directed. The fairy scrambled gratefully aboard.

The ground shook again. A fragment turned under the Siren's foot, and she went down. Smash caught her, lifted her high, and saw that her ankle was twisted. He would have to carry her.

Now the volcano rumbled again. It might be in its offphase, but it wasn't entirely helpless. A new fissure opened in its side, and bright red lava welled out, like fresh blood. It spilled down toward them, shifting channels to orient accurately.

"It's coming for us!" Tandy cried, alarmed. "This land doesn't like us!"

Smash looked northeast. The goblin territory was far across the treacherously shifting rocks. Already the lava plain was humping like a slow ocean swell, as if trying to break free of its cool crust. Smash knew that if much more fragmentation occurred, they would all fall through that crust into the liquid lava below.

"Too far!" Tandy cried despairingly. "We can't make it!"

"North!" Chem said. "It's better to the north!"

They scrambled north, though that horizon looked like a wall of fire. The lava crust broke into big plates that, in turn, fragmented into platelets that slowly subsided under the weight of the party. Red lava squeezed up around the edges and leaked out onto the surface. Meanwhile, the fresh lava from the fissure flowed down to join the turbulent plain, further melting the platelets. There was now no retreat.

"Spread out!" Goldy cried. "Not too much weight on any one plate!"

They did it. The goblin girl was the most agile, so she led the way, finding the best plates and the best crossing places. Tandy followed, glancing nervously back at Smash as if afraid he would be too clumsy. She did care for him; it was obvious, now that Blythe had given him the hint. But that was hardly worth worrying about at this moment. They might all soon perish.

Next in line was Chem, carrying John on her back, her hooves handling the maneuvering well. Then came Smash, holding the Siren in his arms. Her feet had converted back to the tail; evidently that alleviated the pain in her ankle. However, her tail form was also her bare-top form, and the sight of all that juggling flesh made him ravenous again. He hoped he never got so hungry that he forgot these were his friends.

The edges of the plates depressed alarmingly as they took Smash's weight, for it was concentrated in a smaller area than was the centaur's. Once a plate broke under his weight, becoming two saucers, and he had to scramble, dipping a toe in red lava; it hurt terribly, but he ran on.

"Your toe!" the Siren exclaimed. "It's scorched!"

"Better that than falling in," he grunted.

"In case we don't make it," she said, "I'd better tell you now. You're a lot of creature, Smash."

"Ogres are big," he agreed. "You're a fair morsel of creature yourself." Indeed, she had continued to grow more youthful, and was now a sight to madden men. Or so he judged, from his alien viewpoint.

"You're more than I think you know. You could have been where you're going by now if you hadn't let the rest of us impose."

"No. I agreed to take Tandy along, and the rest of you have helped. I'm not sure I could have handled the dragons alone, or gotten out of the gourd."

"You never would have gotten into the gourd alone," she pointed out. "Then you could have avoided the dragons. Would another ogre have taken Tandy along?"

He laughed. He did that a lot since the advent of the Eye Queue, for things he wouldn't have noticed before now evinced humorous aspects. "Another ogre would have eaten the bunch of you!"

"I rest my case."

"Rest your tail, too, while you're at it. If I fall into the lava, you'll have to walk alone."

It was her turn to laugh, somewhat faintly. "Or swim," she said, looking down at the lava cracks.

Now they were at the border. The wall of fire balked them. Goldy stood on the plate nearest it, daunted. "I don't know how much fire there is," she said. "Goblin legend suggests the wall is thin, but—"

"We can't stay here," Tandy said. "I'll find out." And she took a breath and plunged into the fire.

The others stood on separate plates, appalled. Then Tandy's voice came back: "It's all right! Come on through!"

Smash closed his eyes and plunged toward her voice. The flame singed his fur and the flowing hair of the mermaid; then he was on firm ground, coughing.

He stood on a burned-out field. Wisps of smoke rose from lingering blazes, but mostly the ashes were cool. Farther to the north a forest fire raged, however, and periodically the wind shifted, bringing choking smoke and sprinkling new ashes. To the west there seemed to be a lake of fire, sending up occasional mushroom-shaped masses of smoke. To the east there was something like a flashing field of fire, with intermittent columns of flame.

Chem and John landed beside Smash. The fairy was busy slapping out smolders in the centaur's mane. "This is an improvement, but not much of one," Chem said. "Let's get off this burn!"

"I second the motion," Tandy agreed. She, too, had suffered during the crossing; parts of her brown hair had been scorched black. Goldy appeared, in similar condition. None of the girls was as pretty as she had been.

They moved east, paralleling the thin wall of fire. This was the Region of Fire, but since fire had to have something to burn, they were safe for the moment.

Then a column of white fire erupted just ahead of them. The heat of it drove them back—only to be heated again by another column to the side.

"Gas," the Siren said. "It puffs up from fumaroles, then ignites and burns out. Can we tell where the next ones will be?"

They watched for a few moments. "Only where they've been," Chem said. "The pattern of eruption and ignition seems completely random."

"That means we'll get scorched," the Siren said. "Unless we go around."

But there was no way around, for the forest fire was north and the lava flows were beyond the firewall to the south.

Also, new foliage was sprouting through the ashes on which they stood, emerging cracklingly dry; it would catch fire and burn off again very soon. It seemed the ashes were very rich fertilizer, but there was very little water for the plants, so they grew dehydrated. Here in the Region of Fire, there was no long escape from fire.

"How can we get through?" Tandy asked despairingly.

Smash put his Eye Queue curse to work yet again. He was amazed at how much he seemed to need it, now that he had it, when he had never needed it before, as if intelligence were addictive; it kept generating new uses for itself. He was also amazed at what his stupid bonemuscle ogre brain could do when boosted by the Queue and cudgeled by necessity. "Go only where they've been," he said.

The others didn't understand, so he showed the way. "Follow me!" He watched for a dying column, then stepped near it as it flickered out. There would be a little while before it built up enough new gas to fire again. He waited in the diminishing shimmer of heat, watching the other columns. When another died, next to his own, he stepped into its vacated spot.

The other members of the party followed him. "I'll assume this is wit instead of luck," the Siren murmured. Smash was still carrying her, though now she had switched back to legs and dress, in case he had to set her down.

As they moved to the third fumarole, the first fired again. These flares did not dawdle long! Now they were in the middle of the columns, unable to escape unscathed. But Smash stepped forward again into another dying flame, panting in the stink of it, yet surviving unburned.

In this manner the party made its precarious and uncomfortable way through the fires, and came at last to the east firewall. They plunged through—and found themselves in the pleasant, rocky region of the goblins.

"What a relief!" Tandy exclaimed. "Nothing could be worse than that, except maybe what's inside a gourd."

"You haven't met the local goblins yet," Goldy muttered.

There was a small stream paralleling the wall, cool and clean. They all drank deeply, catching up from their long engagement with the heat. Then they washed themselves off and tended to their injuries. The Siren bound her ankle with a bolt of gauze from a gauze-bush, and Tandy tended to Smash's scorched toe.

"Goldy will find her husband here," Smash said as she worked. "Soon we may find a human husband for you." He hoped he was doing the right thing, bringing the matter into the open.

She looked up at him sharply. "Who squealed?" she demanded.

"Blythe said you were looking for—"

"What does she know?" Tandy asked.

Smash shrugged awkwardly. This wasn't working out very well. "Not much, perhaps."

"When the time comes, I'll make my own decision."

Smash could not argue with that. Maybe the brass girl had been mistaken. Blythe's heart, as she had noted, was brass, and perhaps she was not properly attuned to the hearts made of flesh. But Smash had a nagging feeling that wasn't it. These females seemed to have a common awareness of each other's nature that males lacked. Maybe it was just that they were all interested in only one thing. "Anyway, we'll deliver Goldy soon."

They found no food, so they walked on along the river, which curved eastward, north of the mountain range that separated this land from that of the dragons. The goblins had to be somewhere along here, perhaps occupying the mountains themselves. Goblins did tend to favor dark holes and deep recesses; few were seen in open Xanth, though Smash understood that in historical times the goblins had dominated the land. It seemed they had become less ugly and violent over the centuries, and this led inevitably to a diminution of their power. He had heard that some isolated goblin tribes had become so peaceful and handsome that they could hardly be distinguished from gnomes. That would be like ogres becoming like small giants—astonishing and faintly disgusting.

The river broadened and turned shallow, finally petering out into a big dull bog. Brightly colored fins poked up from the muck, and nostrils surmounting large teeth quested through it. Obviously the main portions of these creatures were hidden beneath the surface. It did not seem wise to set foot within that bog. Especially not with a sore toe.

They skirted it, walking along the slope at the base of the mountain range. The day was getting late, and Smash was dangerously hungry. Where were the goblins?

Then the goblins appeared. An army of a hundred or so swarmed around the party. "What are you creeps doing here?" the goblin chief demanded with typical goblin courtesy.

Goldy stepped forward. "I am Goldy Goblin, daughter of the leader of the Gap Chasm Goblins, Gorbage," she announced regally.

"Never heard of them," the chief snapped. "Get out of our territory, pasteface."

"What?" Goldy was taken aback. She was very fair for a goblin, but it wasn't merely the name that put her at a loss.

"I said get out, or we'll cook you for supper."

"But I came here to get married!" she protested.

The goblin chief swung backhanded, catching the side of her head and knocking her down. "Not here you don't, foreign stranger slut." He turned away, and the goblin troops began to move off.

But Tandy acted. She was furious. "How dare you treat Goldy like that?" she demanded. "She came all the way here at great personal risk to get married to one of your worthless louts, and you—you—"

The goblin chief swung his hand at her as he had at Goldy, but Tandy moved faster. She made a hurling gesture in the air, with her face red and her eyes squinched almost shut. The goblin flipped feet over ears and landed, stunned, on the ground. She had thrown a tantrum at him.

Smash sighed. He knew the rules of interspecies dealings. How goblins treated one another was their own business; that was why these goblins had left Smash and the rest of his party alone. Their personal interplay was rough, but they were not looking for trouble with ogres or centaurs or human folk. Unlike the prior goblin tribe, this one honored the conventions. But now Tandy had interfered, and that made her fair game.

The goblin lieutenants closed on her immediately—and Tandy, like an expended fumarole, had no second tantrum to throw in self-defense. But Chem, John, and the Siren closed about her. "You dare to attack human folk?" the Siren demanded. She was limping on her bad ankle but was ferocious in her wrath.

"You folk aren't human," a goblin lieutenant said. "You're centaur, fairy, and mernymph—and this other looks to be part nymph, too, and she attacked our leader. Her life is forfeit, by the rules of the jungle."

Smash had not chosen this conflict, but now he had to intervene. "These three with me," he grunted, in his stress reverting to his natural ogre mode. He indicated Tandy with a hamfinger. "She, too, me do."

The lieutenant considered. Evidently the goblins were hierarchically organized, and with the chief out of order, the lieutenant had discretionary power. Goblins were tough to bluff or back off, once aroused, especially when they had the advantage of numbers. Still, this goblin hesitated. Three or four females were one thing; an ogre was another. A hundred determined goblins could probably overcome one ogre, but many of them would be smashed to pulp in the process, and many more would find their heads embedded in the trunks of trees, and a few would find themselves flying so high they might get stuck on the moon. Most of the rest would be less fortunate. So this goblin negotiated, while others hauled their unconscious leader away.

"This one must be punished," the lieutenant said. "If our chief dies, she must die. So it is written in the verbal covenant: an eyeball for an eyeball, a gizzard for a gizzard."

Smash knew how to negotiate with goblins. It was merely a matter of speaking their language. He formed a huge and gleaming metal fist. "She die, me vie."

The lieutenant understood him perfectly, but was in a difficult situation. It looked as if there would have to be a fight.

Then the goblin chief stirred, perhaps because he was uncomfortable being dragged by the ears over the rough ground. He was recovering consciousness.

"He isn't dead," the lieutenant said, relieved. That widened his selection of options. "But still she must be punished. We shall isolate her on an island."

Isolation? That didn't seem too bad. Nevertheless, Smash didn't trust it. "Me scratch," he said, scratching his flealess head stupidly. "Where catch?"

The goblin studied him, evidently assessing Smash's depth of stupidity. "The island sinks," he said. "You may rescue her if you choose. But there are unpleasant things in the bog."

Smash knew that. He didn't want to see Tandy put on a sinking island in that bog. Yet he did not have his full strength, and hunger was diminishing him further, and that meant he could not afford to indulge in combat with the goblins at this time. In addition, his Eye Queue reminded him snidely, Tandy *had* attacked the goblin chief, and so made herself liable to the goblin's judgment. The goblins, if not exactly right, were also not exactly wrong.

The goblin lieutenant seemed to understand the struggle going on in the ogre's mind. Goblins and ogres differed from one another in size and intelligence, but were similar in personality. Both sides preferred to avoid the mayhem that would result if they fought. "We will give you a fair chance to rescue her."

"Me dance," Smash said ironically, tapping the ground with one foot, so that the terrain shuddered. "What chance?"

"A magic wand." The lieutenant signaled, and a goblin brought an elegant black wand.

"Me no fond of magic wand," Smash said dubiously. He continued to use the ogre rhymes, having concluded that stupidity, or the appearance of it, might be a net asset.

"All you have to do is figure out how to use it," the goblin said. "Then you can draw on its magic to help the girl. We don't know its secret, but do know it is magic. We will help you figure it out, if you wish."

That was a considerable risk! He had to figure out the operative mechanism of a wand that had so baffled the goblins that they were willing to help him use it to defeat their decree of punishment. They would have spent days, months, or years on it; he might have minutes. What chance would a smart man have, let alone a stupid ogre? What person of even ordinary intelligence would agree to such a deal?

Why would the goblins risk such a device in the hands of a stranger, anyway? Suppose he did figure out the operation of the wand by some blind luck? He could be twice as dangerous to them as he already was.

Ah, but there was the answer. An ogre was stupid, almost by definition. He could be far more readily conned out of his advantage than could a smart person. Also, the activated wand might be dangerous, acting against the user. Of course they would help him solve its secret; if it destroyed the user, no loss! Only an absolutely, idiotically, calamitously stupid or desperate creature would take that risk.

John sidled up to Smash. "Goblins are cunning wretches," she whispered. "We fairies have had some dealings with them. I think they mistreated Goldy deliberately, to get you into this picklement."

"I'm sure of it," Goldy agreed. A bruise was showing on her cheek, but she seemed otherwise all right. "My own tribe is that way. My father threatened to eat you all, when he doesn't even like ogre or centaur meat, just to force you to take me here."

"It does seem to be an effective ploy," Smash whispered back. "But we would have taken you anyway, had we known you."

If brass girls could blush copper, goblin girls blushed tan. "You mean you folk like me?"

"Certainly we do!" Tandy agreed. "And you helped us cross the lava plates, leading the way. And you told us a tremendous lot about the hypnogourds, so that Smash knows how to save his soul."

"Well, goblins aren't too popular with other creatures," Goldy said, wiping an eye.

"Nor with their own kind, it seems," Tandy said.

"Because the chief hit me? Think nothing of it. Goblin men are just a little bit like ogres in that respect. It makes them think they run things."

"Ogres aren't too popular with other creatures, either," Smash said. "They beat up their wenches, too."

"This lesson in comparative romance is fascinating," John said. "Still, we're in trouble."

"Pick Tandy up and run out of here," Goldy advised. "That's the only way to deal with our kind."

But Smash knew that the other girls would pay the penalty for that. He had fallen into the goblin's trap; he would have to climb out of it. His one advantage was that he was, thanks to the curse of the Eye Queue, considerably smarter than the goblins thought. "Me try to spy," he told the lieutenant.

"Very well, ogre," the lieutenant said smugly. "Take the wand, experiment with it, while we place her on the island."

Goblins grabbed Tandy and hustled her into a small wooden boat. She struggled, but they moved her along anyway. She sent a betrayed look back at Smash, evidently feeling with part of her mind that he should fight, and he felt like a betrayer indeed. But he had the welfare of the entire party in mind, so he had to act with un-ogrish deliberation. This grated, but had to be. If the wand didn't work, he would charge through the bog and rescue her, regardless of the fins. Even if the fins proved to be too much for him, he should be able to toss her to the safe bank before going under.

They dumped her on an islet that seemed to be mostly reeds. As her weight settled on it, the structure hissed and bubbled from below, and slowly lowered toward the liquid muck surface. A purple fin cruised in and circled the pneumatically descending isle.

Smash concentrated on the wand while goblins and girls watched silently. He waved it in a circle, bobbed it up and down, poked it at imaginary balloons in the air, and shook it. Nothing happened. "Go, schmoe!" he ordered it, but it ignored even that command. He bent it between his hands; it flexed, then sprang back into shape. It was supple and well made, but evinced no magic property.

Meanwhile, Tandy's isle continued to sink. The purple fin cruised in tighter circles. Tandy stood in the spongy center, terrified.

But he couldn't watch her. He had to concentrate on the wand. It was evident that his random motions weren't being successful. What was the key?

Eye Queue, find the clue! he thought emphatically. It was high time he got some use from this curse when it really counted.

The Queue went to work. It considered mental riddles a challenge. It even enjoyed thinking.

Assume the wand was activated by motion, because that was the nature of wands. They were made to wave about. Assume that trial-and-error motion wouldn't do the trick, because the goblins would have tried everything. Assume that the key was nevertheless simple, so that the wand could be readily used in an emergency. What motion was both simple and subtle?

A signature-key, he decided. A particular motion no one would guess, perhaps attuned to a particular person. But how could he guess its nature?

Tandy's isle was almost down to muck level, and the circling fin was almost within her reach, or vice versa. Smash could not afford to ponder much longer!

"Goblin man, help if can," Smash called. After all, the goblins wanted to know the secret, too.

"All we know, ogre, is that it worked for the crone we stole it from," the lieutenant replied. "She would point it at a person or thing, and the object would levitate. That is, rise." The goblin thought Smash would not know the meaning of the more complicated term. "But when we tried it—nothing."

Levitation. That would certainly help Tandy! But he needed to get it started in a hurry.

"Crone so smart, how she start?"

"She looped it in a series of loops," the goblin said. "But when we made the same loops, nothing happened."

Tandy's feet were now disappearing into the muck. Only the submerged mass of the isle balked the fin—for now.

"Give poop. What loop?" Smash demanded.

"Like this." The goblin described a partial circle with a tuck in it.

"That looks like a G," John remarked. Apparently fairies were literate, too.

G. A letter of the human alphabet? Suddenly Smash's intellect pounced. What was a signature except a series of letters? A written name? John's own case illustrated the importance of a name; her entire mission was simply to locate her correct one. One could not choose just any name, because only the right one had power. This should apply for wands as well as for fairies, here in Xanth. Maybe it was different inside the gourd, where names could be changed at will. "What name of dame?"

"Grungy Grool," the goblin answered. "She was a witch."

A witch with the initial G G. Suppose the wand tuned in to the signature of its holder? Smash described a big, careful S.

Nothing happened. Holding his disappointment in check, he described a matching O. Smash Ogre—his initials.

Still nothing. The wand remained quiescent in his hamhand. What now?

Tandy screamed. Her isle was giving way, and she was toppling into the muck.

Smash aimed the wand like an arrow, ready to hurl it at the fin.

Tandy's fall stopped midway. She hung suspended at an angle above the bog, right where Smash was pointing.

"The wand is working!" John cried, amazed and gratified.

Slowly Smash tilted the wand up. Tandy floated, remaining in its power. Of course the activated wand had not moved in his hand before; that wasn't the way it worked. *He* had to move it—to make some other object respond.

"I'm flying!" Tandy cried.

"He made it work!" the goblin lieutenant exclaimed.

Smash guided Tandy carefully to land and set her down. Her feet were muddy and she was panting with reaction, but she was otherwise unharmed. He knew a spunky little girl like her would rebound quickly.

The goblin lieutenant rushed up. "Give me that wand, ogre!"

"Don't do it!" John cried.

But Smash, ever the stupid ogre, blithely handed over the wand. "It is goblin property," he murmured, forgetting to rhyme.

The goblin snatched the wand, pointed it at Smash, and lifted it. Smash did not rise into the air. The wand was not attuned to the goblin. It remained useless to anyone else, exactly as it had been when taken from its witch-owner. Smash had suspected this would be the case.

"But you made it work!" the goblin protested angrily.

"And you tried to turn it against him!" Goldy cried. "Do you call that goblin honor?"

"Well, he's just a stupid ogre," the goblin muttered. "What does he know?"

"I'll tell you what he knows!" Goldy flashed. "He's a lot smarter than—"

"Me smart, at heart," Smash said, interrupting her.

Goldy paused, then exchanged a glance of understanding with him. "Smarter than the average ogre," she concluded.

The goblin lieutenant formed a crafty expression, too subtle for the average ogre to fathom. "Very well, ogre. Teach *her* how to work the wand, if it's not a fluke." He gave the wand to Goldy.

So the goblins figured to get the secret from her. Smash understood perfectly. But he smiled vacuously. "Happily, me teach she."

"Me?" Goldy asked, surprised. "Smash, you don't really want to—"

Smash put his huge mitt on her hand. "You have a mind of your own, chief's daughter," he murmured. "Use it." Gently he moved her hand, making the wand ascribe the letters G G, her initials. Then he stepped back.

"I don't understand," Goldy said, gesturing with the wand.

Three goblins sailed into the air as the moving wand pointed at them.

"She's got it!" the goblin lieutenant exclaimed. "Good enough! Give it here, girl!" He advanced on her.

Goldy pointed the wand at him and lifted it. He rose up to treetop height. "Give what where, dolt?" she inquired sweetly.

The lieutenant scrambled with hands and feet, but merely made gestures in the air. "Get me down, wretch!" he screamed.

She waved the wand carelessly, causing him to career in a high circle. "Do what, who?"

"You'll pay for this, you bi—" The goblin broke off as he was pitched, upside down, just clear of the bog. A blue fin cut across and began circling under his nose.

"Smash," Goldy said sweetly, "why don't you and your friends have a good meal while I try to get the hang of this wand? I might need some advice, to prevent me from accidentally hurting someone." And the goblin lieutenant spun crazily, just missing a tree.

"Feed them! Feed them!" the goblin cried. "This crazy sl—young lady goblin will be the death of me!"

"I might, at that, if I don't learn to manage this thing better," Goldy agreed innocently. The wand quivered in her hand, and the goblin did a bone-rattling shake in the air, almost dropping to within reach of the slavering blue fin.

The goblins hastily brought out food. Smash stuffed himself in excellent ogre fashion on strawberry-flavored cavern mushrooms and curdled sea-cow milk while the goblin girl experimented with the wand, lifting first one goblin, then another.

"Let someone else try it!" a goblin suggested craftily. Goldy glanced at Smash, who nodded. Then she handed the wand to the first taker.

The wand went dead again. Several goblins tried it, without result. It occurred to Smash that if one of them should have the initials G G, as was hardly beyond the reach of coincidence, the wand might work—but that never happened. Probably it was not only the key, but the particular person signing it. Another G G goblin would have to make his own G G signature. That was a pretty sophisticated instrument!

"Give me that," Goldy said, taking it back. It still worked for her. Once the wand was keyed to a particular person, it stayed that way. Since the goblins were illiterate, they never would catch on to the mechanism, most likely.

The meal concluded. Smash rubbed his belly and let out a resounding belch that blew the leaves off the nearest bush.

"Well, I can't say it hasn't been fun," Goldy said, offering the wand back to Smash.

Smash refused it, wordlessly.

"You mean I can keep it?" she asked, amazed.

"Keep it," the Siren said. "I think you will have no trouble getting a suitable husband here now. Probably a chief. Whatever you choose."

Goldy considered, contemplating the wand. "There is that. Power is a language we goblins understand somewhat too well." She faced Smash again. "Ogre, I don't know what to say. No goblin would have done this for you."

"He's no ordinary ogre," Tandy said, giving Smash's arm a squeeze. "Keep the wand. Use it well."

"I will," Goldy agreed, and there seemed to be an ungoblinish tear in her eye. "If any of you folk ever have need of goblin assistance—"

"Just in getting out of here," Chem said. "Any information on the geography to the north would be appreciated."

Goldy gestured toward the lieutenant with the wand. "Information?"

Hastily the goblins acquainted Chem with what they knew of the reaches to the north, which wasn't much.

Well fed, the party set out as dusk fell, following the bog to the river, and the river until it petered out. They camped near the firewall, snacking on some leftover mushroom tidbits Goldy had arranged to have packed. They would have to cross the Region of Fire again to get where they were going, as the goblins had assured them that it went right up to the land of the griffins, which beasts were hostile to travelers.

"That was a generous thing you did, Smash," the Siren said. "You could so readily have kept the wand, especially after they tried to trick you out of it and use it against you."

"Goldy had better use for it," Smash said. "Why should an ogre crave more power?"

"One thing I don't understand," John said. "You say you were victimized by the Eye Queue vine. That makes you smarter than an ordinary ogre, whose skull is filled with bone."

"Correct," Smash agreed uncomfortably.

"But that does not account for your generosity, does it? You have let the rest of us impose on you, and you did something really nice for Goldy, and I don't think another ogre would, not even a smart one. Goblins are like ogres, only smaller and smarter, and they don't do anything for anybody."

Smash scratched his head. Still no fleas. "Maybe I got confused."

"Maybe so," the fairy replied thoughtfully. Tandy and Chem and the Siren nodded, smiling with that certain female knowingness that was so annoying.

Chapter 11

Heat Wave

Smash's Eye Queue would not leave well enough alone; that was its most annoying trait. He greeted the next morning with doubts. "How do we know the griffins are unfriendly?" he asked. "Can we trust the information of the goblins? We do know the fire is dangerous, on the other hand."

"We certainly do!" John agreed. "My wings will never grow back if I keep singeing them! But griffins are pretty violent creatures and they do eat people."

"Let's travel near the firewall," the Siren suggested. "That way we can cross over and risk the fire if the griffins turn out to be too ferocious."

They did that. But soon the bog closed in, squeezing them against the firewall. The colored fins paced them eagerly.

Chem halted. "I think we have to make a decision," she said as she updated her map-image.

"I'll check the other side," Smash said, setting down the Siren. He stepped across the firewall.

He was at the edge of the fumaroles, amidst fresh ashes. Not far north the forest fire continued to rage. There was no safe passage here!

He saw a shape in the ashes. Curious, he uncovered it. It was the burned-out remnant of a large tree trunk, still smoldering. The fall of ashes had smothered it before it finished its own burning. Smash wondered when a tree of this size ever had a chance to grow here. Maybe it had fallen across the firewall from the other side.

Then he had a notion. He put his gloved hamhands on the charred log and heaved it back through the firewall. Then he stepped through himself. "A boat," he announced.

"A boat!" Tandy exclaimed, delighted. "Of course!"

They went to work with a will, scraping out ashes and burned-out fragments and splinters. Then they launched the dugout craft in the muck. Smash ripped out a sapling to use as a pole so he could shove their boat forward. He remembered traveling similarly with Prince Dor. But this was more challenging, because now he had responsibility for the party.

The colored fins crowded in as the craft slid through the bog. At length Smash became annoyed, and used the tip of his pole to poke at the nearest fin. There was a chomp, and the pole abruptly shortened.

Angry, Smash reached out with a gauntleted hand and caught hold of the offending fin. He heaved it out of the water.

The creature turned out to be fishlike, with strong flukes and sharp teeth. "What are you?" Smash demanded, shaking it. The thing was heavy, but Smash had over half his ogre strength back now and was able to control his captive.

"I'm a loan shark, idiot!" the fish responded, and Smash did not have the wit, until his Eye Queue jogged him snidely later, to marvel that a fish spoke human language. "Want to borrow anything? Prompt service, easy terms."

"Don't do it!" John cried. "You borrow from one of of them, it'll take an arm and a leg in return. That's how they live."

"You have already borrowed part of my pole," Smash told the shark. "I figure you owe me. I'll take a fin and a fluke."

"That's not the way it works!" the shark protested. "No one skins sharks!"

"There is always a first time," Smash said. He had a fundamental understanding of this kind of dealing. He put his other hand on the thing's tail and began to pull.

The shark struggled and grunted, but could not free itself. "What do you want?" it screamed.

"I want to get out of this bog," Smash said.

"I'll get you out!" The shark was quite accommodating, now that it was in a bad position. "Just let me go!"

"Don't trust it any farther than you can throw it," John advised.

Smash was not about to. He used one finger to poke a hole in the shark's green fin and passed Chem's rope through it. Then he heaved the creature forward. It landed with a dull muddy splash before the dugout, the rope pulling taut. "That's as far as I can throw it," Smash said.

The shark tried to swim away, but as it moved, it hauled the boat along behind. It was not trustworthy, but it seemed to be seaworthy. Or bogworthy.

"Now you can swim anywhere you want to, Sharky," Smash called to it. "But I'll loose the rope only when we reach the north edge of this bog."

"Help! Help me, brothers!" the shark called to the other fins that circled near.

"Are you helpless?" one called back. "In that case, I'll be happy to tear you apart."

"Sharks never help each other," John remarked. "That's why they don't rule Xanth."

"Ogres don't help each other, either," Smash said. "The same for most dragons." And he realized that he had suffered another fundamental revelation about the nature of power. Human beings helped each other, and thus had become a power in Xanth far beyond anything that could be accounted for by their size or individual magic.

Meanwhile, the loan shark got the message. It was living on borrowed time, unless it moved. It thrust north, and the bog fairly whizzed by. Soon they were at the north bank.

They climbed out, and Smash unthreaded the rope. The shark vanished instantly. No one sympathized with it; it had for once been treated as it treated others.

But now the griffins came. Probably another shark had snitched, so the griffins had been alert for the party's arrival. Since the creatures probably intended no good, Smash stepped quickly across the firewall for a peek at that situation. He found himself in the middle of the forest fire. No hope there!

The great bird-headed, lion-bodied creatures lined up, inspecting the motley group. The monsters were the color of shoe polish. Then they charged.

Smash reacted automatically. He swung his pole, knocking the first griffin back. Then he dived across the firewall, ripped a burning sapling out of the ground, dived back, and hurled the flaming mass at the remaining griffins. The sapling was of firewood, which burned even when green; in a moment the wing feathers of the griffins were burning.

The monsters squawked and hurled themselves into the bog to douse the flames. The colored fins of the sharks clustered close. "You're using our muck!" a shark cried. "You owe us a wing and a paw!"

The griffins did not take kindly to this solicitation. A battle erupted. Muck, feathers, and pieces of fin flew outward, and the mud boiled.

Smash and the girls walked northwestward, following the curve of the firewall, leaving the violence behind. The landscape was turning nicer, with occasional fruit and nut trees, so they could feed as they traveled.

The Siren, rested by her tour in the boat and periodic dippings of her tail, found she could walk now. That lightened Smash's burden.

There were birds here, flitting among the trees, picking at the trunks, scratching into the ground. The farther the party went, the more there were. Now and then, flocks darkened the sky. Not only were they becoming more numerous, they were getting larger.

Then a flight of really large birds arrived—the fabulous rocs. These birds were so big they could pick up a medium-sized dragon and fly with it. Was their intent friendly or hostile?

A talking parrot dropped down. "Ho, strangers!" it hailed them. "What melodies bring you to Birdland?"

Smash looked at the parrot. It was all green and red, with a downcurving beak. "We only seek to pass through," he said. "We are going north."

"You are going west," the bird said.

So they were; the gradually curving firewall had turned them about. They reoriented, bearing north.

"Welcome to pass through Birdland," the parrot said. "There will be a twenty per cent poll tax. One of your number will have to stay here."

"That isn't fair!" Tandy protested. "Each of us has her own business."

"We are not concerned with fairness," the poll replied, while the horrendously huge rocs drifted lower, their enormous talons dangling. "We are concerned with need. We need people to cultivate our property so there will be more seeds for us to eat. So we hold a reasonable share of those who pass."

"A share—for slavery?" Tandy demanded, her spunky spirit showing again.

"Call it what you will. One of you will stay—or all will stay. The tax will be paid." And the rocs dropped lower yet. "Poll your number to determine the one."

Smash knew it would be useless to fight. He might break the claws of one roc, but another would carry away the girls. The big birds had too much power. "We'll see," he said.

Tandy turned on him. "We'll *see?* You mean you'll go along with this abomination?"

"We don't have much choice," Smash said, his Eye Queue once again dominating his better ogre nature. "We'll just have to cross this land, then decide who will remain."

"You traitor!" Tandy flared. "You coward!"

The Siren tried to pacify her, but Tandy moved away, her face red and body stiff, and hurled an invisible tantrum at Smash. It struck him on the chest, and its impact was devastating. Smash staggered back, the wind knocked out of him. No wonder the goblin chief had fallen; those tantrums were potent!

His head gradually cleared. Smash found himself sitting down, little clouds of confusion dissipating. Tandy was beside him, hugging him as well as she could with her small arms. "Oh, I'm so sorry, Smash. I shouldn't have done that! I know you're only trying to be reasonable."

"Ogres aren't reasonable," he muttered.

"It's just that—one of us—how can we ever callously throw one to the wolves? To the birds, I mean. It just isn't right!"

"I don't know," he said. "We'll have to work it out."

"I wish we had the wand," she said.

The Siren came to them. "We do have the Ear," she reminded them.

"There is that," Tandy agreed. "Let me hear it." She took the Gap Dragon's Ear and listened carefully. "Silent," she reported.

Smash took it from her and listened. For him, too, it was silent. Chem had no better result. "I fear it has gone dead—or we have no future," she said. "Nowhere to go."

John was the last to listen. Her face brightened. "I hear something!" she exclaimed. "Singing—fairies singing. There must be fairies nearby!"

"Well, that's what you're looking for," the Siren said. "Let's see if they're within Birdland. Maybe we can get some advice on how to proceed."

There seemed to be nothing better to do. Smash lurched to his feet, amazed at the potency of Tandy's tantrum; he still felt weak. An ogress could hardly have hit him harder! Yet more than that, he marveled at her quick reversal of mood. She had been almost savagely impetuous—then humanly sorry. Too bad, he mused, she hadn't been born an ogress. That tantrum—it also reminded him a bit of one of his mother's curses.

He shook his head. Foolish fantasy was pointless. He had to clear his reeling noggin, and get moving, and find Tandy a good human-type husband so the demon wouldn't bother her any more. Good Magician Humfrey must have known that there would be a suitable man for her somewhere in this wilderness, a man she would never encounter unless she traveled here. Since Smash was passing this way anyway, it had been easy enough to take her along. The truth was, she was nice enough company, tiny and temperamental as she was. He had not had much company like that before and was becoming acclimated to it. He knew this was un-ogrish; maybe such ridiculous feelings would pass when he got rid of the Eye Queue curse.

They proceeded on, following John, who used the Ear to orient on the fairies. The rocs paced them; they would not be able to depart Birdland without paying their poll toll. One body . . .

Actually, Smash might have a way around that. If he went back into the gourd and fought the Night Stallion and lost, his soul would be forfeit pretty soon, and there would be no point in proceeding north. So in that event, he might as well stay here himself. The only problem was, how would the others survive without him? He had no confidence that they were beyond the worst of the dangers of central Xanth.

As they continued, they saw more and more birds. Some were brightly plumed, some drab; some large, some small; some ferocius of aspect with huge and knifelike beaks, some meek with soft little feathers. There were bright bluebirds, dull blackbirds, and brightly dull spotted birds. There were fat round robins and thin pour-beakers.

They went on. There were ruffled grouse, angrily complaining about things, godwits making profane jokes, sandpipers playing little fifes on the beach, black rails lying in parallel rows on the ground, oven birds doing the morning baking, mourning doves sobbing uncontrollably, goshawks staring with amazement, a crane hauling up loads of stones, and several big old red barn owls filled with hay. Nearby were grazing cowbirds and cattle egrets, and a catbird was stalking a titmouse, tail swishing.

"Birds are funny folk," the Siren murmured. "I never realized there was so much variety."

In due course they came to the palace of the Kingbird. "Better bow good and low," the parrot advised. "His Highness the Bird of a Feather, the ruler of Xanth, First on the Pecking Order, doesn't appreciate disrespect from inferiors."

"Ruler of Xanth!" Chem cried. "What about the centaurs?"

"What about King Trent?" Tandy asked.

"Who?" the parrot asked.

"The human ruler of Xanth, in Castle Roogna."

"Never heard of him. The Kingbird governs."

Smash realized that to the birds, the bird species dominated Xanth. To the goblins, the goblins governed. The same was probably true for the dragons, griffins, flies, and other species. And who could say they were wrong? Each species honored its own leaders. Smash, an ogre, was quite ready to be objective about the matter. When in Birdland, do as the birdbrains did.

He bowed to the Kingbird, as he would have done to the human King of Xanth. To each his own mark of honor.

The Kingbird was reading a tome titled *Avian Artifacts* by Ornith O'Logy, and had no interest in the visitors. Soon Smash's party was on its way again.

They came to a large field filled with pretty flowers. "These are our bird-seed plants," the parrot explained. "We have wormfarms and fishfarms and funnybonefarms, and make periodic excursions to Flyland for game, but the bulk of our food comes from fields like this. We are not apt at cultivation—birdshot doesn't seem to do well for us—so we draw on the abilities of lesser creatures like yourselves."

Indeed, Smash saw assorted creatures toiling in the field. There were a few goblins, an elf, a brownie, a gremlin, a nixie, and a sprite. They were obviously slaves, yet they seemed cheerful and healthy enough, acclimated to their lot.

Then Smash had a notion. "John, listen to the Ear again."

The fairy did so. "The waterfall noise almost drowns it out, but I think I hear the fairies close by." She oriented on the sound, going in the direction it got louder, the others following. They rounded a gentle hill, descended into a waterfall-fed gully, and came across the fairies.

They were mending feathers. It seemed some of the birds were too impatient to wait for new feathers to grow, so they had the damaged ones repaired. Only fairies could do such delicate work. Each had a little table with tiny tools, so that the intricate work could be done. And most of them had damaged wings.

"The birds—" Tandy said, appalled. "They crippled the fairies so they can't fly away!"

"Not so," the parrot said. "We do not mutilate our workers, because then they get depressed and do a poor job. Rather, we offer sanctuary for those who are dissatisfied elsewhere. Most of these fairies were cast out of Fairyland."

Tandy was suspicious. She approached the nearest working fairy. "Is this true?" she asked. "Do you like it here?"

The fairy was a male, finely featured in the manner of his kind. He paused, looking up from his feather. "Oh, it's a living," he said. "Since I lost my wings, I couldn't make it in Fairyland. So I have to settle for what I can get. No monsters attack me here, no one teases me for my wing handicap, there's plenty of food, and the work is not arduous. I'd rather be flying, of course—but let's be realistic. I'll never fly again."

Smash saw one fairy down the line with undamaged wings. "What about him?" he asked. "Why doesn't *he* fly away?"

The fairy frowned. "He has a private complaint. Don't bother him."

But Smash was in pursuit of his notion. "Would it relate to his name?"

"Look," the fairy said, "we aren't trying to aggravate your condition, so why do you bother us? Leave him alone."

John had caught on. "Oh, Smash—I'm afraid to ask!"

"I'm an insensitive ogre," Smash said. "I'll ask." He tromped over to the fairy in question. "Me claim he name," he said in his stupid fashion.

The fairy naturally assumed the ogre was as dull as he was supposed to be. It was all right to tell secrets to stupid folk, because they didn't know enough to laugh. "I am called Joan," he said. "Now go away, monster."

Smash dropped his pretense. "That must be as embarrassing for you as intelligence is for an ogre," he said.

Joan's eyes widened and his wings trembled, causing the cloud pattern on them to roll. "Yes," he agreed.

Smash signaled to John. Diffidently, she approached. "Here is the one who got your name, or one letter of it," Smash said. "Trade him your H for his A, and both of you will be restored."

The two fairies looked at each other. "Joan?" John asked. "John?" Joan asked.

"I suspect the two of you are the same age, and took delivery of your names by the same carrier," Smash said. "Probably the Paste Orifice; it always gums things up. You should compare notes."

Joan reached out and took John's hand. Smash was no proper judge of fairy appearance, but it seemed to him that Joan was quite a handsome young male of his kind, and John was certainly pretty, except for her lost wings. Here in Birdland that particular injury did not count for much.

The two of them seemed almost to glow as their hands touched.

Chem and Tandy and the Siren had joined Smash. "What is that?" Tandy asked. "Is something wrong?"

"No," Chem said. "I've read of this effect, but never hoped to see it. It's the glow of love at first touch."

"Then—" Smash said, in a burst of realization that he had suppressed until this moment. "They were destined for each other. That's why their names were confused. To bring them eventually together."

"Yes!" the centaur agreed. "I think John—I suppose it's Joan now—will be staying here in Birdland."

So the fairy's solution was the group's solution! One of their number would remain—happily. How neatly it had worked out. But of course that was the way of destiny, which was never the coincidence it seemed.

They made their acknowledgments of parting and left their fairy friend to her happy fate. The birds, satisfied, let them go.

Their best route north, the parrot assured them, was through the Water Wing. There were very few monsters there, and the distance to the northern border of Xanth was not great.

They agreed to that route. They had already encountered more than enough monsters, and since the birds assured them there were no fires or earthquakes in the Water Wing, the trek should be easy enough. Besides, the Ear had the sound of rainfall, which suggested their immediate future.

John/Joan hurried up as they were about to cross the border. "Here is a heat wave," she said. "My fiancé had it for when he left Birdland, but now he won't be needing it. Just unwrap it when the time comes."

"Thank you," Smash said. He took the heat wave. It seemed to be a wire curved in the shape of a wave, and was sealed in a transparent envelope.

The girls hugged their friend good-bye, and Smash extended his littlest hamfinger so the fairy could shake hands with him Then they stepped across the border, braced for anything.

Anything was what they got. They were in a drenchpour. Not for nothing was this called the Water Wing by the birds! There was ground underfoot, but it was hard to see because of the ceaseless blast of rain.

Chem brought out her rope, and they tied themselves together again— centaur, Tandy, Siren, and ogre, sloshing north in a sloppy line. Smash had to breathe in through his clenched teeth to strain the water out. Fortunately, the water was not cold; this was a little like swimming.

After an hour, they slogged uphill. The rain thinned as they climbed, but the air also cooled, so they did not gain much comfort. In due course the water turned to sleet, and then to snow.

The poor girls were turning blue with cold. It was time for the heat wave. Smash unwrapped the wire. Immediately heat radiated out, suffusing the immediate region, bringing comfort to each of them. The fairy's present had been well considered, for all that it had been an accident of circumstance.

Slowly the snow stopped falling, but the climb continued. This was a mountain they were on, blanketed with snow. By nightfall they still had not crested it, and had to camp on the slope.

They were all hungry, and Smash was ravenous, so he gave the Siren the heat wave and headed out into the snow to forage. He found some flavored icicles in a crevice-cave and chased a snow rabbit, but couldn't catch it. So he headed back with the icicles; they were only a token, but somewhat better than nothing. They would have to do.

It was colder out here then he had figured. His breath fogged out before him, and the fog iced over and coated him, making him a creature of ice. His feet turned numb, and his fingers, too. He hardly knew where his nose stopped and the ice began; when he snorted, icicles flew out like arrows.

Now he slowed, feeling lethargic. Wind came up, cutting into his flesh, buffeting him about so that he stumbled. He dropped cumbersomely to the ground, his fall cushioned by the snow. He intended to get up, as it was now far downhill to their camp, but it was more comfortable just to lie there for a little longer. His Eye Queue cried warning, but after a while that, too, faded out, and Smash slept.

He dreamed he saw Tandy's father, the soldier Crombie, whirling around in his fashion and pointing his finger. The finger stopped, pointing north. But what was it pointing to? Smash remembered Crombie had said Tandy would lose three things; that must be where it would happen.

Then Smash was being hauled awake. That was much less comfortable than drifting to sleep had been. His extremities hurt, burning like fire and freezing like ice simultaneously; his head felt like thawed carrion, and his belly was roasting as if he were mounted on a spit over a fire. He groaned horrendously, because that was what ogres did when roasted on a spit over a fire.

"He's alive!" a voice cried joyfully.

As Smash recovered more fully, he learned what had happened. He had frozen on the slope. Alarmed at his failure to return, the girls had organized a search party and located him. He was as stiff as ice, because that was what he had become. They had feared him dead, but had put the heat wave on his belly and thawed him. Ogres, it seemed, were freeze-storable.

Now that he was awake, it was time to sleep. They settled down around the heat wave, Tandy choosing to rest her head against Smash's furry forearm. Ah, well, that was harmless, probably. "I'm glad we got you thawed, monster," she murmured. "I'm not letting you out alone again!"

"Ogres do get into trouble," he agreed. It was strange to imagine anyone watching out for him, and stranger yet to imagine that he might need this attention, but it seemed he did, on occasion.

In the night there was a horrendous roar. Smash, dreaming again—he tended to do that when asleep—thought it was an ogress and smiled a huge grimace. But the three girls bolted up, terrified.

"Wake up, Smash!" Tandy whispered urgently. "A monster's coming!"

But Smash, in a dream-daze, hardly stirred. He had no fear of the most horrendous ogress.

The monster stamped near, eyes glowing, teeth gleaming, breath fogging out in dank, cold clouds. It was pure white, and every hair seemed to be an icicle.

"Smash!" Tandy hissed. "It's an abom—abom—an awful Snowman! Help!"

The Snowman looked over them, as pale as a snowstorm. It reached out to grab the nearest edible thing. The girls cowered behind Smash, who was mostly covered by a nice snow blanket, so that little of him showed. This snow was not nearly as cold as that of the rest of the mountain, because this was near the heat wave; he was comfortable enough. But it deceived the Snowman, who caught hold of Smash's nose and yanked.

Ouch! Suddenly Smash woke up all the way. A truly ogrish rage shook him. He reached up one huge, hairy arm and grabbed the snow monster by the throat.

The Snowman was amazed. He had never encountered a worse monster than himself before. He had not known anything like that existed. He did not know how to deal with this situation.

Fortunately, Smash knew how to deal with it. He stood up, not letting go, and shook the hapless monster. "Growr!" he growled, and dropped the creature on top of the heat wave.

There was a bubbling and hissing as the Snowman's posterior converted from ice to steam in one foop. The monster sailed into the air and shot out of there like a gust from a gale. Smash didn't bother to pursue; he knew better than to stray from the vicinity of the heat wave again. He was no Snowman!

"It will be a long time before that creature bothers travelers again," Chem remarked with private satisfaction.

"Yes, we have a worse monster on our side," Tandy said, patting Smash's knee. She seemed to like the notion.

Smash was just glad he had enough of his strength back to handle such things as snow monsters. But soon he would have to meet the Night Stallion and put it all on the line. He had better get the girls beyond these dangerous wilderness regions of Xanth first, just in case.

Once more they settled down to sleep, grouping closely around the heat wave. By morning it had melted them deep into the snow, so that they were in a cylindrical well. There seemed to be no bottom to this layer of snow;

was the whole mountain made of it? That could be, since this was the Water Wing, and snow was solidified water.

Smash bashed out a ramp to the surface, and the party resumed the trek. They were all hungry now, but had to be satisfied with mouthfuls of snow.

As they entered the icy ridge of the mountain, the sun melted the remaining clouds and bore down hard on the snow. The snow began to melt. Smash put the heat wave back in its envelope, but soon they were sloshing through slush anyway.

Then the slush turned to water, and the slope became a river flowing over ice. They tried to keep to their feet, but the entire mountain seemed to be dissolving. The treacherous surface gave way beneath them and washed them all helplessly along in the torrent.

Chem seemed to be able to handle herself satisfactorily in the water; and, of course, the Siren assumed her mermaid form and swam like a fish. But Tandy was in trouble because of the sheer rush of water. She could swim well enough in level water, but this was a cataract.

Smash tried to swim to her, but got bogged down himself. He was not really a strong swimmer; he normally waded or whomped through water. But right now he was not at full strength and had been frozen and thawed. This water was becoming too deep and violent for him.

Too much indeed! Smash gulped for air—and got water instead. He coughed and gasped and sucked in a replacement lungful—only to fill up the rest of the way with water.

This was awful! He clawed at his throat, trying foolishly to clear the water while his body struggled for air. But it was no good. The torrent was all about him, finding excellent purchase against his brute body, and he could not breathe.

The agony of suffocation became unbearable. Then something snapped, like the lid of his head, and half his consciousness departed. Smash gave himself up for lost. But it seemed to him that it had been more comfortable to be frozen than to be drowned.

Then he was calm, accepting the inevitable. It was, after all, halfway pleasant doing without air. Maybe this wasn't really worse than freezing. He drifted with the slowing current, relieved, feeling like loose seaweed. How nice just to float forever free.

Then something was tugging fretfully at him. It was the mermaid. She wrapped her arms about one of his and threshed violently with her tail, drawing him forward. But his mass was too much for her. Progress slowed; she needed air herself, with all this exertion. She let him go, and Smash sank blissfully to the depths while she shot up toward the surface.

Slowly he became aware of more tugging, this time on both arms. He tried to shake himself free, but his arms did not respond. He watched himself being drawn upward from the gloom to the light. There seemed to be two figures drawing him, one on each arm, each with a fish-tail—but maybe he was seeing double.

Smash was not sure how long or far he was dragged; time was compressed or dilated for him. But he became aware that he was on a sandy beach, with a nightmare tromping her hooves on his back. He was mistaken. It was a filly centaur; Chem was treading the water out of his body. The experience was almost as bad as vomiting out all the Stallion manure, after that sequence in the gourd. Almost.

In due course Smash recovered enough to sit up. He coughed another bucket or two of water out of his lungs. "You rescued me," he accused the Siren.

"I tried," she said. "But you were too heavy—until Morris helped."

"Morris?"

"Hi, monster!" someone called from the water.

It was a triton. Now Smash understood why there had seemed to be two merfolk hauling him along. The Siren and Morris the Merman.

"We lost the Ear and the heat wave, but we saved you," the Siren said. "And Chem rescued Tandy."

Now Smash saw Tandy, who was lying face-down on the sand. The centaur was now kneading her back, using hands instead of hooves. "You breathed water, too?" Smash asked.

Tandy raised her head. "Ungh," she agreed squishily. "Did you—float?"

"When I sank," he answered. "If that's what dying is like, it's not bad."

"Let's not talk about death," Chem said. "This is too nice a place for that. I'm already upset about losing the Ear."

"Not more upset about that than I am with me for losing the heat wave," the Siren said.

"Maybe you should have thrown Smash and me back and saved the magic items," Tandy said, forcing a watery smile.

"It was fated that we lose them," Smash said, remembering his dream. "Soldier Crombie said Tandy would lose three things, and our loss is her loss."

"That's true!" Tandy agreed. "But what's the third thing?"

Smash shrugged. "We don't have any third thing to lose. Maybe two covers it."

"No, my father always points things out right. We've lost something else, I'm sure. We just don't know what it is."

"Maybe one of you should stay and look for the lost items," the merman said. He was a sturdy male of middle age, roughly handsome. It was evident that he could not make legs and walk on land the way the Siren could; he was a full triton.

"Maybe one of us should," the Siren said thoughtfully.

After that, it fell naturally into place. This was a pleasant region on the fringe of the Water Wing, where the drainage from the snow mountain became a lake that spread into the mainstream wilderness of Xanth. There was a colony of merfolk here, mostly older, scant of maids. It looked very promising for the Siren.

Chapter 12

Visible Void

The three of them—Smash, Tandy, and Chem—proceeded north to the border of the Void, the last of the special regions of central Xanth. "There is great significance to these five elemental regions," Chem said. "Historically, the five elements—Air, Earth, Fire, Water, and the Void—have always been mainstays of magic. So it is fitting that they be represented in central Xanth, and I'm extremely gratified to get them on my map."

"These have been good adventures," Smash agreed. "But just what is the Void? The other elements make sense, but I can't place that one."

"I don't know," the centaur admitted. "But I'm eager to find out. I don't think this region has ever been mapped before by anyone."

"Now is certainly the time," Tandy said. "I hope it's not as extreme as the others were."

Chem brought out her rope. "Let's not gamble on that! I should have tied us when the snow mountain turned to slush, but it happened so fast—"

They linked themselves together as they approached the line. It was abrupt. On the near side the pleasant terrain of the merfolk's lake spread southward. On the far side was nothing they could perceive.

"I'm the lightest," Tandy said. "I'll go first. Pull me back if I fall into a hole." She smoothed back her slightly scorched and tangled brown hair and stepped across the formidable line.

Smash and Chem waited. The rope kept playing out, slowly; obviously Tandy was walking, not falling, and not in any trouble. "Is it all right, Tandy?" the centaur called rhetorically.

There was no answer. The rope continued to moved. "Can you hear me? Please answer," Chem called, her brow wrinkling.

Now the slack went taut. Chem stood her ground, refusing to be drawn across the line. Smash tried to peer into the Void, but could see nothing except a vague swirl of fog, from this side.

"I think I'd better pull her back," Chem said, swishing her brown tail nervously. It, too, was somewhat bedraggled as a result of their recent adventures. "I'm not sure anything is wrong; maybe she just doesn't hear me."

Chem hauled. There was resistance. She hesitated, not wanting to apply unreasonable force. "What do you think, Smash?"

Smash put his Eye Queue to work, but it seemed sluggish this time. His logic was fuzzy, his perception confused. "I don't—seem to have much of an opinion," he confessed.

She glanced back at him, surprised. "No opinion? You, with your unogrish intelligence? Surely you jest!"

"It best me jest," Smash agreed amicably.

She peered closely at him. "Smash—what happened to your Eye Queue? I don't see the stigma on your head."

Smash touched the fur of his scalp. It was smooth; there was no trace of roughness. "No on; it gone," he said.

"Oh, no! It must have been washed out when you nearly drowned! That's the third thing we've lost—your intelligence. That certainly affects Tandy's prospects here. You're back to being stupid!"

Smash was appalled. Just when he needed intelligence, he had lost it! What would he do now in a crisis?

The centaur was similarly concerned, but she had an answer. "We'll have to use my intelligence for us both, Smash. Are you willing to follow my lead, at least until we get through the Void?"

That seemed to make sense to Smash. "She lead, me accede."

"I'll try to haul her back." Chem drew harder on the rope, and, of course, she had the mass to do it. Suddenly it went slack, and the loose end of it slid back across the line.

"Oh, awful!" the centaur exclaimed, dismayed. She switched her tail violently in vexation. "We've lost her!"

seeming to move because of the expansion of the map. "Hey, it's not supposed to do that!" she protested. "It's turning life-size!"

Obviously the map was careering out of control. Smash wondered why that should happen here. If only he had his Eye Queue back, he would be able to realize that this was surely no coincidence, and that it related in some fundamental way to the ultimate nature of the Void. He might even conjecture that the things of the mind, whether animated in the form of a map or remaining inchoate, had considerable impact on the landscape of the Void. Perhaps the interaction between the two created a region of animated imagination that could be a lot of fun, but might also pose considerable threats to sanity if it got out of control. Perhaps no purely physical menace lurked within the Void, but rather, the state of mental chaos that might prevail when no aspects of physical reality intruded upon or limited the generation of fanciful imagery. But naturally a mere stupid ogre could in no way appreciate the tiniest portion of such a complex conjecture, so Smash was oblivious. He hoped this foolish oblivion would not have serious consequences. Ignorance was not necessarily bliss, as any smart creature would know.

Chem, confused by her map's misbehavior, turned it off. Then she tried it again, concentrating intently. This time it expanded from its point source, then contracted to pinpoint size, gyrating wildly, until it steadied down around the size she wanted it. She was learning new control, and this was just as well, for lack of discipline might be extraordinarily troublesome here.

"See, there are the grazing centaurs," Chem said, pointing ahead.

Smash looked. He saw a tribe of grazing ogres. Again, if only he had retained the curse of intelligence, he might have comprehended that another highly significant aspect of this region was manifesting. Chem perceived one nonsensical thing, and he perceived another. That suggested that the preconceptions of the viewer defined in large part what that viewer saw; there was not necessarily any objective standard here. Reality, literally, was something else. In this case, perhaps, a herd of irrelevant creatures was grazing, neither centaurs nor ogres.

If this were so, he might have continued his thought, how could they be certain that anything they saw here was not a kind of illusion? Tandy could be lost in a world of altered realities and not realize it. Since Chem and Smash also were in altered states of perception, the problem of locating Tandy might be immensely more complicated than anticipated. But he, a dull ogre, would merely blunder on, heedless of such potential complications.

"Something funny here," Chem said. "We know centaurs don't graze."

"It seem a dream," Smash said, trying vainly to formulate the concept he knew he could not master without the curse of intellect.

"Illusion!" Chem exclaimed. "Of course! We're seeing other creatures that only look like centaurs." She was smart, as all centaurs were; she caught on quickly.

But she didn't have it all yet. "Me no see centaur she," he said clumsily.

"You see something else? Not centaurs?" Again her brow furrowed. "What do you see, Smash?"

Smash tapped his own chest.

"Oh, you see ogres. Yes, I suppose that makes sense. I see my kind, you see yours. But how can we see what is really there?"

This was far too much for him to figure out. If only he had his Eye Queue back, he might be able to formulate a reversal of perspective that would cancel out the mind-generated changes and leave only the undisturbed truth. Perhaps a kind of cross-reference grid, contrasting Chem's perceptions with his own, eliminating the differences. She saw centaurs, he saw ogres—obviously each saw his own kind, so that was suspect. Both saw a number of individuals, so there the perceptions aligned and were probably accurate. Both saw the creatures grazing, which suggested they were, in fact, grazing animals, equine, caprine, bovine, or other. Further comparison on an organized basis, perhaps mapping the distinctions on a variant of Chem's magic map, would in due course yield a close approximation of the truth, whatever it might be.

Of course, it might be that there was nothing. That even their points of agreement were merely common fancies, so that the composite image would be that illusion that was mutually compatible. It just might be, were the fundamental truth penetrated, that what remained in the Void was—nothing. The absence of all physical reality. Creatures thought, therefore they existed—yet perhaps even their thinking was largely illusion. So maybe the thinkers themselves did not exist—and the moment they realized this, they ceased to exist. The Void was—void.

But without his mental curse he wouldn't see any of that, and perhaps this was just as well. If he were going to imagine anything, he should start with the Eye Queue vine! But he would have to use it cautiously, lest the full power of his enhanced intellect succeed only in abolishing himself. He needed to preserve the illusion of existence long enough to rescue Tandy and get them out of the Void, so that their seeming reality became actual. "Me need clue to find Eye Queue," he said regretfully.

Chem took him literally, which was natural enough, since she knew he now lacked the wit to speak figuratively. "You think there are Eye Queue vines growing around here? Maybe I can locate them on my map."

She concentrated, and the suspended map brightened. Parts of it became greener than others. "I can't usually place items I haven't actually seen," she murmured. "But sometimes I can interpolate, extrapolate from experience and intuition. I think there could be such vines—here." She pointed to one spot on her map, and a marker-glow appeared there. "Though they may be imaginary, just ordinary plants that we happen to see as Eye Queues."

Smash was too stupid to appreciate the distinction. He set off in the direction indicated by the map. The centaur followed, keeping the map near him so he could refer to it at need. In short order he was there—and there they were, the dangling, braided eyeball vines, each waiting to curse some blundering creature with its intelligence and perception.

He grabbed one and set it on his head. It writhed and sank in immediately. How far had he sunk, to inflict so eagerly this curse upon himself!

His intelligence expanded, much as the centaur's map had. Now he grasped many of the same notions he had wished to grasp before. He saw one critical flaw in the technique of using a cross-reference grid to establish reality: turned on his own present curse of intelligence, it would probably reveal his smartness to be illusion. Since Smash needed that intelligence to rescue Tandy, he elected not to pursue that course. It would be better to use the devices of perspective to locate Tandy first, then explore their unreal mechanisms when the loss of such mechanisms no longer mattered. It would also be wise not to ponder the intricacies of his own personal existence.

What would be the best way to find her? If her footprints glowed, it would be easy to track her. But he was now far too smart to believe that anything so coincidentally convenient could exist.

The centaur, however, might be deceivable. "I suspect there could be some visible evidence of the passage of outsiders," he remarked. "We carry foreign germs, alien substances from other magic regions. There could be interactions, perhaps a small display of illumination—"

"Smash!" she exclaimed. "It worked! You're smart again!"

"Yes, I thought it might."

"But it's illusion. The Eye Queue is only imaginary! How can it have a real effect?"

"What can affect the senses can also affect the mind," Smash explained. She had seemed so smart a moment ago. Now, from the lofty vantage of his restored intelligence, she seemed a bit slow. Certainly it was stupid of her to attempt to explain away his mental power, for that would put them right back in the morass of incompetence. He had to persuade her—before she persuaded him. "In Xanth, things are mostly what they seem to be. For example, Queen Iris's illusions of light enable her to see in the dark; her illusion of distant vision enables her to see people who are otherwise too far away. Here in the Void, in contrast, things are what they seem not to be. It is possible to finesse these appearances to our advantage, and to generate realities that serve our interests. Do you perceive the footprints?"

She looked, dismayed by his confusing logic. "I—do," she said, surprised. "Mine are disks, yours are paw-prints. Mine glow light brown, like my hide; yours glow black, like yours." She looked up. "Am I making any sense at all? How can a print glow black?"

"What other color befits an ogre?" he asked. He did not see the prints, but did not remark on that. "Now we must cast about for Tandy's prints." He cracked the briefest smile. "And hope they do not wail."

"Yes, of course," she agreed. "They must originate where we crossed the line: that's the place to intercept them." She started back—and paused. "That's funny."

"What's funny?" Smash was aware that the Void was tricky and potentially dangerous. If Chem began to catch on to its ultimate nature, he would have to divert her in a hurry. Their very existence could depend on it.

"I seem to be up against a wall. It's intangible, but it balks me."

A wall. That was all right; that was a physical obstacle, not an intellectual one, therefore much less dangerous. Much better to wrestle that sort of thing. Smash moved to join her—and came up against the wall himself. It was invisible, as she had suggested, but as he groped at it he began to discern its rough stones. It seemed to be fashioned of ogre-resistant stuff, or maybe his weakened condition prevented him from demolishing it properly. Odd.

His Eye Queue had another thought, however. If things in the Void were not what they seemed to be, perhaps this was true of the wall. It might not exist at all; if he could succeed in disbelieving in it, he could walk through it. Yet if he succeeded in abolishing a wall this tangible by mental effort, what then of the other things of the Void, such as the Eye Queue? He might do best not to disbelieve.

"What do you perceive?" Chem asked.

"A firm stone wall," he said, deciding. "I fear we shall find it difficult to depart the Void." He had thought that intellectual dissolution, or the vacating of reality, might cause the demise of intruders into the Void; perhaps it was, after all, a more physical barrier. He would have to keep his mind open so as not to be trapped by illusions about these illusions.

"There must be a way," she said with a certain false confidence. She suspected, as he did, that they could be in worse trouble right now than they had been when the Gap Dragon charged them or the volcano's lava flows began breaking up under them. Mental and emotional equilibrium was as important now as physical agility had been then. "Our first job is to catch up with Tandy; then we can tackle the problem of departure."

At least she had her priorities in order. "Certainly. We can intercept her footprints by proceeding sidewise. We now have a notion why she did not return. This wall must be pervious from the edge of the Void, impervious from the interior. A little like a one-way path through the forest."

"Yes. I always liked those one-way paths. I don't like this wall quite as well." Chem proceeded sidewise, following the wall. She did not see it or really feel it, yet it balked her effectively. Meanwhile, Smash did not see the glowing footprints, but knew they would lead the two of them to Tandy. There seemed to be more substance to these illusions than was true elsewhere. The illusions of Queen Iris seemed very real, but one could walk right through them. The illusions of the Void seemed unreal, yet prevented penetration. Would they really all dissipate at such time as he allowed himself to fathom the real nature of the Void? If nothing truly existed here, how could there be a wall to block escape? He kept skirting the dangerous thoughts!

Soon Chem spied Tandy's footprints—bright red, she announced. The prints were headed north, deeper into the Void.

They followed this new trail. Smash checked every so often and discovered that the invisible wall paced them. Any time he tried to step south, he could not. He could only go north, or slide east or west. This disturbed him more than it might have when he was ogrishly stupid. He did not like traveling a one-way channel; this was too much like the route into the lair of a hungry dragon. The moment he caught up to Tandy, he would find a way to go back out of the Void. Maybe he could break a hole in the wall with a few hard ogre blows of his fist.

Yet again his Eye Queue, slanted across with an alternate thought. Suppose the Void were like a big funnel, allowing people to slide pleasantly toward its center and barring them from climbing out? Then the wall would not necessarily be a wall at all, merely the outer rim of that funnel. To smash it apart could be to break up the very ground that supported them, and send them plunging in a rockslide down into the deeper depth. No percentage there!

How could he arrange to escape the trap and take his friends with him? If no one had escaped before to give warning, that was a bad auspice for their own chances! Well, he intended to be the first to emerge to tell the tale.

Could he locate a big bird, a roc, and get carried out by air? Smash doubted it. He distrusted air travel, having had a number of uncomfortable experiences with it, and he certainly distrusted birds as big as rocs. What did rocs eat, anyway?

What else was there? Then he came up with a notion he thought would work in the Void. This would use the properties of the Void against the Void itself, rather than fighting those properties. He would try it—when the time came.

"There's something ahead," Chem said. "I don't know what it is yet."

In a moment they caught up to it. It was an ogress—the beefiest, fiercest, hairiest, ugliest monster he had ever seen, with a face so mushy it was almost sickening. Lovely!

"What's another centaur doing here?" Chem asked.

Instantly the Eye Queue analyzed the significance of her observation. "That is another anonymous creature. We had better proceed cautiously."

"Oh, I see what you mean! Do you think it could be a monster?" The centaur, delicately, did not voice the obvious fear—that the monster could have consumed Tandy. After all, it stood astride her tracks.

"Perhaps we should approach it from opposite sides, each ready to help the other in case it should attack." He wasn't fully satisfied with this decision, but the thought of harm to Tandy made the matter urgent.

"Yes," Chem agreed nervously. "As I become acclimated to this region, I like it less. Maybe one of us can draw near her and the other can hide, ready to act. We can't assume a sleek centaur filly like that is hostile."

Nor could they afford to assume the ugly ogress was *not* hostile! They had to be ready for anything. "You hide; I will approach in friendly fashion."

The centaur proceeded quietly to the west, and in a moment disappeared.

Smash gave her time to get properly settled, then stomped gently toward the stranger. "Ho!" he called.

The hideous, wonderful ogress snapped about, spying him. "Who you?" she grunted dulcetly, her voice like the scratching of harpies' talons on dirty slate.

Smash, aware that she was not what she seemed, was cautious. Names had a certain power in Xanth, and he was already below strength; it was best to remain anonymous, at least until he was sure of the nature of this creature. "I am an inquiring stranger," he replied.

She tromped right up to him and stood snout to snout, in the delightful way of an ogress. "Me gon' stir he monster," she husked in the fascinatingly unsubtle mode of her apparent kind, and she clinked him in the puss with one hairy paw.

The blow lacked physical force, but Smash did a polite backflip as if knocked heels over head. What a romantic come-on! He remembered how his mother knocked his father about and stepped on his face, showing her intimidating love. How similar this ogre-she was!

Yet his Eye Queue cautioned caution, as was its wont. This was not a real ogress; she might just be roughing him up for a meal. She might not be nearly as friendly as she seemed. So he did not reciprocate by smashing her violently into a tree. Besides, there was no suitable tree handy.

He used un-ogrish eloquence instead. "This is a remarkably friendly greeting for a stranger."

"No much danger," she said. "He nice stranger." And she gave him a friendly kick.

Smash was becoming much intrigued. He was sure this was no ogress, but she was one interesting person! Maybe he should hit her back. He raised his hamfist.

Then a third party appeared. This was another ogress. "Don't hit her, Smash!" she cried. "I just realized—"

"Smash?" the first ogress repeated questioningly. She seemed amazed.

"We must all describe exactly what we see," the second ogress said. She, too, was no true ogress, for her speech did not conform—unless she had blundered into some Eye Queue vines—but that hardly seemed likely. "You first, Smash."

Confused by this development, he obliged. "I see two attractively brutal ogresses, each with a face mushier than the other, each hunched so that her handpaws reach almost down to her hindpaws. One is brown, the other red."

"And I see two centaurs," the second ogress said. "A black stallion and a red mare."

Oho! That would be Chem, seeing her own kind. Once she had separated from him, her own perceptions had taken over, so that she saw him falsely.

"I see a handsome black human man and a pretty brown human girl," the first ogress said.

"Then you are Tandy!" Chem exclaimed.

"Tandy!" Smash repeated, amazed.

"Of course I'm Tandy!" Tandy agreed. "I always was. But why are you two dressed up like human people?"

"We each perceive our own kind," Chem explained. "Each person in-stinctively generates his or her own reality from the Void. Come—take hands and perhaps we can break through to reality."

They took hands—and slowly the alternate images dissipated, and Smash saw Chem in her ruffled brown coat and Tandy in her tattered red dress.

"You were awful handsome as a man," Tandy said sadly. "All garbed in black, like a dusky king, with silver gloves." Smash realized that his orange jacket had become so dirty it was now almost indistinguishable from his natural fur. "But why did you fall down when I tried to shake your hand?"

The Eye Queue provided the insight to cause him embarrassment. "I misunderstood your intent," he confessed. "I thought you were being friendly."

"I *was* being friendly!" she exclaimed indignantly. "You were the first human being I was able to get close to in this funny place. I thought you might know some way out. I can't seem to go back myself; I bang into an invisible hedge or something. So I wanted to be very positive, and not scare you away. After all you might have been lost too."

"Yes, of course," Smash agreed weakly.

"But you acted as if I'd hit you, or something!" she continued indignantly.

"This is the way ogres show affection," Chem explained.

Tandy laughed. "Affection! That's how human beings fight!"

Smash was silent, horribly embarrassed.

But Tandy would not let it go. "You big oaf! I'll show you how human beings express affection!" And she grabbed Smash's arm, pulling him toward her with small human violence. Bemused, he yielded, until his head was down near hers.

Tandy threw her arms around his furry neck and planted a firm, long, hot-blooded kiss on his mouth, moving her lips against his.

Smash was so surprised he sat down. Tandy followed him, still pressing close, locking his head to hers. He fell all the way back on the ground, but she stayed with him, her brown hair flopping forward to cover his wildly staring eyes as she drove home the rest of the kiss.

At last she released him, as she needed a breath. "What do you think of that, ogre?"

Smash lay where she had thrown him, unable to make sense of the experi-ence.

"He's overwhelmed," Chem said. "You gave him an awfully stiff dose for his first such contact."

"Well, I've wanted to do it for a long time," Tandy said. "He's been too stupid to catch on."

"Tandy, he's an ogre! They don't understand human romance. You know that."

"He's an ogre with Eye Queue. He can darned well learn."

"I'm afraid you're being unrealistic," the centaur said, talking as if Smash were not present. Perhaps that was the case, mentally. "You're a spunky, pretty human girl. He's a hulking jungle brute. You can't afford to get emotionally involved with a creature like that. He just isn't your type."

"And just what is my type?" Tandy flared defiantly. "A damned demon intent on rape? Smash is the nicest male creature I've met in Xanth!"

"How many male creatures have you met in Xanth?" the centaur inquired.

Tandy was silent. Of course her experience had been quite limited.

Smash at last essayed a remark. "You could visit a human village—"

"Shut up, ogre," Tandy snapped, "or I'll kiss you again!"

Smash shut up. She was not bluffing; she could do it. She still had her arms looped around his neck, since she lay half astride him, holding him down, as it were.

"You have to be realistic," Chem said. "The Good Magician sent you out with Smash so the ogre could protect you while you searched for a husband. What good will it do you to find the destined man, as John and the Siren and maybe Goldy did, if you foolishly waste your love on an inappropriate object? You would be undermining the very thing you seek."

"Oh, phooey!" Tandy exclaimed. "You're right, centaur, I know you're right, centaurs are always right—but oh, it hurts!" A couple of hot raindrops fell on Smash's nose, burning him with an acid other than physical. She was crying, and he found that even more confusing than the kiss. "Ever since he rescued me from the gourd and got me back my soul—"

"I'm not denying he's a good creature," Chem said. "I'm just saying, realistically—"

Tandy turned ferociously on Smash. "You monster! Why couldn't you have been a *man?*"

"Because I'm an ogre," he said.

She wrenched one arm clear of him and made as if to strike his face. But her hand did not touch him.

The Void spun about him, dimming. Smash realized she had hit him with another tantrum. That, ironically, was more like ogre love. Why couldn't she have been an ogress?

An ogress. Now, his mind shaken by the double whammy of kiss and tantrum, Smash floated, half conscious, and realized what he had been missing. An ogress! He, like every member of his party, could not exist alone. He needed a mate. That was what had brought him to Good Magician Humfrey's castle. That had been his unasked Question. How could he find his ideal mate? Humfrey had known.

And of course there would be ogresses at the Ogre-fen-Ogre Fen. That was why the Good Magician had sent him to seek the Ancestral Ogres. He would be able to select one who was right for him, knock her about in ogre fashion, and live in brutal happiness ever after, exactly as his parents had. It all did make sense.

He drifted slowly to earth as the horrendous impact of the tantrum eased. "Now I understand—" he began.

"I warned you, oaf," Tandy said. She leaned over and plastered another big kiss on him.

Smash was so dazed that he almost grasped the nature of the kiss, this time. Perhaps it was the effect of the Void, making things seem other than they were. It was as if she were punching him in the snoot—and with that perception she became much more alluring.

Then she broke, and the odd perspective ended. She became a girl again, all soft and pretty and nice and wholly inappropriate for romance. It was too bad.

"Oh, what's the use," Tandy said. "I'm a fool and I know it. Come on, people; we have to get out of this place."

"That may not be readily accomplished," Chem said. "We can travel in deeper, or edge sideways, but we can't back out. I'm sure it's like a whirlpool, drawing us ever inward. What we shall find in the center, I hesitate to conjecture."

"Oblivion," Tandy said tightly. She, too, had caught on.

"A maw," Smash said, climbing unsteadily to his feet. "This land is carnivorous. It gives us respite only because it doesn't need to consume us instantly. It has herds of grazing creatures to eat first. When it gets hungry, it will take us."

"I fear that is so," the centaur agreed. "Yet there must be some way for smart or creative people to escape it. There is so much illusion here, maybe we could fool it."

"So far, it's been fooling us, not we it," Tandy said. "Unless we can wish away that wall—"

But Smash's Eye Queue had been cogitating on this problem, and now it regurgitated a notion—the one he had flirted with before. "If we could escape into another world, one with different rules—"

"Such as what?" Chem asked, interested. "Have you got something on your hairy mind?"

"The hypnogourd."

"I don't like the gourd!" Tandy said instantly.

"And the fact is, even if we all entered the gourd, our bodies would remain right here," the centaur pointed out. "The gourd is a trap itself—but if we did get out of it, we'd still be in the Void. A trap within a trap."

"But the nightmares can go anywhere," Smash said. "Even to Mundania—and back."

"That's true," Tandy agreed. "They can go right through walls, and I think some can run on water. So I suppose they coud run through the Void, and out again. They're not ordinary mares. But they're very hard to catch and hard to ride, and the cost—" She smiled ruefully. "I happen to know."

"They would help us if the Night Stallion told them to," Smash said.

"Oh, I forgot!" Tandy exclaimed. "You still have to fight the Night Stallion! You sacrificed your soul for me—" She clouded up. "Oh, Smash, I owe you so much!"

The centaur nodded thoughtfully. "Smash placed his soul in jeopardy for you, Tandy. I can appreciate how that would affect you. But I'm not sure you interpret your debt correctly."

"I was locked into that horror, deprived of my soul!" Tandy said. "I had no hope at all. The lights had gone out on my horizon. Then he came and fought the bones and smashed things about and brought out my soul, and I lived again. I owe my everything to him. I should give back my soul—"

"No!" Smash cried, knowing that she could endure no worse horror than the loss of her soul again. "I promised to protect you, and I should have protected you from the gourd, instead of splashing in the lake. I'll fight this through myself."

Chem shook her head. "I do see the problem—for each of you. I wish I perceived the answers as clearly."

"I have to meet the Stallion anyway," Smash said. "So when I have conquered him, I'll ask him for some mares."

"That's so crazy it just might work!" Chem said. "But there's one detail you may have overlooked. We have no hypnogourds here."

"We'll use your map again," he said.

The centaur considered. "I must admit it worked for your Eye Queue replacement vine, and our situation is desperate enough so that anything's worth trying. But—"

"Replacement?" Tandy demanded.

"Chem will explain it to you while I'm in the gourd," Smash said. "Right now, let's use the map to locate a gourd patch."

The centaur projected her map and settled on a likely place for gourds while Tandy watched skeptically. Then the party went there, though the way took them deeper into the Void.

And there they were—several nice fat hypnogourds with ripe peepholes. Smash settled himself by the largest. "You girls get some rest," he advised. "This may take a while. Remember, I have to locate the Stallion first, then fight him, then round up the mares."

Tandy grabbed his hamhand in her two delicate little hands. "Oh, Smash—I wish I could help you, but I'm terrified to go into a gourd—"

"Don't go in a gourd!" Smash exclaimed. "Just stay close so you don't get walled off from me and can't bring me out in an emergency," he said gruffly.

"I will! I will!" Tandy's eyes were tear-bright. "Oh, Smash, are you strong enough? I shouldn't have hit you with that tantrum—"

"I like your tantrums. You just rest, and wait for the nightmares, by whatever route they come."

"I know I'll see nightmares," she said wanly.

Smash glanced at Chem. "Keep an eye on her," he said, disengaging his hand from Tandy's.

"I will," the centaur agreed.

Then Smash put his eye to the peephole.

Chapter 13

Souls Alive

He found himself emerging from the cakewalk onto a vast empty stage. He landed gently. There was no vomit. There was a new scene.

The floor was metal-hard and highly polished; his feet left smudge marks where they touched. The air was half lit by a glow that seemed inherent. There was nothing else.

Smash peered about. It occurred to him that if the Night Stallion were here, he could spend a long time looking, as this place seemed infinitely extensive. He had to narrow its compass, somehow.

Well, he knew how to do that. He started tromping, unreeling his string behind him. He would crisscross this region for as long and as far as it took him.

Smash advanced. The string became a long line, disappearing in the distance behind. It divided the plain into two sections.

This could take even more time than he had judged, he realized. Since the girls were waiting outside the gourd in the Void and would not be able to go in search of food or water, he wanted to get on with it quickly. So he needed some way to speed things up.

He cudgeled his Eye Queue again. How could he most efficiently locate a creature that didn't want to be located?

Answer: what about following its trail?

He applied his eye to the floor. Now that he concentrated, he saw the hoofprints. They crossed his projected line, coming from the right rear and proceeding to the left front. There would be no problem following that!

But his curse, in its annoying fashion, caused him to question the simplicity of this procedure. The hoofprints were suspiciously convenient, crossing his line just at the point he thought to look, almost as if they were intended to be seen. He knew that tracking a creature was not necessarily simple, even when the prints were clear. The trail could meander aimlessly, looping about, getting lost in bad terrain. It could become dangerous if the quarry knew it was being tracked—and the Dark Horse surely did know. There could be tricks and ambushes.

No, there was no sense playing the game of the Night Stallion. The trail was not to be trusted. It was something set up to delude an ordinary ogre. Better to force the Stallion to play Smash's game—and if the Horse did not know of Smash's hidden asset of intelligence, that could be a counter ambush. A smart ogre was quite different from a stupid one.

Smash stomped on, following his straight line, halving the territory. This should also restrict the range of the Stallion, since it could not go any place Smash had already looked—as he understood the rules of this quest—and therefore could not cross the line.

Yet the territory still seemed to be infinitely large. He might tromp forever and never come to the far side. For that matter, he hadn't started at the near side, either; he had simply appeared within the range and begun there. He also realized that halving the total territory did not necessarily cut the area remaining to be searched. Half of infinity remained infinity. Also, unless he knew which half the Stallion was in, he had gained nothing; he could spend all his time searching in the wrong half, his failure guaranteed.

Smash pondered. His Eye Queue was really straining now, and probably the eyeballs of it were getting hot in their effort to see the way through infinity. One thing he had to say for the curse: it certainly tried to help him. It never really opposed its will to his own; it sought instead to call his attention to new aspects of any situation encountered, and to provide more effective ways of dealing with problems. He had discovered how useful that was when he had tried to function without its aid. Now he needed it again. How could he figure out a sure, fast way to proceed?

The vine came up with a notion.

Smash put the ball of string into his mouth and bit it in half. He now had two balls, each smaller than the first but magically complete. He took the first and rolled it violently forward.

The ball zoomed straight on, unrolling, leaving its straight line of string. Since it had an infinite length, it would proceed to the infinite end of the plain. Infinity could be compassed by infinity; even an ordinary ogre might grasp that! This process would complete the halving of the Stallion's range.

Now Smash set his ear to the floor and listened. Yes—his keen ogre hearing heard a faint hoofbeat in the distance, to the forward right. The Stallion was up there somewhere, moving clear of the rolling string. Now Smash had the creature partially located. He had done something unexpected, forced his opponent to react, and gained a small advantage.

Smash bit the remaining ball in half and shaped the halves into new balls. He hurled one to the east, establishing a pie-section configuration that trapped the Stallion inside. Then he listened again, determining in what quadrant the creature lurked, and pitched another half-ball in a curve. This wound grandly around behind the Stallion's estimated location, cutting off its retreat. For, though Smash had not tromped personally wherever the string went, the string remained his agent and surely counted. He was using a sort of leverage, and the Horse could not cross his demarcation, lest the animal break its own rule of being only in the last place Smash looked.

He put his ear to the floor again. The beat of hooves had ceased. The Stallion had either gotten away or stopped running. Since the former meant a loss for Smash, he did the expedient thing and decided on the latter. He had at last confined his target!

Smash stomped into the string-defined quadrant. If the Stallion were here, as he had to be, he would soon be found.

In due course Smash spied a blotch on the horizon. He stomped closer, alert for some ruse. The blotch grew as he approached it, in the manner that distant objects did, since they did not like to appear small from up close. It took the form of an animal, perhaps a lion. A lion? Smash didn't want that! He refused to have a mundane monster foisted off on him in lieu of his object. "If it's a lion, it's a Stallion!" he muttered—and of course as he said it, it was true. A single, timely word could make a big difference.

It was a huge, standing, wingless horse, midnight black of hide, with eyes that glinted black, too. This was surely the Night Stallion—the creature he had come to settle with, the ruler of the nightmare world.

Smash stomped to a halt before the creature. He stood taller than it, but the animal was more massive. "I am Smash the Ogre," he said. "Who are you?" For it was best to be quite certain, in a case like this.

The creature merely stood there. Now Smash saw that there was a plaque set up at its forefeet, and the plaque said: TROJAN.

"Well, Trojan Horse," Smash said, "I have come to redeem the lien on my soul."

He had expected the animal to charge and attack, but it did not move or respond. It might as well have been a statue.

"How do I do this?" Smash demanded.

Still no response. Evidently the creature was sulking, angry because he had caught it.

Smash peered more closely at the Stallion. It certainly seemed frozen! He tromped forward and put out a hamhand to touch it.

The body was metal-cold and hard. It was indeed a statue.

Had he, after all, located the wrong thing? That would mean he had been deceived by a decoy and would have to do his search all over again. Smash didn't like this notion, so he rejected it.

He looked at the floor. Behind the statue were hoofprints. The thing might be frozen now, but it had not always been. Probably its present stasis was merely another device to interfere with Smash's quest. This was one devious beast!

Well, there was one way to take care of that. He stood before the Stallion and hoisted a hamfist. "Deal with me, animal, or I will break you into junk."

The midnight orbs seemed to glitter ominously. Trojan did not like being threatened!

Smash found himself alone, on a lofty, windy, rainswept pinnacle.

He looked around. The top ledge was just about big enough for him to stretch out on, but almost featureless. The flat, slick rock terminated abruptly at the edge, plunging straight down to a smashing ocean far below. There were no plants, no food, no structures of any kind—just the tug of the wind and the roar of the ocean beneath.

The Night Stallion had done this, of course. It had spelled him to this desolate confinement, getting rid of him. So much for fair combat.

The storm swirled closer. Storms really liked to get a person stranded in a situation like this! A bolt of lightning crackled down, striking the pinnacle. A section of rock peeled off in a shower of sparks and collapsed, falling with seeming slowness to the distant water.

Smash stood at the steaming brink and watched the tiny splash. The rock had been a fair chunk, massive, yet from this vantage it looked like a pebble.

This was a really nice vacation spot for an ogre. But he didn't want a vacation; he wanted to fight Trojan. How could he get back into the action?

Now his perch was too small to stretch out on. About a quarter of it had fallen. The wind intensified, taking hold of his fur, trying to move him off. He wanted to travel, but not precisely this way! What kind of a splash would he make?

Rain splatted in passing sheets, making the surface doubly slick. The water coursed around his feet, digging under his calloused toes, trying to pry him from the rock so that he would be carried with it as it flowed over the brink in a troubled waterfall. Such a drop did not hurt water, but his own flesh might be less fortunate.

A huge wave surged forward, below, taking dead aim at the base of the rock column. The wave smashed in—and the entire column trembled. More layers of stone peeled and fell. For a moment Smash thought the whole thing was coming down, but about half of it withstood the violence and held its form. However, it was obvious that this perch would not endure much longer.

Smash considered. If he stood here, the column would soon collapse, dropping him into the ravenous ocean. He was an ogre, true, but he lacked his full strength; he would probably be crushed between the tumbling rocks in the water. If he tried to climb down, much of the same thing would happen; the column would collapse before he got below. Ogres were tough, but the forces of nature operating here were overwhelming; he had no realistic chance.

He saw that the ocean waves developed only as they got close to the tower. His Eye Queue concluded that this meant the water was much deeper away from this structure, because deep water didn't like to rouse itself from its stillness. That meant that region was safe to plunge into.

Good enough. He hated to leave this pleasant spire, but discretion urged the move. He leaped off the brink, sailing out in a clumsy swan dive toward the deep water.

Then he remembered he couldn't swim very well. In a calm lake he was all right; in a raging torrent he tended to drown.

He eyed the looming ocean, surging deep and dark. It was no mere torrent; it was an elemental monster. He had no chance at all. Too bad.

He faced the horse-statue. There was no tower, no ocean. It had all been a magic vision. A test, perhaps, or a warning. Obviously he had wiped out. He felt weak; he must have lost a chunk of his soul.

But now he knew how it worked. The Night Stallion did not fight physically; the creature simply threw turbulent visions at him, the way Tandy threw tantrums and cursefiends threw curses. The ocean tower had been sort of fun. So were those tantrums, he realized; when Tandy hit him with one of them . . . But that was nothing to speculate on right now.

"Try it again, horseface!" he grunted. "I still want my soul back."

The Stallion's dark eyes flashed malignantly.

And Smash stood in the center of a den of Mundane lions—real lions this time, not stal-lions or ant-lions. He felt abruptly weaker; this must be a Mundane scene, beyond the region of magic, so that his magic strength was gone.

The lions snarled like mammalian dragons, lashed their tufted yellow tails, and stalked him. There were six of them: a male, four females, and a cub. The females seemed to be the most aggressive. They began sniffing him, trying to determine how dangerous he might be and how edible.

Ordinarily, Smash would have liked nothing better than to mix with a new crowd of monsters in sublime mayhem. Ogres lived for the joy of bloody battle. But two things militated against his natural inclination—his Eye Queue and his weakness. According to the pusillanimous counsel of the first, it was best to avoid combat when the outcome was uncertain; and according to the second, the outcome was highly uncertain. He would do better, his cowardly intelligence informed him, to flee immediately.

But two things were wrong with that course. There was no place to flee to, because he was in a walled arena with wire mesh over the top, so he could not escape, and the lions had him surrounded anyway. He would have to fight unless he could bluff them.

He tried the bluff. He raised his hamfists, though they were unprotected by his centaur gauntlets, and bellowed defiance. This was a stance that would frighten almost any creature of Xanth.

But the lions were not creatures of Xanth. They were from Missouri, Mundania. They had to be shown. They pounced.

Ordinarily, Smash would have been able to mince the mere six monsters with so many blows of fists, feet, and head. But with his strength reduced to Mundane normal, all he could handle was one. While he was pulping that one, the other five were chomping him.

In a moment they had bitten through the hamstring tendons of his arms and legs, making his hamhands and hamfeet useless. They chomped through the nerve channel of his neck, making his head slightly less functional than before. He was now mostly helpless. He could feel, but could not move.

Then they gnawed at him, taking their time, one female on each extremity, the male clawing out his belly for the tasty guts. The pulped cub roused itself enough to commence work on Smash's nose, biting off small bites so as not to choke on its meal. It hurt horribly as the monsters chewed off his hands and feet and delved for his kidneys, and it wasn't much fun when the cub scooped out an eyeball, but Smash didn't scream. Noise seemed pointless at this point. Anyway, it was hard to scream properly when his tongue was gone and his lungs were being chewed out. He knew that when the beasts got to his vital organs, sensation would end, so he waited.

But the lions were sated before then, for Smash was a lot of creature. They left him, delimbed and eviscerated, and piled themselves up for a family snooze. Now the flies appeared, settling in swarms, and every bite was a new agony. The sun shone down through the mesh, cooking him, blazing into his other eye, which paralysis prevented him from closing. Soon he was agonizingly blind. But he still felt the flies crawling up his nose, looking for new places to bite and lay their maggots. It was going, he knew, to be an exceedingly long haul.

How had he gotten himself into this fix? By challenging the Night Stallion to recover his soul and to obtain help to rescue Tandy and Chem from the Void. Was it worth it? No, because he had not succeeded. Would he try it again? Yes, because he still wanted to help his friends, no matter how much pain came.

* * *

He was back before Trojan, whole of limb and gut and eye. It had been another test case, and obviously he had lost that one, too. He should have found some way to destroy the lions, instead of letting them destroy him. But it seemed he still had most of his soul, and perhaps the third trial would enable him to win the rest of it back.

"I'm still game, master of nightmares," he informed the somber statue.

Again the eyes flashed cruelly. This creature of night had no sympathy and no mercy!

Smash was standing at the base of a mountain of rocks.

"Help!" someone cried. It sounded like Tandy.

How had she gotten here? Had she disobeyed his instruction and entered the gourd, following his string to locate him? Foolish girl! Smash looked about, but found no one.

"Help!" she cried again. "I'm under the mountain!"

Smash was horrified. He had to get her out! There was no passage, so he started lifting and hurling away the boulders. He had most of his strength now, despite his prior losses, so this was easy enough.

But there were many boulders, and somehow Tandy's voice always came from under the highest remaining pile. Smash was making progress leveling the mountain, but still had far to go. He was tiring.

Gradually the pile of rocks behind him loomed higher than the pile before, but the cries continued to come from beneath. How had she gotten herself in so deep? He no longer had the strength to hurl the boulders away, but had to carry them with great effort. Then he could no longer lift them, and had to roll them.

At last the mountain had been moved, and the ground was level. But now the voice came from deep below. This was, in fact, a pit the size of an inverted mountain, filled with more boulders—and Tandy was at the bottom.

His body was numb with fatigue. It was a labor just to move himself now. In this respect his agony was worse than it had been in the lions' den, for there all he had to do was lie still and wait. Now he had to cudgel his reluctant muscles to perform, inflicting the torture of exertion on himself. But he kept going, for the job remained to be done. He shoved and heaved and slowly rolled the boulders out.

The deeper he got, the worse the chore became, for now he had to shove the boulders up out of the deepening pit. Still her voice cried despairingly from below. Smash staggered. A boulder slipped from his falling grasp and rolled down to the lowest point. He lumbered after it, hearing her faint sobs. She seemed to be fading as fast as he was!

But his strength had been exhausted. He could no longer move the boulder far enough, strain as he might. Still trying, he collapsed, and the big stone rolled over him.

* * *

Again he faced the Night Stallion, his strength miraculously restored. He realized that Tandy had never been there in the vision, only her voice, used to goad him into an impossible effort.

"I'm still going to save my soul and my friends," Smash said, though he dreaded whatever the Dark Horse would throw at him next. Tandy might not have been literally below that mountain of rocks, but his success in these endeavors had a direct bearing on her fate, so it was the same thing. "Trojan, do your worst."

The evil eyes flashed horrendously, darkening the entire area.

Smash was in a compound with assorted other creatures. It was a miserable place, stinking of poverty, doom, and despair. Jets of bright fire shot from cracks in the ground, preventing escape. Harpies and other carrion birds wheeled above, watching for food.

"Slop time!" a guard called, and dumped a pail of garbage into the compound. A gnome, an elf, and a wyvern pounced on the foul refuse. But before they got more than a few stinking scraps, the harpies swooped down in a squadron and snatched it all away, leaving only a pile of defecation in its place. The prisoners squabbled among themselves in angry frustration. Smash saw that all were emaciated; they had not been getting enough food. Small wonder, with those harpies hovering!

What was to be his torture this time? For Smash realized now that these scenes were supposed to be extremely unpleasant, even for an ogre; each was awful in a different way. As he considered, the sun moved rapidly across the pale sky, as if time were accelerating, for normally nothing could prevail on the sun to hurry its pace one bit. Smash's hunger accelerated, too; it took a lot of food to maintain a healthy ogre.

"Slops!" the guard called, and dumped the pail. There was another scramble, but the wyvern wasn't in it. That noble little dragon was now too far gone to scramble. In any event, the harpies got most of the slop again. Smash felt a pang; even garbage looked good now, and he had gotten none. Of course he wouldn't touch anything a harpy had been near, anyway; they spoiled ten times as much as they ate, coating their discards with poisonous refuse. Harpies were the world's dirtiest birds; in fact, real birds refused to associate with these witch-headed monsters.

The wyvern belched out a feeble wisp of fire and collapsed. Smash crossed over to it, moved by un-ogrish compassion. "Anything I can do for you?" he asked. After all, it took one monster to understand another. But the wyvern merely expired.

Immediately the other prisoners converged, working up what slaver they could; dragon meat was a lot better than starvation. Affronted by the notion of such a fine fighting animal being consumed so indelicately, Smash hefted a fist, ready to defend the body. But the vultures descended in a swarm, gouging the corpse to pieces from every side so swiftly that Smash could do nothing; in moments, nothing but bones was left. His efforts, perhaps pointless from the beginning, had been wasted. Smash returned to his place.

The sun plopped behind a distant mountain, throwing up a small shower of debris that colored the clouds briefly in that vicinity. It really ought, he thought, to be more careful where it landed! The stars blinked on, some more alertly than others. The nocturnal heavens spun by, making short work of the night.

By morning Smash was ravenous. So were his surviving companions. They eyed one another covertly, judging when one or the other might be unable to defend himself from consumption. When the guard came with the slops, the gnome stumbled forward. "Food! Food!" he croaked.

The guard paused, eying the gnome cynically. "Are you ready to pay?"

"I'll pay! I'll pay!" the gnome agreed with uncomfortably guilty eagerness.

The guard reached through the bars of fire and into the gnome's body. He hauled out the gnome's struggling soul, an emaciated and bedraggled thing that slowly coalesced into a pallid sphere. The guard inspected it briefly to make certain it was all there, then crammed it indifferently into a dirty bag. Then he set the pail of slop down and waved the hovering harpies away. They screamed epithets of protest, but obeyed. One, however, so far lost control of herself as to loop down close to the tantalizing garbage. The guard's eyes glinted darkly, and the harpy screeched in sudden terror and pumped back into the dingy sky, dropping several greasy feathers in her haste. Smash wondered what it was that had so cowed her, for harpies had little respect for anything and the guard was an ordinary human being, or reasonable facismile thereof.

The gnome plunged his head into the bucket and greedily slurped the glop. He guzzled spoiled milk, gulped apple and onion peels, and crunched on eggshells and coffee grounds in a paroxysm of satiation. He had his food now; he had paid for it.

The guard turned to gaze at Smash. There was a malignant glitter in the man's eye. Smash realized that he was, in fact, an aspect of the Night Stallion, on his rounds collecting more souls.

Now Smash understood the nature of this trial. He resolved not to purchase his sustenance at that price. If he lost his soul here, he lost it everywhere, and would not be able to help Chem and Tandy escape. But he knew that this would be the most difficult contest yet; each time the Stallion came, Smash would be hungrier, and the pail of slops would lure him more strongly. How could he be sure he would hold out when starvation melted his muscles and deprived him of willpower? This was not a single effort to be made and settled one way or the other; this was a dragging-out siege against his hunger—and the hunger of an ogre was more terrible than his strength.

The sun shoved rapidly across the welkin, looking somewhat undernourished and irritated itself. It kicked innocent clouds out of the way, burning one, so that the cloud lost continence and watered on the ground below. It was an evil day, and Smash's hunger intensified. He had to escape before he succumbed.

He got up, dusted off his bedraggled and filthy hide, and approached the burning barrier. These jets were unlike those of the firewall in Xanth or the jets of the Region of Fire, for they were thicker and hotter than the first and steadier than the second. But perhaps he could cross them. Certainly he had to try.

He held his breath, closed his eyes and charged across the barrier of flames. After all, he had done this in the real world; he could survive a little additional scorching.

He felt the sudden, searing heat. His fur curled and frizzled. This was worse than he had anticipated; his hunger-weakened body was more sensitive to pain, not less. Then the fire passed. He screeched to a halt on singed toes and opened his clenched eyelids.

He was in the prison chamber, the bars of flame behind him. He had blackened stripes along his fur, and his skin smarted—but it seemed he had gotten turned about. What a mistake!

He turned, gulped more air, screwed his orbs shut again, and leaped through the burning bars. Again the pain flared awfully. This time he knew he hadn't turned; he had been in midair as he crossed the flame.

But as he unscrewed his vision, blinking away the smoke from his own eyelashes, he found himself still in the cell. Apparently it was not all that easy to escape. He had to go by the rules of the scene.

Nevertheless, he readied himself for a third try, because an ogre never knew when to quit. But as he oriented on the bars, he saw the guard standing just beyond them, with a glittering gaze. Suddenly he did know when to quit; he turned about and went back to his original spot in the compound and squatted there like a good prisoner. He didn't want to go near the Dark Horse until this struggle was over.

The sun plunged. Another poor creature yielded his vital soul to the Stallion in payment for food. Two more perished of starvation. Smash's firewounds festered, and his fur fell out in stripes. His belly swelled as his limbs shriveled. He became too weak to stand; he sat cross-legged, head hanging forward, contemplating the tendons that showed in high relief on his thighs where the hair had fallen out. He did not ask for food, though he was now being consumed by his own hunger. He knew the price.

Slowly, while the days and nights raced across the sky, he starved. He realized, as he sank into the final stupor, that when he died, the Stallion would have his soul anyway. Somehow he had misplaced this one, too.

Once more he stood before the Stallion statue. Still he had some of his soul, and would not yield. Apparently there was a limit to how much of a soul could be taken as penalty for each loss, and ogres were ornery creatures. "I'll fight for my soul as long as any of it remains to fight for," Smash declared. "Bring on your next horror, equine."

The eyes glinted. Then the Night Stallion moved, coming alive. "You have fought well, ogre," it said, speaking without difficulty through its horse's mouth. "You have won every challenge."

This was completely unexpected. "But I died each time!"

"Without ever deviating from your purpose. You were subjected to the challenge of fear, but you evinced no fear—"

"Well, ogres don't know what that is," Smash said.

"And to the challenge of pain, but you did not capitulate—"

"Ogres don't know how," Smash admitted.

"And to the challenge of fatigue—"

"How could I stop when I thought my friend was caught?"

"And to the challenge of hunger."

"That was a bad one," Smash acknowledged. "But the price was too high." His Eye Queue curse had made him aware of the significance of the price; otherwise he almost certainly would have succumbed.

"And so you blundered through, allowing nothing to sway you, and thus vacated the lien on four-fifths of your soul. Only one more test remains—but on this one depends all that you have gained so far. You will win your whole soul here—or lose it."

"Send me to that test," Smash said resolutely.

The Stallion's eye flickered intensely, but the scene did not change. "Why did you accept the lien on your soul?" the creature asked.

Smash's Eye Queue warned him that the eye-flicker meant he had been projected to another vision and was being tested. Since the scene had not changed, this must be a different sort of test from the others. Beware!

"To save the soul of my friend, whom I had promised to protect," Smash said carefully. "I thought you knew that. It was your minion of the coffin who cheated her out of it."

"What kind of fool would place the welfare of another before his own?" the Horse demanded, ignoring Smash's remark.

Smash shrugged, embarrassed. "I never claimed to be other than a fool. Ogres are very strong and very stupid."

The Stallion snorted. "If you expect me to believe your implication, you think *I'm* a fool! I know most ogres are stupid, but you are not. Why is that?"

Unfortunately, ogres were not much given to lying; it was part of their stupidity. Smash had been directly asked; he would have to answer. "I am cursed with the Eye Queue. The vine makes me much smarter than I should be and imbues me with aspects of conscience, aesthetic awareness, and human sensitivity. I would rid myself of it if I could, but I need the intelligence in order to help my friends."

"Fool!" the Stallion roared. "The Eye Queue curse is an illusion!"

"Everything in the gourd and in the Void is illusion of one sort or another," Smash countered. "Much of Xanth is illusion, and perhaps Mundania, too. It might be that if we could only see the ultimate reality, Xanth itself would not exist. But while I exist in it, or think I do, I will honor the rules of illusion as I do those of reality, and draw on the powers my illusory Eye Queue provides as I do on those my real ogre strength provides."

The Stallion paused. "That was not precisely what I meant, but perhaps it is a sufficient answer. Obviously your own intelligence is no illusion. But were you not aware that the effect of the Eye Queue vine is temporary? That it wears off in a few hours at most, and in many cases provides, not true intelligence, but a vain illusion of it that causes the recipient to make a genuine fool of himself, the laughingstock of all who perceive his self-delusion?"

Smash realized that the creature was indeed testing him another way—and an intellectual test was most treacherous for an ogre. "I was not aware of that," he admitted. "Perhaps my companions were too kind to think of me in that way. But I believe my intelligence is real, for it has helped me solve many problems no ordinary ogre could handle, and has broadened my horizons immeasurably. If this be illusion, it is tolerable. Certainly it lasted me many days without fading. Perhaps it works better on ogres, who can hardly be rendered more foolish than they naturally are."

"You are quite correct. You are no ordinary ogre and you are smart enough to give me a considerable challenge. Most creatures who place their souls in peril do so for far less charitable reasons. But, of course, you are only half-ogre."

Naturally the Lord of Nightmares knew all about him! Smash refused to lose his temper, for that surely was what the Stallion wanted. Lose temper, lose soul! "I am what I am. An ogre."

The Stallion nodded as if discovering a weakness in Smash's armor. He was up to something; Smash could tell by the way he swished his tail in the absence of flies. "An ogre with the wit and conscience of a man. One who makes the Eye Queue vine work beyond its capacities, and makes it work again even when the vine itself is illusory. One who maintains a loyalty to his responsibilities and associates that others would fain define as entirely human."

"I also made the gourd work in the Void, when it was illusory," Smash pointed out. "If you seek to undermine my enhanced intelligence by pointing out that it has no basis, you must also concede that your testing of me has no basis."

"That was not precisely my thrust. Similar situations may have differing interpretations." He snorted, clearing his long throat. "You have mastered the four challenges without fault and are now entitled to assume the role of Master of Challenges. I shall retire from the office; you shall be the Night Ogre."

"The Night Ogre?" Smash, despite the Eye Queue, was having trouble grasping this.

"You will send the bad images out with your night ogresses and collect the souls of those who yield them. You will be Master of the Gourd. The powers of the night will be yours."

"I don't want the powers of the night!" Smash protested. "I just want to rescue my friends."

"With the powers of the night, you can save them," the Stallion pointed out. "You will be able to direct your night creatures to bear them sleeping from the Void to the safety of the ordinary Xanth jungle."

But Smash's Eye Queue, illusory though it might be, interfered with this promising solution. "Would I get to return to the world of the day myself?"

"The Master of Night has no need to visit the day!"

"So you are prisoner of the night yourself," Smash said. "You may capture the souls of others, but your own is hostage."

"I can go to the day!" the Stallion protested.

Again the Eye Queue looked the horse's gift in the mouth. It was full of dragon's teeth. "Only if you collect enough souls to pay your way. How many does it take for an hour of day? A dozen? A hundred?"

"There is another way," the Stallion said uncomfortably.

"Surely so. If you arrange a replacement for yourself," Smash said. "Someone steadfast enough to do the job according to the rules, no matter how unpleasant or painful or tedious it becomes. Someone whom power does not corrupt."

The Dark Horse was silent.

"Why is it necessary to send bad dreams to people?" Smash asked. "Is this only a means to jog them from their souls?"

"It has a loftier rationale than that," the Stallion replied somewhat stiffly. "If no one ever suffered the pangs of conscience or regret, evil would prosper without hindrance and eventually take over the world. Evil can be the sweet sugar of the soul, temptingly pleasant in small doses, but inevitably corrupting. The bad dreams are the realizations of the consequence of evil, a timely warning that all thinking creatures require. The nightmares guard constantly against spiritual degradation—that same corruption you have withstood. Take the position, ogre; you have earned it."

"I wish I could help you," Smash said. "But my life is outside the gourd, in the jungles of Xanth. I am a simple forest creature. I must help my friends survive the wilderness in my own fashion, and not aspire to be more than any ogre was ever destined to be."

The Stallion's eyes dimmed. "You have navigated the final challenge. You have avoided the ultimate temptation of power. You are free to return to Xanth with your soul intact. The lien is voided."

Suddenly Smash felt completely strong again, his soul restored. "But I need help," he said. "I must borrow three of your nightmares to carry my party out of the Void."

"Nightmares are not beasts of burden!" the Stallion protested, scraping the ground with a forehoof. It seemed this creature, if not actually piqued by Smash's refusal to take over the proffered office, was still less cooperative than he might have been. When one scorned an offer of any nature, one had to bear the penalty.

"The nightmares alone can travel anywhere, even out of the Void," Smash said, knowing he had to find some way to gain the assistance he needed. "Only you can help us."

"They could if they chose to," the Horse agreed. "But their fee is half a soul for each person carried."

"Half my soul!" Smash exclaimed. "I don't have enough for three!"

"Half *a* soul, not necessarily your own. But it is true you do not have enough. Nightmare rides come steep."

Smash realized that he was right back in the dilemma he thought he had escaped. He had placed his soul in jeopardy to rescue Tandy from the gourd; now he would have to do it again to rescue Tandy and Chem from the Void. But if he rescued both, he himself would be lost, for the Eye Queue informed him that two halves of a soul amounted to the whole soul.

Of course, he could rescue only Tandy, the one he had agreed to protect. But he could not see his way clear to leave Chem in the Void. She was a nice creature with a worthy mission. She did not deserve to be deserted. And he had more or less agreed to protect her, too, when her brother Chet had delivered her to him at the brink of the Gap Chasm. "I will pay the price," he said, thinking of the gnome begging for slops.

"Do you realize that you could rescue them and retain your soul by becoming the Master of Night?" the Stallion asked.

"I fear I must go to hell in my own fashion," Smash said regretfully. The Horse obviously thought him a smart fool, and his Eye Queue heartily endorsed the sentiment, but somehow his fundamental ogre nature shied away from the responsibility for damning others. Better to be one of the damned.

"Even in sacrifice, you are ogrishly stupid," the Stallion remarked with disgust. "You are obviously unfit for duty here."

"Agreed," Smash agreed.

"Go negotiate directly with the mares," the Horse snorted. "I'll have no part of this." His eyes flared with their black light.

Then Smash found himself on the plain of the mares. The dark herd charged toward him, circling him in moments, as was their wont. Then they recognized him and hesitated.

"I need two of you to carry my friends to safety," he said. "I know the price."

"Naaaay!" one cried. Smash recognized her as the one he had tried to befriend, the one who had carried Tandy to the Good Magician's castle. That had been involuntary, without a fee—until the coffin had claimed a double fee retroactively. Obviously none of that payment had gone to the mare; it had been a gyp deal all around. But she certainly knew how to carry a person. He was sorry he had not been able to figure out what she wanted from Xanth.

"I must rescue Tandy and Chem," Smash said. "I will pay the fee. Who will make the deal?"

Two other mares volunteered. Smash wasn't sure what use they would have for the halves of his soul, but that was not much of his business. Maybe half souls were bartering currency within the gourd, accounting for status in the nightmare hierarchy. "S.O.D.," he said, cautioned by his Eye Queue. "Soul on Delivery."

They nodded, agreeing. "Can you find them?" he asked. When they nodded naaay, he realized he would have to go with them, at least to where the girls were. "Well, we'd better introduce ourselves," he said. "I am Smash the Ogre. How shall I know the two of you?"

One of the two struck the ground with a forehoof. She left a circular impression in the dirt, with little ridges, dark spots, and pockmarks. Smash peered at it closely, struck by a nagging familiarity. Where had he seen a configuration like that before? Then he grasped it; this was like a map of the moon, with the pocks like the cheese holes. One of the dark areas was highlighted, and he saw that there was lettering on it: MARE CRISIUM.

"So you're the mare Crisium," he said, making the connection. "Mind if I call you Crisis?"

She shrugged acquiescently. Smash turned to the other. "And who are you?"

The other stomped a forehoof. Her moon-map was high-lighted in another place: MARE VAPORUM.

"And you're the mare Vaporum," he said. "I'll call you Vapor."

The befriended mare now came forward, nickering, offering to carry him. "But I have no soul left over to pay you," he protested. "Besides, you're far too small to handle a monster like me."

She walked under him—and suddenly he found that he had shrunk or she had grown, for now he was riding her comfortably. It seemed nightmares had no firmly fixed size.

"Then tell me your name, too," he said. "You are doing me an unpaid favor, and I want to know you, in case I should ever be able to repay it. I never did discover what you wanted from Xanth, you know."

She stamped her hoof. He leaned down over her shoulder, hanging on to her slick black mane that flowed like a waterfall, until he was able to read her map. It was high-lighted at a large patch labeled: MARE IMBRIUM.

"You I will call Imbri," he decided. "Because I don't know what your name means."

The three mares galloped across the plain, leaving the herd behind. Little maps of the moon formed the trail wherever their feet touched. It made him hungry to think about it. Too bad the maps weren't real, with genuine cheese!

Soon they passed through a greenish wall and out into the Void. It was the rind of the gourd, Smash realized. They were large and the gourd was small—but somehow it all related. He kept trying to forget that size and mass hardly mattered when magic was involved.

They looped once around—and there was the brute ogre, staring into the gourd's peephole. Until this moment, Smash had not quite realized that his body had not accompanied him inside. He had known it, of course, but never truly *realized* it. Even his Eye Queue had never come to grips with the seeming paradox of being in two places at the same time.

Then he spied Tandy and Chem. They were asleep; it was night, of course, the only time the nightmares could go abroad.

"We'll have to wake them," Smash said, then paused. "No—a person has to be asleep to ride a nightmare; I remember now. Or disembodied, like me. I'm really asleep, too. I'll put them on you asleep." He dismounted and went to pick Tandy up.

But his hands passed right through her. He had no physical substance.

He pondered. "I'll have to wake myself up," he decided. "Since my soul is forfeit anyway, I should be able to stay near the nightmares. They aren't going to depart before they get their payment." It was a rather painful kind of security, however.

He went to his body. What a hulking, brutish thing it was! The black fur was shaggy in some places, unkempt in others, and singed from his experiences with the firewall in yet others. The hamhands and hamfeet were huge and clumsy-looking. The face was simultaneously gravelly and mushy. No self-respecting creature would be attracted to the physical appearance of an ogre—and, of course, the monster's intellect was even worse. He was doing Tandy a favor by removing himself from her picture.

"Come on, ogre, you have work to do," he grunted, putting out a paw to shake his shoulder. But his hand passed through himself, too, and the body ignored him, exactly like the stupid thing it was.

"Enough of this nonsense, idiot!" he rasped. He put a hamfinger over the peephole. He might be insubstantial in this form, but he was visible. The finger cut off the view. The effect was similar to the removal of the gourd.

Suddenly Smash was back in his body, awake. The phantom self had vanished. It existed only when he peered into the gourd, when his mental self was apart from his physical self.

The three mares stood watching him warily. Ordinarily, they would have fled the presence of a waking person, but they realized that this was a special situation. He was about to become one of them.

"All right," he said quietly, so as not to wake the girls. "I'll set one girl on each of you volunteers. You carry them north, beyond the Void, and set them down safely. Then you split my soul between you. Fair enough?"

The two mares nodded. Smash went to lift Chem, gently. She weighed as much as he, but he had his full strength now and could readily handle her mass. He set her on Crisis. Chem was bigger than the mare, but again the fit was right, and the sleeping centaur straddled Crisis comfortably.

He lifted Tandy next. She was so small he could have raised her with one finger, as he had Blythe Brassie, but he used both hands. With infinite care he set her on Vapor.

Then he mounted his own mare, Imbri, who had come without the promise of payment. Again the fit was right; anybody could ride any nightmare, if the mare permitted it. "I wish I knew what you want from Xanth," he murmured. Then he remembered that this was irrelevant; he would not be returning to Xanth anyway, so could not fetch her anything.

They moved on through the Void, traveling north. This was the easy part, descending into the depths of the funnel, and Smash saw that the center of the Void was a black hole from which nothing returned, not even light. This the mares skirted; there were, after all, limits.

They galloped as swiftly as thought itself, the mares as dark as the awful dreams they fostered. Smash now had a fair understanding of the origin and rationale of those dreams; he did not envy the Dark Horse his job. If it was bad to experience the dreams, how much worse was it to manufacture them! The Stallion had the burden of the vision of evil for the whole world on his mind; no wonder he wanted to retire! What use was infinite power when it could be used only negatively?

They climbed the far slope of the funnel, leaving the brink of the dread black hole behind, unobstructed by the invisible wall, in whatever manner it existed. In another moment they were out of the Void and into the night of normal Xanth.

Smash felt a horrible weight departing his shoulders. He had saved them; he had gotten them out of the Void at last! How wonderful this normal Xanthian jungle seemed! He looked eagerly at it, knowing he could not stay, that his soul was now forfeit. The mares had delivered, and it was now his turn. Perhaps he would be allowed to visit this region on occasion, in bodiless form, just to renew the awareness of what he had lost, and to see how his friends were doing.

They halted safely beyond the line. Smash dismounted and lifted Chem to the ground, where she continued sleeping, feet curled under her, head lolling. She was a pretty creature of her kind, not as well developed as she would be at full maturity, but with a nice coat and delicate human features. He was glad he had saved her from the Void. Someday she would browbeat some male centaur into happiness, exactly as her mother had done. Centaurs were strong-willed creatures, but well worth knowing. "Farewell, friend," he murmured. "I have seen you safely through the worst of Xanth. I hope you are satisfied with your map."

Then he lifted Tandy. She was so small and delicate-seeming in her sleep! Her brown hair fell about her face in disarray, partly framing and partly concealing her features. He deeply regretted his inability to see her through her adventure. But he had made a commitment to the Good Magician Humfrey, and he was honoring that commitment in the only fashion he knew. He had seen Tandy through danger, and trusted she could do all right now on her own. She had fitted a lot of practical experience into this journey!

In a moment, he knew, he would not care about her at all, for caring was impossible without a soul. But in this instant he did care. He remembered how she had kissed him, and he liked the memory. Human ways were not ogre ways, of course, but perhaps they had a certain merit. Through her he had gleaned some faint inkling of an alternate way of life, where violence was secondary to feeling. It was no life for an ogre, of course—but somehow he could not resist returning the favor of that kiss now. He brought her to his face and touched her precious little lips with his own big crude ones.

Tandy woke instantly. The two mares jumped away, afraid of being seen by a waking person not of their domain. But they did not flee entirely, held by the incipient promise of his soul.

"Oh, Smash!" Tandy cried. "You're back! I was so worried, you stayed in the gourd so long, and Chem said she thought you weren't ready to be roused yet—"

Now he was in trouble. Yet he was obscurely glad. It was better to explain things to her so that she would not think he had deserted her. "You are free of the Void, Tandy. But I must leave you."

"Oh, no, Smash!" she protested. "Don't ever leave me!"

This was becoming rapidly more difficult. Separating from her was somewhat like departing the Void—subtly awkward. "The mares who carried you out of the Void, in your sleep—they have to be paid."

Her brow furrowed, in the cute way it had. "Paid how?"

He was afraid she wouldn't like this. But ogres weren't much for prevarication, even in a good cause. "My soul."

She screamed.

Chem bolted awake, snatching up the rope, and the mares retreated farther, switching their tails nervously. "What's the matter?"

"Smash sold his soul to free us!" Tandy cried, pointing an accusing finger at the ogre.

"He can't do that!" the centaur protested. "He went to the gourd to win back his soul!"

"It was the only way," Smash said. He gestured to the two mares. "I think it is time." He looked behind him, locating Imbri. "And if you will kindly carry my body back into the Void afterward, so it won't get in anyone's way out here—"

The three mares came forward. Tandy screamed again and threw her arms about Smash's neck. "No! No! Take my soul instead!"

The mares paused, uncertain of the proprieties. They meant no harm; they were only doing their job.

Tandy disengaged herself and dropped to the ground. Her dander was up. "My soul's almost as good as his, isn't it?" she said to the mares. "Take it and let him go." She advanced on Crisis. "I can't let him be taken. I love him!"

She surely did, for this was the most extreme sacrifice she could make. She was deathly afraid of the interior of the gourd. Smash understood this perfectly; that was why he couldn't let her go there. But if she refused to let him go in peace, what was he to do?

Chem interceded. "Just exactly what was the deal you made, Smash?"

"Half my soul for each person carried from the Void."

"But three were carried, weren't they?" the centaur asked, her fine human mind percolating as the fog of sleep dissipated. "That would mean one and a half souls."

"I am returning with the mares," Smash said. "I don't count. Imbri carried me as a favor; she's the one who carried Tandy to the Good Magician's castle a year ago. She's a good creature."

"I know she is!" Tandy agreed. "But—"

"Imbri?" Chem asked. "Is that an equine name?"

"Mare Imbrium," he clarified. "The nightmares come out only at night, so they never see the sun. They identify with places on the moon."

"Mare Imbrium," she repeated. "The Sea of Rains. Surely the raining of our tears."

So that was what the name meant; the education of the centaur had clarified it. Certainly it was appropriate! Imbri was reigning over, or reining in, the rain of tears. But it could be said in her favor that she had not done anything to cause those tears. She had charged no soul.

"Not *my* tears!" Tandy protested tearfully. "Smash, I won't let you go!"

"I have to go," Smash said gently. "Ogres aren't very pretty and they aren't very smart, but they do do what they agree to do. I agreed to see the two of you safely through the hazards of Xanth, and I agreed to parcel my soul between the two mares who delivered you from the Void."

"You have no right to sacrifice yourself again for us!" Chem cried. "Anyway, it won't work; we'll perish alone in the wilderness of northern Xanth."

"Well, it seemed better to get you to Xanth instead of the Void," Smash said awkwardly. Somehow the right he thought he was doing seemed less right, now. "Near the edge of Xanth the magic begins to fade, so it's less dangerous."

"Ha!" Tandy exclaimed. "I've heard the Mundane monsters are worse than the Xanth ones!"

"It may be less dangerous only if you accompany us," Chem said. She considered briefly. "But a deal's a deal; the mares must be paid."

"I'll pay them!" Tandy offered.

"No!" Smash cried. "The gourd is not for the like of you! It is better for the like of me."

"I don't think so," Chem said. "We have all had enough of the gourd, regardless of whether we've been inside it. But there are three of us. We can pay the mares and retain half a soul each. Three fares, so Smash can be free, too."

"But neither of you has to give any part of her soul for me!" Smash objected.

"You were doing it for us," the centaur said. "We can get along on half souls if we're careful. I understand they regenerate in time."

"Yes," Tandy said, grasping this notion as if being saved from drowning. "Each person can pay her own way." She turned to the nearest mare, who happened to be Crisis. "Take half my soul," she said.

Chem faced the second, Imbri. "Take half of mine."

The mare of Rains hesitated, for she had not expected to be rewarded, and she had not carried Chem.

"Take it!" the centaur insisted.

The mares, glad to have the matter resolved, galloped past their respective donors. Smash saw two souls attenuate between girls and mares; then each one tore in half, and the mares were gone.

Smash was left standing by the third mare, Vapor. He realized that he could not do less—and of course Vapor was supposed to have a half soul. In fact, she had been promised half of his. Now she would get it, though she had not carried him. "Take half of mine," he said.

Vapor charged him. There was a wrenching and tearing; then he stood reeling. Something awfully precious had been taken from him—but not all of it.

Then he saw the two girls standing similarly bemused, and he knew that something even more precious had been salvaged.

Chapter 14

Ogre Fun

I n the morning they woke, having suffered no bad dreams. The nightmares were not about to venture near them now, for that might give them the opportunity to change their minds about their souls. Also, what dreams could they be served, worse than what they had already experienced?

Xanth was lovely. The green trees glistened in the fading dew, and flowers opened. White clouds formed lazy patterns around the sun, daring it to burn them off, but it ignored their taunts. The air was fragrant. Mainly, it was a joy to be alive and free. Much more joy than it had been before Smash discovered that such things were by no means guaranteed. He had died in a great dark ocean, under the teeth of lions, under a rock he was too fatigued to move, and of starvation in prison. He had won back his soul, then given it up again. Now he was here with half his soul and he really appreciated what he had.

For some time they compared notes, each person needing reassurance because of the lingering ache of separated souls. But gradually they acclimated, finding that half a soul was indeed much better than none.

Smash tested his strength—and found it at half-level. He had to use both hands instead of one to crush a rock to sand. Until the other half of his soul regenerated, he would be only half an ogre in that respect. But this, too, seemed a reasonable price to pay for his freedom.

"I think it is time for me to go my own way," Chem said at last. "I think I have had about as much of this sort of adventure as I can handle. I have it all mapped; my survey is done. Now I need to organize the data and try to make sense of it."

"Magic doesn't have to make sense," Smash said rhetorically.

"But where will you go?" Tandy asked.

The centaur filly generated her map, with all of northern Xanth clearly laid out, their travel route neatly marked in a dotted line. "It is safe for my kind around the fringes of Xanth," she said. "Centaurs have traded all along the coasts. I'll trot west to the isthmus, then south to Castle Roogna. I'll have no trouble at all." Her projected route dotted its way down the length of northern Xanth confidently. She seemed to have forgotten her protestation of last night about how they would perish without Smash's protection, and Smash did not remind her of it. Obviously it had been his welfare, not her own, she had been concerned with.

"I suppose that's best," Tandy said reluctantly. "I really liked the company of all you other creatures, but your missions are not my mission. Just remember, you're not as strong as you should be."

"That's one reason I want to get on home," Chem said. "I'd recommend the same for both of you, but I know your destiny differs from mine. You have to go on to the Ogre-fen-Ogre Fen, Smash, and take what you find there, though I personally feel that's a mistake."

"Me make mistake?" Smash asked. The things of the Void had faded in the night, since they had left it, and now he found it easier to revert to his normal mode of speech. There was no hypnogourd and no Eye Queue vine, so he was not smart any more.

"Smash, you're half human," Chem said. "If you would only give your human side a chance—"

"Me no man, me ogre clan," he said firmly. That faith had brought him through the horrors of the gourd.

She sighed. "So you must be what you must be, and do what you must do. Tandy—" Chem shook her head. "I can't advise you. I hope you get what you want, somehow."

The two girls embraced tearfully. Then the centaur trotted away to the west, her pretty brown tail flying at half-mast as if reflecting the depressed state of her soul.

"I'm as foolish as you are," Tandy said, drying her eyes, so that the blue emerged again like little patches of sky. "Let's get on to the Fen before night, Smash."

They moved on. Smash, now so near his destination, found himself strangely uneasy. The Good Magician had told him he would find what he needed among the Ancestral Ogres; Humfrey had not said what that would be, or whether Smash would like it.

Suppose he didn't like what he needed? Suppose he hated it? Suppose it meant the denial of all that he had experienced on this journey with the seven girls? The Eye Queue had been a curse, and surely he was well rid of it—yet there had been a certain covert satisfaction in expressing himself as lucidly as any human being could. Facility of expression was power, too, just as was strength of muscle. The gourd had been a horror—yet that, too, had had its fine moments of exhilarating violence and deep revelation. These things were, of course, peripheral, no concern of a true ogre—but he had felt something fundamentally good in them.

He struggled through his annoying stupidity as he tromped on toward the Ogre Fen. Exactly what had made his journey so rewarding, despite its nuisances and problems? Not the violence, for he could have that any time by challenging stray dragons. Not the intelligence, for that was no part of an ogre's heritage. Not the exploration of the central mysteries of Xanth, for ogres were not very curious about geography. What, then?

As the day faded and the sun hurried down to the horizon so as not to be caught by night, Smash finally broke through to a conclusion. It wasn't a very original one, for ogres weren't very original creatures, but it would do. He had valued the camaraderie. The seven girls had needed him, and had treated him like a person. His long association with the human beings and centaurs of Castle Roogna had acclimated him to company, but this time he had had the wit to appreciate it more fully, because of the Eye Queue curse. Now he was cursed with the memory of what could not be again. Camaraderie was not the ogre way.

At dusk they reached the dismal fringe of the Ogre-fen-Ogre Fen. The swampy marsh stretched out to the east and north as far as the eyeball could peer, riddled with green gators and brown possums and other half-fanciful denizens. Were the Ancestral Ogres also here?

"Look!" Tandy cried, pointing.

Smash looked. There were three ironwood trees braided together. That was a sure signal of the presence of ogres, since no other creature could do such a thing.

"I guess you'll get what you want tomorrow," Tandy said. "You'll meet your tribe." She seemed sad.

"Yes, me agree," he said, somehow not as overjoyed as he thought he should be. His mission was about to terminate; that was what he wanted, wasn't it?

He twisted a coppertree into the semblance of a shelter for her and spread a large leaf from a table tree over it. In the heyday of his strength he could have done better, but this would have to do for tonight. But it didn't matter; Tandy didn't use it. She curled up against his furry shoulder and slept.

What was her destiny? he wondered before he crashed into his own heavy slumber. He now understood that she was looking for a human husband and was destined to find one on this journey—but time was running out for her, too. He hoped whoever she found would be a good man who would appreciate her spunky qualities and not be bothered by her tantrum-talent. Smash himself rather liked her tantrums; they were a little like ogre love taps. Perhaps his first inkling of liking for her had been when she threw a tantrum at him. She wasn't really a bad-tempered girl; she just tended to get overly excited under extreme stress. There had been some of that on this journey!

Too bad, he thought again, that she couldn't have been an ogress. But, of course, ogresses didn't have magic tricks like tantrums, or cute little ways of expressing themselves—like kissing.

He shook his head. He was getting un-ogrishly maudlin! What could an ogre know of the refined raptures of human love? Of the caring that went beyond the hungers of the moment? Of the joy and sacrifice of helping the loved one regardless of the cost to oneself? Certainly not himself!

Yet there was something about this foolish, passionate, determined girl-human creature. She was so small she was hardly a good morsel for a meal, yet she was precious beyond the comprehension of his dim ogre wit. She had shown cunning and courage in catching and riding a nightmare to escape her amorous demon, and other excellent qualities had manifested since. He would miss her when she found her proper situation and left him, as had the other girls.

He thought to kiss her again, but the last time he had tried that, she had awakened instantly and things had gotten complicated. He wanted her to complete her sleep in peace this time, so he desisted. He had no business kissing a human girl anyway—or kissing anything, for that matter.

A drop of rain spattered on her forehead. No, not rain, for the night was calm and the nightmare of Rains was nowhere near. It was a tear, similar to the ones she had dropped on him when she had so angrily demonstrated how human beings expressed affection. A tear from his own eye. And this was strange, because no true ogre cried. Perhaps it was her own tear, recycled through his system, returning to her.

Carefully he wiped away the moisture with a hamfinger. He had no right to soil her pretty little brow with such contamination. She deserved much better. Better than an ogre.

The tromp of enormous, clumsy feet woke them in the morning. The ogres were coming!

Hastily Smash and Tandy got up. Smash felt a smidgen stronger; perhaps his soul had grown back a little while he slept. But he was nowhere near full strength yet. Knowing the nature of his kind, he worried some about that.

The Ogres of the Fen arrived. Small creatures scurried for cover, and trees angled their leaves away. No one wanted trouble with ogres! There were eight of them—three brutish males and five females.

Smash gazed at the ogresses in dim wonder. Two were grizzled old crones, one was a stout cub, and two were mature creatures of his own generation. Huge and shaggy, with muddy fur, reeking of sweat, and with faces whose smiles would stun zombies and whose frowns would burn wood, they were the most repulsive brutes imaginable. Smash was entranced.

"Who he?" the biggest of the males demanded. His voice was mainly a growl, unintelligible to ordinary folk; Smash could understand him because he was another ogre. Smash himself was unusual in that he could speak comprehensibly; most ogres could communicate verbally only with other ogres.

Suddenly Smash was fed up with the rhyming convention. What good was it, when no one who counted could understand it anyway? "I am Smash, son of Crunch. I come to seek my satisfaction among the Ancestral Ogres, as it is destined."

"Half-breed!" the other ogre exclaimed. "No need!" For Smash's ability to talk unrhymed betrayed his mixed parentage.

Smash had never liked being called a half-breed, but he could not honestly refute it. "My mother is a curse-fiend," he admitted. "But my father is an ogre, and so am I."

One of the crones spoke up, wise beyond her years. "Curse-fien', human bein'," she croaked.

"Half *man!*" the big male ogre grunted. "We ban!"

"Might fight," the child ogress said, eyes lighting.

It was true. An ogre could establish his place in a tribe by fighting for it. The male grunted eagerly. "He, me!" He naturally wanted to be the first to chastise the presumptuous half-breed.

"What are they saying?" Tandy asked, alarmed by the increasingly aggressive stances of the Fen Ogres.

It occurred to Smash that she would not approve of a physical fight. "They merely seek some ogre fun," he explained, not telling her that this was apt to be roughly similar to the fun the lions of the den had had with him. "Fun in the Fen."

She was not fooled. "What ogres call fun, I call mayhem! Smash, you can't afford any trouble; you're only at half-strength."

There was that. Fighting was fun, but getting beaten to a pulp was not as much fun as winning. If anything happened to him here, Tandy would be in trouble, for these ogres were not halfway civilized, as Smash himself was. It was galling, but he would have to pass up this opportunity. "No comment," he said.

The ogres goggled incredulously. "Not hot?" the male ogre demanded, his hamfists shuddering with eagerness to pulverize.

Smash turned away. "I think what I want is elsewhere after all," he told

Tandy. "Let's get away from here." He tried to keep the urgency suppressed; this could get difficult in a moment. At least he was not caged in, the way he had been with the lions.

The male made a huge jump, landing directly before Smash. He poked a hamfinger at Smash's soiled orange centaur jacket. "What got?" he demanded. This was not curiosity but insult; any creature in clothing was considered effete, too weak to survive in the jungle.

Smash raged inwardly at the implication, but had to avoid trouble. He stepped around the ogre and went on north, toward the Fen.

But again the male leaped in front of him. He pointed at Smash's steel gauntlets, making a crudely elaborate gesture of pulling dainty feminine gloves on his own hairy meat hooks. The humor of ogres was necessarily crude, but it was effective on its level. Smash paused.

"Me swat he snot!" the ogre chortled, aiming a wood-sundering blow at Smash's head. Smash lifted a gleaming fist of his own, defensively.

"No!" Tandy screamed.

Again Smash had to avoid conflict. He ducked under the blow in a gesture that completely surprised the ogre and continued north, inwardly seething. It simply wasn't an ogre's way to accept such taunts and duck away from a fight.

Now one of the mature females barred his way. Her hair was like the tentacular mass of a quarrelsome tangle tree that had just lost a battle with a giant spider web. Her face made the bubbling mud of the Fen seem like a clear mirror. Her limbs were so gnarled she might readily pass for a dead shagtree riddled by the droppings of a flock of harpies with indigestion. Smash had never before encountered such a luscious mass of flesh.

"He cute, cheroot," she said.

That was a considerable come-on for an ogress. Since there were more females than males in this tribe, there was obviously a place for Smash here, if he wanted it. Good Magician Humfrey had evidently known this, and known that Smash needed to settle down with a good female of his own kind. What the aging Magician had overlooked was the fact that Smash would arrive at half-strength, and that Tandy would not yet have found her own situation. Thus Smash could not afford to accept the offer, however grossly tempting it might be, because he could not fight well and could not afford to leave Tandy to the ogres' mercies. For a female went only to the winner of a fight between males. So once again he avoided interaction and continued on north.

Then the male ogre had an inspiration of genius for his kind. "Me eat complete," he said, and grabbed for Tandy.

Smash's gauntleted fist shot forward and up, catching the ogre smack in the snoot. The gauntlet made Smash's fist harder than otherwise and increased the effect of its impact. The creature rocked back, spitting out a yellow tooth. "Delight!" he cried. "He fight!"

"No!" Tandy yelled again, despairingly. She knew as well as Smash did that it was too late. Smash had struck the ogre, and that committed him.

Quickly the other ogres circled him. Tandy scooted to a beerbarrel tree, getting out of the way.

Smash had never before fought another ogre and wasn't quite sure how to proceed. Were there conventions? Did they take turns striking each other? Was anything barred?

The ogre gave him no chance to consider. He charged, his right fist swinging in a windmill motion, back and up and forward and down, aimed for Smash's head. Smash wished he had the Eye Queue so that he could analyze the meaning of this approach. But dull as he was now, he simply had to assume that it meant anything went.

Smash dodged, ducked down, caught the ogre's feet, and jerked them up to head height. Naturally the ogre flipped back, his head smacking into the ground with a hollow boom like thunder, denting a hole and shaking the bushes in the neighborhood. The watching ogres nodded; it was a good enough counter, starting things off. But Smash knew that he had substituted guile for force, to a certain extent, finding a maneuver that did not require his full strength; he could not proceed indefinitely this way.

The ogre bounced off his head, somersaulted backward, and twisted to his big, flat feet. He roared a roar that spooked a flock of buzzards from a buzzard bush and sent low clouds scudding hastily away. He charged forward again, grabbing for Smash with both heavy arms. But Smash knew better than to wait for an ogre hug. His orange jacket would protect him from most of its crushing force, but he would not be able to initiate much himself. He jumped high, stomping gently on the ogre's ugly head in passing.

The stomp drove the ogre a small distance into the ground. It was the first motion of the figure called the Nail. The ogre had to extricate his feet one by one, leaving deep prints. Now he was really angry. He turned, fists swinging.

Smash parried with one arm, using a technique he had picked up at Castle Roogna, then sent his gauntleted fist smashing into the ogre's gross mid-gut. It was like hitting well-seasoned ironwood, in both places; his parrying arm was bruised, and his striking fist felt as if it had been clubbed. This ogre was stupid, so that his ploys were obvious and easily avoided, but he was also tough. Smash had held his own so far only because he was less stupid and had the protection of his centaur clothing. If jacket and gauntlets failed him—

The ogre caught Smash's parrying arm in a grip of iron or steel and hauled him forward. Smash parried again by placing his free fist against the ogre's snoot and shoving. But he quickly became aware of his liability of half-strength; the other ogre could readily outmuscle him.

Worse, the ogre also became aware of this. "Freak weak," he grunted, and lifted Smash into the air. Smash twisted trying to free himself, but could not. Now he was in for it!

The ogre jammed him down on his feet, so hard it was Smash's turn to sink into the ground. He shot a terrible punch at Smash's chest—but now the jacket did protect Smash from most of the effect. Centaur clothing was designed to be impervious to all stones, arrows, pikes, teeth, claws, and other weapons; an ogre's fist was, of course, more than it was designed to withstand, but the jacket was much better than nothing. Meanwhile, Smash countered with another strike to the ogre's face, beautifying it by knocking out another tooth. He had good defense and good offense, thanks to the centaurs—but otherwise he remained treacherously weak.

The ogre windmilled his fist again, this time holding Smash in place so that he could not escape the blow. The fist sledgehammered down on the top of his head, driving Smash another notch lower. He tried to parry but could not; the ogre countered his counter. Another hammer blow landed on his noggin, driving him down yet more. This was the Nail again—and this time Smash was the Nail.

"Don't hurt him!" Tandy screamed, coming down from her tree. "Eat me if you must, but let Smash be!"

"No!" Smash cried, knee-deep in the ground. "Run, Tandy! Ogres don't honor deals about food!"

"You mean he'll destroy you anyway, after—?"

"Yes! Flee while you can, while they're watching me!"

"I can't do that!" she protested. Then she screamed, for the child ogress, larger than Tandy, had pounced on her.

Tandy threw a tantrum. Once more her eyes swelled up, her face turned purple, and her hair stood out from her head. The tantrum struck the little ogre, who fell, senseless, to the ground. Tandy retreated to her tree, for it took her some time to recharge a tantrum. She was now as helpless as Smash.

The ogre had paused, watching this byplay. The typical ogre was too stupid to pay attention to two things at once; he could not watch Tandy while pounding Smash. Smash, similarly, had been too dull to try to extricate himself while watching Tandy, so had not taken advantage of his opportunity. Now the ogre resumed his effort, completing the figure of the Nail. Smash had somehow left his arms by his sides, and now they, too, were caught in the ground, pinned. He knew he would never have allowed himself to get into this situation if he had retained his Eye Queue! Almost any fool would have known better.

Knocks on the head were not ordinarily harmful to ogres, because there was very little of importance in an ogre skull except bone. But the repeated impacts did serve to jog loose a few stray thoughts, flighty fancies not normally discovered in such territory. Why had Tandy tried so foolishly to help him? It would have made far more sense for her to flee, and she was smart enough to have seen that. Of course her loyalty was commendable—but was largely wasted on an ogre. As it was, both would perish. How did that jibe with the Good Magician's Answers? Two people dead . . .

One answer was that the Magician had grown too old to practice magic any more, had lost his accuracy of prophecy, and had unwittingly sent them both to their doom. It was also possible that the Magician was aware of his inadequacy and had sent them to the wilds of interior Xanth in order to avoid giving real Answers. He could have suspected, in his cunning senility, that they would never return to charge him with malpractice.

No, Smash remained unwilling to believe that of Humfrey. The man might be old, but the Gorgon had invigorated him somewhat, and he still might know what he was doing. Smash hoped so.

Soon the ogre had him waist-deep in the ground, and Smash could not retaliate. He lacked the strength. Yet if he had not yielded up half his soul, someone would have had to remain in the Void, and that might not have been much of an improvement over the present situation.

Still the blows descended, until he was chest-deep, and finally neck-deep. Then the ogre began to tire. Instead of using his fist, he gave his big horny feet a turn. He stomped on Smash's head until it, too, was buried in the packed dirt.

The figure of the Nail was complete. Smash had been driven, like a stake, full-length into the ground. He was helpless.

Satisfied with his victory, the ogre stomped toward the beerbarrel tree where Tandy hid. Smash heard her scream in terror; then he heard a fist crash into the trunk of the tree. He heard beer swish out from the punctured barrel and smelled its fumes as it coursed across the ground toward him. He was in a dent in the ground formed by the ogre's pounding; he would soon be drowned in beer, if he didn't manage to drink it all, and Tandy would be dipped in beer and eaten by the victor.

Then he heard the patter of Tandy's feet coming toward him. She was still being foolish; she would be much easier to catch here. The earth about his face became moist as the beer sank in, and he heard it splashing when her feet struck it. He hoped her pretty red slippers didn't get soiled. Meanwhile, the ground shuddered as the other ogre tromped after her, enjoying the chase.

Then she was over Smash, scraping out the ground about his head with her feeble little human hands, uncovering his buried eyes. Foaming beer from the tree swirled down, blearing his vision but softening the dirt somewhat so she could better excavate. But this was useless; she could never hope to extricate him herself, and already the ogre was looming over her, amused at the futility of her effort.

"Smash!" she cried. "Take my half soul!"

In Smash's dim, beer-sotted mind, something added up. One half plus one half equaled something very much like one. Two half souls together—

He saw her half soul dropping toward him, a hemisphere like a half-eaten apple, bisected with fair precision. Then it struck his head, bounced, and sank in, as the Eye Queue had done. He became internally conscious of it as it spread through him. It was a small, sweet, pretty, innocent but spunky fillet of soul, exactly the kind that belonged to a girl like her. Yet as it descended and joined with his big, brutish, homely, leathery ogre half soul, it merged to make a satisfying whole.

At this point, in the Night Stallion horror visions, this would have been the end. But here in real life, with a full soul pieced together, it just might be the beginning. Smash felt his strength returning.

The ogre lifted Tandy into the air by her brown tresses. He slavered. Smash's sunken orbs perceived it all from their beer-sodden pit in the ground.

The girl tried to throw a tantrum, but she was mostly out of the makings. She was terrified rather than angry, her tantrum-energy had recently been expended, and she had no soul. Her effort only made the ogre blink. He opened his ponderous and mottled jaw and swung her toward his broken teeth.

Smash flexed. He had a full soul, of sorts, now; his strength was back. The ground buckled about him. One hamhand rose up like the extremity of a zombie emerging from a long-undisturbed grave, dripping beer-sodden dirt. It caught the hairy ankle of the ogre.

Smash lifted. He was well anchored in the ground, so all he needed was power. He had it. The ogre rose into the air, surprised. But he did not let Tandy go. He continued to bring her to his salivating maw. First things first, after all.

Smash brought the foot belonging to the ankle he held to his own mouth. He opened his own dirt-marbled jaws. They closed on the ogre's horny toes. They crunched, hard.

Folklore had it that ogres were invulnerable to pain because they were too tough and stupid to feel it. Folklore was in error. The ogre bellowed out a blast of pain that shook the welkin, making the sun vibrate in place and three clouds dump their water incontinently. He dropped Tandy. Smash caught her with his other hand, after ripping it free of the ground with a spray of dirt that was like a small explosion. He set her gently down. "Find shelter," he murmured. "It could become uncomfortable in this vicinity."

She nodded mutely, then scooted away.

Smash spit out three toes, watching them bounce across the dirt. He waved the ogre in the air. "Shall we begin, toadsnoot?" he inquired politely.

The ogre was no coward. No ogre was, since an ogre's brain was too obtuse to allow room for the circuitry of fear. He was ready to begin.

The battle of ogre *vs.* ogre was the most savage encounter known in Xanth. The very land about them seemed to tense expectantly, aware that when this was over, nothing would be the same. Perhaps nothing would be, period. The landscape of Xanth was dotted with the imposing remnants of ancient ogre fights—water-filled calderas, stands of petrified trees, mountains of rubble, and similar artifacts.

The ogre began without imagination, naturally enough. He drove a hamfist down on Smash's head. This time Smash met it with his open jaws.

The fist disappeared into his mouth, and his teeth crunched on the scarred wrist.

Again the ogre bellowed, and the sun shook in its orbit and the clouds soaked indecorously. One downpour spilled onto the sun itself, causing an awful sizzle.

The ogre wrenched his arm up—and popped Smash right out of the ground in the process, for naturally Smash had not let go. Beer-mud flew outward and rained down on the watching ogres, who snapped at the blobs automatically.

The ogre slammed his two fists together hard. Since one fist was inside Smash's mouth, this meant Smash's head was getting doubly boxed. Vapor shot out of his ears. He spit out the fist, since he was unable to chew it properly, and freed his head.

Now the two combatants faced each other, two hulking monsters, the one covered with dirt and reeking of beer, the other minus two teeth and three toes. Both were angry—and the anger of ogres was similar to that of volcanoes, tornadoes, avalanches, or other natural calamities—apt to destroy the neighborhood indiscriminately.

"You called me half-breed," Smash said, driving a gauntleted fist into the other's shoulder. This time the blow had ogre force; the ogre was hurled sidewise into the trunk of a small rock-maple tree. The tree snapped off, its top section crashing down on the ogre's ugly head.

He shrugged it off, not even noticing the distraction. "He go me toe," he said, naming his own grievance, though unable to count beyond one. He fired his own fist at Smash's shoulder. The blow hurled Smash sidewise into a rock-candy boulder. The boulder shattered, and sugar cubes flew out and descended like hailstones around them.

"You tried to eat my friend," Smash said, kicking the ogre in the rear. The kick sent the monster sailing up in a high arc, his posterior smoking. Then, to make sure the ogre understood, Smash repeated it in ogrish: "He ea' me she."

The ogre landed bottom-first in the Fen, and the water bubbled and steamed about him. He picked himself up by hauling with one hamhand on the shaggy nape of his neck, then stomped the bog so that the mud flew outward like debris from a meteoric impact and ripped a medium-sized hickory tree from its mooring on an islet. The tree came loose with an anguished "Hick!" and hicked again as the ogre smashed it down across Smash's head, breaking it asunder. Smash felt sorry for the ruined tree, probably because of the influence of the sweet girl's half soul he had borrowed.

The two ogres faced each other again, having now warmed up. There was a scurrying and fluttering in the surrounding jungle as the creatures of the wild who had remained before now fled the scene of impending violence. There were also ripples in the swamp and the beat of dragons' wings, all departing hastily. None of them wanted any part of this!

Now that Smash had his full strength and had interacted with the other ogre, it was his judgment that he was the stronger of the two and the smarter. He believed he could beat this monster—and it was necessary that he do it to protect Tandy. But a lot of battle remained before the issue would be resolved.

Smash leaned forward, threw his arms around the ogre, picked him up, and charged toward the dense, hard walls of a big walnut tree. The ogre's head rammed right through the wood and was buried inside the wall-trunk, his body dangling outside.

Then there was a chomping sound. The ogre was chewing his way out, despite his missing teeth. Soon his snout broke through the far side of the wall, then chomped to the left and right. He spit out wall-nuts as he went, and they formed little walls around the tree where they fell. Then the tree crashed to the ground, its trunk severed. The ogre returned to the fray.

He ripped a medium rosewood tree from the ground and hurled it at Smash. Smash threw up a fist to block it, but the trunk splintered and showered him with splinter-roses.

Smash, in turn, swung a fist through a sandalwood trunk, severing it. He grabbed the loose part and hurled it at the ogre, who blocked it. This time there was a shower of sandals and other footwear.

The ogre took hold of a fat yew tree, twisting it around and around though it bleated like a female sheep, until the trunk separated from the stump. "Me screw with yew," he grunted, ramming the twisted trunk at Smash's face.

"That is un-ogrammatical," Smash said. "Ogres always say he or she, not you." But he ripped off a trunk of sycamore and used it to counter the thrust. "Syc 'em!" he cried, bashing at the yew. "Syc 'em more!" he cried, bashing again. And because this was the nature of that tree, it sycked 'em more.

Both trunks shattered. Trunks were really better for containing things than for fighting. Some trunks were used for trumpeting. Still, these were the most convenient things to use for this battle.

The ogre tromped into the deeper forest to the south, where larger trees grew. He chopped with both fists at a big redwood trunk. Smash stomped to a bigger bluewood and began knocking chips out of it with his own fists. Soon both trees came crashing down, and each ogre picked one up.

The other ogre was the first to swing. Smash ducked, and the redwood whistled over his head and cracked into a sturdy beech tree. The encounter was horrendous. The red was knocked right out of the redwood, and the sand flew from the beech. A cloud of red-dyed sand formed, making a brief but baleful sandstorm that swirled away in a series of diminishing funnels, coating the other trees.

Now Smash swung his bluewood. The ogre ducked behind a butternut tree. The trunk clobbered the tree. Blue dye flew out, and butter squished out. Blue butter descended in a gooky mass, coating everything the red sand had missed, including a small pasture of milkweed plants. Blue buttermilk formed. All the spectator ogres turned from dry red to dripping blue. It did improve their appearance. *Anything* was better than the natural hue of an ogre.

The ogre bent to rip out a boxwood tree. This time Smash was faster. He sliced off a section of trunk from a cork tree and rammed that at the exposed posterior. The cork shoved the ogre right into the box, where he was stuck bottom-up, corked.

Now the ogre was really angry. He bellowed so hard the box exploded and the cork shot up toward the sun with a loud Bronx cheer. When it hit the sun it detonated, and a foul cloud eclipsed the orb, turning a clear day to the smoggiest night ever to clog the noses of the jungle. Creatures began coughing and choking all around, and a number of plants wilted as the stench spread out like goo.

In the cloying darkness, the ogre retreated. he had had enough of Smash's full strength. But Smash was not through with him. He pursued, following the ogre into the deepest jungle by the sound of his tromping.

Something struck Smash's arm, temporarily numbing it. It was an ironwood bar. In the dark the ogre had harvested another tree and had hurled it from ambush. Some might consider this to be a cowardly act, but ogres did not know the meaning of cowardice, so it must have been some other kind of act. Ogres did comprehend cunning, so perhaps that was it.

Smash picked up the bar, started to twist it into a harmless knot, reconsidered and started to hurl it violently back, reconsidered again, and hung on to it. It would make a decent spear.

He listened, trying to locate the ogre. He heard the *sproing!* as another ironwood sapling was harvested. He charged that spot—and tripped over a fallen log. Naturally the log splintered into a storm of toothpicks that shot out like shrapnel, making pincushions of the surrounding vegetation. Smash lost his balance. He windmilled an arm and a leg.

Now the ogre knew Smash's location more accurately. The other spear came whistling at him as if it had not a care in the world and caught his outflung foot. That smarted! Smash rolled back, got his feet properly under him, limped, and struck back where his keen ogre hearing indicated the other ogre was.

Unfortunately, he had not realized that dirt remained in his ears, from the time he was spiked into the ground. His blow was countered, being off target, and the other bar clonked him on the side of the head.

This turned out to be a serendipitous blessing, for the clonk knocked out most of the dirt. Now he could hear properly! He reoriented and swung hard and accurately at the other—and missed, for the other was retreating.

The smog was beginning to clear. Smash pressed forward, striking repeatedly at the dim shape before him. The counterings grew fewer and weaker as the enemy retreated. Smash accelerated—and the figure ducked aside, put out a foot—and Smash tripped over it and stumbled headlong into a dropoff.

In midair he realized he had been tricked. The ogre, familiar with the terrain while Smash was not, had led him to the cliff. Smash should have been more suspicious of the sudden, seeming weakness of his opponent. But of course, without his Eye Queue, he was no smarter than any other ogre.

He landed on a bed of sharp gravel. Something yiped. Great yellow eyes opened. A jet of flame illuminated the area. Smash got a clear view of his situation.

Oops! He had fallen directly into a dragon's nest! This was the lair of a big surface dragon, open to the day because such a monster feared nothing, not even ogres. The dragon wasn't here at the moment, but its five cubs were.

In a moment all of them were up and alert. They were large cubs, almost ready to depart the nest and start consuming people for themselves. They were all as massive as Smash, with coppery snouts, green metal neck scales, and manes of silvery steel. Their teeth glinted like stars, and their tongues slurped about hungrily. As the light returned, all recognized him as an enemy and as prey. What a trap this was!

The ogre looked over the brink of the pit. "Ho ho ho ho!" he roared thunderously, causing the nearby trees to shake. "Me screw he blue!" For Smash stood on blue diamonds that made up the nest, which he had taken for gravel. All dragons liked diamonds; they were pretty and hard and highly resistant to heat. Because dragons hoarded diamonds, the stones assumed unreasonable value, being very rare elsewhere. Smash understood this extended even to Mundania, though he wasn't sure how the dragons managed to collect the stones from there.

Dragons were not much for ceremony. All five pounced, blasting out little jets of flame that incinerated the vegetation around the nest and heated the diamonds at Smash's feet, forcing him to jump.

Smash, angry at himself for his stupidity in falling into this mess—imagine being outwitted by a dull ogre!—reacted with inordinate, i.e., ogrish, fury. He just wasn't in the mood to mess with little dragons!

He put out his two gauntleted hands and snatched the first dragon out of the air. He whipped it about and used it to strike the second in mid-pounce. Both dragons were knocked instantly senseless. Weight for weight, no dragon was a match for an ogre; only the advantage of size put the big dragons ahead, and these lacked that.

Smash hurled both dragons at the other ogre, who stood gloating, and grabbed for two more. In a moment both of these were dragging, and the dragging dragons were hurled up to drape about the ogre.

The fifth dragon, meanwhile, had fastened its jaws on Smash's legs. They were pretty good jaws, with diamond-hard teeth; they were beginning to hurt. Smash plunged his fist down with such force that the skull caved in. He ripped the body away and hurled it, too, at the other ogre.

The smog had largely cleared, perhaps abetted by the breeze from Smash's own activity. Now an immense shadow fell across them. Smash looked up. It was the mother dragon, so huge her landbound bulk blocked off the light of the sun. Not all big dragons were confined to Dragonland! It would take a whole tribe of ogres to fend her off—and the tribe of the Ogre-Fen Ogres would certainly not do that. Smash had been tricked into this nest because the other ogre knew it would be the end of him.

But Smash, having cursed the darkness of his witlessness, now suffered a flashback of dull genius. "Heee!" he cried, pointing a hamfinger at the other ogre.

The dragoness looked. There stood the ogre, in mid-gloat, with the five limp, little dragon cubs draped around his body like so much apparel. He had been so pleased with his success in framing Smash that he had not thought to clear the debris from himself. The liability of the true ogre had betrayed him—his inability to concentrate on more than one thing at a time. Naturally the dragoness assumed that he was the guilty creature.

With a roar so horrendous that it petrified the local trees and caused a layer of rock on the cliff to shiver into dust, several diamonds to craze and crack; and a blast of fire that would have vaporized trees and cliff face, had the one not just been converted from wood to stone and the other not just powdered out, she went for the guilty ogre.

The ogre was dim, but not that dim, especially as a refracted wash of fire frizzled his fur. While the dragoness inhaled and oriented for a more accurate second shot, he flung off the little dragons and dived into the nest-pit, landing snoot-first in the diamonds. The contrast was considerable—the sheer beauty of the stones versus the sheer ugliness of the ogre. It looked as if he were trying to eat them.

Smash hardly paused for thought. At the moment, the dragoness was a greater threat to his health than the ogre. He wrestled a boulder out of the pit wall and heaved it up at the dragoness, while the other ogre struggled to his feet, shedding white, red, green, blue, and polka-dot diamonds. The dragoness turned, snapped at the boulder, found it inedible, and spit it out.

Smash realized that the other ogre had disappeared. He checked, and saw a foot in a hole. The boulder he had thrown had blocked a passage, and the ogre was crawling down it, leaving Smash to face the fire alone. Smash didn't appreciate that, so he grabbed the foot and hauled the ogre back and out. Several more diamonds dropped from crevices on the creature's hide— black, yellow, purple, plaid, and candy-striped. In a moment Smash had the ogre in the air, swinging him around by the feet in a circle.

The dragoness was pumping up for a real burnout blast. Such an exhalation could incinerate both ogres in a single foop. She opened her maw, letting the first wisps of superheated steam emerge, and her belly rumbled with the gathering holocaust.

Smash let go of the ogre, hurling him directly into the gaping maw, headfirst.

The dragon choked on her own blocked fire, for the ogre's body was just the right size to plug her gullet. The ogre's feet, protruding slightly from the mouth, kicked madly. Then the ogre's broken teeth started working as he chewed his way out. The dragoness looked startled, uncertain how to deal with this complication.

Smash wasn't sure how this contest would turn out. The dragoness' fire was bottled, and her own teeth could not quite get purchase on the ogre in her throat, but she did have a lot of power and might be able to clear the ogre by either coughing him out or swallowing him the rest of the way. On the other hand, the ogre could chew quite a distance in a short time. Smash decided to depart the premises with judicious dispatch.

But where could he go? If he scrambled out of the nest, the dragoness might chase after him, and he would be more like a sitting duck than a running ogre, in the open. If he remained—

"Hssst!" someone called. "Here!"

Smash looked. A little humanoid nymph stood within the hole left by the boulder.

"I was raised in the underworld," she said. "I know tunnels. Come!"

Smash looked back at the dragoness, who was swelling with stifled pressure, and at the kicking ogre in her throat. The former was about to fire the latter out like a missile. He had sympathy for neither and was fed up with the whole business. What did he want with ogres anyway? They were dull creatures who crunched the bones of human folk.

Human folk. "Tandy!" he cried. "I must save her from the ogres!"

The nymph was disgusted. "Idiot!" she cried. "I am Tandy!"

Smash peered closely at her. The nymph had brown hair, blue eyes, and a spunky, upturned little nose. She was indeed Tandy. Odd that he hadn't recognized her! Yet who would have expected a nymph to turn out to be a person!

"Now get in here, you oaf!" she commanded. "Before that monster pops her cork!"

He followed Tandy into the tunnel. She led him along a curving route, deep down into the ground. The air here turned cool, the wall clammy. "The dragon mines here for diamonds that my mother leaves," she explained. "There would be terrible disruption in Xanth if it weren't for her work. The dragons would go on a rampage if their diamonds ran out, and so would the other creatures if they couldn't get their own particular stones. It certainly is nice to know my mother has been here! Of course, that could have been a long time ago. There might even be an aperture to my home netherworld here, though probably she rode the Diggle and left no passage behind."

Smash just followed, more concerned about escaping the dragon than about the girl's idle commentary.

There was a sound behind them, like a giant spike being fired violently into bedrock. The dragoness had no doubt disgorged the ogre from her craw and now was ready to pursue the two of them here. Though the diameter of the tunnel was not great, dragons were long, sinuous creatures, particularly the wingless landbound ones, who could move efficiently through small apertures. Or she could simply send a blast of flame along, frying them. Worse yet, she might do both, pursuing until she got close, then doing some fiery target practice.

"Oh, I'm sure there's a way down, somewhere near," Tandy fussed. "The wall here is shallow; I can tell by the way it resonates. I've had a lot of experience with this type of formation. See—there's a fossil." She indicated a glowing thing that resembled the skeleton of a fish, but it squiggled out of sight before Smash could examine it closely. Fossils were like that, he knew; they preferred to hide from discovery. They were like zombies, except that they didn't generally travel about much; they just rested for eons. He had no idea what their purpose in life or death might be. "But I can't find a hole!" Tandy finished, frustrated.

Smash knew they had to get out of this particular passage in a hurry. He aimed his fist and smashed a hole in the wall. A new chamber opened up. He dropped through, carefully lifting Tandy down.

"That's right!" she exclaimed. "I forgot about your ogre strength! It's handy at times."

A rush of fire flowed along the tunnel they had quitted. They had gotten out just in time!

"This is it!" Tandy cried. "The netherworld! I haven't been in this section before, but I recognize the general configuration. A few days' walk, and I'm home!" Then she reconsidered. "No, there isn't any direct connection. The—what's that thing that cuts Xanth in half? I can't remember—"

"The Gap Chasm," Smash said, dredging it out of his own fading memory. In his ogre personality, he was too stupid to forget things as readily as Tandy could.

"Yes. That. That would cut off this section from the section I live in, I think. Still—"

She led him through a dark labyrinth, until the sounds of the enraged dragon faded. They finally stood on a ledge near cool water. "She'll never find us here. It would douse her fire."

"I hope you'll be able to find our way out. I'm lost." Ogres didn't care one way or the other about the depths of the earth, but did like to be able to get around to forage for food and violence.

"When the time is right," she said. "Maybe never."

"But what of our missions?" Smash demanded.

"What missions?" she asked innocently.

Then Smash remembered. She no longer cared about seeking fulfillment. She had given up her soul.

Chapter 15

Point of View

But in a moment he realized this was not serious. "I have your half soul," he said. "Take it back." He put his huge paw on his head and drew out the fillet. It adhered to his own soul, with which it had temporarily merged; evidently the two souls liked each other, different as they were. At last her soul rested in his palm.

Then he moved the faintly luminous hemisphere to her head and patted it in. The soul dissolved, flowing back into her. "Oh, that feels so good!" she exclaimed. "Now I know how much I missed my soul, even the half of it!"

Smash, back to his own half soul, suddenly felt tired. He sank down on the rock where he was resting. It was dark here, but he didn't mind; it was easy to rest in this place.

Tandy sank down beside him. "I think my soul feels lonely," she said. "It was half, and then it was whole with yours, and now it's half again, with maybe the better half missing."

"Yours is the better half," he said. "It's cute and spunky and sensitive, while mine is gross and stupid."

"But strong and loyal," she said. "They complement each other. A full person needs strength *and* sensitivity."

"An ogre doesn't." But now he wondered.

She found his hamhand with her own. "Okay, Smash, I remember our missions now. I wanted to find a good husband, and you—"

"Wanted a good wife," Smash finished. "I didn't know it, but the Good Magician evidently did. So he sent me where I could find one. But somehow the notion of sharing the rest of my life with an ogress no longer appeals. I don't know why."

"Because true ogres and ogresses are brutes," she said. "You really aren't that kind, Smash."

"Perhaps I wasn't when I had the Eye Queue curse. But when I lost it, I reverted to my natural state."

"Are you sure your natural state is brutish?"

"I was raised to be able to smash ironwood trees with single blows of my horny fist," he said. "To wrestle my weight in dragons and pulverize them. To squeeze purple bouillon juice from purple wood with my bare hands. To chew rocks into sand. To—"

"That's impressive, Smash. And I've seen you do some of those things. But are you sure you aren't confusing strength with brutishness? You have always been very gentle with me."

"You are special," he said, experiencing a surge of unfamiliar feeling.

"Chem told me something she learned from a Mundane scholar. Chem and I talked a lot while you were in the gourd, there in the Void, because we didn't know for sure whether we would ever get free of that place. The scholar's name was Ichabod, and he knew this little poem about a Mundane monster resembling a tiger lily, only this one is supposed to be an animal instead of a plant."

"I have fought tiger lilies," he said. "Even their roots have claws. They're worse than dandy-lions."

"She couldn't remember the poem, exactly. So we played with it, applying it to you. 'Ogre, ogre, burning bright—' "

"Ogres don't burn!"

"They do when they're stepping across the firewall," she said, "trying to fetch a boat so the rest of us can navigate past the loan sharks. That's what reminded Chem of the poem, she said. The flaming ogre. Anyway, the poem tells how they go through the jungle in the night, the fiery ogres, and are fearfully awful."

"Yes," Smash said, becoming pleased with the image.

"We had a good laugh. You aren't fearful at all, to us. You're a big, wonderful, blundering ball of fur, and we wouldn't trade you for anything."

"No matter how brightly I burn," Smash agreed ruefully. He changed the subject. "How were you able to function without your soul? When you lost it before, you were comatose."

"Partly, before, it was the shock of loss," she said. "This time I gave it away; I was braced, experienced."

"That shouldn't make much difference," he protested. "A soul is a soul, and when you lose it—"

"It does make a difference. What a girl gives away may make her feel good, while if the same thing is taken by force, it can destroy her."

"But without a soul—"

"True. That's only an analogy. I suppose I was thinking more of love."

He remembered how the demon had tried to rape her. Suddenly he hated that demon. "Yes, you need someone to protect you. But we found no man along the route, and now we are beyond the Good Magician's assignment without an Answer for either of us."

"I'm not so sure," she said.

"We're drifting from the subject. How did you survive, soulless? Your half soul made me strong enough to beat another ogre; you had to have been so weak you would collapse. Yet you didn't."

"Well, I'm half nymph," she said.

"Half nymph? You did seem like a nymph when—"

"I always thought of myself as human, just as you always thought of yourself as ogre. But my mother is Jewel the Nymph. So by heredity I'm as much nymph as girl."

"What's the difference?" He knew there was a difference, but found himself unable to define it.

"Nymphs are eternally young and beautiful and usually none too bright. They are unable to say no to a male for anything. My mother is an exception; she had to be smart and reliable to handle her job. She remains very pretty, prettier than I am. But she's not as smart as I am."

"You are young and beautiful," Smash said. "But so is Princess Irene, and she's a human girl."

"Yes. So that isn't definitive. Human girls in the flush of their young prime do approach nymphs in appearance, and have a number of nymphal qualities that men find appealing. But Irene will age, while true nymphs won't. She loves, while nymphs can't love."

"Can't love?" Smash was learning more than he had ever expected to about nymphs.

"Well, my mother does love. But as I said, she's a very special nymph. And my father Crombie used a love-spell on her. So that doesn't count."

"But some human people don't love, so that is not definitive, either."

"True. It can be very hard to distinguish a nymph from a thoughtless human girl. But one thing is definitive. Nymphs don't have souls."

"You have a soul! I am absolutely certain of that! It's a very nice little soul, too."

He could feel her smile in the dark. Her body relaxed, and she squeezed his paw. "Thank you. I rather like it myself. I have a soul because I'm half human. Just as you do, for the same reason."

"I never thought of that!" Smash said. "It never occurred to me that other ogres wouldn't have souls."

"They're brutes because they have no souls. Their strength is all magic."

"I suppose so. My mother was a variety of human, so I inherited my soul from her."

"And it gave you strength to make up for what you lost by being only half ogre."

"Agreed. That answers a mystery I was never aware of before. But you still haven't explained how you—"

"Functioned without a soul. Yes. It was simply a matter of how I thought of it. You see, human beings have always had souls; they have no experience living without them. Other creatures never had souls, so they have learned to cope. My mother copes quite well, though I suppose some of my father's soul has rubbed off on her." Tandy sighed. "She's such a good person, she certainly deserves a soul. But she *is* a nymph, and I am half nymph. So I can function without a soul. All I had to do, once I realized that, was to think of myself as a nymph. It made a fundamental difference."

"But I think of myself as an ogre—yet I have a soul."

"Maybe you should try thinking of yourself as a man, Smash." Her hand tightened on his.

"A man?" he asked blankly. "I'm an ogre!"

"And I'm a girl. But when I had to, I became a nymph. So I was able to operate without sinking into the sort of slough I did before, in the gourd. I was able to follow your fight, and to step in when I needed to."

"A man!" he repeated incredulously.

"Please, Smash. I'm a half-breed, like you. Like a lot of the creatures of Xanth. I won't laugh at you."

"It's impossible! How could I ever be a man?"

"Smash, you don't talk like an ogre any more. You're not stupid like an ogre any more."

"The Eye Queue—"

"That vine faded a long time ago, Smash! And the one you got in the Void—that never existed at all. It was sheer illusion. Yet it made you smart again. Did you ever consider how that could be?"

It was his turn to smile in the dark. "I was careful not to think that one through, Tandy. It would have deprived me of the very intelligence that enabled me to indulge in that chain of thought, paradoxically."

"You believe in paradox?"

"It is an intriguing concept. I would say it is impossible in Mundania, but possible in Xanth. I really must explore the implications further, when I have leisure."

"I have another hypothesis," she said. "The Eye Queue was illusion, but your intelligence was not."

"Isn't that a contradiction? It's illogical to attribute an effect as significant as intelligence to an illusion."

"It certainly is. That's why I didn't do it. Smash, I don't think you needed the Eye Queue vine at all, ever. Not the illusory one *or* the original one. You always had the intelligence. Because you're half human, and human beings are smart."

"But I was never smart until the Eye Queue made me so."

"You were smart enough to fool everyone into thinking you were ogrishly stupid! Smash, Chem told me about the Eye Queue vine. Its effect wears off in hours. Sometimes its effect is only in self-perception. It makes creatures think they're smart when they aren't, and they make colossal fools of themselves without knowing it. Like people getting drunk on the spillage from a beerbarrel tree, thinking they're being great company when actually they are disgusting clowns. My father used to tell me about that; he said he'd made a clown of himself more than once. Only it's worse with the vine."

"Was I doing that?" Smash asked, mortified.

"No! You really *were* smart! And it didn't wear off, until you lost the vine in the flood. And it came back the moment you got a new vine, even though you only imagined it. Doesn't that suggest something to you, Smash?"

He pondered. "It confirms that magic is marvelous and not entirely logical."

"Or that you became smart only when you thought you ought to be smart. Maybe the Eye Queue showed you how, the first time. After that you could do it any time you wanted to. Or when you forgot to be stupid."

"But I'm not smart now," he protested.

"You should listen to yourself, Smash! You've been discoursing on the nuances of paradox and you've been talking in a literate fashion."

"Why, so I have," he agreed, surprised. "I forgot I had lost the Eye Queue."

"Precisely. So where does your intelligence come from now, ogre?"

"It must be from my human half, as you surmise. Like my soul. I just never invoked it before, because—"

"Because you thought of yourself as an ogre, until you saw what ogres really were like and started turning off them. Now you are sliding toward your human heritage."

"You see it far more clearly than I do!"

"Because I'm more objective. I see you from the outside. I appreciate your human qualities. And I think the Good Magician Humfrey did, too. He's old, but he's still savvy. I ought to know; I cleaned up his castle for a year."

"It didn't look cleaned up to me. I could hardly find a place to stand."

"You should have seen it before I cleaned it up!" But she laughed. "Actually, I didn't touch his private den; even the Gorgon leaves that alone. If anyone ever cleaned up in there, no one would know where all his spells and books and things were. He's had a century or so to learn their locations. But the rest of the castle needs to be kept in order, and they felt the Gorgon shouldn't have to do it, since she's married to him now, so I did it. I cleaned off the magic mirrors and things; some of them had pretty smart mouths, too! It wasn't bad. And in that year I came to understand that behind the seeming absent-mindedness of Humfrey there lies a remarkably alert mind. He just doesn't like to show it. He knew all about you, for example, before you approached the castle. He had you marked a year in advance on his calendar, right to the day and hour of your arrival. He watched every step of your progress. He chortled when you came up against those ogre bones; he'd gone to a lot of work to get those set up. That man knows everything he wants to know. That's why he keeps the Gorgon in thrall, instead of she him; she is in complete awe of his knowledge."

"And I thought he was asleep!" Smash said ruefully.

"Everyone does. But he's the Magician of Information, one of the most powerful men in Xanth. He knows everything worth knowing. So he surely knew how much of a mind you had and crafted his Answer accordingly. Now we know he was correct."

"But our missions—neither is complete! He didn't know we would fail, did he?"

She considered, then asked, "Smash, why did you fight the other ogre?"

"He annoyed me. He insulted me."

"But you tried to avoid trouble."

"Because I was at half-strength and knew I'd lose."

"But then you slugged him. You knocked out a tooth."

"He was going to eat you. I couldn't allow that."

"Why not? It's what ogres do."

"I had agreed to protect you!"

"Did you think of that when you struck him?"

"No," Smash admitted. "I popped him instantly. There was no time for thought."

"So there was some other reason you reacted."

"You're my friend!"

"Do ogres have friends?"

He considered again. "No. I'm the only ogre who ever had friends—and they were mostly human friends. Most ogres don't even like other ogres."

"Unsurprising," she said. "So, to protect me, twice you risked your soul."

"Yes, of course." He wasn't certain of the point of her comment.

"Would any true ogre have done that?"

"No true ogre. Of course, since ogres don't have souls, they would never be faced with the choice. But still, if they did have souls, they wouldn't—"

"Smash, doesn't it seem, even to you, that you have more human qualities than ogre qualities?"

"In this circumstance, perhaps. But in the jungle, alone, it would be otherwise."

"Why did you leave the jungle, then?"

"I was dissatisfied. As I said before, I must have needed a wife, only I didn't know it then."

"And you could have had a nice brute of an ogress, with a face whose full glare would have made the moon rot, if you'd reacted more like an ogre. Are you sorry you blew it?"

Smash laughed, becoming more conscious of her hand on his. "No."

"Do ogres laugh?"

"Only maliciously."

"So you've thrown away the Answer you worked so hard for, you think. Are you going back to the lonely jungle now?"

Strangely, that also did not appeal. The life he had been satisfied with before seemed inadequate now. "What choice do I have?"

"Why not try being a man? It's all in your viewpoint, I think. The people at Castle Roogna would accept you, I'm sure. They already do. Prince Dor treated you as an equal."

"He treats everybody as an equal." But Smash wondered. Would Prince Dor have been the same with any of the Ogre-Fen Ogres? This seemed questionable.

Then something else occurred to him. "You say I was able to make the illusory Eye Queue vine work in the Void because I always did have human intelligence, so there was no paradox?"

"That's what I say," she said smugly.

"Then what about the gourd?"

"The gourd?" she asked faintly.

"That was illusory, too, in the Void, and it had nothing to do with my human nature, yet it also worked."

"Yes, it did," she agreed. "Oh, Smash, I never thought of that! But that means—"

"That illusion was real in the Void. That what we thought was there really *was* there, once we thought it, such as gourds and glowing footprints. So there is no proof I'm smart without the vine."

"But—but—" She began to sniffle.

Smash sighed. He hated to see her unhappy. "Nevertheless, I admit to being smart enough now to find the flaws in your logic, which, paradoxically, proves your case to that extent. Probably we're both right. I have human intelligence, and the Void makes illusion real." He paused, yet again aware of her hand on his. What a sweet little hand it was! "I have never in my life thought of myself as a man. I don't know what it could accomplish, but at least it might be a diversion while we wait for the dragoness to stop searching for us."

Her sniffles abated magically. "It might be more than that, Smash," she said, sounding excited.

Smash concentrated. He imagined the way men were: small and not very hairy and rather weak, but very smart. They used clothing because their natural fur didn't cover the essentials. They plucked shoes from shoe trees and socks from hose vines. He had a jacket and gloves; that was a start. They lived in houses, because wild creatures could otherwise attack them in their sleep. They tended to congregate in villages, liking one another's company. They were, in fact, social creatures, seldom alone.

He imagined himself joining that company, walking like a man instead of tromping like an ogre. Resting on a bed instead of on the trunk of a tree. Eating delicately, one bite at a time, chewing it sedately, instead of ripping raw flesh, crunching bones, and using sheer muscle to cram in whatever didn't conveniently fit in his mouth. Shaking hands instead of knocking for a loop. But the whole exercise was ridiculous, because he knew he would always be a huge, hairy, homely monster.

"It isn't working," he said with relief. "I just can't imagine myself as—"

She set her other hand on his gross arm. Now he felt the touch of her soul, her half soul, for he was attuned to it after borrowing it. There seemed to be a current of soul traveling along his arm between her two tiny hands. He had rescued that soul from the gourd, and it had helped rescue him from the ogres.

He also remembered how quick she had always been in his defense. How she had kissed him. How she had stayed with him, even when he went among the ogres, even when she lacked her soul. Suddenly he wanted very much to please her.

And he began to get the point of view. He felt himself shrinking, refining, turning polite and smart.

Suddenly it opened out. His mind expanded to take in all of Xanth, as it had when he first felt the curse of the Eye Queue. This time it was no curse; it was self-realization. He had become a man.

Tandy's hands remained on his arm and hand. Now he turned to her in the dark. His eyes saw nothing, but his mind more than made up the difference.

Tandy was a woman. She was beautiful in her special fashion. She was smart. She was nice. She was loyal. She had a wonderful soul.

And he—with the perspective of a man he saw her differently. With the mind of a man he analyzed it. She had been a companion, and he realized now how important that had become to him. Ogres didn't need companions, but men did. The six other girls had been companions, too, and he had liked them, but Tandy was more.

"I don't want to go back to the jungle alone," he murmured. His voice had lost much of the ogre guttural quality.

"I never thought you belonged there, Smash." Oh, how sweet she sounded!

"I want—" But the enormity of the notion balked him.

It didn't balk Tandy, however. "Smash, I told you before that I loved you."

"I have human perception at the moment," he said. "I must caution you not to make statements that are subject to misinterpretation."

"Misinterpretation, hell!" she flashed. "I knew my mind long before you knew yours."

"Well, you must admit that an ogre and a nymph—"

"Or a man and a woman—"

"Half-breeds," he said, half bitterly. "Like the centaurs, harpies, merfolk, fauns—"

"And what's wrong with half-breeds?" she flared. "In Xanth, any species can mate with any other it wants to, and some of the offspring are fine people. What's wrong with Chem the Centaur? With the Siren?"

"Nothing," he said, impressed by her vehemence. Moment by moment, as she talked and his manhood infiltrated the farthest reaches of his awareness, he was warming to her nature. She was small, but she was an awful lot of small.

"And the three-quarter breeds, almost identical to the humans, like Goldy Goblin and Blythe Brassie and John the Fairy—"

"And Fireoak the Hamadryad, whose soul is the tree," he finished. "All good people." But he wondered passingly why, since nymphs were so nearly human, they didn't have souls. Obviously there was more to learn about the matter.

"Consider Xanth," she continued hotly. "Divided into myriad Kingdoms of people and animals and in-betweens. We met the Lord of the Flies and the Prince of Whales and the Dragon Lady and the Kingdoms of the goblins, birds, griffins—"

"And the Ancestral Ogres of the Fen," he said. "All of which believe they dominate Xanth."

"Yes." She took a breath. "How can Xanth be prevented from fragmenting entirely, except by interaction and cross-breeding? Smash, I think the very future of Xanth depends on the half-breeds and quarter-breeds, the people like us who share two or more views. In Mundania, no species breeds with another—and look at Mundania! According to my father's stories—"

"Awful," he agreed. "Mundania has no magic."

"So their species just keep drifting farther apart, making that land more dreary year by year. Xanth is different; Xanth can reunify. Smash, we owe it to Xanth to—"

"Now I understand what men object to in women," Smash said.

She was startled. "What?"

"They talk too much."

"It's to fill in for inactive men!" she flared.

Oh. He turned farther toward her in the dark, and she met him halfway. This time there was no confusion at all about the kiss. It was a small swatch of heaven.

At last they broke. "Ogre, ogre," she murmured breathlessly. "You certainly are a man now."

"You're right. The Good Magician knew," he said, cuddling her close to him. In the dark she did not seem tiny; she seemed just right. As with riding the nightmares, things were always compatible. He had known Tandy was very feminine; now this quality assumed phenomenal new importance. "He sent me to the ogres—to find you."

"And he sent me to find you—the one creature rough enough to drive off the demon I fled, while still being gentle enough for me to love."

Love. Smash mulled that concept over. "I cried for you last night," he confessed.

"Silly," she teased him. "Ogres don't cry."

"Because I thought I would lose you. I did not know that I loved you."

She melted. "Oh, Smash! You said it!"

He said it again. "I love you. That's why I fought for you. That's why I bargained my soul for you."

She laughed, again teasingly. "I don't think you know what love is."

He stiffened. "I don't?"

"But I'll show you."

"Show me," he said dubiously.

She showed him. There was no violence, no knocking of heads against trees, no screaming or stomping. Yet it was the most amazing and rewarding experience he had ever had. By the time it was done, Smash knew he never wanted to be anything but a man and never wanted any woman but her.

They found another way out of the netherworld, avoiding the lurking dragon, and trekked south along the east coast of Xanth. Smash, by the light of day, was smaller than he had been, and less hairy, and hardly ugly at all. But he didn't really mind giving up his previous assets, because the acquisition of Tandy more than made up for them. She sewed him a pair of shorts, because men wore them, and he did rather resemble a man now.

They traveled quietly, avoiding trouble. When this threatened to rankle his suppressed ogre nature, Tandy would take his hand, and smile up at him, and the rankle dissipated.

The trip took several days, but that didn't matter, because it was sheer joy. Smash hardly noticed the routine Xanth hazards, since most of his attention was on Tandy. Somehow the hazards seemed diminished, anyway, for news had spread among the griffins, birds, dragons, goblins, and flies that Tandy's companion was best left alone, even if he didn't look like much. It seemed that a certain ogre of the Fen had staggered out of the jungle with a headache, and though he had not given any details, it was evident that he had been roughly treated by the stranger he had fought. Even the crossing of the Gap, which Smash had almost forgotten until he encountered it again, was without event. The Gap Dragon, reputed to have a sore tail, stayed clear.

At length, they drew near the entrance to Tandy's home region. The route was through a chasm guarded by a tangle tree. It was a big, aggressive tree, and Smash knew he could not overcome it. So he drew on his human intelligence and harvested a number of hypnogourds, intending to roll them down to the tree. If it made the mistake of looking in a single peephole—

But as they carried two gourds from the patch, a cloud of smoke formed before them. This coalesced into a dusky demon.

"Well, my little human beauty," the demon said to Tandy, switching his barbed tail about. "You were lost, but now are found. I shall have my will of you forthwith." He advanced on her, grinning lasciviously.

Tandy screamed and dropped her gourd, which shattered on the ground. "Fiant!"

So this was the demon who sought to rape her! Smash set his own gourd down carefully and stepped forward. "Depart, foul spirit!" he ordered.

The demon ignored him, addressing Tandy instead. "Ah, you seem more luscious than ever, girl-creature! It will be long before I tire of you."

Tandy backed away. Smash saw that she was too frightened even to throw a tantrum. The demon had come upon her so suddenly she had not been able to brace emotionally for the assault.

Smash interposed himself between demon and girl. "Desist, Fiant," he said.

The fat demon put out a hand and shoved him. Smash tripped on a stone and tumbled to the ground ignominiously. The demon stepped on his stomach and advanced on Tandy. "Pucker up, cutie; your time has come at last."

Smash was becoming perturbed. Tandy might believe in crossbreeding as the hope of Xanth, but she had not chosen to do it with the demon. As she had explained, there was a considerable difference between what was given voluntarily and what was forced. Smash scrambled to his feet and hurried after Fiant, catching him on the shoulder.

The demon swung about almost carelessly, delivering a brain-rattling slap across Smash's cheek. Smash fell back again, reeling.

Now Fiant shot out a hand and caught Tandy by the hair. She screamed, but could not pull away.

Smash charged back into the fray—only to be met with a careless straight-arm that nearly staved in his teeth. Now the demon deigned to notice him, momentarily. "Get lost, lout, or I'll hurt you."

What was this? Fiant seemed to be stronger than Smash!

The demon drew Tandy in to him by the hair, reaching with the clawed fingers of his other hand to rip off her blouse.

Smash charged again, fists swinging. He caught the demon on his pointed ear.

This time Fiant became annoyed. "You seem to be a slow learner, creep." He loosed the girl, spun about, and struck Smash with a lightning-fast one-two combination punch on chin and stomach. Smash went down, head fogging, gasping for breath. "No man can stand against a demon," Fiant said arrogantly, and turned again to Tandy.

But the brief respite had given her a chance to work up some spunk. She dived for Smash. "Take my soul!" she cried, and he felt its wonderful enhancement infusing him. He had forgotten how weak he was with only half a soul.

Then she was yanked away by the hair. Fiant held her up, her feet dangling. "No more Mr. Nice Guy," he said. "Off with your skirt." On the trip down, Tandy had remade the tatters of her red dress into a good skirt, and completed her wardrobe and Smash's by sewing material from cloth bushes.

Smash leaped up and tackled the demon. Now he had his strength! But Fiant poked two fingers at his eyes. Painfully blinded, Smash fell to the ground again. He had a full soul again; why couldn't he prevail?

It was Tandy who came up with the answer. "Smash, you're too much of a man now!" she cried from her dangle. "Too gentle and polite. Try thinking of yourself as an ogre!"

It was true. Smash had spent several days becoming manishly civilized. As Fiant had said, no man was a match for a demon.

But an ogre, now . . .

Smash thought of himself as an ogre. It wasn't hard. He had spent his life indulging in just such thinking; the old thought patterns were strong. He visualized the ground trembling at his stomp, trees being ripped from their moorings, boulders being crushed to sand by single blows of horny fists.

Hair sprouted on his arms. Muscles bulged horrendously. His height jumped. His orange jacket, which hung on him loosely, abruptly became tight. His shorts split apart and fell off. His hands swelled into hams. His bruised eyeballs popped into awful ogre orbs. *Ogre, ogre* . . .

Smash put one hamfinger to the ground and lifted his whole body into the air; then he flipped neatly to his rock-calloused feet. He roared—and the leaves of the nearest trees swirled away. So, unfortunately, did Tandy's clothes, such as remained; they were not constructed for hurricane winds.

She swung in dainty nudity by her hair. "Go get him, ogre!" she cried, and kicked the demon on the nose.

Fiant looked at Smash—and gaped. Suddenly he faced a monster far worse than himself. He dropped the girl and turned to flee.

Smash bent down, hooked his fingers in the turf, and yanked. The turf came toward him in a rug, dumping the demon on his horns. Smash took one tromp forward and launched a mighty kick at Fiant's elevated rump. The kick should have propelled the demon well toward the sun.

But Smash's foot passed right through Fiant. Smash, thrown off balance by the missed kick, did a backward flip and whomped on his head. That hardly mattered to an ogre, but it gave the demon a chance to get organized.

Fiant realized that the ogre could not really hurt him, thanks to his ability to dematerialize at will. This restored his courage marvelously. Bullies always got brave when the odds were loaded on their side. He got up, strode toward Smash, and punched him in the gut. It was a good, hard blow—but now Smash shrugged it off as the trifle it was and countered with a sweep of his arm that was so swift and fierce it caused a contrail behind it.

But this blow, too, passed through the demon without effect.

"He's dematerializing!" Tandy cried. "You can't hit him!"

Unconvinced, Smash plunged his fist at the demon's head from above. This blow should have driven the demon halfway into the ground. Instead, it passed the entire length of Fiant's body without impediment and struck the bare rock beneath, where the rug of turf had been removed. The rock cracked apart and powdered into sand, naturally. Then Smash rammed a straight punch at Fiant's belly—and only succeeded in sundering the tree behind him. Smash was tearing up the landscape to no avail.

But the demon could hit Smash, by rematerializing his fists just before they struck. The blows didn't really hurt, but Smash was annoyed. How could he pulverize a creature who could not be hit back?

He tried to grab Fiant. This worked slightly better. The demon's body was as diffuse as smoke to his touch, but Smash's spread hamhands had more purchase, and he was able to guide the smoke as long as he handled it carefully. Unfortunately, the demon's fists remained material, and they now beat a brutal tattoo on Smash's face. His nose and eyes were hurting anew.

"Use your mind, Smash!" Tandy called.

Smash held the demon in place, enduring the facial battering while he put his natural Eye Queue intellect to work. What would deal with such a demon once and for all? It would not be enough merely to drive Fiant off; he had to fix it so the demon could never again bother Tandy. If Tandy had a notion how he should proceed, why hadn't she simply screamed it out?

Because if the demon heard, he would act to negate it. Smash had to do whatever it was by surprise.

He glanced at Tandy—and saw her sitting on the gourd he had carried. Suddenly he understood.

He snapped at the demon's fists, using his big ogre teeth. "Oh, no, you don't, monster!" Fiant exclaimed. "You can't get me that way!" Sure enough, he punched Smash on the tongue, and when Smash's teeth closed on the fist, it dematerialized and withdrew unhurt.

But meanwhile, Smash was carrying the demon toward the gourd. When he got there, he slowly tilted Fiant down toward the peephole Tandy had been sitting on. The demon was about to face the gourd. If Fiant saw it too soon, he would strike it and shatter it, ruining the ploy.

Fiant, intent on punching Smash's snout into a pulp, did not spy the gourd until he was abruptly face to face with it. "No!" he cried, realizing what it was. He jammed his eyes closed so he could not look, and dematerialized.

"Yes!" Smash grunted. He shoved the demon headfirst at the gourd. Because Fiant was dematerialized, he passed right through the peephole, headfirst. Suddenly Smash remembered the bottle ifrit inside this same gourd. Wasn't the gourd another kind of container? "You want to force your way into something? This is a good place." Smash fed the rest of the demon through, arms, torso, legs, and feet, until all of him was gone.

"Let him find his way out of *that!*" Tandy cried jubilantly. "Oh, this really serves him right!"

Smash put his ear to the peephole. He heard a faint, angry neighing, as of an aroused stallion, and a startled scream. It seemed the demon could not dematerialize very effectively in a world where everything was already immaterial. Then the beat of hooves faded away in the internal distance.

Smash smiled. As Tandy had suggested, it would be long before the demon found his way out of that situation!

He drew forth Tandy's fillet of soul and handed it back to her. Suddenly he felt his full strength return, and saw Tandy brightening similarly. Their two half souls had been returned!

Smash realized what it was. The nightmares had made a fair exchange for the two halves of Fiant.

Smash straightened up, keeping his eye averted from the peephole. He squinted at Tandy, perceiving her disheveled but pert nudity. "Ogre confess, like she dress," he said.

"Oh, you're a sight for sore eyes yourself!" Tandy said in nurselike fashion, wiping Smash's battered face. "And sore nose, too! But do you know something? I love you just as much in the ogre view."

He kissed her then, using his sore lips, not caring what point of view it might be. Love was, after all, blind.

Night Mare

For our Mare
Sky Blue
and her girl Penny
our Heaven-cent daughter

Contents

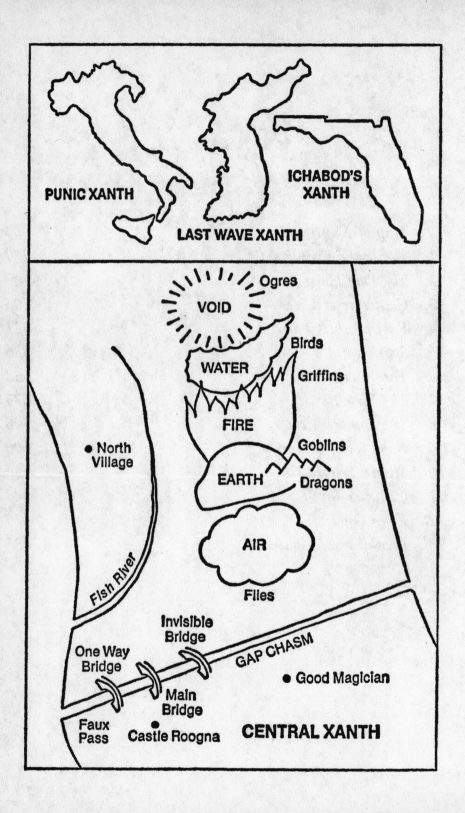

Chapter 1

To See the Rainbow

The stork glided to a landing before Stunk's residence and squawked for attention.

"No, it can't be!" the goblin cried in panic. "I'm not even married!"

" 'Snot that," the stork said through his long bill. "In the off-season I deliver mail." He produced an official-looking letter.

"Off-season for what?" the goblin demanded.

"You wouldn't understand. Take the missive. I have other idiots to bug."

"But I can't read!" Stunk protested, his panic shifting to embarrassment. Few goblins could read, but like most illiterates, they didn't like this advertised.

"I will read it to you, bulbnose." The stork opened the envelope and oriented an eye on the document inside. "Greetings."

"Same to you, birdbrain," Stunk said politely. Goblins had excellent manners, though for some reason other creatures seemed unable to appreciate them.

"Don't answer back, dolt," the stork said. "I'm reading the letter, not talking to you. Don't you know what 'Greetings' means?"

Stunk didn't answer.

"Hey, stupid, I asked you a question," the stork said, irritated.

"I thought you were reading the letter, needlebeak, so I didn't answer back. I'm trying to be polite to one not worth the effort. Of course I know what it means. It's an ungoblinish salutation."

"Salutation, ha! You dope, it means you have been drafted!"

"What? I wasn't aware of any draft. It's a very quiet day; no breeze at all."

"Abducted into the army, moron! Caught by the official press gang. Your happy civilian life is over."

"No!" Stunk cried, appalled. "I don't want to fight. Not that way, with weapons and rules and things. Tell me it isn't true!"

"I'll bet you wish you'd had the baby instead, huh, goblin!" the stork gloated, cradling the letter with his wings.

"Why would I be summoned to war? We're at relative peace with the dragons and the griffins!"

"It's the Mundane invasion, oaf. The Nextwave of conquest. The horrible Mundanes are coming to make dragon stew and goblins too."

"No! No!" Stunk screamed, his horror growing by stumbles and lurches and faltering footsteps. "I don't want to be goblin stew! I'm only a young, ignorant lout! I have my whole ornery life ahead of me! I won't go!"

"Then you are a draft evader or a deserter," the stork said, licking his beak with an orange tongue. "Do you know what they do to deserters?"

"I don't want to know!"

"They feed them to dragons." The stork was gloating; waves of gloat radiated out from him like ripples on a greasy puddle. Behind him a dragon loomed, snorting up little warm-up snorts of purple smoke.

"They'll never get me alive!" Stunk cried, working up to a superior degree of cowardice. He charged out of his hole in the wall, fleeing the draft notice. But already the dragon was pursuing him hungrily, pumping up extra-purple smoke, the kind that not only roasted goblins, but smelled pretty bad, too. Salivary smoke.

Stunk fled screaming, feeling the monster's fire hot at his back. He paid no attention to where his feet were going. He was beginning to outdistance the dragon, but knew he was not yet out of its range; that tongue of flame could reach him any time.

Suddenly he was at the brink of a ledge, unable to stop. His horror doubled as he fell off. He saw the hard rock of the bottom of a canyon rushing up at him as his stubby arms windmilled futilely. Better the dragon than this, and better the draft than the dragon—but now it was too late for either.

It was too much. Bawling out his terror, he woke.

* * *

Imbri leaped through the wall, phasing into intangibility. She had misjudged the client's reaction to the dream and had almost been caught visible. It was very bad form for any night mare to be seen by a waking person, even one as insignificant as a goblin. She galloped out into the night, leaving only a single hoofprint behind as a signature. That signature was important; Imbri was a perfectionist, and liked to put her personal stamp on every bad dream she delivered.

Dawn was threatening. Fortunately, this was her last call; now she could go home and relax and graze for the day. She galloped across the land, passing through trees and bushes, until she came to a patch of hypnogourds. Without pause she dived into a ripe gourd—a feat that would have surprised anyone who was not conversant with magic, as horses were much larger than gourds—and was instantly in an alternate world.

Soon she was on the dusky plain, with the other mares of the night mare herd converging, all returning from duty. Their hoofprints bore maps of the moon, with its green cheese and holes, and the names of the individual mares highlighted thereon. MARE HUMERUM, MARE NUBIUM, MARE FRIGORIS, MARE NECTARIS, MARE AUSTRALE—all her old immortal friends, all with seas of the moon named after them, in honor of their nocturnal performance over the centuries.

Another mare galloped up to intercept Imbri. It was Crisium, serving as temporary liaison to the Night Stallion. She projected a dreamlet the moment she came within range. It was the scene of an elf, waving his arms in animated speech. "Imbri!" the elf exclaimed. "Report to Trojan right away!" The brief dream faded.

A summons from the Dark Horse himself? That was not to be ignored! Imbri whirled on a hoof and charged across the plain, heading for the stable. Her relaxation would have to wait.

The Night Stallion was awaiting her. He stood huge and handsome, midnight black of hide and mane and tail and hoof in the same fashion as all the mares, but on him it was more impressive. *Any* male was impressive in the realm of equus, for the real power lay with the few stallions.

Trojan projected a dream set in a lush human edifice chamber, in which Imbri took the form of an elegant human person lady, and he was a grayhaired human creature King.

"You are not doing well, Mare Imbrium!" the Horse King said. "You have lost that special spark that truly terrifies. I am dissatisfied."

"But I just drove a goblin to distraction!" Imbri-Lady protested.

"After hauling in the dragon and the unforeshadowed cliff," Trojan retorted. "You should have had him terrified into oblivion before he ever left the house. Dream dragons must not be brought in promiscuously, or the dreamers will become acclimated to them and desensitized. That ruins it for the other mares. You must avoid overexposure of emergency elements."

Imbri realized it was true. The nucleus of the dream had been the horror of the draft that was supposed to chill the spine of the client and make him shiver. She had lost her competitive edge and made clumsy what should have been precise. "I will try to do better," her lady form said penitently.

"That is not enough," he replied. "The edge is not entirely a matter of trying. It is inherent. Once you lose it, it's gone. I'm going to have to trade you, Mare Imbrium."

"But this is the only work I know!" she protested, stricken. She felt as the goblin had when receiving a dread notice. After more than a century of dream duty, during which time she had earned and held her designated moon sea, she wasn't ready for anything else.

"You can learn new work. There are daydreams—"

"Daydreams!" she repeated with contempt.

"I believe you have the inclination."

"Inclination?" She was stunned. "I never—"

"You were recently caught and ridden by a client," he said firmly. "No night mare can be caught unless she tacitly acquiesces."

"But—"

"Why would you accede to being caught by a client?" The King held up a hand to forestall her protest. "I will tell you why. You saw, in the memory of another client long ago, the image of a rainbow. You were fascinated by this vision; you wanted to see the reality for yourself. But you knew you could never do that as a night mare, for the rainbow shuns the night. It is a phenomenon of day."

"Yes . . ." she agreed, realizing it was true. The vision of the multicolored rainbow had haunted her for years. But no night mare could go abroad by day; the radiation of the sun caused her kind to fade rapidly. So it had always been a futile notion, and she had been quite foolish to let it distract her.

"As it happens, you possess half a soul," the Stallion continued. "You carried an ogre out of the fringe of the Void and accepted in payment half the soul of a centaur, when all you really wanted was the chance to see a rainbow. Logic has never been the strong point of females."

She remembered it well. The ogre had wanted to do her a return favor, but she had not felt free to converse with him in dreamlet fashion and had been unable to convey her interest in the rainbow to him otherwise. He had been a decent sort, for an ogre and for a male. The two concepts overlapped significantly.

"As it happens," the Dream King continued, "that soul has further dulled your edge, interfering with your dream performance. It is difficult to be truly brutal when you have a soul; that is contrary to the nature of souls."

"But it's only a half soul," Imbri protested. "A mere fillet of soul. I thought it wouldn't hurt."

"Any portion of a soul hurts in this business," he said. "Are you ready to give it up now?"

"Give up my soul?" she asked, appalled for a reason she could not define.

"As you know, most mares who earn half souls soon turn them in to me for storage, so that their edge will not be dulled, and they receive bonus-credit for extraordinary service to the cause. Souls are extremely valuable commodities, and we grasp and hold any we can. You alone retained your share of soul, passing up the advantage you could have had by cashing it in. Why?"

"I don't know," Imbri admitted, ashamed.

"I *do* know," Trojan said. "You are a nice personality, and you have grown nicer over the decades. You don't really enjoy causing people misery. The soul enhances that liability."

"Yes . . ." she agreed sadly, knowing that she was confessing a guilty secret that could indeed wash her out as a bearer of bad dreams. "I have drifted along an errant path."

"This is not necessarily wrong."

Her ears perked forward—an incongruous thing, since she remained in lady image in the dream. "Not wrong?"

"It relates to your destiny. It will one day enable you to see the rainbow."

"The rainbow!"

"You are a marked mare, Imbrium, and you will set your mark on Xanth. That time is near."

Imbri stared at him. The Night Stallion knew more than any other creature in the World of Night, but seldom told it. If he perceived a pattern in Imbri's incapacities, he was surely correct. But she dared not inquire about it, directly.

"Imbrium, I am transferring you to day mare duty. A more horrendous mare will assume your night duties."

"But I can't go into day!" she protested with fearful hope. She knew how brutal and awful some mares were, with wild eyes and wilder manes; they had absolutely no mercy on sleepers. It bothered her to think of her clients being placed in the power of such a creature.

"One of the distinctions between night mares and day mares is the possession of souls. The creatures of night have no souls; those of day have no bodies. You will actually be a halfway creature, with half a soul and a half-material body. I shall enchant you to be able to withstand the light of the sun."

"I can go abroad in the real world by day?" The hope became less fearful, for when the Stallion neighed, all mares believed.

"You will serve as liaison between the Powers of the Night and the powers of day during the crisis."

"Crisis?" Imbri thought she was confusing the term with her friend Mare Crisium.

"It is essential that the enemy not know your nature, or enormous peril may arise. They must perceive you as a simple horse."

"Enemy?"

"It was in the dream you delivered. You have become careless about such details."

Imbri tried to review the details of the last dream, but before she could make progress, the Dark Horse continued. "Therefore you will report to Chameleon, to be her steed."

"To whom? To be what?"

"She is the mother of Prince Dor, Xanth's next King. She is part of the key to Xanth's salvation. She will need transportation and the kind of guidance and assistance only a night mare can provide. Guard her, Imbrium; she is more important than anyone suspects. You will also bear her this message for King Trent: BEWARE THE HORSEMAN."

"But I don't understand!" Imbri exclaimed, the dream background shaking.

"You aren't meant to."

"I don't even know Chameleon or King Trent! I've never had to take a dream to either of them! How can I deliver a message?"

"Your present image is that of Chameleon," the Stallion said, producing a mirror from air so she could look at herself in the dream. Imbri was not a phenomenal judge of human appearance, but the image appeared quite ugly. Chameleon was an awful crone. "Use your dreamer-locater sense; it will operate by day as well as by night. And if you need to meet King Trent directly—he is my present image." The Stallion's dream form was handsome in an aged sort of way—the very model of a long-reigning King.

"But I understand so little!" Imbri protested. "This is like a bad dream."

"Granted," the Stallion said. "War is very like a bad dream. But it does not pass with the night, and its evil remains long after the combat has abated. War is no warning of ill; it is the ill itself."

"War?"

But the Stallion's kingly eyes flashed, and the dream faded. Imbri found herself standing at the edge of the broad grazing plain, alone. The interview was over.

Imbri traveled the realm of the night, making her farewells to its denizens. She went to the City of Brass, threading her way between the moving buildings, meeting the brass folk. Brassies were just like human folk, only made of metal. The males wore brassards and the females wore brassieres. The brass folk were activated when particular dreams had to be mass-produced; they were very good at mechanized manufacturing. Imbri had been here often before to pick up specialized dreams, and they were always well crafted.

One brassie girl approached Imbri. "You do not know me, mare," she said. "I understand you are going dayside. I was dayside once."

Imbri remembered that a brassie had briefly joined the party of the ogre. "You must be Blyght!" she sent.

"I am Blythe. I changed my name. I envy you, mare; I wish I could visit dayside again. The light doesn't hurt me, and some of the people are very nice."

"Yes, they are. If I ever have occasion to bring a brassie there, it will be you, Blythe," Imbri promised, feeling a kind of camaraderie with the girl. Perhaps Blythe, too, wanted to see the rainbow.

Imbri went on to bid farewell to the paper folk and the ifrits in their bottles and the walking skeletons of the graveyard shift and the ghosts of the haunted house. All of them contributed their special talents to the manufacture of frightening dreams; it was a community effort.

"Say hello to my friend Jordan," one of the ghosts told her. "He haunts Castle Roogna now."

Imbri promised to relay the message. She went finally to mix with her friends, the other mares, with whom she had worked so closely for so many years. This was the saddest of her partings.

Now it was time to go. Imbri had used up the day and grazed the night, preparing for the awful transition. She did like her work as a bearer of bad dreams, even if she was no longer good at it. It was exciting to contemplate going into day, but awful to think of leaving the night. All her friends were here, not there!

She trotted out toward the rind. No creature could escape the gourd unaided except a night mare. Otherwise all the bad stuff of dreams would escape and ravage Xanth uncontrolled—a natural disaster. So the gourd had to be limited, a separate world of its own, except for those whose business it was to deliver its product. Some few people foolish enough to attempt to glimpse its secrets by peeking into the peephole of a gourd found themselves trapped there for an indefinite period. If one of their friends interfered with their gaze at the peephole, then they were freed—and seldom peeked again. It was always wisest not to peek at what concerned one not, lest one see what pleased one not.

The Stallion was right: Imbri had lost her touch with the dreams. She carried them, she delivered them—but the goblin's draft notice had not been her first clumsy effort. She no longer had the necessary will to terrify, and it showed. It was indeed best that she go into another line of work, difficult as the transition might be.

She focused on the positive side of it. She would at last get to see Xanth by day. She would see the rainbow at last! That would be the fulfillment of her fondest suppressed ambition.

And after that, what? Could the sight of the rainbow be worth the loss of her job and her friends? That seemed a little thin now.

She came to the rind and plunged through it. She didn't need to will herself immaterial; that came automatically. In a moment she was out in the night of Xanth.

The moon was there, exactly like one of her hoofprints, its sea and craters etched on the surface of its cheese. She paused to stare at it, spotting her namesake, Mare Imbrium, the Sea of Rains. Some called it the Sea of Tears; she had always taken the name as a punnish play on concepts. The Land of Xanth was largely fashioned of puns; they seemed to be its fundamental building blocks. Now, with her half soul and her new life ahead, the Sea of Tears seemed to have more significance.

She backed off and looked at one of her hoofprints. It matched the visible moon, as it always did, even to the phase. The prints of night mares became obscure as the moon waned, unless a mare made a special effort, as for a signature. Imbri had never liked dream duty when the moon was dark; her feet tended to skid, leaving no prints at all. But there was no such problem tonight; the moon was full almost to the bursting point.

She trotted on through the Xanthian night, just as if bearing a fresh load of dreams to sleeping clients. But this time her only burden was her message: beware the Horseman. She didn't know what that meant, but surely the King would. Meanwhile, her equine heart beat more strongly with anticipation as the dread dawn gathered itself. Always before she had fled the rising sun, the scourge of day; this time she would face the carnage it did to the darkness.

The stars began to fade. They wanted no part of this! Day was coming; soon it would be light enough for the sun to climb safely aloft. The sun hated the night, just as the moon despised the day; but Imbri understood the moon had the courage to encroach on the edges of the day, especially when fully inflated and strong. Perhaps the lady moon was interested in the male sun, though he gave her scant encouragement. As long as the moon was present, a night mare could travel safely, though perhaps uncomfortably, even if the edge of day caught her. But why take chances?

Still, Imbri had to brace herself as the light swelled ominously. She knew the spell of the Night Stallion and the presence of her half soul would enable her to survive the day—but somehow it was hard to believe absolutely. What would happen if the spell were faulty? She could be destroyed by the strike of a deadly sunbeam, and her sea on the moon would fade out, unremembered. She trusted the Stallion, of course; he was her sire and he ruled the Powers of the Night. yet surely the sun was an aspect of the powers of the day, and perhaps did not know she was supposed to be exempt from its mischief. Or if it knew, maybe it refused to recognize the fact. "Oops, sorry, Horse; you mean *that* was the mare I was supposed to spare? Fortunately, you have others . . ."

The brightening continued inexorably. Now was the time; she would have to stand—or break and run home to the gourd. Her legs trembled; her nostrils dilated. White showed around the edges of her eyes. Her body was poised for flight.

Then she remembered the rainbow. She would never see it—unless she faced the sun. Or faced away from it; it was always a creature's shadow that pointed to the rainbow, she understood; that was one of the special aspects of the magic of Xanth, that secret signal. But the sunlight had to fall on that person to make the shadow appear—shadows were reputed to be very strict about that—so the shadow could perform.

The mare Imbri stood, letting the dread sun ascend, watching its terrible beams lance their way cruelly through the mists of morning. One launched itself right toward Imbri, amazingly swift, and scored before she could react.

She survived. The only effect was a shine on her coat where the beam touched. The protective spell had held.

She had withstood the awful light of the sun. She was now a day mare.

After the tension of the moment, Imbri felt an enormous relief. Never had she suspected the Night Stallion of seeking to eliminate her by tricking her into braving the sunbeam, yet she realized now that some such suspicion had made an attempt to harbor itself deep in her being. How glad she was that her trust had been justified!

She took a step, feeling the soundness of her legs, the solidity of the ground, and the springiness of the air she breathed. Not only did she seem whole, she seemed twice as real as before. She was now conscious of the weight of her body, of the touch of weeds against her skin, and of the riffle in her mane as a teasing breeze sought it out.

OUCH!

She made a squeal of protest and swished her tail, slapping her own flank smartly. A fly buzzed up. The brute had bitten her!

She had become a creature of the day, all right! No fly could bite a true night mare. Few flies abounded at night, and the mares were solid only when they willed themselves so. Now it seemed she was solid and bitable—without effort. She would have to watch that; getting chomped by a bug wasn't fun. Fortunately, she had a good tail; she could keep the little monsters clear.

There was a certain joy in solidity. Now the sunbeams were bathing the whole side of her body, warming it. The heat felt strangely good. She was more alive than ever. There was something about being all-the-way solid that was exhilarating. Who would have believed it!

She walked, then trotted, then pranced. She leaped high in the air and felt the spring of her legs as they absorbed her shock of landing. She leaped again, even higher—

Something cracked her down in mid-prance. She dropped to the ground, bright white stars and planets orbiting her dazed head. Those stellar objects had certainly found her quickly! What had happened?

As her equilibrium returned, accompanied by a bruise on her head, Imbri saw that nothing had struck her. Instead, she had struck something. She had launched into a pomegranate tree, cracking headfirst into its pome-trunk, jarring loose several granate fruits. She was lucky none of those rocks had hit her on the way down!

Now she understood on a more basic level the liabilities of being substantial all the time. She had not watched where she was going, because she usually phased through objects automatically. As a day mare, she could not do that. When solid met solid, there was a brutal thump!

She walked more sedately after that, careful not to bang into any more trees. There was nothing like a good clout on the noggin to instill caution! Though muted, her joy remained; it merely found less physical ways to express itself, deepening and spreading, suffusing her body.

But it was time to go about her business. Imbri oriented—

And discovered she had forgotten what her business was.

That knock on the head must have done it. She knew she was a night mare turned day mare, and that she had to go see someone, and deliver a message—but who that person might be, and what the message was, she could not recollect.

She was lost—not in terms of the geography of Xanth, which she knew well, but in terms of herself. She did not know where to go or what to do—though she knew it was important that she go there and do it promptly, and that the enemy not discover whatever it was she had to do.

Imbri concentrated. There was something—ah, yes! That was it! The rainbow! She had come to see the rainbow. That must be her mission—though where the rainbow was at the moment, and what she was supposed to say to it, and why this was important to the welfare of the Land of Xanth—these things remained opaque.

Well, she would just have to look for it. Eventually she would find the rainbow, and perhaps then the meaning in this mission would become apparent.

Chapter 2

The Day Horse

Mare Imbri was hungry. There had always been plenty of grazing in the gourd, but she had been too busy and too immaterial to graze while on dream duty and evidently had not consumed enough during the past night to sustain the elevated material pace of the real world. Now she had to graze—and didn't know where to find a decent pasture, here in dayside Xanth.

She looked about. She was in the deep jungle forest. Dry leaves coated the forest floor; there were few blades of grass, and those that she found were wiregrass, metallic and inedible. No doubt this was where the brassies harvested some of the wire for their constructions. She was roughly familiar with this region, of course, since she had been all over Xanth on dream duty—but by day it looked different, and now that she was fixed solid, it felt different.

She had never paid much attention to the potential grazing here. Where would there be a decent pasture?

Well, this was not far west of Castle Roogna, the humanfolk capital. She recalled that there was a large clearing north of here, and that should have plenty of excellent grazing. The problem was, there was a minor mountain range between herself and that pasture, and in her present solid state it would be at best tedious and at worst dangerous to climb over that range.

There was good pasturage at the castle, however. But she had seldom gone there, as the bad dreams for the royal human personages were generally carried by night mares with seniority, those who had been in the business for three centuries or more. Imbri would be likely to blunder in that vicinity, especially by day, and she didn't want to do that.

But she remembered that there was a pass through the mountains, little known but adequate. It had a mildly interesting history—

She paused in her thought. There was a nice patch of grass, superverdant! She could graze right here, after all.

She trotted to it and put her nose down. The grass reached up and hooked in her tender nostrils and lip.

Imbri vaulted backward, her nose getting scratched as the awful greenery ripped free. That was carnivorous grass! She couldn't go near that; instead of being eaten by her, it would eat her.

No help for it. She would have to cross the mountains. She set off at a trot, bearing north. She skirted tangle trees and danglevines and the lairs of dragons, griffins, basilisks, nickelpedes, and other ilk, knowing they were now dangerous to her. She had, after all, illustrated such hazards in the dreams she delivered to deserving creatures often enough. Soon she came to the mountains.

Now where was that pass? A little westward, she recalled. She trotted in that direction. She knew the general lay of the land, but exact details of placement were vague, since material things not relating to clients had not had much importance to her before.

Something was coming toward her. Imbri paused, not frightened but careful. She realized that she was now vulnerable to monsters, though she had confidence she could outrun most of them. Few things moved faster than a night mare in a hurry! But there were so many things to remember when one's body was stuck solid.

The reality was a pleasant surprise. It was a magnificent white horse, trotting eastward along the range. He had a fine white mane, a lovely tail, and his appearance was marred only by a thin brass band about his left foreleg, at ankle height. Imbri had never heard of a horse wearing a bracelet—but, of course, the only horses she knew were those of the gourd.

He halted when he spied Imbri. She became conscious of the distinction between them: she was a black mare, he a white stallion. She had understood there were no true horses in Xanth, only part equines like the sea horses, horseflies, and centaurs. Her kind, the night mares, existed separately in the gourd and did not roam freely when not on business. There were also the daydream mares, but they were completely invisible and immaterial, except to others of their kind. What was this creature doing here?

She decided to ask him. She could have neighed, but wasn't sure she could define her question well enough that way. So she stepped forward somewhat diffidently and projected a small dream. It was technically a daydream, since this was day—a conscious kind of imagining, much milder in content and intensity than the night visions she normally carried. It was also less perfectly structured, since she had no original text to work from. Anything could happen in an extemporaneous dream!

In this dream she assumed a talking form, that of a young human woman garbed in black, with lustrous long black hair in lieu of a mane and a skirt instead of a tail. Skirts weren't as useful as tails, since they were no good for swatting flies, but did serve to render mysterious that portion of the anatomy that profited by such treatment. Human people almost always wore clothing over their functional parts, as if they were ashamed of such parts; it was one of a number of oddities about them. "Who are you?" the dream girl inquired with a fetching smile.

The white horse's ears flattened in dismay and suspicion. He wheeled and bolted, galloping away back west.

Imbri sighed through her nose. He had been such a handsome creature! But apparently he was afraid of human people. Had she known, she would have projected something else, such as a talking bird. If she should encounter him again, she would be much more careful.

She proceeded west and in due course located the pass. And there, standing within it, was a man. He was of good stature for his kind, with pale hair and skin, with muscle on his limbs and handsomeness of his face in the humanoid manner. Naturally no human person was as handsome as a horse; that was another of the discomforts the human species seemed to have learned to live with.

"I say, pretty mare," the man called when he saw her. "Have you seen a runaway white stallion? He is my steed, but he bolted. He wears my circlet on his foreleg." And the man held aloft his left wrist, where there was a similar short circlet. There could be little doubt he was associated with the horse.

Imbri projected a dreamlet: herself in woman form, again garbed in black, her female parts carefully covered. She did not want to scare off another creature! "I saw him shortly ago, man, but he bolted from me, too. He ran in this direction."

The man looked startled. "Is that you in my mind, mare, or did I imagine it?"

"It is me, man," she said, continuing the daydream for him. "I am a dream equine. I project dream visions to your kind, but by day they lack the conviction they have at night." She had not realized it before, but obviously there was no qualitative difference between the dreams of night and those of day. It was just that the conscious minds of waking people were much less credulous, so the impact was less. They could readily distinguish fancy from reality. But the dreams remained excellent for communication.

"Ah. And did you project such a dream to my steed, the day horse? No wonder he spooked!"

"I fear my visions can frighten creatures who are not prepared," she projected, her woman image spreading her hands in the human signal of gentle bewilderment. If only she had been able to inspire such fright in her bad dream duty! "I am the night mare Imbrium, called Imbri for brief."

"A night mare!" he exclaimed. "I have often met your kind in my sleep. But I thought you could not go abroad by day."

"I am under special disposition to the day," she said. "But I do not remember my mission, except perhaps to see the rainbow."

"Ah, the rainbow!" he exclaimed. "And a worthwhile goal that is, mare! I have seen it many times and have always marveled anew!"

"Where is it?" she asked eagerly, so excited she almost forgot to project it in dream form; when she did, her dream girl was in partial dishabille, like a nymph. Quickly she patched up the image, for the dream man was beginning to stare. "I know my shadow points to it, but—"

"There must be sun *and* rain to summon the rainbow," the man said.

"But don't clouds blot out the sun during rainfall? There can't be both at once."

"There can be, but it is rare. The rainbow formation is exceedingly choosy about when and where it appears, lest familiarity make it change from magic to mundane. You will not see it today; there is not rain nearby."

"Then I shall go and graze," she said, disappointed.

"That is surely what my steed is doing, though I feed him well," he said. "His appetite is open-ended; sometimes I think he processes hay into clods without bothering to digest them in passing. Left to his own devices, he eats without respite. But he's a good horse. Where could he have gone? He did not pass by me, and I have been walking east until I heard your hoof-falls."

Imbri studied the ground. Horseprints curved into the gap between mountains. "He seems to have gone through the pass," she projected.

The man looked. "I see his tracks now. That must be it. Had I been a little swifter, I should have intercepted him." He paused, looking at Imbri. "Mare, this may be an imposition, but I am not much afoot. Would you give me a lift through the mountains? I assure you I only want to catch up to my errant steed. Once I see him and call to him, he will come to me; he's really an obedient mount and not used to being on his own. He may even be looking for me, but have lost his way; he is not as intelligent as you are."

Imbri hesitated. She had been ridden before, but preferred freedom. Yet she would like to meet the day horse again, and if she was going this man's way anyway—

"Or if you would like to come home with me," the man continued persuasively, "I have plentiful grain and hay, which I keep for my own horse. He is of Mundane stock, you know; what he lacks in wit he makes up for in speed and power. But he is very shy and gentle; not a mean bone in his body. I fear he will come to harm, alone in this magic land."

Mundane stock. That would explain the presence of the horse. Some Mundane animals did wander into Xanth, randomly. Of course, it was not safe for such creatures here. Even Imbri herself, a creature of an aspect of Xanth, could have trouble here by day; there were perils all about. That was probably why the true daydream mares were intangible; it was a survival trait not to be able to materialize by day. "I will take you through the pass," she projected.

"Excellent," the man said. "And in return, I will show you a rainbow, the very first chance I get." He approached, his voice continuing softly, soothingly. She stood still, with a certain nervousness, for ordinarily no waking person could touch a night mare. But she reminded herself firmly that she was now a creature of the day and touchable.

The man sprang on her back. His boots hung down on either side, around her barrel, and his hands gripped her mane. He had ridden a horse before; if she had not known the day horse was his steed, she could have told by his balance and confidence.

She started through the pass, the man riding easily, so that she was hardly aware of his weight. The ground was firm and almost level, and she was able to trot.

"This is a strange configuration," the man said as they passed almost beneath the looming rocky cliffs of the sides of the pass. "So steep above, so level below."

"This is the Faux Pass," Imbri sent in a dreamlet. "Centuries ago the giant Faux was tramping north, and there were clouds about his knees, so he did not see the mountain range. He caught his left foot on it and tripped and almost took a fall. He was a big giant, and such a fall would have wreaked enormous destruction in Xanth. But he caught himself, and his misstep merely kicked out a foot-sized piece of the range, creating a gap that ordinary creatures could use to get through. Thus it came to be named after him, though now people tend to pronounce it rather sloppily and just call it 'Fo Pa.'"

"A most delightful story!" the man said, patting Imbri on the shoulder. She felt good, and felt foolish for the feeling. What did she care for the opinion of a human man? Perhaps her new solidity made her more susceptible to the opinions of solid creatures. "This is a fascinating derivation. Faux Pass—the giant misstep. I suspect that term will in due course enter the language, for many people make missteps of one nature or another."

They emerged to the north. The plain spread out, filled with lush tall grass. Imbri was delighted; here she could graze her fill.

"I think I see a print," the man said. "Over there." He made a gesture.

Imbri hesitated, uncertain which way he meant, as his gesture had been confusing. She did want to find the day horse; he was such a handsome animal—and he was also male. She veered to the left.

"No, wrong way," the man said. "There." He gestured confusingly again.

She veered right. "No, still wrong," he said.

Imbri stopped. "I can't tell where you mean," she projected, irritated, her dream girl frowning prettily through strands of mussed-up hair.

"Not your fault," the man said. "I love your little imaginary pictures; *you* have no trouble communicating. My verbal directions are too nonspecific, and you evidently are not familiar with my human gestures. But I think I can clarify them." He jumped down, removing something from his clothing. It was a little brass stick with cords attached to each end. "Put this in your mouth, behind your front set of teeth." He held the stick up to her face, sidewise, nudging it at her mouth, so that she had either to take it or to back off. She opened her mouth doubtfully, and set it in, between her front and back teeth, where there was the natural equine gap. Human beings did not have such a gap, which was another one of their problems; they could not chew nearly as well as horses could, since everything tended to mush up together in their mouths, unappetizingly.

"Now I will tug on these reins," he explained. "That will show you exactly where to go. Here, I'll demonstrate." He jumped on her back again and got the two cords reaching from the metal bit to his hands. "Turn that way," he said, tugging in the right rein.

The bit pulled back against her hind teeth uncomfortably. To ease the pressure, Imbri turned her head to the right. "You've got it!" the man cried. "You are a very smart horse!"

It had not been intelligence; it had been discomfort. "I don't like this device," Imbri projected.

"You don't? I'm so sorry. Let's turn to the left now." He tugged at the other rein, sending a twinge to that side of her jaw.

But Imbri had had enough. She balked, planting all four feet firmly on the ground and trying to spit out the brass bit. It tasted awful, anyway. But the reins held it in place, annoyingly. She sent a fierce dream at him, of her dream girl self gesturing in righteous ire, tresses flouncing. "Get off my back, man!"

"You must address me by my proper title," the man said. "I am known as the Horseman."

The Horseman! Suddenly Imbri's misplaced memory returned. Her message was "beware the Horseman"—and now she had an inkling of its meaning.

"Beware the Horseman, eh?" the man repeated, and Imbri realized she had spoken her thought in the dream. Angrily she exploded her dream girl image into a roil of smoke, but this did not daunt the man. "So you carry a message of warning about me! What a fortunate coincidence this is, mare. I certainly can not afford to let you go now. I must take you home with me and keep you confined so that you can not betray me."

Imbri did not know what to do, so she continued to do nothing. She had unwittingly put herself in the power of the one person she should have avoided!

"Time to go home," the Horseman said. "I'll come back and catch the day horse later; you are too valuable a captive to let escape. I understand you night mares can pass through solid rock at night, and even turn invisible. That means I must get you safely corralled before darkness comes. Move, move, mare!"

Imbri refused to move. It was true; he could not hold her at night even if he remained awake and alert. If he slept, she would send him a dream so bad he would be paralyzed. Time was on her side. But she had no intention of obliging him one moment longer than necessary. Her feet would remain planted here until she figured out how to dump him.

"I have another little device that may amuse you," the Horseman said. "It makes horses go." And he banged his heels into her flanks.

Pain lanced through her. There were knives on his boots! Imbri was leaping forward before she realized it, jolted by the shock. A horse's natural response to fright or pain was to bolt, as running was normally the most effective defense.

"You appreciate my spurs?" the Horseman inquired. He drew on the left rein, forcing her to curve around that way.

Imbri tried to slow, but the spurs stung her again, making her run faster. She tried to veer right, but the bit in her mouth cut cruelly and she had to go left. The Horseman had subjected her to his awful will!

No wonder the day horse had fled this terrible man! If only she had realized the Horseman's nature! If only she had not foolishly forgotten her warning message!

But these things had come to pass, and she was paying the price of her neglect. If she ever got out of this fix, she would be a wiser mare!

The Horseman rode her back through the Faux Pass and west along the south side of the mountain range. Imbri stopped fighting her captor and found it amazingly easy to yield to his directives. The Horseman did not hurt her unless she resisted.

Imbri cursed herself for her inability to resist. But she was rapidly becoming conditioned to the will of the Horseman. When she tried to resist, he punished her; when she obeyed, he praised her. He seemed so sure of himself, so reasonable, so consistent, while she seemed, even to herself, like a poorly mannered animal. For now, until she figured out an effective course of independence, she had to go along.

But capitulation was not enough. He wanted information, too. "Who gave you that warning to beware of me?" he asked.

Imbri hesitated. The Horseman touched her sore flanks with his awful spurs—they weren't actually knives, they just felt like it—and she decided that there was no harm in answering. She sent a dreamlet, representing herself in woman form, in shackles, her side bleeding from abrasions, and with a brass bar in her mouth. "Ve commands va Fowers of va Night," the woman said around the bit.

"Do not tease me, mare," the Horseman said, touching her again with the spurs. "Your dreams can speak clearly."

She had to give up that ploy. "He commands the Powers of the Night," she repeated clearly. "The Night Stallion. He assigns the dreams to be delivered. He sent the message."

"The Night Stallion," the Horseman repeated. "Naturally you equines revert to the herd in the wild state. But he is confined to the night?"

"To the gourd," she clarified. "It keeps us secure by day." Now she wished she had never left it!

"Explain," he said. "The only gourd I know is the hypnogourd that has a little peephole. Anyone who sets eye to that is instantly hypnotized and can not move or speak until someone else breaks the connection."

"That is the same," Imbri's tattered dream girl said, looking woeful. She hated giving so much information to the enemy, but didn't see how this particular news would help this man. He already knew better than to peek into a gourd, unfortunately. "We night mares are the only creatures who can pass freely in and out of the gourd. All gourds are the same; all open onto the same World of Night. When a person looks into any gourd, his body freezes but his spirit takes form inside and must thread its way through our labyrinth of entertainments. Those who remain too long risk losing their souls; then their bodies will never be functional again."

"So it's a kind of trap, a prison," he said thoughtfully. "I suspected some such; I'm glad you are choosing to tell me the truth, mare. How many spirits can it contain?"

"Any number. The gourd is as large as Xanth in its fashion. It has to be, to contain dreams for every person in Xanth, every night, no two dreams the same. To us in the gourd, the rest of Xanth seems small enough to carry under one of your arms."

"Yes, I see that now. Very interesting. We can carry your world around, and you can carry ours around. It's all relative." After a moment he had a new question. "To whom were you to deliver your message?"

Now Imbri resisted, being sure this would affect the conduct of the war. But the Horseman dug in his spurs again, and the pain became so terrible she had to tell. She had never had to endure pain before, for it didn't exist in immaterial form; she couldn't handle it. "I was to go to Chameleon with the message for the King."

"Who is Chameleon?"

"The mother of Prince Dor, the next King. She is an ugly woman."

"Why not take the message directly to the King?" The spurs were poised.

"I don't know!" The dream girl flinched, putting her hands to her sides.

The spurs touched. Desperately, Imbri amplified. "My mission was to be secret! Maybe it was a ruse, to report to the woman, who would relay the message to the King. No one would suspect I was liaison to the gourd."

"The King is important, then? Nothing can be done without his directive?"

"The King rules the human concerns of Xanth," Imbri agreed. "He is like the Night Stallion. His word is law. Without his word, there would be no law."

"Yes, that makes sense," the Horseman decided, and the spurs did not strike again. "If you reported directly to the King, the enemy might catch on, and know the warning had been given. That could nullify much of its effect. Still, I think it better yet to nullify *all* its effect by preventing the message from being delivered at all. Because, of course, it is an apt warning; your Night Stallion evidently has good intelligence."

"He is the smartest of horses," Imbri agreed in a fragmentary dreamlet. "He knows more than he ever says, as does Good Magician Humfrey."

"Intelligence, as in gathering data about the enemy," the Horseman clarified. "This is the activity I am currently engaged in. But, of course, your Stallion has the night mare network. You mares were peeking into our brains as we slept, weren't you? No secrets from your kind."

"No, we only deliver the dreams," Imbri protested, her pride in her former profession overriding her wish to deceive the Horseman. "We can't tell what's in people's minds. If we could, I would never have let you put this bit in my mouth." That brass tasted awful, and not just physically!

"How, then, did you know about me? I know you knew, because of your message of warning about me."

"*I* don't know. The Night Stallion knows. He has a research department, so he can tell where to target the bad dreams. But he can't usually tell waking people. There's very little connection between the night world and the day world."

"So I now understand. Many secrets are buried in the depths of night! But what of this Good Magician, who you say also knows a great deal? Why hasn't he warned Xanth about me?"

"Magician Humfrey only gives information in return for one year's service by the one who asks." Imbri said. "Nobody asks him anything if he can help it."

"Ah, zealously guarded parameters," the Horseman said, seeming to like this information. "Or the mercenary motive. So for the truth about Xanth's situation, a person must either pay a prohibitive fee or peer into the peephole of a gourd—whereupon he is confined and can not extricate himself by his own effort. It is a most interesting situation. The people are almost entirely dependent on the King for information and leadership. If anything were to happen to King Trent—" He paused a moment. "His successor, Prince Dor— is he competent?"

"All I know is what I have picked up from people's dreams," Imbri temporized.

"Certainly. And their dreams reflect their deepest concerns. What about Prince Dor?"

"He has hardly had any experience," she sent unwillingly. "When he was a teenager, about eight years ago, King Trent went on vacation and left Dor in charge. He had to get his friends to help, and finally the Zombie Master had to come and take over until King Trent returned. There were a lot of bad dreams then; we mares were overloaded with cases and almost ran our tails off. It was not a very good time for Xanth."

"So Prince Dor is not noted for competence," the Horseman said. "And next in the line of succession is the Zombie Master, whom the people don't feel comfortable with. So there really is no proper successor to King Trent." He lapsed into thoughtful silence, guiding Imbri by nudges of his knees. When he pushed on one side, he wanted her to turn away from that side. He was not wantonly cruel, she understood; all he required was the subordination of her will to his in every little detail.

That was, of course, one thing she couldn't stand. At the moment she could not escape him, but she would find a way sometime. He couldn't keep the bit and spurs on her forever, and the moment he slipped, she would be gone—with a whole lot more news about him than she had had originally. Beware the Horseman, indeed!

They came to the Horseman's camp. There were two men there, Mundane by their look. "Found me a horse!" the Horseman called jovially.

"Where's the other horse?" one asked.

"He bolted. But I'll get him tomorrow. This one's better. She's a converted night mare."

"Sure enough," the Mundane agreed uncertainly, eyeing Imbri. It seemed he thought the reference to night mare was a joke. Mundanes could be very stupid about magic.

"Better off without the white horse," the other Mundane said. "For all the riding you get on him and all the feeding you give him, he's never around when you need him."

"He's got spirit, that's all," the Horseman said with a tolerant gesture. "I like a spirited animal. Now put a hobble on this one; she's a literal spirit, and she's not tame yet."

One of the henchmen came with a rope. Imbri shied away nervously, but the Horseman threatened her again with his awful spurs, and she had to stand still. The henchman tied the rope to her two forefeet, with only a short length between them, so that she could stand or walk carefully but could not run. What a humiliating situation!

They put her in a barren pen where there was a grimy bucket of water. They dumped half-cured hay in for her to chew. The stuff was foul, but she was so hungry now that she had to eat it, though she feared it would give her colic. No wonder the day horse had bolted!

All day she remained confined, while the Mundanes went about their brutish business elsewhere. Imbri drank the bad water, finished off the bad hay, and slept on her feet in the normal manner of her kind, her tail con-stantly swishing the bothersome flies away. She had plenty of time to consider her folly. But she knew the night would free her, and that buoyed her spirit, her half soul.

Now she meditated on that. Few of her kind possessed any part of any soul, and those who obtained one generally didn't keep it, as the Night Stallion had reminded her. Yet she clung to her soul as if it were most important. Was she being foolish? Imbri had carried the half-human Smash the Ogre out of the gourd and out of the Void, but it was not any part of his soul she had. It was half the soul of a centaur filly. That soul had changed her outlook, making her smarter and more sensitive to the needs of others. That had been bad for her business and had finally cost her her profession. But as she gradually mastered the qualities of the soul, she became more satisfied with it. Now she knew there was more to life than feeding and sleeping and doing her job. She was not certain what more there was, but it was well worth searching for. Perhaps the rainbow would have the answer; one look at the celestial phenomenon might make her soul comprehensible. Yet that search had led her into the privation of the moment.

As evening approached, the Horseman and the two henchmen appeared and started hauling firewood logs from the forest. The wood fairly glowed with eagerness to burn. They threw a flame-vine on the pile, and burn it did. The fire blazed high, turning the incipient shadows to the brightness of day.

Suddenly Imbri realized what they were doing. The Mundanes were keeping the pen too light for her to assume her nocturnal powers! As long as that fire burned, she could not escape!

With despair she watched as they hauled more logs. They had enough wood to carry them through the night. She would not be able to dematerialize.

The sun tired and dropped at last to the horizon, making the distant trees blaze momentarily from its own fire. Imbri wondered whether it descended in the same place each night, or whether it came down in different locations, doing more damage to the forest. She had never thought about this before, since the sun had been no part of her world, or she would have trotted over there and checked the burned region directly.

The fire blazed brighter than ever in the pen, malevolently consuming her precious darkness. It sent sparks up into the sky to rival the stars. Perhaps they were stars; after all, the little specks of light had to originate somewhere, and new ones would be needed periodically to replace the old ones that wore out. The Mundanes took turns watching Imbri and dumping more wood on the fire as it waned.

Waned, she thought. That jogged a nagging notion. She wished it had waned this night, putting out the fire. Waned? *Rained;* that was it. If only a good storm would come and douse everything. But the sky remained distressingly clear.

Slowly the henchman on guard nodded. He was sleeping on the job, and she was not about to wake him—but it didn't matter, because the fire was more than bright enough to keep her hobbled, whether he woke or slept. She might hurl a bad dream at him, but that would only bestir him with fright, making him alert again. She would have to deal with that fire first. But how, when she was hobbled?

Then she realized how to start. She approached the fire and put her front feet forward, trying to ignite the rope that hobbled her. But the blaze was too fierce; she could not get close enough to burn the rope without burning herself.

She turned about and tried to scrape dirt onto the blaze with a hind hoof. But the ground was too solid; she could not get a good gouge. She seemed helpless.

Then a shape appeared. Some large animal was stomping beyond the wall of the pen, out of the firelight. A dragon, come to take advantage of a horse who could only hobble along?

She sent an exploratory dreamlet. "Who are you?"

"Is it safe?" an equine thought came in the dream.

It was the day horse! Imbri quelled her surprise and pleasure at his presence and projected another dreamlet. "Stay clear, stallion! The Horseman is looking for you!"

"I—know," the horse replied slowly. She wasn't certain whether it was dullness or caution that made him seem less than smart. She understood that Mundane animals were not terrifically intelligent, and the Horseman had said as much.

"He wants to catch you and ride you again," she sent, making her dream image resemble a centaur, so as to seem more equine while retaining the ability to speak clearly. Of course horses had their own language, but overt neighing and other sounds might wake up the henchman.

"I—hide," the day horse replied, beginning to catch on to this mode of dialogue. He stepped up to the fence and looked over, his head bright in the firelight.

"Well, go hide now, because if that henchman wakes—"

"You—greet me," he said in the dream, awkwardly. "I run. You—caught by man. My fault. I came—free you."

Imbri was moved. She had pictured him in the dream as a white centaur, and he seemed to like the form. She had made sure it was a very muscular and handsome centaur, knowing that males tended to be vain about their appearance. Males of any species were foolish in a number of respects. But what would Xanth be like without them?

"I can't get away as long as that fire burns," her dream filly image said. "I had hoped there would be a rainstorm, but—"

"Rainstorm?"

"Water, to douse the fire," she explained. Sure enough he was the strong, handsome, amiable, stupid type. Fortunately, stallions didn't need brains; they were attractive as they were.

"Douse fire!" he said, understanding. "Make water." He jumped over the pen wall, landing with such a thump that Imbri had to jam a dream of an earthquake at the sleeping henchman to prevent him from being alarmed. Of course he was alarmed, but then she modified the dream to show that the earthquake had been weak and brief, and had cracked open the ground in front of him to reveal a treasure chest filled with whatever it was he most desired. The henchman quickly opened the chest, and out sprang a lovely nude numph. He would remain asleep for a long time!

The day horse walked over to the burning logs, angled his body, and urinated on the flames. Clouds of steamy smoke flared up as the fire hissed angrily. It certainly did not appreciate this treatment!

The new noise disturbed the henchman despite his dream. He started to awaken. This time Imbri sent a mean dream at him, showing the merest suggestion of a basilisk the size of a horse, swinging around to glare at the man. The Mundane immediately squinched his eyes tightly closed; he knew what happened when one traded gazes with a bask! He did not want to wake and see the monster. Imbri let him drift off again, returning to his treasure-chest nymph; Imbri was as relieved as he to see him sleep.

In a moment the fire had sizzled down enough to let the shadows reach out to Imbri. She phased through her hobbles and the wall of the pen. The day horse leaped to follow her.

They ran through the forest. "Come with me to Castle Roogna!" Imbri projected, her filly image smiling gladly and swishing her black tail in friendly fashion.

But the day horse faltered. The handsome centaur image frowned. "Night—tire quickly—creature of day—must give it up." He stumbled. "By night I sleep."

She saw that it was so. "Then we'll hide, so you can rest," she sent.

"You go. I came only to free you," he said, speaking more clearly now. He might be slow, but he did catch on with practice. "Pretty mare, black like deepest night."

Imbri was flattered and appreciative, though he was only telling the truth. She was as black as deep night because she was a night mare. But any notice by a stallion was a thing to be treasured.

Nonetheless, she did have a mission and had to complete it without delay. "When will I see you again?"

"Come to the baobab at noon," he said. "Nice tree. If I am near, I will be there. Do not betray me to the human kind; I do not wish to be caught and ridden again."

"I'll never betray you, day horse!" she exclaimed in the dream, shocked. "You freed me! I'll always be grateful!"

"Farewell," his dream image said. He turned and walked north as the dreamlet faded out. Imbri saw the brass circlet on his foreleg glint faintly in the moonlight.

"The baobab tree!" Imbri sent after him. She knew of that growth from her dream duties; sometimes human people camped out there, and it was conducive to bad dreams at night, a little like a haunted house. It was at the edge of the Castle Roogna estate, out of sight of the castle but impossible to overlook. She would certainly be there when she had the chance.

Chapter 3

Centycore et Cetera

By midnight Imbri reached Castle Roogna. She skirted it and went to Chameleon's home, which was a large cottage cheese. Imbri had once delivered a dream here to Chameleon's husband Bink; it had been a minor one, for the man did not have much ill on his conscience, but at least she knew her way around these premises despite lacking the seniority required to bring dreams to Kings. She phased through the hard rind and made her way—should that be whey, in this house? she wondered—to Chameleon's bed.

But a stranger occupied that bed. Chameleon, according to the image the Night Stallion had formed, was a crone; this person was a lovely older woman of about fifty. Had she come to the wrong address?

"Where is Chameleon?" Imbri inquired in a pictureless dreamlet. Maybe this woman was visiting, and would know.

"I am Chameleon," the woman replied in the dream.

Imbri stood back and considered. The reply had been direct and honest. The Night Stallion must have made an error, forming the image of some other woman. Imbri had never known him to make an error before, but obviously it was possible.

Something else bothered her. Chameleon was sleeping alone, yet she was a family person. Where were her husband and son?

Imbri projected a dream. It was of herself as another centaur filly, standing beside the bed. "Chameleon, I must give you a message."

The woman looked up. "Oh, am I to have a bad dream? Why do they always come when my family's away?"

"No bad dream," Imbri reassured her. "I am the night mare Imbri, come to be your steed and bear a message for the King. When you wake, I will remain. I will talk to you in your sleep, as now, or in daydreamlets."

"No bad dreams?" The woman seemed slow to understand.

"No bad dreams," Imbri repeated. "But a message for the King."

"The King's not here. You must seek him at Castle Roogna."

"I know. But I can not go to him. I will give you the message to relay to him."

"Me? Repeat a dream?"

"Repeat the message." Imbri was getting impatient; the woman seemed to have very little wit.

"What message?"

"Beware the Horseman."

"Who?"

"The Horseman."

"Is that a centaur?"

"No, he's a man who rides horses."

"But there are no horses in Xanth!"

"There is one now, the day horse. And there are the night mares, like me."

"But then people don't need to fear him. Just horses should fear him."

That might be true; certainly Imbri would never again be careless about the Horseman. But it was irrelevant; she had to get the message through. "That is for the King to decide. You must give him the message."

"What message?"

"Beware the Horseman!" Imbri's image shouted, frustrated.

Chameleon's image looked around nervously. "Where is he?"

What was this? Was the woman a complete idiot? Why had the Night Stallion sent Imbri to such a creature? "The Horseman is west of here. He may be hazardous to the health of Xanth. The King must be warned."

"Oh. When my husband Bink comes home, I'll tell him."

"When will Bink be back?" Imbri inquired patiently.

"Next week. He's up north in Mundania, working out a new trade agreement with Onesti, or something."

"I certainly hope he works on it with honesty," Imbri said. "But next week's too long. We must warn the King tomorrow."

"Oh, I couldn't bother the King! He's seventy years old!"

"But this affects the welfare of Xanth!" Imbri protested, getting frustrated again.

"Yes, Xanth is very important."

"Then you'll warn the King?"

"Warn the King?"

"About the Horseman," the centaur filly said, keeping her tail still and her face straight with an effort.

"But the King is seventy years old!"

Imbri stamped a forefoot angrily, in both her dream form and her real form. "I don't care if he is a hundred and seventy years old! *I* am! He's still got to be warned!"

Chameleon stared at the filly image. "You certainly don't look that old!"

"I am a night mare. We are immortal, at least until we die. I have a soul now, so I can age and breed and die when I'm material, but I never aged before, once I matured. Now, about the King—"

"Maybe my son Dor can tell him."

"Where is your son now?" Imbri asked warily.

"He's south at Centaur Isle, getting the centaurs to organize for possible war. Because Good Magician Humfrey says there may be a Wave. We don't like it when Waves are made. But I don't think the centaurs believe it."

"A Wave?" It was Imbri's turn to be confused. She knew the woman wasn't talking about the ocean.

"The Nextwave," Chameleon clarified unhelpfully.

Imbri let that go. She had seen the Lastwave, but that had been a long time ago. "When will Dor be back here?"

"Tomorrow night. Just in time for the elopement."

Somehow the woman's ingenuous remarks kept making Imbri react stupidly, too. "Elopement?"

Chameleon might not be smart, but she had a good memory. "Dor and Irene—she's King Trent's daughter, a lovely child with the Green Thumb, only it's really her hair that's green—have been engaged for eight years now, a third of their lives. They could never decide on a date. We think Dor's a little afraid of the responsibility of marriage. He's really a very nice boy." Obviously "nice" meant "innocent" in this connection. Imbri was surprised to learn that any innocent males remained in Xanth; perhaps this was merely the fond fancy of a naive mother. "Irene is twenty-three now, and she's getting impatient. She never was a very patient girl." This seemed to mean that the other woman in Chameleon's son's life was not viewed with entire favor, but was tolerated as a necessary evil. In this attitude, Chameleon was absolutely typical of the mothers of sons. "So she's going to come here at night and take Dor away and marry him in an uncivil ceremony, and then it will be done. Everyone will be there!"

So the pleasure of a wedding ceremony overwhelmed the displeasure of turning her son over to an aggressive girl. This, too, was normal, except—

"For an elopement?" Imbri felt more stupid than ever. Was this a human folk custom she had missed? She had understood that elopements were sneak marriages; certainly she had delivered a number of bad dreams relating to that.

"Oh, they'll all be in costume, of course. So Dor won't know, poor thing. Maybe Irene won't know either. It's all very secret. Nobody knows except everybody else."

Imbri realized that she had again been distracted by an irrelevancy and was getting ever more deeply enmeshed in the confusions of Chameleon's outlook. "Two days is too long for my message to wait. The Horseman is within range of Castle Roogna now, spying on the Xanth defenses. Anyway, it seems that Prince Dor will be too busy to pay attention to it. You must go to the King first thing tomorrow morning."

"Oh, I couldn't bother the King. He's—"

"Seventy years old. He still needs to know. The Horseman is dangerous!"

The dream Chameleon looked at the dream Imbri with childlike seriousness. "Why don't *you* tell him, then?"

"I can't. My mission here must be confidential."

Then Imbri paused, startled. Confidential? From whom was the secret of her nature to be kept? The Horseman already knew! He had ridden her and intercepted her message and forced her to tell him everything!

"I'll go tell him right now!" Imbri said, cursing her own foolishness.

"But it's night! The King's asleep!"

"All the better. I'm a night mare."

"Oh. That's all right then. But don't give him any bad dreams. He's a good man."

"I won't." Imbri trotted through the rindwall of the cottage, letting Chameleon lapse into more peaceful slumber. She hurried to Castle Roogna, hurdled the moat with one prodigious leap, and phased through the massive outer wall. This would be no easy castle to take by storm! She passed through the somber, darkened halls and passages, until she came to the royal bedchamber.

The King and Queen had separate apartments. Both were safely asleep. Imbri entered the King's chamber and stood over him, exactly as if she were on dream duty.

Even at seventy, which was old for a mortal man, he was a noble figure of his kind. The lines of his face provided the appearance of wisdom as much as of age. Yet it was clear he was mortal; she detected infirmities of system that would in due course bring him to a natural demise. He had reigned for twenty-five years; perhaps that was enough. Except that if he lacked a competent replacement in Prince Dor . . .

She entered his mind in dream form, this time assuming the likeness of a nymph, bare of breast and innocent of countenance, symbolic of her intention to conceal nothing from him. "King Trent!" she called.

He had been dreaming he was sleeping; now he dreamed he woke. "What are you doing in my bedroom, nymph?" he demanded. "Are you one of my daughter's playmates? Speak, or I will transform you into a flower."

Startled, Imbri did not speak—and suddenly, in the dream, she was a tiger lily. She growled, baring her petals in a grimace.

"All right—I'll give you another chance." King Trent did not make any gesture, but Imbri was back in nymph form. Even in dreams, the King's magic was formidable!

"I bring you a message," she said quickly through the mouth of the nymph. "Beware the Horseman."

"And who is the Horseman—a kind of centaur?"

"No, sir. He is a man who rides horses. He rode me—" She paused, realizing this statement did not make much sense while she was in nymph image. "I am a night mare—"

"Ah, then this is, after all, a dream! I mistook it for reality. My apology."

Imbri was embarrassed that a King should apologize to a dream image. "But it is real! The dream is only to communicate—"

"Really? Then I had better wake."

The King made an effort and woke. Imbri was amazed; in all her one hundred and fifty years' experience in dream duty, after her youth and apprenticeship, she had not seen anyone do this so readily.

"So you really *are* a mare," King Trent said, studying her in reality. "Not a nymph sent to tempt me into foolish thoughts."

"Yes. Not a nymph," she agreed, projecting a spot dreamlet.

"And you do not fade in my waking presence. Interesting."

"I am spelled to perform day duty," she explained. "To bring my message."

"Which is to beware the Horseman." The King stroked his beard. "I don't believe I know of him. Is he by chance a new Magician?"

"No, sir. I think he is a Mundane. But he is clever and ruthless. He hurt me." She nodded at the scrapes on her flanks.

"You could not phase away from him, mare?"

"Not by day. I am now mortal by day."

"Would this relate to the invasion the Mundanes are supposed to be mounting?"

"I think so, sir. The Horseman has two Mundane henchmen and a Mundane horse."

"Where did you encounter this cruel man?"

"Two hours' trot west of here."

"South of the Gap Chasm?"

"Yes, your Majesty. At Faux Pass."

"That's odd. My scouts should have spotted any crossing of the Chasm, or any sea approach. You are sure of the location?"

"Quite sure. I made a bad misstep there."

"That happens at Faux Pass."

"Yes." Imbri was embarrassed again.

"Then they must have found a way to sneak in." The King pondered a moment. "Ah—I have it. A quarter century ago, Bink and Chameleon and I entered Xanth below the Gap when we departed from the region of the isthmus, far northwest of here. We somehow traversed in perhaps an hour a distance that should have required a day's gallop by your kind. Obviously there is a magic channel under water. The Horseman must have found it and somehow gotten by the kraken weed that guards it. We shall have to close that off, devious though it may be. There are merfolk in that vicinity; I shall notify them to investigate." He smiled. "Meanwhile, a lone man and two henchmen and a Mundane horse should not present too much of a threat to Xanth."

"The horse is not with them any more, your Majesty. He is the day horse who fled his master and helped me escape."

"Then we must reward that horse. Where is he now?"

"He does not want to meet with human folk," she explained. "He is wary of being caught and ridden again."

Again the King smiled. "Then we shall ignore him. True horses are very rare in Xanth, for there is no resident population. He might be regarded as a protected species. That will help him survive in what might otherwise be a hostile land."

King Trent had a marvelous way of solving problems! Imbri was grateful. "I am also to serve as liaison to the gourd—the realm of the Powers of the Night and to the folk of Xanth," Imbri said in another dreamlet, maintaining her nymph image for the purpose. "And I am to be the steed of Chameleon. But I don't know why; she seems not very smart."

"An excellent assignment!" King Trent said. "Evidently you do not properly comprehend Chameleon's nature. She changes day by day, becoming beautiful but stupid, as she is at the moment, then reversing and turning ugly but intelligent. She is alone because of the exigencies of this presently developing crisis, and that is unfortunate, because someone really should be with her at her nadir of intellect. You can be with her and nudge her from danger. In a few days she will become smarter, and in two weeks she will be so smart and ugly you can't stand her. But she is a good woman, overall, and needs a companion in both phases."

"Oh." Now the Night Stallion's assignment made more sense. It also explained his seeming error: he had shown an image of ugly Chameleon, but meanwhile her aspect had changed.

"Return to her now," King Trent said. "I will have a new assignment for you both by morning."

How thoroughly the King took over, once he tackled something! Imbri trotted through the wall and jumped down to the ground outside. Actually, she landed in the moat, but it didn't matter because she was immaterial; she didn't even disturb the moat monsters. Soon she was back with Chameleon, now understanding this woman better. Appearance and intelligence that varied in a monthly cycle—how like a woman!

Imbri checked in with a reassuring dreamlet, then moved back outside to graze on the excellent local grass. She slept while grazing, comfortably, suspecting she would need all her energy the next day.

A tiny golem appeared at the cottage in the morning. "Oh, hello, Grundy," Chameleon said. "Do you want a cookie?"

"Yes," the miniature figure said, accepting the proffered delicacy. It was an armful for him, but he chewed bravely into the rim. "But that's not why I'm here. King Trent says you must ride the night mare to Good Magician Humfrey's castle and ask his advice for this campaign."

"But I couldn't bother the Good Magician!" Chameleon protested. "He's so old nobody knows!"

"The King says this is important. We have a crisis coming up in the Nextwave and we don't want to misplay it. He says Humfrey should see this mare. Get going within the hour."

Imbri snorted. Who was this little nuisance, to order them about?

The golem snorted back—speaking perfect equine. "I'm Grundy the Golem, and I'm on the King's errand, horseface."

"So you can communicate in nonhuman languages!" Imbri neighed. That was quite a talent! She didn't even have to project a dreamlet at him. Still, she didn't like the insulting inflection he had applied to the uninsulting "horseface," so she sent a brief dream of the fires of hell at him.

The golem blanched. "That's some talent you have yourself, mare," he concluded. He departed with dispatch.

Chameleon looked at Imbri. "But I don't know how to ride a horse," she said. She seemed very unsure of herself in her stupid phase, but she was certainly an excellent figure of a woman of her age.

"Use a pillow for a cushion, and I will teach you how," Imbri projected, her dreamlet showing Chameleon seated confidently and somewhat regally on the dream horse's back, her lovely hair flowing down about her.

Chameleon got a pillow and followed instructions. Soon she was precariously perched, her legs dangling awkwardly, her arms rigid. This was an immense contrast to the evil expertise of the Horseman! But Imbri moved carefully, and the woman gradually relaxed. It really was not hard to ride a horse, if the horse was willing.

They moved east through field and forest, toward the Good Magician's castle. Because Imbri had been almost everywhere in Xanth in the course of her century and a half of dream duty, she needed no directions to locate it. She stayed clear of dragons, tangle trees, and similar hazards and reached the castle without untoward event late in the day. Imbri could have covered the distance much faster alone, but Chameleon would have taken much longer by herself, so it was a fair compromise. They had paused to eat along the way and had taken turns napping; Imbri carried the woman carefully while she slept, then had shown her how to guide the snoozing mare away from holes in the ground and other nuisances by the pressure of knees on sides. Chameleon was quite surprised that a creature could walk while sleeping. She was stupid, but she had a sweet personality and followed directions well; she was learning to be a helpful rider.

As the castle came into view, both mare and woman were startled. It was a monstrous circle of stones set within a moat. Each stone was too huge to be moved physically and stood upright. On top were set enormous slabs of rock, so that the whole formed a kind of pavilion. There was no sign of the Good Magician.

"I am not very smart, of course," Chameleon said, "but I don't understand this at all. That megalith looks many centuries old!"

Imbri was reasonably smart, but she was similarly baffled. She had been by this castle several times in the past, and though it had always looked different, it had never been *this* different. "We shall have to go in and look," she projected. "Maybe there is some sign of what happened to the Good Magician."

"Maybe he moved," Chameleon suggested.

They approached the moat. By night Imbri could have hurdled it or trotted across the surface of the water, but now she had to wade and swim, since she did not want to delay unnecessarily.

The moment her hoof touched the water, a fish swam up. It changed into a naked man before them. "Halt! You can't pass here!"

"Oh, dear," Chameleon said.

Imbri recognized the type. "You're a nix," she projected.

The man shifted form again, partway, adopting the tail of a fish. "Well, mare!" he said. "What else would you expect to find guarding a moat?"

"At Castle Roogna there are nice moat monsters," Chameleon said.

"I *am* a moat monster!" the nix declared. "And you can't pass unless you know the password."

"Password?" Chameleon was plainly perplexed. So was Imbri. Why should they be allowed to pass it they knew a word, if their merit was not otherwise apparent? This did not seem to make sense.

Imbri tried to evoke the word from a dream, but the nix was too canny for that. Dreams were aids to communication and often evoked deep feeling, but were not for mind reading.

"We'll just have to cross despite him," Imbri projected privately to Chameleon, with a dream picture of woman and horse forging across the moat while the nix protested helplessly. After all, the creature carried no weapon and was not physically imposing in either its fish or man form. Also, they had the right and the need to cross; they were on the King's business.

"Yes, we must cross," Chameleon agreed. She hiked up her skirt so that it would not get wet, though of course Imbri was likely to sink low enough in the water to wet the woman's legs to the thighs anyway. They were excellent limbs, considering her age. Perhaps even not considering her age. Water would hardly hurt them.

This was not lost on the nix. He whistled lewdly. "Look at those gams!" he exclaimed.

"Ignore him," Imbri said in the dream image, for she saw that the dream girl Chameleon was blushing. It seemed that despite a quarter century of marriage, Chameleon remained fundamentally innocent. That probably accounted for her son's innocence. Imbri found herself liking the woman even more and felt protective toward her. Chameleon was as esthetic emotionally as she was physically, almost too nice to be true.

They plunged into the water. "Nix, nix!" the nix cried. "You shall not pass without the word! I will freeze your tracks!" He pointed—and the water abruptly congealed about Imbri's legs.

Imbri stopped, perforce. She stood knee-deep in ice! The nix did have power to stop her progress.

"What do you think of that, nag?" the nix demanded with insolent satisfaction. He was now back in fish form, able to speak that way, too. "No password, no passing. I told you! Did you think the rule was passé?"

Chameleon fidgeted helplessly, but Imbri struggled to draw one foot and then another from its mooring. Ice splintered as her hooves came free. Soon she stood on the frozen surface and began to walk forward.

"Nix! Nix!" the sprite cried, back in man form, pointing again with a finlike arm. The ice melted instantly, and Imbri dropped into deeper water with a splash. The nix chortled.

Well, then she would wade again. One way or another, she would cross this moat.

The nix froze the water again—and again Imbri struggled to the top. He melted it, plunging her down. This was awkward, but she continued to make progress. The nix could not actually stop her.

Then she reached the deep where she had to swim. The water came almost to the top of her back. Chameleon hiked her skirt up over her waist. "Oh, it tickles!" she protested.

The nix gloated, now faintly resembling a satyr. "Where does it tickle, wench? *I'll* give you a good tickle, if that's what you like." This caused the dream girl to blush furiously again. But she wouldn't let her dress get wet. Actually, it was a fairly simple outfit in shades of gray, the parts neither matching nor clashing; it was she herself who made it attractive.

"Hey, I never knew a doll could blush that far down," the nix said evilly.

Imbri nosed a splash of water at him, but continued swimming. If the nix remained distracted by the woman's exposure and embarrassment long enough, they would be across. That should embarrass *him*. He certainly deserved it.

Alas, the nix was not that foolish. "Nix, nix!" he cried, pointing again.

This time the freezing was incomplete. The water thickened into cold sludge, but Imbri was able to forge through it. It seemed there was too much volume here to freeze enough to immobilize her submerged body, so the effect was diluted.

"Well, then, nox!" the nix cried angrily. "Nix, nox, paddywox, live the frog alone!"

This nonsense thawed the water, then thinned it farther. Suddenly it was too dilute to support the mare's swimming weight. She sank down over her head.

This was like phasing through solids—with one difference. She could not breathe. The water was now too thin to swim but too thick to breathe, and its composition was wrong.

Imbri's feet found the bottom. This was solid. She turned hastily about and walked the few paces needed to bring her high enough for her head to break the surface. Now she could breathe.

She projected a dreamlet to Chameleon: centaur filly shaking a spray of water out of her hide. "Are you all right, woman?"

"My dress is soaked—I think," Chameleon lamented. "The water isn't very wet."

That was good enough for Imbri. "Take a deep breath, and I will run all the way across the moat on the bottom. With thin water we can do it."

"That's what you think, night nag!" the nix cried, evidently catching part of the dream. He was swimming along, his forepart that of a fish, his hind part that of a man. The water was abruptly fully liquid again. "Try to run through that!"

Imbri realized that it could be dangerous to try. If she swam and the nix vaporized the water, she would sink without a breath and have to turn back. Chameleon could panic and possibly drown. Imbri wasn't certain whether Chameleon could swim, and now was not the time to inquire.

She paused to consider. Alone, she could probably forge through despite the mischievous nix. But with Chameleon, it was harder. Too bad the woman was so stupid; Imbri had to do all the thinking. How could she get them both across with minimum risk?

Then she had a notion. She projected a new dream to Chameleon, a scene of herself in mare form and the woman in woman form, exactly as they were in life. But the nix was there, too, eavesdropping. Whatever they tried, he would foil.

The dream mare projected a dream within the dream to Chameleon. This one bypassed the snooping nix, who did not realize the complex levels available in dream symbolism. In that redistilled dream, Imbri was a woman in black and Chameleon a woman in white. "Trust me," she said to the dream-in-dream girl, who looked slightly startled. "We shall cross—but not the way we seem to. Follow what I say, not what I do. Can you do that?"

The dream-in-dream girl blinked uncertainly. "I'll try, Imbri," she agreed. "That *is* you?"

Oh—it was the human guise that confused her. "Yes. I can take any form in dreams, but I usually am black or wear black, because that's night mare color."

The Chameleons on the three levels of reality, dream, and dream-dream smiled, getting it straight.

Now they returned to focus on the outer dream. "Hang on, Chameleon," the mare cried. In real life Imbri could not physically talk human language, but dreams had different rules. "I'm swimming across now."

"Swimming across," the woman agreed, hiking her skirt high again. Her limbs were just as shapely in the dream as in reality.

"You'll get your no-no wet!" the nix cried, evilly teasing her.

Chameleon blushed yet again—she seemed to have an excellent supply of blush, as pretty women did—but held her pose. The dream mare moved into deep water, swimming across. The real mare did likewise.

"Nix! Nix!" the sprite cried, caught halfway between fish and man forms. He vaporized the water.

The real mare and woman sank—but the dream pair continued swimming. "It's not too deep here," the dream mare called. "We can run along the bottom and still breathe. In just a moment we'll be across!"

"Hey!" the nix exclaimed angrily. "Nix, nix, I'll nix you!" And he froze the water.

Now the real mare was able to slog upward through the cold slush and get her head and the woman's above water so they could breathe again. She plowed clumsily forward.

But the dream mare was stuck. "I can't move!" that mare cried. "We're frozen in tight!"

"Serves you right, nocturnal nag!" the nix shouted jubilantly. "You can't cross without the password!"

"We must turn back!" the dream mare said despairingly.

"Yes, turn back," dream Chameleon agreed, though she did not seem fully convinced.

"You're doing well," the dream-in-dream Imbri woman figure reassured her on that level.

Meanwhile, the real mare pulled free of the slush and swam on toward the megaliths. Progress was faster as the water cleared.

"We'll never get across!" the dream mare wailed.

"Never!" the dream girl agreed enthusiastically.

But the nix was not completely gullible. "Hey—those are your dream images! Real mares can't talk!" He blinked, orienting on the real-life situation—and discovered how they had tricked him. He had been so busy snooping on the supposedly private dream that he had neglected reality, as Imbri had intended. "Nix! Nix! Nix!" he screamed from a fish mouth set in a human face, hurling a vapor spell. The water thinned about them, dropping them down—but now they were close to the far side, and the moat was becoming shallow.

Imbri galloped up the slope, and her head dipped under water only momentarily. The nix froze the water; the mare scrambled up on top of it, as here in the shallower region the freezing was solid.

"Can I breathe now?" the dream Chameleon pleaded.

"Breathe!" Imbri responded, clambering to shore. They had made it!

Behind them, the nix sank wrathfully into a region of vaporizing ice, his human head set on a fish's body. "You females tricked me!" he muttered. Then, looking at the forming cloud of ice vapor: "I never did believe in sublimation."

"It is the nature of males to be gullible," Imbri agreed in a dreamlet, making a picture of the nix formed as a human being with the head of a fish, wearing a huge dunce cap, while an ice storm swirled about him.

They climbed out of the moat and stood wetly before the stone structure. It was immense. Each vertical stone was the height of an ogre, crudely hewn, dauntingly massive.

They had little time to gawk. A monster came charging along the inner edge of the moat. The creature was horrendous. It had horse-hooves, a lion's legs, elephantine ears, a bear's muzzle, a monstrous mouth, and a branching antler projecting from the middle of its face. "Ho, intruders!" the beast bellowed in the voice of a man. "Flee as well as you can so I may have the pleasure of the hunt!"

Imbri recognized the monster. It was a centycore. This was a creature without mercy; no use to reason with it. They would need either to stop it or to escape it.

Imbri ran. She was a night mare; she could outrun anything. She left the centycore behind immediately.

Chameleon screamed and almost fell off. She was still an inexpert rider, not at all like the cruel Horseman, and could readily be dislodged by a sudden move. Imbri had to slow, letting the poor woman get a better hold on her mane. Then she accelerated again in time to avoid the monster.

Soon she had circled the region enclosed by the moat, being confined— and there was the monster again, facing her from in front. Imbri braked and reversed, angling her body to prevent Chameleon from being thrown off, and took off the other way. But she realized that this was no real escape; she would not be able to concentrate on anything else, such as exploring the megalithic structure and searching for clues to the whereabouts of the Good Magician's castle, until she dealt with the centycore.

She slowed, letting the thing gain, though this terrified Chameleon, who was clinging to Imbri for dear life. Imbri hurled back a dreamlet picture of herself as a harpy hovering low, calling, "What are you doing here, monster?"

"Chasing you, you delectable equine!" the centycore bellowed back, snapping his teeth as punctuation.

Ask a foolish question! "We only came to seek the Good Magician," Imbri sent.

"I don't care what you seek; you will still taste exactly like horsemeat." And the centycore lunged, his antler stabbing forward with ten points.

"Oh, I don't like this!" Chameleon wailed. "I wish my husband Bink were here; nothing too terrible ever happens to him!"

That was surely an exaggeration, but Imbri understood her feeling. She accelerated, putting a little more distance between herself and the predator. How could she nullify the centycore? She knew she couldn't fight it, as it was a magic beast, well able to vanquish anything short of a dragon. Even if she were able to fight it, she could not safely do so while Chameleon rode her; the woman would surely be thrown off and fall prey to the monster.

"Run through a wall!" Chameleon cried, sensing the problem.

"I can't phase through solid things by day," Imbri protested, her dreamlet showing herself as a mare bonking headfirst into a megalithic column and coming to a bonejarring stop. She felt Chameleon's sympathetic hand pressure, though the accident had been only a dream; the woman tended to take the dreams too literally. "Only at night—and we have at least an hour of day left." It seemed like an eternity, with the centycore pursuing.

But the description of the problem suggested the answer. Suppose they somehow made it prematurely dark? Then Imbri would be able to phase. For it wasn't night itself, but darkness, that made her recover her full night mare properties; otherwise the Horseman's fire would not have been able to hold her. The Powers of the Night came to whatever night there was, natural or artificial, whatever and whenever it was, for night was nothing but an extensive shadow. Just as day was nothing more than a very large patch of light.

How could they make it dark? Sometimes, Imbri understood, the moon eclipsed the sun, rudely shoving in front of it and blocking it out. But the sun always gave the moon such a scorching on the backside when the cheese did that, that the moon hardly ever did it again soon. There was very little chance of it happening right at this moment; the moon wasn't even near the sun.

Sometimes a big storm blotted out most of the light, turning day to night. But there was no sign of such a storm at the moment. Count that out, too.

There was also smoke. A bad, smoldering blaze could stifle the day for a time. If they could gather the makings of a fire, then start it going—

"Chameleon," Imbri sent in a dreamlet. "If I let you off behind a stone, so the monster doesn't see you, could you make a fire?"

"A fire?" The woman had trouble seeing the relevance, naturally enough.

"To stop the centycore."

"Oh." Chameleon considered. "I do have a few magic matches that I use for cooking. All I have to do is rub them against something rough, and they burst into flame."

"Excellent. Make a big fire—" Imbri projected a sequence in pictures: Chameleon hiding behind a stone column, dashing out when the monster wasn't near, gathering pieces of wood and dry moss and anything else that might blaze. "A big, smoky fire. Keep it between you and the centycore." Actually, the monster could go around the fire to get at the woman, but that wasn't the point. The fire was merely the mechanism to generate smoke.

"I can do that," Chameleon agreed. Imbri accelerated, leaving the centycore puffing behind, veered near a megalithic column, and braked as rapidly as she could without throwing her rider. Why hadn't she tried a fast deceleration, or bucking, when the Horseman had ridden her? Because she, like a dumb filly, hadn't thought of it. But she suspected it wouldn't have worked anyway; the man understood horses too well to be deceived or outmaneuvered by one. Hence his name—the man who had mastered the horse.

Chameleon dismounted and scurried behind the megalith while Imbri galloped ostentatiously off, attracting the monster's baleful attention. It worked; the centycore snorted after her, never glancing at the woman. It probably preferred the taste of horsemeat anyway. Imbri was relieved; if the monster had turned immediately on the woman, there could have been real trouble.

Imbri led the monster a merry chase, keeping tantalizingly close so as to monopolize its attention. Meanwhile, Chameleon dashed about, diligently gathering scraps of wood and armfuls of dry leaves and grass.

In due course the blaze started. A column of smoke puffed up.

"Ho!" the centycore exclaimed, pausing. "What's this?"

Imbri paused with him, not wanting him to spy the woman behind the column. "That's a fire, hornface," she projected. "To burn you up."

"It won't burn me up!" the centycore snorted, the tines of his antler quivering angrily. "I will put it out!"

"You couldn't touch it," Imbri sent, her dreamlet showing the monster yelping as he got toasted on the rump by a burning brand.

"So you claim," the centycore muttered, glancing at his posterior to make sure there was no burning brand being shoved at it. He approached the flame. Imbri skirted it to the other side and reached Chameleon, who climbed eagerly on her back. The woman evidently had been afraid, with excellent reason, but had performed well anyway. That was worth noting; she might not be smart, but she had reasonable courage.

The centycore kicked at the fire. A piece of wood flew out, starting a secondary blaze a short distance away. "You won't put it out that way, bearsnoot," Imbri projected with a picture of a burning branch falling on the monster's antler and getting caught in it. The dream centycore shook his head violently, but the brand only blazed more brightly, toasting his snoot. In a moment the antler began to burn.

"Stop that!" the monster snapped, shaking his antler as if it felt hot.

"You'll burn to pieces!" Imbri dreamed, causing the image's antler to blaze more fiercely. Jets of flame shot out from each point, forming bright patterns in the air as the monster waved its antler about. The patterns shaped into a big word: FIRE.

"Enough!" the centycore screamed. He leaped for the moat and dunked his horn. That doused the dream flame; reality was too strong for it. But Imbri did manage to dream up a subdued fizzle where the points entered the water.

"Hey!" the nix protested, picking up the dream image. He froze the water around the antler, trapping the centycore head-down. The monster roared with a terrible rage and ripped his head free, sending shards of ice flying out. The nix changed to a fish and scooted away, daunted.

Now the centycore scooped icy water toward the fire with his antler. But the fire was too big and too far away; only a few droplets struck it, with furious hissing. Hell had no anger like that of a wetted fire, as Imbri knew from experience.

The centycore considered. Then he scooped up a hornful of muck from the edge of the moat and hurled that toward the fire. There was a tremendous hiss as the blob scored, and a balloon of steam and smoke went up.

"Ha, ha, mare, he's putting it out!" the nix called from a safe distance across the moat. Apparently he felt that it was best to join sides with the monster. "I guess that knots your tail!"

"You shut up!" Imbri projected in a dream that encompassed both nix and centycore. "He won't get it all!"

"That's what you think, horsehead!" the nix cried.

Encouraged by this, the monster indulged in a fever of mudslinging. His aim was good; more gouts of smog ballooned out. The fire was furious, but was taking a beating.

"Curses, he's doing it!" Imbri projected with wonderfully poor grace.

Indeed he was. Soon the fire was largely out and smoke suffused the entire region, making them all cough. The light of the sun dimished, for sunrays didn't like smelly smog any better than anyone else did.

Was it dark enough? Imbri wasn't sure. "If this doesn't work, we're finished," she projected privately to Chameleon. "Maybe you should dismount."

"I'll stay with you," the woman said loyally. Imbri chalked up one more point for her character, though she realized it might be fear of the monster that motivated Chameleon as much as support for Imbri.

Now the centycore reoriented on them. "You're next, mareface!" he cried, and charged.

Imbri bolted for the megalith nearest the fire, where the smoke hovered most thickly. The centycore bounded after her. He was sure he had her now.

The mare leaped right into the stone column—and phased through it. Chameleon, in contact with her, did the same. The darkness was deep enough!

The monster, following too closely, smacked headfirst into the column. The collision jammed several points of his antler into the stone, trapping him there. He roared and yanked, but the stone was tougher than the ice had been, and he could not get free. That particular menace had been nullified.

Actually, Imbri now recognized an additional concern she hadn't quite thought of before. She had not been certain she could phase a rider with her. She had brought the ogre out of the gourd, but he had already been in it, his body separate. She had carried the girl Tandy once, but that had been in genuine night. When she phased out of the Horseman's pen, she had left the hobble behind, and it had certainly been in contact with her body. So the precedents were mixed. Apparently she could take someone or something with her if she wanted to, and leave it behind if she chose. It was good to get such details straight; an error could be a lot of trouble.

Now they could explore the center of the stone structure. They moved in cautiously.

There was a rumble, as of a column wobbling in its socket and beginning to crumble. Some sand sifted down from one of the elevated slabs. Both mare and woman looked up nervously. What was happening?

The noises subsided as they stood. Apparently it was a random event, possibly the result of the heat or smoke of the recent fire.

Imbri took another step forward. There was a long, moaning groan to the right, causing their heads to snap about. It was just another massive stone column settling, doing nothing.

Again Imbri stepped forward. The huge rock slab above slipped its support and crunched down toward them.

Imbri leaped backward, whipping her head around and back to catch Chameleon as the woman tried to fall off. The massive stone swung down where the two of them had been the moment before, thudding into the ground with an awesome impact.

"This place is collapsing!" Chameleon cried. "Let's get out of here!"

But Imbri's memory was jogged by something. "Isn't it strange that it should collapse the very moment we enter it, after standing for what seems by the cobwebs and moss to have been centuries?" Actually, cobwebs could form faster than that, but Imbri wasn't concerned about minor details. "This resembles the handiwork of the spriggan," she concluded in the dream.

"Spriggan?"

"Giant ghosts who haunt old castles and megalithic structures. They are destructive in nature; that's why old structures eventually collapse. The spriggan keep shoving at columns and pulling at cross pieces, until there is a collapse."

"But why right now?" Chameleon asked, since Imbri hadn't directly answered her own question. A creature had to make things quite clear for this woman.

"To stop us from proceeding farther. Don't you remember the nature of Magician Humfrey's castle?"

"Oh, yes. I had to ask him a Question once, before I married Bink, and it was just awful getting in! But not like this."

"His castle is different each time a person comes to it. I've seen it on my way to deliver dreams. Never the same."

"Yes, I remember," she agreed. "He must spend a lot of time getting it changed."

"So this is Humfrey's castle *now*. A megalithic structure. We have passed two hazards and are encountering the third—the spriggan. They are preventing us from advancing by shoving the stones down in our path."

"Oh." Chameleon was not entirely reassured. "But we don't have a Question. We're on the King's business."

"Yes, I understand the Good Magician is not supposed to charge for official business. He must not have realized we were coming."

"But he's supposed to know everything!"

"But he's old and absent-minded and set in his ways," Imbri's dream image reminded her. Still, she was not pleased at having to run this gauntlet. "So we must find out how to get past the ghosts," Imbri concluded. "Then we will be able to consult the Magician despite his forgetfulness."

"The ghosts at Castle Roogna are friendly," Chameleon said, evidently not liking the spriggan.

"No doubt. I am supposed to convey greetings from the ghosts of the haunted house in the gourd to one of the ghosts of Castle Roogna. I haven't yet had the opportunity."

"Who?"

"One named Jordan. Do you know him?"

"Not well. He keeps mostly to himself. But I do know Millie, who is not really a ghost any more. They're all pretty nice, I think, except for the six-year-old ghost, who—" She hesitated, not wishing to speak evil of the dead.

"Who is a brat?" Imbri supplied helpfully.

"I suppose. But the others are nice."

"Spriggan are not. They are to nice ghosts as ogres are to elves."

"That's awful!"

Evidently Chameleon was not going to be much help on this one. Imbri skirted the fallen stone and started forward once more. There was another groan, this one to the left. Imbri shied right—and the column there began to crumble threateningly.

"Oh, I don't like this!" Chameleon cried.

Imbri paused. She didn't like this either. But there had to be a way through. There always was. This was the nature of the Good Magician's defenses. He did not like to be bothered by frivolous intrusions, so he set up challenges; only smart, determined, and lucky petitioners could get through. Imbri knew King Trent would not have sent them here if the matter had not been important, so they had to conquer the challenges. Too bad the smoke had dissipated so she could no longer phase them through solid obstacles. That would have made it easy. But already the shadows were lengthening; soon it would be dusk, and that would solve her problem. All she had to do was keep from getting squished under a rock before then. She really would have been smarter to wait for night before trying to enter the castle, but now she was in it and would carry through with marish stubbornness.

She thought about the spriggan. They were distantly related to night mares, being both material and immaterial. In their natural forms they were invisible, but they could solidify their mouths to issue groans, and their hands to shove stones. They never touched living creatures directly, however; contact with warm flesh discombobulated them, and it took them a long time to get recombobulated.

There might be the answer! All Imbri had to do was make the giants show themselves, then advance on them. Maybe.

"I'm going to try something risky," Imbri projected to Chameleon. Her dreamlet showed herself charging directly at a horrendous ghost. "Would you like me to set you down outside the megaliths, where it is safe?"

Chameleon was frightened but firm. "It's not safe. The centycore is there. Maybe he's gotten unstuck from the column. I will stay with you."

Good enough. "Now we must provoke the ghost-giants into showing themselves. When they do, you must act terrified."

A touch of humor penetrated the woman's naiveté. "I will."

Imbri nerved herself and took a step forward. There was an immediate warning groan. She projected a dream to the vicinity of the sound. "You're pretty bold, hiding behind big stones," her dream image said with an expression of contempt. "You wouldn't scare anyone if you were visible."

"Oh, yeah?" the sprig she had addressed responded. "Look at this, mare!"

The ghost took form before her. He was the size of a man, but his arms were huge and hairy, and his face was dominated by two upcurving tusks. "Groooaan!" he groaned.

Chameleon shrieked in presumably simulated terror. But Imbri moved directly toward the ghost.

The sprig, startled, shrank to the size of a midget. Then, catching itself, it expanded to the size of a giant. "Booooo!" it boooooed, shoving at a ceiling stone. The stone budged, sending down a warning shower of sand. Chameleon screamed again. It seemed she didn't like sand in her hair.

But as the mare neared the ghost, the sprig jumped out of the way, avoiding contact. They passed right through, and Imbri knew she and Chameleon had penetrated well in toward the castle.

There was another invisible groan, from another sprig. Imbri charged it, though another column was crumbling. Her ploy worked; the column crashed the other way, not striking her. The ghosts never pulled columns down upon themselves; thus where the spriggan stood was the safest place to be, despite the scary noises they made. All she had to do was keep charging them, and she would be safe.

It worked. Columns and ceiling stones tumbled all around her, but Imbri navigated from the groan to groan and threaded the dangerous maze successfully.

Abruptly they were inside the castle proper.

Chapter 4

Forging the Chain

"Well, hello Chameleon!" the Gorgon said. She was a mature, almost overmature woman, whose impressive proportions were verging on obesity. Life had evidently been too kind to her. Her face was invisible, so that there was no danger from her glance. "And the mare Imbrium, too! Do come in and relax."

"We are here to see Good Magician Humfrey," Chameleon said. "King Trent sent us."

"Of course he did, dear," the Gorgon agreed. "We have been expecting you."

Chameleon blinked. "But you tried to stop us!"

"It's just Humfrey's way. He's such a dear, but he does have his little foibles. Those creatures wouldn't really have hurt you."

Imbri snorted. She was not at all sure of that!

"You both must be hungry," the Gorgon continued blithely. "We have milk and honey and alfalfa and oats in any combination you two may desire."

"Milk and oats," Chameleon said promptly.

"Honey and alfalfa," Imbri projected in a dreamlet.

"Ah, so it is true!" the Gorgon said, pleased. "You really are a night mare! What a cute way of talking!" She led them to the dining room, where she brought out the promised staples. Chameleon's oats were cooked over a little magic flame, then served with the milk and a snitch of honey from Imbri's soaked alfalfa. It was an excellent dinner.

Then they were ushered into the surly presence of Good Magician Humfrey. He had a tiny, cluttered study upstairs, stuffed with old tomes, multi-colored bottles, magic mirrors, and assorted unclassifiable artifacts. Humfrey himself hunched over an especially big and ancient volume. He was gnome-like, with enormous Mundane-type spectacles and wrinkles all over his face. He looked exactly as old as he probably just might be. "Well?" he snapped irritably.

"Chameleon and the mare Imbrium are here for advice," the Gorgon said deferentially. "You have them on your calendar."

"I never pay attention to that bit of paper!" the Good Magician grumped. "I'm too busy." But he looked at a chart on the wall. There, in large letters, was the note FAIR & MARE. "Oh, yes, certainly," he grumbled. "Well, let's get on with it."

There was a pause. "The advice," the Gorgon reminded the Magician gently.

"Have they paid the fee?"

"They're on the King's business. No fee."

"What is Xanth coming to?" he mumbled ungraciously. "Too many creatures expecting a free lunch."

"That was dinner," Chameleon said brightly.

Again there was a pause. The Gorgon touched Humfrey's elbow.

He looked up, startled, almost as if he had been dozing. "Of course. Beware the Horseman." His old eyes returned to his book.

"But we've already had that message," Imbri protested in a dreamlet.

Humfrey's brow corrugated yet farther. Such a thing would have been impossible without magic. "Oh? Well, it remains good advice." He cogitated briefly. "Break the chain." He looked at his tome again.

"I don't understand," Chameleon said.

"It isn't necessary to understand Humfrey's Answers," the Gorgon explained. "They are always correct regardless."

Imbri wasn't satisfied. "Don't you folk realize there's a war on?" she projected in an emphatic dream. Her picture showed brutish Mundanes tromping like ogres through the brush, frightening small birds and despoiling the land with sword and fire. The image was taken from her memory of the Lastwave. "We have to find out how to defend Xanth!"

Humfrey looked up again. "Of course I realize! Look at my book!"

They crowded closer to peer at his open tome. There was a map of Xanth with portions marked in color.

"Here is where the Mundanes are invading," Humfrey said, pointing to the northwestern isthmus. "They have not yet penetrated far, but they are well organized and tough and determined, and the auspices are murky. Divination doesn't work very well on Mundanes, because they are nonmagical creatures. But it seems the Nextwave of conquest is upon us. It will be the end of Xanth as we know it, unless we take immediate and effective measures to protect our land."

"The Nextwave!" Chameleon repeated, horrified.

"We knew there would be another Wave sometime," the Gorgon said. "All through the history of Xanth there have been periodic Waves of conquest from Mundania. All human inhabitants derive from one Wave or another, or did until very recently. But each Wave sets Xanth back immeasurably, for the Mundanes are barbaric. They slay whatever they do not understand and they understand very little. If this Wave succeeds in conquering Xanth, it will be a century before things return to normal."

"But how do we stop it?" Chameleon asked.

"I told you," Humfrey snapped. "Break the chain."

Imbri exploded with full night marish ferocity. Storm clouds roiled in her dream image, booming hollowly as they fired out fierce jags of lightning. "This is no time for cute obscurities! We need a straight Answer to a serious problem! Do you have an Answer or don't you?" A jag struck near Humfrey.

Humfrey gazed soberly at her, one hand idly swatting away the jag of lightning, though it was only a dreamlet image. "There are no simplistic Answers to a complex problem. We must labor diligently to piece together the best of all possible courses, or at least the second best, depending on what is available."

The mare backed off. She did realize that some answers could not be simple or clear. Magic often had peculiar applications, and predictive magic was especially tricky, even when Mundanes weren't involved.

"Night nears," the Gorgon said gently. Indeed, the cluttered scrap of a window showed near-blackness outside. "You will be able to travel more freely then. We must let Magician Humfrey labor in peace." She led them to another room, where there was a couch. "You will want to rest first. I will wake you at midnight."

That was good enough. There were sanitary facilities and a pleasant bed of straw. Imbri lay down and slept. She could rest perfectly well on her feet, but suspected the Gorgon would worry about hoofprints and droppings and such, so lying down was best. Actually, there was hardly any place in Xanth that could not be improved by a nice, fertilizer-rich dropping, but human beings tended not to understand that.

A night mare visited her, of course. Imbri recognized her instantly. "Mare Crisium!" she exclaimed in her dream. "How is everything back home?"

"The Dark Horse is worried," Crises said. She, like Imbri, could speak in the human language in the dream state. "He says the menace advances, and you are the only one who can abate it, and you have fallen into the power of the enemy."

"I did, but I escaped," Imbri replied. "I delivered the message to King Trent. Now I'm on a mission for him."

"It is not enough. The King is about to be betrayed. You must tell him to beware the Horseman."

"I told you, I told him that!" Imbri flared.

"You must tell him again."

Imbri changed the subject. "Where's Vapors?" She had a special affinity for both Crises and Vapors, for those two mares had picked up half souls at the time Imbri got hers. But the others had not retained them. Their halves had been replaced by the halves from a demon, cynical and cruel, which gave them a certain competitive edge: their bad dreams were real terrors, and they got the most challenging assignments. Even so, they had not been satisfied and had finally turned the half souls into the central office. So Imbri was now the only night mare with any part of a soul. But still, she felt closer to those other two; they understood the impact a soul could have.

"Vapors is with Chameleon. In a moment the woman will wake screaming; then you both must go and warn the King."

Imbri started to protest, but then Chameleon's scream sounded, and both woman and mare were jolted rudely awake. Instantly Vapors and Crises bolted, leaving only their signature hoofprints. Imbri was saddened; she was now considered a mortal creature, who was not permitted to see a night mare in the waking state. That wrenched at her, for she had spent most of her long life in the profession. How quickly the prerogatives and perquisites of employment were lost, once a creature retired! But that was the price she paid for the chance to see the rainbow.

She went to Chameleon, who clutched at her hysterically. "Oh, it was awful, Imbri! Such a bad dream! Is that really what you used to do?"

"Not that well," Imbri sent, with a tinge of regret. Obviously Mare Vaporum retained the terrifying touch that Imbri had lost. "What did you dream?"

"I dreamed King Trent was close to death, or something almost as awful! We must go right back and warn him!" She was still breathing raggedly, her lovely hair in disarray.

A simple premonition of danger to another person—and the client was in shambles. Imbri realized that she had retired none too soon; she would have had to bring in a firebreathing sea monster to achieve a similar effect. She was just too softhearted.

"Get on my back, woman," Imbri projected. "We'll ride immediately."

The Gorgon appeared, carrying a lighted candle that illuminated her empty head oddly, showing the snakelets that were her hair from the inside surface. "Midnight," she said. "Time to—oh, I see you're ready. Do come again soon!"

"We will!" Chameleon called, her mood lightening because of the contact with the familiar facelessness of a friend. Then Imbri plunged through the wall and they were off.

This time there was no trouble from the spriggan, centycore, or nix. Imbri was in her night mare form, phasing through everything, and Chameleon phased with her because that was the nature of night mare magic. They galloped in a straight line toward Castle Roogna, passing blithely through trees and rocks and even a sleeping dragon without resistance. Chameleon was pleasantly amazed; she was a good audience for this sort of thing, and that made Imbri's mood improve.

"Oh, no!" Chameleon exclaimed suddenly. "I forgot the elopement!"

That was right—this was the scheduled night for the marriage of Prince Dor. Chameleon was the mother of the victim; of course she wanted to attend. "We can make it," Imbri sent."

"No, we can't," Chameleon said tearfully. "It was to happen at midnight, and we're hours away, and it's past midnight now!"

Imbri hated to have this lovely and innocent woman unhappy. "We can travel faster—but it's a route you may not like."

"Anything!" Chameleon exclaimed. "If we can even catch the end of it— my poor baby boy—I know he'll be so happy!"

Imbri had a certain difficulty following the woman's thought processes this time, but decided Chameleon had mixed feelings about her son and his marriage. Mothers were notorious for that sort of thing. "Then hold on tight and don't be afraid of anything you see." Imbri galloped into a patch of hypnogourds and plunged into a gourd.

It was dark as they phased through the rind and became part of the gourd world. Of course they were *not* part; they were alien visitors who normally would have found access only by looking through a peephole, instead of passing physically through. This was a gray area of magic, possible only because of Imbri's special status as an agent of liaison.

Then they were in a graveyard. "Oh, are we there already?" Chameleon asked. "The zombie cemetery?"

"Not yet," Imbri projected. "Stay on me!" For if the woman ever set foot inside the world of the gourd alone, she would not readily get free. That was the nature of the region of night.

A walking skeleton appeared. It reached for Chameleon, its hollow eye sockets glinting whitely. "Go away!" the woman cried, knocking the bony arm away. "You're no zombie. You're too clean." Startled, the skeleton retreated.

"They are a lot more cautious about visitors since an ogre passed through and intimidated them," Imbri sent. It had taken weeks after the ogre's departure for the skeletons to get themselves properly organized, since their bones had been hopelessly jumbled together. Probably some of them were still wearing the wrong parts.

Imbri charged into the haunted house. A resident ghost loomed, flaring with awesome whiteness at Chameleon. "Are we back at Castle Roogna already?" she asked. "I don't recognize this ghost." Disgusted, the ghost faded out, thinking it had lost its touch. Imbri knew the feeling; there were few things as humiliating as having one's efforts unappreciated when one's business was fear.

Now Imbri shot out the front wall of the house. She galloped along a short walkway, then out through the decorative hedge. She emerged into a bleak moor. The ground became soggy, opening dark mouths to swallow intruders, but the night mare hurdled them handily. The terrors of the World of Night were for others, not herself. She might be retired, but she was not yet that far out of it.

She passed on to a mountain shaped like a burning iceberg, galloping up its slope. Amorphous shapes loomed, reaching for Chameleon with multiple hands and hungry snouts. Misshapen eyes glared.

Now the woman was frightened, for she had had no prior experience with this type of monster. Zombies and ghosts were familiar, but not amorphous monsters. She hunched down and hid her face in Imbri's mane. That was another trait of human folk: they tended to fear the unfamiliar or the unknown, though often it was not as threatening to them as the known.

Then they were out through the rind of another gourd, their shortcut through the World of Night completed. They emerged from a gourd patch much nearer Castle Roogna. Night mares could travel almost instantly anywhere in Xanth, simply by using the proper gourds. This route was not available to Imbri by day, since she was solid then; fortunately, it was now night.

Chameleon's fright eased as she saw that she was back in the real world of Xanth. "Is that really where you live?" she asked. "Among the horrors?"

"Daytime Xanth seems far more hazardous to me," Imbri projected. "Tangle trees and solid boulders and the Mundanes—those are monsters enough!"

"I suppose so," Chameleon agreed doubtfully. "Are we near the cemetery?"

"Very near." Imbri veered to head directly toward it.

"Wait!" Chameleon cried. "We must go in costume!"

"Costume?" What was this creature thinking of now?

"We must look like zombies so no one will know."

Evidently so. Imbri humored her, since it was difficult to argue with a person of such low intelligence and sweet personality. They stopped, and the woman found stinkvines and ink pots, which she used to make each of them look and smell rotten. Her artistry was reasonably good; Chameleon did indeed resemble a buxom, flesh-loose zombie more than the lovely older woman she really was. Imbri looked like a half-dead nag.

Now they continued to the cemetery, where it lurked in the lee of Castle Roogna. The zombies were up and about in strength. Not many things stirred them, but marriage was in certain ways akin to death in its finality and disillusion. "We conspired with the Zombie Master," Chameleon whispered to one of Imbri's perked furry ears. "He roused his minions for the occasion, though he could not attend himself. One of the zombies is a justice of the peace. I don't know what that is, but it seems he can marry them." She was all excited with anticipation.

Zombies were loosely formed creatures, so naturally would have a justice of the piece, Imbri realized. It was not too great a stretch of the rationale to extend the authority to restore lost pieces of zombie to the union of full creatures of flesh. Marriage, in Xanth, was whatever one made of it, anyway; the real test of it would be the acceptance by the partners in it and by the wider community, rather than any single ceremony.

As they stepped onto the graveyard grounds, things changed. Suddenly the zombies were twice as ghastly as before, dressed in tuxedos and gowns that concealed much of their decay but made the parts that showed or fell off more horrible in contrast. All were standing quietly between the gravestones, facing the largest and dankest crypt at the north end, where an especially revolting zombie stood with a tattered book in his spoiled hands.

A female zombie came up. Her eyeballs were sunken, and parts of her teeth showed through her worm-decimated cheek. Her low décolletage exposed breasts like rotten melons. "Are you a centaur?" she inquired in a surprisingly normal voice.

"I'm Chameleon, your Majesty," Chameleon said, dismounting, evidently recognizing the voice. "And this is the mare Imbri, who brought me back in time for the wedding. Have we missed anything?"

"Wonderful, Chameleon!" Queen Iris cried, embracing her with a sound like funguses squishing. "Take your place in the front row, by the chancel; you're the mother of the groom, after all. You haven't missed a thing; these events always run late."

"And you're the mother of the bride," Chameleon said, happy at the way this was working out.

The Queen Zombie turned to Imbri, her rotten body rotating at differing velocities. Her illusion was a morbid work of art! "You really are a mare?" she asked. "Yes, I see you are. Since you're not related to the principals, you should stand in back."

"But Imbri's my friend!" Chameleon protested loyally.

"I'll stand in back," Imbri projected quickly. She knew little about human folk ceremonies and much preferred to be out of the way.

"Oh, my, that's interesting magic!" the Queen said. "Almost like my illusion, only yours is all inside the head, or do I mean all in the mind? I didn't know animals could do magic."

"I am a night mare," Imbri clarified.

"Oh, that explains it, of course." The Queen turned away, going to greet other arrivals.

Chameleon went dutifully to the front, while Imbri made her way back. She came to stand between two zombies. It seemed the lucky couple for whom this ceremony was waiting had not yet arrived, so there was time to talk.

"Hello," she projected to the one on the left.

The answer was an awful morass of foulness, resembling a blood pudding riddled with maggots. This was a true zombie, who might have been dead for centuries; she had just glimpsed its actual brain. Imbri was not unduly finicky, for every monster was allowed its own style in Xanth, but she was accustomed to the clean bones of the walking skeletons in the gourd. She tried not to shy away from this person, for that would be impolite, but she did not attempt to communicate with it again.

Imbri tried the figure on the right. "Are you a zombie, too?" she sent tentatively.

This person was alive but startled. "Did you address me, or was I dreaming?"

"Yes," Imbri agreed.

He turned to peer more closely at her. "Are you a person or a horse?"

"Yes."

"I'm afraid I'm not used to this concentration of magic," he said. "I may have made a faux pas."

"No, that's west of here," Imbri corrected him.

"It's true! You are a horse, and you did address me!"

"Yes. I am the night mare Imbrium."

"A literal nightmare? How original! One never knows what to expect next in Xanth! I am Ichabod the Archivist, from what you term Mundania. My friend the centaur Arnolde—he is currently in Mundania, as that's his office, liaison to that region—brought me here so I could do research into the fantastic and, ahem, pursue a nymph or two."

"That is what nymphs are for," Imbri agreed politely. She knew it was a very popular human entertainment. But his reference to Mundania alarmed her; was he one of the enemy?

"Oh, no, I'm no enemy!" Ichabod protested, and Imbri realized she had forgotten to separate her private thought from the formal dreamlet. She would have to be more careful about that, now that she was among waking people. "Mundania is many things—you might say, all things to all people. It seems Mundania has extremely limited access to Xanth, while Xanth has virtually unlimited access to Mundania. This includes all the historical ages of our world. Therefore Xanth is but an elusive dream to the Mundanes, most of whom do not believe in it at all, while Mundania is a prodigious reality to Xanthians, who are very little interested in it. Am I boring you?"

He was doing that, of course, but Imbri had the equine wit not to say so. "I deal in dreams, and I am elusive, so I am certainly a creature of Xanth."

"Really? You mean you are a dream yourself? You're not really there?" He reached out a hand, tentatively, to touch her shoulder.

"Not exactly." She phased out, and his hand passed through her.

"Fabulous!" he exclaimed. "I must put you in my notebook. You say your name is Imbrium? As in the Sea of Rains on the visible face of the moon? How very intriguing!"

He might be Mundane, but she saw that he was not entirely ignorant. "Yes. They named the Sea of Rains after my grandam, who lived a long time ago. I inherit my signature from her and the title to that portion of the moon." She phased back to solid and stamped a forehoof, making a moonmap imprint with her own name highlighted.

"Oh, marvelous!" Ichabod cried. "I say, would you do that on a sheet of my notebook? I would love to have a direct record!"

Imbri obligingly stamped his page. The map showed up very clearly on the white paper, since of course there was a coating of good, rich, cemetery dirt on her hoof.

"Oh, thank you, thank you!" the Mundane exclaimed, admiring the print. "I have never before encountered a genuine nightmare—not in the flesh, so to speak. It is not every Mundane who receives such an opportunity! If there is any return favor I might possibly do you—"

"Just tell me who is here and how the ceremony is to proceed. I have never attended an elopement."

"I shall be delighted to, though my own understanding is far from perfect. It seems that Prince Dor and Princess Irene—their titles are similar but have different derivations, as he is the designated heir to the throne, while she is merely the daughter of the King—both of whom I met eight years ago in Mundania, are at last to achieve nuptial bliss, or such reasonable facsimile thereof as is practicable."

Imbri realized that Mundanes had a more complex manner of speaking than did real people; she cocked one ear politely and tried to make sense of the convolutions.

"But he seems not yet to be aware of this, and she is supposedly not aware that virtually everyone in Castle Roogna or associated with it is attending. It is supposed to be an uncivil ceremony, performed in the dead of night by a dead man—i.e., a zombie. A most interesting type of creature, incidentally. Queen Iris has cloaked all visitors with illusion—she does have the most marvelous facility for that—so they seem to be zombies, too, and she has mixed them in with the real zombies so that no one not conversant with the ruse is likely to penetrate it. Oh, what a tangled web we weave, when first we practice to deceive! That is a Mundane quotation from—"

He broke off, for there was a stir to the south. Just in time, for he had been about to bore Imbri again. He did seem to have a formidable propensity for dullness. All the zombies, real and fake, hushed, waiting.

The pale moonlight showed a young woman of voluptuous proportion stepping through the fringe of the Castle Roogna orchard, hauling along a handsome young man. "We'll just cut through the zombie graveyard," she was saying. "We're almost there."

"Almost where?" he demanded irritably. "You're being awfully secretive, Irene. I'm tired; I have just come back from Centaur Isle, where I couldn't make much of an impression; I've consulted with King Trent about the Nextwave incursion and how to contain it; and now I just want to go home and sleep."

"You'll have a good sleep very soon, I promise you," Irene said. "A sleep like none before."

A rock chuckled. "It'll be long before you sleep, you poor sucker!" it said.

"Shut up!" Irene hissed at the rock. Then, to Dor: "Come on; we're almost there."

"Almost where?"

"Don't trust her!" the ground said. "It's a trap!"

Irene stamped her foot, hard. "Oooo!" the ground moaned, hurting.

"I wish you'd just tell me what you're so worked up about," Dor said. "Dragging me out here for no reason—"

"No reason! Hah!" a chunk of deadwood chortled. Irene kicked it into the moat, where there was a brief, wild splashing as a moat monster snapped it up.

"I suppose you do have the right to know," she said as they entered the graveyard. All the guests had abruptly faded into invisibility, thanks to Queen Iris's illusion. "It's an elopement."

"A what?"

"Elopement, idiot!" a tombstone cracked. "Better run before you're lost!"

Irene rapped the stone on the top, and it went quiet. She seemed to have had experience dealing with talking objects. "We're eloping," she said clearly. "I'm taking you secretly away to get married. Then you'll have something nice in bed with you."

"Something nice?" Dor asked, bemused. "You mean you're giving me a pillow?"

This time it was Dor she kicked, as the whole cemetery guffawed evilly. "*Me*, you oaf! Stop teasing me; I know you aren't *that* stupid. I can be very soft and warm when I try."

"Ooooo!" the crypt said in a naughty-naughty voice. "Not many of that kind *here!*"

"But we haven't set the date!" Dor protested.

"That's why we're eloping. We'll be married tonight, before anyone knows. So there won't be any foolishness. The job will be done."

"But—"

She turned and kissed him emphatically. "You have an objection?"

Dor, obviously daunted by the kiss, was silent.

"Marvelous, just marvelous, the way she manages him," Ichabod murmured beside Imbri.

The couple arrived at the crypt. "Zombie justice, where are you?" Irene called.

The officiating zombie appeared, holding his book. Also, slowly, the rest of them phased into dim view, under the continued glow of the moon.

"We're going to be married by a zombie?" Dor demanded weakly. "Won't the union fall apart?"

"Ha. Ha. I have laughed." She shook her head, so that her green hair flounced darkly in the limited light. "It's the only person I could get without alerting Mother," Irene explained. There was a choked snort of mirth from the depths of the audience. Irene looked around and spied the crowd. "Well, all you zombies didn't have to rip yourselves from your graves," she said in a spooks-will-be-spooks manner. "But I suppose some witnesses are in order."

"I didn't know there were this many zombies buried here," Dor said.

"There aren't, you poor stiff," the crypt said. "These are—"

"Quiet!" the Queen Zombie snapped.

Now Irene was suspicious. "That voice is familiar."

"Of course it is, you luscious dummy!" the crypt said. Then a black cloud roiled out of nowhere and emitted a roll of thunder that drowned out whatever other information the crypt disgorged.

"There's something very funny about this," Dor said, squinting at the loud cloud.

Irene reverted to first principles. "What's funny about zombies? They love grim occasions. Let's get on with it."

The zombie magistrate opened his book. A page fell out; the volume was as decrepit as the zombie.

"Oh, how I hate to see a book mistreated," Ichabod breathed beside Imbri.

"Wait a moment," Dor protested. "You tricked me out here, Irene. I didn't agree to get married tonight."

"Oh? Well, I intend to marry someone! Should it be one of these zombies?"

"Now that's a bluff I can call," Dor said.

Irene stood in silent but almost tangible grief. Her shoulders shook. Tears plopped into the sod at her feet. Dor, aided by a touch of the Queen's illusion, assumed a form somewhat like the hinder part of a giant's boot: a first-class heel. "Ah, well—" he mumbled inadequately.

Irene flung her arms about him and planted another kiss that made the audience murmur with envy. Even the zombies seemed moved. When she was through, Dor stood as if numbed, as well he might.

"Classic!" Ichabod whispered. "That girl has absolutely mastered the art!"

The zombie magistrate mumbled something unintelligible. He had no tongue, and he was reading from the pageless book, with empty eyeball sockets.

"I do," Irene said firmly.

The zombie mumbled something else as his nose fell onto the book.

"He does," Irene said, nudging Dor.

The zombie made a final effort, causing several loose teeth to dribble out of his mouth.

"I've got it," Irene said. She produced a ring with an enormous stone that glowed in the moonlight so strongly it seemed to illuminate the graveyard. "Put it on me, Dor. No, not that finger, idiot. *This* one."

Dor fumbled the moonstone onto the designated finger.

"We're married now," Irene said. "Now you can kiss me."

Dor did so, somewhat uncertainly. The audience broke into applause.

The remaining illusion faded, revealing the zombies and people standing throughout the graveyard. Irene's gaze swept across the crowd. "Mother!" she exclaimed indignantly. "This is your mischief!"

"Refreshments are served in the Castle Roogna ballroom," Queen Iris said, controlling a catlike smirk. "Come, dears—mustn't keep the King waiting."

Dor came out of his trance. "You made King Trent fetch refreshments?"

"Of course not, Dor," Queen Iris said. "I supervised that chore myself yesterday. My husband refused to participate in this little charade, the spoilsport. But I know he'll want to congratulate you."

"He should congratulate *me*," Irene said. "*I* landed Dor, after all these years."

"In the whole castle, one honest person," Dor muttered. But he did not seem unhappy. "I knew the King would not betray me."

"Well, you're married now," Queen Iris said. "At last. Now come on in before the food spoils."

The zombies stirred. They liked the notion of spoiled food.

Soon all the living people were across the moat, where sleepy moat monsters made only token growls of protest, and inside Castle Roogna, where food and drink had been set out. Imbri found herself near the beverage table. Since she did not drink human-style drinks, and did not much care for human-style treats, she was satisfied to watch.

Ichabod, still beside her, felt otherwise. "I love to eat," he confided. "It is my inane ambition eventually to become obese." He took a buttercup filled with a sparkling brown liquid. "This looks suitably calorific." He tilted it to his mouth.

As the liquid passed his lips, Ichabod made a funny little jump. Brown fluid splashed over his face. "I say!" he sputtered. "Why did you do that, mare?"

"Do what?" Imbri projected.

"Kick me!"

"I did not kick you!" she protested.

"I distinctly felt a boot in my posterior!" Then he cocked his head, looking at her feet. "But you don't wear boots!"

"If I kicked you, you would have a map of the moon on your rump," Imbri sent.

Ichabod rubbed the affected portion. "True. It must have been an hallucination." He tipped the remaining liquid to his mouth.

Again he jumped. "Someone *did* kick me!" he exclaimed. "But there was no one to do it."

Imbri got a notion. "Let me sniff your drink," she sent.

Ichabod held down the cup for her. Imbri sniffed—and felt a slight shove at her tail. "I thought so. This is the rare beverage Boot Rear, distilled from the sap of the shoe-fly tree. It's the drink that gives you a real kick."

"Boot Rear," Ichabod repeated thoughtfully. "I see." He picked up another cup. "Perhaps this differs. It seems effervescent, but colorless." He put it cautiously to his lips, paused, and when no suggestion of a kick manifested, gulped it quickly down.

Shining bars formed about him, enclosing him so tightly that he yelped with discomfort. "Let me out!" he cried.

Imbri quickly put a hoof on a nether bar and used her nose to shove the higher bars apart. In a moment Ichabod was able to squeeze out, his suit torn, abrasions on his body. "I suppose that was the result of the drink, too?" he asked irritably.

Imbri sniffed the empty cup. "Yes. That's Injure Jail, a concoction of incarcerated water," she reported.

"I should have guessed." But the man hadn't given up. He took a third drink, sipped it with extreme caution, paused, took a deeper sip, waited, and finally swallowed the rest. "This is excellent."

Then he fidgeted. He reached inside his jacket and drew out a card. "Where did this come from?" He found another up his sleeve, and a third dropped out of his pant leg.

Imbri sniffed the cup. "No wonder. This is Card Hider," she reported.

"This begins to grow tiresome," Ichabod said. "Imbri, would you do me the immense favor of locating me a safely sedate beverage?"

Imbri obliged, sniffing her way along the table. "Seam Croda," she sent. "Poot Frunch. June Pruice."

"I'll take that last," Ichabod said. "That sounds like my style. I think it is presently June in my section of Mundania."

Chameleon came to join them. "Wasn't that a wonderful wedding?" she asked, delicately mopping her eyes. "I cried real tears." She picked up a drink.

"Wait!" Imbri projected and Ichabod cried together. It was an unclassified beverage.

But Chameleon was already sipping it. It seemed she had to replace the fluid lost through her tears. Then her feet sank into the floor. "Oh, my—I'm afraid I took a Droft Sink!" she exclaimed. "I'm sinking!"

Imbri and Ichabod managed to haul her back to floor level. "I wouldn't want to seem to criticize the Queen, who I am sure put a great deal of attention into this spread of refreshments," Ichabod said. "But in some quarters it might be considered that certain types of practical jokes become, shall we say, tiresome."

Now the Queen herself approached. "Have you taken any of these drinks?" she inquired brightly. She had clothed herself in a fantastically bejeweled royal robe that was perhaps illusory. "I trust you find them truly novel and not to be taken lightly or soon forgotten. I want this occasion to make a real impression on the guests."

Mutely, the three nodded. The drinks were all that the Queen described.

Queen Iris picked one up herself and sipped delicately.

Then she spit it out again, indelicately. Her pattern of illusion faltered, revealing a plain housedress in lieu of her robe. "What's this?" she demanded.

"A truly novel beverage that makes a real impression and is not soon forgotten," Ichabod murmured.

"Don't get flip with me, Mundane!" the Queen snapped, a miniature thundercloud forming over her head. "What's in this cup?"

Imbri sniffed. "Drapple Ink," she projected.

"Drapple Ink!" the Queen exclaimed, her gems reforming and glinting furiously. "That's meant for signing official documents indelibly! What's it doing on the refreshment stand?"

Ichabod picked up another cup of Boot Rear. "Perhaps this one is better, your Majesty," he suggested, offering it to her. "It certainly made an impression on me."

The Queen sniffed it. She took a step forward, as if shoved from behind. "That's not what I ordered!" she cried, and now her gems shot little lances of fire. "Some miscreant has switched the drinks! Oh, wait till I get my claws on that chef!"

So Queen Iris had not been responsible for the joke. Chameleon looked relieved.

The Queen paused, turning back. "Oh—Chameleon," she called. "I really came to ask if you had seen my husband the King. He doesn't seem to be here. Would you look for him for me, please?"

"Of course, your Majesty," Chameleon agreed. She turned to Imbri. "Will you help me look, please? He might be in a dark room, meditating."

"And we have another message to give him," Imbri reminded her, remembering. "Beware the Horseman, or break the chain."

"If only we knew what chain." Chameleon sighed. "I haven't seen any chains."

"I'll help, too," Ichabod said. "I do love a mystery."

They looked all through the downstairs castle, but could not find the King. "Could he be upstairs, in the library?" Ichabod asked. "That's a very nice room, and he is a literate man."

"Yes, he is often there," Chameleon agreed.

They went upstairs, going to the library. A ghost flitted across the hall, but was gone before Imbri could send a dreamlet to it. If she ever had a moment when she wasn't busy, she would catch up to a ghost and inquire where Jordan was, so she could give him the greeting from the ghosts of the haunted house in the gourd world.

The library door was closed. Ichabod knocked, then called, but received no answer. "I fear he is not in," he opined. "I do not like to enter a private chamber unbidden, but we should check."

The others agreed. Cautiously they opened the door and peeked in. The room was dark and quiet.

"There is a magic lantern that turns on from a button near the door,"

Chameleon said, fumbling for it. In a moment the lantern glowed, illuminating the room.

There was King Trent, sitting at the table, an open book in front of him. "Your Majesty!" Chameleon cried. "We have to tell you—"

"Something is wrong," Ichabod said. "He is not moving."

They went to the King. He sat staring ahead, taking no notice of them. This was odd indeed, for King Trent was normally the most alert and courteous person, as men of genuine power tended to be.

Imbri projected a dream to the King's mind. But his mind was blank. "He's gone!" she sent to the others, alarmed. "He has no mind!"

The three stared at one another with growing dismay. Xanth had lost its King.

Chapter 5

Sphinx and Triton

By morning the new order had been established. King Trent had been retired to his bedroom for the duration of his illness, and Prince Dor had assumed the crown and mantle of Kingship and sat momentarily on the throne, making it official. For Dor was the designated heir, and Xanth had to have a King. He had vaulted in one strange night from single Prince to married King.

If there was to be a visible transformation in the young man, it had not yet materialized. He called a meeting of selected creatures after breakfast. The golden crown perched somewhat askew on his head, and the royal robes hung on him awkwardly. These things had been fitted for King Trent, who was a larger man, and it seemed King Dor preferred to wear them unaltered, so that they could be returned when King Trent recovered.

The shadows of Dor's eyes showed that he had not slept. Few of them had;

the joy of the elopement had shifted without pause to the horror of involuntary abdication. Indeed, King Trent had lost his mind while the others were celebrating in the zombie graveyard. It was hard not to suspect that the two events were linked in some devious way. The new Queen Irene evidently thought they were; she had lost a father while in the process of gaining a husband.

"We have a crisis here at Castle Roogna," King Dor said, speaking with greater authority than his appearance suggested. Queen Irene stood at his side, poised as if ready to catch him if he fell. Her eyes were dark and red, and not from any artifice of makeup or magic. How well she knew that it was the misfortune of her father that had catapulted her to replace her mother as Queen; this was hardly the way she had wanted it. Former Queen Iris was upstairs with King-emeritus Trent, watching for any trifling signal of intelligence. No one knew what had happened to him, but with the Mundane invasion, they could not wait for his recovery.

The King turned to a blackboard that his ogre friend had harvested from the jungle. On it was a crudely sketched map of Xanth, with the several human folk villages marked, as were Centaur Isle and the great Gap Chasm that severed the peninsula of Xanth but that few people remembered. "The Mundanes have crossed the isthmus," Dor said, pointing to the northwest. "They are bearing south and east, wreaking havoc as they progress. But we don't know what type of Mundanes they are, or how they are armed, or how many there are. King Trent was developing that information, but I don't know all of what he knew. I will consult with the Good Magician Humfrey, but that will take time, as we don't have a magic mirror connecting to his castle at the moment. The one we have is on the blink. We shall try to get it fixed; meanwhile, we're on our own."

That reminded Imbri. "Your Majesty," she sent in a dreamlet. "We have Magician Humfrey's message for the King. In the excitement we forgot—"

"Let's have it," Dor said tiredly.

"It was 'Beware the Horseman'—which we had already told King Trent. And 'Break the chain.' That was his other message."

Dor's brow wrinkled. He had a full head of intermediate-shade hair that was handsome enough when disciplined, but it was now a careless mop. Were it not for the crown, he would have been easy to mistake for some weary traveler. "I don't understand."

"Maybe my father would have understood," Irene murmured. "He could have had dialogue with the Good Magician. Maybe there's a chain in the armory whose magic will be released when it is broken."

"Sometimes Humfrey's obscure Answers are more trouble than they are worth," Dor grumbled. "Why can't he just come out and say what he means?"

"I can perhaps explain that," the Mundane Ichabod said. "First, he may believe he is speaking plainly, since he knows so much more than others do. Second, prophecy tends to negate itself when made too obvious. Therefore it has to be couched in terms that become comprehensible only when conditions for fulfillment are proper."

"Maybe so," Dor said. "Or maybe Humfrey is getting too old to give relevant Answers any more. If we don't find a chain in the armory, we'll just have to wage this war ourselves. The first thing we have to do is get good, recent information. I'll have to send a party I can trust to scout the Mundanes—"

"I'll go," Chameleon said.

King Dor smiled. "Even a King does not order his own mother into danger. Especially when she is as pretty as mine." Imbri exchanged a glance with Ichabod, aware that what Dor really meant was that Chameleon was well into her stupid phase, a probable disaster on a reconnaissance mission. "At any rate, I doubt you could travel fast enough to—"

"I mean with Imbri," Chameleon said. "Anyone is safe with her."

"Ah, the night mare." Dor considered. "Is it true, mare, that you can move as fast as thought itself?"

"Yes, King," Imbri replied. "When I use the gourd. But that's only at night."

"And you can keep my mother safe, even by day?"

"I think so."

King Dor paced the floor, the oversized robe dragging. "I don't like this. But I've got to have better information, and my mother is one person I trust absolutely. I think I'd better send Grundy the Golem along, too, to question the plants and animals. I'd go myself, to question the stones, if—"

"You must stay here and rule," Irene said, holding his arm possessively.

"Yes. I really wish we could include an expert in the party who would know exactly what to look for. It's so important that we know precisely what we're up against. Mundanes are not all alike."

Ichabod coughed. "Your Majesty, I fancy myself something of an expert in Mundane matters, since I am of Mundane persuasion myself. I should be glad to go and identify the invading force for you."

Dor considered. "Ichabod, I have known you for eight years, intermittently. You have done excellent research on the magic of Xanth, and your information has been invaluable when we have needed to research Mundania. You enabled us to locate and rescue King Trent when he was captive in Mundania. I do trust you, and value your information, and know King Trent felt the same. That's why he gave you free acess to all the things of Xanth and allowed you to research in the castle library. But you *are* Mundane; I can not ask you to spy on your own people."

"My people do not ravage and pillage and slaughter wantonly!" Ichabod protested. "Do not judge all Mundanes by the transgressions of a few."

"Those few may be enough to destroy Xanth," King Dor said. "Yet you make a good case. But you would need a steed to keep up with the night mare, and I do not think any of our available creatures are suitable. A centaur might help, but most of them are down at Centaur Isle, organizing for the defense of their Isle. I should know; I just returned from there! So—"

"The day horse might help," Imbri projected.

"The day horse?" King Dor asked.

"I met him in the forest. He was Mundane steed for the Horseman, but he escaped and helped me escape. He doesn't like the Mundanes. He might be willing to carry Ichabod, though, if no bit or spurs were used, if he knew Ichabod was not one of the enemy Mundanes." Imbri twitched her skin where her own sore flanks were healing. "I am to meet him at the baobab tree at noon."

King Dor considered briefly. "Very well. I don't like organizing such an important mission so hastily, but we can't defend Xanth at all unless we get that information. If you meet this day horse, and if he agrees to help, Ichabod can ride him. But you, Mother, will be in charge of the mission. Only please listen to Grundy—"

Chameleon smiled. "I have been stupid since before you were born, Dor. I know how to get along. I will listen to Grundy."

Now the golem appeared. He was as tall as the length of a normal hand and resembled the wood and rag he had originally been fashioned from, though now he was alive. Most people of Xanth had magic talents; he was a talent that had become a person. "We'll get along fine," he said. "I care about Chameleon."

"I know you do," King Dor said.

"I was Dor's guide when he wasn't even a Prince," Grundy said, asserting himself. "I know Chameleon from twenty-five years back. Can't say the same for this nag, though."

Imbri's ears flattened back in ire. She sent a dreamlet of a thousand-toothed monster chomping the golem.

"Then again," Grundy said, shaken as he had been the last time they clashed, "maybe I've met her in my dreams."

Chameleon smiled in an inoffensive way. "Night mares are very scary in dreams, but nice in person."

"Take care of yourselves," King Dor said gravely. He seemed quite different from his petulance and indecision of the prior evening, as if the responsibility of leadership had indeed brought out a new and superior facet of his character. "There is not one of you I would care to lose." He smiled, to show there was a modicum of humor there, though it wasn't really necessary.

"We must say good-bye to Queen Iris," Chameleon said. She led the way upstairs, and Imbri and Grundy followed, not knowing what else to do.

The King's bedroom had become an enormous dark cave, with stony stalactites depending from the domed ceiling and deep shadows shrouding the walls. Muted wailing sounded in the background. Fallen King Trent had the aspect of phenomenal grandeur, while Queen Iris was garbed in the foulest rags. The setting was illusion, courtesy of the Queen's talent, but the sentiment was real.

"I just wanted to say, your Majesty, that we miss the King and will try our best to help," Chameleon said, standing on a rocky escarpment.

Queen Iris looked up. She saw how lovely Chameleon was, and knew what it meant. "Thank you, Chameleon. I'm sure your son will make a good King," she said, speaking slowly and clearly so the woman would understand. Of course there was no assurance that Dor would be able to handle the job, let alone the Mundanes, but this was not the occasion for the expression of such doubts.

"I'm going north now with Mare Imbri and Grundy and Ichabod maybe, to spy on the Mundanes."

"I'm sure you will spy well." Queen Iris's gaze dropped; her politeness was almost exhausted.

"Good-bye, your Majesty," Chameleon said.

The Queen nodded. Then the visitors left the gloomy cave and found the stairs leading down.

They grabbed some supplies, reviewed the map, selected a promising day-time route, and moved out. Imbri galloped ahead to the baobab tree, for it was coming on to noon and she didn't want to miss the day horse. She carried Grundy, who could talk to any living thing and would not seem like a human person. Ichabod and Chameleon followed more slowly on foot.

The baobab was a monstrous tree. It towered above the jungle, its apex visible from far away. The oddest thing about it was the fact that it grew upside down. Its foliage was on the ground, and its tangled roots were in the air. A space around it was clear, for the baobab didn't like to be crowded, and used hostile spells to drive away competitive plants.

Imbri poked her nose in the foliage. Was the day horse here? He hadn't specified which day; he might be elsewhere this noon.

The golem made a windy, whispering sound. The tree replied similarly. "Bao says the horse's waiting inside," Grundy reported.

Imbri nosed her way to the tremendous, bulbous trunk. There was a split in it wide enough to admit a horse. She entered cautiously.

Inside it was like a cathedral, with the dome of the tree rising high above. Wooden walls convoluted down to a tesselated wooden floor. From inside, the tree looked right side up. Perhaps that was illusion.

There in the center stood the handsome day horse, shining white. His mane and tail were silken silver, and his hooves gleamed. His small ears perked forward alertly on either side of his forelock. He was almost the prettiest sight she had seen.

"Now there's a horse you can call a horse," Grundy murmured apprecia-tively. "No fish-tail, no unicorn-horn, no shady colors, no bad dreams. The Mundanes may not be good for much, but they certainly know how to grow horses!"

Imbri could only agree, despite the golem's obliquely derogatory reference to herself—the implication that Xanth could not grow good horses. The only male of her species she had known before was the Night Stallion, who was her sire. The dark horses had been closely interbred for millennia, but now they seldom bred at all because the relationship was too close. New blood was needed—but what was she thinking of? This was a Mundane horse, not really her kind. Her new solidity was giving her new sorts of reaction.

The day horse made a nicker. "He says come forward so he can see you in the light, black mare," Grundy translated unnecessarily. Of course Imbri understood equine talk! She stepped forward. She hadn't seen the day horse more than fleetingly by day before and was now as skitterish as a colt. The sheer masculinity of him had a terrific impact on her.

"You are lovely as the night," the day horse nickered.

"You are handsome as the day," Imbri nickered back. Oh, what a thrill to interact with such a stallion!

"I just hate to interrupt this touching dialogue," Grundy cut in with a certain zest. "But you do have business, you know."

Imbri sighed. The confounded golem was right. Quickly she projected a dream of explanation, describing what she wanted from the day horse.

He considered. "I don't like going near Mundane human folk," he said in the dream. "They might capture me again." He stomped his left foot nervously, making the brass circlet on it glint. "Then I would never get away."

Imbri well understood. Once he was tethered, he would not be able to phase away by night, as Imbri could, for he was not magic. Like the Mundane human beings, he was limited to Mundane devices. This was the terrible curse of all Mundanes. *They could not do magic.* Most of them did not even believe in magic, which might be a large part of their problem. Fortunately, their offspring in Xanth soon became magical. That was why the Mundane conquests never lasted more than a generation or so; the intruders stopped being Mundane.

"You don't have to go near them," Grundy said in equine language. "All you have to do is carry Ichabod close enough so *he* can look at them. He's Mundane himself, so he knows—"

"Mundane!" the day horse neighed, his nostril's dilating and white showing around his eyes.

"But he's a tame Mundane," the golem continued. "Loyal to Xanth. He doesn't want to see it despoiled. He likes the wild nymphs too well."

"What does he do with nymphs?" Imbri asked, curious.

"Mostly he just looks at their legs," the golem explained. "He's too old to chase them very fast. I'm not sure he would know what to do with one if he caught her, but he likes to dream. No offense to you, night mare." Grundy was getting more civil as he became better acquainted with her.

"No offense," she sent. "That's not the kind of dream I carry, anyway."

The day horse was shaking his head and scuffling the floor with his hooves. "I don't like Mundane men. I know about them. They can't be trusted."

"Say, that's right!" Grundy said. "You came with them! You can tell us all about them. What time and region of Mundania are they from?"

"Time? Region?" The day horse seemed confused.

"Mundania is all times and all places," Grundy said with assumed patience. "Thousands of years, and more territory than in all Xanth. We need to know when and where you come from so Ichabod can look it up in his moldy tomes and find out how to fight the men."

"I don't know anything about that," the day horse neighed. "All I know is how the Horseman put the bit in my mouth and the spurs to my sides and made me go." Imbri nickered with sympathy; she understood exactly.

"You've got to know!" the golem cried. "How can you spend your whole life among the Mundanes and not know all about them?"

The day horse just looked at him, ears angling back.

Imbri caught on. "Mundane animals are stupid, like Chameleon," she projected to the golem in a private dreamlet. "He never noticed the details of the Mundane society. He was probably kept in a stable and pasture."

"That must be it," Grundy agreed, irked. "He probably couldn't even talk until he came to Xanth." Then he brightened, speaking inside the private dreamlet so that the day horse would not overhear. "At least *he* can't betray us to the Mundanes. He won't understand our mission either."

"Yes," Imbri acknowledged sadly. "He's such a fine-looking animal, but not a creature of Xanth." Not like the Night Stallion, who was every bit as intelligent as a human being. It was really too bad.

They returned their attention directly to the mission. "Somehow we've got to convince you to help," Grundy told the day horse. "Otherwise the Mundane Wave may wash right across Xanth. Then you won't have anywhere to escape to; Mundanes will control everything."

That daunted the creature. "I don't want that!"

"Of course, you might hide from them easier if you took off that brass circlet you wear," the golem said.

The day horse glanced down at his foreleg where the band clasped it. "Oh, no, I couldn't do that!"

"Why not? As long as you wear it, the Horseman knows you're his horse. If you took it off, he might think you were some other horse, especially if you got your coat dyed black."

The day horse communicated slowly and with difficulty, but with certainty. "If I take off the circuit and they catch me, they will know I am a deserter and will butcher me for horsemeat. If I leave it on, they may think I only got lost and will not treat me so bad."

Grundy nodded. "Not a bad effort of logic, for you," he admitted. "So the band represents, ironically—for all that it's brass, not iron—a kind of insurance. Because they believe you're too dumb really to try to escape—and the fact that you don't remove it confirms that belief."

The day horse nodded back. He was not, indeed, quite as stupid as he seemed.

"But if you give Ichabod a ride, and then are later caught by the Mundanes, they will believe that you were captured by the other side and had no choice. You did not return to the Mundanes because the enemy wouldn't let you. That's insurance, too."

The day horse considered. Slowly the sense of it penetrated. "Does this renegade Mundane of yours use spurs?"

"No. Ichabod is an old man who has probably never ridden a horse before in his life. A centaur, maybe, because the centaur archivist Arnolde is his closest friend, but that's not the same. You'd have to step carefully to prevent Ichabod from falling off."

The day horse digested that. Certainly Ichabod did not sound like much of a threat. "No bit?"

"We don't use that sort of thing in Xanth. Creatures carry people only when they choose to. Imbri, here, is giving me a ride because she knows I can't get about the way she can. You don't see any bit in her mouth, do you?"

In the end, the day horse was swayed by the golem's persuasion and agreed to carry Ichabod, on condition that there be no direct contact between him and the Mundanes. "I don't even want to *see* a Mundane," he insisted. "If I saw them, they might see me, and if they see me, they will chase me, and they might catch me."

"You could outrun them!" the golem protested.

"Then they would shoot me with arrows. So I don't want to go near them at all."

"Fair enough," the golem agreed.

They departed the tree, picked up the archivist, and headed north. Sure enough, Ichabod was unsteady on horseback and had to hang on to the day horse's mane to stop from sliding off one side or the other. But gradually he got used to it and relaxed, and the horse relaxed also. The lack of a bit and reins made all the difference. Soon they were able to pick up speed.

Imbri became aware of another aspect of group interaction. She picked up Chameleon without thinking, but realized by the reaction of the day horse that the woman had not been mentioned before. At first the day horse had hesitated; then, when he saw how pretty Chameleon was, he watched her with interest. If it had been Chameleon who had needed the ride, it would have been easier to persuade this animal!

The day horse was a fine runner, making up in brute strength what he lacked in intellect, and Imbri found herself reacting on two levels to him. She liked his body very well, but was turned off by his slow mind. Yet, she reminded herself, she liked Chameleon well enough despite her slowness. Maybe it was that Chameleon was not a potential breeding object.

Yes, there it was. The presence of a fine stallion meant inevitable breeding when Imbri came into season. As a night mare, she had been immortal and ageless and never came into season, or at least not seriously. But as a material animal, she was subject to the material cycle. She would age and eventually die, and so there would be no one to carry on her work and maintain title to her sea of the moon unless she had a foal. Material creatures had to breed, just to maintain their position, and she would breed if she had the opportunity. This was no imposition; she wanted to do it.

But she also wanted to produce a handsome and smart foal. The day horse was handsome but not smart. That boded only half a loaf for the foal. Yet the day horse was probably the only other possible stallion extant in Xanth, in or out of the gourd; without him there would be no breeding at all, unless she searched out one of the winged horses of the mountains. She understood those types hardly ever deigned to associate with earthbound equines, however. That kept the options severely limited and made the decision difficult.

Would there be a decision? When a mare came into season—and this was a cyclical thing not subject to her voluntary control when she was material— any stallion present would breed her. Nature took it out of the province of individual free will, perhaps wisely. Human folk were otherwise; they could breed at any time, and the complexities of their individual natures meant that often they bred at the wrong time, or to the wrong person, or did not breed at all. That probably explained why horses were so much stronger and prettier than human beings. But humans were generally more intelligent, probably because it required a smart man to outsmart and catch a difficult woman, or a smart woman to pick out the best man and get him committed to the burden of a family. The midnight scene in the graveyard had illustrated that! Prince Dor had no doubt played innocent to avoid getting married, but had this time been outmaneuvered. And unless Imbri found a way to control her own breeding, she would have a stupid foal. So if she didn't want that, she would have to place distance between herself and the day horse when her season came on. Fortunately, that would not occur for a couple of weeks; she would have time.

Soon they arrived at the great Gap Chasm, which separated the northern and southern portions of Xanth. Few people knew about the Gap because of the forget-spell on it; it didn't even appear on many maps of Xanth. Since they were on the King's business, they had access to the invisible bridge that spanned it. Most people forgot about the bridge along with the Chasm, but it was there for those who knew how to find it. Imbri, as a night mare, felt very little effect from the forget-spell, so had no trouble.

The day horse, however, was hesitant. "I don't see any bridge," he neighed.

"No one can see the bridge," Imbri projected. In her daydreamlet she made the bridge become visible as a gossamer network of spider-silk cables. In her night dream duty she had not needed to use the bridge, but had known of it and the two others, as well as the devious paths down and through the Gap. She had perfect confidence in all the bridges, and in the charms that kept monsters off the paths, though she would be wary of descending into the Gap when the Gap Dragon was near. No spell ever stopped that monster; it ruled the Chasm deeps. That was another thing normally forgotten, which meant the dragon caught a lot of prey that didn't know it existed—until too late.

"It's all right, day horse," Ichabod said reassuringly. "I have been across it before. I know magic seems incredible to Mundane folk, such as are you and I, but here in Xanth it is every bit as reliable as engineering in our world. I have no fear in crossing."

Encouraged by that, and by now well aware that Ichabod was Mundane yet harmless but not stupid, the day horse followed Imbri out into midair over the Chasm. "Don't worry," Grundy called back. "You can't fall. It has rails on both sides. Except for the center, where a stupid harpy crashed through them and left a blank stretch."

The day horse stumbled, horrified, for he was now approaching the center. The golem laughed.

"It's not true," Imbri projected immediately. "Don't listen to the golem. He has an obnoxious sense of humor."

The day horse recovered his balance. He glared at Grundy, his ears flattening back. He dropped a clod on the bridge, a symbol of his opinion. Grundy had made an enemy, foolishly. It was one of his talents.

They got across without further event and trotted on north. They still had a long way to go, and would not reach the region of the Mundane line this day.

Now the terrain became rougher, for they were traveling cross-country. Northern Xanth was less populated by human folk than was central Xanth, so there were fewer people paths. One good trail led directly to the North Village, where Chameleon's husband Bink had been raised. But they intended to avoid human settlements, to keep their mission secret; the Mundanes surely had spies snooping near the various villages, Ichabod warned. So they went east of the North Village, threading the jungle between it and the vast central zone of Air in the center of northern Xanth.

The jungle thinned to forest, with clusters of everblues, everyellows, and evergreens, and then diminished to wash and scrub. As if to compensate, the ground became rougher. Their trot slowed to a walk, and the walk became labored. Both horses shone with sweat and blew hot blasts from dilated nostrils. Chameleon and Ichabod, unused to such extended travel, were tired and sore, and even the obnoxious golem was quiet, riding in front of Chameleon where he could hang on to Imbri's mane. The trouble with travel was that it was wearing.

In addition, it was hungry business. Horses had to eat a lot, and it was hard to graze while trotting. They would have to stop at the next suitable field and spring they found. But there was no suitable spot here; the land was pretty much barren. Certainly there was no spring on the hillside, and no river.

"Maybe we should cut west, toward the North Village," Grundy said. "Much better terrain there."

"But it would delay us, and perhaps expose our mission," Ichabod protested. "There must be a better alternative."

Imbri reflected. She had not been to this region recently, because there were very few people in it, and therefore few calls for bad dreams. "There are some lakes scattered through this region, with lush vegetation around them, but I can't place them precisely," she projected to the group. "The local plants and animals should know where they are, however." She gave her mane a little shake, waking Grundy, who, it seemed, had had the indecency to nod off during her reflection.

"Huh?" the golem said. "Oh, sure, I can check that." He began questioning the bushes they passed. Soon he found a fruitfly who had been seeded at a lake to the north. "But the fly says to beware the sphinx," the golem reported. "The sphinx got a sunburn and is very irritable this week."

"Beware the sphinx?" Chameleon asked. "I thought we were to beware the Horseman."

"That's good advice!" the day horse neighed. "How often have I felt that monster's spurs!"

"You mean like Imbri's flanks?" the golem asked. "I find it hard to believe anyone would want to poke holes in the hide of a living horse. What kind of a monster is this Horseman?"

The day horse did not like Grundy, but this question mellowed him somewhat. "A human monster."

"Spurs are an indefensible cruelty," Ichabod commented. "The typical horse will perform to the best of his ability for his rider. Spurs substitute the goad of pain for honest incentive, to the disadvantage of the animal."

The day horse nodded, evidently getting to like the archivist better. There was always something attractive about a well-expressed amplification of one's own opinion.

Imbri agreed emphatically. "And the bit is almost as bad," she sent.

"I don't see any scars on your flanks," Grundy said to the day horse.

"I learned long ago to obey without question," the day horse replied. "He hasn't used the spurs on me in some time; the scars are now so faint as to be invisible. But if he caught me now, after I escaped him, it would be terrible. There would be blood all over my hide."

Imbri visualized bright red blood on the bright white hide and flinched. What horror!

"Surely so." Ichabod nodded. "Man has a very poor record in his treatment of animals. In Xanth it is not as bad, for animals are much better able to defend themselves."

"Dragons are!" Grundy agreed, laughing. "And ant lions and basilisks and harpies."

They were mounting a steep, bald hill that barred their way north. Aggressive carnivorous vines and nettles to east and west made this the best route, laborious as it was. But soon they would be over it and might be able to relax a little going down the other side, where the sweet lake was supposed to be. Imbri and the day horse dug their hooves into the reddish turf, scuffling the sparse dry grass aside. The slope was spongy and warm from the sun.

Suddenly the bank exploded into a bunch of sticks. Chameleon screamed. Both horses reared and plunged to the sides, startled.

"Flying snakes!" Grundy cried. "Fend them off! I recognize this species; they're mean and unreasonable and some of them are poisonous. No use to try to talk to them; they only respect a clout on the snoot."

Chameleon and Ichabod had staffs they had harvested from a forest of general staffs. They had been using these to brush away clinging vines and such. Now they used them in earnest as the snakes darted through the air, jaws gaping. They were not big serpents, but they might be poisonous, as Grundy had warned. Imbri dodged away from them as well as she could, avoiding a green one and a red one, but a yellow one got through and bit her on her left front knee. She reached down with her own teeth and caught it behind the head and tore it loose, but the punctures hurt. She had never had to worry about this sort of thing as a full night mare!

A few moments of vigorous action got them away from the snakes, who could not fly very fast. Air simply was not as good to push against as ground. They resumed plodding up the hill.

"It is strange that both the Night Stallion and the Good Magician provided the same warning," Ichabod reflected aloud. It was one of his annoying habits. He talked a great deal about obscure aspects of situations, boring people. "Since the Horseman is an obvious enemy and perhaps a leader of the invading Mundanes, naturally loyal Xanth citizens should avoid him. Why waste a prophecy belaboring the obvious?"

"I fell into his power anyway," Imbri confessed. "I carried the warning, but I did not recognize the Horseman when I met him. If the day horse hadn't helped me escape—"

"I couldn't stand to see a mare as pretty as you in the power of a man as cruel as that," the day horse said in the community dream Imbri was providing. "I was terribly afraid to come so close to his camp."

"You didn't seem at all afraid," Imbri returned, complimenting him.

"Thank you," the day horse said. "I look bolder than I am, I suppose."

That seemed to be true. The day horse's fear of the invading Mundanes amounted almost to a fetish. Imbri felt he was overreacting. But outside of that, he did look bold, with his brilliant white coat and flaring mane and tail and muscular body. All factors considered, it remained a pleasure being with him.

With a final effort, they crested the red knoll. Now the Land of Xanth spread out around them in a sufficient if not marvelous panoply, like the clothing of an ill-kempt giant. In the distance to the south was the barely visible crevice of the Gap Chasm; to the west was a faint tail of smoke rising from the cookfires of the North Village; to the north—

"A lake!" Ichabod exclaimed happily. "With rich green color around it, surely suitable grazing for the equines and fruits for the unequines. There's our evening campsite!"

So it seemed. "But there's an awful mess of corrugations between us and it," Grundy said.

"I can travel a straight line to it," Imbri sent. "I am used to holding a straight course, regardless of the view, once I know where I'm going."

"Good enough," Grundy said.

Imbri started down the slope, leading the way—and stumbled. She went down headfirst, and Grundy and Chameleon were thrown off. They all went rolling down the rough slope helplessly, until they fetched up in a gully on the side of the knoll.

Grundy picked himself up, shedding red dust and bits of grass. "What happened, horseface?" he demanded grumpily. "Put your foot in it?"

"My knee gave way," Imbri projected, abashed. "That never happened before."

Chameleon righted herself. Even dirty and disheveled, she looked lovely. It was not necessarily true that women grew ugly as they aged; she was the impressive exception. "Is it hurt?" she asked.

Imbri rolled over, got her forefeet placed, and heaved herself up front-first in the manner of her kind. But she immediately collapsed again. The knee would not support her weight under stress.

Chameleon looked at it as she might inspect the scrape on the leg of a child. She was not bright, but that sort of thing did not require intelligence, only motherly concern. "You were bitten!" she exclaimed. "It's all swollen!"

The day horse arrived, picking his way carefully down the slope. "Bitten?" he neighed.

"So those snakes *were* poisonous!" Grundy said. "Why didn't you tell us one got you? We could have held it for interrogation and maybe found the antidote."

"Horses don't complain," Imbri sent. She had never been bitten before and had not properly appreciated the possible consequence. Her leg had hurt, but she had assumed the pain would ease. It had done so—but the extra strain of the downhill trek had aggravated what she now realized was not a healing but a numbness. Her knee had no staying power.

"I will carry all the people," the day horse offered. "I can handle it."

After a brief consultation, they acceded. The stallion was tired and sweaty, but still whole and strong; he could bear the burden. Chameleon and Grundy joined Ichabod on the day horse's broad back. It was a good thing he was along; the whole party would have been in trouble had it been Imbri alone for transportation.

Now it was up to Imbri to get herself on her feet. She set her good right leg under her and heaved herself up. Now that she wasn't depending on her left knee, it couldn't betray her.

She tried her left leg, but the numbness remained. It was better to hold it clear and hop along on the other three. It was possible to walk, jerkily, slowly, this way.

"Perhaps we could fashion a splint," Ichabod said. "To keep your knee straight so you can at least put weight on it."

That was an apt notion. They scouted around and found a projecting ledge from which several fairly stout poles sprouted. Ichabod dismounted and took hold of one, but though it wiggled crazily under his effort, it did not come loose from the ground.

"Cut it," Grundy said.

Chameleon had a good knife. Where she kept it Imbri wasn't sure, for it had not been evident before, but this suggested the lovely woman was not entirely helpless. She stooped beside the pole, applied her blade, and sawed at the base.

The ground shook. There was a rumble. Chameleon paused, looking askance at the others. "No meaning in a rumble," Grundy said. "Except to get out of here before an earthquake decides to visit."

"Earthquakes don't decide to visit," Ichabod protested. "They are natural, inanimate phenomena—merely the release of stresses developing within or between layers of rock."

There was another rumble, closer and stronger. "Not in Xanth," the golem said. "Here the inanimate has an ornery personality, as is evident when King Dor converses with it. Everything has its own individuality, even a quake."

The archivist had to step about to keep his feet during the second shaking. "There is that," he agreed nervously.

Chameleon sawed again at the pole. Her blade was sharp, but the pole was tough; progress was slow. A gash appeared, from which thick red fluid welled.

"I wonder what kind of plant that is?" Grundy said. He made some noises at it, then shook his head. "It doesn't answer."

"Maybe we can break it off now," Ichabod said, becoming increasingly uneasy. He wrenched the pole around more violently than before.

Suddenly the entire horizontal ridge of poles lifted up. A slit opened in the ground beneath them, revealing a moist, glassy surface crossed by bands of white, brown, and black. It was pretty enough for a polished rock formation.

"That's an eye!" Grundy exclaimed.

Ichabod, hanging from the pole, looked into the monstrous orb, aghast. "What's a hill doing with an eye?" he demanded. "And what am I suspended by?"

"An eyelash," the golem said. "I should have realized. It's alive, but it's not a plant. I was trying to talk to the eyelash of an animal. Naturally it didn't answer; eyelashes don't."

Ichabod dropped to the lower eyelid. One foot jammed accidentally into the eye. The eye blinked; the lid smashed down like a portcullis. The man wrenched out his foot and scrambled away.

"Get on the horse!" Grundy cried. "Get out of here!"

The three of them scrambled aboard the day horse, who moved out rapidly. Imbri hobbled after them.

Suddenly Imbri caught on. "The sphinx!" she broadcast. "This is the sphinx!"

"We were warned to beware of it," Grundy agreed. "As usual, we walked right onto the danger without recognizing it."

The ground shook again and buckled. The monstrous face of the sphinx was opening its mouth. A tremendous bellowing roar came forth in a hurricane blast of air.

"When it pains, it roars!" Grundy cried.

"Oh, for pity's sake!" Ichabod grumbled. "This is no time for idiotic puns."

"Xanth is mostly made of puns," the golem told him. "You have to watch where you put your feet, or you end up stepping on puns."

"Or something," Chameleon said, noting where some horse clods had fallen.

Meanwhile, the day horse was galloping off over the flexing cheek of the monster toward the shoulder. The tremendous sphinx was reclining, its face tilted back, so that the slope was by no means vertical. The pink knoll they had climbed was its sunburned pate. Every hoofprint must have aggravated the monster, but it had not become truly aroused until its eyelash had been attacked.

"Imbri!" Chameleon called from far ahead, realizing that the mare was not maintaining the pace.

"Keep going!" Imbri projected. "I'll follow!"

But she could not follow well on three legs, with the face of the sphinx shaking all over. She lost her footing and rolled toward the mouth, which was now sucking in a gale of breath. She scrambled desperately and managed to avoid it—but then rolled helplessly across the cheek in the wrong direction. Now the mouth was between her and her friends.

She fetched up against another projection. It was the huge, curving outcropping of the ear. Beyond it the face dropped unkindly far to the cracking and shuddering ground.

Imbri decided to stay where she was. At least the ear could not chomp her.

But what about her friends? They could be caught and tromped! They were on the dangerous part of the face.

Then she had a notion. She pumped her dream projection up to maximum strength and sent the sphinx a vision of absolute peace and contentment. Imbri wasn't expert at this sort of dream; all her experience had been with the other kind. But she did have half a soul now, and it was a gentle soul, and it helped her fashion a gentle dream.

Slowly the irritated sphinx calmed. It submitted to the dream of soft, sunny pastures with little sphinxes gamboling on the green. Cool mists wafted across its burning pate. Its eyes closed, broken eyelash and all, and the rumbling diminished.

Carefully Imbri left the cavern of the ear and hobbled back along the huge cheek toward real ground. But her hooves irritated the sunburned skin, resuming the waking process. The monster was not nearly as deeply asleep as it had been before; any little thing could disturb it now. A creature of such mass had considerable inertia, whether heading into sleep or out of it, and at the moment it was almost in balance. She had to retreat to the safe ear.

Unable to depart during daylight, Imbri settled down for a nap herself. She kept the sphinx passive by projecting a nominal sweet dream, just enough to lull it back to sleep when it thought about waking. Fortunately, sphinxes liked to sleep; that was why they were very seldom seen wandering around Xanth. There was a myth about one who had retreated to Mundania to find a suitably quiet place, and who had found a nice warm desert and hunkered down for a nap of several thousand years. The ignorant locals thought it was a statue and knocked off its nose. There would be an awful row when it woke and discovered that . . .

Meanwhile, it was easy for this one to doze off when no one was trotting on its face or blasting off its nose. This was just as well, considering the situation of Imbri's party.

When she woke, it was dark. Now she could move freely. Her bitten leg did not need to support any weight, now that she was able to dematerialize. She got up and galloped through the sphinx's head, where sweet dreams still roamed; her hooves got coated with sugar and honey. She emerged from the other ear and moved on north toward the lake. Soon she found it, trotted across it, and found the camp of the others.

Chameleon was the first to spy her. "Mare Imbri!" she screamed joyfully. "You got away!" She hugged Imbri fiercely, and the mare remained solid for the occasion. It was easy to like Chameleon despite her intellectual handicap, especially at a time like this. No creature except a basilisk would object to being hugged by a person of Chameleon's configuration.

"She wanted to return for you," Grundy said, "but we told her no. All we could have done was get ourselves in trouble and maybe make things worse for you."

"My son the King told me to listen to the golem," Chameleon said apologetically, her lovely face showing her distaste.

"It was best," Imbri agreed in a general dreamlet. "I hid in the sphinx's ear until night, then shifted to immaterial form."

"Your leg seems better," Ichabod observed.

"It isn't. But it's no worse. Maybe it will improve by morning."

They settled down for the remainder of the night. Chameleon, Grundy, and Ichabod slept, while the day horse and night mare grazed on the rich pasturage and snoozed. Imbri had to go solid to crop the grass, but she could phase out while chewing it, and she moved slowly enough so as not to aggravate her knee. And indeed, as the pleasant nocturnal hours passed, the numbness faded and strength returned. She had at last thrown off the lingering effect of the snake's venom.

In the morning, rested, they all were feeling fit. Chameleon stripped and washed in the shallow edge of the lake; Ichabod turned his back self-consciously, but Grundy openly goggled. "Age sure comes gracefully to some folk," he remarked. "But you should see her in her off-phase."

"I have," Ichabod said stiffly. "She has the most remarkably penetrating mind I have encountered."

"And the aspect of the most horrendous hag," the golem said, smirking.

"She merely manifests the properties of all women, with less ambiguity. They all begin lovely and innocent, and end ugly and smart."

"I guess that's why you like looking at nymphs," Grundy retorted. "They don't have minds, so there's nothing to distract you from their important points."

"Oh, I don't look at the points," Ichabod protested. "I look at their legs."

"Why don't you look at Chameleon's legs? They're as good as any and better than most."

"Chameleon is a person and a friend," the archivist said severely.

"Oh, she wouldn't mind." The golem was enjoying himself, needling the man. "Hey, doll, is it all right if Ichabod looks?"

"Silence!" Ichabod hissed, flushing.

"Certainly," Chameleon called back. "I'm under water."

"She was under water all the time!" Ichabod said, catching on as the golem rolled on the ground with mirth. "There was nothing to see!"

Something stirred across the lake. There seemed to be a cave just below water level. Now several heads showed.

"Tritons!" Grundy said. "Stand back from shore; they can be ornery."

Indeed, the mermen approached with elevated tridents. Chameleon tried to rise, then remembered her nakedness and settled back in the water, not smart enough to realize that her modesty could be fatal. Imbri charged back to guard her, and the day horse joined them.

Three tritons drew up just beyond the kicking range of the horses. "Ho! What mischief is this?" one cried. "Do you come to muddy our waters?" His three-pointed spear was poised menacingly.

Imbri broadcast a pacifying dreamlet. She was getting better at this with practice. "We only pass by, meaning no harm," her dream figure of a black mermaid said. "We did not know this lake was occupied by your kind."

Now the triton peered at Chameleon, whose torso he had briefly glimpsed when she started to stand. "That one must have nymphly blood," he remarked appreciatively.

But several mermaids had followed the tritons from the cave. "That's a human woman," one said. "Leave her alone."

The triton grimaced. "I suppose these people are all right. They haven't littered the grounds."

"Say," Grundy asked as the tension eased, "do you folk know the Siren? She settled in a lake somewhere in this general region several years back."

"The half-mer? Sure, she comes by here sometimes. She can split her tail into legs, so she can cross between lakes when there's no waterway. She married Morris, and they've got a halfling boy like her, part human but okay. Nice people."

"I know the Siren from way back," Grundy said. "And her sister the Gorgon, who married Good Magician Humfrey." He relaxed, seeing the tritons relax. "Where is the Siren now? Maybe we can pay her a visit."

"They live by the water wing," a mermaid said. "I don't think your kind could get there safely. You have to swim, or go through the zone of Fire."

The golem shrugged. "So we can't get there from here. It was a nice thought, anyway."

"Do you know any special hazards north of here?" Imbri asked in another dreamlet.

"Dragons on land, river monsters in the water, man-eating birds in the air—the usual riffraff," the triton said carelessly. "If you got by the sphinx, you can probably handle them."

"Thank you. We'll try to avoid them," Imbri sent, and let the dreamlet fade.

The group organized, once Chameleon had gotten dressed, and trotted north. Imbri had no further trouble with her knee; the toxin had dissipated, leaving no permanent damage, and she carried woman and golem as before.

They kept alert, avoiding the dragons, river monsters, and predator birds, and by evening arrived near the Mundane front. The invaders had penetrated well into Xanth, which shortened the trip; the fleeing animals gave Grundy horrendous reports of their violence. It seemed the Mundanes were using fire and sword to lay waste to anything they could, and were such deadly warriors that even large dragons were getting slain. This did not bode well for the defense of Xanth.

"I think my turn has come," Ichabod said. "I must actually see the soldiers to identify them specifically; there should be details of armor and emblem that will enable me to place them, if not immediately, then when I return to my references. Already I know they are medieval or earlier, since they employ no firearms. That's fortunate."

"Firearms?" Chameleon asked, looking at her own slender limbs as if afraid they would flame up. Her gesture was touching in its innocence.

"Those are weapons utilizing—something like magic powder," Ichabod clarified. "Imagine, well, cherry bombs shot like arrows from tubes. I hope Xanth never encounters that sort of thing. I wish *my* world had never encountered it." He looked around. "Suppose I ride Imbri, while Chameleon rides the day horse? I don't believe King Dor intended his mother to expose herself to extreme danger."

"I'm sure he didn't!" Grundy agreed emphatically. "It was bad enough when she exposed herself to the tritons. That's why he sent me along."

"To look at his mother bathing?" Ichabod inquired with a certain faint malice. Grundy got on everyone's nerves.

"Go with the day horse, Chameleon," Grundy said, ignoring the gibe. "We'll spy on the Mundanes and rejoin you later."

"We?" Ichabod asked, frowning, and the day horse's ears flattened back. Neither of them was thrilled by the prospect of the golem's company.

"I'm coming with you. I can learn a lot by talking with the plants and animals—maybe enough to spare you the natural result of your own heroics."

Ichabod smiled with certain scholarly resignation. "There is indeed that. I confess to being somewhat of a Don Quixote at heart."

"Donkey who?" Chameleon asked, blinking.

"Donkey Hotay, to you," the archivist said, smiling obscurely. "It is not spelled the way it sounds, even here in Xanth. He was an old Don, a Mundane scholar, buried in his books, exactly as I was before Dor, Irene, Grundy, the ogre, and Arnolde the Centaur rousted me out of my sinecure and opened a literally fantastic new horizon to my perspective. Don Quixote set himself up as a medieval knight in armor and rode about the Iberian countryside, having adventures that were far more significant for him than for the spectators, just as I am doing now. There was an encounter with a windmill, a truly classic episode—"

"What kind of bird is that?" Chameleon asked.

"Oh, a windmill is not a bird. It is—"

"We had better get going," Grundy interjected impatiently.

"Yes, indeed," Ichabod agreed. "We shall locate the two of you by asking the plants your location when we return. Do stay out of danger, both of you."

The day horse neighed. "You can be sure of that!" Grundy translated for him.

Chapter 6

The Next Wave

Imbri carried the golem and the Mundane scholar toward the terrible Mundane front. Xanth had not suffered a Wave invasion in a century and a half; this was an awesomely significant event.

"I believe I perceive some tension in you, Imbri," Ichabod said. "Am I imposing on you?"

"I was thinking how long it has been since the Lastwave," Imbri sent. "I was young then, only twenty years old, but I remember it as if it were last year."

"You were there?" Ichabod asked, surprised. "That's right—I forgot that you are one hundred and seventy years old. Since the Lastwave, as I reconstruct it, was one hundred and fifty years ago—" He paused. "I have, of course, researched this historically, but have talked with no eyewitnesses. I would dearly love to have your personal impressions."

"Well, I only saw bits of it at night, on dream duty," Imbri demurred. "The big battles were by day, and I could not go abroad by day then."

"Still, I would be fascinated!" the scholar said. "Your impressions, in the context of historical detail, would help complete the picture."

"Maybe you had better give that context," Grundy said, getting interested in spite of himself, "so we all know exactly what we're talking about." The golem, of course, had not been around for the Lastwave and hated to admit ignorance on anything.

"Certainly," Ichabod said. Historical detail was dear to his old heart. "My friend Arnolde Centaur provided some considerable information. It seems that the Firstwave of human colonization occurred over a thousand years ago. Before that, there were only the animals and hybrids, such as the centaurs. They have a touching story about the origin of their species—"

"Get on with the recent stuff," Grundy said.

"Um, yes, of course," Ichabod agreed, irritated. "There were a number of Waves, perhaps a dozen, most of them quite brutal, as the Mundanes invaded and ravaged Xanth. After each Wave conquered the land and settled down, the children would turn up with magic talents, becoming true citizens of Xanth. Then in fifty or one hundred years, another Wave would come, destroying much of what the prior Wave had accomplished. Finally, one hundred and fifty years ago, the Lastwave was so savage that the people of Xanth decided to prevent any future invasions. Once things settled down, in about fifteen years, a Magician King adapted a magic stone of great potency to project a deadly shield that destroyed anything crossing through it, and set that shield entirely around Xanth. The shield kept Xanth safe from intrusions for one hundred and ten years, until King Trent, who had spent time in Mundania, assumed power after the demise of the Storm King and abolished the shield. It seemed that mankind had been diminishing in the absence of immigration. So it was better to risk another invasion than to suffer certain extinction of the human species in Xanth by stiflement. Thus for the past quarter century there has been no shield—and now the consequence would seem to be upon us. King Trent refused to reinstate the magic shield, preferring to fight off the invaders, and perhaps with his power of transformation he could have done it. But now—"

"Now King Trent is out of the picture, and King Dor doesn't know how to set up the shield," Grundy finished. "Anyway, the Mundanes are already inside Xanth, so that's no answer."

"I am not certain it ever was an answer," Ichabod said. "I believe King Trent was correct; there has to be freedom of the border and commerce between Xanth and Mundania. Unfortunately, not all Mundanes come in peace. The Lastwavers, as I understand it, were Mongol Mundanes, of our thirteenth century A.D., circa 1231, if I do not misremember my Asiatic history. They believed they were invading the peninsula of Korea. Today Korea is severed by a line very like the Gap Chasm, with a major city where Castle Roogna is, suggesting a most intriguing parallelism—" He noted

Grundy's open yawn and broke off that conjecture. "But that's irrelevant to the present reprise. The Mongols were truly savage conquerors, and I can well understand the Xanthians' decision to have no more of that." He shook his head. "But it was Imbri's impressions I wanted. How did the Mongols look from this side, mare?"

"In the bad dreams I had to deliver, they were savage, flat-faced people," Imbri projected. "They killed all who opposed them, using arrows and swords. They rode horses—all those horses were killed, after the Wave was stopped, because of the terror the people of Xanth had for my kind after that. That was the equine tragedy; horses never intended mischief for Xanth."

"I am sure they didn't," Ichabod said consolingly. "The innocent often suffer most from the rigors of war. That is one of the appalling things about violence."

Imbri was getting to like this man. "Some of the dreams I delivered were to the Lastwavers. We night mares have always been fair and impartial; we deliver our service to all in need, no matter how undeserving. The Wavers suffered fears and sorrows, too, especially when their drive began to falter. They killed animals without compunction or compassion, yet they cared about their own families, left behind in Mundania, and about their comrades-in-arms. They saw Xanth as a terrible magic land, with deadly threats everywhere—"

"Well, of course it is, to Mundanes," Ichabod said. "Yet a person of Xanth would have similar difficulty going about in my own portion of Mundania, particularly if he did not know the patterns of highway traffic. Had I not been protected by my friends when first invited here, I would not have survived long. My first day in Xanth, I almost walked into a nickelpede nest. I thought the nickelpedes were units of currency."

"Xanth natives avoid such things routinely," Grundy said. "But I do remember those metal dragons in your land, shooting smoke out of their tails and carrying people around inside them for hours before digesting them. It was awful! When a person gets into unfamiliar territory, he's in much danger. We walked right onto that sphinx's head, for example—and we had been warned to beware the sphinx."

"And to beware the Horseman," Ichabod added. "And to break the chain. The trouble with these warnings is that we seldom understand them until it is too late."

"I don't even know where the chain is, let alone how to break it," Grundy said. "Fortunately, that's not my worry. King Dor is no doubt pondering that question now. I somehow doubt there is any chain in the Castle Roogna armory."

Ichabod returned to the subject. "Are you saying, Imbri, that you found the Mundane invaders—the Mongols—to be human beings, that is to say, feeling creatures, like the rest of us? You know, I'm fascinated to converse with a person who shared, as it were, the same stage with the Mongols, who were centuries before my time."

"That was the strangest thing about it," Imbri admitted in the dream. "Among themselves, they were perfectly decent creatures. But in battle they thought of people as they did dragons and basilisks and salamanders. They actually liked slaying them."

"It is an unfortunately familiar pattern in Mundania," Ichabod said. "First one group dehumanizes another, then it destroys it. In Xanth no real line between human and creature exists; many animals are better companions than many human folk." He patted Imbri's flank. "And how are we to define the centaurs, who have aspects of both? But Mundania has no recognized magic, so all animals are stupid, unable to speak the language of man. This leads to terrible wrongs. I much prefer Xanth's way."

"Yes, it is handy for communication," the golem agreed. "Here the animals and plants speak different languages, while human folk speak only one. Vice versa in Mundania. So animals don't really speak the language of men; it's just that some have learned it, as you have. No one has ever figured out what enchantment makes all human folk intelligible to each other here, even invading Mundanes. It just seems that the moment any human type steps into Xanth, the language matches."

"There is much remaining to learn about the magic of Xanth," Ichabod said. "I only hope I live long enough to fathom some significant part of it."

Imbri's ears perked forward. She sniffed the breeze. "Mundanes!" she projected.

Instantly the others were alert. Soon they all perceived the smoke of a burning field. "Why do they destroy so wantonly?" Grundy grumbled. "They can't use burned-out land any better than we can."

Ichabod sighed. "I'm afraid I can answer that. The point of such destruction is not to preserve land for one's own use, but to deprive the opponent of its produce, to diminish his capacity for war. Starving creatures can't fight effectively. Since there is magic everywhere in Xanth, and the Mundanes have none, they hurt Xanthians much more than themselves by ruining the land for everyone. It is an unkind but effective ploy."

"We have to stop them," Grundy said.

"Of course. But it will not be easy. We must spy out their nature, then organize to contain them. That is why our mission is so important. A side can not prevail, militarily, without good information about the enemy."

Imbri continued forward, carefully watching for the dread Mundanes. There was a slight wind from the north, whipping the fire south, and small creatures were fleeing it. But fire was hardly unknown in Xanth; fire-breathing dragons, fireflies, firebirds, and salamanders started blazes all the time. So this one would burn out in due course, since rivers and dense, juicy vegetation were all over Xanth and did not ignite well. Possibly the fire would be put out when it irritated a passing storm cloud and got rain dumped on it. The Land of Xanth put up with many indignities, but once properly aroused, it could find ways of dealing with nuisances. It seemed to Imbri that the Mundane Nextwavers had just about worn out their presumed welcome.

The trouble was, to remain downwind of the fire was to suffer the discomfort of heat and smoke. To cross to the upwind side was to risk discovery by the enemy. This scouting was awkward in practice, however necessary it was in theory.

"This will never work," Ichabod said, coughing, as a curl of smoke teased him. "I fear we are in an untenable situation. I don't like to counsel delay, but perhaps we should wait till evening—"

"Wait!" Grundy cut in. "I think I see an errant gust."

Imbri looked. Terns were wheeling to the west, first one and then another, taking turns in the manner they were named for. From the way they maneuvered and coasted and floated in the sky, she could tell the direction of the wind they rode. It was bearing north. It was indeed an errant gust, going counter to the prevailing wind. Probably it was a young breeze, not yet ready to settle down and pull with its elders.

"While the tern is wheeling, I'll not dream of squealing," the golem said in singsong. "Know what will happen when that gust dusts the fire?"

Ichabod, who had been wincing at something he must have taken as another pun, caught on. "Thick smoke—back in their faces, blinding them— and can you phase through it, Imbri?"

"Yes, I can phase through smoke when it's thick enough," Imbri projected. That was what she had done to escape the centycore at Magician Humfrey's castle. "But it's unreliable. When it thins, I'll turn solid again."

"Once we see them clearly, we can depart in utter haste," Ichabod said. He was now taut with nervousness, well aware of the danger they faced. "They may have horses; can you outrun your own kind?"

Imbri considered. "If they're like the day horse, they can match my pace by day. Not by night."

"Better not risk it," Ichabod said. "We are in no condition to oppose armed men."

"But with the smoke, we won't have to!" Grundy protested.

"Why don't we find a region where they have been, one that has not yet been burned?" Imbri projected. "Grundy can question the grass there and get a description."

"Excellent notion," Ichabod agreed.

"There is that." The golem liked a job that made him important.

The errant gust arrived at the fire. The flames swirled gleefully and reversed their angle, and the smoke poured north. There was dismay among the ranks of the Mundanes as it enveloped them. They coughed and gagged in a minor cacophony.

Imbri picked her way along the edge of the reversed fire, looking for a good route north. Suddenly men rushed out of the smoke, coming south.

"Oops," Grundy said. "A small miscalculation."

Imbri bolted. She ran south—but an arm of the fire had made its way there, and its smoke now came back toward her. It was not thick enough for concealment or phasing, though. She veered east, not wanting to leap through the flames unless she had to—and came up against the Mundanes. They had quickly taken advantage of the change in the wind to overrun this region. They held spears and swords at the ready, and some had bows. There were too many of them to permit escape.

The Mundanes closed on Imbri and her party, carefully. They were a fairly motley bunch, with different types of armor and clothing, but they were evidently disciplined.

"This has the aspect of a mercenary force," Ichabod murmured. "Little better than brigands. Pre-Christian era, European. Gaul or Iberia, I surmise."

"You a Roman or a Punic?" a soldier demanded.

"Roman or Punic!" Ichabod repeated under his breath. "That's it! The Romans used citizen-soldiers, at least at first; later they became, in fact, professional soldiers, landholders in name only. But the Punic forces—that's a contraction of 'Phoenician'—were known to make open and extensive use of mercenaries. Carthage—these would likely be Carthaginian mercenaries, circa 500 to 100 B.C."

"Speak up, old man!" the soldier cried, making a threatening gesture with his sword.

"Oh, I am neither," Ichabod said hastily. Quietly, to Grundy and Imbri, he murmured: "They assume I'm the only intelligent person. I think it best to deceive them, much as I detest the practice of prevarication."

"Yes," Imbri projected. "Grundy can pretend to be a doll, and I will be a stupid animal."

"You don't look like much," the Mundane said. "Where'd you steal the fine horse?"

"I did not steal this horse!" Ichabod protested. "I borrowed her from a friend."

"Well, we'll borrow her from you. Dismount."

"We shouldn't be separated," Imbri sent in a worried dreamlet. She remembered her prior capture by the Horseman and did not relish a repetition of that experience.

"This is not a completely tame animal," Ichabod said. "I ride her without saddle or reins, but she would not behave for a stranger."

The soldier pondered. Evidently he had had experience with half-wild horses. He put his hand on Imbri's shoulder, and she squealed warningly and stomped a forefoot, acting like an undisciplined animal. "All right. You ride her for now. We're taking you to Hasbinbad for interrogation."

Hasbinbad was evidently a leader, for he had a comfortable tent to the rear. He emerged fully armed and armored, with a shaped breastplate, a large, oblong shield, and an impressive helmet. He was a gruffly handsome older man on the stout side. His face was clean, his beard neatly trimmed.

"My troops inform me you were lurking south of our clearance blaze," Hasbinbad remarked. "What were you doing there?"

"You're a true Carthaginian!" Ichabod exclaimed.

"All my life," Hasbinbad agreed with an ironic smile. "Are you a native of this region? I am prepared to offer a fair reward for good information."

Imbri did not trust this urbane Mundane leader. But she had to let Ichabod handle the interview.

"I am a visitor to this land, but I have traveled a fair amount," Ichabod replied carefully. He seemed more intrigued than concerned now. Apparently he liked meeting what were to him historical figures. "I saw your fire and came to investigate—and your ruffians quickly made me captive."

"They are instructed to kill all strange animals and take prisoner any men they encounter," Hasbinbad said. "Strange things have happened since we crossed the Alps and entered Southern Gaul. This is much wilder country than Hispania."

"It certainly is!" Ichabod agreed emphatically. "This would be about the year 210 or 215 B.C., in the Po valley, and—" He paused, and Imbri sent a questioning dream.

"You speak strangely," Hasbinbad said. "Where did you say you were from?"

"Horrors!" Ichabod said to Imbri in the dream. "I am speaking nonsense! I can't refer to pre-Christian dates; these people of course have no notion of their future! And I can't tell him where I'm from, or *when* I'm from; he would think me a lunatic."

"Tell him you are a lunatic from Castle Roogna yesterday," Imbri suggested, not following all of the man's confusion. She had thought it was only Chameleon who became convoluted in her thoughts, but perhaps it was a general human trait.

"From Castle Roogna, in central Xanth," Ichabod said to the Mundane, following the suggestion.

"You are Roman, then?"

Ichabod laughed. "Not at all! This isn't Italy!"

Hasbinbad elevated an eyebrow. He was fairly good at that. "It isn't? Where, then, do you claim it is?"

"Oh, I see. You crossed from Spain to France, then through the Alps to the Po valley—"

"Bringing twelve hundred men and nine elephants to the aid of my leader, Hannibal, who is hard-pressed by the accursed Romans," Hasbinbad finished. "But we have not yet located Hannibal."

"I should think not," Ichabod agreed. "I fear you have lost your way. Hannibal was—is—in Italy, during the Second Punic War, ravaging the Roman Empire. This is, er, present-day Xanth, the land of magic."

"Xanth?"

"This is Xanth," Ichabod repeated. "A different sort of land. No Romans here. No Hannibal either."

"You are saying we do not know how to navigate?"

"Not exactly. I'm sure you followed your route exactly. You must have encountered a discontinuity. It is complicated to explain. Sometimes people step through accidentally and find themselves here. It's generally sheer fluke. It is much easier to leave Xanth than to find it, unless you have magic guidance."

The Carthaginian leader puffed out his cheeks, evidently humoring the crazy man. "How should we find Rome?"

"Turn about, leave Xanth, then turn about again." But then Ichabod reconsidered. "No, perhaps not. You would probably be in some other age and place of Mundania if you went randomly. You have to time it, and that's a rather precise matter. I suppose if you tried several times, until you got it just right—"

"I'll think about it," Hasbinbad said. "This is an interesting land, whatever it is."

"What do you think?" Imbri asked Grundy and Ichabod in a dreamlet. "I distrust this person's motive."

"Yes, he's lying," Grundy said in the dream. In life he was lying on Imbri's shoulder, playing the part of a lifeless doll. "He knows this isn't Rome, or wherever he was going. He's testing you, maybe to see if you're lying to him."

"If you don't find your way to Italy," Ichabod said aloud to the Carthaginian, "Hannibal will not have the reinforcements he needs and will be hard-pressed. We could help you find the way."

"If, as you claim, this is not Italy," Hasbinbad rejoined, "then perhaps it is still ripe for plunder. My troops have had a hard journey and need proper reward. Who governs you?"

"King Trent," Ichabod said. "I mean, King Dor."

"There has been a recent change?" the Mundane asked alertly.

"Uh, yes. But that is no concern of yours."

"Oh, I think it is my concern. What happened to the old King?"

Ichabod obviously was not adept at deception. It was part of the foolish yet endearing nature of the man. "He suffered a mishap. Perhaps he will recover soon."

"Or perhaps King Dor, if he proves competent, will suffer a similar mishap," Hasbinbad murmured.

"He definitely knows something," Imbri sent. With an effort, she kept her ears from flattening back so that she would not give away the fact that she understood the dialogue.

"What can you know of our Kings?" Ichabod demanded, though technically he was not a citizen of Xanth.

Hasbinbad shrugged. "Only that they are mortal, as all men are." He looked meaningfully at Ichabod. "Now what should I do with you, spy? I shall retain your horse, of course, but men are more difficult to manage, and you do not appear to be very good for hard labor."

"We must get out of here!" Ichabod said to Imbri in the dream. The man was getting really worried.

"Do you think your King Window would pay a decent ransom for you?" the Punic leader inquired.

"That's King Dor, not Window," Ichabod muttered. "Ransom is a Mundane concept; he would not pay."

"Then I suppose we'll just have to sacrifice you to Baal Hammon, though he prefers the taste of babies. Even our gods have to go on less succulent rations in the field."

Ichabod tried to run, but Hasbinbad snapped his fingers and Mundane soldiers charged up. They seized Ichabod and dragged him away. Imbri tried to follow, but they threw ropes about her, tying her. Resistance was futile; the Mundanes bristled with weapons.

Imbri was hustled to a pen and left there. Fortunately, the Mundanes did not know her nature and did not realize that the golem was a living creature. The two remained together, but Ichabod was imprisoned separately. "Maybe we can rescue him tonight," Imbri sent in a dream.

"I hope so," Grundy replied. "He's a decent old codger, even if he is Mundane. But that Mundane chief certainly knows more than he's letting on. He knew King Trent was out of the picture. There's a conspiracy of some nefarious sort here, and it's not just the Nextwave conquest."

Then a man approached the pen. "Why, it is the dream horse!" he exclaimed.

Imbri looked at him—and her heart sank down to her hooves. It was the dread Horseman!

"Oh, don't pretend you don't know me, mare," the Horseman said. "I don't know how you managed to escape me before—well, I do know, but don't see how you doused the fire. I was so angry when in the morning I discovered you were gone that I almost slew my henchmen, but then I realized that none of us had really come to terms with the notion of a horse as smart as a person. My horse certainly isn't smart! The fool's probably half starving by this time. So I chalked up my experience with you as a lesson in underestimating my opposition, and I shall not do that again." The Horseman grinned with a somewhat feral edge. "I'll make you a deal, mare: tell me the secret of your escape, and I will take you for my own now, sparing you the brutality of the Punics. I'll let you go, once I recapture my regular steed, the day horse. *Him* I can confine, once I have possession. Fair enough?"

"I won't deal with you!" Imbri sent tightly.

"You don't believe I have power here? I am second in command to Hasbinbad and can take what steed I choose. I am a good deal more than a spy."

"I believe you," Imbri sent. "That's why I will not cooperate with you."

"I'm really not such a bad fellow," the man continued persuasively. "I treat my steeds well, once they know their place. All I require is absolute obedience."

"Spurs!" Imbri sent in a dream like a blast of dragonfire.

"Hotter than the breath of Baal, your thought! But I don't use the spurs, once my steed is tame," he argued. "There are no fresh cuts on the hide of the day horse, I'll warrant, unless he got himself caught in one of those prehensile bramble bushes. The ungrateful animal! He'll perish in that jungle alone; he's not smart enough to survive long. So he needs me—and I need him. The Punic horses are lean and tired from their arduous trek over the cold mountains; the best food was reserved for the elephants. I had to subdue a centaur to make my way up here, once the forces of Xanth started closing in on me south of the—I misremember, but I think there was some kind of barrier—"

"The Gap Chasm," Imbri sent, then cursed herself; she should have let him forget it entirely.

"Yes, that. You told the King of my presence, didn't you?"

"Of course I did!" Imbri sent viciously, with the image of two hind feet kicking him in the face.

The Horseman jerked back involuntarily before controlling his reaction to the dreamlet. "So you won't tell me how you doused the fire? Well, I can conjecture. The guard was nodding, and you sent a bad dream at him that he was on fire, so he fetched a bucket of water—something like that? I deeply regret underestimating your talent there."

Now why hadn't Imbri thought of that? She probably *could* have tricked the guard into something like that! Meanwhile, she refused to implicate the day horse, who, it seemed, was one or two iotas smarter than his master credited.

"Still, I can't really fault you for fighting for your side," the Horseman continued. "I am fighting for my side, after all. So let's call it even: I caught you, you escaped, you betrayed me to the Xanth King. But now you have been caught again, and because I appreciate your full spirit and powers, I want you more than ever for my steed. You and I could go far together, Imbri! On the other hand, my friends the Punics would be very interested to know exactly what kind of horse you are, and how to prevent you from escaping at night. Should I tell them?"

Imbri stiffened. He could make her truly captive! That would strand Ichabod and Grundy, too, and leave Chameleon in a very awkward situation, for she was no smarter than the day horse. Grundy might escape, since he continued to play the rag-doll role and the Horseman did not know about him, but what could the tiny man do alone in the jungle of Xanth?

She would have to deal with this horrible man, appalling as the very thought was. She forced her ears up and forward, instead of plastered against her neck the way they wanted to be.

"I see you understand, Imbri," the Horseman said. "You should, as you are the smartest horse I have ever encountered. But you refuse to cooperate. Very well, I am a reasonable man. I am prepared to compromise. I will exchange information for noninformation: you tell me exactly how you escaped before, so I know who or what betrayed me, and I will not provide any part of the information to the Punics. It will all be privileged communication. What will happen will happen."

Imbri was in a quandary. Could she trust the Horseman to keep his word? Was it fair to betray the day horse? What should she do?

"You don't trust me, I can see," the man said. "Indeed, you have no reason to. But trust must begin somewhere, mustn't it? Try me this time, and if I betray you, you are no worse off than otherwise. All you are really gambling is some information that won't change anything now. I simply want to profit from a past mistake. I try never to make the same error twice. Since it profits me nothing if the Punics destroy you and your scholarly friend, I am not gambling much either. We each stand to lose if we do not cooperate, regardless of our opinion of each other. I'd rather have you loose and living, so that there is hope to capture you fairly at some future date. My education for your freedom, no other obligation. I don't see how I can proffer a more equitable deal than that."

"What should I do?" Imbri queried Grundy in a dreamlet.

"This is bad," the golem replied therein. "This character is insidious! He's trying to get you to trust him. That's the first step to making you his steed for real, to convert you to his side and betray Xanth. Think of the damage he could do if he could phase through walls at night on your back! So you can't afford to trust him."

"But if he tells Hasbinbad my nature, I'll be trapped and Ichabod will be sacrificed to Baal Hammon!"

"That's bad, all right," Grundy agreed. "I guess you'll have to go along with him. Just don't trust him! Beware the Horseman!"

Imbri decided she would have to accept the deal. She stood to lose too much otherwise, and her friends would suffer as well, and her mission would be a failure and Xanth would pay the consequence. "The day horse freed me," she sent reluctantly to the Horseman, hating him for what he was making her do.

"Ha! So he was close by all the time? What did he do?"

"He—doused the fire."

"But a horse has no hands! He can't carry water. He—" The Horseman paused. Then he laughed. "Oh, no! He didn't!"

"He did."

"That animal is smarter than I thought, for sure! Must have been the presence of a fine mare that spurred him to his finest performance. He never paid such attention to any ordinary mare, I'm sure. So you ran off with him— but I gather you did not stay with him. Where is he now?"

"I don't have to tell you that!" Imbri sent, simultaneously angry at the way the Horseman had made her reveal a secret and flattered at his assessment of the day horse's opinion of her. Any female was delighted at the notion that an attractive male found her interesting. Even if she wasn't sure she wanted anything to do with him, she still wanted to be considered worthwhile by him. It gave her a certain social advantage.

The Horseman frowned. "No, I suppose you don't. That wasn't part of our deal, this time. But I'm sure that stallion didn't do such a risky favor just from the equine goodness of his heart. Women make fools of men, and mares make fools of stallions! He must have been attracted to you even then, and surely more so now."

Better and better! But Imbri was careful not to react.

"So if you're here, he can't be far distant. You probably see each other often, and maybe travel together. That way you repay him for helping you, and he gets shown where to graze and how to survive on his own in Xanth. That's why I wasn't able to find him, and why he didn't return from sheer hunger and thirst. It was probably just chance that the Punics caught you instead of him."

The man was uncomfortably sharp! Imbri did not respond.

"Very well," the Horseman said. "You have answered my question, perhaps more completely than you intended, and I believe you. I will leave you in peace. We shall surely meet again." He turned and walked away.

Imbri hardly dared relax. "Do you think he will keep his bargain?" she sent to Grundy.

"We'll find out," the golem replied. "I can see why you fear him; he's a keen, mean basilisk of a man! But in his arrogance, he just might be sincere. His perverted standard of honor may mean more to him than the opinion of one mare, and he does hope to use you to locate the day horse. He'll probably try to follow you when you escape. At least he doesn't know about me. I can untie the ropes and scramble out of the pen and probably free you even if they light fires."

"Save that for the last resort," she suggested. "If the Horseman honors his word, for whatever reason, I won't need it."

"But I can go scout out where they have Ichabod," the golem said. "That will facilitate things, so we can act fast when night comes."

"Yes," she agreed, her confidence beginning to recover from the bruising the Horseman had given it. "But we must play dumb until then."

"Oh, sure." But though the golem lay like a limp doll, he used his special skill to interrogate the plants and creatures nearby. There was a blade of grass growing at the edge of the pen that had somehow escaped the attention of whatever horse had been penned here before. Grundy told it that he would have his friend the mare chomp it off flat if it didn't answer his question, and the grass was intimidated. Grundy was forcing it to cooperate the same way the Horseman had used leverage against her. That made her wonder whether there was really any difference between them in ethics, and she was distressed but did not protest.

The blade of grass told Grundy all it knew of the Mundanes of the Nextwave—which was not very much. They had camped here two days ago, and called themselves Punics, though they were mostly recruits from Iberia and Morocco, wherever those places were. Many of them had sore feet from their arduous march through the mountains, so were resting now.

Grundy questioned a spider who had a small web against the wall of the pen. The spider said the Mundanes had carried Mundane lice and fleas along with them, and that these parasites were fairly fat and sassy and made pretty good eating. The spider had made it a point to learn the language of its prey, so as to be able to lure the bugs into its web; thus it had picked up some of the Mundane-bug gossip.

The trek over the mountains had been truly horrendous. It seemed the Mundane seasons were more rigorous than those of Xanth, and the high mountain passes were covered with magic masses of ice called glaciers that made the passage treacherous. They had started with twelve hundred men and nine elephants; they had lost a third of the men and two-thirds of the elephants. Hasbinbad, for payroll reasons (whatever a payroll might be; none of them could guess), refused to acknowledge the missing men. They had also started with two hundred horses, of which only fifty remained, and some of those had run away when they came to Xanth.

"The day horse," Imbri projected.

"Yes, one of a number," Grundy agreed. "The spider doesn't know the horses by name, of course, but that fits the pattern. The day horse was smart for a Mundane animal, so must be doing better than the other escapees. Most of them are probably inside dragons by now."

That saddened Imbri, but she knew it was likely. "What do the soldiers think of Xanth?"

Grundy questioned the spider. "They grumble a lot," he reported in due course. "They have not been paid, so they must plunder. Paid—hey, that must be what the payroll is! What Hasbinbad owes the soldiers! Many of them have died as they blundered into tangle trees, dragon warrens, and monster-infested waters. Some have been transformed to fish because they drank from an enchanted river; the spider got that from a flea who jumped off a man just in time. Others pursued nymphs into the jungle and were never seen again. Perhaps two hundred have been lost to the hazards of Xanth. So now they are proceeding very carefully, and doing better. They have slain several dragons and griffins and roasted and eaten them. But they are nervous about what else may lie ahead."

"Justifiably," Imbri sent. "They have antagonized all creatures of Xanth by their carnage. They should march back out of Xanth before they do any more damage."

"They won't as long as there is plunder to be had," Grundy said. "The spider confirms what we have seen ourselves: these are tough creatures, dragons in human guise, with a cunning and ornery leader. Only force will stop them. That's the way Mundanes are."

"Except for Ichabod," Imbri qualified.

"He's not a real Mundane," the golem said, irked at having been caught in an unwarranted generalization. "He's greedy for information, and his head always was full of fantasy, and he has an eye out for nymphs, too."

A Mundane guard came and dumped an armful of fresh-cut hay into Imbri's pen. Hay was best when properly cured, but naturally the ignorant Mundanes didn't know that, and this was better than nothing. She munched away, like the stupid animal she was supposed to be. Then she snoozed on her feet, patiently awaiting the fall of night.

At dusk, when deepening shadows offered concealment, Grundy the Golem slipped out to scout the region. His ability to converse with all living things enabled him to get information wherever he went.

By the time it was dark enough for Imbri to phase through her confinement and free herself, Grundy was back. "I've found him," he whispered. "I'll show you where." He jumped onto her back—and fell right through her to the ground.

Oops. She was insubstantial. She phased back to solidity, let him mount, then phased out again, taking him with her. Then she followed his directions to find Ichabod.

The scholar was in a separate pen, guarded by an alert swordsman. The area was lighted; Imbri could not safely go in.

"I'll distract the guard," Grundy said. "You go in solid, pick him up, and charge out. It'll be chancy, and they'll be after us—but they can't do a thing when you're phased out."

Imbri was not sanguine about this, but saw no better course. Soon they would discover her absence from her own pen and be after her anyway, so she had to hurry. "Go ahead," she projected. The golem jumped down, turning solid as he left her ambience, and made his way behind the guard.

"Hey, roachface!" Grundy called from a region not far back. His tone was exquisitely insulting.

The man glanced about, but could not spy the hidden golem. "Who's there? Show yourself."

"Go show your own self, snakenose," Grundy replied. Cheap insults were his forte; he was surely enjoying this.

The soldier put his hand on his sword. "Come out, miscreant, or I'll bring you out!"

"You can hardly bring out your own sloppy dank tongue, monstersnoot!" Grundy retorted.

The man whipped out his sword and stalked the sound. He was as vain about his appearance as any true monster, with as little justification. The moment his back was turned, Imbri walked quietly into the pen. "Get ready!" she sent to Ichabod in a dream.

The scholar had been snoozing uncomfortably. Now, in his dream, he reacted with startled gladness. "My hands are tied," he said. "I can't mount."

Imbri applied her teeth to the rope binding his hands and chewed. She had good teeth, and soon crunched through it. But the delay was fatal; the guard turned around and spied them.

"Ho!" he bellowed, charging forward with sword elevated. "Prison break!"

Ichabod jumped onto Imbri's back. She leaped away, avoiding the descending sword. But she remained in the lighted enclosure, still solid, and therefore vulnerable.

Grundy ran up. "Move out, mare!" he cried, leaping to her neck and clutching her mane.

The soldier swung his sword again, clipping a few hairs from her tail. Imbri leaped over the wall of the pen, escaping him.

But the Mundane's cry had roused the camp. Hundreds of torches were converging, lighting the area, preventing Imbri from phasing out. She had to gallop in the one direction that remained open: east.

"Shoot them down!" a voice commanded. It sounded like Hasbinbad himself.

Arrows sailed toward them. Ichabod jumped and groaned. "I'm hit!"

"Keep going!" Grundy cried. "We're doomed if we stop now!"

Imbri kept going. The torches fell behind. Those soldiers were afoot, not having had time to get to their own horses, so they could not keep the pace. But the pattern of lights was such that she still could not veer south to rejoin Chameleon and the day horse. So she raced on east. As she got beyond the torchlight, she phased into unsolid form, so that the arrows could no longer hurt them, and became invisible to the Mundanes. But they retained a fair notion of where she was, and the pursuit continued. Since she was pure black, she tended to disappear in darkness anyway, and they probably assumed this was why they couldn't actually see her. Some of them were now on horses and could keep the equine pace.

But a night mare in dream form could outrun any ordinary equine. Imbri left them behind and ran on into the night, through trees and small hills, getting as far clear as she could.

"How are you doing?" she sent to Ichabod.

There was no answer. She phased back to solid and queried him again, in case he hadn't heard her in the phased-out state. Now she felt the warm blood on her back. The man was losing blood and was unconscious; only the fact that he had no more mass in the phased-out state than Imbri herself did enabled him to remain mounted. He had sunk so far he no longer dreamed. This was worse than she had feared!

"We've got to get magical help for him," the golem said, worried. "Fast, before he sinks entirely. Some healing elixir."

"We don't have any," Imbri sent.

"I know that, mareface!" he snapped. "We'll have to take him to a spring, or to Castle Roogna, where they have some stored."

"Too far. He may be dead before we get there."

"Find a closer place, then!"

"Maybe the Siren has some," Imbri suggested. "She lives in the water wing, and we're not far from it."

"Move!" Grundy said. "Get him there before it's too late! He's no young squirt, you know."

She knew. She moved. She came to the wall that confined the water wing and plunged through. Beyond it was water, a sea of it, with a storm raining thickly down to add to the total. It was one of the seven natural wonders of Xanth, though creatures could not agree just which the seven were. But the water passed through them as Imbri galloped along the surface. She wished there had been a gourd patch handy so that she could use the gourd network in this emergency. But of course there were no gourds in the lake. The water wing was all water.

Fortunately, she was able to travel at maximum velocity across the sea. In a much shorter time than any ordinary horse could manage, she reached the home region of the Siren.

It was night, but the merfolk colony was awake, nightfishing. Several of them had strings of nightfish already. "Where is the Siren?" Imbri sent in a broadband dreamlet.

A mermaid swam up. "Hello, Grundy," she called. "Why do you seek me?"

The golem jumped off Imbri's back, turning solid and splashing into the water, where the buxom creature picked him up. "My friend Ichabod is wounded and dying. My friend the night mare brought him here. Have you any healing elixir?"

"We do," the Siren said. "Carry him to land at the edge of the wing; Morris will bring the elixir."

Imbri trotted to the shore. The Siren got the elixir from her husband, then emerged from the water, her tail splitting into two well-fleshed legs. She sprinkled a few drops on Ichabod.

To Imbri's dismay, there was no immediate effect. "It's not working!" she projected.

"This is a dilute elixir," the Siren explained. "We don't have any really potent springs here in the water wing. They're under the water, you see, so it's hard to capture the essence. But this will work in a few hours—faster, if he can drink some."

They set the unconscious man up and poured a few drops in his mouth. Then Ichabod stirred. His eyes opened and he groaned.

"He lives!" Grundy exclaimed joyfully. "I was really worried about the old codger."

"Get that arrow out of his back!" Morris called from the lake. He was a full merman, so could not go on land. "The healing can't be complete with the arrow in him!"

That was obvious; they had been so concerned about the bleeding that they had not paid attention to the wound. But this remained a problem. The arrow was barbed, and they could not dislodge it without inflicting terrible new pain and damage that might kill the man despite the elixir. Magic did have its limits.

"Maybe if you phase it out—" Grundy suggested.

Imbri tried this. She took the shaft of the arrow in her teeth, then phased into insubstantiality and backed away. The arrow phased with her, and the spaced-out head of it moved without resistance through the man's body until it was free. She hurled the arrow away, gratified; she had removed it without hurting Ichabod at all!

Now the gaping wound started visibly healing. All they had to do was wait.

In half an hour, Ichabod was whole once more. "I hope I never have to go through that particular experience again!" he said. "Thank you, lovely maiden, for your timely help."

The Siren smiled, pleased. She was middle-aged, and evidently appreciated being called a maiden.

"She's no maiden," Grundy said, with his customary etiquette. "She's the Siren."

"The Siren?" Ichabod asked, growing if anything more interested. "But does she lure sailors to their doom?"

"Not any more," the Siren said with a frown. "A centaur smashed my magic dulcimer, and that depleted my power."

"Oh." Ichabod pondered. "You know, if you had your power again, you could do a lot of good for Xanth. You could lure the Mundanes—"

"I really don't want to harm people, not even Mundanes," she said. "I'm a family woman now. Here is my son Cyrus." She introduced a small boy who smiled shyly, then dived into the lake, his legs changing in mid-dive to the tail of a triton.

"Nobody likes killing, of course," Ichabod said. "But perhaps you could lure them to some isolated island in waters infested by sea monsters so that they could not do anyone any harm."

"Yes, that would be all right," she agreed. "Or lure them to my sister the Gorgon, who could change them to stone. Such statues can be restored with the right magic, or when returned to Mundania, where the spell would be broken, so it's not quite the same as death." She shrugged. "But I fear my power is gone forever, as only the Good Magician knows how to restore the instrument, and he wouldn't do it even if I were willing to pay his fee of one year's service. So it really doesn't matter. I think I'm much happier now than I ever was when I had my power, frankly." But she looked pensive, as if aware of the enormous ability she had lost.

Ichabod spread his hands. "One can never tell. I am on good terms with Good Magician Humfrey, having provided him with a number of excellent Mundane research tomes, and perhaps I can broach the matter. I suspect you have just saved me at least a year of life by your assistance. At any rate, I certainly appreciate what you did for me." He turned to Imbri. "And you and Grundy, of course. Now we really must rejoin Chameleon."

He was right. The night was passing entirely too rapidly. They bade farewell to the Siren and the friendly merfolk and headed southwest. They had to get out of the water wing before Imbri turned solid again, for she could not gallop across the water by day.

They made it through the perpetual storm at the edge of the water wing and out into normal Xanth terrain before the sun rose. Imbri invoked her person-locating sense, which she had used during her decades of dream duty to find the sleepers on her list, and oriented on Chameleon. The Night Stallion had always provided the addresses of the sleepers as part of the labeling on their dreams, but she could tune in on people she knew well and who were thinking of her. At least she hoped so; she had not tried it when the location of the person was unknown.

It worked. In this manner they caught up to Chameleon and the day horse. The woman was sleeping in a cushion bush, while the horse grazed nearby. Apparently they had scouted the area and made sure it was safe. Chameleon seemed to have a good sense for safety, despite her stupidity. Of course, while no place in Xanth was completely safe, many were safe enough for those who understood them. A Mundane in this area would probably have fallen prey to a patch of carnivorous grass or a tangle tree or the small water dragon in the nearby river; Xanth natives avoided these things without even thinking about them. Perhaps it was the complex of dangers here that made it safe from Mundanes.

Chameleon woke as they approached. "Oh, I'm so glad you're safe!" she exclaimed. "I had a night mare visit—I thought at first it was you, Imbri, but it wasn't—with a horrible dream about Ichabod getting badly wounded. I'm so glad to see it wasn't true!"

"It was true," Ichabod said. "That's why our return was delayed."

"We got caught by the Mundanes," Grundy said.

"Oh, now I remember; that was in the dream, too. How perfectly awful!"

The day horse approached, ears perking up. "How glad I am to have had this horse near," Chameleon said, patting him on a muscular shoulder, and the day horse nickered. Obviously he liked Chameleon, as did all people who knew her in her lovely phase.

"We were using the smoke of that brush fire for cover, but the wind shifted," the golem continued. "They surrounded us. We talked to their leader, Hasbinbad the Punic. Then the Horseman came—"

The day horse snorted.

"I tell you he was there," Grundy insisted. "Said he forced a centaur to carry him north, since things got hot near Castle Roogna. We don't know what happened to the henchmen Imbri told us about; maybe a dragon got them. Good riddance! He wanted to know how Imbri escaped from him before—"

"And I had to tell him," Imbri sent apologetically. "He promised to let us go, and I think he kept his word."

"If he kept his word, it was only because he had no reason to keep you there!" the day horse insisted in the dream Imbri provided. "I know that man! He never does anything for anyone unless he stands to gain!"

"Well, he did let us go," Grundy said. "Maybe it was a plot to follow us back to you. But we foiled that! We went through the water wing to see the Siren and get Ichabod healed, and the Mundanes couldn't follow. So maybe we outsmarted the Horseman after all."

"I doubt it," the day horse said in the dream. "He has levels and levels of cunning. He probably wanted to let you go, for some devious reason of his own. Maybe he knew the Mundanes wouldn't let him have Imbri for himself, so he saw to it they couldn't keep her either. He's like that. He spites people in subtle ways so the mischief can't be traced to him. He wants everything his own way. But he surely knows just about where we are now. We must flee south immediately."

"That's for sure," Grundy agreed. "We've got our information; we know who the Mundanes are. Now we have to get it to King Dor as fast as we can, so he can figure out how to break up the Wave."

That made sense. Imbri was amazed at the expressiveness of the day horse, who hardly seemed stupid at all now. His points about the Horseman were well taken. But if the man had wanted them free, knowing they would go straight to King Dor, what was his rationale? He was an enemy who would only suffer if the King organized a good defense. Something important was missing, and it made her uneasy.

They set off south. Chameleon was satisfied to continue riding the day horse, so they left it the way it was. All day they galloped, avoiding the problems of the journey up, and made such good progress that by nightfall they had crossed the invisible bridge and were back at Castle Roogna.

The day horse, wary of populated places, begged off entering the castle itself. "People tend to want to catch me and pen me," he explained in equine language that Grundy translated for the nonequines.

Chameleon was sympathetic. "I understand," she said. "The Mundanes penned Imbri." She dismounted, then threw her arms about the horse's sweaty neck, giving him an affectionate hug. "Thank you so much, day horse!" She kissed his right ear.

Horses did not blush, but this one tried. He wiggled his ear, snorted, and scuffled the ground with a forefoot. He flicked his tail violently, though there were no flies near. Then he turned on two hooves and trotted away, seeking his own place to graze and rest.

"It's easy to like a pretty woman," Grundy remarked somewhat wistfully. "Even if you are a horse."

And easy for a mare to like such a horse, Imbri thought to herself. He was such a beautiful, nice, helpful animal. If only he were smarter!

Chapter 7

The First Battle

King Dor was waiting for them. He listened gravely to their report, making careful note of the numbers and armament of the enemy as Ichabod reported them. Imbri was amazed to discover how observant the Mundane scholar had been; he had noted everything relevant, and was able to fill in from his wide background information. It seemed Xanth now knew more about the Mundanes than the Mundanes knew about Xanth.

"The Carthaginian mercenaries were—are—redoubtable fighters," Ichabod concluded. "They had excellent leadership, and were accustomed to carrying on on their own with very little support from the home city. They dominated the western half of the Mediterranean Sea, and even the Romans were unable, generally, to match them in battle." He broke off. "But I wander too far afield, as is my wont. My point is that these are formidable foemen who are prone to feed captives to their bloodthirsty god Baal Hammon. You must not give them any quarter. I dislike advocating violence, but I see no peaceful way to abate this particular menace. Fortunately, they have no weapons with which you are unfamiliar, except perhaps that of treachery."

Dor shook his head heavily. He seemed to have aged in the three days Imbri's party had been away, though he had caught up on his sleep. "I had hoped it would be otherwise, but a Wave is a Wave. We shall fight with what resources we have. So there are about six hundred Nextwavers remaining, armed with swords, spears, and bows. This is too great a number for us to handle by ordinary means. I have marshaled the old troops of King Trent's former army, but I am skeptical about their combat readiness. What we really need is the help of some of Xanth's more ferocious animals, such as the dragons. In Xanth's past they have been known to help us out of bad situations. But so far, this time, they have rejected my overtures. I think they might have been more positive toward King Trent, as his power is more compelling than mine. The dragons seem to feel that if men wish to kill men, this will make things easier for dragons."

"Wait till the Nextwavers ravage Dragon Land," Grundy muttered. "Then the beasts will take notice."

"That may be too late for us," Dor said. "In any event, it is not just the dragons. The goblins, who really are more manlike than beastlike, told our messenger to go soak his snoot."

"The goblins don't want to get drafted for war," Imbri sent, remembering the last bad dream she had processed.

King Dor concentrated on a map of Xanth before him. "We expect the Mundanes to drive for Castle Roogna first. That is where the Mundane city of Rome is in the land they thought they were invading, so naturally they see it as the target. Unfortunately, they are correct; if they conquer or destroy Castle Roogna, Xanth will have no central focus for resistance. Dragon land and Goblin land are in central Xanth; if the Nextwave flows down the west coast, it will miss those regions. So the dragons and goblins are not worrying. Since the main human regions are in the west, we must bear the brunt." He ran a hand over his hair, which seemed already to be thinning. "I wish King Trent were well; he has the tactical ability to handle this sort of thing."

There it was again. Even King Dor lacked confidence in his ability. The loss of King Trent had been a terrible blow to Xanth—as it seemed the enemy leader Hasbinbad was well aware. The Horseman had done a good reconnaissance.

"The Gap Chasm will stop them," Grundy said.

"It may, if we take down the magic bridges. I don't want to do that except as a last resort. Those bridges are hard to restore. Good Magician Humfrey supervised the installation of the main one, and he's not young any more."

"He never was young," Grundy said. "I think he was born a wrinkled, hairless gnome. But you do have a point. I think the Gorgon pretty well runs his castle now. I'm not sure I'd trust a bridge whose construction he supervised today."

"So I shall lead King Trent's old army to intercept the Mundanes north of the Gap—"

"Not you, Dor!" Chameleon exclaimed, alarmed.

"But, Mother, I'm the King!" he protested somewhat querulously. "It's my job to lead the troops."

"It's your job to govern Xanth," Grundy said. "If you go foolishly out to battle and get yourself killed, where is Xanth then?"

"But—"

"Listen to them, your Majesty," a voice said from the doorway. It was Queen Iris, garbed in black. "I know what it is like to be halfway widowed; I don't want my daughter to learn."

Dor smiled wanly. "I'll try to hang on to my life. I'll stay out of the actual battle. But I must be there with the troops. I can not do less than that."

As anticipated, the Nextwave flowed down the western side of Xanth, avoiding the deadly central region and the monsteriferous coastal region. The Horseman, obviously, had scouted out their best route—the enchanted path that trade parties used to reach the isthmus that was the only access to Mundania. Now that enchantment was helping the enemy force to drive directly for Castle Roogna.

Most creatures of Xanth thought of the historic Waves as sheer ravening hordes of Mundanes, and the current Wave resembled that notion closely enough. But it was evident that this force had considerable expertise supporting its violence. The Mundanes were quickly learning how to handle the hazards of Xanth and how to use beneficial magic.

The quiet North Village had to be evacuated hastily before the Wave swamped it, and the centaur village south of it was similarly abandoned. These local centaurs were less prudish about magic talents than were those of distant Centaur Isle and were quite helpful to the human Villagers, carrying the aged and infirm. In return, the human folk used their magic talents to facilitate the travel of the centaurs, conjuring food and tools as needed. It was a fine cooperative effort. Imbri knew that Dor's paternal grandparents lived in the North Village, and the sire and dam of Chet and Chem Centaur lived in the centaur settlement, so this effort was important to those who were at Castle Roogna in a personal as well as a tactical sense. Faces were turning grim at the notion of handing these areas over to the enemy, but it was a necessary evil.

Queen Iris was deputized by King Dor to supervise the evacuation of those regions. She spent day and night in the bedroom with unconscious King Trent, using her enormous powers of illusion on behalf of the welfare of Xanth in the manner King Trent would have asked her to. She projected her image to every household of the Village, warning each person of the danger and making sure that person left. Iris could actually perceive these people, and they could perceive her; to that extent her illusory images were real. It was indeed difficult to ascertain exactly where illusion left off and reality began. She spoke calmly but certainly, making sure that important belongings were taken and that nothing of possible advantage to the Mundanes was left behind. Because she could also perceive the progress of the Wave, though this was at the fringe of her range, the people had the confidence to evacuate in an orderly manner, not rushing wastefully, while also not delaying overlong.

But the Queen was working too hard. Her use of illusion at such range was like a horse galloping cross-country; it required a lot of concentration and energy. Iris would not rest herself at night, insisting on checking and rechecking every detail. Her illusion-figures were blurring. Iris was no longer in the flush of youth; she was as old as King Trent. This enormous effort without respite was apt to put her into a state no better than that of Trent.

Finally King Dor sent Imbri in to her, carrying a basket of food and drink, with instructions to make the Queen take a needed break. King Dor did not feel right about giving orders to his mother-in-law, which was why he asked Imbri to handle it. His reason for choosing her was seemingly superficial—her ability to project dreams resembled the Queen's ability to project illusions. Perhaps there would be rapport. Imbri was glad to try.

Imbri entered the bedroom and set the basket down, releasing the strap she had held in her teeth. "Queen Iris, I have brought refreshment," she sent. "You must eat and drink."

Iris paused in her labor of illusion. "Don't try to fool me, mare," she snapped. "There's sleep potion in that beverage."

"So there is," Imbri agreed. "Your daughter put it in. But she says she will watch her father while you rest, if you are willing."

"Her place is with her husband, the new King," Iris said, softening. "I know she loves her father. She doesn't have to prove it to me."

"Please—take the rest. The Villagers can travel now without you, and your talent may be needed later. There are people in charge like Dor's grandfather Roland, of the Council of Elders, and Chester and Cherie Centaur, who tutored King Dor in literacy and martial art. They can handle it now."

"In fact, Irene loves Trent more than she loves me," Iris grumbled. But she ate the cake and drank the coconut milk provided, and allowed herself to get sleepy. "*You* watch the King," she said. "And don't send me any bad dreams! I have more than enough already."

"No bad dreams," Imbri agreed.

But she did send the Queen a good dream, of the Villagers and centaurs arriving safely south of the Gap Chasm and finding temporary homes in other villages and on other ranges.

"Don't try to fool me!" Queen Iris said in her sleep, catching on. "I deliver illusions to others; I prefer reality for myself."

"You are brave," Imbri sent.

"I'll have none of your false flattery either!" the Queen retorted, threatening to wake up.

"I didn't say you were nice," Imbri said in the dream, taking the form of an older woman, one with whom the Queen might be comfortable. "I said you were brave."

"It takes no courage to project pictures to others; you should know that."

"To seek reality," Imbri clarified. "I send my images inside the minds of others, rather than outside, as you do, but I, too, prefer to know the truth, which may not be at all like a dream. Many people do prefer illusion, however."

"I appreciate your effort," the Queen said. "You're trying to keep me asleep, and I suppose I do need it. I can't serve Xanth well if I am overtired." Then she brought herself up short. "Xanth? Whom am I fooling? I said I sought reality, but this is illusion! I never cared for the welfare of Xanth! I always wanted to rule it, which is an entirely different matter. But no Queen is permitted to rule Xanth, no matter what her talent."

"Ichabod says Xanth is a medieval Kingdom," Imbri's image said. "He thinks that eventually it will progress to equal rights for women."

"Is the King all right?"

Was this a deliberate shifting of subject, or merely the meandering of an overtired mind? Imbri checked King Trent. "He is unchanged."

"Do you know, I only married him so I could be Queen. If one can not rule, the next best thing is to be married to the one who does. It was a marriage of convenience; we never fooled each other that there was love between us. He had to marry because the Council of Elders who made him King required it; he married me so as to eliminate Magician-level dissension."

"But surely—" Imbri started to protest.

"I have my faults, and they are gross ones, but I was never a hypocrite," the Queen insisted. "I craved power more than anything else, and Trent craved power, too. But he did not want to remarry, and when he saw he had to, he refused to marry for love. So he made the deal with me, as I was unlovable. That was perhaps almost as potent an asset as my magic; if his dead Mundane wife was watching, she would have known I was not capable of replacing her in his esteem. He was, in fact, punishing himself. I knew it—but the truth is, I wasn't looking for love either. So I was happy to prostitute myself for the appearance of power and distinction—though it wasn't prostitution in any literal sense. He had no physical desire for me."

Imbri was embarrassed by these revelations, but knew the Queen was unwinding in her sleep. Long-buried truths were bubbling to the surface. It was best not to interfere. "Horses don't look for love either," she said. "Just companionship and offspring and good pasturage."

The Queen laughed. "How well you define it, night mare! That was what I sought, in addition to power. And King Trent gave me all those things, in his fashion; I can not complain. He was known in his youth as the Evil Magician, but he was in fact a good man. *Is* a good man."

"And a good King," Imbri agreed. "I understand this is the best age of Xanth since King Roogna's time."

"True. King Roogna fought off the Fourth or Fifth Wave, I misremember which, and ushered in the golden age of Xanth. He built this fine castle. We call the present the silver age, but I suspect it is as gold as the other was." She paused reflectively. "It is strange how things work out. I married Trent from contempt, thinking to use him to achieve subtle power for myself. But he was stronger and better than I thought, and instead of dominating him, I was dominated by him. And strangest of all, I discovered I liked it. I could have loved him . . . but the one love of his life died before he returned to Xanth. He had had a son, too. Some alien disease took them both; he never spoke about it. He would have felt guilty if he ever loved again. So he was true to his design, while I was not. How I envied that unknown, deceased Mundane woman!"

"But you have a child by him!" Imbri protested.

"That signifies less than it might," the Queen said. "Xanth needed an heir, in case there should be no Magician when Trent died. Someone to fill in, to occupy Castle Roogna until a Magician showed up. So Trent had to come to me. He was so disturbed by it that I had to invoke my illusion to make it appear to be two other people, not him and me. *That* was how we conceived Irene."

Imbri was shocked. "A mating of convenience?"

"Again you phrase it aptly. It was real for me, but not for him; he was only doing his duty. But after Irene came—not even a Sorceress, and not male, a double failure—I think there was no conflict there. He could love another child, for it is possible for a man to have several children without denying any of them. The girl was no threat to his memory of his son. He loved Irene. And sometimes, I think, he almost loved the mother of Irene."

"Surely so!"

"And now he is gone, or temporarily incapacitated—that is one illusion I must cling to!—and I can play the role I am supposed to: that of the grieving, loyal wife. Because it is true. A marriage of convenience turned secretly real—for me, at least. And I can do what I can for the good of Xanth, because that is what *he* would be doing, and now I can only realize myself through him." She grimaced. "I, the original feminist! How utter was my fall, the worse because it is unrecognized."

"I don't see that as a fall," Imbri said.

"You are a mare." But the Queen smiled, accepting the comfort. "I would give anything to have him back, on any basis, or to join him in his ensorcellment. But it seems that is not my decision to make, any more than any of the other crucial decisions of my life have been."

Queen Iris sank then into a deeper sleep, and Imbri let her descend below the threshold of dreams, gaining her precious rest. Imbri had not suspected the depth and nature of Iris's feeling and had not sought such knowledge, but was glad she had learned of it. Truly, human folk were more complex than equine folk!

* * *

In the same period of a few days, King Dor's hastily marshaled and outfitted army prepared to meet the enemy onslaught. Everyone knew that King Trent could have organized an effective campaign—but King Trent was sadly out of it. People lacked confidence in Dor—but he was the only King Xanth had. Was he enough?

Dor accompanied the army north, along with his private bodyguard composed of long-term boyhood friends. He rode Chet Centaur, who was armed with a fine bow, spear, and sword, and who could magically convert boulders to pebbles, a process he called calculus. Chet's sister Chem was along, too, for her magic talent of map projection was invaluable for charting the postions of Xanth and Nextwave troops. Chem carried Grundy the Golem, whose ability to converse with living creatures complemented King Dor's ability to talk with inanimate things; together they could amass a lot of information in a hurry. Smash the Ogre also came. He now resembled a large, somewhat brutish man, for he was half man by birth. But when the occasion required, he could still manifest as the most fearsome of ogres. Since he could not readily keep pace with the centaurs afoot in man form, Imbri served as his steed. She knew Smash from the time he had visited the world of the gourd. He had terrorized the walking skeletons, but had been gentle with her, and in a devious manner she owed her half soul to him.

Of course, Imbri knew Chem in an even closer manner. It was half of the centaur filly's soul she had. This was the first time Imbri had encountered her since that exchange.

They trotted side by side, following King Dor and Chet. Chem was a pretty brown creature with flowing hair and tail and a slender, well-formed human upper torso. Imbri liked her, of course, but felt guilty about the soul. So as they moved, she conversed by dream privately with the filly.

"Do you remember me, Chem? I have half your soul."

"I remember. You helped us escape the Void. Without you, we would have been doomed, for nothing except night mares can travel out of that awful hole. Now you are helping Chameleon, aren't you?"

"She doesn't like battle, but wants to safeguard her son Dor, so she delegated me to carry the ogre. I think that makes sense, in her fashion."

"Yes, I know. My folks wanted me to stay at Castle Roogna with the wives—Queen Iris, Queen Irene, Chameleon, and Smash's wife Tandy, who is as nice a girl as I know. But I'm not married, and I don't feel quite at home with the wifely types. They live mostly for their males."

Imbri remembered her conversation with Queen Iris. "They seem to like it that way."

"I can't see it. So I persuaded King Dor he needed me at the front."

Imbri's mental image of another female centaur laughed. She liked this creature better than ever! "Now that I'm a day mare, I suppose I should return your soul—"

"No, it was a fair exchange, as these things go," Chem said. "As I said, without your help, and the help of those other two night mares, Crises and

Vapors—without them, Smash, Tandy, and I would not have been able to resume our normal lives. My half soul is regenerating nicely now, and I hope your half soul is doing the same."

"It may be," Imbri said. "I don't know how to judge. I was always a soulless creature before."

"Some of the best creatures are soulless," Chem said. "I don't know why souls should be limited to human and part-human creatures. Some dragons are more worthy than some Mundanes." Her gaze flicked to Imbri's rider. "And even some ogres are good people."

"I caught that!" Grundy exclaimed. "They're talking about you, Smash, in dreams."

"And why not?" Smash inquired mildly. "They're friends of mine."

"Aw, you don't even think like an ogre any more. You're no fun," the golem complained. The others laughed.

"And there may be some reason for you to have that half soul," Chem concluded privately in Imbri's dream. "Often these things turn out to have greater meaning or direction than we at first appreciate. I like to think that someday my shared soul will help you as greatly as your assistance helped me. Obviously it won't rescue you from the Void, but—"

They spied a harpy sitting on a branch of a pepper tree. The marching troops had skirted this tree generously, so as not to catch the sneezes. The harpy seemed to be immune, perhaps because she was already fouled up with dirt. "Hey, birdbrain!" Grundy called in his usual winning manner. "How about doing some aerial reconnaissance for us?"

"For you?" the harpy screeched indignantly. She had the head and breasts of a woman and the wings and body of a buzzard. This one was fairly young; were it not for the caked grime, her face and form might have been tolerable. "Why should I do anything for your ilk, you blankety blank?"

Imbri and Chem stiffened, the latter's delicate shell-pink ears reddening, and Smash turned his head, for the blanks had not been exactly blank. Harpies were as foul of mouth as they were of body, and that was about the limit of foulness in Xanth.

"For the greater good of Xanth, fowlmouth," Grundy called back, being the fastest to recover from the verbal horror that had spewed like festering garbage from the harpy's mouth. Indeed, he seemed to be mentally filing the terms for future use, though there were few if any occasions where he might safely do so. "To help stop the invading Mundanes from ravaging everything."

"The greater good of Xanth can go blank up a blankety blank, sidewise," the harpy retorted. "It's no blankety doubleblank to me."

Again it took a moment for the terminology to clear. Even the pepper tree was turning red. If there was one thing harpies were good at, it was bad language.

"There will also be a lot of carrion after the battle," Grundy said. "Gooey, gooky corpses steaming in the sun, swelling and popping open, guts strewn about—"

The harpy's eyes lighted with dismal fires. "Oh, slurp!" she exclaimed. "It makes me unbearably hungry!"

"I thought it might," Grundy said smugly. Strangely enough, no one else looked hungry. "All you have to do is fly by the enemy positions and report where they are and how many—"

"That's too much blank blank work!"

"Spiked eyeballs, chopped livers, severed feet—"

"I'll do it!" the harpy screeched, licking her dirty lips. She launched from the tree, stirring up a huge cloud of pepper, and flapped heavily north.

"But the Mundanes may shoot her down with an arrow," Chem protested without much conviction.

"The smell will keep them beyond arrow range," Grundy said facetiously. It occurred to Imbri, however, that he might be right; it took some time to get used to harpy scent.

Now they came to the Gap Chasm and proceeded across. This was the only visible two-way bridge, so was the most used; it would have to be the first to go if the Mundane Wave got this far.

The Gap Dragon was present; it raged and reached upward, but the Gap was too deep to make this a serious threat. "Go choke on your own tail, steamsnoot!" Grundy called down to it, and dropped a cherry bomb he had plucked carefully from the Castle Roogna orchard tree. The dragon snapped at it and swallowed it whole. There was a muffled boom as the bomb detonated, and smoke shot out of the dragon's ears. But it seemed to make no difference; the monster still raged and pursued them. The Gap Dragon was tough, no doubt about it!

By the time they were across, the harpy was back. "There are about three hundred of them," she reported. "They're headed toward the nickelpede crevices. I don't like that; the nickels don't leave anything behind worth eating."

Chem concentrated, and her magic map formed. It showed the nickelpede crevices, a minor network of cracks in the ground. "Where exactly are the Mundanes?" she asked.

The harpy gave her the specifics, and Chem plotted them on her map. Then the harpy flew off, explaining that she had trouble with the smell of the human folk. Now they had a clear notion of the disposition of the enemy troops. "But there are only three hundred of them here," Chem remarked. "That suggests they are holding back half their force, perhaps as a reserve."

They drew abreast of King Dor to advise him. "Yes, we'll try to drive them into the nicklepede crevices," he agreed. "If they take cover there, they'll regret it."

But Dor's troops were out of condition and not young; their average age was near fifty. Progress was slow. They would not reach the Mundane Wave before it cleared the nickelpede region. Such a fine opportunity lost!

"We shall have to establish our position and wait for them," King Dor decided. "As I recall, there's a love spring north of the Gap—"

"There is," Chem agreed, projecting her map. "Right here." She pointed to the spot. "We're already past it, and the path by it is one-way; we can't reach it from here."

"That's fine; I don't want to reach it. I want to avoid it. I don't want my troops drinking from it."

Grundy laughed. "That's for sure! But maybe if we fetched some of that water for the Mundanes, they'd immediately breed with any female creature they saw—"

"No," Dor said. "That's not funny, Grundy. We won't fight that way."

The golem scowled. "You can be sure the Mundanes would fight that way! They have no civilized scruples. That's what makes them so tough."

"But we do have civilized scruples," King Dor said. "Perhaps that is what distinguishes us from the Mundanes. We shall maintain that distinction."

"Yes, your Majesty," the golem agreed with disgust.

"What other difficult aspects are there between us and the Nextwave?" King Dor asked Chem.

"There's a river that changes anyone who drinks from it into a fish," she answered, pointing it out on the map. "From what Ichabod said, I think they've encountered an arm of that river farther north, but they may not realize it's the same. And over here is the Peace Forest, where people become so peaceful they simply lie down and sleep forever—"

"That won't give the Mundanes any trouble," Grundy said. "They're not peaceful at all!"

"But we should keep our troops clear of it," King Dor said. "And the river. We'll have to find a safe supply of water. Anything else?"

"Just the nickelpedes," Chem answered. "But the Mundanes will be past that region and the peace pines. The river is probably where we'll meet them."

King Dor sighed. "So be it. I hope we can stop them without too much bloodshed."

No one replied. Imbri knew they shared one major concern: did this young, untried King have what it took to halt the devastating incursion of a Mundane Wave of conquest? They would know the answer all too soon.

To the gratified surprise of all, King Dor did seem to know what he was doing. He ranged his troops along the river, having them dig trenches and throw up embankments with brush piled up in front so that the archers could sight on the enemy without exposing themselves. He had the spearmen ranged in front of the archers, to protect them from charging enemy troops, and the swordsmen in front of the spearmen. "Do not break formation until your captains give the order," King Dor concluded. "They outnumber us; they may try a false retreat, to draw us out, so they can fall on us in the open. Beware! Do not assume that those who lack magic are not dangerous."

The men chuckled. They were all former Mundanes and lacked magic themselves. The King had paid them a kind of compliment.

Now they just had to wait for the arrival of the enemy. The harpy, eager for the spoils of battle, continued her spy overflights, so everyone knew the Mundanes were not trying anything fancy. They were marching straight down the main path, without any attempt at secrecy. They had no advance scouts and sent no detachments out to flank a potential enemy force. In this respect they were indeed merely a horde charging down the route of least resistance, at greatest speed. Their progress was marked by flame and smoke; they left mainly ashes in their path. The North Village was gone, and it would be long before the centaur range was green again.

Imbri hurt, thinking of all that wanton destruction of excellent pasture. Yet she could understand the Mundanes' rationale; the fire destroyed the unknown threats of magic and routed hiding magic creatures, making the Mundanes feel more secure.

"I don't trust this," Chet Centaur said. "Either they're criminally careless or they have no respect at all for the opposition. Or it's a ruse of some sort. Where are the rest of their troops?"

"Maybe they plan to take Castle Roogna before we know they're coming," King Dor said, perplexed. "Mundanes are unsubtle folk, but we can't afford to underestimate them. All I want is to stop them today. If they have to forage in their own burned-out territory, they'll soon be hungry."

"And thirsty,"Grundy added, eyeing the river.

"I suppose transformation is kinder than slaughter," King Dor agreed with a sigh. "Certainly King Trent believed that it was."

It was late in the afternoon when the Nextwave arrived. The motley crew forged up to the river, not even noticing the embankments beyond it. There was no action by Dor's army; his captains would give the attack order only on his signal. Imbri was much impressed; the young King had amazing grasp of the strategy of battle. It was almost as if he had fought Mundanes before— and of course that was impossible, as there had been no Wave in his lifetime, or in the lifetimes of his parents or grandparents. Only Imbri herself had ever seen a Wave surge into Xanth, as far as she knew, though maybe Good Magician Humfrey was old enough. Well, there were the zombies and ghosts, who had existed in their ageless manner for centuries, but they didn't really count.

The first Mundanes threw themselves down beside the river and slurped up the sparkling water. They converted instantly to fish, who leaped and flipped with amazement and discomfort until they splashed into the water and disappeared.

The standing Wavers stared. But they were not completely dull; very soon they caught on to the nature of the enchantment, realizing that this was the same river they had encountered before. Immediately they cried the alarm to their companions.

Some of these were skeptical. They had not seen the transformations of their leading comrades, and suspected some crude Mundane practical joke was being played to aggravate their thirst. So one dropped down to guzzle water—and turned into another fish while all were watching.

That did it. Guards were posted along the river to warn the others, and the Mundane losses were cut. Perhaps a dozen had become fish; the great majority remained.

The Mundanes pushed on past the river, obviously wanting to find a better place to camp for the night. Then they spied the barricades.

"We should give them fair warning," King Dor said.

"Fair warning!" Grundy expostulated. "You're crazy!" Then the golem looked abashed, remembering to whom he was talking. "Figuratively speaking, your Majesty."

"Opinion noted," King Dor remarked dryly, and in that moment he reminded Imbri of King Trent. "Imbri, can you project a warning dream that far?"

"It would have to be very diffuse and weak," she sent. "They would probably shrug it off as of no consequence."

King Dor nodded. He spoke to the leader of the Xanth army. "Ask for a volunteer to stand up and warn the Mundanes not to proceed farther."

"I'll do it myself, sir," the man said, saluting. He was a balding, fattening, middle-aged man, but he had done good work organizing the troops and handling the logistics of feeding and moving so large a force—one hundred men—on such short notice.

The man lumbered down the back slope of the hill on which King Dor was situated, so as not to give away the King's location. He circled to the rear of the barricade and mounted a convenient boulder. Then he cupped his mouth with his hands and shouted with excellent military volume: "Mundanes! Halt!"

The leading Mundanes looked up, then shrugged and marched on, ignoring him.

"Halt, or we attack!" the Xanth leader cried.

The leading Mundane brought his bow about, whipped an arrow out of his quiver, and shot it at the Xanth general. The other Mundanes charged toward him.

"Well, we tried," King Dor said regretfully. He signaled the general, who had dodged the first arrow and now was taking cover behind the boulder.

The general gave the order. The Xanth archers sent their first shafts flying. Most of them missed, either because the archers were long out of practice or because their hearts weren't in it. For over two decades they had opposed monsters, not men, or indulged in elaborate war games whose relation to actual warfare was questionable. One arrow did strike a Mundane, more or less by accident.

"Blood!" the harpy screeched hungrily.

The Mundanes finally realized they were under attack. They retreated across the river, protecting their bodies with their shields. A couple of them tripped as they stepped backward through the water, fell, gulped, and became fish.

Now the Mundanes were angry, as perhaps they had reason to be. They lined up along the river and shot off a volley of arrows. But these did not have much effect, because of the embankments and brush that protected the Xanth troops.

Then Hasbinbad, the Carthaginian leader, appeared at the front, splendidly armed and armored in the grand Punic tradition. He was a considerable contrast to the motley assortment of archers and spearmen he commanded. Imbri could not overhear his words, but the effect on the Mundanes was immediate. They formed into a phalanx, shields overlapping, and marched back across the river. The Xanth defenders were astonished, but a few of them knew of this type of formation, and word quickly spread. The Mundanes were now virtually impervious to arrows.

But the Xanth commander knew about this sort of thing. At his orders, crews of strong men heaved at boulders that had been scouted and loosened earlier, starting them rolling grandly down the slope. One crunched directly toward the phalanx. The Mundanes saw it coming and scattered, their formation broken. That threat had been abated.

Maybe the Nextwave would be contained, Imbri thought. They had to pass this spot to get to Castle Roogna, and they weren't making headway yet. Soon night would fall, and the nocturnal creatures would emerge, forcing the enemy to seek cover.

But the Mundanes who remained beyond the river had been busy. They had a big fire going—they certainly liked to burn things!—and now were poking their arrows into it. Were they destroying their weapons? That did not seem to make much sense!

Then they stood and fired their burning arrows at the brush barriers of the defenders. "Trouble!" Chet Centaur muttered. "We should have anticipated this."

Trouble indeed! The dry brush blazed up quickly, destroying the cover. Men ran to push out the burning sections, but during this distraction the entire Mundane army charged in a mass. The Xanth archers sent their arrows more seriously now, bringing down a number of the enemy, but this was only a token. Soon the Mundanes were storming the barricades, brandishing their weapons, and the Xanth troops were fleeing in terror. A rout was in the making.

"I won't put up with this!" King Dor cried. "Take me there, Chet!"

"But you could be killed!" the centaur protested.

"I have faced death before," the King said seriously. "If you don't carry me, I'll go afoot."

Chet grimaced, then drew his sword and galloped forward. "Idiocy!" Chem muttered, taking her coil of rope and pacing her brother, carrying the golem.

Imbri agreed with her—and bore Smash right behind them. One thing was certain, there were no cowards in the King's bodyguard, but plenty of fools.

They charged to the burning barricades, where the Mundanes were making their way through. Suddenly the flames began talking, as the King exerted his talent. "I'm going to destroy you, Mundane!" one cried as it licked close. "I'll really burn you up!"

A number of Mundanes whirled, startled. "Yes, you, armorface!" the flame taunted. "I'll scorch the skin off your rear and boil you in your own fat! Beware my heat!"

Some Mundanes hastily retreated, but others leaped out the near side. They closed on the King's party. "Get him!" one cried. "That's their King!"

But now Smash the Ogre went into action. He swelled up monstrously, bursting out of his human trousers, until he was twice the height and six times the mass of a man. He no longer sat astride Imbri; he stood over her. He roared, and the blast of his breath blew the leaves off the nearest trees and bushes and shook the clouds in their orbits. He ripped a small tree from the ground and swung it in a great arc that wiped a swath clear of enemy personnel. It seemed the Mundanes had not before encountered an angry ogre; they would be more careful in the future.

King Dor and Chet trotted on, and where they went the ground yelled threats at the Mundanes, and the stones made crunching noises as if a giant were tromping near, and dry sticks rattled as if poisonous. The Mundanes were continuously distracted, and more of them retreated in disarray. Any who sought to attack Dor were balked by the sword and rope of the two centaurs, and many of the rest were terrified by the charging ogre. The Punics seemed daunted as much by the strangeness of this new opposition as by its ferocity.

The Xanth troops rallied and came back into the fray. Blood had been shed; now they knew for certain that this was serious business. Long-neglected skills returned in strength. Soon the Mundanes were routed, fleeing across the river and north as dusk came. King Dor called off the chase, not wanting to risk combat at night.

The harpy had her heart's desire: there were some fifty Mundane corpse left on the battlefield. But there were also twenty Xanth dead and twice that number wounded. The brief action had been mutually devastating. This was every bit as bad as the terrible dreams Imbri had delivered during the campaign of the Lastwave! Still, it was a technical victory for the home team, an the pain of the losses was overbalanced by the satisfaction of successful turning back the Nextwave.

"This is internecine warfare," Chet said. "It does great harm to both side I wish there were some more amicable way to deal with this problem."

"It isn't ended," King Dor said. "They'll return tomorrow, and they st outnumber us. We have barely forty men in fighting condition. We must up new boulders and make a rampart that is impervious to fire. We'll haul supplies of river water, which no one must drink, and drill on targets for b

and arrow accuracy. We can hold them if we work at it, but it still will not be easy."

"And if we hold them for another day or so," Chem added, "they should lose interest in fighting and gain interest in feeding themselves. Then it may be possible to negotiate an end to hostilities, and the Wave will be over."

Imbri hoped it would be that easy. She had a deep distrust of the Mundanes and knew how devious they could be.

The troops were allowed to eat and sleep in shifts, while others labored all night on the defenses. The walking wounded were encouraged to walk south, back across the bridge over the Gap, as this was safer than remaining for tomorrow's renewed battle. If the Mundanes were hurting as badly as the Xanthians, they would not renew the attack, but that was uncertain.

The two centaurs, the golem, the ogre, and Imbri ranged themselves about King Dor's tent and slept by turns also. There was no trouble; evidently the Mundanes were no more eager to fight by night than were the Xanthians.

"Did you notice," Chet said at one point, apparently having cogitated on the events of the day, "there are no Mundane horses here? They must all be with their reserves."

Imbri hadn't noticed, but realized it was true. She should have been the first to make that observation! If the Punics had wanted to move rapidly, why hadn't they used their horses? "Maybe they did not have enough horses for every man," she sent, "and could not take time to let the horses graze, so could not use them here. An all-horse mounted party would have been too small to capture Castle Roogna. But surely those horses will be used later."

"Quite possible," Chet agreed. "But I also wonder whether the missing horses and the missing men can be doing an encirclement, planning to attack where we least expect, while our attention and all our troops are concentrated here."

"We had better tell the King in the morning," Imbri sent. "He will want to set a special guard about Castle Roogna in case the Mundanes do try that! Fifty horses and riders could take Castle Roogna if our forces were elsewhere."

Reassured that they had anticipated the Mundane ploy, they relaxed.

The Mundanes, amazingly, attacked again at dawn. They formed another phalanx, this time maneuvering skillfully to avoid the rolling boulders.

"Your Majesty!" Grundy called. "The enemy is attacking!"

There was no response from the tent. Chet swept the flap aside and they all peered in.

King Dor lay still, his eyes staring upward. But he was not awake.

Chet drew the King to a sitting posture. Dor breathed, but did not respond. His eyes continued staring.

Imbri flicked a dream at him and encountered only blankness.

"He has gone the way of King Trent!" Chem exclaimed, horrified.

After that, it was disaster. The Mundanes rapidly overran the Xanth defenses. The surviving home troops fled, and this time there was no one to

rally them. The centaurs tied the King to Imbri's back, then guarded her as she carried their fallen leader back to Castle Roogna. Seeming victory had become disaster.

And what would they tell Queen Irene, Dor's brand-new wife and widow?

Chapter 8

The Zombie Master

"Somehow I knew it," Irene said. "A nightmare told me Dor would not come back." She was dressed in black. "I blotted the dream from my mind, thinking to escape the prophecy, but when I saw your party coming, I remembered." She looked at King Dor, suppressing her expression of grief for the moment. "Take him to the King's chamber."

They took King Dor up to join King Trent, and Irene remained there. There was nothing more to say to her at the moment.

"Who is the next King?" Grundy asked. "It has to be a Magician."

"That would be the Zombie Master," Chet said. "Magician Humfrey is too old, and he doesn't participate in contemporary politics. When King Trent was lost in Mundania eight years ago and King Dor had to go look for him, the Zombie Master reigned for a couple of weeks quite competently. When there was a quarrel, he would send a zombie to break it up; pretty soon there were very few quarrels." Chet smiled knowingly.

"But the Zombie Master is off in the southern unexplored territory," Chem protested. "He likes his privacy. I don't even have him on my map."

"And the magic mirror's still out of commission," Grundy said. "We can't call him."

"We should have had that mirror fixed long ago," Chem muttered. "But it seemed like such a chore when we didn't have any emergency."

"Life is ever thus," Chet said. "We've got to reach him. He's got to be King again, at least until King Dor gets better, and he'll have to stop the Nextwave from crossing the Gap Chasm."

"Dor's not getting better," Grundy said. "Queen Iris tried everything to bring King Trent around, but the healer says it's an ensorcellment, not an illness, and we don't know the counterspell."

"I can reach the Zombie Master," Imbri projected. "I have been to his castle before, delivering dreams to his wife."

"His wife is Millie the Ghost!" Chet protested. "Surely she doesn't have bad dreams!"

"She worries about the mischief her children may get into," Imbri sent.

"Now that's worth worrying about!" Chem agreed. "They visited Castle Roogna some years back, and I'm not sure the place has recovered yet. Those twins must drive even the zombies to distraction!"

"We have to get news to the Magician that the onus has fallen on him again," Grundy said. "He won't believe Imbri alone. He doesn't know her, and will think it's just another bad dream."

"He'll believe Irene," Chet said. "But I don't know whether she—"

"She's all broken up right now," Chem said. "I don't think she can handle it."

"There's Chameleon," Chet said. "But she's lost her son—"

Chem shook her head. "There's more to Chameleon than shows. But she's not yet out of her pretty phase. That means—"

"We all know what that means!" Grundy cut in. "But maybe it's better for her to be busy while her husband is away in Mundania."

"Cynically put," Chem said. "Still, we could ask her. The need is pressing."

They asked her. Chameleon, pale from reaction to her son's sudden fate, nevertheless did not hesitate. "I'll go."

Just like that, Imbri and Chameleon were traveling again, this time without other companions. They had delayed three hours until nightfall, for that was the night mare's best traveling time, and with the gourds, the distance did not matter. Imbri filled up on hay and oats, and Chameleon forced herself to eat, too, preparing herself for the excursion.

At dusk they went out, going to the nearest patch of hypnogourds. As darkness thickened, Imbri phased through the peephole and galloped across another segment of the gourd world. She regretted she couldn't stop to check in with the Night Stallion and report on her recent activities. But he surely knew, and he could send another night mare to contact her any time he needed to.

The gourds ushered any ordinary peeper into a continuing tour, locked to the particular person. If someone broke eye contact, he reverted immediately to the world of Xanth, but if he looked into any gourd again, he would find himself exactly where he left off. Imbri was not bound by that; she was passing strictly from one gourd to another, and the terrain was incidental. But she was carrying Chameleon, and this influenced the landscape; they were in the region they had left before—the burning iceberg.

But the amorphous entities that reached for Chameleon no longer frightened her. "I have lost my son," she said simply. "What worse can the likes of you do to me?"

Imbri realized that the woman was smarter than she had been. She was also less lovely, though still quite goodlooking for her age. Every day made a difference with her, and several days had passed since their last journey together.

The amorphous shapes gaped and grabbed, but were helpless against the woman's disdain. Also, Imbri and her rider were not completely solid here; nothing in the gourd could touch them physically.

Imbri galloped on over the iceberg and down the far slope. Now they came to the stonemasons' region. The stonemasons were made of stone, and worked with wood and metal and flesh, as was reasonable. Some were fashioning a fancy backdrop set painted with horrendous fleshly monsters, the stage scenery for some of the worst dreams. There was, of course, no sense wasting effort bringing in real monsters when they weren't going to be used; the pictures were just as good in this case.

Chameleon stared at these with dull curiosity. "Why do they work so hard to make dreams people don't like?" she asked.

"If people didn't suffer bad dreams, they would never improve their ways or prepare for emergencies," Imbri explained. "The dreams scare them into behaving better and warn them about possible calamities. There's a lot of evil in people, waiting to take over unless they are always on guard against it."

"Oh. Like not fixing the magic mirror."

Well, that was close enough. Probably a warning dream should have been sent about that, but of course it was hard for the Night Stallion to keep up with every minor detail of a crisis. People did have to do some things on their own initiative, after all.

They moved on past the stonemasons and into a region of boiling mud. Green and purple masses of it burst out in messy bubbles, and bilious yellow currents flowed between them. Imbri's hooves didn't even splash, however; she didn't need a mud bath. "What's this for?"

"This is the very best throwing-mud," Imbri explained. "It is impossible to hurl a glob of it without getting almost as much on yourself as on your target. Most people, after a messy experience with this, start to mend their ways."

"Most?"

"A few are addicted to mud. They wallow in it constantly."

"They can't have many friends."

"That's the funny thing! They have almost as many friends as the clean people. The trouble is, the friends are all the same kind of people."

"But who would want that kind of friend?"

"Nobody. That's the beauty of it."

Chameleon smiled. She was definitely getting smarter.

They raced on through a tangle of carnivorous vines and out another peephole. They were back in Xanth proper, in sight of the Zombie Master's new castle.

It looked just about the way an edifice constructed by zombies should look. The stones were slimy green and crumbling; the wood was wormy and rotten. The hinges on the door and the bars on the windows were so badly rusted and corroded they were hardly useful or even recognizable. The moat was a putrid pool of gray gunk.

"This is certainly the place," Chameleon remarked.

Imbri picked her way through the surrounding gravesites and across the bedraggled drawbridge. She remained phased out, so that she had virtually no weight; otherwise it could have been a risky crossing.

A zombie guard met them at the main entrance. "Halsh!" it cried, losing part of its decayed epiglottis in the effort of breath and speech.

"Oh, I never liked zombies very well," Chameleon said. But she nerved herself to respond to the thing. "We came to see the Zombie Master. It's urgent."

"Thish waa," the zombie said. It turned, dropping a piece of its arm on the ground. Zombies had the ability to lose material continually without losing mass; it was part of their magic.

They followed it into the castle. Once they got past the decrepit outer wall, an amazing change occurred. The stone became firm and clear and the wood solid and polished. Healthy curtains draped the hall. There was no further sign of rot.

"Millie must have laid down the law," Chameleon murmured. "He has his way outside, she has it her way inside. A good compromise, the kind men and women often arrive at."

"Eh?" something inquired.

They both looked. A huge human ear had sprouted from the wall, and a mouth opened to the side.

Chameleon laughed. "Tell your mother she has visitors, Hi," she said.

Imbri remembered now: the Zombie Master had twin children, eleven years old, named Hiatus and Lacuna.

"Then sign in, dummy," the lips said.

There ahead of them was a big guest book. Chameleon dismounted, going to the book. "Oh, see who has signed in before!" she exclaimed. "Satan, Lucifer, Gabriel, Jack the Ripper, King Roogna—"

"Lacky's talent is changing print," Imbri reminded her in a dreamlet.

"Oh, of course; I remember," Chameleon said. She signed the book, watching to make sure her signature didn't change to something awful. Then Imbri set her right forehoof on the page, imprinting her signature-map of the moon, with MARE IMBRIUM highlighted.

"Chameleon! I'm so glad to see you again!" It was Millie, no longer a ghost. Her talent was sex appeal, and, like Chameleon, she remained true to her nature as she matured. She was now about eight hundred and forty years old, with only the forty really counting, and looked as pretty as her visitor.

The two women hugged each other. "It's been so long!" Chameleon exclaimed. "Hasn't it been eight years since you visited Castle Roogna?"

"And then only because Jonathan had to be King for a while. That was simply awful! He doesn't like indulging in politics."

Chameleon sobered. "I have bad news for you, Millie."

Millie looked at her, quickly turning serious herself. "You came on business!"

"Terrible business. I apologize."

"The King—"

"Is ill. Too ill to rule."

"Your son Dor—"

"Is similarly ill."

"Chameleon, that's horrible! But—"

"The Zombie Master must be King now, as he was before, until the crisis is past."

Millie looked stricken. "King Trent—he was getting old—we knew that sometime he would—but your son is in his prime—"

"He was ensorcelled."

Millie stared at her for a long moment. Then her face began losing its cohesion, as if she were becoming a ghost again. "I was Dor's governess! I always liked him—and he rescued Jonathan for me. He fetched the elixir that made Jonathan whole. And in doing that, he gave me back my happiness. I really owe him everything. How could something like that happen to him?"

"He got married. Then he was King. Then he won a battle against the Nextwave. Then he—"

"Oh, Chameleon!" Millie cried, horror-stricken.

Now at last Chameleon collapsed, her burden shared. "My son! What will I do without my son? I was ready to, to let him be married, but this—he's almost dead!" She was crying openly now.

Millie embraced her again, joining her in tears. "Oh, I know what it is to be almost dead! Oh, Chameleon, I'm so sorry!"

Imbri did not wish sorrow on anyone; that was part of what had made her lose her effectiveness on dream duty. It seemed she had been thrust into a reality with horrors worse than those of dreams. She had worried about Chameleon's lack of reaction to Dor's loss. Now she realized that Chameleon had come to the right place; Millie the Ghost had known Dor almost as closely as his mother had. Shared grief was easier to bear than isolated grief.

A man appeared in the far doorway. He was of middle age, dourly handsome, and wearing a black suit. He was the Zombie Master, the Magician from Xanth's past.

"You are a night mare," the Zombie Master said to Imbri. "I am familiar with your kind. Speak to me in your fashion."

Imbri realized that it would be some time before the women were able to communicate intelligibly. Quickly she sent a dream that summarized the situation, showing pictures of Kings Trent and Dor lying mindlessly on beds in Castle Roogna, with the grieving widows sitting beside them. Xanth needed a new King.

"I had hoped this type of crisis would not come again," the Zombie Master said gravely. "I have seen prior Waves, in life and death. This one must be abated. I will go with you to Castle Roogna tonight. Chameleon can remain here with my family."

"But you must bring your zombies!" Imbri sent.

"I fear there is no time for that. At any rate, most of them are already at Castle Roogna. They will have to do the job."

"But how will Chameleon get home, when—?"

"We have Magician Humfrey's magic carpet here, on loan but never returned. She can use that when she is ready. But she will be more comfortable here for the time being, I believe."

"I don't know—" Imbri demurred.

"If what you tell me is true, I am now King Pro Tem. Balk me not, mare."

That was the truth. King Jonathan the Zombie Master bade farewell to his wife and children, then mounted Imbri, who trotted out into the night. She returned to the gourd patch, warned the Zombie Master not to be alarmed at what he might perceive, and dived in.

This time they entered Phantom Land. The phantoms swooped in, howling.

"Say, haven't I seen you before?" the Zombie Master asked, looking directly at one phantom. The thing paused, startled.

"They are trying to scare you," Imbri sent.

"Naturally. I am in the same business." He concentrated on the phantom. "Beside Specter Lake, about seven hundred years ago. I was the zombie Jonathan, keeping company with a ghost. You—"

The phantom brightened, literally. It remembered.

"But that was in Xanth," the Zombie Master continued. "How did you get in here?"

The phantom made a gesture of holding an object and of looking closely at it.

"Oh—you peeped into a gourd," the Zombie Master said. "And got trapped inside."

The phantom nodded.

"But I suppose one place is as good as another for your kind," the Zombie Master concluded. "You can operate here as readily as in Xanth, and you have companions of your own kind. And the useful occupation of acting in cautionary dreams."

The phantom made a gesture of appreciative agreement. Someone understood! Then it moved on, evidently having business elsewhere. Dreams were too important to be delayed by social meetings.

Imbri moved on also. She should have known that the Magician would not be frightened by routine horrors!

They passed through a region of spinning nebulae, avoiding the brightest and hottest of them. Then on into a forest so thick with giant spiders that Imbri had to weave between their legs to get through. Then on out the peephole of a gourd near Castle Roogna, and to the castle itself.

"You certainly have an efficient mode of travel," the Zombie Master remarked.

The two widows were grieving by the two Kings, dry-eyed and sleepless, exactly as Imbri had shown them in her dream for the new King. Imbri brought the Zombie Master right into the bedroom where both Kings lay like corpses, side by side.

The Zombie Master dismounted and approached. "This ascension is not of my choosing," he said to the women. "Allow me to verify their condition. Perhaps they can be revived."

He put his hand on Dor's forehead. "He does not respond to my power. He is not dead."

"No, not dead," Irene agreed in a whisper. "Ensorcelled."

"Of course. We shall track down the source of that ensorcellment," the Zombie Master said. "Magician Humfrey surely can do that. But at the moment we must stop the advance of the Nextwave, about which the good mare Imbri has kindly informed me. I have fought a Wave before, in my prior life; my zombies alone are not sufficient, but, abetted by a formidable natural barrier such as—what is it, something that crosses Xanth—"

"The Gap Chasm," Irene said. "You moved too far from it, so have almost forgotten it because of the forget-spell on it."

"Just so. The Gap Chasm. My zombies can guard the bridges and destroy them if necessary. I shall need a lieutenant who is familiar with Castle Roogna and the recent events. I can not afford to waste time updating myself about recent changes in the castle."

"Grundy the Golem," Irene said. "And Ichabod the Mundane; he knows all about the enemy. And Chet and Chem Centaur. And, of course, Mare Imbri."

"Indeed," the Magician agreed dourly, and left the room. Imbri followed.

Soon there was another council of war. Grundy and Ichabod reported all relevant details of their spy mission, and Chet Centaur gave the details of the battle with the Punics and the manner in which King Dor had been enchanted.

The Zombie Master pondered. "There seems to be a pattern here," he remarked. "In each case the King was alone, though seemingly well guarded. In each case the enchantment occurred by night. I suspect we have a nocturnal enemy who can strike at a moderate distance, or who is able to pass guards unobserved. Whom do we know who could do that?"

"A night mare," Imbri said in a general dreamlet. "My kind can become insubstantial and invisible by night and can project dreams from a small distance. But we can't ensorcell."

"A night mare," the King repeated, removing the crown. It fitted him well enough, but he evidently was not comfortable with such trappings and preferred to dispense with them. "Could there be a renegade, one with special powers?"

"I know of no renegade among residents of the gourd," Imbri sent. "The Night Stallion has special powers—but he is loyal to Xanth and never leaves the gourd. All other dark horses lack mental powers, other than dream projection, and regular horses lack even that. There are only the Mundane horses anyway, completely unmagical."

"There's the day horse," Grundy said. "But he's stupid."

"Not completely stupid," Imbri sent. "He seems smarter as he becomes accustomed to our ways. Still, I don't see how he could be the sorcerer, even if he had night power. Twice he helped us against the Mundanes. He freed me from the Horseman and carried Chameleon on the spy mission."

"I did not mean to implicate horses," the Zombie Master said. "Could some other creature develop similar powers?"

Chet shrugged. The gesture started at his human shoulders and rippled down along his equine forepart. "Anything is possible. Perhaps a variant of a basilisk, who stuns instead of kills. Or a groupie-fish, stealing souls. Obviously *some* creature or person can destroy Kings."

"One smart enough to recognize a King, since they're the only ones taken," Grundy put in.

"Precisely," the Zombie Master said. "And I am surely the next target. There is one thing you should know about me: I was a zombie for eight hundred years. I was restored to life by a special elixir Dor obtained, and I owe him an eternal debt of gratitude. I retain the power to animate myself as a zombie, should I suffer an untimely demise. So if the mysterious enemy should strike me down and I die, you must locate my zombie and question it. Perhaps the identity of the mysterious enchanter will be revealed."

They all nodded sober agreement. What a grim way to locate an enemy!

"Now I must rouse the Castle Roogna guardian zombies and march them tonight to the Chasm. It is surely our only chance to get there before the Nextwave does. Timing is critical."

"The zombies are already mostly roused," Grundy said. "Dor and Irene got married less than a week ago in the zombie graveyard."

"That would rouse them," the Zombie Master agreed with a gaunt smile. "Zombies love weddings and similar morbidities. Now I must go organize them into an army. The rest of you get some sleep. Report to the Chasm at dawn, armed. I may need some of you living folk to be captains, as zombies do not think too well." He left the room, going to gather his forces.

"Captain of a zombie troop!" Grundy said. "Well, why not? Zombies aren't bad people, once you get used to the smell."

Imbri remembered the brief dream contact she had had with one zombie at the wedding: maggoty blood pudding. Zombies might not be bad people, but they were hardly pleasant companions. Still, as warriors against the Mundanes, the zombies had definite promise.

At dawn, imperfectly rested, they reported as directed. The King had already ranged his zombies along the Chasm and behind trees. The Mundanes could cross only where the bridges were, and since one bridge was one-way from south to north and another was invisible, the third was the obvious choice. It was visible and solid, with a well-worn path to it.

The Mundanes had had a full intervening day to regroup and travel, and they had not wasted it. At midmorning they arrived at the Gap Chasm, following the main path. They had evidently learned that straying from the path was to invite assorted and awful hazards. The wilderness of Xanth had ways to enforce its strictures.

Immediately the zombies closed on them, throwing chunks of rotting flesh and fragments of bone in lieu of missiles.

The Nextwavers reacted exactly as they were supposed to. They screamed and retreated in confusion. Mundanes were prejudiced against zombies, as they were against ghosts, ghouls, vampires, werewolves, and similarly innocent creatures, and tended to avoid physical contact with them.

Then Hasbinbad appeared, gesticulating. Again he rallied his errant army. The potency of a good leader was manifest; the motley crew became a determined force. The Mundanes began attacking the zombies, shooting arrows into them. Naturally the arrows had no effect; they could not kill what was already dead. Other Mundanes hacked at the zombies with their swords. This was more effective, for Zombies could not function well without limbs or heads.

But the Mundane's aversion to the zombies handicapped them, and many living men were brought down by the walking dead. Soon the ground was littered with bones and flesh, fresh-dead mixed with un-dead.

Now Hasbinbad led a charge to the main bridge. His surviving men followed in a hastily formed phalanx, their overlapping shields brushing aside the zombies. The Mundanes were winning the battle.

"We have to deal with that leader," the Zombie Master muttered. "Without him, they are nothing; with him, they will prevail."

Imbri had to agree: leadership made all the difference. Had King Trent remained active, the Wave would not have gotten this far. King Dor, too, had been winning. How could Xanth defend itself when it kept losing its leaders just as they got the hang of it?

A picked squad of zombies guarded the bridge. These were zombie animals, more formidable than zombie people.

Hasbinbad came up against a zombie wyvern. The small dragon was in bad condition, even for its kind, and shed scales and flesh with every motion. The Mundane chief hacked at its snout with his sword. The snout exploded like a rotten log; teeth, tongue, nostrils, and eyeballs showered down around the Mundanes. Then the wyvern fought back, exhaling a belch of fire. The fire was as decrepit as the creature, drooling out greenishly and licking at Hasbinbad's feet. It was hot, though; the Mundane danced back out of the way with a green hotfoot.

When the gasp of fire faded, the Nextwaver advanced again. He lopped off the rest of the wyvern's head. Ears, brains, and tonsils flew up in slices, showering the Mundanes again. But the bare neck thrust forward, jamming into Hasbinbad's face, squirting candy-striped pus, forcing him to retreat a second time.

Again the man struck. Vertebrae, muscles, and stringy nerves flung out, festooning the Waver's sword arm. But still the man pressed forward—and received a faceful of watery blood that pumped out of the truncated torso. He shook himself off as if not quite believing this was happening, wiped the gook out of his eyes with the back of his left fist, then slashed some more, heedless of the guts and tatters of skin that burst out and wrapped about his body. He now resembled a zombie himself.

"That Mundane is determined," the Zombie Master remarked.

"He's the one who brought them through the snowcovered Mundane mountains of Halp," Grundy said. "From Ghoul to Hitaly. He's one smart, ruthless cuss."

A zombie ant lion pounced at the Mundane leader. This was a relatively new zombie, not very far decayed. The lion-head roared, showing excellent teeth, and the ant-body had six healthy legs and a stinger. The creature was alert to the strikes of the sword, dodging out of the way. Few zombies had any sense of self-preservation; even Hasbinbad recognized this as unusual.

Another Mundane emerged from the phalanx, aiming an arrow at the ant lion. But three zombie goblins charged at him, grabbing for his legs.

Then the other Mundanes got into the action. Soon they had dispatched the ant lion and goblins, together with zombie frogs, rabbits, and a watery-eyed hydraulic ram. As the ram fell into the Gap, the gore- and rot-strewn men stood at the very edge of the bridge.

On the bridge, however, was a zombie python, buttressed by zombie roaches, a zombie flying fish, and a zombie cockatrice. The Mundanes concentrated on the python, apparently not recognizing the genuinely dangerous monster, the cock. Hasbinbad tackled the snake's head, distracting it so that two other Mundanes could skirt it and start across the bridge.

"That chief's valor has just preserved his life," the Zombie Master murmured.

The two Wavers on the bridge trod diligently on the roaches, which popped and squished with assorted ghastly sounds, depending on their state of preservation. The Wavers swished their swords at the flying fish, who darted around their heads, squirting mouthfuls of stagnant water. Then the first Mundane came face to snoot with the cockatrice.

There was a moment's pause before the Mundane dissolved into green goop and slurped off the bridge. A living cockatrice could convert a living creature to a corpse by the mere force of its gaze, but a zombie cockatrice lacked full power. Instead it halfway melted creatures to muscle rot.

The second Mundane charged the little monster—and he, too, melted into putrescence and plopped into the Chasm. There was a choking sound from below; the Gap Dragon had arrived on the scene and snapped up the gob. Now the poor dragon had mild indigestion.

"Avert your gaze! Use your shields!" Hasbinbad bawled, so loudly that Imbri heard it all the way across the Chasm.

One brave Nextwaver obliged. The man pulled his helmet over his eyes, raised his shield, and edged out onto the bridge, guided by the guardrails. Listening to yelled instructions from his leader, he oriented on the cockatrice and finally used the bottom edge of his shield to sweep the little monster off the bridge.

The cockatrice fell, and the Gap Dragon had recovered enough to snap it up. There was a gulp, then a kind of stifled belch. Now the dragon had a real pain in the gut.

"I don't like this at all," the Zombie Master muttered. "Those Nextwavers are too strong for us. We may be forced to destroy the bridge."

"I can bring them down singly as they cross," Chet said, holding his bow ready.

The Zombie Master considered. "It seems worth a try, though I am skeptical of its eventual success. There are quite a number of Mundanes who have not yet seen battle; the bridge is too small a compass. We have held them so far only because they can not bring their full force to bear, but they will surely overwhelm us before long."

Hasbinbad had by now dispatched the zombie serpent. Now the Nextwave started across the bridge, single file.

Chet nocked an arrow, aimed, and let fly. The shaft arced across the gulf, then thunked into the face of the leading Mundane. The man collapsed and fell into the Chasm.

The second Nextwaver elevated his shield to protect his face. The centaur's second arrow struck him on the exposed thigh. The man screamed, lost his balance, and fell.

The third Nextwaver held his shield low, but waited until the centaur aimed, watching closely. When the arrow flew at his head, he used his shield to intercept it—and got caught by Chet's second arrow, aimed at his leg.

In this manner, Chet methodically dispatched six Mundanes, using as many arrows on each as were necessary to do the job. Then he ran out of arrows.

this better than she might have before she left dream duty. There was a special intensity to physical existence that insubstantial creatures could not experience.

Then an eye popped open in the nearby wall. Print appeared beside it. MUSH! MUSH! YUCK!

"Go to your room, children!" the Zombie Master snapped. "Go make your own dreams!"

Cowed, the eye and print faded. The Zombie Master kissed his wife, who responded passionately. If there was one thing Millie was really good at, it was passion.

Then the Magician's eyes went blank. He froze in place.

"Jonathan," Millie asked, alarmed, "what's the matter?"

But the Zombie Master did not respond. He simply stood there, staring through her.

Imbri was abruptly out of the dream—for there was no longer a mind to receive it. "He's been taken!" she sent to Grundy. "Right while he was dreaming!"

"But no one's here but us!" the golem protested. "Imbri, you didn't—?"

"No! I don't do that to people! I can't. And wouldn't if I could. This was not the work of any night mare. I would have recognized any who came, and none came, anyway!"

"I'll investigate this," Grundy said. "Make us solid, quickly."

She materialized, there in the tent. Grundy jumped down. He made a whispering, rustling sound, talking to a patch of grass within the tent. "The grass didn't see anything," he said.

"Maybe outside the tent—"

Grundy lifted up the flap and scrambled out. Imbri phased through the wall and trotted to Chet. "The King's been ensorcelled!" she sent to the centaur. "Just now!"

"But Grundy was on guard!" he cried, snapping alert.

"So was I. But the King went from right under my nose—in the middle of a dream I sent!"

"Hey, I've got it!" Grundy cried from the tent area. "This tree says there was a man here a moment ago. He climbed in the tree, then jumped down and ran away."

Chet galloped over to the golem. "Who was it? Anyone we know?"

"The tree can't identify him," Grundy said. "All men look alike to trees. Anyway, it was dark, and he seems to be a stranger to this glade. He could be anyone, Xanthian or Mundane."

"He must be Xanthian," Imbri sent. "Obviously he has magic: he threw a spell to blank out the King, then ran away."

"Why didn't it blank us out, too?" Grundy asked.

"We weren't material. The spell must have passed right through us."

"Or it was aimed specifically at the King, as the other spells were," Chet said. "I agree; it has to be Xanthian. Someone with the power to cloud men's

Now the Mundanes double-timed across the bridge, one after the other. They had taken the unavoidable losses and finally were charging to victory. Their depth of numbers, so feared by the Zombie Master, was taking effect.

"The bridge!" the Zombie Master snapped.

Chet brought out his sword and hacked at the cables that supported the bridge. They severed, but the walk held, so he chopped into that, too.

"Hold!" the first Mundane bawled, seeing what was happening. Of course Chet continued desperately chopping. Chem swung her rope, looping the first Mundane just before he reached solid ground, and yanked him off the walkway.

Still the tough planks of the bridge resisted Chet's sword. This was a job for an axe, and they had none. Imbri wished that Smash the Ogre were here—but he had been delegated to defend Castle Roogna itself, in case of complete disaster, since the palace guard of zombies was no longer there. The Zombie Master had been warned about the missing reserve force of Mundanes, which might even now be circling to take Castle Roogna from the rear. The ogre was also on the lookout for who ever or whatever lurked in the vicinity, enchanting the Kings. So it was a necessary post, and Smash could not be spared for action farther afield.

The next Nextwaver leaped across the opening crevice in the bridge—only to be met by the Zombie Master's own sword. Stabbed neatly through the heart, he died, falling headlong on the ground.

The Zombie Master bent to touch the dead man—and this Mundane revived. He stood up, blood dripping from his chest. "Master!" he rasped.

"Guard this bridge," the Zombie Master ordered him. "Let no living creature pass."

The new zombie faced the Chasm, sword in hand, while Chet continued chopping. As the next Mundane came across, the zombie drove fiercely at him with that sword.

"Hey!" the next one cried. "You're on our side!"

"No more," the zombie Mundane grunted, and slashed again. The other warrior danced aside, startled—and stepped off the bridge.

Now at last Chet got through the final board. The weight of the crossing soldiers snapped the remaining tie. The bridge pulled away from its mooring and flopped down into the Gap Chasm. Screaming, a dozen Mundanes fell with it.

Hasbinbad stood at the far side. "That won't stop me!" he bawled. "I'll cross anyway and wipe you out! You're finished, King Zombie!"

Imbri swished her tail in fury, but the Zombie Master turned away. "My proper business is reanimating the dead, not killing the living," he said. "I have been responsible for destroying more lives this day than ever elsewhere in my life. I concede the necessity but detest the reality. Pray that the Chasm holds them back, sparing us further malice."

"We'll have to watch them, though," Grundy said. "To be sure. I don't trust Hasbinbad."

"My minions will watch." The Zombie Master walked away from the Chasm. "But we shall be near to reinforce them, until we know the Nextwavers have given up."

Imbri looked back. Hasbinbad the Carthaginian still stood at the brink of the Chasm, yelling and shaking his fist. ". . . take you out, too, Zombie King!" his voice came faintly. "Just like the Transformer and Firetalk Kings . . ."

So the attacks on the Kings were definitely connected to the Mundane invasion! But *how?* Until they had the answer, they could not even take reasonable precautions against it.

They found a tent in the forest near the Chasm that a large tent caterpillar had left. This was the very best natural shelter available, fashioned of the finest silk; tent caterpillars made themselves very comfortable before they magically transformed themselves to winged form and took off. The King retired for necessary sleep, as he had not rested the prior night. Chet and Grundy stood guard by the tent, beating a path around it in a circle, watching for any possible sign of intrusion, while Chem galloped back toward Castle Roogna with news of the battle.

Imbri found a forest glade close by that had good pasturage. She grazed and slept, for it had been long since she had eaten and rested properly, and this constant physical existence was wearing. No wonder the material creatures soon aged and died; they simply wore out!

After an hour's munching and cogitation—grazing was always the best time to chew on concepts, between snoozes—Imbri became aware of the approach of another animal. It was the day horse. She nickered to him gladly, discovering that she had missed him these past two hectic days. "Where have you been?" she projected.

"Staying well away from the Mundanes," he replied in the dream. "They have been coming south, frightening me; I think they are chasing me down."

"You're beautiful, but not bold," she informed him. "We had two battles with them, and have halted them only at the Gap Chasm."

"I know. I heard the clamor. Have you really stopped them?"

"I think so. We cut the main bridge across the Chasm, and they don't know about the invisible bridge to the east. If they try to climb down through the Gap, the Gap Dragon will get them. They've already lost about forty more men today."

"Xanth won't be safe until all of them are gone, especially the Horseman."

Imbri remembered the double warning to beware the Horseman, and understood the horse's personal concern. She had felt those spurs herself! Still, she wasn't sure he was the worst threat. For one thing, there had been no sign of him among the Mundanes recently; he must be with the reserve force, way up in northern Xanth, so was no present threat. "Especially Hasbinbad, too," she amended.

"He's just a brute man. He drives straight ahead and hacks away at any-

thing. But the Horseman is devious and clever; he is the true leader and your real enemy."

The day horse certainly was hung up on that! "But we haven't seen him since we escaped the Punics."

"That means he's up to something. Until you nullify him, you'll never sleep securely."

Imbri didn't argue further. If the Night Stallion and Good Magician Humfrey both felt the Horseman was the real danger, he probably was. But in what way? That wasn't clear at all. What could even the smartest, least scrupulous Mundane do to harm a Kingdom of magic?

They grazed together for an hour. Then, as night came on, the day horse departed, traveling south, away from the Mundanes, seeking his safe haven. Imbri snorted indulgently to herself. He was excellent company, but he had his idiosyncrasies. The Mundanes couldn't get him as long as they were north of the Chasm. And if they came south of it by some infernal miracle, all he had to do was run; no man afoot could gain on a healthy horse, and the trees of the jungle would block an attack by bows and arrows.

Imbri returned to the Zombie Master's tent at night, phasing through trees and hillocks. She found Grundy alert; he spotted her the moment she turned to material form. "You don't catch me sleeping on the job, mare!" he said, smirking. "Though if you stayed invisible, I'd have a problem. I'll admit that much."

"Perhaps I should maintain invisible guard," Imbri sent.

"No, you have to graze and rest yourself," the golem said, perhaps wanting to share the honor of guarding the King.

"I could check invisibly every hour or so."

"Well—" Then Grundy had a notion. "Could I go with you when you—"

"Certainly. You would be invisible, too."

"Goody! Let's check now."

Imbri let him jump on her back. Then she phased out of sight and walked through the tent wall. The Zombie Master was sleeping peacefully. Imbri sent a dream into his mind. "Hello, your Majesty," she said in her dream form, this time a reasonably well-preserved female zombie. "It's only Mare Imbri. Are you comfortable?"

"Quite comfortable, thank you, mare," the King replied. "Except I miss my family. Do you think you could put them in this dream?"

"Certainly," Imbri said, her zombie image shedding a hank of moldy hair in approved fashion. She concentrated, and in a moment Millie the ghost appeared, somewhat faintly, but quite beautiful, radiating sex appeal.

"Oh, Jonathan!" Millie said. "I love you so much!" She opened herself to him.

"Now this is what I call a good dream!" the Zombie Master exclaimed, encompassing her. Their love had endured the eight hundred years when he was a zombie and she a ghost; evidently the flesh had not weakened it. She, having recently made the transition to mortality herself, could under-

minds. A traitor among us, taking out our Kings in the midst of a crisis so we can't organize a good defense against the Nextwave."

"Exactly as Hasbinbad threatened," Imbri sent. "This is no coincidence; this is enemy action."

Grundy was pursuing the trail, questioning grass, bushes, and trees. But soon the path crossed a rocky region that led into a river, and was lost. "King Dor could have handled this; he talks to the inanimate. But—"

"But King Dor has already been taken," Chet finished. "Oh, we're in terrible trouble! What will we say to the others?"

"The truth," Grundy said. "We were watching the King, instead of the surroundings, and we got skunked. We need a new King—again."

"I'll go!" Imbri sent. "I can reach Castle Roogna quickly. The Queens must be told."

"Take me with you," Grundy said, leaping onto her back. "Chet, you notify the zombies. They'll have to defend the Gap Chasm as well as they can without their master."

"Yes," the centaur agreed. "I fear the Punics will pass the Chasm. But we should have a few days to prepare for their next onslaught." He looked at the fallen King. "And I'll carry him back to Castle Roogna."

This was becoming almost commonplace, this disposition of the Kings of Xanth! Imbri felt the shock, but not as hard as it had been when King Trent and King Dor were taken.

Imbri phased out and charged through the night toward the nearest gourd patch. She knew the location of most of the hypnogourds of Xanth, since the night mares used them for exits. "Brace yourself for a strange environment," she warned the golem.

"It can't be worse than what we know now in Xanth," Grundy muttered.

Imbri feared he was right. The Kings were being taken faster now; where would it end? How could the loyal defenders of Xanth stop it, when the sorcery could happen right while they were watching?

Chapter 9

Good King Humfrey

Queen Iris met them at Castle Roogna. "Somehow I knew it," she said. "Every time we get our defense going well, we lose our King. I have been mourning for my husband when I should have been protecting his successors. You two go directly to Good Magician Humfrey; he must be the next King. Don't let him put you off; the old curmudgeon can't refuse this time! I'll send word to Millie the Ghost, if a regular night mare hasn't beaten me to it, and will organize things here at the castle. Tell Humfrey this is pre-emptive; he's the last male Magician of Xanth and must assume the office immediately, and no gnomish grumbling."

Imbri realized that the old Queen still had considerable spirit and competence. Now that the crisis was deepening, she was putting aside her personal grief and shock to do what needed to be done. She was providing some leadership during the vacuum. Grundy had commented with innocent malice on the uselessness of the Queen, whom King Trent had married mainly out of courtesy; now Imbri knew directly that there was much more to it than that. Queen Iris's grief was genuine, but so was her mettle.

Fortunately, Imbri's century and a half of night labors had inured her somewhat to busy nights. The golem remounted and they galloped for the Good Magician's castle. She used the same gourd patches she had taken with Chameleon, but her rider was different and so the gourd terrain differed. This time they charged through a region of carnivorous clouds that reached for them with funnel-shaped, whirling, sucking snouts and turbulent gusts. They whistled with rage when unable to consume this seeming prey. Clouds tended to be vocally expressive.

Then there was a forest of animate trees whose branches clutched at them and whose leaves slurped hungrily, but these, too, failed. Finally they threaded through a field of striking weapons—swords, clubs, and spears moving with random viciousness, nooses tightening, and metallic magic tubes belching fire, noise, and fragments. Yet again they passed through safely, for Imbri was long familiar with this region. The world of the gourd had to supply everything that was required for bad dreams, and weapons were prominent.

"This is a fun scene you have in your gourd," Grundy remarked, relaxing once he realized they were safely through.

They emerged near the Good Magician's castle and charged through its walls and into its halls. Humfrey was in his study, as usual poring over a huge tome. He looked up glumly as Imbri and Grundy materialized. "So it has come at last to this," he muttered. "For a century I have avoided the onerous aspect of politics, and now you folk have bungled me into a corner."

"Yes, sir," Grundy said. The golem was halfway respectful, for Humfrey had enabled him to become real, long ago when he had been unreal. Also, Humfrey was about to come into considerably more power. "You have to bite the bullet and be King."

"Xanth has no bullets," Humfrey grumped. "That's a Mundane anachronism." He scowled as his old eyes scanned a shelf on which sat a row of magic bullets, giving him the lie. "I'm not the last Magician of Xanth, you know."

"Arnolde Centaur doesn't count," Grundy said. "His talent only works outside Xanth, and anyway, he's not human."

"Both arguments are specious. His turn will come. But first must come Bink; he will be King after me."

"Bink?" the golem cried incredulously. "Dor's father? He has no magic at all! King Trent had to cancel the rule of magic for citizenship, just so Bink could stay in Xanth."

"Bink is a Magician," Humfrey insisted. "Possibly the most potent one alive. For the first quarter century of his life, no one knew it; for the second quarter, only a select few knew it. Now all Xanth must know it, for Xanth needs him. Bear that in your ugly little mind, golem, for you will have to pass the word. Perhaps Bink will break the chain."

"Breaking the chain!" Imbri sent. "That's your advice for saving Xanth from the Nextwave!"

"Yes, indeed," Humfrey agreed. "But it is proving hard to do. I shall not succeed, and I am unable to prophesy beyond my own doom. But I think Bink is the one most likely to break it—or perhaps his wife will."

Golem and mare exchanged a glance. Had the Good Magician lost what few wits remained to him?

The Gorgon appeared in the doorway. A heavy opaque veil covered her face completely. "I have packed your spells and your lunch, my love," she murmured.

"And my socks?" Humfrey snapped. "What about my spare socks?"

"Those, too," she said. "I might forget a spell, but never something as important as your spare socks." She smiled wryly under the veil and set a tied bag before him on the desk.

"Not on the open tome!" he exclaimed. "You'll muss the pages!"

The Gorgon moved the bag to the side of the book. Then she dropped to her knees before Humfrey. "Oh, my lord, must you go into this thing? Can't you rule from here?"

"What's this 'my love, my lord' business?" Grundy demanded. "The Gorgon kneels to no one!"

Humfrey picked up the bag. "What must be must be," he said. "So it is written—there." He jammed a gnarled finger on the open page of the tome.

Imbri looked. The book said: IT IS NOT FOR THE GOOD MAGICIAN TO BREAK THE CHAIN.

The Gorgon's veil was darkening as moisture soaked through it. Imbri was amazed; could this fearsome creature be crying? "My lord, I implore you—at least let me come with you, to petrify your enemies!"

Grundy looked at her with sudden, horrified understanding. "To petrify—and she wears a concealing veil she wouldn't need for an invisible face. The Gorgon's been loosed!"

"Her power must not be loosed prematurely," Humfrey said. "Not till the King of Xanth so directs, or it will be wasted and Xanth will fall. She must fetch her sister for the time when the two of them are needed."

"But how will we know?" the Gorgon demanded. "You restored the Siren's dulcimer and have it waiting for her here. But we may not even *have* a King of Xanth, let alone one who knows what to direct!"

"Someone will know," Humfrey said. "Mare Imbrium, I must borrow you until I recover my flying carpet. Golem, you must baby-sit this castle until the girls return."

"Me? But—"

"Or until need calls you elsewhere."

"What need?" the golem asked, baffled.

"You will know when it manifests." Humfrey cocked a forefinger at the miniature man. "Do not diddle with my books. And leave my spells bottled."

"But suppose I'm thirsty?"

"Some of those bottled spells would turn you into a giant—"

"A giant!" the golem exclaimed happily.

"—purple bugbear," the Gorgon concluded, and the golem's excitement faded.

The Magician climbed onto Imbri, using a corner of his desk as a stepping block. He was small, old, and infirm, and Imbri was afraid he would fall. Then he hauled up the heavy bag of spells and almost did fall as it overbalanced him. "I'd better use a fixative spell," he muttered. He opened the bag and rummaged in it. He brought out a bottle, worked out the cork, and spilled a plaid drop.

A plaid banshee formed and sailed out through the ceiling with a trailing wail.

"Wrong bottle," the Gorgon said, standing. "Here, let me get it." She reached into the bag and drew forth a white bottle. She popped the cork and spilled out a drop. Immediately it expanded into a white bubble that floated toward Imbri and the Magician, overlapped them, and shrank suddenly about them, cementing Humfrey and his bag firmly to the mare's back.

"You see, you do need me," the Gorgon said. "I know where every spell is packed."

"Stay," Humfrey said, as if addressing a puppy. "Move out, mare."

Imbri moved out, phasing through the wall and leaping down to the ground beyond the moat. In her insubstantial state, such leaps were safe.

They were on their way to Castle Roogna, but Imbri was dissatisfied. "Why didn't you let her be with you?" she sent reprovingly to the Magician. "The Gorgon really seems to care for you."

"Of course she cares for me, the idiot!" Humfrey snapped. "She's a better wife than I deserve. Always was."

"But then—"

"Because I don't want her to see me wash out," he said. "A man my age has few points of pride, and my doom will be ignominious."

That seemed to cover it. Humfrey loved the Gorgon; his way of showing it was subtle. Still, Imbri had a question. "If you know you will fail, and are only going to your doom, why do you go at all?"

"To buy time and allow my successor to return from Mundania," Humfrey replied. "Xanth must have a King, a Magician King, and Bink is the next. But he is in Mundania. Without a King, Xanth will fall to the Nextwave."

"But to go to your death—"

"It is not death, precisely," Humfrey said. "But since I can not be sure it will not in due course become death, I do not care to temporize. My wife will perform better if not handicapped by hope. I have locked up hope."

"That is a cruel mechanism," Imbri sent, shuddering as they entered the eye of a gourd.

"No more cruel than the dream of night mares," he retorted.

The raw material of those bad dreams now surrounded them. Mirrors loomed before them, distorting their reflections, so that Humfrey resembled now a goblin, now a squat ghoul, now an imp, while Imbri passed through stages of bovine, ursine, and caprine resemblances. They entered a region of paper, where nothing existed that was not formed of painted paper, and the birds and animals were folded paper.

"This is fascinating," Humfrey said. "But I have more immediate business. Mare, I mean to unriddle the identity of the hidden enemy before he takes me out. I will record his name on a magic slate and hide it in a bottle he can not find. You must salvage that bottle and recover that Answer so that my successor may have it."

"You are the Magician of Information," Imbri sent. "How is it you do not know the Answer?"

"Some knowledge is self-destructive," Humfrey replied. "Some Answers I could fathom, but my fathoming would cause the situation to change, perhaps creating uglier Questions than the ones answered. But mainly, I can not accurately foretell a future of which I am an integral part, and the discovery of the identity of the ensorceller is in that future. Answers might seem valid but be false, because of my conflict of interest."

Imbri could not quite understand that, but decided it probably made humanish sense. After all, the Good Magician was supposed to know.

They emerged from the gourd in the patch nearest to Castle Roogna and trotted toward the castle. Dawn was threatening, for Imbri's travels did take a certain amount of time. But she phased through the stone ramparts and delivered the Good Magician to the throne room, where Queen Iris awaited him.

"Excellent," she said. "The resources of this castle and of Xanth are at your disposal, Good King Humfrey."

"Naturally," Humfrey grumped. "Just let me dismount."

But he was unable to dismount, for the adhesion spell held him securely on Imbri's back. He had to fish in his bag for an antidote. He did not get it right the first time, instead releasing a flock of green doves, then a fat book titled Mundane Fatuities; remarking that that had been lost for some years and would now be useful for entertainment reading, which was probably why the Gorgon had packed it, he then brought out a rolled pair of polka-dot socks. The Gorgon had indeed remembered! Finally he found the antidote and was free to return to his own two feet.

"Now let's review the situation," King Humfrey said. "We've lost five Kings, with five to go—"

"What?" Queen Iris asked, startled.

"Five Kings," he repeated, irritated.

"What five?"

"Bink, Humfrey, Jonathan—"

"You're counting backward," Queen Iris said. "And you and Bink haven't been lost yet—" She paused. "Bink?"

"I just told you, Iris!" Humfrey snapped.

"It was me you told, Magician," Imbri sent hastily. "Bink is to succeed you as King."

"Same thing. You're both females. How can I remember you apart? Now, the essential thing is to beware the Horseman and break the chain. Bink is the one most likely to—"

"But Bink has no magic!" Queen Iris protested.

"Stop interrupting, woman!" Humfrey snapped.

The Queen's notorious ire rose. Her standard evocation of temper, black thunderclouds, boiled in the background, split by jags of lightning. This was impressive, since they were inside the castle. Imbri liked to generate similar storms when she herself was angry, but hers remained within the dreamer's mind. "Whom do you suppose you are addressing, gnome?"

"*King* Gnome," Humfrey corrected, reaching into his bag. He withdrew a vial, removed the cork, and shook out a drop that scintillated at the lip of the container. As it fell, the drop exploded in heat and light. The Queen's storm cloud sizzled and shrank as if being fried in a hot pan, and the lightning jags drooped limply. The Queen's display of temper subsided. The Magician had made his point. He had destroyed illusion.

"King Gnome," she repeated sullenly.

"The nature of Bink's talent is this," Humfrey said. "He can not be harmed by magic. Since the Mundanes represent a nonmagical menace, he may not be able to stop them—but he may be able to break the chain of lost Kings—"

"The chain of lost Kings!" Queen Iris exclaimed. "*That* was what you meant!"

"And thereby provide essential continuity of government for Xanth. Given that, the Mundane menace can be contained."

The Good Magician paused. When Queen Iris saw that he had finished, she ventured another question. "Why wasn't Bink's magic known before? He should have been King by now—"

"If it had been generally known that he was secure from the threats of magic, his enemies would have turned to nonmagical means to harm him," Humfrey explained. "Therefore his magic would betray him after all. So it protected him by protecting itself from revelation, making his immunity from magical harm seem coincidental. Only King Trent knew the secret, and he protected it rigorously, lest Bink's talent turn against him as a magical enemy. For Bink's magic is powerful indeed, however subtle its manifestation; in fifty years of his life, nothing magical has ever harmed him, though often it seemed to, or was aborted only by apparent coincidence. I myself was unable to fathom his secret."

"But obviously you know it now!" the Queen protested.

"I was able to penetrate it when he went to Mundania," Humfrey said smugly. "That temporarily nullified his power. I knew he had magic all along; I simply had not known its nature. But even after I ascertained this, I couldn't tell anyone. Until now, when he is away again—and must be recognized as the legitimate heir to the throne of Xanth."

"He shall be recognized," Queen Iris said grimly. "But how can there be five more Kings after him if he is to break the chain of Kings?"

"That detail is unclear to me," the Good Magician confessed. "Yet my references suggest it is so."

"How can there be five more Kings when there are no more Magicians in Xanth?" the Queen persisted.

"There is one more—Magician Arnolde," Humfrey said.

"But he's a centaur!"

"Still a Magician."

"But his magic operates only beyond Xanth. Inside Xanth he has no power!"

"The law of Xanth does not specify what type of magic a Magician must have or where it should operate," Humfrey reminded her. "After Bink, Arnolde will be King."

"And after Arnolde?"

Humfrey spread his hands. "I would like to know that myself, but my references were opaque. If the full chain of future Kings were known, our hidden enemy might nullify them in advance; paradox preserves the secret."

Queen Iris shrugged. She evidently suspected Humfrey was getting senile, but didn't want to say it. "What can I do to help save Xanth, your Majesty?"

"Bide your time, woman. Acclaim each King as he comes. When the chain is broken, you will have your reward. The single thing you most desire."

"I've been biding my time while three Kings have been lost!" she exclaimed. Then, as an afterthought: "What single thing?"

"You don't know?"

"I asked, didn't I?"

"I don't remember. Whatever it is, you'll get it. Maybe before the chain breaks. Meanwhile, these are difficult times." Humfrey yawned. "Now let me sleep; later in the day I must bait my trap." He sighed. "Too bad it won't be effective." He reached into his bag again, brought out a small, folded wallet, and unfolded it lengthwise and breadthwise again and again, until it became a small folding cot. He lay down on this and commenced snoring.

Queen Iris shook her head. "Difficult times indeed!" she repeated. "They don't make Kings the way they used to. Humfrey always was the most annoying man."

There was a noise outside as the sun came up. Queen Iris walked to the largest window and opened it. The magic carpet sailed in and landed neatly on the floor. Chameleon was on it, slightly less pretty than before. "I just had to come," she said apologetically. "My husband is due home from Mundania tonight, and I have to be here to meet him."

Queen Iris greeted her with open arms. Imbri noted that human women did a lot more hugging than did other creatures. "My dear, I have a lot to tell you, not much of it good." They moved into another room.

Imbri went down and out to the deserted zombie graveyard to graze and sleep on her feet. The best grazing was always around graves. She knew Magician King Humfrey would summon her when he needed her.

At noon Good King Humfrey summoned her back to the castle. "Carry me to the baobab tree," he said. "I shall set my trap there."

The baobab! That was where she had gone to meet the day horse! Would he be there today?

Chameleon appeared. "Your Majesty—may I go now to meet my husband? I want to be sure he does not blunder into the Mundanes, who are between him and here."

"He's due in the isthmus tonight," Humfrey said. Now that he was King, he did not seem at all vague or confused, though he remained stooped by age. "Imbri will fetch him then, when she can travel swiftly and safely."

"But I want to go with her," Chameleon said. "I've lost my King, my son, and my friend the Zombie Master; I must see to my husband myself."

Humfrey considered. "Perhaps this is wise. The Night Stallion believes you are important in coming events. There will be much to prepare Bink for, in the short time remaining to him. But you will need another steed. Arnolde will be with him, but the centaur will be tired; he is almost as old as I am, you know."

Imbri, of course, was older than either. But night mares were eternal. "The day horse!" she sent. "He helped before. He meets me at the baobab tree. He can be the second steed."

Humfrey's brow wrinkled even more than normal. "The day horse? I have not researched that one. Is he magic?"

"No, he's an escaped Mundane horse," Chameleon explained. "He is very nice. He would be an excellent companion."

The Magician shrugged. "As you wish." He loaded himself and his bag of tricks onto Imbri and spelled the works into place.

"We'll be back for you tonight!" Imbri sent in a dreamlet to Chameleon. Then she headed off, carefully using the doors and stairs, since this was solid day.

She trotted out to the baobab. She did not see the day horse—but of course he would hide from the Magician, being very shy of strangers. "Day horse!" Imbri sent. "It is all right! This is Good Magician King Humfrey."

The day horse came out from behind the upside-down tree. "He's not Mundane?" he asked within the dreamlet.

"Far from it! He's a great Magician. He knows everything."

The day horse stepped back, alarmed.

"Not everything," Humfrey grumped. "Only what I choose to research—and I haven't researched Mundane horses and don't have time now. Come on—we have to set up my spells."

The day horse hesitantly followed them inside. Humfrey spelled himself free of Imbri's back, then began setting out his devices. Bottles and vials and packages and books emerged from his bag in bewildering number and variety, until the volume of them was obviously more than the bag could have enclosed. Naturally the Magician used a magic bag that held an impossible amount.

"What are these things for?" Imbri asked in a dreamlet, her equine curiosity getting the better of her. She wasn't sure the Magician would deign to answer.

"It's best that you know," he said, surprising her. "First, I need to keep informed of the progress of the Nextwavers. Therefore I shall release these Spy I's." He opened a metallic container by rolling up its top on a kind of key. This seemed like an absolutely senseless way to package anything, but of course the Good Magician had his own ways of doing things. Inside were packed a score of white eyeballs. He shook the can, and several popped out and hovered in the air uncertainly.

"Go peek at the Gap Chasm," he directed them. "Snoop on the Mundanes. Set up a regular schedule of reports."

The balls flew off in a line. "Eye Spy!" they whistled as they departed.

Now Humfrey brought out a bundle of paper-thin doll cutouts. "I must also lure them to this spot so as not to endanger Castle Roogna," he said. He untied the string binding the cutouts, and the first ones began peeling off. As they did, they expanded and filled out. Hair unstuck itself and billowed about the head-sections; breasts popped forward from the upper torso-frames, and legs rounded from the lower portions. The dolls became floating, air-filled nymphs, lovely in the manner of their kind, but fundamentally empty. They hovered, bounced, and jiggled expectantly.

"Follow the Spy I's," Humfrey directed them. "Put on your airs on the return trip, staying just ahead of those who pursue you. Any of you who get caught are apt to get punctured." He smiled obscurely.

Silently the nymph shapes flew away.

"But if the Mundanes come here, they'll attack you!" Imbri sent protestingly.

"Naturally," Humfrey agreed. "And I shall destroy them with my remaining spells." He seemed to have forgotten his earlier remark about his plans being doomed to failure. He reached in the bag again and drew forth a wet-looking loop of substance. "Now pay attention, mare, in case I need your help, though obviously I won't need it." He held up the loop. "This is the River Elba, conveniently coiled." He hung it on his right arm, demonstrating its convenience. "It says 'Able was I ere I saw elbow,' close enough. If you untie the cord binding it, Elba will be unbound and will flood out the region. Do not free the river unless you have the enemy in a floodable region."

The day horse snorted. Humfrey's nose wrinkled. "You doubt me, horse? Note this." He took hold of a single strand of the loop and broke it where it passed under the binding cord. This enabled him to separate the strand from the main loop. He tossed it at the day horse.

The loop-strand expanded in midair, becoming a torrent of water. The day horse was soaked. The water splashed down his legs to his hooves and flowed on out of the baobab tree, tapering off as its volume diminished. It was indeed part of a fairly substantial river.

"Well, you did snort!" Imbri sent mirthfully. The day horse shook himself, not particularly pleased. He did not snort again.

Humfrey brought out a box. Lettering across the top spelled PANDORA. "My secret weapon, more potent than any other. Pandora was a charming girl who really didn't want to give this up," he said, smiling with an ancient memory. "But I knew she'd open it if I didn't get it out of her hands." He set the box down.

Imbri wondered what the Good Magician's relationship with Pandora had been, and what had happened to the girl. Probably she had died of old age long ago. What was in that box? Imbri experienced an intense female curiosity, but decided not to inquire. She would surely find out in due course.

"Box of quarterpedes," the Magician said, setting out another item.

"Quarterpedes?" Imbri sent inquiringly.

"Very rare cousins of the nickelpedes," Humfrey explained. "They are five times as bad. They gouge out two bits at a time."

Imbri had no further curiosity about that. Nickelpedes were ferocious little creatures, five times as fierce as centipedes. Anything worse than that was too dangerous to loose upon Xanth. It was a doomsday weapon.

"Dirty looks," Humfrey said, setting out a biliously swirling bottle. "Jumping beans. Enormous squash." Other items appeared.

"Isn't a squash something to eat?" the day horse ventured within the dream Imbri maintained for him on standby.

"This one is to your Mundane vegetables as a hypnogourd is to a pumpkin," the Good Magician said with a certain relish. "Which is not to say that the pumpkin does not have its place. I remember a pumpkin carriage a young woman used—or was that a glass slipper? At any rate, this particular vegetable is not edible. It likes to squash things."

The day horse twitched his white ears, obviously impressed.

"Now here is the higher power armament," Humfrey said, bringing out a small book. "Herein are listed selected Words of Power. Anyone can use them to excellent effect. Of course, it is necessary to pronounce them correctly." He continued setting out items, humming to himself.

"What do you think?" Imbri asked the day horse in the dream. "Can Magician Humfrey stop the Mundanes?"

"Yes," the animal answered, awed.

"Can he stop the Horseman?" she persisted, though she was not yet clear what threat the Horseman represented, aside from his position as second in command to Hasbinbad.

The day horse backed up a few steps, skitterishly. "No, I don't think so."

"But the Horseman can't put spurs to the Good Magician!"

"Stay clear of the Horseman!" the day horse insisted, breathing harder.

Obviously some element of this puzzle was missing. Imbri had glimpsed only a part of the Good Magician's array of spells, but was satisfied that they could quickly ruin an army. Humfrey, like the preceding Kings, was stronger than anticipated. Yet the day horse thought the Horseman could prevail.

The first Spy I returned. "What have you glimpsed?" Humfrey asked it.

The seeing eyeball hovered before a wall. It projected a beam of light. Where the light struck the wall, a magic picture appeared. It showed the Mundanes using ropes to lower themselves down the wall of the Chasm. Some men were already down; these were using drawn swords and spears to fend off the Gap Dragon. A number of them were lying in blood on the ground of the Chasm floor, but the dragon was suffering, too. Some of its scales were missing, and it was limping. As more Mundanes joined the first ones, the dragon would suffer more.

Humfrey, Imbri, and the day horse watched, fascinated, as the procession of Spy I balls constantly updated the newsreel report. The tough Mundanes drove the Gap Dragon back until at last the poor thing turned a battered tail and fled. Imbri had known of the activities of the Gap Dragon and its predecessors for all her life; it was a merciless monster who destroyed all those creatures misfortunate enough to blunder into the Chasm. But now she felt sorry for the monster. The Mundanes were worse.

As the afternoon declined, the Mundanes crossed the bottom of the Chasm and set their ropes for climbing the south wall. A few zombies remained to guard the Chasm; they flung down the ropes, preventing any anchorage from being achieved. Mundane archers ranged along the north side to shoot arrows at the zombies. These scored, but of course did not have any significant effect. But the arrows trailed cords that dangled down into the Chasm. The Wavers below grabbed the ends and yanked the zombies down. Then they chopped the zombies into pieces too small to continue fighting. The Punics had certainly gotten over their initial horror of the un-dead!

Now the Mundanes flung anchors up and, when the ropes were firmly caught, hauled themselves up hand over hand. The process was time-consuming but inevitable. By nightfall the entire Punic army, as much as remained of it, would be on the south bank of the Gap. Xanth's greatest natural barrier had been conquered by the enemy.

Humfrey made a note. "Two hundred and five surviving Mundanes," he said. "A number of those are wounded. No horses or elephants. More than enough to swamp Castle Roogna. But my bag of tricks can accommodate them. The problem will be the other band of Nextwavers who remain in norther Xanth—the reserves. We have no such reserves."

"The other band remains north?" Imbri asked. She had been afraid they were circling south.

"You did not suppose that six hundred troops could dwindle to two hundred merely by marching down the length of Xanth?" the Magician inquired curtly, missing the point. "Hasbinbad wisely divided his forces. The Horseman commands the reserve contingent, though he seems to have delegated the routine to a lieutenant. That is the force we must fear, for it is whole and fresh, while our defense has been decimated. They have been using their horses to carry messengers back and forth, so the second force knows what happens to the first, and where and of what nature the hazards of Xanth are. These are experienced troops, tough and cunning."

The Good Magician's talent for information was manifesting, Imbri realized. Humfrey had an excellent grasp of the tactical situation. Why, then, was he so certain he would not survive the encounter? Why was he so carefully explaining things to her? She knew this was not his nature. Normally the Good Magician was very tight with his information. It was as if he thought *she* would have to invoke many of these spells, or show someone else how to do it. That belief of his, if such it was, was unnerving.

The Spy I balls showed the Nextwavers making camp and foraging for food and drink. They were catching on to the bounties of Xanth and now, instead of burning out the region, they were hammering out chocolate chips from an outcropping of chocolithic rock and tapping beer-barrel trees for flagons of foaming natural brew, to which they seemed to be quite partial.

"The nymphs travel slower than the I balls," Humfrey remarked. "I had thought they would lead the Wavers here tonight, but it will be noon tomorrow before they arrive. My error; I misread my prophecy." He frowned. "I'm not quite as young as I used to be. I'm making foolish mistakes. That must be why I'm doomed to ignoble failure."

"But, your Majesty!" Imbri protested in a dreamlet. "You have an excellent program of defense! When you bring the Punics here and loose your spells against them—"

Humfrey shook his head. "Don't try to flatter an old curmudgeon, mare! You're a few years older than I am! Certainly my program is good; I researched it years ago from a tome describing how best to wash out Wavs. But I am about to make a single colossal, egregious, flagrant, and appalling oversight whose disastrousness is exceeded only by its irony."

"What oversight?" Imbri asked, concerned.

"I am going to overlook the single most phenomenal flaw in my plan—the one that completely nullifies all the rest. It is ironic because it is a flaw that I would readily have perceived in my younger years, when I was more alert than I am now."

"But surely if you know there is a flaw—"

"I'm too dull and corroded to find it now," he said. "I have cudgeled my ailing brain, but I can not detect it. The thing is so obvious any fool could see it—except me. That is my undoing. That is why I forbade my wife, the lovely Gorgon, to accompany me. I am ashamed to have any human being witness my final folly. And I charge you, you animals, not to embarrass me after my failure by blabbing the truth in this respect. Just tell the world that I did my best and it wasn't sufficient."

"But *I* can't see the flaw either!" Imbri protested.

"Because you are blinded by your own marish folly," he said. "At least you will have a chance to redeem yours, at the cost of great heartbreak."

"What folly is this?" she asked, curiosity warring with distress.

"If I knew that, it would provide the key to my own folly," he said. "Swear to me now that you will protect my guilty secret when finally you fathom it."

Disturbed, Imbri yielded to his entreaty. "I so swear," she sent. Then she put it to the day horse, in a separate dreamlet.

He, too, swore. "No one shall know his folly from me."

Humfrey smiled grimly. "At least I salvage that foolish fragment from the yawning abyss of my indignity." He lifted a small bag. "Here is another potent weapon—the bag of wind. Loose it when only enemy troops are near, for it is dangerous to all. Brace yourself well, lest you, too, be blown away." Then he looked at the magic sundial on his wrist, which showed him the time even when no sun was shining. "Ooops—it is time for you to go pick up Chameleon. Then you will have to teach your stallion friend how to remain in contact with you while you phase through the World of Night, lest he get lost forever in the gourd. Go to it, hoofmates."

"Hoofmates!" Imbri was startled and embarrassed by the appellation. But the fact was, she did like the day horse, and knew that it showed, and soon she would be coming into season. If she did not wish to mate with him, she would have to come to a decision and take action soon. Human females could be choosy and difficult about mating and usually were; mares had no such option. If she were near the stallion at the key time, she would mate. The day horse, obviously, was aware of that, which was one reason he was indulging her by assisting in activities of little interest to him, such as the Good Magician's setting up of spells.

The day horse was looking at her curiously. Imbri fought back her half-guilty thoughts, perked her ears up straight, and formed a dream for him to step into, one with innocent open pasture for a background and absolutely clear of any suggestion of mating. She doubted she was fooling him, but had to maintain the pretense.

But his curiosity was unrelated. "Phase through the night?" he asked in the dreamlet.

"Oh, I forgot to ask you," she sent, relieved. "Will you come with me again, to carry Ambassador Bink home from the isthmus? He is to be the next King of Xanth, so must be brought safely past the Mundanes."

"The Mundanes!" he reacted, alarmed.

"They won't see us in the night," she sent reassuringly. "I want to carry his wife Chameleon there to meet him, so we need another steed."

"Chameleon!" he said gladly. "She is a nice woman."

"You seem to like her better than me!" Imbri snorted, her dream mare turning green with jealousy.

"Well, she *is* human, therefore a creature of power—"

He really had an obsession about human beings, whether negative or positive! In the dream, Imbri shifted to human form—jet-black skin, a firm, high bosom, and with a regal flow of hair from her head. "How do you like me now?" she demanded.

He snorted with mirth. "I like you better equine. I can't touch a dream girl."

"That's what you think!" she said, her dream form striding lithely forward.

"You're wasting time," Humfrey snapped. "Save your flirtations for the journey. There's a war on."

The dreamlet puffed into confused vapor. Imbri was glad horses couldn't blush; otherwise she would now be solid red. She had indeed been flirting, when she had resolved not to; the presence of a handsome male brought out this aspect of her nature.

She walked somewhat stiffly out of the baobab tree. There was a small spring beside it; she went to it and drank deeply, knowing it might be long before she drank again. Water was very important to horses! Especially when they were burning with embarrassment. Also, she was giving the day horse time to come join her. She was sure he would, though his own equine dignity required that he not seem eager. After all, he was a stallion, and stallions did not leap to the bidding of mere mares.

In a moment, to her relief, he did emerge. He, too, took a long drink. In this subtle way he had committed himself to the journey; he had taken the first step.

She set off for Castle Roogna, and the day horse paced her. He was truly magnificent in the lessening light, his white coat standing out bravely, while her black coat made her almost invisible. Truly, they were like day and night! It was as if he epitomized the male of any species, bright and bold, while she was the essence of the female, dark and hidden.

He glanced sidelong at her, perking his ears forward, and she knew he was giving her the horselaugh inside. She had certainly been making a foolish filly of herself, parading in the dream as a woman! She was indeed somewhat smitten with the stallion, the first she had known who was not her sire, and knew she would not flee him when the season came upon her and would not retreat to some far, inaccessible region before that time to avoid the compulsion of nature. Far region? She had only to step into any gourd! But would not. He knew it, too, and knew she knew. No artifice for equines!

"The World of Night?" he inquired in neightalk, for she had shut down the dreams.

She relented and opened her dream to him. "I can enable creatures in direct contact with me to phase through objects at night and to use the gourd bypass for rapid travel. But it is dangerous, for there are spooky things within the world of the gourd. You may not want to risk it."

"And if I don't," he asked cannily, "where will you be when you come in season?"

She hadn't thought of it quite that way, at least not consciously. Of course she had a certain leverage of her own! Any normal mares in Xanth were in the hands of the Mundanes, so he couldn't chance that, and no other night mare was accessible. He was the only male—but she was the only female. Stallions did not govern the times for mating, but they were always interested. Naturally he would seek to please her, even at some inconvenience to himself. He did not know her cycle; for all he knew, she might come into season tomorrow. He had to stay close to her when opportunity came, lest he miss it.

So she could be difficult and choosy, too, in the manner of the human women! She could turn her favor on and off capriciously, driving the male to distraction. That promised to be fun—except that she really did have important business to attend to. She had to fetch Bink to Castle Roogna before Good King Humfrey made his abysmal blooper and wiped out, so Bink could be King and take over the campaign before the Nextwave swamped the last bastion of Xanth. How important her participation had become!

"My season is not yet," she returned. Of course that did not answer his question; she was not about to yield her newfound advantage by committing herself prematurely. "I must train you in continuous contact now, while some light remains. Then we'll use the gourds to go to the isthmus with Chameleon during darkness."

"I like the sound of this," he nickered.

So did she, actually. Horses were not as free about bodily contact as human beings were, but they did indulge in it. "You must remain touching me continuously, for my phase-magic extends only to those in contact with me. We must match strides exactly so we can run together without separating."

"Like this?" he asked in the dream, and in the flesh he moved over until his side squeezed against her. His flesh was soft and warm and firm; he had a nice, smooth coat and excellent musculature that made contact a pleasure.

"Like this," she agreed, feeling guilty again for enjoying the sensation so much. What was there about pleasure that so readily inspired guilt? She had associated with human beings so much, recently, that she was starting to react in the same confused way they did!

Imbri and the day horse walked in contact, then shifted together to a trot. Now the beats of their eight hooves become two, as one front hoof and one rear hoof struck the ground together for each of them. BEAT-BEAT, BEAT-BEAT! There was something very fulfilling about such a cadence, and even more pleasant about matching cadences; the measured fall of hooves was the very essence of equine nature.

Then, all too soon, Castle Roogna hove into view. The day horse sheered away, breaking contact. "I'll not go there!" he snorted, his abiding fear of human places taking over.

Imbri sighed, but understood. "I will bring her out. You wait here." It was a good place for a horse to wait, for the castle orchards had extremely lush grass.

She left him grazing and trotted on into the castle. Chameleon was waiting, eager to join her husband. It was a feeling Imbri was coming to understand much better, now that she had a male interest of her own.

Chameleon seemed to have become less pretty, even in the few hours of this day, and now was hardly out of the ordinary in appearance. But Imbri knew she was correspondingly smarter. Maybe she wanted to meet Bink before she lost too much of her charm; it was a natural enough concern. A human woman without charm was the least fortunate of creatures.

The woman mounted and they moved out. The day horse was waiting, grazing dangerously near a pinapple tree that he evidently didn't recognize. Darkness was closing, but still his white hide showed up clearly.

"Oh, I'm so glad to see you, day horse!" Chameleon exclaimed with girlish enthusiasm.

The horse lifted his head, startled. He breathed hard, half snorting.

Imbri caught on. "This is Chameleon," she sent to him. "She changes each day, getting less pretty, more intelligent. You saw her several days ago, in her most beautiful stage—but she really is the same woman."

"Of course I am the same woman," Chameleon said. "You and I stayed in the forest while Imbri and Grundy and Ichabod encountered the Nextwavers and Hasbinbad and the Horseman. We had such a nice time together."

The day horse softened, allowing himself to be persuaded. His ears perked forward. Chameleon stroked his nose. Now he was sure of her. He nickered.

"But I am different in my fashion," Chameleon acknowledged. "Not as pretty—and I will become less pretty yet, until you can't stand me at all. I also have a sharp tongue when I'm smart, as women do; nobody can stand me then."

The day horse snorted. He would not be that fickle, surely, he thought.

"You'll see," Chameleon said sadly. "The stupidest thing a woman can do is to be too smart. Give it another week, maybe less. If you can tolerate me then, I'll gladly ride with you again."

They trotted toward the nearest gourd patch. Chameleon became nervous. "Will we be passing the place where . . . ?" She trailed off, unable to finish.

"We will not pass the place where your son was taken," Imbri sent in a gentle dream that could not entirely eschew the horror connection. Chameleon was standing up well; perhaps Millie the Ghost had talked with her and put things in perspective. Millie had eight hundred years' perspective! But as Chameleon became more intelligent, Dor's loss would strike her more profoundly. That was probably another reason she wanted to rejoin her husband—especially since he was now in line to become King himself. She was not going to be absent when the second of the two men in her life was in peril.

As if to distract herself from the looming grief, Chameleon chatted innocently enough to the day horse. "Back when I was young, I lived in a village on the north edge of the Gap Chasm, and I had a separate name for each phase of my cycle. I was Wynn when I was pretty, and Dee when I was normal, and Fanchon when I was ugly. The villagers knew how it was and treated me like three different people, and that made it easier. But though they all liked Wynn—especially the young men!—and half of them liked Dee, nobody could stand Fanchon. Since anyone who married me would get all three, I was doomed to spinsterhood. Then I met Bink, who seemed like such a nice man, though he lacked magic, and I thought that if I didn't let him find out my nature . . . I was foolish, but I had an excuse, as I was stupid at the time. Wynn was the first me he encountered. So I thought maybe I could find a spell to make me normal all the time. Good Magician Humfrey told me no spell would do it, but that all I had to do was go to Mundania, and when my magic faded I would be Dee, permanently. So I tried, but somehow things got tangled up, and in the end Bink liked me as I was, so he unspinstered me." She laughed. "No spell for Chameleon! I didn't need magic, just the right man."

And if she lost Bink, Imbri thought gloomily, she would be in deep, deep trouble.

They arrived at the gourd patch. "Now get in step and in contact with me," Imbri sent to the day horse. "Do not heed anything you see within the gourd. If you break contact, you are lost."

The day horse moved close, but Chameleon's right leg got in his way. "I'll ride sidesaddle," she said, shifting her posture though there was no saddle. She was quicker to catch on to both problem and solution than she would have been before. "And I'll hold on to a strand of the day horse's mane, to be sure there's contact." She caught his mane, which was conveniently on the left side, while Imbri's was on the right. "Oh, it's like silk!" she exclaimed.

This was a gross exaggeration; his mane was more like flexible white wires, beautiful but tough. The mane and tail of a horse were designed by nature to swing about and slap flies stingingly, and were effective in that capacity. But the day horse nickered appreciatively. He had liked Chameleon in her pretty-stupid guise; he seemed to like her better in her neutral state. She was, certainly, a nice if ordinary woman now.

They matched step and plunged into the gourd. Obviously the day horse was no coward about new experiences; it was only strange people he was wary of. The green rind passed by them; then they were in a region of massive wooden gears that turned slowly and ground exceeding fine. Now the day horse snorted with alarm, but maintained contact with Imbri. Together they charged between the gears, Imbri directing their progress through a continuing dreamlet. She showed an image of the gourdscape, with a dotted yellow line marking their route. She ran just to the left of that line, he to the right. It worked well enough, for she was familiar with this region, as she was with all of the gourd.

"What are these wheels for?" Chameleon asked. She had visited the gourd before, so was no longer frightened.

"They measure out the time for every event in every dream," Imbri explained. "There are hundreds of people and creatures having thousands of dreams every night; if the length and placement of each dream were not precise, there would be overlapping and gaps and fuzziness. Each night mare has a schedule; she must deliver each dream on time. These gears measure out those times more accurately than any living creature could do. Even so, there are many small jumps and discontinuities in dreams, as the timing and placements get slightly out of synch."

"Thousands of dreams each night," Chameleon breathed, awed. "I never realized there was such precision behind the few little dreams I have!"

"You have dreams all night," Imbri returned. "But most of them you forget by morning. Most of them are probably good dreams, for you are a good person; those ones emanate from another source. The true day mares are invisible horses who carry the daydreams and the pleasant night dreams; they don't keep good accounts and don't seem to mind if their dreams are misplaced or forgotten. They are happy, careless creatures." She realized she might be unfairly condemning the day shift, perhaps from ignorance; the day mares were probably quite decent when one knew them. "Still, their time slots have to be allocated, and they must be integrated with the serious dreams we working mares deliver. The coordination is complex."

"I just never knew there was so much inside the gourd!" Chameleon said.

"Few people do," Imbri sent. "They assume things just happen coincidentally. There is very little coincidence in Xanth. It is a term used to hide our ignorance of the true causes of things."

On they went through the labyrinth of grinding gears, leaping over small ones, skirting big ones, and jumping through holes in the hollow ones. The gears were all different colors and turned at different rates, in a bewildering array.

At last they came to a new region. This was watery, and huge fishlike shapes swam through it. Loan sharks and card sharks and poor fish crowded the channels, powering toward the team of horses, then banking off with a great threshing of flukes. No one in the gourd could touch a night mare or her companions; any who did would answer to the Night Stallion, and he was not a forgiving creature. These fish were denizens of the gourd and could be dispatched to inclement assignments, such as desert duty—most unpleasant for a fish. All who molested night mares had long since gone to the most hellish spots, with the hoofprints of the Dark Horse branding their posterior regions forever. Nevertheless, the fish could bluff, and this they were doing now.

The travelers came to a third region. Here coruscating beams of light sliced crisscross in every direction plus one. Some were burning red, scorching what they touched; others were searing white, vaporizing their objects. Black ones turned things frigidly cold; green ones made them sprout leaves.

"Oh, I know what these are for!" Chameleon exclaimed. "They make things hot or cold or bright or dull or clean or dirty or anything!" She was certainly getting smarter.

"Yes," Imbri agreed, discovering new interest in these things that were long familiar to her. "If Xanth dreams were left to themselves, they would be horribly bland. They have to be touched up so that there is good contrast. A great deal of art goes into dreams to make them properly effective."

"Then why do we forget most of them?" Chameleon asked. "It seems like such a waste!"

"You don't really forget them," Imbri qualified. "They remain in your experience, the same as does every tree you see every day, every bug you hear buzzing, and every gust of breeze your body feels. All of these things influence your character, and so do the dreams."

"It's amazing!" Chameleon said, shaking her head. "There is so much more to life than I thought. I wonder if the Mundanes have similar things to influence their characters?"

"I doubt it," Imbri sent. "After all, look at how brutish and bad they are. If they had proper dreams, they wouldn't degenerate like that."

Now they reached another rind and burst out of the gourd. They were in the isthmus of Xanth, the narrow corridor of land that led to Mundania. This was where Bink and Arnolde would be arriving, having completed another diplomatic mission. Imbri and the day horse separated; it really was easier to run separately. "You came through that very well," Imbri complimented him.

"I just concentrated on my running," he replied tightly in the dream. "I knew if I looked about too much, I'd lose my step and get separated."

They entered a plain, where the flat, hard ground was illuminated by the faint light of the waning moon and running was excellent. Imbri loved to run and knew the day horse did, too; horses had been created to do most of the quality running in Xanth. She tried to imagine the bad dreams being carried by lumbering dragons, and suffered a titillation of mirth. No, it had to be done by true night mares!

Then a shape appeared in the moonlight, like a low-flying cloud. It was flat on the bottom and lumpy on top. It swooped toward them.

Imbri phased into intangibility, protecting herself and her rider from hostile action. "Hide!" she sent to the day horse.

But a voice from the cloud hailed them. "Imbri! Chameleon! It's me—Grundy the Golem!"

So it was. Imbri phased back. "Whatever are you doing here?" she sent indignantly. "You're supposed to be watching King Humfrey's castle while the Gorgon is away."

"Emergency," he said, coasting down beside them. "I used one of Humfrey's bottled spells to summon the magic carpet and buzz right over here. You certainly move fast! I tore through the night so swiftly that I've got shatters of cloud on me! Glad I caught you in time."

"In time for what?" Chameleon asked.

Suddenly the golem was oddly diffident. "Well, you have to know, before—"

"What's that?" Imbri projected—and as she touched Grundy's mind, she became aware of a maelstrom within it. The golem was generating his own bad images!

"I had to tell you—about the Good Magician. I activated a magic mirror—all it took was the right anti-glitch spell; it could have been done any time before, and we could have had good communications—I got the spell from a book the Gorgon left for me in case I needed magic for an emergency—and tuned him in, or tried to—"

"Have the Mundanes attacked already?" Chameleon asked, worried.

"No, not exactly. Yes, I guess so. That is, it's a matter of definition. He's gone."

"What?" Chameleon's confusion was Imbri's, too. "You mean the Good Magician left the baobab tree?"

"No, he's there. But not there."

"I don't—"

"Humfrey's been taken!" Grundy cried.

"No!" Chameleon protested. "It's too soon!"

"He's gone, just like the others. Staring into nothing! Bink has to be King right now! That's why I had to reach you, before the Mundanes get to the baobab tree and wipe out all the bottled spells or use them against us!"

Chameleon put her hand to her eyes, stricken. "Already! I won't have my husband at all, any more than Irene had Dor!"

"Bink can take the carpet!" Grundy said. "He's got to get to Castle Roogna right away!"

"No," Chameleon demurred. "Bink knows nothing about being King. He has to be prepared."

"There's no time! The Mundanes will be marching in the morning, and we're halfway through the night now!"

"Imbri and I will bring him back," she said firmly. "We'll prepare him on the way. We'll catch him up on all the recent details he's missed by being away. By the time he arrives, he will be ready. I hope."

Grundy shook his little head dolefully. "You're the Queen now, you know. But if Xanth has no King when the Mundanes reach Castle Roogna—"

"Xanth will have a King," Chameleon said.

"On your head be it," the golem muttered.

Chapter 10

Magic Tricks

The Good Magician's prophecy of the moment of Bink's arrival in Xanth was accurate. In the early wee hours of the morning, Bink and Arnolde walked out of drear Mundania. Chameleon ran to embrace her husband, while Imbri and the day horse exchanged diffident glances with the centaur. Grundy performed introductions.

"You're just the way I like you, Dee," Bink remarked after their kiss. He was a fairly solid, graying man who had been physically powerful in his youth. Imbri remembered him now; she had on occasion brought him bad dreams.

"Dee?" Grundy asked.

Bink smiled, confirming what Chameleon had already told the others. "My changeable wife has a private name for each phase. Dee is ordinary, not too much of anything. I don't know why I pay attention to her." He kissed her again.

Arnolde was an old, bespectacled centaur who seemed out of place in the forest. He was by training and temperament an archivist, like his friend Ichabod, one who filed books and papers in obscure chambers, for what purpose no one understood. But he was also a Magician, his talent being the formation of an aisle of magic wherever he went, even in the most alien reaches of Mundania. This greatly facilitated contact and trade with that backward region. He had no apparent magic in Xanth itself, which was why his status had been unknown for most of his life. In this respect he resembled Bink, and the two males seemed to enjoy each other's company.

"Might I inquire the reason for this welcoming party?" Arnolde asked. "We expected to sleep the rest of the night here at the fringe of Xanth, then take two more days to travel south to the North Village."

"Ha!" Grundy said. "There *is* no—"

"Please," Chameleon said, interrupting the golem. "I must tell him in my own way."

"But Humfrey told *me* to tell him!" Grundy protested competitively.

The centaur interceded benignly. "May I suggest a compromise? Let the golem make one statement; then Chameleon can tell the rest in her own manner."

Chameleon smiled fleetingly. "That seems fair."

"Okay," Grundy grudged. "Bink, you're King. You have to get back to Castle Roogna right away. You can use the magic carpet; it will get you there in an hour."

"King!" Bink exclaimed. "What happened to King Trent? I'm not in line to be King of Xanth!"

"King Trent is ill," Chameleon said.

"Then our son Dor should take over."

"Dor is ill, too," she said very gently.

Bink paused, his face freezing. "How ill?"

"Too ill to be King," she replied. "It is an enchantment. We have not yet found the countercharm."

"Surely Good Magician Humfrey can—" Bink saw her grave expression. "Him, too? The same enchantment?"

"And the Zombie Master. But Humfrey told us that you are, in fact, a Magician who can not be harmed by magic, and that you have the best chance to break the chain of lost Kings, though he feared you would not. You must be King and stop the Mundanes—"

"The Mundanes! What's this?"

"The Nextwave invasion," Grundy put in.

Bink laughed mirthlessly. "I see there is indeed much for me to catch up on. Is the magic carpet big enough for two? You and I, Chameleon, could—"

"No," Grundy said. "It won't support two full-sized people; it's a single-seater model. And you can't take two days riding south. You'd get there after Castle Roogna falls to the Mundanes, and anyway, the main bridge across the Gap is down, and Wavers are all over the place, and—"

"I won't let you go alone!" Chameleon protested, showing some fire. She was not nearly as accommodating to the notions of others as she had been in her lovely stage. "I've lost my son, so soon after he was married. I won't let it happen to you!"

"But Xanth must have a King," Bink said. "Though I'm incompetent in any such activity, I must try to do my duty. How else can I get there in time?"

"Imbri can take you," Chameleon declared with sudden inspiration. "She's a night mare; she can get you there by morning—and she can tell you everything you need to know and help you manage. That way you'll be properly prepared."

"I find this mostly incomprehensible," Bink said. "But I'm sure you know best, Dee. I had had another kind of meeting with you in mind—"

"So did I," she said bravely. "By the time I catch up with you, I'll be well on toward ugly."

"You are never ugly to me," he said with a certain gallantry. But he could not quite conceal his disappointment. He had been some time away from her, and obviously she was a woman who needed to be appreciated at the right time.

"Go with Imbri," she said. "The rest of us will follow at our own pace."

They embraced again. "Can the rest of you travel safely?" Bink asked as he went to Imbri.

"Oh, sure," Grundy said. "The day horse knows how to stay clear of Mundanes, and I've got the flying carpet for emergencies. I'll ride Arnolde and keep him out of mischief."

"Indubitably," the centaur said, smiling wryly.

"I've got to fill you in on everything before I fly back to Humfrey's castle," Grundy continued. "You'll be King after Bink, Arnolde."

Chameleon frowned. "Grundy, you are a perfect marvel of diplomacy," she said with gentle irony.

"I know it," the golem agreed smugly.

Bink mounted Imbri and waved farewell to his wife. Imbri could tell by the way he sat that he had had some experience riding animals, unlike his wife. The centaurs probably accounted for that. Bink had traveled to Mundania many times, and perhaps had encountered Mundane horses there, too.

Imbri sent a dream of sad parting to the others, seeing them as a pretty picture—the old centaur appaloosa carrying the golem, and the magnificent white stallion bearing the sad woman. Yet it was true that Arnolde, too, needed to be updated in detail for when he would be King. If nothing else, he would need time to ponder whom to designate as his successor, since things tended to move too rapidly for the Council of Elders to deliberate and decide.

Imbri set off for the nearest gourd patch. "What's this about my son Dor getting married?" Bink asked her.

Imbri sent him a small dream showing the elopement wedding in the zombie graveyard. She followed that with their discovery of the fate of King Trent. The dream became a full-fledged narrative, so that Bink hardly noticed when they plunged into the gourd and charged through the maelstrom of the raw stuff of real dreams. By the time they emerged from the gourd near Castle Roogna, Bink had become acquainted with everything relevant that Imbri knew.

"You are some mare, Imbri!" he said as the castle came into sight. They were just in time; dawn was threatening; had it arrived while they were in the gourd, they would have been trapped within the World of Night for the day. Imbri's night powers existed only at night, as always.

They entered the castle. Queen Iris met them. "Thank fate you're here, Bink; we just discovered King Humfrey has been taken. You—"

"I am King," Bink said with surprising certainty. He had assimilated Imbri's information readily and now was taking hold in a much firmer fashion than Imbri had expected. Bink had been a kind of nonperson in Xanth, considered to be a man without magic and therefore held in a certain veiled contempt; that contempt had been undeserved. Imbri suspected that even Grundy and Chameleon and the day horse expected little of Bink; already it was evident that he would surprise them. Xanth's recent Kings had not lasted long, but each had shown competence and courage in the crisis. Yet how long could this continue, in the face of the terrible enchantment that persisted in striking each King down?

They went to the room where the enchanted Kings were laid out. The Zombie Master and Good Magician Humfrey had been added to the collection. Chet and Chem Centaur had evidently been out to the baobab tree and carried in the latest victim.

Irene remained by her husband. She looked up. "Bink!" she said, rising and going to him. "Did you know that he—we—"

Bink put his arm around her. "The mare Imbri told me everything. Congratulations! I'm only sorry you did not have more time together."

"We had no time at all!" she complained, making a moue. "The Kingship monopolized him. Then he was ensorcelled." She choked off, her eyes flicking toward her supine husband.

"Somehow we'll find the counterspell," Bink said reassuringly.

"They say you—that it can't happen to you—"

"It seems my secret is out at last. Your father knew it always. That is why he sent me on some of the most awkward magical investigations. But I am not invulnerable; the Mundanes represent as much of a threat to me as to anyone else. But perhaps I can deal with this mysterious enemy who has enchanted these four Kings. I shall go immediately to the baobab tree and try to use Humfrey's bag of tricks to stop the Nextwave."

"You seem remarkably well informed," Queen Iris remarked.

"Yes. Only a man of my talent can safely use Humfrey's spells. Only those spells can stop the Mundanes at this point—which, of course, is the reason Humfrey was ensorcelled before he could use them. I will use them, and I want that enchanter to come to me. His magic won't work—and then I'll be able to identify him. That's why Humfrey thought I might break the chain of enchantments—if I can prevent the Mundanes from taking me out physically."

"Then it is victory or real death for you," Irene said.

"Yes, of course. This is why Magician Humfrey could not foresee my future; my talent prevents him, and neither he nor I can handle the Mundane element as a matter of divination." He paused. "It is odd, however, that he, the most knowledgeable of men, was taken out by enchantment, not by a Mundane weapon."

"He knew it was coming," Imbri sent. "He said he was overlooking something important, perhaps because he couldn't foresee his own future." That was as much as she could impart without abridging her promise not to reveal the ignominious nature of the Good Magician's fall—though it did not seem ignominious to her. Obviously the enemy enchanter had waited till Humfrey was alone, then struck stealthily. The shame should attach to the enchanter, not to Humfrey.

"Take me there," Bink told her. "And the rest of you—let it be known that I am alone at the baobab tree. I want the enemy enchanter to get the news." He looked down at his enchanted son. "I will set things right for you, Dor. I promise. And for the others who so bravely served. The enchanter shall undo his mischief." Bink's hand touched the hilt of the sword he wore with a certain ominous significance. Imbri had not thought of him as a man of violence, but she realized now that he would not hesitate to do whatever he felt was required to accomplish his purpose.

Imbri took him to the baobab. Chem Centaur was there, guarding the Good Magician's spells. Everything seemed undisturbed.

"How was he found?" King Bink asked.

"He was sitting on the floor here, holding this bottle," Chem said, picking up a small red one. "He must have been setting it up with the others when—"

"Thank you," Bink said, taking the bottle. "You may trot back to Castle Roogna—no, just one moment." He popped the cork.

Red vapor swirled out. "Horseman!" the Good Magician's voice whispered. Then the vapor dissipated, leaving silence.

"He bottled his own voice!" Chem exclaimed.

"Now we know who enchanted him," Bink said. "The Horseman. Humfrey promised to tell us who, and he did—just before he was taken himself."

"Beware the Horseman!" Imbri sent in a nervous dreamlet. "That was his earlier warning!"

"It suggests the Horseman is near," Bink said. "That is what I want. He will come to me when I am alone." He waved Chem away. "Humfrey was true to his promise. He has produced the key information. Go inform the others. I think we are on the way to breaking the chain. At least we now know the meaning of the two prophecies. We know whom to stop and why."

"I don't like this," Chem said, but she trotted obediently out of the tree.

"I remember when she was a foal," Bink remarked. "Cute little thing, always making mental maps of the surroundings. She's certainly a fine-looking filly now!" He turned to Imbri. "I said I would be alone, but I wasn't thinking of you. I hope you don't mind remaining, though I know you fear the Horseman."

"I don't fear the Horseman," Imbri protested. "It's the day horse who fears him. If that horrible man comes near me, I'll put a hind hoof in his face and leave my signature on the inside of his skull."

"Good enough," the King agreed with a grim smile. "But it may be better to leave him to me, as he is obviously no Mundane, and you may be vulnerable to his magic. What does he look like?"

Imbri projected a dream picture of the Horseman. She was shaking with abrupt rage. Of course the man was no Mundane! He had deliberately deceived her so she would not know in what manner he was a threat to Xanth. And she had allowed herself to be fooled! This was the sort of indignity Humfrey must have felt, overlooking the obvious.

"That's very good, Imbri. You have a nice talent there. If you weren't a night mare, it would be a double talent—dream projection and the ability to dematerialize at night. But I suppose both are really part of your nature, not considered talents at all." He shook his head. "Magic is funny stuff; I have never been certain of its ramifications. Whenever I understand it, some new aspect appears, and I realize that I don't understand it at all."

Imbri found herself liking this man in much the way she liked his wife Chameleon. He was a nice person, no snob, intelligent and practical, with a certain unpretentious honesty. "Magic seems natural enough to me," she ventured. "What is so hard to understand about it?"

"For one thing, the distribution and definition of magic talents," he said. "For centuries we men believed that all creatures either had magic talents or were themselves magical. Thus men *did* magic, while dragons *were* magic. Then we discovered that some centaurs could do magic, too. So we have a magical species performing magic, fudging the definition. Now we have you night mares bridging the definition also. If we assume you are natural horses who possess magic talent, we run afoul of the double-talent problem, for only one talent goes to any one person. We had thought every talent was different, but then we discovered the curse fiends, who all have the same talent—but at least that does not violate the one-talent-per-person limit. But you—"

"I see the problem," she agreed. "All night mares can phase out and project dreams. Maybe a creature *can* have two talents."

"Or a magical creature, who phases through objects at night, can have the single talent of sending dreams," he said. "We can make it fit our present definitions—barely—but the suspicion remains that someday we will discover some form of magic that does not. Consider this Horseman: he's obviously a man with the ability to ensorcell other men. That's not remarkable in itself; my father Roland can stun people, and, of course, King Trent transformed them. But how does the Horseman get around so handily without being observed? Does he have a second talent, perhaps similar to your of the night? We don't know, but must be prepared for that possibility."

"Now I understand your doubt," she said. "Magic is more complicated than I thought."

"I would like you to review your knowledge of the whereabouts of the Horseman each time a King was enchanted," Bink continued. "Obviously he was there to do his foul deed, but he has also been associated with the Mundanes when they were far distant. The manner of his travel may give us some hint how to balk him. He must be a man of Xanth, helping the Mundanes for personal advantage. Evidently they made him second in command in exchange for his help, but he does not help them too much. He let you escape them, knowing you were helping Xanth, and that would have the effect of evening the contest and making his service more valuable."

"The rogue!" Imbri sent emphatically, with the image of the moon colliding violently with the sun and showering Xanth with fragments of burning cheese. "If the Mundanes and Xanthians destroy each other, he can take over himself!"

"Such is the way of rogues," King Bink agreed. "His power is to banish the minds of people, but it may not be inherent in him. Perhaps he has a bottle full of minds, the same way Good Magician Humfrey has bottles of everything else. Maybe it is the bottle that does the magic, sucking in the Kings. But surely he had to approach his victims to do this. We must not assume we know the precise nature of his magic."

Imbri concentrated. She had actually met the Horseman only twice—once near Castle Roogna, just before King Trent was taken, and once in Hasbinbad's camp in northern Xanth. She had not seen him when King Dor was taken, or when the Zombie Master went, though it was obvious in retrospect that he had been the man in the tree.

"So he could have been there with the Mundane army, then," Bink said. "The Mundanes were not far away, just across the river, while King Dor slept. You did not see the Horseman because he was hiding, skulking around, waiting for his chance."

Imbri had to agree. In the confused situation of the battlefield, it would have been easy to sneak up close to the King's tent at night.

"And the next time, the Zombie Master was in the field, too," King Bink persisted.

Imbri reviewed the scene for him, showing how the Zombie Master had been sleeping, enjoying a dream Imbri had brought him. How Grundy had tracked a man to a river and lost him, after the King had been taken.

"So we know he does not have to touch his victim physically," Bink concluded. "He can be a short distance away, perhaps out of sight. That's an important point—no direct visual contact needed. He could have come here to this tree and hidden in a recess; perhaps he was here when you were and simply waited until Magician Humfrey was alone. It could have happened soon after you departed. How many more of Humfrey's spells have been set out since then?"

This was a most methodical approach! Imbri studied the bottles and boxes, trying to remember how many had been out of the bag before. "Not many more," she said.

"The Horseman wouldn't have had reason to travel far in the night," Bink continued. "Though I doubt he remained here in the tree. For one thing, he did not disturb Humfrey's spells. Not even the bottle that named him—surely a prime target! He must have been nervous about discovery and not delayed one moment after doing his deed. That suggests he can not enchant someone who is on guard, or perhaps can take only one person at a time, so must catch his victim alone and may be vulnerable for a period thereafter. So he left quickly, lest someone else arrive on the scene. Smash the Ogre's little wife Tandy is like that; once she stuns someone with a tantrum, she can not do so again for some time."

Again Imbri had to agree. It made her nervous to think that the dread Horseman lurked close by. By daylight she could not dematerialize, and that increased her nervousness.

"You surely need to rest and graze, Imbri," Bink said. "Go out and relax, but check on me every hour or so. The pseudonymphs aren't due to bring the Mundanes here until noon. I think the Horseman will try to strike before then, for he surely knows these spells of Humfrey's are dangerous to his allies, the Mundanes. If I have miscalculated in any way, I'll need you to carry the message to Castle Roogna."

Imbri nodded, both reassured and worried. King Bink was several times the man she had first taken him for—but it seemed that the Horseman was similarly more devious. She went out to graze, but the grass didn't taste very good. She watched for the possible approach of the Horseman, fearing that he would somehow sneak past unobserved, as it seemed he had done before. The Horseman had been making fools of them all so far!

Every hour she checked, but King Bink was all right. Noon came, and all remained well. Imbri was almost disappointed; she certainly wished no ill to the King, but she hated this tension of waiting. Suppose Bink were not invulnerable to the enchantment? Or suppose the Horseman wanted to reduce the force of Mundanes some more, keeping the sides even, so planned to let King Bink fight a while, using the spells, before taking him out? Or had the Horseman already tried and failed, unbeknownst to them? Where did things really stand?

Right on schedule, the first of the floating nymphs arrived, hotly pursued by a slavering Mundane.

Imbri had relayed all she had learned about the Good Magician's spells. Now Bink picked up one of the unidentified ones. "Stand well clear, Imbri," he warned. "This spell will not hurt me, but it might hurt you. I'm going to experiment while I'm not hard-pressed. I can still use my sword if a single Mundane comes at me. When too many come, I'll draw on the heavy stuff."

Imbri stood back. It seemed to her he was taking a considerable risk—but she realized that he was immune to magical danger and knew it, so could afford to gamble in a way no other person dared. This was safer for him than trying to take on all the Mundanes physically! Perhaps that was another reason Good Magician Humfrey had publicized Bink's secret talent. Bink was the only one who could safely play with unknown killer-spells, so had to be the one to succeed Humfrey himself and had to use those spells when no friends were close enough to be hurt by them. It was amazing how carefully Humfrey had planned every detail, his own failure included.

The nymph floated up, looking devastatingly winsome by human standards. Imbri had seen the creatures as they were first inflating, dead white and bulging. The night air must have done them good, for now there was color and bounce to match the buoyancy, and intricate little jiggles in private places as they moved. No wonder the Mundane was in sweaty pursuit!

Now the Mundane spied King Bink. "Oh, no, you don't! She's mine!" he cried, drawing his sword. "I chased that divine dream half the night and day!"

"In all fairness, I must tell you two things," Bink said. "First, the nymph is not real. She is a shape from a spell, with no mind at all—"

"I don't care where she's from or how smart she is!" the Mundane said, licking his brute lips. "I'm going to give her the time of my life—right after I get rid of you." He advanced, sword poised.

"Second, I am holding the spell of a Magician," Bink continued, backing off. "It may hurt you or even kill you, if—"

The Mundane leaped, his sword swinging viciously. Bink popped the cork on the vial, pointing the opening at him.

A green fireball shot out, expanding as it moved. It was head-sized as it struck the Mundane in the chest.

The man screamed. The fire burned into his chest with terrible ferocity, consuming it. In a moment the Mundane fell, his chest mostly missing.

Bink stared, looking faint. "Humfrey wasn't playing idle games," he whispered. "He was set to destroy the enemy army!"

Imbri agreed. That had been one deadly weapon! "But it was a choice between the enemy or you," she sent in a supportive dreamlet, glad she had taken the advice to stand well clear. "He tried to kill you when you tried to be reasonable with him."

"Yes. I have steeled myself to that," Bink said. "Still, the stomach is weak. I have seldom killed before, and most Mundanes are not like him. They can be quite civilized . . . though I admit this one wasn't."

Already a second pseudonymph was coming, leading another brute Mundane. Bink snatched up another vial. "Halt, Mundane!" he cried. "I have slain your companion!"

"Then I'll slay you!" the Mundane cried. He carried a bow; now he brought out an arrow and nocked it, taking aim.

Bink opened and pointed the vial, as he had the first. Something sailed out of it as the arrow flew toward him. The arrow struck the object and went astray, missing Bink's head by the span of a hand and plunking into the wall behind him.

Imbri looked at the thing skewered on the shaft of the arrow. It was a bean sandwich. The Mundane had just shot Humfrey's lunch.

The Mundane stared for a moment. Then he emitted a great bellow of a laugh. "You're fulla beans!"

Bink took a third vial. As the Mundane drew another arrow and aimed, Bink pointed and opened it.

This time smoke issued from the container. It shaped into a huge face. The face laughed. "Ho ho ho!" it roared. It was laughing gas.

But the Mundane's sense of humor was limited to laughter at others, not at himself. He shot an arrow through the face at Bink, barely missing. He drew a third. Imbri grew more nervous; these spells were not doing the job reliably.

Bink gave up on the spells for the moment. He ducked through the smoke, drawing his sword, and charged at the Mundane.

The Mundane, realizing that his bow was useless at close quarters, hastily drew his own sword. The two met in personal combat—but the Mundane was much younger and faster.

Imbri stepped forward, knowing she could not stand by and let the King be killed. But as the laughing gas dissipated, a third Mundane appeared, carrying a spear. He closed on the other two people, seeking an opening to dispatch the King.

Imbri charged across, spun about, and flung out a kick with her two hind legs. This caught the spearman in the chest and smashed him back. Imbri knew she had either killed the man or hurt him so badly he would not fight again for a long time. She now had blood on her hooves.

She turned again to help Bink, but he had dispatched his opponent. It seemed he knew how to handle a sword; his skill had bested the Mundane speed.

But already three more Mundanes were entering the tree, weapons drawn. Now the Punic army was arriving in force! Pseudonymphs floated all about, dancing just out of the grasp of the men, jiggling remarkably, causing the Punics to become more aggressive than ever.

"I have to return to magic," King Bink said. "I can't take on the whole Nextwave with my lone sword!" He glanced at the one Imbri had dispatched. "And I can't ask you to risk your hide, either. But it's no longer safe for you to stand away from me; soon there'll be many more Mundanes. So you had better stay close to me; that way the magic is less likely to backlash against you, and may protect you exactly as it protects me."

Imbri did not see that the magic had helped the King much. Protection against being harmed by magic was not the same as being protected by magic. But she agreed; she would be better able to help him if she were close. She could carry him out of the tree if the Mundanes became overwhelming.

Bink picked up a package and tore it open. A score of large rubber bands fell out. Now at last he showed some ire. "What good are these?"

Imbri touched one with her hoof. Instantly it climbed up her foot and tightened about her ankle. It hurt; she had to lift her foot to her teeth to rip it off. Then it tried to clasp her nose.

"Oho!" Bink exclaimed. He stooped to pick one up. It writhed in his hand, but could not manage to close on his wrist. He flipped it at the nearest Mundane.

The band slid over the man's head and constricted about his neck. Suddenly he was choking, turning purple in the face.

"A weapon indeed!" Bink said. He flipped two more chokers at the other Mundanes. One looped about a man's arms, binding him awkwardly; the other caught its man around the waist, squeezing his gut. The bands might be small and harmless when Bink handled them, but were savage when they touched any other flesh!

More Mundanes appeared. Bink tossed the rest of the chokers, then picked up another vial. A knife flew from it, transfixing the Punic. But more was needed, so Bink opened a large, wide-mouthed bottle.

The bottle did not eject anything. Instead it expanded rapidly, until it was big enough to admit a man standing upright. On its side were printed the mystic words CAVE CANEM. Imbri wasn't sure what that signified, but it seemed vaguely threatening.

"So it's a cave," Bink said. "Maybe it will serve. Hey, nymphs—fly in here!" He pointed to the opaque glass cave.

Obligingly, the buoyant nymphs flew inside. The Mundanes who were able charged in after them. Six men disappeared into the cave.

There was a horrendous growling deep inside, and a medley of screams. Imbri, startled, projected in an inquiring dreamlet—and discovered that the minds of the Mundanes had become truly animalistic, like those of vicious dogs.

"The cave of canines," Bink said. "Remarkable device!"

"Beware of the cave!" Imbri agreed. She didn't like canines; they tended to nip at equine heels and were difficult to tag with swift kicks.

Before long, the glass cave overflowed. Mundanes spilled back out, doggedly running on four feet, yelping. Their faces looked more canine than human, though Imbri wasn't sure this was very much of a change. The dogfaces scrambled out of the tree, tails between their legs.

Tails? Imbri looked again—but too late. The creatures were gone.

Still the Mundane menace grew. The rest of their army seemed to have arrived in more or less of a mass, and individual vials were not enough. Some men were distracted by the fleeing canines, and some appeared to have been bitten by those, but there were too many intact Mundanes to stop.

"Time for the ultimate measures," King Bink said. "Stand by to carry me to safety, Imbri; this may be worse than we anticipated."

Imbri stood by. Bink lifted the bag of winds and started to untie it.

A huge Mundane charged at the King, slashing downward with his sword.

He missed Bink, who had alertly dodged, but scored on the bound river. The tie was severed cleanly.

Instantly the coil sprang outward as the water was released. The floor flooded, the liquid getting deeper moment by moment. There was a lot of fluid in a river! The Mundanes cursed as their feet were washed out from under them. The one trying to attack the King was dumped and carried away by the torrent.

Then the string tying the mouth of the windbag came loose. The winds roared out of confinement. They swirled around the chamber of the baobab tree and whipped the surface of the rising water into froth. It became hard to stand, and not much fun to breathe.

Imbri tried to find King Bink, but he had been swept by the swirl, along with the Mundanes. Apparently the river, once released, had become a nonmagical force, so could act on him. Perhaps it was merely moving him without hurting him. No two-footed creature could keep on his feet in this! That was yet another inherent human liability—lack of a sufficient number of feet on the ground. Imbri did not care to gamble that Bink would not drown.

No—as she reviewed what she had been told of his talent, she decided he would not drown, because that fate would have been set up by magic—after all, the river had been magically bound—and therefore his drowning forbidden. But there were Mundanes mixed in that soup with him, and one of them certainly might hurt him, since they had been trying to do that regardless of magic. So her help was definitely needed.

She forged through the frothing water, squinting her eyes against the whirling wind. She did not know in what direction the wind wanted to go, because here in the tree it was still looking for the exit. She found the King. He was holding on to the edge of the Canem Cave. She nudged him, and he shifted his grip to her. He was carrying something that hampered him, but Imbri floated up under him and got him halfway clear of the violent torrent.

Now she half swam, half drifted with the current, moving out of the tree. Mundanes were also being carried along, burdened by their weapons and armor, gasping and drowning in the River Elba. Humfrey had prophesied correctly; able were they ere they saw Elba. She wasn't sure she had the phrasing quite right, but certainly the elements from coil and bag were devastating an army.

Outside the tree, the tide diminished. Imbri found her footing and forged toward higher ground. A few Mundanes were doing likewise. At last Imbri stood on an elevated ridge overgrown with quaking aspen; the timid trees were fluttering with apprehension as the water surged toward their roots. "Are you all right?" she sent to King Bink.

"Tired and waterlogged," he replied. "But whole. However, the battle is not yet over." For more Mundanes were straggling up to the ridge.

"We can outrun them," Imbri sent.

"No. They would only reorganize and march on Castle Roogna, where the women are. It has neither human nor zombie defenses any more. The ogre is there, but he can not be in all places at once. I don't want our loved ones subject to the will of the Punics, treated like pseudonymphs. I must deal with the enemy here, now; I shall not return to Castle Roogna until the threat has been entirely abated."

Imbri could appreciate his sentiment and admire his courage. But Bink was only one man against what appeared to be about twenty surviving Mundanes. He was fifty years old, which was getting along, physically, for a male of his species. He was likely to get himself killed—and his prospective successor, Arnolde Centaur, was still far away. Yet Bink was the King, and his decision counted.

"I see you have doubts," he said, smiling grimly. "You are a sensible mare. But I am not yet entirely dependent on my own resources. I salvaged the Good Magician's book of Words of Power."

"I hope they are good ones," she sent. "Here come two Mundanes!"

King Bink opened the book as the Mundanes approached him, spears poised. He fixed on the first one. "Oops—I don't know how to pronounce it," he said.

"Try several ways!" Imbri sent, for behind the two spearmen other Mundanes were coming, just as ugly and determined. One thing about these Punic mercenaries—they never gave up! If the King didn't use magic to protect himself, the nonmagical assault of the enemy would quickly finish him.

"SCHNEZL!" Bink read aloud, with a short E.

Nothing happened. The Mundanes drew nigh.

"SCHNEZL!" he repeated, this time using a long E.

The two Mundanes broke into uncontrollable sneezing. Their eyes watered, their breath got short, and they doubled over in nasal convulsions, trying vainly to blow their lungs out through their noses. Their buttons popped off, their belts snapped, and their eyes bugged in and out. They dropped their spears and staggered into the murky water, still firing out achoos. The other Mundanes paused in wonder and admiration at the cannonade. It seemed the King had pronounced the Word correctly the second time. Even Imbri felt an urge to sneeze, but she hastily suppressed it and stood closer to Bink. That helped; he did seem to have an ambience of immunity.

"Odd," Bink remarked. "The print has faded from the page. That Word is no longer written there."

"It must be a one-shot spell," Imbri sent. "How many more do you have?"

Bink flipped through the pages of the book. "There must be hundreds here."

"That should be enough." She was relieved.

Another Waver was charging up, sword swinging. Bink read the next Word. "AmnSHA!" he cried, accenting the second syllable.

The Mundane did not sneeze. He continued charging.

"AMNsha!" Bink repeated, this time accenting the first syllable.

Still the Mundane came, seemingly unaffected.

"AMNSHA!" Bink cried, with no accenting and hardly more than one syllable. And ducked as the man's sword whistled at his head. The blow missed.

The Mundane stopped and turned. He looked perplexed. "What am I doing here?" he asked. "Who are you? Who am I?"

"The Word made him lose his memory!" Imbri sent in a pleased dreamlet. "Too bad all the remaining Mundanes weren't within range of it!"

"Good thing you were in contact with me so it didn't catch you," King Bink responded. "Humfrey would have made better use of it and harmlessly abated the entire Mundane threat. My son Dor reported a similar use of a forget-spell eight hundred years ago at the Gap Chasm."

That was another mystic reference to something Dor obviously could not have been involved in. Maybe it was a memory of a dream. "We had better deal with the Mundane," Imbri reminded him in a dreamlet.

King Bink addressed the soldier. "You are an immigrant to the Land of Xanth. You will find a good homestead and a willing nymph, and will settle down to be a productive citizen. Congratulations."

"Yeah, sure," the man said, dazed. He lumbered off in search of his homestead.

But three more Mundanes were coming, and these did not look at all forgetful. The last Word had faded from the page. Bink turned the leaf and read the next one. "SKONK!"

There was a sudden terrible odor. The stench spread out from the sound of the Word, forming a bilious cloud that drifted in the path of the enemy soldiers. Unheeding, they charged into it. They had learned to be concerned about tangible magic, but to ignore mists and apparitions.

Immediately they scattered, coughing and holding their noses. They had received the brunt of the stench, though the peripheral wash was enough to make Imbri gag. That was bad, because horses were unable to regurgitate. A coincidental drift of wind had carried the mist away from the King, so he did not suffer. Coincidental?

The three Mundanes plunged into the water, trying to wash away the smell. A murk of pollution spread out from them, and small fish fled the region. It seemed it would take a long time for the men to cleanse themselves.

Yet another Mundane was attacking as the fog dissipated. This one paused just beyond it, fitting an arrow to his bow.

The King consulted the book. "KROKK!" he yelled at the bowman.

The Mundane changed form. His jaw extended into a greenish snout bulging with teeth. His limbs shrank into squat, clawed extremities. His torso sprouted scales. Unable to hold on to his bow or maintain his balance, he fell forward, belly-flopping on the ground with a loud whomp. He scrambled to the water and paddled away, propelling himself with increasing efficiency by means of a massive green tail that sprouted from his hind part.

"He turned into a gator," Bink remarked, impressed. "I didn't know the Good Magician had any transformation spells."

"He collected all kinds of information," Imbri sent. "Many people owed him favors for his services, and he knew exactly where to find useful bits of magic. He's been accumulating things for over a century. Once I brought him a bad dream about a box of quarterpedes, and he promptly woke and fetched it from the place the dream identified it. I didn't even know what they were and had forgotten the matter until that box turned up in his collection of spells in the baobab tree. He never missed a trick."

"I should have rescued that box," Bink said regretfully. "Maybe when the water subsides—"

Another Mundane charged. He swung a battle-axe with hideous intent. Bink quickly glanced at the book again. "BANSH!" he cried.

The Mundane disappeared, axe and all. These were certainly useful spells, when they worked!

But about a dozen Punics remained on the ridge. They now formed into an organized company and advanced slowly on the King. This was a more serious threat.

Bink leafed through the book, looking for a suitable Word. "If only there were definitions given!" he complained.

A spear sailed at the King. "Dodge!" Imbri sent.

Bink dodged. But the spear caught the open book and knocked it out of his hand. He regained his balance and dived for it, but the volume fell in the water. The crockagator forged up and snapped the book into its big mouth with an evil chuckle, carrying it away. The King had been abruptly deprived of his magic defense by nonmagical means. True, the crock had been magically transformed—but an untransformed Mundane could have done the same thing.

"But see!" he cried, stooping to pick up a floating bottle. It was yellow and warty and somewhat misshapen. "Isn't this the one containing the enormous squash?"

"I believe it is," Imbri agreed. It seemed Bink's talent was helping him compensate for the loss of the remaining Words. Maybe he wasn't being harmed, but just shifted to a more profitable mode, as the Words were highly variable in effect.

"I'll use this; you check the water for any other bottles." King Bink popped the cork, then hurled the bottle at the Mundane formation. The thing grew enormously, as was its nature, until it popped down on top of several Mundanes and squashed them flat.

Imbri found another bottle and fished it out with her teeth. She got some water in her mouth, and it still reeked of Skonk, but that was a necessary penalty. She brought the bottle to the King as the remaining Mundanes skirted the squash and advanced. He opened the bottle immediately and pointed it at the enemy.

A series of specks floated out from it. These expanded, becoming balls. On each ball a face formed, scowling awfully. One directed its glare at Imbri— and suddenly she was coated with grime.

"Oh, I see," the King said. "This is a bottle of dirty looks. Let's get them aimed properly." He reached out and turned each ball so that it faced the Mundanes.

The results were less than devastating, but more than inconvenient. The Punics turned dirty, their clothing badly soiled, their faces and arms gunked with grease and mud and sand. But they had been pretty dirty to begin with, so this was only an acceleration of a natural trend. They hacked and spit, trying to clear filth from their mouths. One aimed an arrow at King Bink, but the slime on his bow was such that the weapon twisted in his hand, fouling his shot. Another tried to draw a knife, but it was stuck in its holster, fastened by dirt and corrosion.

Imbri found two more bottles. One turned out to contain jumping beans. They bounded all over, peppering the Mundanes annoyingly; one man was blinded as the beans happened to score on his eyes, while another got one up his nose. That put him in immediate difficulty, since his nose bobbled about in response to the bean's continued jumping.

But six determined Punics remained, closing in on the King. The odds were still moderately prohibitive.

Bink opened the last bottle. A host of spooks sailed out. "Go get 'em!" the King ordered, and the spooks went after the Punics.

There ensued a fierce little battle. The spooks were supernatural creatures with vaporously trailing nether sections but strong clawed hands and grotesque faces. They pounced on the Mundanes, biting off noses, gouging for livers, and wringing necks. This was a reasonably pointless exercise, as spooks could not digest these tidbits, but old instincts died hard, and the Mundanes did find the approach somewhat disquieting. They fought back with swords and spears, lopping off limbs and transfixing faces. Blood flowed, ichor oozed, and bodies soon littered the ground.

As the sun dipped low, getting clear of the sky before night caught it, the mêlée subsided. All the spooks were gone; one Mundane remained standing.

It was Hasbinbad, the Punic leader, the toughest customer of them all.

"So you are the King of Xanth," Hasbinbad said. "You're a better Magician than I took you for. I knew the Transformer King was deadly dangerous, and I discovered the Thing-Talking King was tough, too; I certainly wanted no further part of the Zombie King, who turned my own dead against me, and the Information King knew entirely too much. But you had the reputation of possessing no magic, so I figured you'd be safe." He shrugged with grim good nature. "We all do make mistakes. I should have taken you out, too, to promote the Centaur King, who I know has no magic power in Xanth."

"You appear to know a great deal about Xanth and the nature of our government," King Bink said.

"And you know a great deal about Mundania, as you term the real world," Hasbinbad rejoined. "Men of age and experience do master the essentials rapidly. It is essential to survival in this business. When we first entered Xanth, I thought it was Italy, but when a roc-bird carried away one of my precious remaining elephants, I realized that something unusual was afoot. So I sent out my spies and in due course learned much of what I needed. I realized very soon that we would have to have magic to fight magic, so the deal we made with the Horseman was fortuitous. This is a better empire than Rome, and I intend to conquer it and become the eleventh King of this siege."

"You will have to deal with the fifth King first," Bink said.

"I intend to. All my committed army is gone, but so is all your magic. Now you must meet me my way, man to man, Mundane fashion. After I dispatch you, I shall return to my reserve force and conquer Xanth without further significant resistance." He advanced, sword ready.

Imbri moved to intercept the Mundane. One swift kick would—

"No," King Bink said. "This is my responsibility. I have borrowed Humfrey's bag of tricks; now it is time I do my own work. You stand clear." He drew his sword.

"Well spoken," Hasbinbad said, unimpressed. He held his own sword casually, obviously not unduly alarmed by the caliber of the opposition. He was, after all, well armored, while King Bink was not, and the Punic was sure of his own skill with the weapon. He was a man of war, while the man of Xanth was a recently drafted King, no warrior.

"There remains one detail you may have overlooked," Bink said, and now his expression was anything but amiable. "One of those Kings you had eliminated by the Horseman was my son." The sword glinted as he stalked the Mundane.

"Ah, your son," the Punic said, taken aback. "Then you have a blood motive." He scowled. "Yet it remains to be seen how much that counts against skill."

The two came together. Hasbinbad swung his blade; Bink countered expertly. "Ah, I see you have learned your craft after all," the Mundane said, becoming impressed. He made a feint, but failed to draw the King out of position.

Then Bink attacked, slicing at the Punic's left arm where the armor did not cover it. Hasbinbad countered, but still got nicked. "First blood!" he exclaimed, and parried with a vicious stroke of his own that did not score.

Bink's lack of armor now showed as an advantage, for there was no extra weight on him to tire him, and his skill was great enough to make armor unnecessary. He pressed Hasbinbad methodically, forcing the man to take defensive measures.

Then the Mundane drew back. "It grows dark," he panted. "I do not like to fight at night. I call for truce till dawn."

Imbri was alarmed. The Mundane was trying to gain time to recover his strength!

Bink shrugged. He had been among Mundanes, so was familiar with their odd customs. "Truce till dawn," he agreed.

Imbri swished her tail in frustration. This was surely folly!

Hasbinbad sheathed his sword and looked about. "I'm hungry," he said. "Want to trade some Mundane travel rations for some good grog? You natives know how to find free-growing juice without getting zapped by a tree, don't you?"

"Yes," Bink agreed.

"I don't like this," Imbri sent in a dreamlet. "That man is not to be trusted. The tide is receding; you can get away from him for the night."

"And risk losing track of him?" King Bink asked in the dream. "He still has half an army up north, and we have no means to stop it if it is competently led. I must deal with the leader now and not let him get away."

"You are honest; he is not. You must not trust him," Imbri urged.

"I know his nature," Bink returned gently.

"Are you conversing with the dream mare?" Hasbinbad inquired. "I'd like to have a steed like that myself. When we captured her up north, I did not know her nature; I'll not make that error again."

"This man knows entirely too much!" Imbri sent urgently. "Your Majesty, he is dangerous!"

"I will keep an eye on him," Bink promised. "You can travel readily at night; go inform the ladies at Castle Roogna of the developments of this day. This war is not over; we must raise new forces to deal with the second Mundane army."

He was the King; she had to obey. With severe misgivings, Imbri phased into nonmateriality and trotted across the ebbing water toward Castle Roogna. As she left, she heard Hasbinbad inquire: "Just who is to be King after the centaur? I thought you were out of Magicians. I inquire purely as a matter of professional curiosity."

"I am not in a position to know," Bink replied. "If I live, there will be no other Kings; if I die, I will not find out. How is it you know as much as we do about these matters?"

Hasbinbad laughed. If he answered, the words were lost in the distance as Imbri moved away. But both questions bothered her: how *did* the Punic know and, after Arnolde, who *would* be King? It seemed that both Xanth and Mundane forces accepted the prophecy that there would be ten Kings before the siege ended. But as was often the case, the specific unfolding of that prophecy was shrouded in alarming mystery.

Chapter 11

Centaur Input

I
mbri reached Castle Roogna quickly, for the baobab tree was not
far from it. She could readily have brought the King back here, had
he been willing to come. But he was determined to finish the action his way
and maybe he was right. Hasbinbad would be much more dangerous at the
head of his second army than he was alone.

The women were alert and worried. Tandy, the ogre's wife, had moved into
the castle, as it seemed she did not like being left alone while Smash guarded
it. Now that Imbri had seen first hand—technically, it was first hoof, but the
human folk would not understand that—the determination and savagery of
the Mundanes, she was sure that one ogre was not enough to stop a siege of
the castle. Quickly Imbri projected a broad dream that summarized the events
of the day, so that they all understood it.

Irene shook her head with sad resignation. Like her mother, she had recovered equilibrium after initial grief. This did not mean that she missed her husband and father less, but that she realized she had to do what she could to prevent the Kingdom of Xanth from being entirely destroyed. Her grief would keep; now was the time to fight. "Bink will not come back," she said. "He is too good a man; that's his fatal fault. I love him as I love my father, but I know him. He has never yielded to reasonable odds; he always follows his course, no matter what it costs. There is something of that quality in Dor, too . . ."

"And a great deal of it in Smash!" Tandy added. She was a girlishly small young woman, dark-haired and cute, hardly the type Imbri would have thought would be attracted to an ogre. But Imbri had interacted with her passingly before, and knew that she needed a really strong husband to protect her from the attentions of a demon. Certainly Smash was strong.

"Do you think we should prepare for the next King?" Queen Iris asked gently.

Imbri did not answer.

"I think so," Queen Irene agreed.

"Then we must impose on Imbri yet again to contact the centaurs," Iris said. She turned back to the mare. "Bink should have come back to organize things; since he did not, we women are forced to do what we can. If a centaur is to be our next King, the folk of Centaur Isle must be advised. They have resisted active participation in this campaign—foolishly, I think. Maybe they'll support one of their own in a way they declined to do for a human King." She sounded bitter.

"Not necessarily," Irene said. "They frown on magic talents in sapient species. They exiled Arnolde when his talent became known. They might treat him worse than a man."

"They exiled a centaur with magic. A centaur King of Xanth could be another matter. If we make the situation quite clear, they should come around. We know they are organized and ready; all they have to do is march."

"Make it clear?" Imbri sent in a query.

"That if they do not support us now, with all our faults as they perceive them, they will have to deal with our successors, the Punics. They have run afoul of Mundanes before, historically; I doubt they will relish the prospect."

"I'll go," Imbri sent. "I'll tell them tonight."

She set off, galloping south. She worried about King Bink, but knew he did not want her to return till morning; his peculiar sense of honor required him to win or lose his battle alone. So the best thing she could do was this, to help prepare Xanth for the next King. This was the stuff of which bad dreams were made; her duties had not changed as much as she had supposed!

The southern wilds of Xanth raced by, replete with garden-variety monsters and monstrous gardens. She had seldom been here because it was thinly populated, and thus few people needed dreams delivered. Now she was passing near the castle of the Zombie Master—

On an impulse she swerved. Millie the Ghost and her two children would be there alone, perhaps not even knowing the Zombie Master was ensorcelled. She had to stop by and say something, though there was little she could do.

She reached the castle, hurdled the gooky moat, penetrated the decrepit wall, and trotted into the clean main hall, where Millie was reading from a book titled *Weird Mundane Tales* to the children by the eerie glow of a magic lantern. All looked up as she entered.

"Imbri!" Millie exclaimed gladly.

"I just wanted to be sure you knew—" Imbri projected, but could not continue.

"We know," Millie said. "No one told us, but we knew when Chameleon left that it would soon be our turn. The chain has not yet been broken."

"You are taking it very well," Imbri sent.

"I was a ghost and Jonathan a zombie for eight hundred years," Millie said. "We have had a lot of experience with death and have learned to be patient. Jonathan has not returned as a zombie, so I know he isn't really dead. When the chain is broken, he will return." She had excellent perspective!

"Bink is King now, and after him will come Arnolde Centaur. Then there may be four more Kings before the chain is finally broken—but we don't know who they may be, for Xanth is out of Magicians."

"Who enchanted the Kings?" Millie asked. "Do you know yet?"

"The Horseman. King Humfrey named him, before he . . . The Punic Hasbinbad pretty much confirmed it."

"Is the Horseman a Magician?"

That made Imbri pause, horrified. "If he's a Magician, he might claim the throne of Xanth!"

"That was my thought," Millie said. "He helps the Mundanes conquer Xanth, then assumes the throne as the last Magician, ending the chain. By Xanth law, we would have to accept him."

"This is terrible!" Imbri projected. "He may be encouraging us to fight the Mundanes; then if he becomes King, he'll start ensorcelling the Mundane leaders so they can't fight any more. He is playing both sides against each other so that he can take over in the end. Beware the Horseman—the chain leads to him!"

"Unless we somehow break it before then," Millie said. She hugged her two children close to her, preventing them from becoming too frightened.

"I am going to Centaur Isle to ask them to support Arnolde when he is King," Imbri sent. "Maybe this will help convince them."

"Let's hope so," Millie said. "Don't let me detain you, Imbri; this is too important. But I do thank you for stopping by."

Imbri turned to go—and discovered an eye in the floor looking up at her, and a print where her hind feet had been, reading: THIS IS A HORSE'S REAR. The children were up to their usual tricks. She stepped over the eye and print and walked on through the wall.

She raced on south, glad she had made the side trip. As it happened, she had gained a valuable if horrible new insight in the process. She had known before that the Horseman was playing his own game, but had not thought of the consequence of his being recognized as Xanth's only surviving Magician. He could accomplish his fell purpose—if they didn't break that chain first. Reality was becoming even more like a bad dream.

It was a long way to the southern tip of Xanth. She had forgotten how much time it would take. It was midnight by the time she arrived. Then she remembered: she should have used the gourds! Her distraction had been such that she had never thought of the obvious!

That reminded her of Good King Humfrey's shame. What obvious thing had he overlooked that should so mortify him before the fact? The Horseman had sneaked up on him, true—but that had happened to every King of Xanth so far.

The centaurs of the Isle were mostly asleep. Imbri had to locate their leader quickly. She projected a dream to the mind of the first sleeper she encountered, a middle-aged female. "Who is your leader?"

"Why, everyone knows that," the centauress said. "Gerome, Elder of the Isle."

"Thank you."

"Since when does a dream thank a person?"

"Anything can happen in a dream."

Now Imbri used her night mare person-locating sense and homed in on Gerome. This centaur was old, his hair and coat beginning to turn gray. She shaped her dream carefully and sent it in to him.

In this dream, she was a female centaur, of middle age and dark of hide. "Elder Gerome, I bring important news," she began.

"Ah, you would be the night mare from Castle Roogna," he said, unsurprised. "We have been expecting you."

Obviously the centaur community had its own sources of information. Centaurs did employ magic; they just didn't like to recognize it in themselves. Those centaurs who developed magic talents were exiled; thus all the ones around Castle Roogna were not welcome here at the Isle. Yet this was the principal bastion of the species and this was where the real help had to come from. "Do you know, then, that Xanth is under attack by the Nextwave of Mundanes?"

"Of course."

"And that one of the human folk called the Horseman has been taking the minds of our Kings—Trent, Dor, the Zombie Master, Humfrey, and maybe Bink?" Imbri didn't really believe that last, but preferred to think of it that way rather than of death at the foul hands of Hasbinbad.

"Bink?"

"He is a human Magician whose talent has been concealed until recently."

"That is in order, then."

"But after him, the King of Xanth will have to be Arnolde Centaur."

"Now that is problematical," Gerome said. "We do not accept—"

"If we do not stop the Nextwave, it will conquer us, as have Waves of the past. You centaurs know what it is like when a new Wave rules Xanth."

Gerome sighed. "We do indeed! Better the obscenity we know than the one we may experience. Very well; we shall treat Arnolde as we might a human King, and answer his call if it comes."

"The Mundanes could overwhelm Castle Roogna before your force arrives," Imbri pointed out. "It would be better to march to Castle Roogna now, to be there at need."

Gerome shook his head. "We dislike this, but acknowledge the merit of the notion. We shall dispatch a contingent by raft in the morning. It will take two days for us to make port near Castle Roogna, and half a day to march inland. Will your forces be able to fend off the Wave until then?"

"Probably," Imbri replied in the dream. "Half the Mundane army has been destroyed; the other half should take two or three days to reach Castle Roogna."

"Very well. You have our guarantee. But there is a price."

"A price?"

"We have *de facto* local autonomy. We want it to become openly recognized by the government of Xanth, henceforth and for all time."

"If Arnolde becomes King, I'm sure he will grant you that."

"See that he does," Gerome said sternly.

That was that. Centaurs were creatures of honor, so she knew they would act as promised. Imbri withdrew from the centaur Elder's dream and let him sleep in peace. But she set a hoofprint in the dirt of his doorway so that he would remember her when he woke.

She trotted out, looking for a gourd patch. But there turned out to be none on the Isle; it seemed the centaurs had methodically stamped them out because of their devastating hypnotic magic. That was understandable but inconvenient. She would have known about this, had this been her beat for dream duty. Now she had either to spend time looking for a gourd on the wild mainland or to race for home directly.

She decided on the latter course. It took more time, but was less frustrating. She raced straight north, through trees and mountains, over lakes and bogs, under low-hanging clouds and the nose of a sleeping dragon, and up to Castle Roogna just as dawn sleepily cracked open an eye. It was good to race flatout for this distance; it made her feel young again.

Inside the castle, she gave her report. "They are sending a detachment, but they want autonomy."

"We can't make that decision," Queen Irene said. She was on duty while her mother slept, awaiting Chameleon's return. "Only the King can do that."

"It's time for me to rejoin King Bink anyway," Imbri sent. *If he still lives,* she thought nervously.

"Yes. He is my husband's father," Irene said. "Bring him back here, however you find him." She had aged rapidly in the past few days and looked more like her mother. Her eyes were deeply shadowed and there were lines forming about her face. She had the reputation of being a beautiful and well-developed girl; both qualities were waning now. Continued crisis was not being kind to her.

Imbri was tired, but she couldn't take time to rest. She trotted on out toward the baobab tree.

King Bink was not there, of course; he had left when the river flooded it out. Now there were only scattered Mundane bodies, forest debris, drying layers of mud, and occasional bottles. Imbri checked one of these, but found it was open, the cork lost, whatever had resided in it wasted, the penalty of the flood. The water was gone, but it would be long before the region recovered.

She made her way to the ridge that had been an island yesterday evening. She found the remnants of a camfire, with two empty T-cups from a T-tree and pots from a pot pie. Bink and Hasbinbad had eaten together. Then what?

Imbri checked for footprints. She sniffed the ground. She listened. She had acute equine senses. She picked up a trail of sorts.

King Bink had located a pillow bush and slept there. But Hasbinbad's traces came there, too. They were fresher; he had come later. The footprints were not straightforward, not those of one who came openly; they were depressed too much on the toes, scuffling too little sand. A sneak approach.

A sneak attack at night, before dawn. Both men gone. Imbri did not like this. Had the Punic leader treacherously . . . ?

But there was no blood. No sign of violence. Hasbinbad had sneaked up—but Bink had not been caught. He had moved away from his bed before that time, perhaps leaving a mock-up of himself behind.

Hasbinbad, it seemed, had attempted treachery, but Bink had anticipated him. The King had indeed been alert and understood the nature of his opponent. Imbri, working it out, was relieved. But what had happened then?

She quested and found two trails in the night. Bink following Hasbinbad. The wronged pursuing the guilty. The truce had been violated, relieving the King of any further need to be trusting, and now the fight had resumed in earnest. Bink had shown himself to be stronger in direct combat, yet had held back for what he deemed to be ethical reasons, without being naive. Hasbinbad had blundered tactically as well as ethically, and sacrificed any respite he might otherwise have claimed.

Imbri followed the trail with difficulty, knowing that she was losing headway. Bink and Hasbinbad had evidently moved rapidly in the predawn hour; Imbri was moving slowly, lest she lose the subtle traces. This was not ideal tracking terrain; there were rocky patches and boggy patches and the crisscrossing tracks of foraging animals, obscuring the human prints.

Her eye caught something in a hollow to the side. Imbri detoured briefly to investigate. It was a corked vial, containing yellowish vapor or fluid. Another of Magician Humfrey's spells, borne here by the transient tide, unbroken. What should she do with it? She did not want to leave it, but would have to carry it in her mouth. That would be awkward, especially if she happened to chew on it and break the glass. Suppose it was an ifrit? Still, there were many dangers in Xanth, and she might need the help of a spell. So she picked it up and carried it carefully with her lips.

The trail seemed interminable. Hours passed as the two men's traces bore north. Imbri was sure now: Hasbinbad wanted to get away, having found King Bink too much for him. The Punic was trying to rejoin his other army, the one nominally commanded by the Horseman, so he could lead another and more devastating thrust at Castle Roogna. The first army had eliminated the opposition; the second would complete the conquest.

There was a hiss. A flying snake was orienting on Imbri, feeling that its territory had been invaded. This was one of the wingless kind that levitated by pure magic, wriggling through the invisible columns of the air. It was a large one, twice Imbri's own length, and poisonous saliva glistened on its fangs. Probably Hasbinbad's passage had roused it, but Bink's presence had balked it. If magic could not harm the King, how could a magical creature? Bink could go anywhere in Xanth with perfect safety as long as he remained careful about nonmagical hazards. Perhaps, ironically, Hasbinbad had been protected by Bink's ambience, as Imbri herself had been protected when she stood close to him. Now it was her misfortune to encounter the serpent fully roused and by day, when she was vulnerable. Yet she could not detour around its territory; she would never be able to locate the fading trail again in time to do any good.

She hesitated, but the snake did not. It hissed and launched itself at her, jaws gaping. Involuntarily, Imbri bared her teeth, bracing for battle—and cracked the vial she had forgotten she held. Immediately she spit it out—but a trickle of fluid fell on her tongue. It was not yellow—that turned out to be the color of the glass—but colorless, and also tasteless. Plain water?

The snake struck, burying its fangs in her neck. Disaster! Imbri felt the poison numbing her, spreading outward much faster than had been the case when she had been bitten on the knee before. This was a larger, more deadly snake. How she hated snakes!

Imbri flung her head and lifted a forehoof, lashing at the snake's body, knocking it to the ground. The reptile hissed and struck at her again, but she stomped its head into the ground, killing it. The thing had been foolish to attack a fighting mare; horses knew how to deal with serpents. But Imbri herself had been critically slow, owing to fatigue and the distraction of the breaking bottle; otherwise the fangs would not have scored.

Now she assessed her situation. She had been bitten, but she was massive enough so that the poison might dilute to a nonfatal level by the time it spread through her body. If it happened to be a poor bite, and if this happened to be a mildly toxic variety of snake instead of a supertoxic one, she would survive. But she would certainly suffer, and would probably lose the trail.

Yet she didn't feel too bad. The numbness was constricting, retreating back around the puncture. Was her body fighting it off? How was that possible?

She had no special immunity; in fact, her condition should have been aggravated by the weapon released from the vial. Too bad it hadn't destroyed the snake!

Weapon? Imbri licked her lips, detecting a faint aftertaste. That was no weapon; that was healing elixir! No wonder she was not suffering; she had blundered into the universal restorative, the one thing that could counter the snake's bite and restore her waning energy. She had had the luck of King Bink!

Luck? In Bink's case it wasn't luck; it was his magic talent. She knew now that it had operated in some extremely devious ways to protect both his health and his anonymity all the prior years of his life. It could not be limited to his direct personal experiences; it had to extend back to affect whatever magic threatened him indirectly. Suppose he was in trouble, and magic was responsible—how would his talent counter the danger by seeming coincidence?

It could arrange to have the vial of elixir float conveniently near, for him to discover when the snake attacked. But the snake had not attacked him; it couldn't, because his magic prevented it more directly. So why the elixir, unused?

This could be operating on a more subtle level. Bink was threatened by a Mundane person—yet in the ambience of magic that was Xanth, Hasbinbad almost had to have had the benefit of some magic, because no one could avoid it here. So in a devious fashion, the threat against Bink was also magical, and therefore his talent would act to protect him against it. But extremely subtly, for this was a borderline case.

His talent just might arrange to have magical help come to him, to protect him from the Mundane. Maybe he would need healing elixir to abate a wound inflicted by Hasbinbad, so here it was. Imbri herself had become a tool of the King's magic, and was being deviously protected by that magic so she could fulfill her mission.

She checked the ground. By an amazing chance, the bottom section of the vial had dropped upright and nestled in the grass, containing some fluid.

Chance?

Imbri found the loose cork, picked it up delicately with her teeth, and set it in the ragged new neck of the vial. She tamped it carefully with her nose. It just fit, sealing in the precious fluid. There was no room remaining inside the truncated container for more than a few drops, but that didn't matter. The amount would be sufficient for its purpose, whatever and whenever that was. She had what King Bink would need.

She moved on, carrying the vial again, feeling more confident. She made better progress, and the trail began to warm. Still, she had a fair amount of time to make up.

It was midafternoon by the time she followed the trail to the Gap Chasm. Here there was a change. There were signs of a scuffle, and some blood soaked the ground, but there were no people.

She sniffed, explored, and formulated a scenario: Hasbinbad had, naturally enough, forgotten the Gap Chasm. Most people did. He had been suddenly balked, and King Bink had caught up. There had been a desperate fight, with one of them wounded—and one of them had fallen into the Chasm.

Anxiously she sniffed in widening half-spirals, since the Chasm was too deep at this point to show any sign of the victim within it, assuming the Gap Dragon had not already cleaned up the mess. Which man had survived? It should be the King, according to her revised theory of his magic—but she was not sure her theory was correct.

She found a trail leading away. Joy! It had the smell of Bink! There was blood on it, and the prints dragged, but the King had won the final contest. He was the lone survivor of this encounter with the Wave.

She followed it on to the west. Bink must be going to intersect the path to the invisible bridge across the Chasm so he could follow it safely back the other way to Castle Roogna. The path was charmed against monsters; Bink might not need that protection, but still, a path was easier to follow than the untracked wilderness, especially when a person was tired and hurt.

Imbri speeded up, no longer sniffing out the specific traces. Now she knew where he was going; she would catch up, administer the healing elixir, and give him a swift ride home. Maybe there had been yet another level to his power: it had preserved her from the flying snake so she could come and help him now, apart from the elixir, by becoming his steed. All would be well; King Bink had survived his campaign and should have centaur support for the next one. The centaurs were excellent archers; if they lined up on the south edge of the Gap, the Mundanes would never get across!

As she neared the invisible bridge, in the last hour of the day, she spied a figure. It was the King, resting on the ground. She neighed a greeting.

But as she came to him, her joy turned to horror. Bink was sitting unmoving, staring at the ground, in a puddle of blood from a wound in his chest. Was he dead?

Quickly she crunched through the piece of vial and smeared the dripping elixir across his wound with her nose. Instantly the gash healed and turned healthy, and the King's color improved. But still he did not respond to her presence, and when she sent him a dreamlet, she found his mind blank.

"But it can't happen to you!" she wailed protestingly in the dream, assuming the image of a weeping willow tree in deep distress. "You are the one person who can not be harmed by magic!"

Yet the fact belied the logic. King Bink had defeated one enemy physically, only to fall prey to the other magically. He had, after all, been taken by the Horseman.

It was night by the time she got him to Castle Roogna, draped across her back. A man might mount an unconscious horse, but it was another matter for a horse to cause an unconscious man to mount.

Arnolde and Chameleon had arrived fortuitously within the hour. The centaur had given her a ride, after the day horse had tired from the night's hard travel. Day horses were not night mares; they had to proceed carefully through darkness, instead of phasing through the vagaries of the terrain. The stallion had stopped at the brink of the Gap Chasm, too nervous to trust the one-way bridge.

"The one-way bridge?" Imbri sent, perplexed. "It is one-way north; how could you use it south?"

"We had to," Arnolde explained. "We knew the main bridge was out."

The answer was simple: Queen Iris had seen them coming, using an illusory magic mirror, and had sent old Crombie the soldier and his visiting daughter Tandy out to meet them. Tandy's husband the ogre had offered to go and hurl the folk across the Chasm, but they declined his helpful notion by pointing out that he was needed to guard Castle Roogna from surprise attack. Tandy had crossed first, making the bridge real before her, stopping just shy of the north anchor. Crombie had stopped just off the south end, keeping the bridge real between himself and his daughter. Arnolde and Chameleon had crossed safely while it was thus anchored. Had Grundy remained with them, they could have used the magic carpet to ferry across, one by one, but the golem had long since flown back to the Good Magician's castle to keep watch until the Gorgon returned with her sister the Siren. Actually, Arnolde confessed, he would hardly have trusted his mass to a carpet designed for human weight. Once the travelers had crossed, Crombie and Tandy had jumped to land at either end, letting the bridge fade. Tandy would walk around to the invisible bridge and return to Castle Roogna later in the night. The day horse, professing to be too tired to go farther, had settled in place to graze and sleep. They had not argued with him; Mundane creatures did tend to be nervous about things they could not see, and he had not wanted to admit his fear of the bridge.

"But Xanth isn't safe at night!" Imbri protested. She was displeased at the day horse's recalcitrance; he was a big, strong animal who should have been able to carry Tandy to the other bridge before retiring. He would have done so for Chameleon, or if Imbri herself had been along. But, of course, Mundane animals were neither the magical nor the social equals of Xanth animals; this was a reminder of that fact. It was useless to be angry at a Mundane creature for not being Xanthian.

"She is the wife of an ogre, and the path is enchanted; even a tangle tree would hesitate to bother her," Queen Iris said, a trifle grimly.

Imbri remembered how Smash the Ogre had torn up the Mundanes in combat. No one with any sense would antagonize an ogre! The Mundanes who had penetrated to this region had all been dispatched. So it was true: Tandy should be safe enough.

But that was the only light note. King Bink had been taken, and Xanth had a new King. Chameleon now had both a son and a husband to mourn. The grief that the Horseman had brought to Xanth in the name of his ambition for power!

"This development was not, unfortunately, unanticipated," Arnolde Centaur said in his didactic way as Queen Iris broached the matter of the crown. "As an archivist, I am conversant with the protocols. Xanth must have a Magician King. It is not specified that the King must be a man."

"He can be a centaur," Queen Iris agreed. "The framers of Xanth law did not anticipate a centaur Magician."

"Perhaps not," King Arnolde agreed. "They may also have overlooked the mischief wrought by the Horseman. That was not precisely my meaning, however. Where is the Council of Elders of human Xanth?"

"Roland is here," Queen Iris said. "Bink's father, Dor's grandfather. He is old and failing, but retains his mind. He was rousted from his home at the North Village when the Mundanes pillaged it. He can speak for the Elders, I'm sure."

"I must talk to him immediately."

They brought Roland, for the King had spoken. Roland was King Trent's age, still sturdy and erect, but he moved slowly and his sight was fading. In the years of relative calm during King Trent's rule, the Council of Elders had had little to do and had become pretty much ceremonial. Roland retained his magic, however; he could freeze a person in place.

"Roland, I have in mind a certain interpretation or series of interpretations of Xanth law," Arnolde said. "I would like your endorsement of these."

"Interpretations of law!" Queen Iris protested. "Why waste your time on such nonsense when there is a crisis that may topple Xanth?"

Arnolde merely gazed at her, flicking his tail tolerantly.

". . . your Majesty," she amended, embarrassed. "I apologize for my intemperate outburst."

"You shall have an answer in due course," the Centaur King said gently. "Roland?"

The old man's eyes brightened. This sounded like a challenge! "What is your interpretation, King Arnolde?"

Imbri noted how careful these people were being with titles, in this way affirming the strength and continuity of the Kingship, so vital to the preservation of Xanth.

"Xanth must have a King who is a Magician," the centaur said. "The definition of the term 'Magician' is obscure; I interpret it to mean a person whose magic talent is more potent by an order of magnitude than that of most people. This is, of course, a relative matter; in the absence of the strongest talents, the most potent of the remaining talents must assume the mantle."

"Agreed," Roland said.

"Thus, in the present circumstance, your own talent becomes—"

"Oh, no, you don't!" Roland protested vigorously. "I see the need to promote new talents to Magician status for the sake of the continuing succession of Kings, and I endorse that solution. But I am too old to assume the rigors of the crown!"

How very clever, Imbri thought. Of course Xanth would find its remaining Kings by this simple device! What a fine perception Arnolde had, and how well he was applying it to the solution of the crisis. It was certainly important that a person be designated to follow Arnolde as King, since Humfrey's prophecy indicated four Kings would follow the centaur. If Arnolde lost his position before attending to that matter, there would be chaos.

"Well, then, the talents of younger people. Irene, for example, should now be ranked a Sorceress, since her magic is certainly beyond the average, and our top talents are gone."

"True," Roland said. "I have privately felt she should have been diagnosed a Sorceress before; certainly her relative talent qualifies her now. But this will not profit the Kingdom, since she is a woman."

Queen Irene was upstairs with Chameleon and their unfortunate husbands; otherwise, Imbri knew, she would have been quite interested in the turn this dialogue had taken. Queen Iris, however, was reacting with amazed pleasure.

"In what way is the power of a Sorceress inferior to that of a Magician?" Arnolde inquired rhetorically.

"No way!" Queen Iris put in. This had been a peeve of hers for decades.

"No way," Roland echoed with a smile.

"Then we agree that the distinction is merely cosmetic," Arnolde said. "A Sorceress is, in fact, a female Magician."

"True," Roland acknowledged. "A Magician. The terminology is inconsequential, a lingering prejudice carrying across from prior times."

"Prejudice," Arnolde said. "Now *there* is a problematical concept. My kind is prejudiced against certain forms of magic; I have experienced that onus myself. Your kind is prejudiced against women."

"By no means," Roland objected. "We value and respect and protect our women."

"Yet you systematically discriminate against them."

"We do not—"

"Certainly you do!" Iris put in vehemently under her breath.

"I stand corrected," the centaur said with an obscure smile. "There is no legal distinction between the human sexes in Xanth."

"Well—" Roland said. He seemed to have caught on to something that Imbri and the Queen had not.

"Then you see no reason," Arnolde continued, "why a woman could not, were she in other necessary respects qualified, assume the throne of Xanth?"

Queen Iris stopped breathing. Imbri, now discovering the thrust of the Centaur King's progression, suffered a dreamlet of a cherry bomb exploding in realization. What an audacious attack on the problem!

Roland squinted at the centaur obliquely. He half chuckled. "You are surely aware that the throne of Xanth is by ancient custom reserved for Kings."

"I am aware. Yet does that custom anywhere define the term 'King' as necessarily male?"

"I have no specific recollection of such a definition," Roland replied. "I presume custom utilizes the masculine definition or designation for convenience, carrying no further onus. I suppose, technically, an otherwise qualified female could become King."

"I am so glad your perception concurs with mine," Arnolde said. Both men understood that they had just played out a charade of convenience, knowing the crisis of Xanth. "Then with the presumed approval of the Elders, I hereby, in my capacity and authority as King of Xanth, designate the line of succession to this office to include henceforth male and female Magicians." The centaur swung to focus through his spectacles on Queen Iris. "Specifically, the Magician Iris to follow me, and her daughter the Magician Irene to follow her, should new Kings of Xanth be required before this present crisis is resolved."

Again Roland smiled. "I concur. I believe I speak for the Council of Elders."

Queen Iris breathed again. Her face was flushed. A small array of fireworks exploded soundlessly in the air around them: her illusion giving vent to her suppressed emotion. She, together with all her sex, had just been at one stroke enfranchised. "One could get to like you, Centaur King."

Arnolde shrugged. "Your husband has always been kind to me. He provided me with a gratifying position when my own species cast me out. You yourself have always treated me with courtesy. But it is logic that dictates my decision, rather than gratitude. An imbalance has been corrected."

"Yes, your Majesty," she breathed, her eyes shining. In that moment Queen Iris resembled a beautiful young woman, like her daughter, and Imbri was not certain this was entirely illusion.

Arnolde turned to Imbri. "Now I must have a conference with you, good mare. I realize you are tired—"

"So are you, your Majesty," Imbri sent.

"Then let us handle this expeditiously so we both can rest before my brethren arrive."

"Of course," Imbri agreed, wondering what he had in mind. The play of his intellect had already dazzled her, and she knew he would be an excellent King, even though he could perform no magic in Xanth.

They retired to a separate chamber for a private conversation. Imbri wondered why Arnolde should wish to exclude the others, such as Queen Iris, who surely needed to be kept advised of official business.

"Does it strike you as odd that King Bink, who was immune to harm by magic, should nevertheless fall prey to the spell of the Horseman?"

"Yes!" Imbri agreed. "He should have been invulnerable! He believed he was! His talent was working with marvelous subtlety and precision. He wanted the Horseman to approach him, believing that—"

"Yet he evidently was not immune," Arnolde said. "Why should this be?"

"He was very tired after fighting Hasbinbad and getting wounded and dragging himself almost to the bridge path. Maybe his talent had been weakened."

"I question that. His talent was one of the strongest known in Xanth, though it *wasn't* known."

"Yet it failed to protect him from magical harm—"

"There is my point. Could it be that Bink was not actually harmed?"

Imbri glanced toward the room where the Kings were lying. "I don't understand. He *was* ensorcelled."

"You assume the enchantment was harmful. Suppose it was not? In that event, Bink would not be proof against it."

"But—" Imbri could not continue the thought.

"Let me approach the matter from another perspective," Arnolde said. "It strikes me that the symptoms of these ensorcelled Kings are very like the trance inspired by the hypnogourd."

"Yes!" Imbri agreed, surprised. "But there is no gourd."

"Now suppose the Horseman has the talent to form a line-of-sight connection magically between any two places," the centaur said. "Such as the eye of a King and the peephole of a gourd. Would that account for the observed effect?"

Imbri was astonished. "Yes, I think it would!"

"Then I suspect we know where to look for the missing Kings," Arnolde concluded. "Would you be willing to do that?"

"Of course!" Imbri sent, chagrined that she had not seen this obvious connection before.

"Rest, then. When you are ready, you may return to the gourd and investigate. Only you can do this."

"I must do it now!" Imbri sent. "If the Kings are there—"

"We still would not know how to get them out," the Centaur King finished. "We must be wary of exaggerating the importance of this notion, which perhaps is fallacious. This is why I have not mentioned it to the grieving relatives. I do not wish to deceive them with false expectations."

Imbri understood. "I shall say nothing to them until we know. Still, I must find out. I can rest after I know and after I report to you." She started out, using the door so as not to appear too excited to the others.

"That is very nice of you," Arnolde said.

Imbri almost bumped into the Mundane archivist, Ichabod, who was on his way in. He had evidently been summoned to the King's presence for another conference. Imbri understood why; Ichabod was Arnolde's closest friend in Xanth, possessing similar qualities of intellect and personality, together with his comprehensive knowledge of Mundanes. He would be an excellent person to discuss prospects with, since he could be far more objective about Xanth matters than the regular citizens of Xanth could. She sent him a dreamlet of friendly greeting, and Ichabod patted her on the flank in passing.

* * *

Imbri found the nearest gourd patch and dived into the World of Night. Because she was alone, there were no special effects. She trotted directly to the pasture of the Night Stallion.

He was waiting for her. "It's high time you checked in, you idiotic mare!" he snorted in an irate dream, the breeze of his breath causing the lush grass to curl and shrivel. "You were supposed to serve as liaison!"

"King Arnolde sent me," she replied, intimidated. "A lot has happened recently, and he—"

"Out with it, mare! Ask!"

"Have the lost Kings of Xanth—?"

"Right this way." The Stallion walked through a wall that abruptly appeared in the pasture, and she followed.

They came into a palatial, human-style chamber. There were all the Kings. King Trent was playing poker with Good Magician Humfrey and the Zombie Master. King Dor was chatting with the furniture, and King Bink, a recent arrival, was asleep on a couch.

"They're all right!" Imbri projected, gratified. "Right here in the gourd! Why didn't you send another night mare out to advise us?"

"It is not permitted," the Stallion replied. "To tell the future is apt to negate it, likewise to divulge what can not be known through natural channels. You were the designated channel; it had to flow through you. There was no other way to handle this situation without supernatural interference, so I had to stand aside and let it proceed undisturbed. All I could safely do was try to warn Xanth about the Horseman."

Imbri snorted. "That didn't make much difference!"

"Precisely. The future was not spoiled, because people seldom believe the truth about it. It shall not be spoiled, though critical revelations remain to be unveiled. Now that a King of Xanth has figured out the riddle of the Kings, that information is no longer privileged. Perhaps he will figure out the rest in time to save Xanth. I leave you to it." He paused, giving Imbri a meaningful stare. "Still, beware the Horseman."

"I *am* wary of him!" Imbri protested. But the Night Stallion walked back through the wall and was gone, leaving her with the uncomfortable feeling that she was missing something vital, as she had done before. Yet what more could she do except watch out for the Horseman and not trust him at all?

The three Kings quickly concluded their poker game—the Magician of Information, naturally, seemed to be well ahead, and had a pile of oysters, bucksaws, and wilting lettuce to show for it—and turned to Imbri. "How goes it Xanthside?" King Trent inquired politely, as if this were a routine social call.

"Your Majesty," Imbri sent, still halfway overwhelmed by this discovery of the lost Kings. "Do you want the whole story?"

"No. Only since Bink was taken. We know it to that point."

Imbri sent out a dream that showed her search for King Bink, their return to Castle Roogna, the ascension of Arnolde Centaur, and his solution of the riddle of Kings and designation of Queen Iris and Queen Irene as the next Kings.

"Marvelous!" the Zombie Master exclaimed. "That is one sensible centaur!"

"That accounts for two Kings to follow him," Humfrey said. "But there is supposed to be a line of ten. Who are the other two?"

King Dor joined them. "The Dark Horse knows," he said. "But he won't tell."

"He is right not to tell," the Zombie Master said. "We must figure it out for ourselves. Only then can we break the chain and finally save Xanth."

"Is there no way to get you back to Xanth?" Imbri asked.

"Not while the Horseman is free," Humfrey answered. "I believe the only way to stop him from enchanting people is to end his life—but even he may not be able to reverse a line of sight he has made. It seems to be a limited talent, one-way, like the one-way bridge across the Chasm. He is not Magician caliber."

"Yet what mischief he causes!" the Zombie Master exclaimed. "As long as a single gourd exists, his power remains. Perhaps we are lucky he did not strike years ago."

"He probably did not know about the gourds," Humfrey said. "Many people don't."

"The gourds!" Imbri sent, appalled. "*I* told him about the gourds, or at least about the World of Night. He thought the gourd was merely an oddity, but after he knew its nature—*I* showed him how to imprison the Kings!"

"This is the nature of prophecy," King Trent said philosophically. "You carried the message, but did not understand the nature of the threat. None of us did. You are no more culpable than the rest of us. You have certainly done good work since, and your Night Stallion seems to feel that you hold the key to the final salvation of Xanth."

"Me!" Imbri sent, astonished.

"But we do not know in what way," Good Magician Humfrey said. "This is an aspect of information that has been denied to me, along with the specific nature of my own colossal folly. Perhaps it is simply in your position as liaison. I dare say the wives will be pleased to know we remember them."

Dor laughed. "Mine may say good riddance! I certainly didn't pay her much attention after we married."

"She won't sulk long," King Trent said. "My daughter is a creature of femalishly mercurial temperament, like my wife." Then he did a double take. "My wife! I referred to Queen Iris!"

Humfrey elevated an eyebrow. "After a quarter century, it's about time, Trent. You can't live in the past forever."

Imbri remembered how King Trent had loved his Mundane wife, not the Queen, and the sorrow this had brought to Iris.

"It may be a bit late for such a revelation, but yes, it is true. It is time to relate to the present, without renouncing the past. Iris has been worthy."

King Trent returned his attention to Imbri. "Please convey that message, Mare Imbri."

Imbri was happy to agree. Then she turned to Humfrey. "How did the Horseman get you and Bink?" she asked the Good Magician. "You recognized him, so should have known how to stop him, and Bink is supposed to be immune from hostile magic."

"That was perhaps part of my blunder," Humfrey said. "I paid so much attention to setting up my spells that I did not see him enter the tree. Suddenly he was standing there. I only had time to whisper his identity before he zapped me. Had I been alert, as I should have been, I could have had a Word of Power ready—" He shook his head, ashamed.

"When did he come?" Imbri asked.

"As I said, I was not paying attention, but I would guess very soon after you and the day horse left. He must have been lurking in hiding, waiting his chance to catch me alone. The cunning knave!"

"And Bink—how did he—?"

"Bink was not harmed by the magic," Humfrey replied, confirming the centaur's diagnosis. "He was only sent to a new awareness, as were the rest of us. We find our present company quite compatible. Therefore his talent was not operative."

Except to the extent of preserving her to rescue Bink's body, Imbri realized. The protective talent had a narrow definition of Bink's welfare; he was in actual physical danger while he was King, and in none thereafter. So it did make sense, though Xanth itself suffered. At least his banishment to the gourd had enabled his successor Arnolde to solve the riddle.

"How can I help?" Imbri asked.

"Just what you plan," the Zombie Master told her. "Liaison. Bear news to the wives. Perhaps we shall have useful advice on the conduct of the war. Tell whatever King is current to request our input if he desires it."

"Or she," Imbri sent. "Queen Iris will be the next King."

The Kings exchanged glances. "We are no longer in direct touch with the situation," Humfrey said. "Perhaps it is best to leave the matter of governance to the centaur; he seems remarkably competent."

"Send my love to my mother and my wife," Dor said sadly. He formed a wan smile. "I'll convey the message to my father myself," he added, glancing at the sleeping Bink.

Imbri bade farewell to the five Kings and set off again for the real world.

She arrived at Castle Roogna near midnight. Some of the people were awake, some asleep. It made no practical difference; she broadcast her glad dream to all. "The Kings are all in the gourd! They are well! They send their love!"

Those who were awake crowded close; those who were asleep woke abruptly. In a moment Imbri was the center of attention. She dispensed all the messages, including King Trent's to the Queen.

Iris seemed stricken. "He said that?" she asked, unbelieving.

"That it is time to live in the present, and you are his wife," Imbri repeated.

"Oh, Mother!" Irene cried, going to Queen Iris and embracing her. "You have become part of the family!" It seemed a strange comment, but Imbri understood its meaning. The tragedy of Xanth was bringing its incidental benefits. Imbri retreated to the castle gardens, where she relaxed, grazed, and slept, catching up on about two days' activity.

Tandy returned safely in the night and was reunited with her ogre husband, who had been pacing the grounds worriedly, idly tearing weed-trees out of the ground and squeezing them into balls of pressed wood. It was a nervous mannerism of his. But all seemed reasonably well for the moment.

In due course the centaur contingent landed, having made excellent time, and Imbri went to lead them in to Castle Roogna. She had thought Chem or Chet would prefer to do it, since they were centaurs, but this was not the case. Chet and Chem were magic-talented centaurs, and the conventional centaurs would not associate voluntarily with their ilk. Chet had actually visited Centaur Isle once; but though he had been treated with courtesy, he had soon gotten the underlying message and had never visited again. In certain respects the separation between magic and non-magic centaurs was greater than that between Xanth human beings and Mundanes. Thus Imbri, no centaur at all, was a better choice; she could keep the pace, she knew the way, and they didn't care if she had magic. In fact, they held her kind in a certain muted awe, since a mare had been the dam of their species. They revered true horses, while not being unrealistic about their properties.

She met them at the beach. The centaurs used magic-propelled rafts that were seaworthy and quite stout. They certainly weren't shy about the use of magic in its proper place. There were exactly fifty of them, all fine, healthy warriors with shining weapons and armor. Imbri wondered whether fifty were enough to handle three hundred Mundanes, however.

"We are centaurs," their leader said proudly, as if that made the question irrelevant. He did not deign to introduce himself. The arrogance of these warriors was unconscious, and she did not allow it to disturb her. She led the contingent to Castle Roogna by nightfall.

"Thanks to the very kind and competent assistance of Ichabod and Queen Iris," Arnolde reported, "we have located the second Mundane army. He analyzed their likely course, and her illusion can project her image briefly to almost any region of Xanth, so that she can see the enemy." It seemed that Queen Iris was going all-out to help the Centaur King, being quite grateful to him on more than one count. "The Horseman is with them, south of the Ogre-fen-Ogre Fen. We do not know how he reached them so rapidly. He did have two days to travel, which would be enough for a healthy and able man who knew the route—but he must have crossed some of the wildest terrain of Xanth to get there. I checked it on Chem's map; there are flies, dragons, goblins, griffins, and ogres, as well as virtually impassable natural regions. I must confess I am at a loss even to conjecture how he managed it."

Imbri shared his confusion. She had been to those regions of Xanth and knew how difficult they were. The Lord of the Flies took his office seriously and was apt to have intruders stung to death, and the other creatures were no less militant. "He must have used his talent to stop any hostile creatures, and maybe to cow a griffin into transporting him. He is a very efficient rider; he can tame anything with his reins and spurs." Oh, yes, she knew!

"That must be it. At least he is no present threat to us here." Arnolde did not comment on the implication that the Horseman believed the Centaur King would be ineffective, therefore was not worth sending to the gourd. Imbri suspected the Horseman had made a bad mistake there.

The centaurs of the Isle contingent declined to enter Castle Roogna. They camped in the gardens, foraging for fruit from the orchard and pitching small tents. They did not need these for themselves so much as for their supplies. "Tell us where the Mundanes are," their leader said coldly. "We shall march there in the morning and dispatch them."

Imbri showed him the enemy location in a dreamlet map, since Chem was not encouraged to approach with her more detailed magic map. The prejudice of the Centaur Isle centaurs against their talented brethren was implacable.

"They are in ogre territory?" he asked, surprised. "The ogres of the fen are wild and hostile; how could mere Mundanes have bested them?"

"These are very tough Mundanes," Imbri explained. "They beat back the Gap Dragon in the Chasm."

"The what in the where?"

It was that forget-spell operating again. "A ferocious monster in a crevice," she sent.

The centaur was unimpressed. "Any of us could do that. More likely the Mundanes made a deal with the ogres, promising them plunder if they joined the invasion."

"Such deals occur," Imbri agreed, determined not to be antagonized. "Such as the promise of autonomy—"

"Are you attempting humor, mare?" he demanded coldly. It seemed the centaurs' reverence for horses had limits. King Arnolde had immediately granted the Isle centaurs local autonomy, remarking that it made no practical difference, but they did not express overt appreciation. Certainly this particular centaur remained prickly!

"Of course not," Imbri demurred, keeping her ears forward and her tail still. She was getting better at such discipline. Social politics made her master new things. "I merely fear that we may be up against more than Mundanes. When the human King of Xanth sought help from the other creatures, most expressed indifference, feeling that it was a human-folk war, not theirs. So there could be a tacit understanding with the Mundanes, in which the Punic army is allowed to pass through monster territory without impediment, provided no damage is done in passing. It is also possible that some animals chose to ally themselves with the Mundanes. In fact, their current leader, the Horseman, did that; he is a Xanthian turncoat."

The centaur spat to the side, contemptuous of any kind of turncoat. "We'll handle it," he decided, with what she hoped was not an unwarranted confidence. "Now leave us; we shall march at dawn."

Imbri retreated to the castle. Chameleon was up and alert now, less pretty and more potent mentally, restored from her grief by the news that her husband and son were well, if enchanted. "Imbri—do you think you could carry a person into the gourd to visit the Kings?"

Imbri paused, considering. "I suppose I could. I hadn't thought of it. Mostly it is only the spirit of a person that goes into the gourd, but I have been carrying people through on the way to far places. I could take you to see your family."

"Oh, I don't mean me, though I certainly would have been tempted in my other phase. I mean Irene."

"Irene?"

"She and Dor were married just before he became King and had to master the rigors of Kingship and take over the campaign against the Mundanes and go to battle. He never had a moment to himself unless he was sleeping. So she was widowed, as it were, almost before she was married."

Oh. Imbri had a little trouble getting adapted to the woman's more intelligent thought processes, for she had been acclimated to the slow, pretty version. But it was true. There had been no wedding night. Imbri knew that sort of thing was important to human people. It was like coming into season and being walled off from the stallion. "I will take her to him," Imbri agreed. "Tonight, before anything else happens."

Chameleon fetched Irene. "Dear, Imbri has somewhere to take you."

The girl shook her head. "I can't leave Dor. You know that. If anything happened to his body, he would never be able to return."

She didn't know! It was to be a surprise.

"I really think you should go, Irene," Chameleon said. "It will do you good to leave the castle for a while. Things may get harder later. I will watch Dor for you."

Irene sighed. She could not refuse Dor's mother the chance to sit by his body. "You're probably right. Very well, I'll take a ride. This time." She mounted Imbri, and they set off.

It was not yet dark, so Imbri took her time, circling the centaur camp and going to the gourd patch indirectly. She could not safely enter the gourd until night.

"Do you know, it *is* good to get out," Irene confessed, looking about. "I haven't ridden a night mare before. Do you really phase through trees and boulders?"

"I really do, at night," Imbri sent, but did not amplify.

"I've been meaning to thank you for all you have done," Irene continued, brightening as the mood of the evening infused her. "You have taken Chameleon everywhere and made things so much easier for Dor."

"We all must do what we can." This reminded Imbri that she was supposed in some way to hold the key to the salvation of Xanth. If only her role were clearer! All she could do now was continue from hour to hour, trying to improve things in little ways. Was that enough? She doubted it.

"Yes," the girl agreed. "All I've been able to do is sit and wait. I curse myself for a fool; I had so many years I could have married Dor and I just waited, thinking it was a sort of game. Now that it's too late, I realize—" She stopped, and Imbri knew she was stifling tears.

There was no point in deception. "I am taking you to him now," Imbri sent.

"Now? But—"

"Inside the gourd. With your father and the other Kings. A visit. But you must return with me before dawn, or you, too, will be trapped in the world of the gourd."

"I can go there? For a few hours?" Comprehension was coming.

"For a few hours," Imbri agreed.

"And I will be real? I mean, I'll seem solid, or the Kings will? Not just diffuse spirits?"

"Yes. Some creatures are there in spirit, some in body. When I enter the gourd, my magic accommodates; it is all right. No one except a night mare can travel physically in and out of the gourd—except those in contact with a phased-out night mare."

"Then by all means, let's go!" Irene exclaimed, gladdening.

Now it was dark. Imbri came to the gourd patch and plunged into the nearest ripe peephole. The rind passed behind them; they then phased through another wall and into the graveyard, where skeletons roamed. One skeleton waved to Imbri in greeting; then she trotted on into the chamber the Night Stallion had reserved for the visiting Kings.

The Kings were alert and waiting, having somehow anticipated this visit. "Irene!" King Dor cried happily.

Irene greeted her father and Dor's father, then turned to Dor. She frowned attractively. "You can't skip out this time!" she said. "We started our marriage in a graveyard, and we'll consummate it in a graveyard."

"The skeletons wouldn't like that," he murmured.

"The skeletons don't have to participate." But she yielded to the extent of allowing Imbri to show them to a private chamber filled with pillows. As Imbri left, they had a full-scale pillow fight going.

Imbri now retired to the graveyard for some good grazing. One of the graves began to shake and settle, but she squealed warningly at it and it desisted. Imbri did not take any guff from graves, just grass.

Well before dawn, Xanthside—dawn never came to the World of Night, naturally—she returned to the chamber of Kings. Dor and Irene were there, talking with the others, looking happy. A number of pillows were scattered about; it seemed the pillow fight had spread, as conflicts tended to. Everyone appeared satisfied.

Irene looked up and saw the mare. "Oh, it's time to go, or Mother will know what mischief I was up to!" she exclaimed. She brushed a pillow feather from her hair, gave King Dor a final kiss, and went to Imbri.

They moved on out, emerging from the gourd before the sun climbed from its own nocturnal hiding place. The sun was afraid of the dark, so never appeared before day came. "Oh, Imbri!" Irene exclaimed. "You've made it so nice, considering . . ."

Considering that the Kings were still prisoners and Xanth was still under siege by the Mundanes. Imbri understood. This had been no more than an interlude. "We must rescue the Kings soon," Imbri sent. "Before their bodies suffer too much from hunger."

"Yes," Irene agreed. "We have to capture the Horseman—soon."

They returned to Castle Roogna. King Arnolde was alert. "Are you rested, Imbri?" he inquired.

Imbri replied that she was; the cemetery verdure was marvelously rich, and her hours of quiet grazing and sleep within the familiar gourd had restored her to full vitality. Perhaps, too, her part in facilitating Irene's reunion with her father and husband had buoyed her half spirit. She was only sorry she had missed the pillow fight.

"Then I must ask you to lead the centaurs to the Mundanes," the King said. "They are not conversant with the specific route, and we don't want them to fall prey to avoidable hazards. I would do it myself, or have Chet or Chem do it, but—"

Imbri understood. The Centaur Isle troops still refused to deal directly with the obscenely talented centaurs. She couldn't approve of their attitude, but knew that there were few creatures as stubborn as centaurs. It was best to accommodate them without raising the issue; they were, after all, here to save Xanth from the ravage of the Nextwave. "I will take them there," she agreed. "Where exactly are the Mundanes now?"

"They are proceeding south, skirting the regions of Fire and Earth, passing the land of the goblins. We sent news to the goblins of the Mundane threat, and they promised to organize for defense, but we're not sure they've gotten beyond the draft-notice stage. We don't even know whether we can trust them. It is difficult to intimidate goblins, but the Mundanes are extremely tough. In past centuries goblins were a worse menace than Mundanes, but they were more numerous and violent then. Chem says she knows one of them, a female named Goldy who possesses a magic wand—but I prefer caution."

Imbri went to join the centaurs, who were organizing efficiently for the march. At dawn their tent stables were folded and packed away.

Imbri led them north along the path to the invisible bridge across the Gap. They were amazed; they had no prior knowledge of this immense Chasm, thanks to the forget-spell on it. They trotted in single file across the bridge and soon were able to regroup on the north side.

Guided by her memory of the map Chem had formed for her before she left, Imbri led the centaurs through the land of the flies; they had suitable insect repellent and knew how to cut through the flypaper that marked the border. The flies buzzed angrily, but could not get close; the repellent caused them to bounce away, no matter how determinedly they charged.

The centaurs were able travelers, and progress was swift. Imbri led them to the fringe of the dragons' territory. "Do not menace the dragons," she sent in a general dreamlet. "I will explain to them." And when the first dragon came, she sent it an explanatory dream, showing brute human folk fighting half-human folk, both of whom might turn against reptile folk at the slightest pretext. The dragon retreated. Dragons were cautious about armed manlike creatures, especially in this number. They had experienced the depredations of magic-talented men and knew how well centaurs could fight. It was better to be patriotic and let the war party cross in peace.

Still, there were pauses along the way, for centaurs had to eat and lacked the ability to graze. More and more it was apparent to Imbri that any deviation from the straight equine form was a liability. The centaurs had to consume huge amounts of food to maintain their equine bodies, but it all had to be funneled through their inadequate human mouths. Fortunately, they had brought concentrated supplies along, but it remained inefficient business.

The route was not straightforward. Between the dragon country and the goblin country there was a jagged mountain range, projecting west into the region of earthquakes; they had to skirt the mountains closely to avoid getting shaken up.

It was there, in the late afternoon, that the Mundanes ambushed them. Imbri cursed herself for not anticipating this—but of course she was not a mind reader, so could not discover their nefarious plots. She only projected dreams and communicated with people by putting herself into those dreams. Had she known the Mundanes were close—but she had not known. She *should* have known, though. She realized this now, for the Mundanes had been marching south; naturally the centaur contingent would encounter them south of the location King Arnolde had described.

The centaurs fought back bravely, but were caught. The Mundanes rolled boulders down the near slope of the mountain, forcing the centaurs to retreat into the region of earthquakes. That was disaster, for the ground cracked open with demoniac vigor and swallowed a number of them whole. The carnage was awful. In moments only ten centaurs remained, charging back out of the trap. Most of them had been wiped out before they could even organize for defense.

But as soon as the centaurs were clear, they halted, consulted, and moved slowly back toward the Mundanes. "What are you doing?" Imbri demanded in a dreamlet.

"Now we have sprung the trap; we shall destroy the enemy," a
replied.

"But there are several hundred Mundanes, protected by the terrain
be slaughtered exactly as your companions were!"

The stubborn creatures ignored her. Weapons ready, they advan
battle.

"This is folly!" Imbri projected, sending a background image of an a
centaurs being washed away by the tide of a mighty ocean. "At least
until darkness; then you can set an ambush of your own. At night I w
able to scout out the enemy positions—"

They walked on, stiff-backed, refusing to be dissuaded from their set co
by marish logic. Centaurs were supposed to be very intelligent, but t
simply did not readily take advice from lesser creatures.

Imbri hung back, knowing she could not afford to throw away her life w
theirs. She had to admire the centaurs' courage in adversity, but also had
disassociate herself from it. She had to return to Castle Roogna to report (
the disaster, in case Queen Iris had not picked it up by means of her illusio

Yet Imbri remained for a while, hoping the centaurs would become sens
ble. They did not; as the Mundanes gathered and charged to attack th
centaur remnant, the ten stalwart creatures exchanged terse commands and
brought their bows to bear. There were now twenty times as many enemy
warriors on the field as centaurs, and more men in reserve; obviously the
Punics believed this was a simple mop-up operation.

It was not. For all their folly, the centaurs were well-trained fighting creatures, with excellent armor and weapons, who now knew exactly what they
faced. Their unexcelled archery counted heavily. In a moment ten arrows
were launched together, and ten Mundanes were skewered by shafts through
their eyes. Even as they fell, another volley of arrows was aloft, and ten more
went down. Every single centaur arrow counted; no target was missed or
struck by more than a single arrow and no Mundane armor was touched. In
the face of marksmanship like this, armor was useless. Imbri was amazed.

The Mundanes, belatedly realizing that they faced real opposition, hastily
formed into a phalanx, their shields overlapping protectively. Still, they had
to peek between the shields to see their way—and through these crevices
passed the uncannily accurate arrows. The leading Mundanes continued to
fall, and none who fell rose again. Now Imbri realized that Chet, a young
centaur, had not yet fully mastered his marksmanship; otherwise he would
have needed no more than a single arrow per Mundane when he had opposed
them on the Chasm bridge. What an exhibition this was!

But once committed to this course of battle on the field, the Punics were as
stubborn as the centaurs. They maintained their phalanx, stepping over their
fallen comrades, and closed on the centaurs. More of them fell, of course, but
the rest pressed on. By this time the centaurs' arrows were running out. It was
coming to sword conflict—and the Mundanes still outnumbered the centaurs
ten to one.

Had all fifty centaurs avoided the ambush, Imbri realized, they could have destroyed the entire Mundane army without a loss. Their confidence had not been misplaced. Of course, the Mundanes would not have met them on the open field if they had been aware of the marksmanship they faced, so it might have been more even. As it was, the centaur disaster had been followed by the Punic disaster; forty centaurs and a hundred Mundanes were dead. And there might still be a good fight—but the centaurs would surely lose, for swords were not as distant and clean as arrows. Imbri turned and galloped away, feeling like a coward but knowing this was what she had to do.

A goblin stepped out before her, waving his stubby arms. Imbri screeched to a halt. "Who are you?" she sent.

"I am Stunk," he said. "You brought me a bad dream once—and then it came true. I got drafted. I should have fled Goblin Land when I had the chance."

After a moment, Imbri remembered. Her last delivery—the one that had shown her inadequacy for the job. "But the goblins didn't fight!"

"All we did was guard our mountain holes," he agreed. "But Goldy, girl-friend of a chief, sent me to intercept you. She says some of her friends are on the human side, so she wants to help—but she's the only one who will. So if the folk at Castle Roogna need her, come and get her. She does have the magic wand and a lot of courage."

"I will relay the message," Imbri sent.

Stunk saluted, and Imbri flicked her tail in response. The goblin turned north, while she continued south. Apparently getting drafted was not nearly as bad in life as in a dream. Of course, it was Stunk's fortune that the goblins had avoided actual combat with the Mundanes.

Night closed. She located a gourd patch and plunged into a peephole. It was too bad she couldn't use this avenue by day; she might conceivably have been able to fetch help for the centaurs in time to do them some good. But if she could not use the hypnogourds by day, at least they could not harm her as they did other creatures. She was a denizen of the gourd world, immune to its effect; but it was pointless to approach a gourd when she couldn't use it.

The Horseman, she remembered—he had actually used the gourd to eliminate the Kings. So if he tried to wield his talent on her, he would fail, and she could destroy him. That, too, was good to know, because she did want to destroy him.

She galloped through the familiar reaches of the dream world. It occurred to her that she could report to the five prisoned Kings on the way and perhaps receive their advice to relay to King Arnolde. She was supposed to serve as liaison, after all. So she detoured toward that section. She wondered briefly whether it would be possible for her to carry one or more of the Kings out, to rejoin his natural body. She had done that for Smash the Ogre once. But she realized immediately that she could not, because she did not know the specific channel that had brought each King into the gourd. Any King she brought out would continue to exist as a phantom; his body would remain

inert. There was nothing but frustration to be gained by that. She had to locate the particular channel that connected the Kings to a particular gourd; only the Horseman knew that key. Naturally he would not give that information simply for the asking.

She entered the chamber of the Kings—and skidded to a halt, appalled.

"Yes, it is I," Arnolde said. "I, too, have now been taken."

Imbri projected a flickering dreamlet, stammering out her news of the fate of the centaurs. This was worse even than that, since the Horseman was still taking out the Kings as fast as they could be replaced. She had thought the Horseman was with the Mundane army, but evidently he hadn't stayed there long.

"It seems that every time a King shows competence," King Trent said, "the Horseman takes him out. At such time as Xanth enthrones an incompetent King, he will surely be allowed to remain until the enemy is victorious. Meanwhile, Imbri, kindly do us the favor of informing my wife, the Sorceress Iris, that she is now King."

"Queen . . ." Imbri sent, numbed.

"King," he repeated firmly. "Xanth has no ruling Queens."

"With my apologies for misjudging the location of the Horseman," Arnolde added. "I told Iris to sleep, since there was no present menace to me. Evidently I was mistaken."

Evidently so, Imbri had to agree. She nodded and trotted on out, feeling heavy-hoofed. When would it end?

Chapter 12

𝕶ing 𝕼ueen

She reached Castle Roogna, unconscious of the intervening journey. The palace staff was sleeping, including the Queens.

Imbri approached Queen Iris and sent her a significant dream: "King Arnolde has been taken; you must assume the Kingship, your Majesty."

"What? Arnolde was quite alert a moment ago!" Iris protested.

"You have slept some time, King Iris."

"King Iris!" the Queen exclaimed, wrenching herself awake. She lurched to her feet and stumbled to the King's apartment. "King Centaur, I just had a bad dream—"

She stopped. Arnolde stood there, staring blankly.

"It's true!" Iris whispered, appalled. "Oh, we should have guarded him more closely!"

"I met him in the gourd," Imbri sent. "He agreed you must be King now. King Trent said it, too. And I have bad news to report to the King."

Iris leaned against the wall as if feeling faint. She was no young woman, and recent events had not improved her health. Only her iron will to carry on as a Queen should had kept her going. "All my life I have longed to rule Xanth. Now that it is upon me, I dread it. Always before I had the security of knowing that no matter how strong my desire, it would never be fulfilled. Women don't really want all the things they long for. All they really want is to long and be longed for. Oh, whatever will I do, Imbri? I'm too old and set in my ways to handle a dream turned so horribly real!"

"You will fight the Mundanes, King Iris," Imbri sent, feeling sympathy for the woman's predicament.

The King's feminine visage hardened. "How right you are, mare! If there's one thing I am good at, it is tormenting men. Those Mundanes will rue the day they invaded Xanth! And the Horseman—when I find him—"

"Stay away from him, your Majesty!" Imbri pleaded. "Until we unriddle the secret avenue of his power, no King dare approach him."

"But I don't need to do it physically! I can use my illusion on him."

Imbri was doubtful, but let that aspect rest. "He may be close to Castle Roogna," she sent. "We thought he was up in Goblin Land . . ."

"He *was* in Goblin Land!" King Iris cried. "I saw him myself only yesterday!"

"But he must have been here to take out King Arnolde."

"Then he found a way to travel quickly. He's probably back with his army by now. I can verify that soon enough." She took a deep breath. "Meanwhile, let's have your full report on the war situation. If I am to do this job, I'll do it properly. After it is over, I shall be womanishly weak, my foolish hunger for power having been expiated, but I can't afford that at the moment."

Imbri gave the report to her, then retired to the garden pasture on the King's order and grazed and rested. She liked running all over Xanth, but it did fatigue her, and she wished it wasn't always because of a new crisis.

In the morning King Iris had her program ready. She had devised a very large array of illusory monsters, which she set in ambush within the dragons' terrain, awaiting the Mundanes' southward progress. The real dragons took one look at the VLA and retreated to their burrows, wanting none of it.

In midmorning the Punic army appeared, still two hundred strong, marching in disciplined formations. Imbri saw that a number of the soldiers were ones who had not participated in the battle with the centaurs; apparently about fifty had held back or been on boulder-rolling duty; these had filled in for the additional fifty the centaurs had wiped out in the final hand-to-hand struggle. An army of three hundred fifty—slightly larger than the Xanth intelligence estimate had thought—had been reduced to somewhat better than half its original size in the course of that single encounter. If only she, Imbri, had been alert to the ambush, so that all fifty centaurs could have fought effectively! But major errors were the basic stuff of war.

King Iris had somehow gotten the magic mirror to work again, perhaps by enhancing its illusion with her own, and focused it on the Mundane army, so Imbri and the others were able to watch the next engagement. An audience was very important for Iris; her sorcery of illusion operated only for the perceiver.

First to pounce were two braces of sphinxes. Each had the head and breast of a man or woman, the body and tail of a lion, and the wings of a giant bird. The females were five times the height of a normal man, the males larger. All four monsters spread their wings as they leaped into the air and uttered harsh screams of aggression.

The Mundanes scattered, understandably. A number of them charged into the bordering zone of Air and were blown away by the perpetual winds there. Some took refuge in the burrow of a local dragon; there was a loud gulping sound, followed by the smacking of lips and a satisfied plume of smoke. Then there was a windy burp, and pieces of Mundane armor flew out of the burrow. Most of the remaining soldiers simply backed up, shields elevated, awaiting the onslaught. They certainly weren't cowards.

The sphinxes sheered off as if deciding the odds were not proper. Of course the real reason was that the illusion would lose effect if the Mundanes ascertained its nature. No illusion could harm a person directly; he had to hurt himself by his reaction to it. If the sphinxes charged through the soldiers and revealed themselves as nothing, the game would be over.

After the sphinxes came the big birds, the rocs. The sky darkened as six of these monsters glided down, casting monstrous shadows. The two remaining Mundane elephants spooked and fled headlong back north, trumpeting in terror; they knew the sort of prey rocs liked to carry off. That set off most of the remaining horses, who stampeded north, too. It would be long before many of these were recovered, if any could be rounded up unscathed.

"Now that's the way illusion should operate," Queen Irene murmured appreciatively. "They'll make slower progress with most of their animals gone."

Each roc held a big bag, and as they passed over the Mundanes they dropped these bags. The bags burst as they struck the ground, releasing yellow vapor that looked poisonous. Bushes and trees within its ambience seemed to shrivel and wilt and turn black, and phantom figures in the likeness of Mundanes gagged and staggered and fell in twisted fashion to the ground.

Imbri made a whinny of admiration for the sheer versatility of the King's performance; she would have been terrified if she faced that apparent threat. She heard someone cough, as if breathing the awful gas. If the illusion had that effect on these viewers, who knew it for what it was and who were not even in it, how much worse it must be for the superstitious Mundanes in the thick of it! Maybe it was possible after all, to wipe out the enemy without touching it physically.

The Punics reeled back, afraid to let the yellow vapor overtake them. Their leader came forward—the Horseman, riding a fine brown horse. Naturally that man had prevented his steed from spooking. Imbri was startled; this meant he *was* with this army and not lurking around Castle Roogna. How had he traveled so fast? He had to have magical means—a carpet, perhaps, or some renegade person of Xanth who enabled him to do it. Someone who could make him fly—but that did not seem likely. The mystery deepened unpleasantly.

The Horseman yelled at the troops, then strode forward into the fog. It did not hurt him. They rallied and stood up to it—and of course it did not hurt them either. The bluff had been called.

After that, the Mundanes ignored the splendid illusions King Iris threw at them. They marched south, toward the Gap Chasm, and it seemed nothing she could do would stop them. But Imbri knew the King wasn't finished. "There's more than one type of illusion," Iris said grimly.

By late afternoon the Punic army was approaching the Gap. It was making excellent time, because no creature of Xanth opposed it and the Horseman obviously had mapped out a good route. But King Iris made the Chasm appear to be farther south than it was. Then she sent a herd of raindeer trotting across the spot where the real Chasm had been blocked out, bringing a small rainstorm with them. Illusion worked both ways: to make something nonexistent take form, and to make something that was there disappear. This combination was marvelously effective. Little bolts of lightning speared out from the rainstorm, and there were boomlets of thunder. Iris was a real artist in her fashion. One might disbelieve the storm—but overlook the nonexistence of the ground it rained on. Water from that storm was coursing over that ground, beginning to flood it. There were even reflections in that water.

The Mundanes, jaded by the displays of the day, charged past the nonexistent deer, right on into the nonexistent storm, across the nonexistent ground—and fell, screaming, into the very real Gap Chasm. The Horseman had forgotten about it, naturally enough, and the Mundanes had never known of it.

The Horseman quickly called a halt and regrouped the Mundanes—but he had lost another thirty men. He was down to a hundred and fifty now, and obviously not at all pleased. He reined his horse before the illusion and shook his braceleted fist.

Imbri was privately glad to see the man had not caught the day horse. He must have pre-empted this one from a lesser officer. Could he have ridden the brown horse to Castle Roogna and back in the night? It seemed unlikely; the horse was too fresh. But since the Mundanes had retained a number of horses, before the Queen spooked them away, he certainly might have used one of those for his purpose, though the best routes for hoofed creatures were not necessarily the shortest ones and certainly not the safest. The best shortcuts were ones only something like a man could take. So there still seemed to be no perfect answer. Yet the major mystery was not how he traveled, but how to abate the enchantment on the six Kings.

"Is that so, you Mundane oaf!" King Iris demanded, in response to the Horseman's fist-shaking gesture. "You can't threaten me, horsehead! I'll use my illusion to chip away your entire army before it reaches Castle Roogna!" And she formed the image of a raspberry bush, which made a rude noise at him.

Contemptuously, the Horseman guided his horse right through the illusion—and smacked into the ironwood tree that Iris had covered up by the raspberry. His horse stumbled, and the Horseman was thrown headlong. He took a rolling breakfall in the dirt and came to rest unhurt but disheveled and furious.

"Oh, Mother, that wasn't nice!" Irene chortled.

King Iris formed the image of her own face there before the fallen man, smirking at him. She could see him through the eyes of her illusion.

The Horseman saw her. He made a swooping gesture with his two hands— and suddenly the illusion vanished.

Queen Irene glanced at her mother, alarmed. "What's the—" Then she screamed.

Now it was evident to them all: King Iris had taunted the dread enemy— and had been taken by his magic.

After a shocked pause, Imbri sent a dreamlet to the girl: "What is your program, King Irene?"

Irene spluttered. "I'm not—I can't—"

"King Arnolde decreed you a Sorceress, therefore a Magician, therefore in the line of succession, and he named you to be the eighth King of Xanth. You must now assume the office and carry on during this crisis. Xanth needs you, your Majesty. At least we know your mother is safe in the gourd."

The girl's wavering chin firmed. "Yes, she is with my father now, perhaps for the first time. As long as we protect her body. But the moment those Mundanes get inside this castle, all is lost. They will slay the bodies of our Kings, and then our people will be forever in the gourd, or worse. Our situation is desperate, for we no longer have magic that can strike down the enemy from a distance." She paused, glancing around the room. "Who will be King after me?"

"Humfrey said there would be ten Kings during this siege," Imbri reminded her. "But you are the last Magician. We can't let the Horseman claim the throne by default. I think you'll have to designate your successor from among the lesser talents, just in case."

King Irene nodded. She turned herself about, surveying the people in the room a second time. Chameleon was helping Crombie the old soldier move King Iris to the chamber where the six previous Kings were kept; she would be the seventh.

"Chameleon," Irene said.

The woman paused. Imbri had to do another mental adjustment, for Chameleon was now far removed from her prettiness of the past. It would have been unkind to call her ugly, but that was the direction in which she was going. "Yes, your Majesty?" Even her words had harshened.

"You will be King Number Nine," Irene said clearly.

"What?" Chameleon used her free hand to brush a straggle of hair back from an ear that should have remained covered.

"You are the mother of a King and the wife of a King and you're just coming into your smart phase. We are out of Magicians; now we have to go with intelligence. King Arnolde showed what could be done with intelligence; he clarified the line of succession and located the lost Kings. He did more to help Xanth than any magic could have done. You will be smarter yet. Maybe you will be able to solve the riddle of the Horseman before—" She shrugged.

"Before he becomes the tenth King," Chameleon said. She was much faster to pick up on other people's thoughts now, after her initial surprise at being designated a prospective King.

Imbri found this steady progression a remarkable thing. She knew Chameleon was the same woman, but most of the identifying traits of the one she had carried north to spy on the Mundanes were now gone. She liked the other Chameleon better.

Tandy went to take Chameleon's place, helping Crombie conduct the former female King to the resting chamber. Chameleon returned to talk with Irene. "I see your logic," Chameleon said. "I am no Sorceress, and there are many people in Xanth with stronger magic than mine, but I believe you are correct. What we most require is not magic, but intelligence—and that, for a time, I can provide." She smiled lopsidedly, knowing better than anyone that if she retained the office of King too long, Xanth would be in an extremely sad state. She would have to wrap up the job during the nadir of her appearance, for there was no intellect to match hers then. "I shall see that the Horseman is not the tenth King, whatever else I do or do not accomplish." She did not bother to argue the unlikelihood of Irene's getting taken; they both knew that this was inevitable as the prophesied chain continued to its end. "But in case you face the Horseman directly, King Irene—"

Irene's brow furrowed. "I'm not sure I follow your implication."

"You are a lovely young woman. He might attempt to legitimize his takeover by taking you in another fashion."

Irene flushed. "I'd kill him!" Then she tilted her head, reconsidering slightly. "I'll kill him anyway, if I get the chance. I owe him for my father, my mother, my husband—"

Again Chameleon smiled. How different this expression was from the one her lovely version had shown. This was a cold, calculating, awful thing. "I am not questioning your personal loyalty to Xanth. I am merely suggesting that it might occur to him to try. It is the kind of thing that occurs to men when they encounter young women of your description. If you could discipline yourself enough to seem to accept his interest, at least until you fathomed his secret—"

Slowly Irene's smile matched that of the older woman. The strangest thing was that it was no prettier on Irene's face than on Chameleon's. Imbri saw, and understood, and was repelled. Human women well knew the advantage they had over human men and used it ruthlessly. What an ugly way to try to save Xanth! Yet if it came to that extreme, was there any better way? What was justified in war? Imbri wasn't sure. Maybe there was no proper answer to this type of question.

Now King Irene went to work organizing her campaign. The magic mirror showed the Mundanes camping for the night; at least there were several campfires. The rest was darkness. If the Punics resumed their march at dawn, it would take them at least two hours to reach the invisible bridge—obviously the Horseman knew about it—and longer to get to Castle Roogna.

Irene turned to Imbri. "The bridge—could you kick that out tonight?"

"I could try," Imbri sent. "But I would run the risk of falling into the Gap, since I can't use a lever or an axe, and would have to stand on the bridge in material form to kick at its supports. This sort of work really requires human hands and tools." It galled her to admit that there was something a human folk person was better at than an equine person, but in this very limited respect it was so.

"I will go with you," Chameleon said. "I'm not strong, but I'm good at that sort of challenge. I have a sharp knife that should cut through the strands."

"But—" King Irene protested.

"There is no danger from the Mundanes by night," Chameleon reminded her. "And none from Xanth monsters when I'm on the enchanted path or on the night mare. If we can take down that bridge quickly, the Nextwave will be stalled at least another day, navigating the Chasm, and we shall be much better able to defend Castle Roogna."

"But if I should be taken during your absence—"

"I'll return promptly. I promise."

The girl spread her hands. "You are correct, of course. I'm afraid to be alone with this responsibility, but that's a luxury I can't afford. Unlike my mother, I never even imagined being King. I shall set up a collection of plants to defend this castle, but I won't make them grow until you are safely back inside."

Chameleon mounted Imbri, and they took off through the wall and headed for the local gourd patch.

"I have another task for you," Chameleon said when they were alone. "I do not believe that either the Gap or Irene's plants can stop the Mundanes for long, and we'll never eliminate the Horseman unless we first trap him and prevent his escape. This will require a lure he can't resist, and some desperate measures on our part."

"I want to kill the Horseman if I find him," Imbri sent. "I'm not sure he'll tell us how to nullify his enchantment. He deceived me once, but he will never trick me like that again." She swished her tail, smashing imaginary flies.

"He is extremely elusive, and I think I know why," Chameleon said. "It would be quite unfortunate if I am wrong—and I'm not yet at my peak of intelligence, so I may be—therefore I will not voice my suspicion. But if I am

right, he will take King Irene, and he will also take me, immediately following. He will suppose that will make him the tenth King, the chain complete,
but we can prevent that by acting first. There must be one more King of
Xanth designated, one he can't send to the gourd. That is the King who can
finally break the chain."

"Yes, Magician Humfrey's prophecy makes the tenth monarch vital," Imbri
agreed, diving into a gourd. Neither of them paid attention to the gourd
world, which now seemed commonplace, being absorbed in their conversation. "But who is it to be? Anyone you select can be enchanted."

"Anyone but one," Chameleon said.

"Who?"

"You."

Imbri veered into the wall of the City of Brass, one of the subdivisions of
the gourd, where the brassies labored on metallic aspects of bad dreams. Of
course the brass wall didn't hurt her, as it was insubstantial in her present
state, but by the time she straightened out, she had startled several of the
laboring brass folk. "Who?"

"Who are you looking for?" a brassie man inquired, thinking she was
addressing him.

Embarrassed, Imbri covered by naming the one brassie she knew of who
had seen the real world. "Blythe."

"You're in the wrong building," the brassie man said. "She's in B-Four."

"Tell her I may need her help soon," Imbri sent, realizing that she might
turn this blunder to advantage. Blythe Brassie just might be able to help in
the crisis of Xanth. "Right now I'm on my way elsewhere."

"Yes, carrying garbage to the dump," another brassie remarked, eying Chameleon.

Imbri hastily trotted on through another wall, feeling an unequine burning
in her ears. "The brass folk are very insensitive," she sent to Chameleon.
"They have no souls and no soft tissues."

"I am used to this sort of thing," Chameleon said. "People assume that
because I am ugly I must be bad, and they treat me that way, then find
confirmation when I do not react with delight. If they approached me in my
off-phase the way they do when I'm pretty, they would find me easy enough
to get along with."

There was much truth in that, Imbri was sure. She remembered how
Smash the Ogre had been considered brutish and violent because of his size
and appearance, when in fact he was a most decent creature. People tended
to become what others deemed them to be. Perhaps that was another aspect
of the magic of Xanth.

Chameleon resumed her discussion. "I am designating you to be the final
King of Xanth, Imbri. If I am correct, and I hope I am, you are the only one
who can do it. This is the real reason the Night Stallion sent you out into the
day. He knew what he was not permitted to tell, so he did what he could to
save Xanth by making it possible. It was a course requiring much grief, in-

cluding Good Magician Humfrey's shame, but the only likely way to save Xanth. You are the key. You must be the tenth King."

"But I'm a horse!"

"Yes, I had noticed. Are you any less a creature of Xanth?"

Imbri snorted. "I think I liked you better when you were beautiful, and not just because of your appearance."

"Everyone does. But on certain rare occasions, intelligence is more valuable to a woman than beauty."

"Oh, of course! I didn't mean—"

"I will be beautiful again, Imbri. I can not afford to remain King then; I would defeat Xanth through sheer stupidity. If the Horseman had the intelligence to banish Irene and keep me in power, he could certainly work his will during my other phase. I must provoke the crisis now, while I have the wit to handle it. Things may move quite rapidly once I return to Castle Roogna. Just you be ready to do your part, mare."

"I don't understand this at all!" Imbri sent in a dreamlet of darkly roiling nebulosities. "You aren't even King yet, but you talk of getting banished to the gourd. If you designate me King, no citizen of Xanth would accept it."

"They won't need to," Chameleon said. "I would explain more thoroughly, but I fear that would disrupt the prophecy. You must tell no one of this—until the time. Meanwhile, after we take down the bridge, you must go and fetch help for Irene's plants. The throne of Xanth has come at last to women; it behooves the women to defend it with greater efficacy than the men did. Go fetch the Siren and the Gorgon from Magician Humfrey's castle and locate Goldy Goblin; we'll need their talents for the final confrontation."

"But if I go there, how will you get back to Castle Roogna?" Imbri had never dreamed such an office would come to her, and as a night mare, she had dreamed a great deal, but did belatedly see the logic of it. She was immune to the Horseman's power, so could stop him in a way no other creature could. But practical details of organization remained. "At least I must take you back there before—"

"We shall see what works out," Chameleon said enigmatically. That was another annoying aspect of her intelligence; obviously there was a lot Imbri was missing.

They plunged out of the gourd near the bridge and galloped to the brink of the Chasm. But there was a problem. The Mundanes had set guards there. Imbri faded back into the dark forest, before the enemy spied her, and halted. "What now? I could approach invisibly, but would have to materialize to attack the bridge."

Chameleon considered, tapping her fingers idly against Imbri's mane. "We'll have to get rid of them. I'll devise a slingshot, and you can power it. Make sure I don't grab the wrong kind of vine."

They quested quickly through the jungle, locating several large elastic bands, which they harvested and tied to firm ironwood trunks, making a huge sling. Chameleon set a big stone in the net, and Imbri drew it back with all the weight of her body. Chameleon had fixed a temporary kind of harness from vines to make this possible.

Following Chameleon's directions, Imbri adjusted her position until the slingshot was aimed right at the Mundanes. At Chameleon's command she phased out, releasing the bands, and the rock hurtled up and across.

It scored a perfect hit on the near side of the bridge, sweeping the two Mundane guards into the Chasm. Chameleon knew exactly what she was doing in this phase! The two of them hurried across and discovered that the stone had also ripped away the bridge. The job was done already!

Two more Mundanes stood across the Chasm. They nocked arrows to strings—but Chameleon jumped on Imbri, and Imbri phased out again, and the arrows passed harmlessly through them. Nevertheless, they retreated from the Chasm, so that there would be no threat.

They heard a noise from the west. "A centaur's coming!" Imbri sent.

"No, I suspect it's a horse."

Indeed, in a moment the white day horse appeared. Imbri projected a dreamlet of greeting to his mind.

"Is the bridge still there?" he asked worriedly. "I heard a crash, so came running. The best grazing is south, but I have a good hiding place on the other side, and it's getting late."

"No bridge," Imbri sent. "We just took it out. You couldn't have used it anyway; the Mundanes had set guards on it."

"The Mundanes!" his dream figure cried. "I understood they were way up north!"

"That was yesterday. Now they are here. Tomorrow they'll be crossing the Chasm, and the day after that they'll be at Castle Roogna."

"I must flee!"

"If I understand his reactions correctly," Chameleon said, "you have informed him of the proximity of the Punic army, and he wants to get away from here."

"Yes," Imbri agreed. "He is very nervous about Mundanes. I can expand the dream to include you so you can talk to him directly—"

"No, don't bother. When I was fair and stupid, I felt at home with the normal equine intellect; now that palls. But I do need transportation. Tell him I shall be the next King of Xanth, the ninth, and ask him if he would like to carry me back to Castle Roogna. That's on his way south, away from the enemy."

Imbri did as she was bidden. "That's Chameleon?" the day horse asked, amazed. The night was dark, since it was no longer a good phase of the moon, but his excellent equine night vision showed him her appearance well enough. "I know she changes, but this creature is ugly, even for the human kind!"

"But she's the same inside," Imbri sent to both.

"The hell I am!" Chameleon snapped.

"And she's going to be Queen of Xanth?" the day horse asked, daunted.

"King of Xanth." Imbri did not have the nerve to say who would follow Chameleon in that office.

The day horse shrugged. "She's ugly, but I liked her once and can carry her, if there are no Mundanes there."

"There are none," Imbri reassured him. "Even Ichabod retired to a human village, after Arnolde the Centaur King got taken out. There are only women inside Castle Roogna now, with King Irene."

The day horse snorted acquiescently. Women were no threat to him. Chameleon mounted, and they set off at a gallop for Castle Roogna.

Imbri headed for Magician Humfrey's castle, via the gourd. As she traversed a fraction of the night world, she wondered idly how Chameleon had guessed she would find convenient transportation back. The woman was hideously smart in her proper phase, but this smacked of prophecy.

Soon she reached the Magician's castle and trotted across its moat and through its wall. "Grundy!" she sent in a general dreamlet. "Is the Gorgon back yet? Tell her not to look at me!"

"I am back," the Gorgon replied in the dream. "The golem returned not long ago to Castle Roogna to help fight the final battle. I am thoroughly veiled. Just let me wake up, and I will introduce you to my sister the Siren and Goldy Goblin, who also returned with me."

So the goblin girl had been serious about helping! "Don't wake up," Imbri sent. "You surely need your sleep, and I already know the Siren. I will talk to you all in one dream." She expanded the dream to include the others, now that she knew their identity.

"Oh, you are the night mare Smash the Ogre knew!" Goldy exclaimed as she saw Imbri. "The Siren told me about you. You carried Smash from the Void."

"Well, not exactly," Imbri demurred, somehow flattered. "But I did help and I received half of Chem Centaur's soul for the service. That enabled me to go dayside."

"I know how that is," the goblin girl said. "The ogre arranged for me to have this magic wand, and that gave me great power among my kind. Soon I will marry a goblin chief. I was down in the mines, picking out a trousseau of precious metals, or I would have come to help the centaurs fight the Mundanes. I didn't know until too late, so I sent a messenger who may not have reached you—"

"He reached me," Imbri sent.

"Then the Gorgon picked me up before I heard from him. *Now* I'm ready." She waved her wand in the dream, and objects flew about, touched by its power of levitation.

"Magician Humfrey told me to fetch my sister," the Gorgon explained. "And she told me that we should gather some of her other friends, so we tried. But Fireoak the Hamadryad can't leave her tree for such a risky venture, and John the fairy is expecting offspring—I don't think you know these

"Best of fortune, King Imbri," King Trent said solemnly. "Xanth is depending on you."

Now Imbri appreciated the full magnitude of the challenge. The tenth King *had* to break the chain—and she was that King.

people anyway—and we couldn't reach Blythe Brassie, and have still to get the word to others like Chem and Tandy—"

"Chem and Tandy are already at Castle Roogna," Imbri sent, flashing an image of the castle in the background. "And I can fetch Blythe any time if she wants to come. She expressed interest before, and I left a message at the City of Brass for her to be ready."

"It would be so nice to get together again," the Siren said. "And to see the ogre again, too; he made it all possible."

"Chameleon asked me to fetch help to defend Castle Roogna," Imbri sent. "I can take you there one at a time."

"No, we'll use the magic carpet," the Gorgon said. "We used a bottled conjure-spell to send the golem back, so we saved the carpet. We can start in the morning and keep whistling it back until all three of us are there. Will that be time enough?"

"It should be," Imbri agreed. "We expect the Mundanes there in two days. King Irene will grow plants to stop them—"

"King Irene!" the Gorgon exclaimed. "What happened to the Centaur King?"

Imbri quickly updated them on recent developments. "So Chameleon will be the next King," she concluded.

"This is moving almost too swiftly for me," the Siren said. "We've got to stop losing our Kings!"

"And stop the Nextwave army," the Gorgon added. "I believe I can do much of that myself, if I can get a good look at them."

"Yes," Imbri agreed. "Take care that no Xanth defenders are near."

The Gorgon nodded. "We certainly shall. You go fetch Blythe; we'll meet you at Castle Roogna."

Imbri let them lapse back into dreamless sleep. She trotted out and to the gourd patch and soon was back at the City of Brass.

All the brassies of Blythe's block were frozen into statue form, which was normal for them when at rest. Imbri pressed the activation button with her nose and they came to life. "Will you come with me to the real world, Blythe?" Imbri asked the pretty brassie girl. "Your friends have asked for you, and you did mention to me—"

"I'd love to!" Blythe exclaimed. "It's a strange place out there, with all its living things, but I liked the ogre and the girls."

"I'll have to clear it with the Night Stallion," Imbri sent. "But I think it will be all right."

Blythe mounted her, and they made an arrangement to have the brassie building turned off again after they departed it, then went on to check on the seven Kings.

Imbri received a shock. Now there were nine Kings. Both Irene and Chameleon had been taken.

"Now it is up to you, King Mare," Chameleon said. "Only you can stop the Horseman."

"But how did he get to you?" Imbri asked, flustered. Chameleon had warned that things might proceed rapidly, but this was hardly to be assimilated.

Chameleon smiled unpleasantly. "I brought him inside Castle Roogna. My plan worked perfectly."

"You what?"

"I confirmed my suspicion and lured him into the trap, using myself as bait. The moment he was inside, we sent all other living occupants of the castle outside, and King Irene grew the plants she had set out, and they quietly confined him to the castle while he was occupied with us." She made that nasty smile again. "For a while he somehow thought Irene found him handsome, but when he realized she was only stalling for time for her plants to complete their growth, he banished her to the gourd. Then I assumed the crown and told him we knew his secret and would never let him escape the castle, and of course he banished me, too. So my tenure as King was very brief: no more than two minutes. He was very angry about being outwitted, particularly by one he had regarded as stupid."

"But he never met you before!" Imbri protested. "You were in the forest with the day horse when Grundy and Ichabod and I met him!"

"Not precisely. Now you must go and dispatch him, and that will not be easy," Chameleon concluded.

"It will be easy!" Imbri sent. "I will gladly kick that monster to death!"

Chameleon shook her head. "No, not easy at all. You can't kill him."

"Certainly I can, King Chameleon!" Imbri sent hotly.

"Because it may be that only he can abate the enchantment he has put all of us under. You must first make him free us—and he won't do that voluntarily."

Of course that was true; they had been over it before. Imbri was letting her equine temper run away with her. "But I can still kick him into submission. Before I finish, he'll be glad to tell me all." But uncertainty was gnawing at her.

"Not so," Good Magician King Humfrey said. "There is an aspect we may have neglected to clarify."

"You see," Chameleon continued, "he is the offspring of a stallion and a human woman. The result of a liaison at a love spring. That's why he calls himself the Horseman. He is a crossbreed, like the centaurs."

"Like the centaurs?" Imbri asked, confused. "But he's a man!"

"He is a werehorse."

Slowly the terrible realization came across Imbri. "The—day horse?"

"The same. His mind could occupy two forms, each one quite natural to him. No one suspected, because no such creature has manifested in recent times."

"Why didn't you tell me?" Imbri sent, appalled. "All this time I—he—"

"I realize that was cruel," Chameleon said. "But I was not quite sure. If I were wrong, I would have maligned a good and innocent animal. If I were

right, it would have been dangerous to inform you, because your reaction could have alerted him and made him avoid our trap. So I had to deceive you, and I regret that."

"All the time, with us—the Horseman!"

"Whose magic talent is to connect a line of sight between any two places—such as a human eye and the peephole of a gourd, as we surmised. That is how he enchanted all of us. But if you try to kick him, he will change into his horse form—and he is more powerful than you."

"Not by night!" Imbri protested. But she remained appalled. She had thought the day horse was her friend! Now she remembered how the animal had always been in the general vicinity of the Horseman. Certainly this had been so when she had first encountered both of them, the one purporting to be fleeing the other. What a cunning camouflage—and she had been completely deceived. The horse had even freed her from captivity by the man—how could she suspect they were the same? Then, when she, Grundy, and Ichabod had spied on the Mundane army, while Chameleon slept, the Horseman had appeared in the Mundane camp. And the Horseman's uncanny ability to travel—naturally he had used his stallion form to gallop in hours what might have taken his human form days, while the man form could navigate the special passes and shortcuts that might have balked the animal form. The best of both forms! As the day horse, pretending to be stupid, he had learned the secrets of Xanth—the invisible bridge, the projected lines of Kings—and they had thought him their ally and had told him everything!

Now, too, she understood the shame of the Good Magician. The day horse had been there when Humfrey had set out his spells and explained them to her! Humfrey could have enchanted the Horseman at any time, had he realized what was in retrospect so obvious. Instead he had allowed himself to be caught in that moment when Imbri had been outside, waiting for the day horse to follow; the stallion had changed to the Horseman, ensorcelled the Magician, changed back, and run with Imbri. If Humfrey was mortified, what, then, of Imbri herself. She had indeed been marishly stupid.

It all fitted so neatly together now. She was sickened. It had taken Chameleon, in her nasty smart phase, to put all the clues together and arrive at the proper conclusion. The Horseman, perhaps becoming contemptuous of his opposition, had been fooled himself. Naturally he had gone with her into Castle Roogna; there was his chance to eliminate the last two Kings expeditiously and take over.

They were all standing there, waiting for Imbri to come to terms with it. King Dor had his arm around King Irene, and both looked pretty well satisfied to be together again. King Trent had taken the hand of King Iris, a seemingly minor gesture of quarter-century significance. All nine Kings appeared to be well enough off here, for the time being—but their bodies were in Castle Roogna, at the mercy of their enemy, the Horseman. They had figured out the truth, and that was essential, but the end of this crisis was hardly certain yet.

Chapter 13

Breaking the Chain

There was no trouble about getting Blythe Brassie released for real-world duty; the Night Stallion had been waiting for the request. Imbri and the brassie girl arrived at Castle Roogna before dawn.

The Gorgon, the Siren, and Goldy Goblin were already there. So were Chem Centaur and Tandy and her ogre husband Smash, who had been faithfully guarding the castle throughout. Other people and creatures had been sent to neighboring villages for their own safety, since it was now known this would be a battle site. The old soldier Crombie had been persuaded by his daughter to march with the others, to protect them on the journey and point the way if any got lost. The truth was, he was no longer in condition to fight Mundanes, but he had indomitable pride. The Siren had organized these things with the tact and sensitivity she possessed.

Blythe was joyed to meet the others. Old friends greeted one another enthusiastically. Then they sobered, knowing that the difficult time was soon to come. Marching from the Gap was one enemy; within the castle was another. Both had to be dealt with—by this pitifully frail-seeming group of females and a single ogre.

"And one golem," Grundy pointed out with grim pride. Obviously he had not departed with the others, though he should have. What he could do to help wasn't clear at the moment, but he was ready to do it.

They looked at Imbri, who suddenly realized it was now her place to give directives, for she was King. "Rest, eat," she sent in a slightly shaky dreamlet. "We don't expect the Mundanes until another day. You'll know what to do."

Imbri faced the castle, a dark silhouette against a sky thinking about brightening. "And I know what I must do first!"

The castle was imposing in a strange new way, as she gradually made out the details. It was almost entirely overgrown by vegetation. Tangle trees braced against its walls, and carnivorous grass sprouted from the crannies. Animate vines dangled from the parapets. Kraken weeds sprouted from the moat, making the normal moat monsters uneasy. King Irene was gone, but her magic remained, and it did indeed seem to be of Magician caliber.

There was no easy way any person could pass in or out of that place. The Horseman certainly was trapped, for a tangler would as quickly gobble a horse as a man. The plants could not invade the interior of the castle, for that was protected by assorted spells that had been in place for centuries, but they certainly lurked for anything outside. Imbri had to enter the castle now, before dawn, or she would not be able to do so until nightfall. Only her immaterial state could pass those savage plants! Chameleon and Irene had certainly set their trap well, and done as much for Xanth in their brief tenures as Kings as any of the prior Kings had.

There was a sound from the north. Chet Centaur came galloping, his fine body sweating from the effort. Imbri marveled at how different the results of crossbreeding could be—a fine centaur on one hoof, the awful Horseman on the other.

"The Mundanes are coming! The Mundanes are coming!" Chet exclaimed breathlessly.

"But we took down the bridge!" Imbri protested.

"I know it. I checked as well as I could without being seen by them. Apparently they sent a man across right after you left. It happened so fast the Gap Dragon didn't have time to get there—though I'm not sure that poor monster is eager to encounter Mundanes again! The man hauled the invisible bridge back up—it's netlike, you know—and tied it in place, and they marched across it at night. Now their vanguard is upon us! I would have discovered it earlier, but I was checking other trails."

"You were on routine night patrol, not expecting anything," Grundy said. "We all knew the one place they would not cross was at the broken bridge. Or thought we knew."

"We have all underestimated the Mundanes," the Siren said. "That's why the war has gone so badly for us. We keep thinking that people without magic can't be much of a threat. That's not true at all; in fact, such people are the most ruthless and depraved, perhaps because of that lack, so are doubly dangerous."

Imbri realized that the Siren, who had been deprived of her own magic talent for more than twenty years, was in a position to appreciate the deleterious social effects of loss of magic. She was a good woman and had survived and perhaps even improved herself during that hiatus, but lesser people could readily do worse.

Imbri, like the others, had made another serious miscalculation. She had assumed that the Mundanes would remain camped for the night, then forge across the Gap Chasm by day in the manner the other army had crossed a few days before, and camp again on the south side. They had outsmarted her, advancing cleverly and rapidly to rejoin their trapped leader. Now the consequence of this misjudgment was apparent; the siege was on before the defense was ready.

The Horseman would have to wait. Imbri had a battle to organize. The Nextwave could not be allowed to capture Castle Roogna, the last solid symbol of Xanth independence, or to rescue the Horseman. If she went inside to deal with him, she would be trapped there by daylight, unable to phase through walls and plants, and thus be unable to deal with the army outside. She might kill the Horseman but lose the battle, so that Xanth would have nothing at all except barbarians overrunning it. Even a bad leader was probably better than none at all. If she dealt first with the Mundanes, the Horseman would remain trapped, and she could deal with him at her leisure.

But that wasn't a perfect answer. Suppose the Horseman got angry and started killing the bodies of the Kings? Could she afford to risk that? Imbri wavered again. The burden of decision making was heavy, for a mistake affected the welfare of many other creatures, and perhaps the entire Kingdom.

"Don't worry," the Siren said, divining her thought. "The Horseman won't hurt the Kings. He is holding them hostage. He knows we could send in a flight of harpies or other deadly creatures to wipe him out, if we weren't concerned about our own people in there. Meanwhile, the Kings are no threat to him. He has everything to gain by taking good care of them—until the Mundanes win this battle and free him. If the Mundanes lose, he'll try to use the Kings as bargaining chips to win his own freedom."

That made sense, Imbri hoped. "We must organize quickly," she sent. "The Gorgon must be where only the enemy can see her, but not where they can shoot arrows at her."

"Fear not," the Gorgon said. "I will remove my veil only in the presence of a Mundane. I can hide behind a tree and peek out—"

"But the others will see what happens to the first," the Siren said. "The Mundanes are very quick to perceive and act against threats to their welfare. But I can help. Magician Humfrey restored my magic dulcimer before he became King; I have it now, and my power has returned. Let me lure them—"

"First we must get all Xanth males clear of the area," Imbri sent.

"Aw, we know about the Gorgon," Grundy protested. "We won't look her in the puss."

"All males must be clear," Imbri insisted. "Beyond hearing, so you won't be lured in by the Siren. You go out and warn them, in the name of the King. Get far away and don't return until one of us finds you and tells you it's safe."

"Oops—Smash went on another patrol through the jungle," Tandy said. "To make sure no Mundanes were sneaking in from any other directions."

"We have to do it, golem," Chet said. "She's the King Mare. And she's right. We must warn everyone as fast as we can, catching any stragglers and getting well away from here ourselves. We can intercept Smash and warn him off."

"We'll give you as much time as possible," Imbri sent. "This is a battle only females can fight, because they are immune to the Siren's song." She turned quickly to the Siren. "That's right, isn't it?"

"That's right," the Siren agreed. "My power is related to that of Millie the Ghost—projected sex appeal. I suppose a male Siren could summon females."

"That would serve them right!" Grundy exclaimed. The Gorgon turned toward him, lifting one hand to her veil. Hastily he mounted Chet, and they galloped off while the Siren chuckled. The Gorgon would not really have lifted that veil!

Imbri remained uneasy. They certainly had an excellent weapon, or combination of weapons, in these two sisters, since the Mundane army was all male. If only they had had more time to work out a really solid defense!

In hurried moments, they set up a crude arrangement, the best they could manage with the disadvantage of their situation. As the sun hauled itself up out of the forest to the east, singeing the leaves of the adjacent trees, the head of the Mundane column marched upon the castle. Light glinted from the Punic shields and helmets as the dread Wave crested a ridge.

Chem Centaur concealed herself in a hollow old beer-barrel tree and projected a large map of what she saw. This identified the position of all the Mundanes in the area in a way that every defender could see. The Punics could see it, too—but no Xanth positions were marked on it, so it didn't help the enemy. The Mundanes peered about, trying to spot the origin of the map, but there were a hundred fat old trees in the vicinity, none of whom cared to help the enemy, and many other features of the terrain to baffle the intruders. So the Mundanes spread out, poking their spears at each tree and getting peppered by supposedly accidental falls of deadwood. Soon they would discover the right one.

But Goldy Goblin, using the projected map for orientation, waved her magic wand. A Mundane flew up in the air, involuntarily, with a startled cry. He sailed in a high arc over the jungle, then plunged, screaming, out of sight.

The Mundanes oriented on this new menace, for the moment forgetting

the map. They located Goldy, perched high in a you-call-yptus tree. They
shot arrows at her, but the tree called out a warning, as was its nature, and
moved its branches to intercept them.

The Mundanes stared, thinking this another coincidence, blaming the
movement on the wind. But as the breeze died, and the tree kept balking
their shots, they realized that it, too, was a combatant. All the trees around
Castle Roogna could move, within reasonable limits, and they were guardians
of the castle. But they could not do much unless the Mundanes came within
reach, and the enemy soldiers were careful to stay clear.

The Mundanes charged the yptus tree. Goldy used her wand to loft another and another over the jungle and into the nearest lake, where hungry
goozlegizzard monsters lurked, but there were too many for her to stop. They
reached the base of the tree and started climbing.

Then Blythe Brassie went into action. She was perched on a lower branch
and had a basket of cherry bombs harvested from the local cherry tree. She
dropped these singly on each ascending helmet. The bombs detonated as they
struck, splattering cherry juice in the enemy faces and making the helmets
clang. The climbing Mundanes fell out of the tree and out of the fight.

The other Mundanes shot arrows at Blythe. They were so close that the
tree's branches were unable to react fast enough to protect her. But the
arrows clanged off her brass body harmlessly. Well, almost harmlessly; each
one left a dent, and she was very sensitive about dents. Furious, she hurled
more cherries at the archers, blasting them out.

Angered in turn, the Punics formed a kind of phalanx, overlapping their
shields above their heads, so the cherry bombs had little effect, and marching
to the base of the tree. Then they used their swords to hack at the trunk.

"OooOooO!" the tree groaned with a sound like that of wind sighing
through its branches. It certainly was hurting.

Blythe dropped down on the top of the phalanx and knelt to locate crevices. Through these she squeezed more cherry bombs. The explosions in the
confined space of the formation caused the overlapping shields to jump and
fall apart. Smoke poured out, assisted by the coughing and hacking of the
people inside the enclosure. Blythe lost her perch and fell down into the
phalanx.

Now the Punics whose bodies remained intact grabbed the brassie girl.
Blythe struggled, but they were too many and too strong for her. "Look what
we've got here!" one gloated. "A golden nymph."

"We know what to do with that kind!" another exclaimed. "Hold her arms
and legs—"

Imbri, seeing this from deeper in the jungle, galloped across to where the
Siren hid. "They've got Blythe!" she sent the moment she came within
range. "They're chopping Goldy's tree! Now it's time for you!"

The Siren nodded. She put her hands to her dulcimer and began to play.
Music sprang out magically, filling the air. Then she sang. Her voice merged
oddly with the notes of the instrument, forming an unusual but compelling

melody. The magic was not entirely in the dulcimer and not entirely in her voice, but together the two formed a powerful enchantment. The sound floated out over the battlefield, suffusing the environment.

The Mundane men reacted in quite a different manner than the Xanth females. The soldiers straightened up, listening, pausing in whatever they were doing. Some had arrows nocked to strings; some were chopping at the you-call tree; some were advancing on the castle; and some were holding Blythe Brassie spread-eagled, preparing for some heinous male act. All froze a moment, then turned and faced the music. Blythe, battered and dented but otherwise undaunted, dropped to the ground; the men had no further interest in her.

There was no formation now, only a somnambulistic shuffling toward the unseen Siren. For almost twenty-five years the merwoman's power had been blunted by the loss of her magic instrument; now it burst forth again in its fantastic compulsion. The Mundane men crowded toward the source of the sound, jostling one another discourteously. They clogged like drifting garbage at the narrow entrance to the glade where the Siren sang and shoved blindly to enter—and of course got shoved back. Everything about the Mundanes was brutish. But slowly the clog cleared, and they funneled in.

Beside the Siren stood the Gorgon. As each man approached, she lifted aside her veil and looked him in the face. He turned instantly to stone, a statue in place. The man following him was not concerned; he simply went around and was in turn converted to stone.

Imbri watched from behind the Gorgon, which was the safest place to be. The Siren's power operated only on men, but the Gorgon's worked on anyone or any creature. The combination of Siren and Gorgon was deadly potent. At this rate, the entire Mundane army would soon be stoned.

Then Imbri's acute equine ears heard a distant call. "Imbri! Trouble!" It was from one of the girls; what was the matter?

Imbri left the garden of statues, careful never to face the Gorgon, though she knew the Gorgon would cover her face the moment any friendly party turned toward her. A night mare might be immune to the Horseman's enchantment, but not to the Gorgon's, which was of a different nature. Imbri galloped on past the heedless Punics.

It was Tandy who was calling. She had been on peripheral duty, watching out for unexpected developments, and she had found one, to her horror. "It's my own husband!" she exclaimed as Imbri joined her. "Smash! He must have missed Chet and Grundy and not gotten the warning to flee! So he came in to report! Now he's caught by the Siren's song, and I can't stop him!"

Indeed, the ogre was tromping along behind the Mundanes, orienting on the hidden glade, captive to the melody. Smash stood twice the height of any of the men and weighed about six times as much; no ordinary person could stop him physically. In addition, he had his magic ogre strength, making him much more dangerous than his size suggested; he could crush rock with his bare hands and squeeze juice from trees. A giant could hardly have stopped him; certainly it was beyond the power of a person Tandy's size.

Imbri tried. "Smash!" she sent in an urgent daydream. "You are caught by the song of the Siren! Block it out, or you will face the Gorgon!"

"Me know; me go," the ogre agreed, reverting to his dull ogrish manner, though his human ancestry gave him intelligence. He tromped on. A couple of objects were clutched in his hamhands.

The lure certainly was powerful! Imbri realized she could not stop Smash. She galloped back to the glade, sending a dream to the Gorgon: "Do not petrify me, friend! I'm coming into sight!"

The Gorgon veiled her face, and Imbri approached her safely, albeit feeling shaky in all four knees. She stopped behind the devastating woman, and the Gorgon resumed flashing at Mundanes, petrifying each in place. The glade was now crowded with statues, and the Siren and the Gorgon had to keep backing away to make room for more. These two were destroying an army that had marched the length of the wilderness of Xanth, cowed griffins and goblins and dragons, and made refugees of whole Xanthian communities. It was surely ironic that the end of the Nextwave should be brought about by two middle-aged and fairly gentle married women.

"The ogre is approaching, and I can not dissuade him," Imbri sent. "Siren, you will have to cease singing for long enough to free him. I'll send him far away; then you can resume."

"But that will also free the Mundanes!" the Siren protested in the dream.

"I know. But the Gorgon can continue petrifying them. They won't know they should flee. The ogre can move very fast; it won't be long."

"As you wish." The Siren stopped singing and playing. "Actually, my fingers are getting tired; I haven't done this in a long time." She flexed them, working the fatigue out, getting limber for the next siege of playing.

"Smash!" Imbri sent to the ogre in a strong long-range dream. "Flee to the jungle as fast as you can! Get out of range of the Siren's voice so you won't get stoned!" She accompanied her words with a picture of the Gorgon petrifying men, including one ogre who was converting slowly to an ugly statue.

"Me flee!" the ogre agreed. "Me leave spells, she use well." He set something on the ground, turned about, picked up Tandy, and charged away, shaking the earth with his tread.

"You, too, Chem!" Imbri sent, realizing that the centaur's map was no longer necessary. "Get away from here and see if you can find other help, in case we should need it. Maybe some of the monsters of the jungle—"

"They're staying out of it," Chem replied, dodging a spear. "They don't want to mix in human business. They don't care who rules Xanth."

"Well, go anyway. I don't want you getting hurt here."

Chem nodded. She was sensible enough to grasp the reality of the situation. It was best to keep all expendable personnel well clear of the moving Gorgon so that no accidents could happen.

The Mundanes, meanwhile, were shaking their heads, reorienting. Some tried to attack the running ogre, thinking he was fleeing them. That foolishness was rewarded immediately; Smash swung his free fist in a surprisingly wide arc, knocking them away. It was an almost idle gesture for him, akin to the swatting of flies, but the Mundanes flew through the air and did not move again after they plowed into the earth.

Other Mundanes returned to their original mission, advancing on the castle. Their numbers had been depleted; there were fewer than a hundred remaining. Some continued on into the glade, trying to ascertain what was happening there, and these the Gorgon quickly dispatched.

Several soldiers stopped to pick up the items the ogre had set down. Imbri had forgotten about those; Smash had called them spells, so he must have believed they were magic that would help in the war effort. She galloped over, but was too late; the Mundanes were already opening one box. Whatever the magic was, the enemy had it. As King, she was not handling such details very well.

There was a scream, followed by frantic activity. The Mundanes started desperately swatting at something, stomping their feet, and fleeing the region. They ignored Imbri.

In a moment she realized what it was. Smash had picked up the box of quarterpedes left by Good Magician Humfrey. It must have washed into the jungle undamaged. The terrible little monsters naturally attacked anything they could reach. They were all over the Mundanes, gouging out two bits of flesh with every pinch, a scourge not even brute soldiers could ignore. In a moment the area was clear—clear of quarterpedes, too, for they were all on the Mundanes. Screams and curses in the distance bespoke the location of the affected individuals. What lucky mischief for the Castle Roogna defenders!

The second box remained. Imbri remembered this one; it was lettered PANDORA. She wondered what was inside, but knew better than to open it herself. She picked it up with her teeth and carried it with her; maybe the Gorgon could identify its contents, since she had packed it for the Good Magician.

Soon Imbri judged the ogre to be far enough away; the sounds of boulders cracking and trees being knocked over had faded in the distance. She wondered idly whether the quarterpedes would have dared to gouge at the ogre, had he opened their box. She trotted back toward the Gorgon's glade circuitously, avoiding Mundanes. "Start again, Siren!" she sent.

There was no response. "Hey, Siren!" Imbri sent again, in a stronger dream.

Still there was nothing. "Gorgon, tell your sister to resume singing," Imbri sent.

After a moment the Gorgon responded in the dream. "My sister has been taken by the Horseman!"

Imbri's confidence collapsed like a wall struck by the ogre. Too late, she realized what had happened. The Horseman, confined to Castle Roogna, had heard the Siren's song, faintly, and felt its compulsion. Since he could not reach her, he had remained partially transfixed, perhaps walking in place against the wall, perhaps in imminent danger of stepping out to be gobbled by a carnivorous plant. The moment the song stopped, he had been freed—so he had acted to eliminate the danger. He must have been able to see the Siren from an embrasure, and could work his magic on whomever he could see. Or perhaps her song had enabled him to focus sufficiently on her. He had connected her to the gourd. She now had joined the Kings.

"We'll have to fight without her," Imbri sent. "Do not be alarmed, Gorgon; she is well enough off in the gourd. Just protect her body from the Mundanes, and we shall rescue her when we rescue the Kings."

"I'll do more than protect her body," the Gorgon said grimly. "I'll petrify every last ilk of a Mundane!" She walked purposefully around the statues, holding her veil away from her face, looking for enemy men. Imbri was glad she had cleared the area of friends; this was certainly dangerous territory now!

But it wasn't the same without the Siren's summoning. The Mundanes were becoming aware of the danger. Some formed a phalanx, not looking out; others located the Gorgon by looking at her in the reflections of their shields. They blindfolded some of their archers and gave them instructions on aiming their bows by using the shield-reflection technique. The first arrows missed, but the Mundanes' aim was improving. They might not be in the centaurs' class as archers, but they were good enough. The Gorgon had to keep moving to avoid getting struck.

"We need to reorganize," Imbri sent. "You must back up against Goldy's tree, Gorgon. Then Goldy can protect you. Blythe can help a lot, too; I don't believe your power affects her, since she is already made of metal."

"My sister mentioned that Blythe was immune to the glare of a basilisk," the Gorgon said. "Mine is no worse than that."

"Get on my back; we must hurry."

Carefully the Gorgon mounted. Then Imbri galloped on, while the Gorgon glared about, leaving a trail of statues in their wake. Many Mundanes had not yet gotten the word; they soon got the look, and that finished them.

A centaur galloped back. It was Chem. "Why isn't the Siren singing?" she called. "Is something wrong?"

Imbri quickly sent her a dream of explanation. "Get away from the Mundanes," she concluded. "They remain dangerous."

"So I see," Chem agreed. "One thing I can do. I can circle around and carry my friend the Siren away to safety."

"An excellent notion," Imbri said, and the centaur galloped away.

They set up by the yptus tree, with Blythe Brassie protecting the Gorgon from hurled spears and close arrows, while Goldy Goblin used her wand to remove any archers whose blindfolded aim became too good.

They settled into a war of attrition, with the numbers of the enemy steadily decreasing, but their alertness increasing. The Punics tried to swamp the Gorgon with another phalanx; Goldy and Blythe disrupted it, loosening it so that some Mundanes inadvertently looked out—and turned to stone. That messed things up for the others, who found themselves in a pileup of mixed living and stone bodies. They tried to charge with a huge tree trunk as a battering ram, but Imbri sent a dream picture of a tree to one side of the real one, and they oriented on that and charged harmlessly by. When they ground to a halt, realizing that something was wrong, and looked back, the Gorgon got them all stoned with a single glance. Others tried to use the stoned bodies of their companions as weapons, picking them up and shoving them toward the tree, but the statues were too clumsy and too easy for Goldy's wand to move away.

It seemed the girls were doing all right, despite their reverses. The Mundanes were down to about fifty and were fazed by the number of their companions who were statues. Soon they would not have enough of a force left to storm the plant-defended castle and rescue their leader. The day was passing; when night fell, Imbri's power would be magnified, for she would be invulnerable to strikes against herself. As it was, only constant vigilance, the proximity of the Gorgon, and the fact that many Mundanes did not know what office Imbri held prevented her from getting wounded. Had the Punics been able to face her and attack, they would soon have prevailed.

Then Imbri realized that she hadn't seen any Mundanes lofted out of the battle for a while. "Are you all right, Goldy?" she sent in a dreamlet to the high branches of the tree.

She encountered only blankness. With a tired and familiar wash of horror, she knew that the goblin girl had been taken. The Horseman had evidently spotted her, concentrated long-distance, and finally managed to reach her. It surely wasn't easy for him to score at this range, but he had nothing to do except try; perhaps he had missed a hundred chances, then eventually scored when conditions were just right. Maybe Imbri had erred again by not going in to deal with him at the outset; he certainly was causing mischief now! Whom would he reach next?

"I think you should get out of the line of sight of the castle," Imbri said to the Gorgon. "Blythe and I are from the World of Night, so can't be enchanted that way; looking into a gourd's peephole does not hypnotize us. But you—"

Hastily the Gorgon edged around the tree until she could no longer see Castle Roogna. But without Goldy's help, their situation was critical. Now the Mundanes could organize a phalanx without having individual members fly out from it. They had shields angled like mirrors in several places so that they could orient specifically on the tree. There would be no stopping this one!

"We have to move," Imbri sent. "They are too much for us."

They moved, Imbri carrying both Blythe and the Gorgon. The double load was awkward, especially since the brassie girl was heavier than flesh, but the phalanx was not able to pursue efficiently, so Imbri did a lumbering gallop and made it to the protection of the main jungle.

Then she felt the Gorgon sliding off. Blythe grabbed the woman to prevent her from falling, but that was only a minor problem.

They had appeared in sight of the Horseman, and he had been ready and had taken the Gorgon. Maybe it had been a lucky score for him, but the damage was critical. Now they had no really good weapon against the Mundanes. All they could do was hide until nightfall, hoping the plants around Castle Roogna would confine the Horseman until then. Imbri was not especially proud of the way she had managed things; she should have realized that the Horseman would strike again the moment he got the chance.

The Mundanes did not pursue them far, perhaps fearing some new trap. They might be satisfied to have routed the defenders, not knowing that the Gorgon could not turn and strike again. Imbri soon was clear of the enemy, moving through the quiet jungle. She and Blythe set the Gorgon in a pillow bush, covered her over with a blanket from a blanket tree, and left her there; she should be safe for a few hours. Most of the predatory creatures of this region had departed when the Mundanes came, as the reputation of the invaders as hunters of monsters had preceded them. Imbri and Blythe went to the edge of the jungle to watch the Mundanes.

Irene's plants remained formidable. The first Mundanes who ventured close to the front gate got snatched and consumed by the vines and tangle trees guarding it. Pieces of Mundane fell to the grass, and it gobbled these just as avidly. Some plopped into the moat, where the moat monsters fought with the kraken weeds to snap them up. That taught the men caution.

The Punics tried another battering ram, charging up to the moat and hurling it across at the wall, but the tentacles snatched it out of the air and dumped it back on the men's heads. A real battering ram, which was a horned and hoofed animal who liked to charge things headfirst, would never have made the mistake of charging a tangler.

The Mundanes consulted, then scattered. "What are they doing?" Blythe asked.

It soon became apparent. They were gathering dry wood. "They're going to use fire," Imbri sent.

"Oh, the plants won't like that!" the brassie girl said worriedly. She had learned about plants during her prior visit to the real world, when she had traveled with the ogre. "But doesn't water stop fire?"

"It does," Imbri agreed. "But the Mundanes have proved to be resourceful before; they must have some way in mind to get around that."

Imbri looked at the sky. The sun was now descending, as it did every day about this time when it got too tired to maintain its elevation. Soon night would come. She doubted the Mundanes could free their leader before the friendly darkness closed. "When night arrives, I will enter Castle Roogna and confront the Horseman," Imbri sent. "You must go then to rescue Goldy Goblin from the yptus tree and bring her to where we have hidden the Gorgon."

"Yes. I will keep them safe," the brassie girl promised.

The Mundanes rolled small boulders into the moat, slowly filling it in at one place and forming a crude causeway. They shoveled dirt and sand into the interstices. The plants and moat monsters were not smart enough to realize what the men were doing, so did not oppose it directly. They tried to grab the men as morsels, but left the boulders alone. In due course the causeway reached the castle wall, so that the Mundanes were able to march up to it, while fighting off attacking tentacles.

Now the Punics brought their collected wood and piled it against the wall where the causeway touched. But the vines grabbed the sticks and hurled them back, perceiving them as useful missiles.

"I could get to like such plants," Imbri sent appreciatively.

This did not balk the Nextwavers for long. They started their fire away from the wall, then drew burning brands from it and threw them at the plants. The plants threw them back, but received a number of scorches in the process. It was evident that before long the Mundanes would be able to clear a section of the wall. They weren't approaching the front gate, for that was guarded by two ornery tangle trees; but here at the ramp, the wall was less heavily defended.

Of course, the wall itself remained behind the plants, and that was excellently solid. They would have to batter a hole in it, which would take time. Imbri judged she would have about an hour to deal with the Horseman after night fell. But she wasn't sure, for the Punics had surprised her before with their savage cunning. Still, these ones must have been active for a day and a night and another day without rest; they were bound to give out eventually.

Darkness closed. "Go about your business, Blythe," Imbri sent, and phased out.

"Good luck!" the brassie called after her.

Imbri started to neigh a response—and discovered that she still held the Pandora box in her mouth. She had been so caught up in events that she had never noticed the way it propped her mouth open. Well, she would simply have to hold on to it a little longer, since she didn't know what it contained. It was bound to be important, though; hadn't Humfrey said his secret weapon, more potent than any other, was locked up in this box? He had been afraid the girl Pandora would take it out prematurely, so had kept the box.

If she opened it herself, something horrible might emerge to destroy her, as the quarterpedes had done to the Mundanes who opened the other box. If she let this item fall into the hands of the Mundanes, some fearsome thing might come forth to aid them. What should she do? It was a problem.

Imbri suspected she would need the luck Blythe wished her. Everything depended on her. If she found herself in real trouble, she would open the box and hope it helped her. But she wouldn't touch it before then, only when she had nothing to lose.

The castle loomed closer. She had not been able to concentrate on this aspect of her challenge. Now, as she galloped invisibly toward the final encounter, seeing the grim wall illuminated on one side by the smoldering blaze of the Mundanes' fire, she realized why: it was because of the day horse.

She had thought the day horse was her friend. Now she knew he was not. He had deceived her from the outset, running from her because he feared she could read his mind, then meeting her in the form of the Horseman and learning more about her, then returning in horse form to ingratiate himself with her by freeing her. What a cynical mechanism to make her feel positive toward him! Thereafter he had used her to find his way conveniently all around Xanth, learning about the enchanted paths, the invisible bridge, and the nature of the Xanth defenses. Thus *she* had been responsible for the ultimate betrayal of Xanth, setting up a series of Kings for confinement in the gourd. All that the day horse had told her about the selfish motives of the Horseman, such as why he had allowed her to escape Hasbinbad's camp, were true; he had been in a position to know. Of course that creature, in either form, had enabled her to remain free; she was far more useful to the enemy than were any of the Mundane spies! Beware the Horseman indeed! If she had known . . .

Now she did know. Now she was the tenth King of Xanth, and she had to atone for her colossal error in judgment. She had to destroy the monster she had so innocently facilitated.

But that wasn't all of the point now. There was something else. Something more fundamental. What was it?

She couldn't kill the Horseman because of his magic, which would probably continue after him, leaving the Kings in dire circumstances. She had to make him tell his secret, which meant she would have to converse with him, and she couldn't do that because—

Because why? Somehow her mind sheered away as if at the brink of the Gap Chasm. But she had to face the truth, for this was the critical encounter. What was that truth?

She snorted hot little snorts and swished her tail violently from side to side, venting her private rage at the cynical way the day horse had maneuvered her, reviewing it once more in order to evoke the elusive thought she knew was so important. The day horse had played the innocent, pretending to be almost stupid, almost cowardly, when he was in fact none of these things. He had given rides or aid to future Kings of Xanth, facilitating their advance, not from any good will to them, but because he judged them to be potentially ineffective rulers against whom the Mundanes could make easy progress. When each new King disappointed him by demonstrating surprising determination and capability, he took out that King to make way for another, weaker one. Ironically, even the less promising of these, the women, became towers of strength for Xanth, until at last the least impressive of all, Chameleon, fathomed his secret and trapped him.

Least impressive? No, that doubtful honor belonged to Imbri herself—not human, not male, and no Magician. Xanth had at last been brought to the indignity of being governed by a night mare. A creature whose life cycles were equine—

Suddenly, as she encountered the dark moat, she suffered her final, horrible realization—the one that had eluded her before; she was coming into season.

It had been developing all along, of course, in the normal equine cycle. As a full night mare, she had never been tied to it, for she had been mostly immaterial. But once she became a day mare, the things of solid existence had loomed larger, and nature had proceeded inexorably. Now nature said it was time for her to mate. Her mind had been distracted by the crisis of the Kings, but her body had never changed its course.

The enemy she faced was, in his fashion, a stallion.

She veered away from the castle. She could not face him now! She could not even go near him! Her equine nature would betray her! It would not permit her to attack him; it would require her to mate with him.

Yet she could not stay away, either, for soon the Mundanes would break open an aperture in the wall and free their leader. Then Xanth would be finished. The Horseman would kill the hostage bodies of the Kings and proclaim himself King, and there would be none but a discredited mare to deny him. If she were going to stop him at all, she had to do it now.

Imbri wavered indecisively. If she went inside Castle Roogna, she would surely betray Xanth to the enemy; if she avoided confrontation, she would let Xanth fall by default. Which way was she to go?

She turned again. Better, at least, to try! She charged toward the castle, determined to do what she had to do. She might be in season, but she had a mind equivalent to that of a human being, and a human woman could pretty well control her mating urges, such as they were. Imbri had to determine, once and forever, whether she was a civilized King—or a simple animal.

She phased across the moat, through the vegetation and the stone of the wall, and into the deep gray matter of the castle. A ghost spied her, waved, and vanished; then all was still. She made her way to the throne room—and there was the Horseman, her foe, sitting slumped on the throne, a golden crown on his head, a scepter in his hand, sleeping. Such ambition!

She materialized and stood looking at him. He was a fairly handsome figure of a man, with curly light hair, good musculature, and that thin brass band on his left wrist, the only jewelry he wore. Yet even though he was in repose, there was a cruel hook to his upper lip. He was not a nice person.

It would be easy to kill him now! This was the enemy who had plagued Xanth generally, and her personally, for he had ridden her and dug his cruel spurs into her flanks. She could dispatch him with perfect joy and justice.

But first she had to force from him his secret so she could free the nine other Kings of Xanth. If she failed, they would all perish as their physical bodies starved, even if the Horseman died first. If the Horseman won, Xanth would be ruled by the tyrant imposter and his Mundane henchmen. She *had* to succeed—but still did not know how to proceed.

As she stood there in unkingly uncertainty, the Horseman woke. His eyes opened, and he spied her.

"Well," he said, seemingly unperturbed. "So you have arrived at last, King Mare."

He seemed so confident! Imbri knew that there was no way this horrible man could get on her back, since she was fully on guard. Even if by some trick he managed to get on her, he could not remain, since she would simply dematerialize. He would have to get off in a hurry, or she would carry him into the gourd and turn him over to the Kings. He would never get to rule Xanth then! She could attack him, while he could not attack her, not even with his special magic talent. She was one of the few creatures naturally immune to his power. That was why she was here now. He had to know that. Why, then, should he appear unconcerned?

"What, no dreams, Imbri?" he asked brightly. "All this trouble to come see me, and no dialogue?"

"I'm here to break the chain," she sent, trying to rid herself of the unreasonable awe of him she felt. "How do I free the Kings from your spell?"

"You don't, Imbri! Those Kings are past; I am the next and final King of Xanth, as you can plainly see."

"Not so. I am the present King of Xanth," she sent, her equine ire rising. "I will kick you to death before I let you usurp the throne!" She took a step forward.

The Horseman waved a hand in a gesture of negligence. "So the issue is which of us is the true tenth King of Xanth. You are bluffing, mare. I know you are immune to my power, and I know I can not ride you or strike you while it is dark. I have seen the night world from which you hail! Nevertheless, you are not about to attack me—because all your prior Kings will die if I do. There will be no one to unriddle the enchantment I made."

"Then you *can* free them, if you choose!" Imbri sent.

"I did not say that," the Horseman replied, as if playing a game.

"Either you can free them or you can't. If you can't, then they are doomed anyway and you have nothing to bargain with. If you can free them, you had better do so, or you will lose your life. I shall not permit you to gain the throne of Xanth by your mischief. Either King Trent returns to power or I shall remain King; in neither case will you assume the office. The question is whether you will free the Kings and live, or fail to free them and die."

The Horseman clapped his hands together in mock applause. "Oh, pretty speech, nocturnal mare! But what if I live, and you die, and I am accepted as the final King of the chain?"

She saw that he had no intention of yielding. He was stalling until his Mundane allies rescued him. She would have to kick him. Perhaps when he was suitably battered, and knew she was serious, his nerve would crack. She braced herself for a charge.

Suddenly the Horseman hurled a spell enclosed in an opaque globe. It bounced against the wall behind Imbri and burst. From it a bright light emerged, illuminating the whole chamber as if it were day. It was a sunspot, one of the spells in the royal arsenal. The Horseman had spent part of his confinement exploring the castle and had, of course, raided its store of artifacts. He was, after all, far from helpless—and she should have anticipated this.

Imbri wrenched her eyes away from the blinding sunspot—but too late to prevent damage. Her vision, adapted to night, was temporarily stunned. Fool! She had allowed herself to be completely vulnerable to surprise!

"What—did that sudden blaze hurt your sensitive evening eyes, mare?" the Horseman inquired with false concern. "Do you have difficulty seeing me, King Equine? Perhaps I can alleviate your indisposition."

Imbri whirled to the side, avoiding his approach—but soon crashed into a wall. The forgotten object in her mouth flung out and clattered across the floor. She could not see—and not only that, she could not phase out, because of the daylight the sunspot generated. The scheming Horseman had hit her with a double penalty. How cunningly he had laid his countertrap, knowing she was coming!

"I dislike this, Imbri," the Horseman said, stalking her. "You're such a beautiful animal, and I really do appreciate fine horseflesh. I am, I think, uniquely qualified to judge the best. But you have placed yourself between me and the throne of Xanth and have cost my *ad hoc* allies an extraordinary amount. So I must congratulate you on the way you organized those females, and dispatch you—"

Imbri lurched away again, caroming off a wall. Her vision was beginning to return, but slowly. Things were still mostly blurry.

"Mare—he's got a magic sword!" a voice warned in her ear.

"Who are you?" Imbri sent to the unknown person. How could there be anyone else in the castle?

"I am Jordan the Ghost," the person whispered, again in her ear. "We ghosts have been watching for the rescue attempt, and I was notified the moment you phased in. I know what you are doing, and the great effort you must make. I have friends within the gourd. I will help you, if you trust me."

"I bear a message of greeting to you from them!" she sent as she continued to move. "I forgot to seek you out before, when I had the opportunity. Of course I trust you!" Now she deeply regretted her neglect. There were half a dozen ghosts in Castle Roogna, and Millie, the Zombie Master's wife, had been one of their number for eight hundred years. Naturally the ghosts supported the legitimate Kings of Xanth! "Help me. Get on my back and guide me till my sight returns."

"I'm on," Jordan said. Imbri felt nothing, but that was normal for a ghost. "One body length ahead, turn right. There's a door. Hurry; he's about to strike at your flank!"

Imbri leaped forward and veered right. She misjudged slightly and banged her shoulder, but got through the doorway.

"Two body lengths," the ghost said. "Turn left."

She obeyed and found another opening.

"It is dark here," Jordan advised her.

Glory be! Imbri phased into immateriality and walked through a wall. She was safe now, thanks to the ghost. "Thank you, Jordan," she sent. "Are you still with me? I mean, now that I'm—"

"Oh, yes, I'm still riding you," he said. "The state of your materiality makes no difference to me."

Now Imbri's sight was firming. "Did the Horseman follow?"

"He did not. He remains in the light, sword ready. He is eyeing the box you brought, but not touching it."

"He doesn't know what's in it," Imbri sent. "Neither do I. It's a complete gamble, which I plan to open only when there is no hope. That way it will be unable to hurt me if it is bad, and may help me if it is good."

"That makes sense. But he has control of the box right now and doesn't dare open it."

"Then we are at an impasse," Imbri sent. "He can't hurt me in the dark, and I doubt I can hurt him in the light. If that's a typical magic sword, it will skewer me before I can hurt him."

"It is," the ghost confirmed. "Of course, you could borrow some other weapon from the arsenal."

That sounded good. Imbri knew she had little time to dispatch the Horseman, for she could hear the Mundanes pounding at the outer wall. "What is there?"

"Oh, lots of things," Jordan said. "Magic bullets—only we don't know what they are or how they are used, whether they are for biting or for making people feel good. Vanishing cream, which we can't see at all, let alone drink. Healing elixir. Fantasy fans—"

"What's a fantasy fan?" Imbri asked.

"A bamboo fan that has a magic picture on it when spread open," Jordan explained. "It also makes you think you're cooler than you are, especially when the picture is of a snowscape. Periodically these fans gather together from all over Xanth for some big convention where they shoot the breeze and blow a lot of hot air and decide who is the secret master of fandom."

Oh. Imbri didn't need any fantasy fans. In fact, none of the items seemed useful for her present situation. "Is there anything to nullify his sword?"

"Oh, yes. Magic shields, armor, gauntlets—"

"I can't use those things! I have no hands!"

"Oh, yes, I see. Xanth hasn't had a handless King before! Let me consider. It's the sword you must be wary of. You can't avoid it; the moment he gets within range, it will strike for the kill. I presume that if it weren't for that, you could dispatch him in the light."

"Yes." Imbri knew that even if the Horseman got on her back and used his spurs, he could not control her now; she would ignore the pain and launch into darkness, where she would be in control in either phase. No, the Horseman would not dare try to ride her this time!

"I've got it!" Jordan cried, snapping his ghostly fingers without effect. "The melt-spell!"

"Will that melt metal?"

"Indubitably. That is what this one is for. The Mundane scholar, Ichabod, was cataloguing the spells of the armory for King Arnolde, and that was an old one he discovered before the men were sent away from this region. Too bad he didn't have the chance to finish the job; there's a lot of good stuff here that even we ghosts don't understand."

They trotted down to the armory. The spell was in a small globe, as many were; Imbri wondered what Magician had packaged such spells, for they seemed to keep forever. She picked the globe up in her mouth, carefully, for the ghost could not carry anything physical. She phased back, phasing the spell with her, and trotted off to the main floor.

She heard the crashing of the Mundanes attacking the wall. By the sound of it, they were making progress. Their ramp and fire had nullified the moat and plants in that vicinity, so they were free to batter the stones as much as they craved. In just a few more minutes they would break in. She had to finish with the Horseman before then, for otherwise the Mundanes could go on the rampage and kill the ensorcelled Kings regardless of the outcome of her conflict. Imbri hurried.

In fact, she thought now, she had better make sure that, if it seemed she would beat the Horseman, she finished him off quickly so that he would have no chance to take the true Kings with him.

She came in to the lighted room, where the Horseman awaited her, sword ready. He looked even more arrogant now, his thin lip curling up from half-bared teeth, his brass bracelet gleaming with seeming malevolence in the light of the sunspot.

She was prepared for the light, and the sunspot was no longer as brilliant, so this time she had no trouble with vision. She turned solid in the room, however; any light stronger than moonlight did that to her.

"Ah, I thought I might see you again, King Mare," the Horseman said with a supercilious sneer. "You must meet me—or forfeit your cause." He strode forward, the sword moving with an expertise that was inherent in it, not in him.

Imbri spit out the spell. It flipped through the air toward the Horseman. The sword alertly intercepted it, slicing it in two—and therein lay the sword's demise. It wasn't intelligent; it didn't know when to desist. Had the spell been allowed to pass unmolested, or had the Horseman simply caught it in his left hand, preventing it from breaking, he would have been all right. But as the globe separated into halves, the vapor of the spell puffed out, clouding about the blade of the sword.

The blade melted. First it sagged, then it drooped, like soft rubber. At last it dripped on the floor. It was useless.

Now Imbri leaped for the Horseman with a squeal of combat, her forehooves striking forward.

The man dodged aside, throwing away the useless weapon. He tried to jump on her back, but Imbri whirled, bringing her head around, teeth bared. Most human beings did not think of equine beings as teeth fighters, but they were. However, all she caught was his sleeve; he was moving too fast for her. He was scrambling onto her, ready to use his awful spurs.

She lunged to the side, slamming into the wall, trying to pin him against it, to crush him and stun him. Again he was too fast; he certainly understood horses! He rolled over her back and off the other side, landing neatly on his feet.

Imbri swung about and lashed out with her hind hooves. The double blow would have knocked his bones from his body, had it scored, but he had thrown himself to the side, anticipating her attack with uncanny accuracy.

But she was a night mare, with a century more experience than he had in life. She knew far more about this sort of thing than had any horse he had dealt with before. She spun on her hind feet as they touched the floor and leaped for him again. She knew she had him now; he could not safely leave the lighted chamber, for in the darkness the advantage would be entirely hers. In moments she would catch him, in this confined space, with hoof or teeth or the mass of her body, and he would be done for.

The Horseman had fallen to the floor, getting out of her way. Sure enough, she had surprised him with her speed and ferocity. He had misjudged her exactly as she had misjudged the day horse, assuming that the personality that showed was the only one inhabiting that body. He was accustomed to tame Mundane horses, who tolerated riders because they knew no better. Now he scrambled on hands and knees as she reoriented for the kill. He was too slow this way; she knew she had him.

Then he transformed into his other form. Suddenly the day horse stood before her, massive, white, beautiful—and male. She had, in a pocket of her mind, doubted that her horse friend and her man enemy could really be the same; now that doubt had been banished.

Imbri hesitated. The masculinity of this magnificent creature struck her like a physical blow. She was in season, ready to mate, and this was the only stallion she knew. If she destroyed him, she might never again have the chance to breed.

He was the enemy; she knew that. Had she retained any doubt, the presence of the brass band on his left foreleg, just above the foot, would have removed it. She had believed that that band was the token of his slavery to the Horseman; now she was aware that it was much more than that. The form of the creature had changed; the form of the inanimate band had not. How ready she had been to believe whatever he told her! She had gone more than halfway to delude herself, wanting to believe that no horse could be evil.

She knew his nature now—but all her being protested against violence in this case. No mare opposed a stallion—not when she was in season. It was as contrary to her nature as it was for a human man to strike a lovely woman. It simply wasn't done. This was no decision of intellect; it was a physiological, chemical thing. With equines, intellect was not allowed to interfere with the propagation of the species. She had always before considered this an advantage. But advantage or disaster, it was so.

The day horse turned toward her, lifting his handsome head high. He snorted a snort of dominance. He recognized his power over her. It did not matter that they both knew him to be her enemy, her deadly rival for the Kingship, or that he was only stalling for time until the Mundanes completed their break-in. The Horseman had occupied her as long as he could, using up precious time; now the day horse was doing the rest of the job. Nature held her as powerless as she had been when blinded.

"Imbri! Don't let him dazzle you!" Jordan the Ghost cried in her ear. He was still with her; she had forgotten him during the intense action. "No male is worth it! I know, for I am a worthless male who ruined a good girl, and now suffer centuries of futile remorse. Don't let it happen to you! Xanth depends on you!"

Still she stood, virtually rooted, smelling the compelling scent of the stallion. She knew she was being totally foolish, as females had always been in the presence of virile males. She knew the consequence of her inaction. Yet she could not act. The mating urge was too strong.

The day horse nipped her on the neck. Imbri stood still. There was pain, but it was exquisite equine pain, the kind a mare not only accepted from a stallion but welcomed. He was dominant, as he had to be, to be a worthy stud.

He marched around her, taking his time. This, too, was part of the ritual. He sniffed her here and there and snorted with affected indifference. Oh, he certainly had her under control! The ghost had given up, knowing Imbri was lost. Her glazing eyes were fixed on the box on the floor, the one that had the word PANDORA printed on it. All it would take would be three steps to reach it and strike it with a forehoof, opening it, releasing whatever it contained—but she could not force herself to take those steps.

There was a loud crash from the distant outer wall. The Mundanes had broken in at last. Imbri quivered, trying to break free of her paralysis, but the stallion snorted, quieting her. She simply could not oppose him, though all her reason protested her folly. She had fatally underestimated the compulsion of her own marish nature.

"Hey, General—where are you?" a Mundane called.

The day horse shifted momentarily into his human form. "Here in the throne room!" he called back.

That broke the spell. Imbri jumped, moving like the released mechanism of a catapult, turning on him. But as she faced him, poised for the strike, he converted back to stallion form. He arched his neck, eyeing her with assurance, completely handsome and potent. He tapped the floor with his left forehoof.

Imbri, in the process of freezing again despite her best resolution, saw the brass band on that leg. The band that advertised exactly who and what he was.

She struck out with a forefoot, catching him on that front leg, attacking the band. The blow was not crippling or even very effective; its significance lay in the fact that she was opposing him. His shift of form, and his direct recognition of alliance with the Mundane enemy, had disrupted the equine mood. He was not a horse in the guise of a man, but a man in the guise of a horse. Imbri did not breed with a man in any guise. Now she knew, subjectively as well as objectively, that he was no friend of hers. All she had to do was look at that band, to see him as he was.

The day horse squealed, more in anger than in pain. He stomped his forefoot again. He was as handsome in his ire as in his dominance.

Imbri refused to be captured again. The brass band remained fixed in her mind. Her head swung about, her teeth biting into his neck just behind the furry white ear. She tore out part of his splendid silver mane. Red blood welled up, staining the shining hide.

Now the day horse fought. He squealed and reared, his forehooves striking out—but she reared, too. She was not as large and powerful as he, so was at a disadvantage, but she was driven by pure outrage and the knowledge that she was fighting not only for her pride, her freedom, and her life, but for the welfare of the nine other Kings and for the Land of Xanth itself. She was the King Mare; she *had* to prevail.

She whirled, her lesser mass giving her greater maneuverability, and launched a rear-foot kick. She scored on his shoulder and felt the bone crumbling under the force of her blow. The day horse stumbled, limping, then righted himself and came at her again. He was indeed a fighting creature and quite unafraid; instead of turning about to orient his powerful hind hooves on her, he used his head. This was the contemptuous nipping approach of the dominant animal.

This time Imbri kicked him in the head.

He collapsed, blood pouring from his nostrils.

Imbri looked at him. Now she was sorry for what she had done, though she knew it was necessary. He had made a fatal tactical error, coming at her in the mode of disciplining rather than in the mode of fighting, and had paid the consequence. Yet the blood on his pretty white coat, gushing over the floor, horrified her.

She knew there was healing elixir in the armory. She could fetch some of that, and in an instant this most beautiful creature could be restored. No stallion should suffer so ignominious a demise!

"Where are you, General?" the Mundane called, approaching the throne room.

Imbri charged for the door, whirled, and caught the man with a hard kick in the chest as he entered. He went down with a broken groan, unconscious or worse.

"Jordan!" she sent. "Will you ghosts help? The Mundanes are said to be superstitious; they're actually afraid of the supernatural. If you show your-selves to them and make threatening gestures, it may scare them away. I've got to protect the dormant Kings while I try to reverse the Horseman's en-chantment on them."

"We'll do our best," Jordan said, and floated swiftly and purposefully away.

Imbri returned to the day horse, determined to force him to divulge the secret. She hated all of this, but if she had to, she would taunt him with the healing elixir, holding it back until he acquiesced.

But she discovered that he had changed again. He had reverted to his human form, in a pool of blood—and the Horseman wasn't breathing. The terrible force of her kick had smashed the bones of his head. She knew at a glance that he was dead.

There was now no way to make him talk. She had in her desperation hit him too hard. She had murdered him.

She stared at the awful sight, her agony for the death of the day horse merging with her grief for the coming loss of the Kings of Xanth. What could she do now? She had squandered Xanth's last chance!

Bleak despair overwhelmed her. She and the ghosts might fight off the Mundanes, but what use was that now? The King Mare had brought doom, exactly as should have been anticipated.

"The box!" Jordan prompted, returning. "Maybe it has a counterspell—"

Listlessly, Imbri put her hoof on the box and crushed it. Thin, translu-cently pink vapor puffed out, expanding into a rather pretty cloud. It encom-passed her, for she made no effort to avoid it. For good or evil, she accepted it.

It certainly wasn't evil. She felt invigorated and positive. Somehow she generated confidence that things would work out after all.

"Hope!" Jordan exclaimed in her ear. "It was hope locked in that box! I feel it, too! Now I believe that my own long morbidity will eventually termi-nate."

Hope. Good Magician Humfrey had mentioned that he had locked up hope. She hadn't realized that it was in the Pandora box. She understood, objectively, that nothing had changed, yet the positive feeling remained. There had to be some way!

Imbri's eye caught the brass circlet on the Horseman's wrist. Something turned over in her mind. Why had he never removed it, though it was an obvious hint of his identity? Surely it had considerable value for him. Could that thing be a magic amulet? Something to enable him to convert from man to horse? No—that conversion was inherent in his nature, just as the Siren's ability to change from legs to tail sprang from her man-mermaid parentage. The Siren needed the dulcimer to do her separate magic.

The band—could it be something like the dulcimer, to amplify or focus his power? If the example of the Siren was valid, these crossbred people did need something extra to bring out their full talents. Part of their magic was their dual nature, so the rest was weaker than it should be. A dulcimer—a thin brass band. The magic of the Horseman could have resided not wholly in him but partly in the amulet.

It was her only remaining chance. She had hope; this could solve the problem of the Kings! She took the brass ring in her teeth and tugged it. It would not pass over his hand, so she used a forehoof to crush the bones of his dead extremity together, pulping the appendage, until there was room for the circlet to pass. Then she took it in her teeth and trotted out of the chamber, to darkness.

"We'll protect the Kings!" Jordan called after her. "As long as we can scare the Mundanes . . ."

She sent a neigh of thanks and phased through the walls and out of the castle. She saw in passing that the ghosts were indeed doing a good job of holding the remaining Mundanes back; with the Horseman and one of their own number dead, and with the ghosts menacing the rest, these troops would be quite wary of penetrating deeper into the castle by night. They would not realize for some time that the ghosts had no physical power. She hoped the Mundanes would be balked long enough; the Horseman had lost, but Xanth would not win until the Kings had been saved.

She shot out into the night, the brass band still firmly in her teeth. She knew one person who was knowledgeable about brass. "Blythe!" she broadcast as powerfully as she could. "Blythe Brassie!"

As she neared the place where she had left the Gorgon, she heard the brassie girl's dream response. "Here, King Imbri!"

In a moment they were together. "Blythe, I have a ring of brass I took from the Horseman. I think it connects to his power, but I don't know how it works. Can you tell?"

Blythe took the band and examined it closely. "Yes, I believe I have encountered something like this before. Note how short it is; very little depth compared with its mass. It is what we call a short circuit."

"A short circuit? What does it do?"

"It's supposed to make a wrong connection, to divert power from its proper avenue—or something. I'm really not clear about the details."

"Could it divert light?" Imbri asked, her new hope flaring again.

"Yes, I think so. It might make a lightbeam go the wrong way."

"Like from a person's eye to the peephole of a gourd?"

Blythe brightened. "The missing Kings!"

Imbri looked through the loop. All she saw was Blythe, on the other side. But of course it required magic to implement the effect—and that was the Horseman's talent. He had somehow used the short circuit to connect the gaze of each King to a gourd's peephole, causing the King to be confined to the gourd. The ring could be a short circuit to the gourd on one side and to the King's eye on the other. "But how could the connection be broken?" Imbri asked.

"You have to shield the circlet," Blythe said. "Ordinary matter won't do it, though. It has to be magic."

"I don't have any such magic—and very little time," Imbri sent desperately. "How can I abate its power quickly? Should I just break it? I'm sure I could crush it under my hoof with just a stomp or two, or have the ogre chew it to pieces."

"Oh, no, don't do that!" Blythe said, alarmed. "That could seriously hurt the Kings, sending them back to the wrong bodies or permanently marooning them in the night world." She paused, smiling fleetingly. "Isn't it funny, to speak of anyone being marooned in our world! But, of course, since they don't have their bodies with them—" She shrugged her metal shoulders. "You must interrupt its power without damaging the brass. That's the way such things work. That will have the effect of cutting off the Kings' view through the peephole, harmlessly."

She ought to know, Imbri realized, since she was of the magic brass region. Desperately Imbri cudgeled her mind. What would do it?

Then she had a notion. "The Void!" she sent. "That nullifies anything!"

"Yes, that's where we send hazardous wastes to be disposed of," Blythe agreed. "Things like used brass spittoons. That should work. Nothing ever returns from there."

Imbri took back the band and launched herself north, toward the Void. Then she remembered to veer to the nearest gourd patch. Obviously it did not affect the band to be within the gourd, since the day horse had been there while wearing it and no prisoned King had been released. But the Void was different. Even the creatures of the gourd world had to be careful of it.

She plunged madly through the night world, heedless of all its familiar scenes, and out of the gourd within the dread Void. She suppressed her growing nervousness. After all, Xanth depended on her performance.

Now she ran straight into the most feared region of Xanth—the center of the Void. The land curved down here, like the surface of a huge funnel, descending to its dread central point. For the Void was a black hole from which nothing escaped, not even light. Only Imbri's kind could safely pass the outer fringe of it—and she had to dematerialize for the inner fringe, lest her physical body be sucked in, never to emerge. She was terrified of this depth, for it was beyond where she had ever gone before—but she had to make sure the brass ring was properly placed, that its effect was absolutely shielded. If she set it rolling or sliding down toward the hole, and if it snagged on the way, the Kings could remain captive for an indefinite future time until the ring completed its journey.

She wasn't even sure a direct placement in the hole would break the spell, but it did seem likely, and it was all she had left to try. It was her only hope. If this did not break the chain, then Xanth was doomed to anarchy, for there would be no way to rescue the Kings, and the Mundanes would ravage Xanth unchallenged. The Horseman was gone, but his mischief would remain after him, causing Xanth to suffer grievously.

She came to the bottom of the funnel. She saw the deepest blackness of the black hole. She was immaterial, yet it seemed to suck her in. It had a somber, awesome latent power. She was extremely afraid of it.

She opened her mouth and dropped the brass band. It plummeted as if gaining weight. In an instant it disappeared into nothingness. There was not even a splash, just a silent engulfment. The deed was done.

Imbri tried to turn and depart the funnel. Her feet moved, but her body made no progress. She had approached too close to the dread maw of the Void! Even dematerialized, she could not escape it.

She scrambled desperately up the side of the funnel, but slowly, inevitably, she slid back. Her hooves had no purchase; *nothing* had purchase here! She had penetrated the region of no return. Her fall accelerated.

With a neigh of purest terror and despair, Mare Imbri fell into the black hole of the Void.

Chameleon seemed to float up, her face and body amazingly ugly, but her spirit beautiful. "Chem! Chem!" she called out over the jungle of Xanth. "Chem Centaur—where are you?"

"Here I am!" Chem cried. "Here with the Gorgon. Don't worry, she's thoroughly veiled!"

"We need your soul," Chameleon said, drifting down to join them.

"I have only half my soul," the centaur said. "Imbri the night mare has the other half."

"No, you have all of it now. Don't you feel it?"

Chem was surprised. "Why, yes, I do! I feel buoyant! But how is this possible? I never begrudged Imbri her half, and my half was regenerating. Now I have more than a full soul; it's too much!"

"Imbri fell into the black hole of the Void," Chameleon explained. "She killed the Horseman and carried his magic talisman to the Void, to free the rest of us from the enchantment, but she couldn't escape it herself."

"The Void! Oh, this is terrible! You mean she's dead, after all she did for Xanth?"

"No. We believe one essential part of her survived. She lost her body in the sacrifice she made to break the chain, fulfilling the prophecy, but her soul remained. No soul is subject to the Void. It's the only thing in Xanth that is not vulnerable to the black hole."

"But it reverted to me! It wasn't her own soul, because the creatures of the gourd don't grow their own souls! They have to borrow from those of us who do. I don't want her half soul! I want Imbri to live! After what she did for Xanth, and the kind of person she was—" The centaur filly was crying human tears of frustration and grief.

"So do we all," Chameleon agreed. "That's why Good Magician Humfrey and I, anticipating this, made plans for such a contingency. We could not act while we were confined within the gourd. But the moment Imbri freed us, Humfrey uttered a spell he knew. A Word of Power. An enchantment to keep a special soul discrete, despite its origin."

"Discreet?"

"Discrete. Separate. So Imbri could live on after her body was lost."

"But how, then—if her soul came back to me—?"

"She came, too. Free her, Chem; the Good Magician's spell enables you to do that, because you have the first claim on that soul."

The centaur concentrated immediately. "Imbri, I love you! I free you! Take your half soul; be yourself!"

Something intangible snapped. Imbri floated free. "Is it true?" she sent. "Am I really alive?"

"Yes, lovely night mare!" Chameleon said. "You are alive in the purest sense. But you have lost your body. You can never again materialize. You are now of the spirit world, like the ghosts."

"But what can I do without my body?" Imbri asked, dismayed. She remembered her awful fall into the Void—and the arrival of Chameleon. Nothing in between.

"That's part of what we arranged," Chameleon said. "Humfrey's spell took care of the paper work, or whatever, so it's all right. We all love you, Imbri, and we all thank you, and we owe our lives and our hopes to you, and we want to be with you often. So you will be a true day mare, carrying daydreams and pleasant evening dreams, much as you have been doing. Only now it is official, and forever. Whenever we daydream, you will be there with your new associates, making sure each dream is properly delivered and enjoyed."

Imbri liked the concept. She no lor.ger liked bad dreams. Still, she was perplexed. "My associates?"

Now several other mares appeared, trotting prettily through the air. They were of pleasant colors—red, blue, green, and orange. "Welcome, black mare," one sent, perking her ears forward in a friendly fashion. "Oh, the Day Stallion will like you! You have such an individual color!"

"The Day Stallion?" Imbri sent, an unpleasant association forming.

A male horse appeared, flying winglessly through the air, bright golden as the sun. "I assign the daydreams," he sent. He swished his tail negligently. He was the handsomest stallion Imbri had ever seen. "But you may choose any you like to deliver. We are very informal here and seldom take things very seriously. This present daydream is an example; we're all linked together in it, and we're all helping with it, so as to introduce you to the nature of your new work gently. All the recent Kings of Xanth and their friends are sharing it. Soon they must revert to normal consciousness, to transform the Mundane Wavers back into men, one at a time—King Trent transformed them all to stinkweeds, and the castle smells awful—to see if they're ready to swear allegiance to the present order, and to see about King Trent's retirement so he can spend more time with his wife, and about King Dor's permanent assumption of the throne of Xanth—these things must, after all, be accomplished with the appropriate ceremony—but first they wanted to see you properly established in your own new employment. We have never had a King among our number before."

"But I'm not King any more!" Imbri protested. "Now that the real Kings have been freed—"

"You will retain the honorary title, King Mare Imbrium," King Trent said with a smile. "You are the one who saved Xanth. We shall fashion a statue in your likeness and never forget you."

There was a murmur of agreement from all the others in the collective daydream—her friends.

Suddenly Imbri knew she was going to like this duty. With that realization, she looked up and saw that it was day. Time had passed between her descent into the Void, the final breaking of the chain of Kings, and her reanimation as a soul-horse. Now the sun was up, but there was a light shower, as if the clouds were shedding tears of joy at the salvation of Xanth. Perhaps it was some weather overlapping from her region of the moon, the Sea of Rains.

There, in the bright misty sky, was the many-colored rainbow she had always longed to see, spanning her horizon.

About the Author

Piers Anthony was born in August, 1934, in England, spent a year in Spain, and came to America at age six. He was naturalized as an American citizen in 1958 while serving in the U.S. Army. He now lives in Florida with his wife Carol and their daughters Penny and Cheryl. His first story was submitted to a magazine in 1954, but he did not make his first story sale until 1962. Similarly, he submitted his first novel, which was also his thesis for his B.A. degree from college, in 1956, but did not sell a novel until 1966. He has written well over 50 books. His first Xanth novel, *A Spell for Chameleon*, won the August Derleth Fantasy award for 1977. His novel *Ogre, Ogre* may have been the first original paperback ever to make the *New York Times* bestseller list. The Xanth series consists of over 16 novels. His house is hidden deep in the forest, almost impossible to find, and he now has a computer in the horse pasture.